The Sarah Roberts Series

Vol. 31-33

by

Jonas Saul

PUBLISHED BY:

Imagine Press Inc.
Ebook ISBN: 978-1-998047-26-0
Print ISBN: 978-1-998047-27-7

The Sarah Roberts Series Vol. 31-33
Copyright © 2023 by Jonas Saul

The Sarah Roberts Series

Dark Visions (One)
The Warning (Two)
The Crypt (Three)
The Hostage (Four)
The Victim (Five)
The Enigma (Six)
The Vigilante (Seven)
The Rogue (Eight)
Killing Sarah (Nine)
The Antagonist (Ten)
The Redeemed (Eleven)
The Haunted (Twelve)
The Unlucky (Thirteen)
The Abandoned (Fourteen)
The Cartel (Fifteen)
Losing Sarah (Sixteen)
The Pact (Seventeen)
The Terror (Eighteen)
The Chase (Nineteen)
The Betrayal (Twenty)
Sarah's Return (Twenty-One)
The Hunt (Twenty-Two)
The Delivery (Twenty-Three)
The Trap (Twenty-Four)
The Ultimatum (Twenty-Five)
The Depraved (Twenty-Six)
The Condemned (Twenty-Seven)
Payback (Twenty-Eight)
The Unknown (Twenty-Nine)
Wrath (Thirty)
The Damned (Thirty-One)
The Game (Thirty-Two)
The Decoy (Thirty-Three)
The Disappearance (Thirty-Four)
The Whole Truth (Thirty-Five)
Alex (Thirty-Six)
Parkman (Thirty-Seven)

Darwin (Thirty-Eight)
Aaron (Thirty-Nine)
Remains To Be Seen (Forty)

The Jake Wood Novels

The Immortal Gene (Book One)
The Immortal Target (Book Two)

Standalone Novels

The Drowning
The Woman in the Woods
The Threat
The Specter
The Mafia Trilogy
A Murder in Time
Frequency of the Dead

Co-Authored Novels

Collision Course (Written with Gary Ponzo)
There Will Be Blood (Written with Rania Stone)
The Soulless (Written with Rania Stone)

Short Story Collections

Twisted Fate (Tales of Horror)
Twists of Fate (Tales of Hope)

The Damned

Book Thirty-One

Chapter 1

THE MILES STRETCHED ON, and no one had died yet.

Sarah Roberts leaned her head back and mused on that. "How is it we haven't killed each other?"

Her boyfriend glanced in the mirror, yawned, and drove without responding. He didn't even shake his head.

"Aaron? Where are we going with this?"

Now, he looked at her; his face scrunched into a frown. "What do you mean? We're going to see your parents in Santa Rosa."

She clucked her tongue and leaned forward to twist in her seat. "No, where are *we* going?"

He leaned forward and turned on the radio, his eyes on the road. Sarah watched Aaron's hand as he flicked through the stations, her eyes focused on his bloodied knuckles. He settled on Lana Del Rey, then eased back into the driver's seat and yawned again, not looking her way once.

Sarah turned off the radio, suppressing the urge to call him out for his apparent rebuff. "Not something you want to talk about?" Soft pellets of rain hit and spread across the windshield.

Aaron set the wipers to intermittent without acknowledging her.

"Aaron?" There was more urgency in her tone now. "Benjamin's gone. I get that. We're all hurting, but it's been several months now. Just tell me how long you need to grieve. That's different for everyone, but how long before you return to work? Alex and Daniel need you. *I* need you."

His hand tightened on the wheel—the scab on his largest knuckle splitting open. There was just enough light from the dashboard for her to see the sparkle of fresh blood seeping out.

She grabbed a tissue from inside the glove box and went to dab at it when he pulled his hand away.

"Don't."

She gawked at him. "You're bleeding."

This time, he looked at her, and she saw the pain in his eyes—it replaced his vacant stare. Then he turned back to the road as the rain came down harder.

"You owe me an answer," she whispered before glancing back at Willow, their daughter, sleeping in the back seat. Luckily, she hadn't seen her dad lose his shit hours ago at the last truck stop when they gave him the wrong change for their coffees. He'd shouted and cursed until the manager gave them the coffee for free as long as they left immediately.

Free wasn't their goal, but honesty was. Being misunderstood and ashamed of losing his temper, he'd punched the brick wall outside the truck stop and mangled the flesh over his knuckles.

"When Willow wakes later tonight or in the morning, she'll see your hand."

"I'll deal with it."

Sarah watched him for a moment. "You're not letting me in. Your appetite sucks. You lash out at others and won't take Benjamin's watch off."

Aaron's lower lip trembled as he looked at the watch on his left wrist.

"Aaron, I don't want to mention the extra drinking to dull the pain. I don't want to evaluate you, but you have to come back to us eventually, and the longer you're gone …" She drifted off when a tear slipped over Aaron's eye and dropped onto his sallow cheek. "Willow needs her dad back. Do it for her if you won't deal with your grief and come back for me."

Sarah turned to face forward in her seat. They passed an exit sign that said East Glenrock.

Aaron hit the blinker and eased onto the exit.

"Where are we going?"

"I need coffee." He snatched a glance at her. "There won't be a fight this time. Even if they steal my change, I'll let them keep it. Honestly."

She exhaled and slumped down in her seat. "I could use a coffee, too."

The clinking of the watchband drew her attention back to Aaron.

"What are you doing?"

"Taking it off." He eased it over his left hand, grasped it in his right hand, and then dangled it over the center console. "Here, you wear it until we get home. Keep it safe for me."

"Are you sure?" She gently took it from him and stared down at the gorgeous face of Benjamin's watch.

"I would hate to lose it."

Benjamin had bought a replica of the Marvels of the World Series watches. He had a depiction of the Great Wall of China on the face of the watch, with blue hands that showed the time. It was quite a stunning piece, even if it only cost him a few hundred dollars.

"The original watches sell for millions." Aaron glanced at her, back to the road, then to the watch. "He loved that thing."

Sarah slipped it onto her wrist. It didn't sit well on her wrist as a large men's watch, but she'd make it work until they got to California.

Aaron adjusted himself in his seat. "We still in Wyoming?"

And will be for a while yet, her sister whispered.

"What?" Sarah gasped. "Why?"

But Vivian was already gone.

"Your sister?" Aaron eased off the gas as they approached a large truck stop on the right.

Sarah nodded but realized he probably couldn't see her gesture in the dark and whispered a short *yes*.

Aaron sneered at her. "Vivian finally stuck her head above the sand? Coming around to let one of us die again?"

There was a hint of animosity in his tone that she didn't like. It wasn't Vivian's fault that Benjamin was dead. Some would argue she could've stopped it, but she didn't commit the act. Therefore, she couldn't be blamed.

"You should be glad when she's not around. It's been months since we've had anything meaningful from her, which means no bad guys, no bullets, and no one's life has been put in danger."

Aaron scoffed. "Whether she's around or not, trouble always finds you."

She snapped her head sideways to glare at him. "I won't let shitty comments slide. I know you're suffering—we're *all* suffering. If you want to be a dick, then be a dick, but not with me, the mother of your child. Remember, I didn't kill Benjamin."

Aaron jerked the car off the road as they entered the truck stop's parking lot.

She'd let it go—for now. They could cool off while he went inside to get them coffee. Then she'd go in and use the bathrooms and stretch her legs.

It was close to nine in the evening. Within a few hours, they'd find a hotel with a vacancy sign and rest for the night, only to wake in the morning and start driving again.

And once they got settled at her parents' place in Santa Rosa, she'd talk with him. It was time. She needed direction in her life, and he was too wayward and childish for her. Maybe it was time for a change after all these years. Or perhaps they just needed a temporary break to sort out their own feelings.

The car came to a stop near the back of the parking lot. Aaron killed the engine, undid his seatbelt, and cracked open his door, pocketing the car keys in one fluid motion. The car remained dark as the interior light option was set to the off position. They didn't want to wake Willow when the doors opened at night.

"Why did you park back here by these trees?" Sarah studied his face, trying to make sense of the man she'd loved and known for a decade. "Were you thinking about sleeping in the car?" She gestured toward the building. "Because there are lots of spots up there."

"I wanted a longer walk to stretch my legs." He got to his feet with a grunt and left his door open to avoid waking Willow with the noise of closing it.

The rain had subsided, so Sarah opened her door softly and pushed it wide. A light, cool breeze wafted through the car.

Aaron was halfway across the parking lot when she realized he hadn't asked if she wanted anything. What if her bladder was bursting? What if she needed chocolate with her coffee? Or a soda instead? With Willow sleeping, someone had to stay behind while the other went inside.

When Aaron was hurting, all he thought about was himself.

Even though her mind whispered *typical man*, she tried hard not to think like that. Aaron wasn't *typical*. He was just stupid sometimes and stubborn.

The engine ticked as it cooled, and the sound of a rig slowing down came through Aaron's open door.

They'd stopped at a regular truck stop and gas station. The neon red light on the overhead roof atop the gas pumps lit up the night like a warning sign.

A warning sign.

What could her sister mean when she said they'd be in Wyoming for a while? It was too cryptic for her liking. Would the car need service? A flat tire? What?

"You haven't come around for several months, Vivian, and now you pop up and tell me some riddle." Sarah glanced around the parking lot, looking at nothing in particular. "Then you don't answer me." Sarah shook her head. "You're acting like Aaron now."

The rain had subsided enough that only a few light drops rested inside the open doors.

Sarah glanced back at Willow. Her daughter was still asleep and likely would be until tomorrow morning when they woke up in whatever hotel they found. It was the same routine as the previous two nights. Willow fell asleep when the sun went down and woke in the morning. Even carrying her into the hotel last night hadn't woken her up. To be a small child again …

Something rustled the leaves behind the car, pulling Sarah's eyes toward the movement.

She blinked several times, then rubbed her weary eyes. Nothing moved behind the car. The breeze was too soft to rustle the leaves, and no car was near theirs.

She spun back around and glanced at the truck stop.

No sign of Aaron yet.

She needed to shut the doors and lock the car until he returned. It would get stuffy without the car keys—the power windows wouldn't work—but he'd be along soon.

"Why park back here?" she muttered as she fumbled with her seatbelt, but it was somehow stuck. She shifted her butt sideways, twisted around, and looked down. A piece of her shirt was jammed in with the clasp. She pulled and yanked, then heard something stumble through the trees behind the car.

An animal? If so, it was heavy.

With both doors open, she had a moment of panic and yanked on the seatbelt harder.

A man shouted a few words from somewhere in the bushes behind the car. She couldn't be sure, but she thought he'd said, *You're dead, bitch.*

Her pulse pounded in her neck; her heart rate doubled; she got the seatbelt undone as Vivian's words rolled through her mind again—they'd be in Wyoming for a while.

That wasn't good. That wasn't part of the plan.

Seatbelt out of the way, Sarah lunged across the front seat. The center console shoved up into her lower ribs hard, but she couldn't reach Aaron's wide-open door.

Before she could adjust herself to climb over the console and grab his door, a woman popped into view.

Sarah let out a small yip at the surprise of seeing the woman standing there, her hands jerking in frantic movements.

Sarah reared back, staring at the woman with something dark covering her face—*blood!*

It streamed from several places on her face—likely from running in the woods in the dark, branches cutting her—and her clothes were torn. The panicked look in her eyes told Sarah everything she needed to know.

This girl was in her mid-twenties; she was scared, afraid, and in trouble.

That man mumbled something from the trees again about catching and killing her.

Before Sarah could utter a word, the woman dropped into the driver's seat, closing the door quietly beside her.

Sarah grabbed the woman's sleeve. "What are you doing?" She kept her voice low, controlled. "My daughter is in the back seat. Get out of my car."

Willow would be awake at any moment and completely disoriented when she saw a bloodied woman in the front seat instead of her dad.

"Pleeaassse." The woman moaned the word, glancing back at Willow. "They'll kill me. We have to get out of here—now. Where are the keys?"

"I don't have them." Sarah shot a glance back at Willow. Her daughter stirred, but then she turned, faced the back of the seat, and curled up in a deep sleep.

Distraught, the woman openly cried, her hands roaming the steering column for keys that weren't there as her shoulders hitched uncontrollably.

Where there wasn't blood on her skin, sweat covered her—the torn shirt was soaked through. The whites of her eyes were clear as she shook her head in frustration.

"With your car doors open like that—" She cut herself off with a gasp, then spun around to look out the back window. "I thought you were here for me."

Their eyes met, the woman openly bawling.

"What is it?" Sarah asked, wondering how she could help and what Aaron would think of this when he returned. "What's going on? Do you need the police?"

The woman grabbed a clump of her hair and pulled it on, muttering something repeatedly. Sarah only caught a few words.

"It's not true. This can't be happening. It's not true. This can't be —"

Her nostrils flared, and she stamped her feet on the floorboards, frustration oozing off her in waves.

"There you are, bitch," a man said behind Sarah's open door.

She spun around and stared up into the eyes of a monster. The man had to be six and a half feet tall, bald, and built like Dwayne Johnson's trainer. He held a wrench the size of an average man's forearm and had a crooked, creepy smile. Only two teeth showed on the far left of his ugly grin.

"What the fuck do you want?" Sarah asked, already looking at him for his weak spots as her stomach dropped in anticipation of a fight. She didn't want this trouble, didn't invite it, and was furious at Vivian for not warning her about it.

But now, she had no choice. She had to stop whatever this was from descending into chaos because she was the only one who could. Aaron wasn't here, and her daughter was still asleep in the back.

Before the man could answer her, the driver's side door was ripped open, shaking the car violently.

For all the subtlety of the hysterical woman moments ago, that couldn't have been her.

Another man laughed.

"C'mere, bitch."

Sarah spun around as a man grabbed the woman's hair and yanked her from the driver's seat. The woman screamed in pain as she dropped out of the car and landed on the wet parking lot on her stomach.

"Hey," Sarah yelled, reaching for the woman but missing her.

Willow would be awake now.

Before she turned back around, something collided with her cheek.

Oh no, went through her mind. *That had to be his fist.*

The man laughed as Sarah's forehead bounced off the top of the glove box, where it said the airbag was stored.

A hand landed on the top of her head, tightened on a clump of her hair, then pulled her halfway out of the car, her butt still in the passenger seat.

"Trying to help that bitch escape us will cost you," the Dwayne Johnson lookalike whispered close to her ear.

"I didn't do anything yet, fuckhead—"

Like a freight train, something large collided with her cheek, cutting off her sentence.

That one didn't just stun her—it felt like it shattered her jawbone and broke a tooth loose. She moved her mouth, relieved her jaw wasn't dislocated. Someone was moaning close by—then she realized it was her.

She fluttered her eyes to get them open, but was so dazed she couldn't get her bearings.

Blood poured from her mouth, and her cheek felt like it was already swelling. The broken tooth passed her lips and dropped to the floor on the passenger side.

The man pulled on her hair again as she tongued the new hole in the right side row of her teeth.

"Yes," she whispered, her lips already swelling. "Lost a fuckin' tooth." Willow popped into her dazed thoughts, and she struggled against the man's enormous strength, trying to angle her head back to check on her daughter.

The man's breath was in her ear again. "That ain't all you'll lose, stupid bitch."

Then he yanked her bodily from the car using her hair alone. The rest of her body smacked onto the pavement. Her hip took its brunt while her scalp was on fire, where the man's hand remained there, his fingers entangled in her thick hair. Like he could conjure fire from the air, the pain at the top of her head grew intense, forcing deep moans from her throat.

She grabbed his wrist, her nails digging in, her vision blurred by tears, and her consciousness wavering.

Where was his groin? She'd mash his balls under her feet. She would stomp on his throat, then pop one of his knees. And if he hurt her baby, she'd gouge out his eyes with her thumbs and tear open his neck with her teeth.

But none of that came to be.

When he released her hair, he had pulled back his cowboy-booted foot and now kicked her in the face so hard she launched sideways, her head connecting with the side of the back door of their car, her shoulder blades bouncing off the bottom ridge of the vehicle before she dropped to the pavement.

Still breathing, barely conscious, Sarah muttered to herself to get up and fight. But nothing was responding correctly.

She whispered Willow's name, her hand clinging to the car to try to get up and check on her daughter.

The fire in her head intensified, and any movement worsened it.

"What about the kid?" a man said.

Nooo, Sarah said, but nothing came out of her mouth besides blood.

"Leave the kid."

"Huh?" the first man said. "All by herself? Dude, that's not cool."

"What, you wanna babysit now?" He grunted. "Daddy will be out soon."

There was a pause, and then the other man said, "Daddy? How do you know that?"

"Holy fuck, are you stupid?"

"Hey, I'm just asking, is all. And don't call me stupid."

"The bitch was in the passenger seat. There's a kid in the back seat. The driver's seat was empty, and the car keys were not there. Otherwise, that bitch would've gotten away."

"Okay. So?"

"That means Daddy is in the truck stop taking a shit or buying food before they hit the road again."

"Ahhh," the other man whispered. "Got it. So he'll be back soon and can take his kid."

Someone snapped his fingers. "Bingo, dingo."

"Hey, stop calling me that."

"Daddy gets his little girl, and we take the women. Once we're done with them, Daddy can have Mommy's used body back when they pull her from the North Platte River."

Sarah got her hands under her and tried to push up, but bumped the car's underside. She had to get to Willow. Protect her baby from these men. Use her body as a shield. Anything other than leaving her behind.

"Damn, check this bitch out. She's a fighter and a beauty. Liam, you'll let me have a go at her, too, right?"

Something whacked hard against flesh.

"Ow," one of them moaned.

"I said no names."

"Does it matter? She's done for now. She's seen our faces."

"Still, stupid, no names."

"Don't call me stupid." The man's voice turned serious yet whiny. "Dingo, I can deal with, but stupid is a whole nother league."

"Fine. Fuck off and help me drag these cunts into the bush."

Someone knelt close to her. She pushed sideways and then up, but couldn't get her leg far enough to rest on her knees.

"Willow," she moaned.

"Hey, Dingo, check out the nice watch on the boss lady here."

Sarah's left arm was yanked up so hard that her shoulder muscles flared in pain. *No, not Benjamin's watch. Please leave that.*

"Gimme that," the other guy said.

The watch was torn from her arm, and then the man twisted her bodily onto her back and lifted his boot over her face.

16

"Lights out, bitch whore."

Sarah tried to move away, but wasn't fast enough.

A glint of light flashed off the length of the wrench as the man's boot dropped down.

Then flames filled her head, and all the lights went out, her last conscious thought being Willow's name.

Chapter 2

AARON STOOD IN LINE behind two men wearing cowboy hats, his foot tapping impatiently. They'd been struggling to figure out their bill for several minutes now, the line behind Aaron steadily growing. The large man on the right felt he'd been overcharged for the peach pie, and now they were examining the menu with the woman at the till.

The people gathered behind Aaron had their bills in hand, waiting to pay for their meals as well. A family of four had a tired boy whining that he wanted to go to the car now, and his mother kept shushing him.

Another family allowed their young son to run up and down the hallway leading from the restaurant to the gas station section, while they attempted to chastise him in a foreign language that Aaron didn't recognize. It was either German or Scandinavian.

He closed his eyes to remain calm. Two coffees and a Coke were all he wanted. If he hadn't gone to the bathroom first, he would've beat these yokels to the register. He still had to gas up before they left, too.

"See the price, sir?" the lady at the till said. "Your bill adds up properly."

"Well, it still seems ten dollars too high."

That was all Aaron could handle. He slipped around the men and sidled up to the counter.

"I'll pay their extra ten bucks. I can't wait any longer. I need to hit the road." Aaron pulled out a twenty and dropped it on the counter. "This should cover my three drinks; any extra can go toward their bill."

The man who had done the complaining righted himself and stared at Aaron, his head tilted back. "Much obliged, friend." His eyes lowered to Aaron's missing finger and bloodied knuckles. The smile disappeared, and the man's face slackened, his eyes deep and serious. He went to slap Aaron on the shoulder with a friendly pat, but Aaron was already stepping away, and the man's hand missed. "Appreciate that," he heard from behind him. "Send our thanks to Cohen."

Cohen? Who the hell was Cohen? Leonard?

Aaron headed for the exit, juggling the drinks and knowing Sarah would wonder what he'd been up to for so long. Those men had argued over their bill for at least four to five minutes, not to mention how long he had to wait for the waitress to return to the kitchen and grab two coffees.

Several times throughout this trip, Sarah had argued with him about his attitude. He was aware it was out of sorts, but couldn't fix it yet, or didn't possess the tools to fix it, and he didn't want to make Sarah think he'd taken his time on purpose.

Just before he exited the building, that kid who'd been running around cut him off and almost made him drop the coffee.

Someone cursed in German behind him—he was sure it was German now—as he caught his breath and secured the beverages.

"Motherfucker," he muttered to himself.

One deep inhale later, he turned around, placed his back against the door, pushed it open, and spun back around to stare at the parking lot.

"Fuck, why did I park so far away?"

After descending the steps, he strolled toward the car, thinking up the best way to tell Sarah about the cowboys and their *supposedly* inflated bill.

Why did the man change his demeanor when he saw Aaron's hand? And who the hell was this Cohen he referred to?

Halfway across the large parking lot, he heard Willow calling his name.

Aaron frowned. Why was she awake? Maybe she had to use the toilet, too. He stared hard at the windshield, but the glare from the parking lot lamps reflected off the slanted glass, and he couldn't see inside the car.

Closer now, he detected something in Willow's voice that he didn't like.

Was that fear like the cry he'd hear from her after a bad nightmare?

He stepped around the open passenger door and glanced inside.

The front of the car was empty.

"You okay, honey?"

Willow nodded, her eyes sleepy and wet from crying.

He set the coffee on the roof and glanced around the parking lot. "Sarah?"

"She's gone, Daddy."

Aaron leaned in the car to look at Willow in the back seat. "Where did she go, honey?"

Willow shrugged. "Something woke me up. Men were talking. Then Mommy was gone."

His stomach dropped as acid filled it. "Men talking?"

Willow nodded in the exaggerated way that kids do.

"Like policemen?"

Willow shook her head. "Bad men, I think."

"What made them bad?"

His voice almost cracked. Sarah wouldn't leave four-year-old Willow alone like this. Willow had to have been dreaming.

"Not sure. They were angry and grunting."

"Grunting?"

Aaron placed a hand on the console to support himself, then jerked it back. He'd touched something wet. When he pulled back out of the car and held his hand up to the light, he saw blood on it.

Rooted to the spot, he froze and stared at the blood, his leg muscles tightening. Sweat broke out on his forehead and neck as he took in the car's interior.

Frantically, he wiped the blood on his gray slacks without thinking, then yanked out his cell phone and flicked on the flashlight app.

He almost dropped to his knees when he shone it on the dashboard and front passenger seat. His free hand kept him upright as he gripped the top of the open doorframe.

"What happened here?" he asked aloud, leaning closer to the floor to examine a small white rock.

A tooth! It was a tooth with the glistening root still attached.

"I don't know what happened, Daddy. I was sleeping."

"No, I'm sorry, honey." He swallowed and then regained his composure. "I was talking to myself."

"Is that blood?" Willow's tone seemed fearful. "Did something happen to Mommy?"

Aaron flicked off the phone and pocketed it. "Come on, Willow. We need to go sit at the truck stop for a bit."

"Is this where our hotel is tonight?"

Aaron opened the back door and waved for her to exit. "C'mon, honey. We'll go find Mommy, then head to a hotel."

Willow nodded as she scooted across the seat, yawning. "I'm tired."

"I know, honey." He collected her in his arms and held her tight as he hustled back to the truck stop.

With that much blood—and a tooth—in their car, he had to call the local cops.

Sarah had been kidnapped.

Chapter 3

LIAM HAD TO DO most of the dragging as Dom wasn't strong enough to get both women through the trees and into the bed of their pickup. Luckily, it wasn't more than a hundred yards.

He'd placed the woman they'd been chasing, Jamie Sutton, over his shoulder because she weighed no more than a hundred pounds wet, and yanked the other woman by the wrist with Dom trying to hold her ankles.

"Hurry, Dingo," Liam said over his shoulder. "This one's a fighter."

"How do you know that?" Dom scoffed. "You smacked her several times, and she was out like a light."

"Fuck, are you stupid sometimes."

"Don't call me stupid."

Liam slowed to catch his breath when the pickup's bumper was sighted. He turned back to face Dom.

"I know I hit her"—he glanced at the woman with his boot print still etched on her cheek—"but she still tried to get up. Even after I knocked out her tooth, she wanted to get up." Liam raised his fist and stared at the large college ring on his finger. It had knocked out many teeth in his time. "I had to step on her head to knock her out." He appraised the woman's body. "She's built, too. Like she could fight if given a chance. We don't want her waking up until we're at the barn."

"Got it." Dom snapped his fingers, something he often did when he was nervous. "No problem there. But if she does wake up, just step on her head again, right?"

"Yeah, sure, with Sutton up on my shoulders. I'm not Superman, Dingo." He turned away, bent at the knees, grabbed the woman's wrist, and dragged her through the underbrush again. "It's not helping that everything's so wet after that rain earlier."

They made it to the tailgate of the pickup. Instead of lifting Sutton, he leaned over the edge of the pickup bed and let her roll off his shoulders into it. There was a dull thud as bones—and her skull—made contact with steel.

"Help me up with this one."

Dom grabbed the woman's legs and Liam her arms.

"I can't deadlift this woman," Dom said, the strain evident on his face, in his corded neck.

"Then rock her like a swing, and we'll toss her in the back."

Dom nodded. "I can do that."

They got her moving like a swing, back and forth, her backside almost at shoulder height when Dom let her go, and the woman flopped to the ground.

"Why'd you let go?" Liam gaped at him.

"She slipped, man. Sweaty and shit."

"For fuck's sake."

Liam got to one knee in front of the woman, grabbed her arms, and placed them over his shoulders. Then he leaned into her gut and pushed up to a standing position. It took considerable effort, but he could get her onto his shoulder like the Sutton woman moments before.

He stumbled a couple of steps toward the pickup, then leaned sideways and shoved their cargo into the back.

Once he retrieved the keys from his pocket, he tossed them to Dom, who missed them.

"You drive. I'll sit in the back with these two in case one of them wakes up."

Dom grabbed the keys off the dirt and headed to the truck's cab without a word.

"Take it easy on the road. I don't want to be thrown around back here."

"It's one mile away. You'll be fine."

"Just don't drive like a maniac, or I'll brain you when we get to the barn."

Dom was already in the cab and closing the door.

Liam hopped up on the gate and then into the truck's bed. He arranged the women so their heads were near him if they woke and wanted to sit up.

The truck's engine turned over, then vibrated as Dom dropped it into gear.

Gravel crunching under the tires made Liam relax. They'd caught up to Sutton in time. That was a close one. So close that he didn't want to tell the boss about it, although he wasn't sure how he *couldn't* tell him. The new woman, with her gorgeous hair and body, had seen their faces. They had to bring her along. It made sense, and that's why their boss had him on these jobs—because he thought well on his feet.

When Sutton's body was discovered in a few days, and that other woman had seen Sutton, she would give the police a sketch of their faces, which would be it for them. Even their boss would feel that sort of heat. So he had to take her, too.

A mistake was made, and Liam rectified it immediately.

It wouldn't happen again.

How could his boss be mad when no actual harm had been done?

Dom slowed at the end of the dirt road, signaled like a good boy, and turned onto East Birch Street. On a Saturday evening, the only traffic was mainly out-of-towners, and hardly any of those were out tonight.

Even so, headlights raced up behind them.

Liam sat lower in the truck's bed as the wind whipped up his hair. By his calculation, Dom would turn off Birch Street in a few hundred yards. Then this asshole behind them could find his speeding ticket up the road at the next radar trap.

Liam glanced down at the women as their hair billowed in the wind, thinking about the crazy things he would do to the new bitch.

That was one of the perks he got from working for his boss. The women were mules. The women made the product and did what they were told, or Dalton gave them to Liam, and Liam could keep them as pets for as long as he wanted.

Sutton had briefly gotten away, but now he might hand off the bitch to Dom for a couple of days. This new woman looked like a lot more fun.

The car behind them flicked on its high beams and moved closer to their bumper.

"Hey," Liam shouted. "Back off."

Red and blue lights flashed once just as Dom slowed to turn onto the road that led to the barn.

Dom pulled in far enough to allow the cruiser room to park off Birch Street.

When the pickup stopped, Liam pushed up to his feet at the exact moment the cruiser's lights went dark.

The door opened, and Officer Kirk Taggart got out of the cruiser. His rounded cheeks and second chin were painted red in the pickup's taillights.

"Hey, Captain Kirk." Liam chuckled. "If you wore red, I'd swear you'd be the perfect fat Santa for the town's Christmas parade."

"Don't call me that. I'm not a captain, and that Santa comment isn't nice." Kirk pointed at him and squinted. "You think you're smart, but ever since high school, I got you beat." He adjusted his uniform, tucked in the bottom of his shirt, and brushed out a wrinkle near his sleeve. "I'm one of four patrol officers with the Glenrock Police Department, soon to make detective, and you'll still be—"

He stopped talking when Liam burst out laughing. With an eye on the two unconscious women in the back, he covered his mouth and shook his head.

"Soon to make detective? You're such a fuckin' idiot, Kirk Taggart. The Glenrock Police Department doesn't employ more than one detective at a time, and that's Detective Billings's job."

The cop shuffled his feet and averted his eyes to look at Dom, who had stepped out of the pickup's cab. "Yeah, well, whatever. I'll be undercover then."

"Undercover what?" Liam looked from Kirk to Dom. "You're too *big* to be undercover anything."

He scoffed, then kicked at the dirt with his polished police boot. "Whatchoo guys doing out here, anyway? I heard Dalton's pissed about something."

His boss was pissed? About what?

Liam glanced at Dom, then down to the women at his feet. Jamie Sutton had escaped, but they'd recaptured her within five to ten minutes. How could Dalton know about that already?

"You find out why he's pissed?"

Kirk shook his head and heaved up his pants, slipping his thumbs inside his beltline. "No idea. Just heard from dispatch."

"Heard what?"

"See, Liam? You're the dumb one here. I just frickin' told you. I heard that Dalton's pissed about something."

He'd let Kirk have his fun. Whatever got Dalton pissed couldn't blow back on him. They needed to secure these girls in the barn and then call Dalton.

"What you got in the back?" Kirk asked, stepping forward.

"Nothing you need to see." Liam raised his hands, but Kirk was already moving forward.

"Shit, man, why you got two bloodied women up there?" Kirk stared up at Liam with a pained expression. "You're gonna get me fired, man. I got a job to do. What do I tell Billings?"

Liam leaned down and braced himself with both hands on the pickup's side, still several feet above Kirk. "You don't tell Detective Billings shit, is what you do. This has nothing to do with *your* job. These girls work for Dalton. We drove them out to the field for their little catfight, and they knocked each other out." He shot a look at Dom, warning him to corroborate his story. "Now we're taking them back to the barn to sleep it off. This has nothing to do with you, the department, or Billings." He quickly checked on the women. Both were still passed out, but they wouldn't be for long. "You wouldn't want Dalton hearing you took two of his employees to the drunk tank when we had it under control, now would ya?"

Officer Kirk Taggart shook his head and took a step backward. "You guys do what you have to do and keep me out of it." Kirk took a few more steps back toward his open door. "I don't never want to get on Dalton's bad side."

"Understood." Liam stood to his full height. "Dom, get back in the truck. We'll tell Dalton that Kirk's one of the good guys."

Kirk stopped at the door to his cruiser, his face contorted in confusion. The man's arm jerked out toward Liam as if some crazy thought hit him at that moment, and Liam could've sworn Kirk was Chris Farley in uniform.

"I'd much prefer if you kept my name out of Dalton's ears. I'm trying to do good things here in Glenrock."

Dom's door closed, and the pickup dropped into gear. Liam lowered to sit on the bed of the truck.

"You don't think Dalton's doing good things?" Liam asked as the truck eased away.

Something like bewilderment crossed Kirk's features before his eyes and mouth shot open, and he pointed skyward.

"I didn't say nothin' of the sort," he shouted.

Liam frowned, and even though he heard every word, he placed a hand behind his ear and tilted his head, mouthing the word *what*.

They were moving away from Kirk, so when Kirk shouted again, he didn't hear him.

Liam turned away from the cop he bullied in high school and stared at the hulking shape of the barn coming up on his right, a solitary light on out front.

It was time to lock these women down and then call the boss to find out what was going on.

He wouldn't sleep tonight without knowing what had angered Dalton. And if he was the source of that anger, he was sure Dalton would let him get the sleep he needed—for a very long time.

Chapter 4

AARON RAN BACK TO the truck stop with Willow in his arms, then set her down. Holding hands, he led her through the restaurant area, where two wait staff tried to offer them seats, looking everywhere for Sarah. Then he walked back out to the convenience store area—she was nowhere in sight.

He stopped in front of the washrooms and dropped to his knees to be at eye level with his daughter.

"Willow, honey, can you tell me everything you saw and heard?"

She glanced around them, a worried expression on her face. As strong as she was at times, with the terrible things she'd already endured in her short life, missing Sarah was the hardest for her. He noticed Willow's lower lip quivering slightly now.

She shrugged once. "There were voices. Tired and sleepy, I turned and put my face against the seat. I thought you and Mommy were arguing. Then something banged as the door shut hard, and the car shook. Or maybe something bumped into the car." She shrugged again, her little hands coming up, palms outstretched. "The doors were open, and you guys were gone. When I sat up, I saw you walking to me, so I called out your name."

"Okay, that's good, baby." He pulled her in for a hug, tapping her back lightly. After a moment, he eased back and looked into her face. "Can you do something for me?"

She nodded, chin to chest, her tiny eyes wide and staring at him.

"Can you go inside the ladies' room and see if Mommy is in there?"

"Sure, but I already know she isn't."

"Do you know where she is?"

Willow shook her head, her brown hair raising at the ends.

"Then how do you know she's not in there?"

Aaron was aware of his daughter's talents. Moving things with her mind came naturally to Willow. But her ability to see the immediate future was incredible. Even though Willow could foresee that she'd enter the bathroom and come out less than a minute later without her mother, it didn't deter Aaron from wanting her to do it still.

"I see myself coming out alone."

Aaron looked at the floor, then back up to Willow. "We've checked everywhere in this truck stop except the employee areas and the bathrooms. I really just want to check it before I call the police to tell them Sarah's gone."

"The police?" Willow echoed, understanding dawning on her face. "And we can't tell them about me, right?"

"Right."

Willow nodded. "I'll be right back, Daddy."

Like a brave version of Sarah, their daughter ran into the women's bathroom and exited twenty seconds later, shaking her head.

"You can call the police now."

Aaron forced a smile for her. She was so strong at such a young age.

He took her hand and led her out of the truck stop, across the parking lot, and back to their car, where the coffees and the Coke were still on the roof.

Sarah hadn't returned.

He checked the time, then rechecked it. She'd been gone for at least ten minutes now.

"Here, honey. Let's put you up on the hood where I can see you."

Aaron grabbed her under her arms, sat her on the car's hood, then scanned the parking lot. Nothing was out of place. It looked like a regular Saturday at any truck stop in America.

Yet there was blood in his car, a tooth on the floorboards on the passenger side, and his Sarah was gone.

She was taken by force. That much was for sure. She would not leave Willow alone in the car at a rest stop when he'd just gone in for coffee. And there was no way she'd walk out on him like that—no way. Not Sarah's style.

He glanced away from Willow to hide the tears filling his eyes.

Oh, Sarah, where are you?

He shook his head slowly to banish the thought that something terrible had happened to her. Wouldn't Vivian warn her, warn them?

Wait, didn't Vivian pop up earlier when they were talking? He couldn't recall what Sarah said about her sister's impromptu visit.

He opened the passenger door and peered inside, taking in the interior with a clear view. He knew what he was looking at, and it scared him.

That tooth had to be Sarah's unless she fought with someone and knocked their tooth out. He knew better than to touch anything in case the authorities wanted to do some forensics on the car.

A sudden heaviness overcame him, a numbness. He grabbed at the doorframe to hold himself up. They'd gone months without any shit in their lives, and now this. But what was *this* exactly?

His limbs tingled with fatigue and worry as his throat tightened. How could he find Sarah while attached to Willow? He'd have to trust the cops, which was always a gray area for them.

Aaron pushed away from the car and surveyed the parking lot one more time. He couldn't tell if it had been ten minutes or half an hour, but he had to call it in.

"You okay, Daddy?"

Willow's tone was fearful. When he looked at her, he saw her chin lowered and her eyes downcast.

"I didn't do anything wrong, did I?"

"Oh, no, honey." He moved closer and embraced her. "You're doing just fine, sweetie. I need you to stay strong, okay?"

"Hmm-mmm." Her little voice was muffled in the folds of his shirt.

He moved back to stare at her. "You know how Mommy has her sister help her occasionally?"

Willow nodded.

"Well, before we stopped here for coffee, Vivian said something to Mommy."

"Is it good or bad?"

"See, I don't know. Mommy didn't tell me. But now Mommy is gone to help someone. I think she'll be back soon, and we'll continue to Grandma and Grandpa's place soon, too, okay?"

Willow nodded again.

"But just to be safe, I'm going to let the police know that we can't find Mommy, and maybe they can recommend a hotel close by until Mommy shows up. Deal?"

"Deal." Willow pasted a smile on her face, even though her eyes bulged with tears.

"It'll be okay, honey. Vivian will help Mommy."

"It's not her I'm worried about."

"Oh?" Aaron pulled out his phone. "You know something you can tell me?"

"I'm worried about you."

Aaron stopped moving, cell phone in hand, and stared at his daughter.

"Me?" He blinked several times. "Why me?"

"Because you're a good person, and you'll do the right thing, but that'll get you in trouble."

He scoffed, then clucked his tongue to cover the sound.

"How could doing the right thing get me in trouble?"

She lifted her right shoulder to her ear in a half-shrug, then dropped it.

"I just don't like the policemen."

Aaron tightened his grip on the cell phone. "What policemen, honey? Were there policemen here earlier?"

She shook her head. "I think Mommy needs us. Please call for help."

Aaron didn't like this at all. What was Willow talking about? She couldn't recall much from when Sarah went missing, and now she's talking about bad police officers.

What other choice did Aaron have, though? He couldn't stand around the truck stop's parking lot all night waiting for Sarah to show up. He'd need local law enforcement to help if she were in trouble.

He stepped away from Willow. "I'll be right over here. Wait for me there."

Willow nodded, and Aaron dialed the emergency services number.

When a dispatcher answered, he got redirected to the police, and a man picked it up.

"You've reached Glenrock Police Department. How can I help you?"

"I think my girlfriend was kidnapped."

"Come again?"

Aaron glanced back at Willow. She was staring over at a large rig entering the gas station area.

"My girlfriend is missing, and there's blood in the car. Send someone to the truck stop off Route 25 in Glenrock."

"You're speaking with Detective Stewart Billings. I'll come myself."

Aaron told him where he was parked and hung up the phone before emotion closed off his throat.

Then he texted Parkman back home to tell him the news.

Sarah was gone.

Aaron and Willow were waiting for the police.

And they were stuck in Glenrock, Wyoming, in the middle of nowhere, losing hope by the second.

Chapter 5

LIAM FINISHED WITH THE duct tape just in time. The pretty one they picked up at the gas station was awake now, and there was a fire in her eyes that would take some time to break.

He'd pegged her right—she was a fighter.

"Now, now," he whispered close to her ear. "You'll enjoy your time with us."

Dom laughed as he yanked a piece of duct tape off the roll. He was on his knees in front of Sutton, securing her ankles to the legs of the chair.

"Women don't *enjoy* their time with you, Liam."

He chose not to chastise the idiot for repeating his name. The women wouldn't leave the barn alive, and there was no fixing stupid.

In a high-pitched voice, Liam shouted, "I'm a lover, not a fighter."

Dom stopped what he was doing and stared at him. "You know how creepy that sounds, right?"

"What?" He caressed the woman's face, and she jerked back, grunting something. He stared into her eyes while responding to Dom. "I don't beat them or torture them. My female captives are treated with respect until I'm bored."

"Yeah, but you fuck them twice a day or more."

Liam lifted his thick shoulders. "And who doesn't like sex? We know women *love* sex. They crave it. Pretending otherwise is bullshit. They moan, open their legs, and practically beg for it." He blew the woman a kiss, and she grunted a bunch of angry-sounding words at him. "So why not fuck like rabbits for a week before they die?"

Dom's phone rang as he was shaking his head. "I don't think all the girls like what you're saying. You do nasty things to their backsides, too …" His words drifted off when he saw the screen of his phone. "It's Dalton."

Liam frowned at the use of Dalton's name. He grabbed his cell phone from his back pocket. "Shit, my battery must have died." He glanced up at Dom. "Answer it."

Dom stared at Liam, his face a mask of fear. He extended the phone to Liam when it was on the fourth ring.

"Fuckin' give it to me, then." Liam snatched the phone from Dom's grip and slapped the answer button.

"It's Liam."

"Where are you?"

"The barn."

"Why aren't you picking up your phone?"

"Battery died."

There was a pause. Liam stared at Dom as that bloody woman grunted again. Now, Sutton was stirring awake.

"We might have a problem."

Kirk's words came back to Liam when he'd pulled them over in the pickup. *Dalton's pissed about something.*

"What do you need from us?"

"Come to the hotel. Conference room one."

The line died.

Liam stared down at the phone and then handed it to Dom.

"What?" Dom said, his voice strained.

"He wants to meet us at the hotel."

"When?"

"Now."

Dom turned toward the door and jogged that way.

"Hey!" Liam shouted.

Dom jumped and spun around. "What?"

"We can't leave until we're sure these two are locked down."

Dom stared at the two women for a moment, then nodded once. "They're fine."

"Go." Liam pointed at the barn door, his eyes on the straw-covered floor of the barn. "Get out of here before I smack you one upside the head. I'll be out in a second."

"What, man?" Dom's voice took on a pleading tone. "They're fine."

"I said *go!*" Liam shouted the order.

Luckily for Dom, he spun around and jogged out of the barn with the fear of invoking Liam's wrath on his face.

"Gotta do everything my fuckin' self," Liam muttered.

He checked the Sutton woman. Satisfied she was locked in tight—

even her circulation appeared to be cut off at the ankles—he moved to the new woman.

"They're going to come looking for you, pretty one." He fingered her lengthy hair, knowing he had to get to the hotel but also knowing he could take an extra couple of minutes. "You walked away from your baby girl. That douchebag husband of yours will want to know where you got to. He'll call the cops." He lowered to his haunches and checked her ankles. "But see, the cops in this town are where they are because of Mr. Dalton. And Mr. Dalton works for some rich philanthropist who wants to stay rich. They do good police work and stop speeders, but no one ever bothers Mr. Dalton or his employees, and they *never* investigate anything on Dalton's properties."

Liam pushed up to his full height when the pickup outside turned on. He touched her hair again.

"You're going to be a lot of fun later tonight." He grabbed his crotch and rubbed himself. "Oh fuck, I can almost feel that ass on me now." He hollered out a yowl, face aimed at the barn's roof.

Then he backed away from her, pointing at her face.

"Later, bitch. You and me. A date it is. Gee, thanks for asking."

He laughed at his wit, then turned and ran for the pickup.

Couldn't keep Dalton waiting much longer.

Chapter 6

AN UNMARKED POLICE CRUISER entered the truck stop parking lot, slowed, and turned in a wide arc, then stopped. After a moment's pause, the driver spun the tires on the wet pavement and raced toward Aaron.

"The police are here, honey."

Even though Willow was worried about her mother, while they waited, she had gotten sleepy and was resting her head on Aaron's shoulder while he held her.

Now, he set her down on the hood of the car as the cruiser came to a stop about ten feet from the front bumper of Aaron's car.

A tall man got out, nodded at him once, then closed his door. The man pasted on a smile, one that reminded Aaron of a man about to try to sell him a magic elixir at a carnival, and strode forward, his hand extended.

"Detective Stewart Billings."

They shook hands.

"Aaron Stevens." He winced when Billings's fingers rubbed the scabs on his knuckles.

The detective must've felt something was off because he glanced down briefly, then released Aaron's hand.

"Hey, sweetie," Billings said in a childlike voice, his head dipped while addressing Willow. "You doing okay?"

Willow nodded. "Yeah. Just want my mom back."

"We'll certainly do our best. I'm going to need to talk to Daddy for a moment. That okay with you?"

Willow kept nodding. "I'll wait here."

"Good girl."

Billings gently touched Aaron's arm and directed him toward the rear of the vehicle.

"Tell me everything you can," he said low enough so that Willow wouldn't hear. "Where are you from? Where are you headed? What happened here? That sort of stuff."

Aaron took a deep breath to collect himself, then started talking, with occasional glances at Willow, whose yawns grew more frequent.

"So you came back out with those drinks still sitting on the roof of your car to find your daughter alone?"

Aaron leaned against the back bumper, his stomach churning with every minute Sarah was gone.

"Something bad has happened, Detective. This isn't like Sarah. She'd never leave her daughter alone like that."

The detective looked over at Willow, then back to Aaron. "Not many mothers would." He pointed at the open passenger door. "Have you touched anything inside the car?"

"Yes. When I came back out, and Sarah was gone, I leaned inside to see if she was in the back seat. You'll see my handprint on the center console. When I discovered the blood, I wiped my pants here." Aaron pointed, directing the detective's eyes. "Then I opened the back door and got Willow out of there."

"Okay, let me look around." The detective stepped back and gestured toward the front of the car. "Can you wait up there with your daughter?"

"Of course."

Aaron moved to the front of the car as the detective slipped on a pair of gloves and pulled out a small flashlight. Then he leaned inside the vehicle and moved the flashlight along the dashboard, the floorboards, the seat, and the driver's side area. After waiting several minutes, he eased back out of the car and flicked off his flashlight.

Willow had lain down on her side and curled up to close her eyes while Aaron placed a hand on her shoulder to comfort her.

"Hmmm." The detective sounded indecisive. "Something doesn't add up here."

Aaron's eyebrows knitted together. High-strung with all the worries about Sarah's whereabouts, he reminded himself of what Willow had said about not liking the policemen. "What doesn't add up?"

"You pull off the highway for coffee, and after buying the drinks, you mosey on back outside to find your girlfriend gone and all this blood in the car, along with that tooth."

The detective's tone annoyed him. "Size it up any way you like, Detective, but that's what happened."

"How long does it take to buy a coffee? You're saying someone attacked your girlfriend and made off with her in under a couple of minutes?"

Aaron schooled himself to remain calm and answer the detective's questions. "More like ten minutes. Maybe longer."

"What were you doing inside for that long, or should I ask?"

"I took a piss," he said, his tone clipped now, "ordered the drinks and went to pay all within five minutes. There was a delay at the till. Two truckers were disputing their bill. A line had formed. I didn't want to upset Sarah, so I paid the discrepancy and came out here to find her gone."

The detective's eyes narrowed as he studied Aaron with his head tilted back slightly. "Didn't want to upset her." The detective moved around the open passenger door and peered over at Willow. He placed his gloved hands on his hips and studied Aaron. "Taking an extra couple of minutes would upset your girlfriend? She doesn't sound like a nice lady."

Anger rose from the pit of his stomach, making Aaron lean forward. The urge to shout at this stupid man overwhelmed him, but he was able to suppress it and lean back.

"She may have needed to use the restroom." He kept his tone even, without emotion. This wasn't an interrogation. He'd done nothing wrong. Sarah was missing, and he needed this man's help. "We didn't want to wake our daughter, so I went first."

The detective raised a finger as if to make a point. "But you said, 'she may have needed to use the restroom.' That made me think you hadn't asked her before you went inside. Did you?"

Aaron stared at him for a long moment, then shook his head. "I did not."

"Why would that be? After a long shift on the road, wouldn't that be the first question at a rest stop?"

Aaron looked away and stared at a pickup truck passing the gas station out on the road. "I was upset about something trivial. I just wanted to piss, get the coffee, then get back on the road." He turned to face the detective, a chill making his shoulders vibrate. "Sarah's a big girl. She would've spoken up if she needed to use the toilet before me."

The detective pasted on that fake smile again, but he accompanied it with a short chortle this time.

"Of course, of course. And understandably, you'd be upset to return to the car to this." He gestured at the interior of the vehicle.

"What's next?" Aaron checked on Willow—she looked asleep. Oh, to be a child again, to sleep when tired—anywhere, anytime.

"Well, for starters, I want to have this vehicle examined. Get samples of that blood—it might come from different people. Bag that tooth, as well."

Aaron nodded. "Thought so."

The detective tilted his head sideways and squinted again. "You're a CSI fan?"

Aaron shook his head and took a deep breath to calm his nerves and keep thoughts of Sarah at bay for now. "I've worked with the authorities in the past."

"You have?" The detective walked around him, stripping the gloves from his hands. "In what capacity?"

"Unofficial, if that's what you mean."

"Unofficial? How so?" He stopped by his cruiser and leaned against it.

"Sarah's gifted." He gestured at his sleeping daughter. "She is, too."

"Gifted?" This time, his chuckle sounded nervous. "How are they gifted?"

"Google Sarah Roberts. You'll see."

Detective Billings stared at Aaron longer, his eyes narrowed, then opened the front door. "I'd rather you told me your version of gifted than see what the internet says." He lifted a radio to his mouth, called an officer to respond to the site, and then set the radio down.

"Sarah can hear the other side."

"Ohhh." He smiled. "You mean like a crystal ball sort of thing?"

"And that's why we don't tell people about her. Better to just google her name. She's worked with several police departments in the past to help locate missing persons."

"Well, I think I'll just deal with a *missing* Sarah Roberts tonight and let all the psychic stuff go for now."

Aaron eyed the man to see if he was mocking him. "You're not a believer?"

Billings angled his head down, shook it back and forth, and then faced the road. "There's us, there's dirt, and there's nothing in between." He gazed at Aaron now, his face slack, emotionless. "I don't believe in much, Mr. Stevens. If there were such a thing as psychic abilities, I'd like to think they would be put to good use."

"If you were to google Sarah, you'd see that that's the case with her."

"Hmph." His radio crackled inside the car. A dispatcher said something Aaron couldn't decipher, then Billings said, "Copy that," and set the radio down. "Mr. Stevens. If your Sarah is psychic, why didn't she see what happened to her coming? Why pull into this gas station for coffee? And why allow you to park all the way in the back near these bushes? It's like she *allowed* you to do these things. I mean, if she's psychic, wouldn't she have warned you?"

Aaron glanced around them, thinking about Sarah's short visit with her sister minutes before they stopped here.

The detective cleared his throat. "Or is there something else at play?"

Aaron shot a glance at the detective, his bullshit radar spiking at the detective's tone. "What is that supposed to mean?"

The detective shrugged. "Could be she wanted to leave you. Could be she *allowed* you to park at the back of a foreign truck stop near bushes to cut herself, bleed in the car, then run."

Now, he was angry, and hiding that level of rage was too challenging even to try. "Now, why would she do that, Mr. Detective?" He knew he sounded pissed off, but this man was jumping to conclusions when Sarah needed him to search for her. "There's no way Sarah would *run* from me—ever. She'd kick my ass, tell me to get out, yell at me, or make it clear she was leaving and on what date. Sarah is no coward who would run off into the night, abandoning her child. You got it wrong, mister. All wrong."

"Really?" He glanced down at Aaron's hand, making himself self-conscious. "Then why is your hand bleeding? Punch anybody lately?"

Aaron lifted his hand to inspect it. The scab over his large knuckle had split, which he was sure had happened when he was driving earlier. "I got angry at something unrelated. Someone was trying to rip me off. I punched a brick wall to let it out." He lowered his hand. "It's totally unrelated to Sarah's disappearance."

The detective nodded. "Of course, it is. Look, let's have samples taken from your vehicle while you and your daughter accompany me to the station, where we'll take your *official* statement. Then, we can have officers scour the area in search of your girlfriend while you get some sleep. If we haven't located Sarah by morning, we'll reconvene and see what else we can do. Sound about right?"

A police cruiser stormed into the lot and raced over to their location.

Leaving an official statement was a good idea. He needed them out there looking for Sarah. Whether this detective dick didn't like Aaron, didn't believe a word of his story, or didn't believe in Sarah's abilities meant nothing to him. They'd find Sarah, or she'd break out of wherever she was and come looking for him. Glenrock was small. This wouldn't last long, and they'd be back on the road to Santa Rosa sooner rather than later.

"That works for me," he mumbled as the police officer stepped from his vehicle.

"Officer Taggart," Billings nodded toward the heavyset cop, "will take you and your daughter to the station. I'll follow along once the samples have been taken from your vehicle."

Without another word, feeling sick, they were leaving the car with Billings and not driving on into the night to some hotel somewhere, Aaron lifted his daughter and carried her toward the police car.

"Mr. Stevens," Billings called to him.

Aaron turned at the back door that the cop had opened for him.

Billings held out his hand. "The keys?"

Aaron held Willow a moment more, staring at the detective. Handing over his keys made this an official investigation. No turning back. The cops would be in possession of their vehicle until all this shit was over.

But something had happened, and there was no denying that Sarah needed help—if she was still alive—which was something he couldn't even contemplate.

His phone buzzed in his back pocket as he set Willow down in the cruiser's back seat, then rummaged for his keys. He tossed them to the detective, who caught them easily, then eased in beside Willow and closed the door gently.

Sure enough, it was Parkman. He wanted to know what was going on.

What happened? he asked.

Sarah's missing in bumfuck, Wyoming. Heading to the police station now to give my statement.

Statement? Missing? What the fuck?

Might need help.

I'll catch the next flight to Wyoming, then rent a car.

After typing the city name, Aaron added, *See you soon.*

He rested his head back and stared at the ceiling of the police car until the mumbled voices of the detective and the cop talking made him look over at them.

They eyed him, whispering to one another.

Things weren't looking good. Not good at all.

Aaron realized he could use all the help he could get.

He placed a hand over his stomach, his worry for Sarah making him physically sick.

The big cop dropped into the driver's seat a minute later, the cruiser vibrating with his bulk.

"Good evening, Mr. Stevens," the cop said. "I'm Patrol Officer Kirk Taggart, and we're going to take care of you and do our best to find your missing Sarah."

"Take care of me?"

"Yes, sir. We've got a nice hotel we can put you in for the night, courtesy of a local philanthropist, a Mr. Martin Cohen."

Cohen. There's that name again. The truckers arguing about their bill mentioned the name, as if Aaron was supposed to know it.

The cruiser got underway, leaving the truck stop.

Aaron looked back over his shoulder.

Detective Billings was leaning against the hood of his unmarked cruiser, his arms crossed, an ugly smirk on his face.

Aaron had a dark feeling in the pit of his stomach that things had gone wrong, and they would only get worse.

He turned back around in his seat and stared at his phone, praying

Sarah got away from wherever she was and called him.

That's all he needed. To end this and leave this damned place.

Something was wrong in Glenrock. Even without any psychic abilities, he could feel that much. Whatever was wrong here was about to spill into their lives.

And there was nothing he could do about it.

Nothing at all.

Chapter 7

"Park on the side, away from those lights." Liam pointed to where he wanted Dom to go.

"Why over there?" Dom sounded dejected, like he'd asked him to do some distasteful task.

"Because dipshit, I said so. And there's blood in the back of this pickup. You wouldn't want some hotel guest asking questions about the blood, now would you?"

Dom laughed. He leaned forward, held his stomach, and snickered as he pulled the truck over and parked.

"Geez," Dom said between breaths. "You're really dumb sometimes, too." He looked at Liam, the top of his head leaning on the steering wheel, a broad smile on his face. "This is a farm truck. We have cattle. There will be blood in the back from time to time." He laughed again, and Liam wanted to smash the man's teeth with his fist but refrained from doing so.

He shouldered his door open, hopped out of the pickup, and slammed the door behind him.

Dom got out the other side. When they met at the hood, he grabbed Dom's lapel and yanked upward.

"I got enough shit to deal with now that Dalton's angry about something. He called this emergency meeting, and you're making jokes, laughing at me." Liam leaned close, his nose almost touching Dom's cheek.

Dom reared back as far as possible, but Liam's grip wasn't offering much leeway.

Liam snorted. "You don't think that sort of behavior might trigger me, set me off?" With a firm shove, he pushed Dom away from him. "Sometimes, I just want to smash my fist so far down your throat I can touch your stomach." He vibrated, attempting to shed the urge to hurt the man. "Laugh and make fun of all you like. I'm trying to think out here. Dalton's angry about something. We already got enough trouble that we don't need a guest at this hotel asking about *our* pickup." He shook his head, fists clenching at his side. "Fuck, are you ever stupid sometimes."

A thick vein pulsed in Dom's pale forehead as he blinked at Liam rapidly, as if he didn't recognize the man. The laugh, the smirk, and the joy were gone. Dom had been brought back to reality. He jammed his hands up into his armpits and turned to look up at the four-story hotel.

Built and paid for by Martin Cohen, it was a great place to stay overnight when in the area. It had four floors, each with ten rooms, and there was talk that Cohen wanted to add more floors. Most people didn't understand that logic since the hotel was never full, but Liam knew why. More rooms meant more fake bookings to help Cohen launder his money.

After glancing up at all the rooms facing the road and only seeing one light on in one room on the second floor, Liam and Dom entered the Glenrock Hotel through a side door, using Liam's master key. Only a few trusted employees were given all-hours access to the hotel, and Dalton ensured one of those men was Liam.

"Are we walking into a trap?" Dom asked.

Liam snapped sideways to glare at Dom. "A trap? Why? You don't think Dalton needs us anymore?" Why did he hang around with this guy so much? Dom drove him crazy. "And what if we were? What would we do? Not go?"

Dom slowed, then stopped in the hallway. "Well, I don't want Dalton mad at me."

"And if he is?" Liam checked the time on his phone. Even though Dom hightailed it to the hotel, it felt like they had kept Dalton waiting too long. Even now, talking in the hallway was keeping Dalton waiting.

Dom shuffled from one foot to the other. "I'm not walking in there if we did something wrong."

"Let me ask you something, numbnuts." He saw that Dom was shaking now. The man's jowls vibrated slightly. "What if you don't go to meet Dalton when summoned? What happens then?"

Dom shrugged and looked away. "Don't know. He calls you on the phone, tells you what he wants?"

Liam shook his head in an exaggerated gesture. "Nope. Wrong answer. He sends a team of men over to break your legs and bring you to meet him in a wheelchair. Then he will be mad at you, too, and you wouldn't want that."

"Listen, man. I just don't want him mad at me tonight, you know."

"Did you do something to make him mad?"

Dom shook his head back and forth violently.

"Then you have nothing to worry about." Liam got moving down the corridor again. "Come or not, it's your funeral."

Dom mumbled something under his breath and ran to catch up. Liam couldn't ignore the twisting in his stomach at this unscheduled meeting and the fact that Captain Kirk Taggart knew Dalton was pissed about something before Liam knew. Wasn't *he* Dalton's right-hand man? How would dumbass Taggart know anything before Liam?

They skirted through the lobby's center, entered a long corridor, and slowed when they saw the men in black suit jackets posted outside the door to conference room one.

"Gentlemen," Liam said, moving closer, his stomach in knots now. "Dalton called us for a meeting."

The man closest to him wasn't as big as Liam, but he looked much deadlier. These guys were Cohen's mercenaries—they had to be lethal.

Did that mean Cohen was here tonight, too?

Shit!

The man jerked his head backward once while staring at Liam's arms.

It was an easy gesture to understand—time to be searched, but Liam had no idea why. This was unprecedented.

There were no niceties involved either. The man's rough hands made Liam jerk left and right to avoid getting a crushed nut.

"Hey, take it easy."

The man didn't seem to hear him as he touched Liam's shoulder and pushed him to the side. The guy's strength surprised him because Liam was well north of two hundred pounds. He'd left his preferred weapon back in the barn—the large wrench—so they'd find nothing on them tonight.

When Liam was done, he moved to the side while Dom was rough-handled.

"What's all this about?" Liam asked.

Neither man answered him.

Dom squirmed like he was under attack by an army of beetles, doing some form of dance to avoid all the touches hitting awkward places, whether Dom liked it or not.

Then it ended.

Cohen's man knocked on the door twice, twisted the knob, and opened it for them.

Liam ignored them. If they weren't going to be professional, respond to him, or act like they're on the same team, then neither would he—fuck 'em.

He moved past the man who'd frisked him, bumped his shoulder solidly, then entered the conference room.

Dalton sat at the end of the long table, conferring with his boss, Martin Cohen. Four other men were in the room, two a few feet from Cohen, standing in the far corners, and the other two on either side of the door Liam had just walked through. They were all wearing identical black suits and white earplugs, as if they were part of the Secret Service, guarding the president. Damn, Cohen had an ego the size of the planet.

What the hell is Cohen doing here at this late hour with six gorillas to guard him?

Liam moved along the extended table to take a seat close to Dalton.

Cohen glanced up, watched Liam briefly, then looked at the door. He kicked his head back once—a signal to shut the door, then waved a hand for Dom to pick a chair.

"We can seat twenty at this table. Any one will do."

Dom stared at Liam for a moment too long, like he'd made a mistake, then hastily pulled out a chair and dropped into it.

Dalton sat up straighter and cleared his throat. "We need to get this meeting underway so Mr. Cohen can go home and get some rest. He has church in the morning."

"Blessed be those who attend church regularly."

Liam nodded at him and looked sidelong at Dom. The man seemed to be getting stupider and stupider. Instead of moving closer to hear better, he sat six chairs away like he didn't belong. But the issue was Dom's face. The man looked positively guilty of something. Liam could vouch for him, but Dom was so afraid that he looked like he was about to shit himself.

"Dom," Liam said. "You can hear everything okay in that hemisphere? You don't want to move closer?"

Dom nodded in two short bursts, got up, and dropped into a chair one away from Liam.

Dalton stared at the two of them with that look the principal used to give Liam back in high school. We'll talk about this later. Or, don't embarrass me in front of my boss. Perhaps he was misreading Dalton altogether, and that look said he was in mortal danger.

When Dalton placed both hands flat on the table, Liam's nerves rattled. They weren't here to kill them. If they wanted him and Dom dead, they wouldn't bring them to the hotel to talk. No, they would've had them come to Cohen's farm. Once they were dead, their bodies chewed up by the pigs, the local authorities would file a missing persons report that was just that—filed. No one would look for them. No one would care.

This meeting was something else entirely.

"We have a problem." Dalton's tone bothered Liam, which meant it had to be freaking out Dom.

"What sort of problem?" Liam asked, his leg tapping Morse code under the table. He placed a hand on it to try to quell the nerves.

"There are rumors of a Satanic cult here in Glenrock. They're calling themselves *The Damned*."

Liam suppressed his laugh, instantly knowing how terrible it would've been had he let it rip out of his chest and mouth because Dalton was dead serious.

"A cult?" Two words. That's all he could manage at the moment. Maybe the urge to laugh came from his relief that they weren't here to discuss some stupid mistake they'd made.

"Let me handle this," Cohen said, laying his Southern accent on strong.

Dalton nodded and leaned back in his chair.

"You boys know I do a lot for this town, right?"

Liam nodded and looked at Dom, who was nodding, too. Good, maybe the idiot wasn't all stupid, just some stupid.

Cohen pushed his chair back and got to his feet, the gold around his neck dangling out over the table momentarily, then slamming back to his chest when he righted himself.

"I built this hotel." Cohen stepped behind Liam, then moved on to stop behind Dom. "I have the biggest farm operation this side of Wyoming, praise the Lord, and I fund the local libraries and schools, not to mention the churches and all we do to feed the homeless."

"Yes, sir," Liam said, then closed his lips when Dalton glared at him.

Dom squirmed in his seat like he was about to be hit on the head, but then Cohen got walking again.

When Cohen was on one of his tirades—sermons—he wasn't to be interrupted. Yet, there was something about the way the man sermonized that made Liam want to get up and clap at appropriate times —this wasn't one of those times.

"I even fund the local police department to ensure it runs smoothly. They need to be able to keep the disaffected wrongdoers out of our daily lives. Even the Good Book talks about punishment and thieves, for when the Lord's son was crucified, there were two thieves right there, crucified alongside him." Cohen had reached the end of the table by the door and circled it to come back behind Dalton. "In the New Testament, he was described as the impenitent thief. In the books of Matthew and Mark, both thieves join the crowd in mocking Jesus." Cohen raised a hand. "But in the Gospel of Luke, one taunts Jesus. The thief asks why Jesus doesn't save himself. The other thief, the penitent one, asks for mercy."

Liam was well aware that Cohen was going somewhere with this, but he had no idea where yet. Could he be saying there was a thief among them? If so, what did the thief steal? The man's wealth and influence were well-known and well-protected. Liam had no idea how anyone could steal from the man.

Cohen moved along the other side of the table, coming back around toward his chair.

"And so I say unto you men this evening, we have a thief among us, and I am to root them out and crucify them."

He stopped behind Dalton, but it didn't seem to faze the man one bit. Seconds ticked by before Cohen moved again to take his seat at the head of the table.

Liam had to suppress another urge to ask what was stolen. This was a don't-speak-until-you're-spoken-to moment if he ever saw one. But would Dom know that? He glanced at Dom quickly. The poor guy had lost all color. If Liam didn't know any better, he imagined Dom shitting his pants right there in the plush seat of conference room one.

"What did they steal would be the next question," Cohen said.

Liam nodded, happy the man continued speaking before his mouth opened and got him in trouble.

"Well, I'll tell you what they stole."

Liam waited, his breath properly bated.

"My reputation, my good name. They stole the image we portray in this wonderful, God-fearing part of Wyoming. They stole my ability to make an honest living without the likes of the IRS breathing down my neck."

If Liam wasn't mistaken, Cohen's lips were trembling now. This event evoked emotion in the man, which Liam had never seen before.

Cohen had paused to catch his breath. He placed a hand on Dalton's arm. "You carry on. Tell them the rest. I'm done."

Dalton leaned forward as Cohen's hand came off his arm. "Gentlemen, we were informed that an outside member of law enforcement will be joining us this week. They may already be here."

"Law enforcement?" Liam's nerves had started to calm, but Dalton's words shook him to the core. "Why would they come here?"

"Those rumors of a cult operating somewhere close by have summoned the authorities, and we must put a stop to it."

Liam frowned. "But there's no cult, sir. Or, at least, none we've seen. I should know. I grew up here. Captain Kirk Taggart—I mean, Patrol Officer Taggart is a high school buddy of mine. He would've told me if something like that was going on."

"Taggart isn't aware of the cult because its members post images online."

"What?" Liam adjusted himself in his chair, completely confused.

"You don't work the farm, Liam, so be quiet a moment and let me explain."

Cohen nodded to Dalton's words as if he were listening to an internal rock album in his head. Liam was sure Cohen was certifiable, but he didn't care. He had an easy job working for Dalton and rarely had to deal with or see Martin Cohen, which was his preference.

"You remember those cows that were killed last week?"

Jamie Sutton came to mind. That's why she had blood on her. He'd found her in the field, slicing up the belly of a pig like she was a deranged lunatic. Something about her mental derangement turned him on, though. What he would do to her before he killed her would be like fireworks in his ball sack.

Instead of admitting to knowing anything, he just nodded and hoped Dom would keep his mouth shut.

"Someone has been killing Mr. Cohen's cattle in some form of ritual sacrifice, taking photos, and then posting them online. They draw Satanic symbols and write out *The Damned* in the animal's blood."

Liam's face dropped, and his mouth gaped.

"No way," Dom said beside him.

Only two words, and they were the wrong two. There was no level of stupidity that Dom wouldn't go to. By saying *no way*, it implied that the information Dalton relayed to them wasn't to be believed. Liam was well aware that Dom likely meant it in *no way, I can't believe it*. However, Dom wasn't bright enough to convey his message clearly to others.

"Can the online source be traced?" Liam asked, hoping they'd let Dom's stupidity go for now.

"We tried that," Cohen said, looking up. "We've tried everything, and now we can't stop what's coming."

Liam was afraid to ask, but did anyway. "What's coming?"

"The authorities, dummy." Dalton tsked his tongue once. "They'll have questions. There'll be an investigation. They will want to look into everyone's business, including Mr. Cohen's here, and they'll want to root out this cult-like David Koresh in Texas. The last thing America wants is another Jim Jones."

"Who's that?" Dom asked, and Liam almost reached across the open space between them to choke the life out of the little bastard. Maybe when they got back to the barn before he fucked that Sutton woman, he'd do just that—strangle Dom until his eyes popped from his head.

Dalton ignored the dumb question, his eyes on Liam. "Here's what will happen going forward. You and Dom will be assigned barn duty for the next week."

"Barn duty? What's that mean?"

"It means you'll be stationed in the barn, and you don't leave for a week or until we tell you the coast is clear. Food and some alcohol will be brought to you. Think of it as a free pass, a barn vacation. Get drunk, eat all you want, and stay out of the public eye for a week."

Liam nodded once, hoping Dom would keep his mouth shut. If that fucker ruined this for him, he'd be pissed. A whole week with two bitches at his disposal, food deliveries, and beer. What a way to make a living. He'd fuck that new girl so many times she'd think she'd gone to cock heaven.

"During your time in the barn, you will be guarding the livestock, watching from the loft for anyone who may be coming onto the land to perform their rituals. If you see anyone, you'll call me, and I'll send a team of men like them"—he gestured at Cohen's four men, who stood dutifully around the room, waiting for orders—"and they will put an end to all this ritual, Satanist shit."

"Hallelujah," Cohen whispered, his head lowered.

"In the meantime, it's business as usual, and our contacts at the police department will work the new arrivals."

Liam frowned and tilted his head. "Wait, sir, didn't you say they may already be here?"

"At this point, we're not sure if that's the case, but we may have a new person in Glenrock passing as a tourist or even a local working undercover and feeding the authorities information."

"An informant," Dom whispered, his tone one of surprise.

Another nail in his coffin.

"Yes, an informant." Dalton nodded. "Which we are looking into at the moment."

"That's it, gentlemen," Cohen snapped, his hands slapping the tabletop.

The meeting was done. They were being dismissed.

Dalton pushed his chair back and got to his feet.

Liam and Dom did the same, with Dom practically running for the door.

"Remember," Dalton said. "Go right to the barn. Sleep there tonight. Do not go home. Do not stop at the truck stop, the minimart, or the liquor store. Go to the barn. Supplies are on their way."

Liam was sick all over again. What if those supplies arrived before they did? What if they found Sutton and that other woman bound in those chairs in the middle of the barn? All his fun would end in a single moment.

"And report to me directly if you see anyone near the cattle. Nobody should be on Mr. Cohen's property for the rest of the week. The word has been put out, and Glenrock doesn't have enough cops to do a stakeout, so you guys are it."

Dom was hopping from foot to foot like he needed to take a piss.

Everyone stared at him. "What is it, Dom?" Dalton asked.

"Report to you if we see someone with a knife on the farm, right?"

Dalton scrunched up his face. "So, you have been listening."

"Right. Well …" Dom glanced at Liam, and Liam knew what he wanted to say. This was a mistake of the highest magnitude. If Jamie Sutton was one of the cult members, she was already being disposed of this week. Telling Dalton and Cohen about it now could get them in trouble—dangerous trouble.

"Spit it out," Dalton boomed in his principal's authoritative voice.

"There was a woman." If Dom didn't calm down and take a couple of deep breaths, Liam was sure the man would faint, which would be a wonderful thing at the moment.

"And?" Dalton prodded.

"We found her tonight, about two hours ago, slicing into the belly of one of the pigs near the farm."

Dalton shot a stern glance at Liam. "What?" His harsh tone made goosebumps rise on Liam's arms. Even two of Cohen's men turned to glare at Liam, then Dom.

Cohen got to his feet. "Are you serious, boy?" The Southern accent disappeared. Cohen's true voice came out, hard and stern.

Dom nodded, shaking his entire upper body with the movement. He tried to smile, to act cool, but it failed miserably. The man was falling apart.

Cohen and Dalton exchanged a glance.

"Where is this woman now?" Dalton asked, facing Liam.

He had to give up Sutton now. "Tied to a chair in the barn." He'd kill Dom later in the week for this. The asshole would not escape his wrath. Not this time. "We just finished tying her up when you called us here."

"And you didn't think to mention this until now?" Dalton's voice rose with each word.

They were in some hefty bag trouble now. Dom was dead. Liam would use a farm accident to dispose of the idiot.

Liam opened his mouth to respond, but Cohen cut him off.

"Gentlemen," Cohen boomed in the room, waving his arms wide. "It appears we're going for a ride to the barn to chat with this woman."

Everyone moved toward the door, with Liam walking on wobbly legs.

Dalton grabbed his arm and yanked him back until Dalton's mouth was close to his ear. "You and I will discuss this later. I should know shit like that. You've embarrassed me in front of Cohen for the last time."

His boss's tone suggested several other things than a calm conversation.

If he survived this debacle, Dom certainly wouldn't.

It was that simple.

They exited the conference room en route to the barn and a grim future.

Chapter 8

OFFICER TAGGART WASN'T TOO talkative in the car, which was fine with Aaron. The cop parked out front of the station and took an extra moment to pull himself out of the car, tuck in his shirt flaps again, and open the back door so Aaron could exit the police cruiser.

Once they entered the small station, Taggart pointed at a row of doors. "This way, sir."

He led him to a room, opened the door, and stood back so Aaron could enter with his daughter in his arms.

"How long will this take?" Aaron asked softly so as not to disturb the little girl. "I want to get my daughter to bed in a hotel room while you guys are out looking for my girlfriend."

Taggart nodded. "It shouldn't take long. Detective Billings is on his way back now. You'll be free to go once he has your official statement." The officer tried for a calming smile, but it wasn't helping the situation.

"Here, one second." Aaron laid Willow down gently on a chair, then stood and pulled out his phone. Opening the photos application, he scrolled to a recent one of Sarah, then held it up for Taggart to see. "Do you need me to send this to a department email so you guys can print it and distribute it to your fellow officers?"

Taggart squinted, then leaned closer to the photo as if he had caught something that had drawn him in.

He blinked, reared back, then stared at Aaron as if he wasn't breathing.

"What?" Aaron lowered the phone. "You recognize her?"

The cop gasped for breath. "Uhm, no, sir. Just thought I did for a second. Look, I have work to do. Go in and sit down. I'm sure Detective Billings will be along shortly."

Taggart went to pull the door closed, but Aaron stuck a foot in front of it.

"Then tell me, what was that reaction to the photo?"

The cop stammered a moment, his fleshy cheeks jiggling like Jell-O. "Uh, she looked like someone I used to know." He lifted one shoulder. "An ex-girlfriend. Not important."

Then he shoved his way past Aaron and moved down the hallway.

Aaron eased his foot back, and the door closed on its own.

"What was that all about?" he whispered, focusing on Willow. "He acted like he knew Sarah."

But how could he? Unless he'd seen her face in the media in the past. However, that didn't make sense. Sarah hadn't been in the media in a while and likely not in the news in the Wyoming area.

The more he thought about it, the more Aaron was sure Officer Taggart knew Sarah or had seen her somewhere earlier that evening.

He sat and fumbled with his phone, texting Parkman for an update. The man had obtained a ticket and would arrive tomorrow, early afternoon.

Finally, something was going their way.

You may have stumbled onto something bad, though, Parkman texted.

Bad how?

There's some cult shit in the area. They claim to be Satanists. A group called The Damned.

Wtf?

Just hold tight. On my way ...

Aaron checked his battery and decided to stop using his phone for a bit. The charger was in his luggage in the trunk of his car, which the Glenrock Police Department had now seized.

Someone knocked lightly on the door, and then it opened. A woman in her mid-forties, dressed in business attire, poked her head in at this late hour.

"Are you a lawyer?" Aaron asked, sure he got it right. "I don't need a lawyer to give my statement."

The woman stepped all the way inside but still held the door open. "I'm with children's services. I've been asked to come and take care of your daughter while you give your statement."

Aaron swallowed a lump in his throat. "Uhm, no. That won't be necessary. Sorry to hear they wasted your time."

"Let me assure you." The woman's voice was velvety soft as she tried to console Aaron. "Your daughter will be in this building the entire time. I'll stay with her until the interview is complete. I've been led to believe it's her mother the police are now looking for." The woman gestured at Willow.

Aaron nodded, not trusting what would come out of his mouth. All they wanted was a coffee break off the highway, and now Sarah's missing, there's blood in their car, and child services wanted to take Willow from him—not happening.

"I'm sorry, sir, but there's no way we can leave your daughter in this room while you give your statement. The officer will require you to be honest about things, which isn't always the best for little ears." She scrunched up her face at those last two words. "I'm sure you understand."

He shook his head and looked down at Willow. "My daughter isn't going anywhere, especially not out of my sight. She was in the car when her mother was taken. She may know something the detectives need to hear."

"I completely understand, and that's why a different officer will speak with your daughter. The statements will need to be given on an individual basis."

Aaron shook his head. "You do what you have to do, and I'll do what I have to do."

She stared at him for a long moment. "What does that mean, exactly?"

Aaron glared back. "I entered Wyoming with my daughter and girlfriend and intend to leave Wyoming the same way. At this point, I've lost my girlfriend. I won't be letting my daughter out of my sight tonight."

The woman slipped a foot in the door and crossed her arms over her chest. "I'm afraid I'm going to have to insist."

"Well, that's nice." He smiled up at her. "You can insist all you want, but kindly do it in another part of the building."

"Teresa," a man called from the hallway. "Happy you could make it in at this hour on a Saturday night."

The door pushed open, and Detective Billings entered the room, but stopped when he saw Willow on the floor near Aaron's feet.

"You just about to take her to the other room?" he asked.

"That was the plan, Detective." Teresa stared at Aaron.

Billings glanced over at Aaron. "*Was* the plan?"

"I won't let my daughter out of my sight." Aaron moved closer to Willow.

"Mr. Stevens. We're not kidnapping your daughter, I assure you. Mrs. Baker here is legitimate. She has ID and everything. Your daughter will be in this building in her care for an hour, maybe more, and then you're off to a complimentary hotel room that we've paid for at the Glenrock Hotel." The detective rubbed his hands together lightly. "Super easy, and everyone's happy."

Aaron looked at Willow, then back up to the detective.

Teresa moved around the detective to stand over Willow. "I'm afraid I have to insist—"

"Right, we've been through that. Not happening."

"Mr. Stevens. This is a police department. What could possibly happen to your daughter?"

Aaron suppressed the urge to laugh. "Detective Billings, I have seen things go bad in police departments in my time. My daughter stays put."

Teresa leaned on the table to be closer to Aaron. "If you persist in this manner, I'll be forced to deem you an unfit parent, Mr. Stevens. Subjecting a young girl of this age to the conversation you're about to have will not go well with local judges. Do not *make* me take her from you. I assure you that your daughter will be waiting for you when the interview is over."

"*Make* you take her?" Aaron's face hardened as he rose to his feet. "I'd like to see you try." He turned to Billings. "Bring more cops. You'll need them."

Chapter 9

"YOU RIDE WITH US," Dalton called over to Liam as he was headed toward the pickup. He slowed his step, then stopped and looked at Dalton's SUV.

Cohen was getting into the rear SUV with three of his men. Dalton and two of Cohen's men were piling into a Land Rover. Weren't there six men in black suits?

"You want Dom to drive alone?"

Dalton nodded at something over Liam's shoulder. He spun around and saw the sixth member of Cohen's black-suited men jumping in the pickup truck beside Dom.

Without another word, Liam made his way to the Rover. He sat in the back beside Dalton, leaving his seatbelt off in case he needed to jump from the moving vehicle. With Dalton, he had no idea what to expect.

"How long have we had this problem?"

Liam turned to Dalton. "The cult issue?"

Dalton stared straight ahead. He didn't acknowledge Liam's question. The man didn't even blink.

"About three weeks." Liam looked out the window. They were edging out onto the highway with the pickup in the lead.

"Haven't I told you to look out for these assholes?"

"Yes, sir, you did."

"And did you?"

"Yes."

"So why am I hearing about it in front of Cohen?" Dalton turned to look at him now, anger radiating from his eyes.

"I'm sorry, sir. We had just secured the woman when you called."

"Why not tell me on the phone?"

"Because we were already coming to see you?" Liam shrugged, hoping it sounded more like the question he intended it to be.

"You know what I think?"

Liam shook his head, now sure whatever he said would come out wrong.

"I think you were going to dispose of her in your own way."

Liam frowned. "My way?"

"You're going to lie about that, too?"

"No, sir."

"Your perversions are common knowledge."

Liam fought the urge to lower the window. He would need it open if he vomited, which he was perilously close to doing. Dalton had disposed of ex-employees horrifically in the past. As long as Liam remained loyal and devoted, he had nothing to fear. But now Dom had stained his record, and he looked inferior to Dalton, less than.

They rode in silence for a mile.

When his phone rang, he jumped, drawing the eyes of one of Cohen's men.

Dalton stared at him on the second ring. "Aren't you going to answer it?"

Liam pulled out the phone. "It's only Taggart calling." He killed the volume and slipped it away. "I can call him back when we're done tonight."

"No." Dalton left no room for leeway in his tone. "Answer the phone."

Liam only paused for a moment, then pulled the phone back out and clicked the button.

"What?"

"Holy shit, dude." Taggart was gasping like he'd tried to run and couldn't get more than ten steps. "What have you done?"

Liam angled away from Dalton to peer out the window. "What do you mean by that?"

"I'm at the barn."

His body temperature dropped as his core froze over. He gripped the phone tightly to avoid dropping it. Captain Kirk was at the barn. With Jamie Sutton and that other woman, he snatched from the truck stop parking lot. How could that be? And what would Cohen and Dalton think when they showed up and saw Glenrock police on site?

"What are you doing there?" He kept his tone calm, clipped.

Taggart was still breathing hard. "You know that woman"—he gasped, swallowed—"you snatched from the truck stop."

"How would you know about that? You only saw them in the back of the pickup ..." his voice trailed off. How much could he say sitting beside Dalton?

Liam wondered if he'd survive the night now. This night had gone from bad to worse. Taggart was in the barn. He'd likely removed the duct tape from the bitch's mouth. He knows about the truck stop because that bitch told him about it.

"What you've done, Liam, is a serious crime—"

"Listen to me, Taggart. You don't know what you've gotten yourself into. Leave it be."

"What's going on?" Dalton asked from beside him.

Liam raised a finger to signal he'd only be a moment more.

"No, you listen, *Liam*." Taggart said the name with disdain. "That woman has a child! Her boyfriend is at the police station. He's giving his statement to Detective Billings as we speak. You can't kidnap mothers and do those," he was panting heavily still, "and do those *things* to them."

"What things are we talking about?"

"She told me." A breeze must've come up as it muffled Taggart's voice. "What you said you would do to them."

Liam glanced over at Dalton and stared at him when he asked Taggart his next question. "Where are you now?"

"Near the pigsty. I can't find that Sutton woman. When I untied her, she bolted out the door."

Liam panicked. Those weren't the words he wanted to hear. Now, he was surely a dead man tonight.

"Taggart," Liam shouted into the phone. "What have you done?"

"On most things, I can look the other way," he muttered. "We're old friends. I get that. But I can't let you kidnap people for your sex slave-deprived fantasies. That's not right."

"Why are they untied?" This wasn't going to land on him. No way. He wouldn't let it. They'd be at the barn in a matter of minutes, and what would they find when they got there—the Sutton woman gone?

After what Dom did by opening his mouth to Cohen and Dalton— this was literally Hell breaking loose.

First Dom, and now Taggart. He was surrounded by incompetence, and Dalton would place all the blame on him.

"When I let that mother go, she told me what you were going to do. She told me that Sutton was running from you. All that mother did was try to help. What was I supposed to do?" Was that panic he detected in Taggart's voice?

"Where is the other woman?"

"I don't know. She was waiting by the cruiser while I looked for Sutton. She's still there, I suppose."

If they were still there, he could salvage this.

"Stay where you are. I'm on my way. We can still fix this."

"I don't think so." Taggart wasn't running anymore—if what he did could be called running—as his breathing was normalizing. "I think that Sutton woman made it to the highway. I see taillights out on the road. She's gone to the wind now, my old friend."

With those final few sentences, Liam *knew* he was dead.

Dalton had killed men for less.

"Listen to me, Taggart. Hold that other woman—"

"The mother? Uh, uh, no way. I'm taking her back to the station, so her family can leave this place and be done with you."

"Listen to me," Liam shouted into the phone. Everyone in the Rover stared at him. Even the driver watched him in the mirror. "Stay where you are and keep that woman there. Do you understand?"

"You're not my boss, *Liam*. You can yell at me like we're back in school, but I'm a cop now. Those days are over—" Taggart grunted.

Something dropped hard, and a thumping sound came through the phone.

"Did you drop the phone?" Liam waited. Nothing. "Taggart? Hello?"

There was a rustling on the other end of the line. Then he heard someone breathing into the phone.

"Taggart? Is that you?"

"You picked the wrong woman to fuck with. I'm going to shut you all down, fuckhead."

The line died.

Chapter 10

"Now, Mr. Stevens." Billings placed both hands out in front of him. "Calling more officers in here won't be necessary. No one will be fighting you and taking your daughter anywhere. Teresa, let's just all calm down. Mr. Stevens has been—"

"Aaron, please. I hate the sound of Mr. Stevens."

Billings nodded. "Aaron has been through a lot tonight. His girlfriend is missing, and there's blood in his car. Understandably, he wouldn't want to be separated from his daughter."

This reminded Aaron of a Mexican standoff without the guns.

"But, Aaron, I need a formal statement, and I can't have your daughter in the room while we do that, so I have a solution."

Aaron nodded for him to continue.

"I'll take your statement in my office, which has windows for walls. No one will hear a word we say to one another, but Mrs. Baker will tend to your daughter beside the window while we're talking. She won't move from your sight the entire time. How's that for a compromise?"

Teresa stood over the sleeping form of Willow, hands on her hips. She nodded at Aaron when he glanced her way. "Works for me," she said. "Take his statement, then Aaron and his daughter can go get some rest."

"Aaron?" Billings stared at him. "Does that work?"

"I'll know when I see your office."

Billings grinned and shot out a hand toward the door. "Right this way."

Aaron collected Willow, held her close to his chest as she stirred, and then followed Billings toward the back of the police station.

As promised, his office was surrounded by windows. There were a few desks on either side of the glass that Teresa could sit at while Willow slept. And if she woke, Teresa would be there to signal Aaron, who could come and deal with her.

He placed her on a small sofa against the back wall, then followed Billings into his office without another word.

Billings closed the door and gestured at a chair. Aaron took the one closest to the window, then dragged it closer to watch the child services woman.

"You're having a hard time tonight, eh?"

Aaron snapped his head toward Billings. "Why don't you tell me what the hell is happening in your town?"

Billings stopped moving as he was about to drop into his chair behind his desk, then slowly tilted his head to look at Aaron.

"What is that supposed to mean?"

"You want the whole list?"

Billings flopped into his chair. "Sure, why not? Tell me what you think is going on in my town. I mean, seeing as you just got here and all."

Aaron ignored the man's sarcasm. He had other things on his mind at the moment. "How is Cohen involved in the Satanic cult that's rumored to be in the area?"

That struck a nerve. Detective Billings's mouth flopped open. Then he snapped it shut and glanced away. Better to hide his face than allow what was on his mind to show through.

"Where are you hearing things like that?" Billings grabbed a pen from a holder on his desk, scratched it on paper until the ink bled, and then looked back at Aaron, his expression blank.

"When I was in the truck stop, I tossed a twenty on the counter behind those two slowpokes I mentioned earlier to cover their discrepancy and my drinks. I couldn't wait any longer. One of the men saw my torn knuckles and said something like, 'Send our thanks to Cohen.' Then, when I got in Officer Taggart's cruiser, he told me the local hotel I'd be staying at was built by a philanthropist named Martin Cohen."

Billings wasn't writing anything down. The man just stared at him as he spoke.

Aaron took a quick peek at Willow. Teresa was on her phone, tapping away at something. He turned back to stare at Billings. "I texted a friend for help. He looked into Glenrock, Wyoming, and texted back that there's some Satanist cult shit going on here. And when Taggart dropped me off in that interview room, I showed him a photo of Sarah. You know, in case he wanted to distribute it around."

They stared at each other for a long moment.

"And?" Billings prodded.

"The man had seen her before. Which is impossible because we just arrived in your town hours ago."

"Is Sarah a celebrity or something?"

Aaron leaned toward the detective. "Your officer had seen her tonight. Sometime within the past two hours, Officer Taggart had seen Sarah, and he panicked when he eyeballed the photo, then bolted from the room."

"Coincidence?"

Aaron peeked at Willow again, then back to the detective. "So, how about you tell me what's going on here tonight? Where's Sarah, and why do your people have her?"

"Now hold on, Mr. Stevens." Billings held up his hands. "That's a mighty big accusation."

"Aaron. The name's Aaron."

"We got that."

"Is it?"

"Is it what?"

"Is it a mighty accusation? Or am I onto something, *Detective*?"

"You can't go around telling law enforcement that they're kidnapping people. Are you out of your mind?"

"I've done it before, and I was right. And from what I've seen tonight, something isn't adding up here."

Billings set the pen down. "Okay, *Aaron*. You've been straight with me. I think it's only fair I be straight with you."

"Please. By all means." Aaron eased back and leaned against the window, his head tilted to stare at Willow, arms crossed over his chest.

"You've been aggressive from the moment I met you. There's blood in your car, and from my trained eye, that spatter came from two different people. Your hand is mashed up, and you deliberately parked at the back of the lot when it had no more than ten cars in it. We have to look at all angles when we get a call that someone's missing or kidnapped. What do you think all that leads me to think?"

Aaron shrugged. "I don't know. That someone tried to carjack us? Sarah fought them off, but wasn't successful? Who knows?"

Billings was trying to bore a hole in him with his stare. "You don't think I'd suspect foul play?" He waited a moment, then added, "On your part?"

Aaron scoffed. "Think what you want, but you're barking up the wrong tree."

"Then convince me otherwise." Billings picked up the pen again and tapped it against the desk blotter. "You're an angry man, Aaron. You called on a station of police officers back there, ready to fight us all —"

He snapped his head to glare at Billings. "I'm a father. I would grievously hurt anyone who came between my daughter and me."

Billings laughed. "Yeah, okay. Convince a jury that a detective in the state of Wyoming, along with a child services representative, was trying to come between you and your daughter. Good luck with that one." The detective shook his head and stared down at his tapping pen. "You don't see the pattern I'm seeing, do you?" He glanced back up. "Because I'll tell you what I'm seeing. There was an angry man before me who was fighting with his girlfriend. Who knows why? Maybe you're breaking up, or maybe it's a custody thing. You're both far from home, and you told me you were heading to Sarah's parents' home in Santa Rosa. Is that the end of the road for you two? Is that why you chose Glenrock to take her out and ditch the body?"

Aaron jumped to his feet. "I've had enough of this hick town and your bullshit. I'll find Sarah myself."

"Sit down, Aaron." Billings's voice took on a seriousness Aaron hadn't detected before. "I said, sit down, or I will make you take a seat."

Aaron moved toward the door. "I don't respond well to threats, Detective Billings." He clutched the doorknob and turned back. "I'll find my own accommodations—"

Billings had a gun out, aimed at Aaron, before he could twist open the door.

From the corner of his eye, he saw Teresa on her feet, her phone gone, her hands out in front of her. She was edging closer to Willow.

"Sit down, Aaron. You're not going anywhere."

He gave his full attention to Billings with a dazed look as he took in the new situation. Aaron's posture was stiff. He eased his hands out from his sides.

"Are you going to shoot an unarmed man in your office, Detective? Hmm? How would that look? Especially after that man came in to report his missing girlfriend."

"Who are you, really? I mean, I know your name is Aaron Stevens, but what agency do you work for?" Billings lowered his arm to rest it on his desk. The gun was still pointed at Aaron's midriff.

"I own a small business in Toronto. My girlfriend is an American citizen, and her parents live—"

"I've heard all this bullshit before. When are you going to start telling me the truth?"

Aaron let his hands ease back to his sides. Teresa hadn't moved, which meant he didn't need to run from the office yet.

"What has got you confused, Detective? Why do you think I'm lying?"

"You know about Cohen, the cult problem we've been having in town. You accused a cop in this station of lying to you about seeing your girlfriend, and you're obviously a fighter of some kind. Is it UFC? Some kind of mixed martial arts?"

"You're taking some serious leaps." The adrenaline was leaking from his system now, leaving him shaking mildly, so he leaned back against the office door to hide it. "I explained how I knew that shit. I've got a text on my phone to prove the link to the cult stuff." He reached for his phone, and Billings raised his arm, the gun aiming at Aaron's face. "Take it easy. I'll leave my phone where it is." Aaron brought his hands around to the front.

Billings lowered his arm to rest on the desk again. "Martin Cohen is our savior. What those Satanists are doing is reprehensible. How that's connected to you isn't clear, but I'll find out soon enough. Now, come back and sit down so we can finish with your statement."

"Then what? I'll be free to go?"

"That depends on how well you convince me you're not lying." Billings shrugged. "How am I supposed to know Canadian laws?"

"Excuse me? What do Canadian laws have to do with this?"

"What if your girlfriend has custody, and you followed her down here to snatch your daughter back from her as she tried to get to her parents' place? When Sarah parked in the back to sleep, you know, to avoid hotels or a cash trail you could trace, you took your chance. If that's what happened, where will we find the body, Mr. Stevens? Hmm? Tell me where Sarah's body is, and this'll go a lot easier on you."

Aaron gawked at him. "You should be a writer. That imagination astounds me." He shook his head. "When you analyze the car, you'll see I've been the one driving it across the country. My luggage is in the trunk, too. Even my charger for my phone. Not to mention I have gas receipts along the way and two hotel receipts where people will either remember us or a camera picked us up together—"

"I have other theories," Billings cut in. "But I'd much rather get to the bottom of what actually happened." Billings used the barrel of the gun to point to a chair. "Take a seat, Aaron. Give me your statement. Prove to me I'm wrong about you."

Torn between wanting to leave and feeling like they were being held hostage, Aaron decided his best play was to keep speaking the truth. But what then? What would Billings do in an hour? Were they going to hold him on suspicion of some trumped-up crime? Would he waste time behind bars, hiring a lawyer to get him out, while Sarah was out there somewhere needing his help?

What was the alternative? Walk out of the building? But how? It wasn't possible at the moment. Billings made that abundantly clear.

Aaron moved back toward the chair. He stared out at Teresa. She calmly sat back down and glanced at Willow, who was still sleeping.

"Now that we're more relaxed." Billings smiled. "Let's talk—man to man. Tell me what happened. Tell me everything. Enlighten me on your suspicions of our little town and Martin Cohen, too." He set the weapon on the desk within his grasp, then leaned back in his squeaky chair and crossed his legs. "I feel by the time the sun rises, we'll have gotten to know one another quite well, Mr. Aaron Stevens."

"I assure you, Detective Billings, I won't be here that long."

Billings quirked up his right eyebrow. "You've got other plans?"

"I'll repeat my statement from beginning to end. Then I'm taking my daughter somewhere safe. Once that happens, I'll be back to find Sarah, and I will damage whoever was involved in her disappearance."

"Those are some strong words, Aaron. You sure you want to be telling an officer of the law something like that?"

"You'd only be offended or concerned if you're involved."

"Whoa, now. No need to shoot out more accusations, mister."

"Are you a father?" Aaron glanced at the man's messy desk but saw no family photos.

Billings stopped moving and narrowed his eyes at Aaron. "Why, yes. I've got two sons. They live with their mother in Casper, a half-hour away."

"Then you'd know why I'm emotional and angry right now. You'd also know that if you had nothing to do with this, if your name and reputation were clean, a statement like the one I just made wasn't an accusation. It was a promise."

"Are you insinuating that I'm involved in some way?" Billings shook his head. "Wasn't I the one who took your call at the station? When my few patrol officers were on the road and busy, wasn't I the one who drove out to talk to you myself, even though I was done for the day and about to head home?"

"As soon as I mentioned Cohen, you took a different look at me. You praised the man and suggested I was the bad guy here. What, is Cohen filling the station's coffers? Paying everyone off? Is he the local bad guy who gets a free pass because he's rich and owns the Glenrock Hotel?"

Billings clutched at his stomach as he laughed, his chest heaving. Aaron looked over at Willow. Teresa was still staring at him, waiting for the chance to steal his daughter from him.

"Wow." Billings managed to squeeze out that one word between laughs. His face had reddened, and veins bulged on his neck. "You've got some big balls. I've never met a man with bigger cojones than you, mister." A short chortle escaped him as the riotous laughing dissolved. Then he righted himself in the chair. "You were about to tell me how your girlfriend was allegedly abducted." Billings picked up the pen and scratched it against the paper again.

"Don't you guys usually record a statement? Or type it up? You're going to use a pen?"

"Look, Aaron, I've had about enough—" His phone rang, cutting him off. He glanced at the number. "Oh, this oughta be interesting. It's

Officer Kirk Taggart himself." Billings held up a finger. "One second, Aaron. Let's take this on speaker."

By the third ring, Billings punched the button on the phone. "Go ahead. You're on speaker."

When only heavy breathing came over the line, Billings looked at Aaron. Both men got to their feet.

The caller cleared their throat.

"Taggart?" Billings said, leaning toward the phone. "Is that you?"

"Taggart won't be available for a while," a woman said, her words spoken as if she had a large candy in her mouth.

"Sarah!" Aaron shouted and ran to the desk. "Oh my fuck, are you okay?"

Billings snatched his gun off the blotter and aimed it at Aaron. "Calm down," he whispered.

"Where are you?" Aaron asked, ignoring the detective and staring at the phone. "Willow and I will come to pick you up."

"Aaron, get Willow somewhere safe, then wait for me. I will join you soon."

Billings was shaking his head back and forth.

"Soon?" Aaron blurted. "Why not now? And what's wrong with your mouth? Are you eating something?"

"Got hit in the face with a wrench by some guy named Liam. Cost me a tooth. Liam will pay for that."

Aaron glared at the detective. "See, asshole? Adds up, no?"

"Detective Billings," Sarah said. "I understand you're taking Aaron's statement at the moment."

Billings frowned. "How would you know that?"

Aaron smirked. "I warned you. She *knows* things sometimes."

Billings kept his eyes on Aaron. "I was trying to take his statement, but your boyfriend is somewhat aggressive."

"You're holding a gun on me," Aaron shouted. "And I'm the aggressive one? Yeah, right!"

"Billings," Sarah's voice came through, muffled like she was now jamming the phone against her lips. "You have two little boys, correct?"

A muscle above Billings's right eye twitched as his jaw tightened. "Carry on," he said, not acknowledging Sarah's question. "What's your point?"

"If something happens to my daughter or Aaron, I'll hold you personally responsible. If you want to see your sons again, if you're not part of Cohen's bullshit, let Aaron leave town with Willow. I'll be gone by tomorrow. Aaron, take care of Willow, and see you soon. I'm about to have a meeting with Martin Cohen."

The line died.

Billings got to his feet and aimed his gun at Aaron's forehead. "I don't respond well to threats either, Mr. Stevens. I want to know who the fuck you people are. Start talking, or you'll spend the night in the hospital." He lifted his right shoulder in a half-shrug. "I don't care which."

Then he adjusted his aim and fired the weapon in the small office.

Chapter 11

Officer Taggart lay at Sarah's feet on a bed of straw.

His Taser and service pistol were in her hands now. She turned off the cop's cell phone and pocketed it. "Tell me more before they get here. Who are these people, and why was Sutton running from them?"

"I already told you. Liam does whatever he wants in this town and gets away with it because he works for Cohen. I knew the guy in high school but avoided him and stayed out of his business."

"Who does he work for again?" Sarah tongued the hole in her mouth. When she hit the nerve, her tongue retreated. Maybe Liam had a few teeth she could remove.

"Cohen, the man's name is Martin Cohen. Everybody works for Cohen." He leaned up on his elbows. "Can I get up now? My head hurts."

Sarah jerked sideways to stare at the side of the barn, where lights flashed through a crack in the wooden wall.

She pushed the officer back down with her foot. "Do you work for Cohen?"

"Not directly."

"What the fuck does that mean?"

"I'm a cop in this town, and he funds the police. So, I guess some of his money finds its way onto my paycheck, but I never see the guy, and I don't take orders from him."

"One more question." She aimed the Taser at Taggart as the vehicle out front stopped. "How many men are coming?"

Taggart exhaled a heavy sigh. "I wish I knew. Liam said he was on his way and that we could fix this."

"And by 'this,' he means me because you told him that Sutton got away."

Taggart nodded. "I guess so."

The vehicle had stopped out front, and then the engine died.

Sarah needed a plan and somewhere to hide, but ideally, she should just get out of there. But when Taggart was untying her, Vivian stopped Sarah from running with eight short words.

Leave now, and hundreds of people will die.

Once Sutton ran out of the barn with Taggart chasing her, Sarah stumbled out after the cop.

Sutton was gone toward the road, lost in the dark once she'd passed the single light at the front of the barn.

Sarah eavesdropped on Taggart's phone call, then punched him in the head hard. When he woke up, she had questions. Where was Aaron? How did he know to come and rescue them? Who was he calling?

Taggart told her that Detective Billings was interviewing Aaron at the station and that the detective was sketchy. Aaron could be in trouble.

Once Sarah got the answers she wanted, she called Billings to warn him off Aaron, but she was more worried now than before the call.

That one line Aaron had said on the phone about Billings holding a gun on him sent chills through her.

What kind of hornet's nest did they disturb in this small town in Wyoming? And why was the church so important? Vivian told her about the church, but it made no sense.

A horn honked outside.

"Captain Kirk?" a man shouted. "You in there?"

Sarah raised a finger to her lips, then whispered, "Why did he call you that? Are you a Trekkie?"

"We're coming in." The voice from outside echoed in the cavernous barn.

In the dim bulbs strung up on a wire fifteen feet above her head, she could see a ladder that led to a loft. It would only be temporary, as Liam and whoever he brought with him would find her—if that was who had arrived.

Did he have men surrounding the building right now? Did she have time to leave through the back? There were too many unknowns, making this a dangerous situation.

Taggart moved, drawing her eye back to him.

"Don't." She lifted the Taser and aimed it at his midsection.

He stopped moving. "Hey, don't forget who cut that duct tape." Taggart positioned himself in a way that he could look up at her. "I helped you escape. You don't want to hurt me."

"You're still helping me escape. I just need you a little while longer."

He stared at her, then his face slackened. "Oh, okay. I get it. I can do that."

Sarah averted her gaze to the front of the barn.

"Why does it always fall on me to handle this shit?" she muttered to Vivian. "Aaron's gonna be pissed."

The creaking noise of the door opening reverberated throughout the barn. It eased open about a foot.

"We're coming in," a man repeated.

"Who is that?" she whispered.

"Liam."

"Who's he with?"

She was in the open area of the barn with no idea what she was dealing with yet, and she'd knocked out a cop. His weapons were in her hands, and—his weapons.

Sarah glanced down at them as two men stepped inside the barn.

With a quick adjustment, she got behind Taggart, dropped to her knees, then lifted the cop's head so it could rest on her thighs.

"What are you doing?" He groaned the words.

She placed the gun barrel against his temple. "Be quiet. You're now my hostage until I get my daughter back."

"Oh, I don't know," Taggart said, looking up at her, his eyebrows raised. "That's not a really good idea for you or me."

"Who's there?" a man called.

Two men, one much taller than the other, had stepped inside. By the man's size alone, she could tell it was the Dwayne Johnson trainer guy who hit her in the face with the wrench.

She leaned down to Taggart's ear. "Is that Liam on the left?"

The cop nodded.

"Who's he with?"

"His lackey, Domenick Miller."

"These the assholes coming after Jamie Sutton?"

Taggart nodded against her thighs.

The taller man had moved toward the chairs that had recently held Sarah and Jamie. "Why'd you release them, Captain Kirk?" He scanned the barn until his eyes seemed to stop in their direction. "Is that you,

Taggart? Lying down on the job?"

"Stop where you are," Sarah said, her mouth aching when she raised her voice. "No need to come any farther."

"Okay, just take it easy." The big man raised his hands to show they were empty. Then he bumped the man beside him, who then did the same. "It was all just a misunderstanding."

"Yeah, right. Those obscenities you whispered into my ear before leaving were meant as a joke? I highly doubt that, you fucking pig."

"Now come on, what kind of man do you think I am?"

"Then explain Jamie Sutton to me. Why was she bleeding like that? Why were you chasing her?"

Liam moved a few steps closer. Now, his face was bathed in the light from a bulb directly above him, suspended from the center of the barn's roof.

"She slaughtered a few of our cattle as some twisted sacrifice. I caught her with the knife in her hand, deep in one of our pigs."

"So, call the cops. Why chase her, grab me, and tie us up in this barn? You ruined a perfectly good road trip." Well, it hadn't been all roses and sunshine, but it was better than this.

Liam moved closer. Domenick sidled up to him. Something was wrong with the smaller man. Sarah squinted in the small amount of light but couldn't read his features well enough.

Liam released a nervous giggle of sorts, glancing down at the barn floor. "You don't understand—"

"Then make me."

He looked up and glared at her. Any sign of humor was erased from his face. "Aren't you even a little worried that you're holding a gun to the head of an officer of the law?"

"I should shoot you with this cop's gun, then leave out the back. You die, and Taggart can make up a story of how you drew down on him."

"So, what, you're some gang bitch from Los Angeles or something? You just happen to be out on vacation with your kid and that little bitch of a man, getting refreshments at a gas station in Wyoming?" He scoffed and moved closer again. Now, he stood less than ten feet from them. "Come on. You're a smart lady. You see how this'll end for you.

Put the gun down and get out of here. This is your only chance."

"And if I don't?"

Domenick glanced past Sarah, then up to the loft over her shoulder.

She studied the man's face. What was he looking for?

Domenick glanced over his shoulder back at the front door they'd entered through.

He's waiting for someone. More people are here.

"You've got a kid to think about—" Liam was saying.

"You threatening my daughter now!" she shouted, then regretted it as the pain in her face throbbed along her jaw and into her head. She tongued the hole in her gums again and tasted blood.

"No, I'm saying you have a daughter to think about. Drop the gun and get out of here, or you may never leave this town."

Sarah changed positions. She placed the Taser against Taggart's scalp, then aimed the gun at Liam.

"Or I could shoot you both before you made the door, Tase this cop until he's unconscious, and leave then. Who'd be the wiser?"

"You better be a good shot. You miss, and I'll murder you slowly."

They eyed each other for a long moment while Sarah called out to Vivian.

What am I doing here?

There was no response.

So, it's like that, huh?

"Trading barbs is juvenile." She jerked the gun toward Domenick, then back to Liam. "We're wasting time. Who else is with you? Your friend there looks like he's expecting company."

Liam's meaty arm swung down fast and thumped into Domenick's chest. The smaller man stumbled backward, then dropped onto his ass.

"He's nervous as fuck. Doesn't like guns."

"Not many people do, but that's not it. You brought others. Why don't you bring them in here so I can meet them?"

Liam scowled at her from ten feet away as Domenick got back to his feet.

After seconds of staring at each other, Liam nodded slowly, the light playing tricks on his lean, muscular face, making him appear healthy, skeletal, and healthy again.

"Miss Jamie Sutton is back in my possession. I didn't want to raise the stakes, but it seems you're determined to hold my old high school buddy hostage."

"Yeah, right. Sutton got away. If you have her, prove it. Bring Jamie in here."

Without another word, Liam spun around and headed back toward the front door, with Domenick pivoting and following him.

"Domenick stays here," she shouted.

The man didn't stop walking.

Sarah fired a round into the roof.

Both men jumped and ducked, arms flailing to cover their heads as Taggart jerked away from her at the sound of the weapon going off so close to him. She pressed the Taser into his neck. "Get back in position."

Taggart moved slowly, hands near his waist, head back on her lap.

"What the fuck, lady!" Liam shouted.

Somewhere high above them, birds had fluttered from their nests.

"Why doesn't anyone take me seriously? I said, *Domenick stays here!*"

The pain in her face had moved to her head like a freight train docking in her forehead. It was tolerable for now, but she'd need painkillers soon.

Liam grunted something, and Domenick stepped back into the light in the center of the barn.

The door opened at the front, then eased shut.

Liam was back outside, and whoever came with him was getting an update.

She could only imagine where this was going and didn't want any part of it, but Vivian insisted she stay.

"You gonna let me go?" Taggart asked, his tone shivering in sync with his body.

"Of course. Just don't do anything stupid. We're almost done."

After a glance up at the loft and then behind her, she was relieved to see no one was advancing on her position.

Taggart adjusted himself and lifted his head to look down the length of his body.

"What's that smell?" Sarah asked.

"I, uh, I pissed myself."

Sure enough, a wet stain had formed in the crotch of his pants.

"Look, Taggart, don't be a hero, and don't be an asshole, and you'll get out of this unscathed. You've nothing to worry about."

He looked up at her, his big eyes pleading. "What's unscathed mean?"

"Just shut up, do what you're told, and no one will get hurt."

"I can do that."

Sarah lowered her center of gravity, adjusting herself deeper into the straw under her butt, wondering what the hell her sister had gotten her into.

Who would die tonight?

It couldn't be her, because she had to go to church tomorrow.

Vivian was firm on that.

Church tomorrow. It would be a Sunday morning. Everything will be clearer tomorrow.

Then the insanity would begin, whatever the hell that meant.

Chapter 12

LIAM SLIPPED OUTSIDE THE barn door and strode up to Cohen's men, who had gathered to wait behind the pickup.

When Taggart alerted him to Sutton getting in a car on the road, Dalton had their vehicle race ahead the last mile to see if they could find out which vehicle she'd gotten into.

Sure enough, the minivan that picked up Sutton was just easing off the shoulder when Cohen's men blocked it in.

Sutton tried to run, but in her exhausted condition, she didn't make it more than ten yards before Cohen's men captured her.

Now, everyone but Cohen and two of his black-suited security guards were stationed behind the pickup, including Sutton, who had a thick piece of tape covering her mouth.

"Who fired that shot?" Dalton said like he was barking at Liam.

"The woman holding Taggart hostage."

"A woman? Come on, man. Can't you handle a woman? What are you doing in there?" Dalton punched a fist into the open palm of his other hand. "End this. Now."

"I'm trying." Liam nodded toward Sutton. "I need her, though."

"Why's that? So this out-of-towner bitch can have two hostages? No fucking way. Sutton stays with us. Cohen needs to speak with her."

Liam faced Dalton, his patience running thin with his boss. The man simply didn't understand how things needed to be.

"Look, the woman in that barn is experienced in some way. She's ex-military or Mossad or some shit, and she means business. She's got Taggart hostage. If I go in with Sutton, it'll give me something to bargain with."

He'd broken out in a full-body sweat and hadn't noticed until stepping back outside in the cool evening breeze. After the rain from earlier, the temperature had dropped several degrees, making him shiver slightly now. Or were his nerves causing him to shake?

Dalton pulled out a Magnum and thrust it under Liam's chin. "You got us in this mess. What's stopping me from killing you and going in there to end this myself?"

His head tilted back as far as it would go, the tip of the weapon pressing hard into the underside of his mouth. He looked down at Dalton over his cheeks and tried not to shit himself in front of soldiers like Cohen's men.

"I will get us out of this mess," Liam said, enunciating each word as best he could with his mouth jammed closed.

The gun fell away, and Dalton stepped back. "Let him take the Sutton woman." He gestured to Cohen's men. "If he fucks it up, shoot Liam in the face and feed him to the pigs." Dalton glared at Liam. "No more fucking around. You're either an asset to Mr. Cohen or a liability, and Cohen has made it clear. No more liabilities."

Cohen's men released Sutton, and she dropped to the ground, whimpering something behind her taped mouth.

Stunned by what Dalton had just said, Liam stepped forward, grabbed Sutton by the arm above the elbow, and yanked her to her feet.

"One more walk into the barn, you stupid bitch, then it'll all be over." He glanced at Dalton. "I'm an asset. You'll see."

When he walked by Dalton, the man grabbed his arm in a vice grip and yanked him to a stop.

"Don't kill her or get her killed." Dalton's tone made it clear there was no room for error. "Cohen needs his time with her. Some questions need answers."

Liam stared straight ahead. All this alpha male shit was getting on his nerves. Dalton would be dead if it were Dalton and him in the ring. But because he was the big, powerful boss, Liam had to bow down and listen to his shit. Just maybe, one day, Liam would make Dalton eat his own shit for a change.

"Is that understood?" Dalton asked, inches from his ear.

Liam clenched his teeth and turned to face Dalton, who eased back some. Maybe Dalton saw the madness in Liam's eyes for the first time and knew to stop poking the bear that could kill and eat him.

"Understood," was all he said.

Dalton's hand dropped away, and Liam dragged the Sutton woman toward the barn door.

Chapter 13

AARON JUMPED BACK FROM the sound of the detective's gun so hard that he bumped into the glass wall and dropped to his knees. He scoured his body, searched for the gunshot wound, and saw where a small bullet hole had punctured the brown wall near the floor.

That bullet missed Aaron's shin by nothing more than mere inches.

He snapped his head up to look into Detective Billings's angry, bulging eyes. The detective had come around from behind his desk and now stood over Aaron.

"The next bullet breaks flesh if you so much as breathe."

Aaron raised his hands, his stomach doing backflips at how dangerously close he came to being shot.

He missed Benjamin so much at that moment. If he were there, he would've made some quip about how bullets always miss Aaron but never him. If Benjamin had been standing there, he would've gone on and on about being shot. There was no way that bullet would've missed his friend.

Billings moved closer and gestured with the gun for Aaron to stand up.

That was a mistake. Aaron only needed to be a few feet closer to disarm the man and break a few bones.

Aaron slowly pushed upward. "Take it easy, Detective." His gaze moved from the gun to Billings, then back to the gun. "We can figure this out."

"There's nothing to figure out. That girlfriend of yours attacked a cop and stole his phone." He gestured wildly with the gun as he talked. "Who knows what she did to the man? Come to think of it, who knows what happened in your car? I look forward to getting the blood samples back in a few weeks. Or maybe it'll take a month."

"And in the meantime?" Aaron had to keep him talking. He needed the man slightly closer—just a smidgen more.

"In the meantime, you'll be my guest in our lovely holding cell."

Billings moved until he was in the correct position. Aaron glanced over to ensure Willow wasn't watching and saw she wasn't there. He turned further. Teresa, the child services woman, was gone, too.

Footsteps pounded the floor as several people ran toward them.

In a fit of rage, Aaron snapped his hands out in a precise move. One hand smacked the gun to the left as he jerked his upper body to the right. The weapon fired, and the sound of the small projectile buzzed past his left ear.

Glass shattered behind Aaron in a violent cascade of noise.

Then Billings's gun hand was twisted upward, pressure mounting on his wrist to the point where it was about to break.

The man shouted in pain as his knees buckled in front of Aaron. The gun snapped out of the detective's grip at the exact moment the office door burst open.

Aaron caught the gun in midair, even though he'd jolted at the sudden movement of the door smashing open. The door flew around in a wide arc and bumped the wall, making him release his grip on Billings out of reflex.

Aaron shot his knee forward into Billings's face to get the detective out of his way, then spun around to defend himself from whatever was coming at him.

The men running toward the office had stepped inside, but Aaron couldn't hear them too well as his ears were still ringing from the gun going off so near his face.

He blinked several times to get the sweat out of his eyes as he raised Billings's gun.

Two uniformed officers were staring him down. A tall, skinny cop with greasy-looking hair dropped to help Billings, and the other cop, a blond, mustachioed older cop, had drawn his sidearm on Aaron.

"Drop it," the mustache man shouted at him.

Aaron saw the man's mouth move and heard the words, but it sounded like he was on the other side of a warehouse rather than the other side of an office.

"You drop it," Aaron shouted back.

The other uniformed officer had helped Billings to lean against the wall. The detective's nose was gushing blood from where Aaron's knee connected with it. He had his head back, but the blood kept flowing over Billings's mouth and down his neck into his shirt.

Mustache Cop was shouting something again, even stepping closer, but Aaron couldn't tell what he was saying.

This wasn't good at all. Willow was gone. He was in a police station with a cop pointing a weapon at him. Sarah was somewhere in town getting into her own trouble. Weren't they on the highway hours ago, minding their own business?

How was this supposed to end? With one of them dead? Or both of them dead?

The tall, skinny cop unclipped his pistol and pulled it out at arm's length to aim at Aaron. The officers moved apart, Skinny to Aaron's left, Mustache to his right, keeping several feet back from Aaron.

The ringing in his ears was subsiding slowly. He could hear them shouting better.

"Drop the weapon. Last chance."

An alarm was going off somewhere in the building. Aaron glanced over at the broken window, looked past it toward the front of the building, and considered firing the gun and making a run for it. He could find Willow and leave Glenrock. Find a place to hide. Vivian could tell Sarah where to find him.

But could he escape without getting shot while two trained officers pointed their weapons at him? And if he were lucky enough to get out of the building without anyone getting shot, the resulting manhunt would never end.

There was no win here.

Billings had backed him into a corner, one he couldn't crawl out of at the moment.

"The detective was trying to kill me," Aaron shouted, then nodded at the bullet hole in the wall. "He shot at me, so I disarmed him."

"Fine," Mustache said. "Then lower the weapon."

Aaron flipped the gun upward and extended his hands.

It was over.

Both officers lunged at him, snatched the gun from his grip, and shoved him to the ground.

A heavy weight dropped onto his back, knocking the wind out of him. He tried to protest, but he couldn't catch his breath.

Then the weight dropped again, and it felt like something broke—

his ribs, maybe. The pain in his back told him something had given way.

Sure, he stole a detective's gun and aimed it in self-defense, but was that enough to kill him?

He tried to turn over but couldn't.

Something large caught his eye as it swung down and collided with his face.

Just before it struck him, he recognized the side of Billings's desk. The assholes had upended the entire desk and dropped it on his head.

Then, the lights went out for Aaron.

Chapter 14

THE BARN DOOR OPENED. Liam was back, and he wasn't alone. This time, he was supporting someone who didn't seem to have the use of their hands.

Sarah lowered her head and stared, squinting into the dark to get a better look. Liam dragged Jamie Sutton into the light a second later, then released her.

So they did nab her again.

The woman dropped to the barn floor and stayed there, a low moan escaping her lips.

Something primal rose within her to hurt Liam, to hurt him badly. She suppressed the urge—for now.

"That wasn't very nice," she said loud enough for Liam to hear. "Didn't your mother teach you how to treat women? Or were you fucking her, too?"

Liam jumped forward several steps, his face twisted up in rage.

Sarah raised the weapon, and the fool stopped. "You're only about eight feet away. You don't want to try your luck? Maybe I miss, maybe I don't."

Liam flexed his chest, his arms moving outward as he took a deep breath. Then his face softened, and he eased back beside Domenick.

"Do not mention my mother again." He spoke through his teeth. "Or I'll yank out your eyes and fuck your skull before killing you."

"You wanna fuck my brains out, is that it? So romantic for a piece of human garbage like you." She shook her head as she lowered her gun arm. "Where do people like you come from? I guess some people didn't evolve from the Paleolithic era."

"Are we going to trade insults all day or get this over with?"

"I'd prefer if you both walked out of here and left Sutton and me alone with Taggart, but that's not going to happen, is it?"

Liam shook his head. "Release Taggart, give me the gun, and we'll avoid the sexual violence and just go straight to violence. That's about all I can offer you."

She looked from Domenick to Liam, then back to Domenick.

"I have to decide which one of you I'm going to kill."

Domenick uttered a short whine, which was cut off by Liam smacking him.

"Shut up." Liam growled the words. "She's bluffing."

"What?" Domenick seemed to have trouble staying on his feet. "How would you know?"

"Because if she were going to shoot one of us, she'd have done it already. This little lady isn't a murderer." Liam took a step closer, a half-grin on his face. "I don't think she can even pull the trigger when it's aimed at someone." He took another step forward. "She's afraid and in way over her head, so she's playing tough. I've seen bitches like that before."

Sutton moaned on the floor, turning to her side and rolling away from the light.

Sarah adjusted herself under the cop's head. "Wow, you are so fucking stupid, Liam. It amazes me."

The man was no more than five feet away now.

Taggart stirred. "Liam, don't." Taggart forced the words out of his tightened lips.

"People get shot all the time." Liam's grin widened. "They survive." He moved to four feet away. Sarah raised the weapon. "Maybe I'll take my chance."

Sarah smiled back at him. She wouldn't miss at this range. "Please, just one more step." She used a soft, pleading tone. "One bullet to the groin is all I need before killing you with one to the brain."

Liam stopped moving, his smile evaporating. "This bravado you're portraying is ridiculous." Liam horked up a wad of saliva and spat on the floor. "What do you expect to gain here today? You won't make it out of this town alive, little girl. You messed with the wrong people." He tilted his head back. "You shoot me, and more will come. You shoot them, even more will come—"

"And I'll keep killing the bad guys until they're all dead, just like cops and robbers when I was a kid. You ever play that?" Sarah shook her head. "Probably not for long. You'd be the bad guy and die first." Now, she smirked at him. "But you're right. Enough of this. Time for you to leave."

Liam glanced down at Taggart. "C'mon, Captain Kirk. Get up. The lady wants us to leave."

Taggart adjusted himself to get up, but Sarah lowered her elbows onto his shoulders and forced him to stay put.

"Taggart remains here with me a little longer. You, on the other hand, are useless to me. So leave and take Domenick with you before I shoot you both out of boredom."

Domenick backed away a few steps while Liam glared at her.

"What, you think this ends here?"

"C'mon, Liam," Domenick pleaded. "Don't push her."

"Shut up!" Liam shouted.

Taggart jerked under her at Liam's booming voice.

Sarah squinted at Liam, adjusting her aim. "You best listen to your friend. I owe you for a missing tooth, and I might want that payment before you leave."

Liam nodded as if he were going to give in and just leave. He backed up a few steps, then turned and walked toward Sutton.

Sarah saw the distinctive bulge in the back of his pants where a gun was concealed, but didn't think he'd be stupid enough to pull it out while a weapon was trained on him.

He got to Sutton, grabbed her feet, and dragged her into the light.

"You want us to leave?" Liam shouted. "I own this town. I tell Taggart what to do and when to do it. Since I was a kid, this has been my town, and it's still my town. There's only one person I look up to, so I do as he says, and that's not you, you stupid bitch." Liam yanked out his weapon and aimed it at Sutton.

Sarah raised her gun and aimed it at Liam's chest. "You die if you pull that trigger."

Liam stared at Sarah, a pained expression on his face, a pleading in his eyes. He held Sutton by one arm, her head lulled to the side, the gun pressing hard at her cheekbone.

"I sure wish we could've worked something out."

A gun went off, and Sarah screamed.

She pulled the trigger twice, then blinked rapidly in the aftermath.

Both of her bullets had entered Liam's chest, the small puncture holes easy to see from where Sarah hunkered a short distance from him.

But those weren't the shots that killed Liam.

There was a large exit wound in the center of his forehead.

Someone had shot Liam from behind.

The big man dropped to his knees, his eyes wide and unseeing, then he fell forward onto his face, his gun having never fired a shot.

Jamie had shouted behind her mask of tape and arched her body to crawl-roll away from the dead man.

Officer Taggart had moved away from Sarah. Exposed and in the open on the barn floor, the ladder to the loft behind her, she took a moment to glance around and see who shot Liam.

Domenick was gone. He either ran for the door and was outside now, or he was hiding in the shadows in one of the corners of the barn.

A single man stood silhouetted to the left of the door at the front, staring in her direction.

Sarah eased backward, watching the man. He didn't make a move. He just stood there. The silhouette was bigger than Domenick and more confident, too, but she couldn't see his face or where he was staring.

By the time she reached the ladder, the man still hadn't moved.

A moment later, two more men slipped inside the barn and moved off to the side shadows.

Sarah ducked down to make herself harder to see.

Then, two more men slipped inside.

Where the hell are they all coming from? Were they with Liam or coming to save Sarah and Sutton? Wait—if they were with Liam, why did they kill him?

Something in her gut told her not to trust anyone at the moment. She couldn't let them see her until she found out whose side these newcomers were on.

She tucked the Taser and the gun away in her beltline, then crawled toward the ladder.

She heard Officer Taggart speaking while climbing the backside, so the wooden ladder would mostly cover her movements in the semi-dark this far back.

She stopped near the top of the ladder and stared out at the barn.

Taggart was speaking with the man who was still standing by the door, unmoving. The man jerked his arm once, and Officer Taggart stumbled out the barn door.

Was that Martin Cohen?

On the last rung from the top, Sarah watched as two men stepped near the glow from the light bulb and helped Sutton to her feet. Then they escorted her toward the door, her feet dragging most of the way.

Movement to her left caught her eye.

The others were still looking for her.

She swung around the ladder as quietly as possible, pulled herself up onto the loft's floor, then rolled onto a bed of hay and stopped.

Someone's phone rang.

A man spoke in low tones while Sarah's heart pounded in her ears.

She needed to leave the barn and the area to find Aaron and wait for Vivian to tell her more.

"Sarah," a man shouted from below. "Hide and seek is over. Come on out, little girl, and have a chat with us."

She got up and stayed low, moving toward the square window on the side wall where the moon was lighting up some hay. They'd come up the ladder and check the loft soon, and she couldn't be there when they did.

"Sarah," the man shouted again. "It's over. We've got Aaron and Willow."

She stopped, her hand on the edge of the window. A sentence like that almost made her turn back and walk up to the man. Then she'd fire a bullet into his brain.

But how would that help anything?

Her freedom allowed her to work on getting them back, and her freedom guaranteed they wouldn't harm her small family—at least until they nabbed her—which she couldn't allow to happen.

Outside the window was a fifteen-foot drop to the ground.

She glanced back over her shoulder. The loft was empty. They hadn't come up the ladder yet.

She grabbed several armfuls of hay and dropped them out the window. If it drew attention outside, there was nothing she could do about it, but it looked like all of Liam's friends—if she could call them friends—were inside the barn at the moment.

She'd piled a small batch of hay directly below the window when she heard someone climbing the ladder.

There wasn't enough time to stand in the window and assess where to land. The man's head would pop over the edge of the loft at any second.

Sarah moved to the side of the window, keeping to the shadows.

When she glanced back, the man's head was on a swivel, moving left and right, stopping on nothing in the loft.

He hadn't seen her.

He climbed the rest of the way, stood to his full height beside the ladder, and flicked on a small penlight.

Shit! Did they bring lights with them?

Moving ever so slowly to avoid crinkling any straw, she eased Taggart's gun out of her belt and brought it around to rest on her bent-up knees, her back still against the barn wall.

When the man made a pass to his left with the light, Sarah caught the edge of steel in his hand. He was armed and ready to shoot her.

What the hell were these guys up to that Jamie Sutton was so important to them? They murdered Liam to keep her alive because it looked to Sarah that Liam was about to shoot Sutton. It mystified her that a team of soldiers or mercenaries was operating in small-town Wyoming. What the hell was going on? Maybe they were a local militia group or something.

The man moved forward, the light coming with him.

When it shone on Sarah's feet, he stopped.

"How about a game of hide and go fuck yourself?" She fired from ten feet away, clipping the man's shoulder at the exact moment his weapon fired.

His bullet thunked into the wood beside her head, making her cringe and collapse into a flat position.

When she brought the gun up again, the man stumbled once, dropped to his buttocks, then rolled over the edge of the loft.

A soft thud confirmed he'd hit the barn floor below.

Men uttered quick orders to one another below her. A weapon fired, then another. Disturbed hay burst skyward five feet to her left, then two feet to her right.

They were randomly shooting up into the loft floor.

Sarah jammed the gun back in her belt, climbed onto the window's ledge, eyed the small bump of hay she'd made on the ground, then pushed off the ledge and out into the open air as multiple weapons fired behind her.

Chapter 15

FBI SPECIAL AGENT ANDREW Newman returned to his hotel room window and stared at the parking lot again. He checked the time. It was after midnight, and there hadn't been much activity since he'd arrived and checked in.

Earlier, a pickup truck had pulled in, and two guys got out, with one looking up at his window before they walked around to the side of the hotel. Shortly after that, three vehicles left, and there'd been nothing since.

What worried him was that Agent Jamie Sutton, his former partner, hadn't shown up at their meeting point. Did he get it wrong? Was he at the wrong restaurant?

They'd agreed to meet at the roadside café and truck stop for dinner so she could brief him on her findings. Sutton had worked only a few cases since graduating from Quantico when she'd mistakenly shot someone.

She had been suspended with pay until the investigation was concluded and had chosen to go home to Douglas, Wyoming, to stay with her mother.

Two weeks in, she had called him to report that Douglas had a drug problem.

"Isn't there a drug problem everywhere nowadays?" he'd asked.

"Not like this. It's available on every street corner in Douglas, Glenrock, and Casper, and the cops are turning a blind eye."

Andrew knitted his brows. "You saw this with your own eyes?"

"I did."

"Then it's not so much a drug problem, it's a cop problem, and it's certainly not an FBI problem."

"But it goes much deeper than that."

"How so?"

Agent Sutton had seen drug deals going down in the open. No one was doing a thing about it. When she witnessed a cruiser in the area, she hung around to watch the bust—but that didn't happen.

When the cop eased by the dealer, they nodded at one another.

Currently suspended from the FBI, she had little recourse, so she called it in and was told someone would look into it.

Weeks passed before she got a call back that agents had gone to Douglas, Glenrock, and even Casper, Wyoming, but had found no wrongdoing.

So she'd called Newman, who was working a case in Nevada. He'd promised to see her as soon as his current case was wrapped up and take a look himself. In the meantime, he warned her to stay out of the way.

"You're currently on suspension, Sutton—"

"*Agent* Sutton. They'll see it was a righteous shooting."

"Fair enough, but while suspended, if they catch wind that you're actively working a case, that shitstorm might not be one you can survive."

"Look, all I want—"

"Let me finish," Andrew cut in. "Leave this alone. Wait for me to come up, spend a couple of days. Show me what you saw. I'll report it and get an investigation on the books."

There was silence on the other end of the line.

Andrew waited, but Sutton didn't respond. "Does that work?"

"That works."

"You'll leave it alone for a while?"

"I'll leave it alone."

They had hung up with that agreed to, and then Andrew read about some Satanic cult sacrificing cattle in the area and called Sutton back. Sutton's mother said it took him a week to reach her—she was always out somewhere—but the woman wasn't too forthcoming.

"Any idea where that Satanic shit is coming from?" he asked Agent Sutton when he got her on the phone.

"Probably some punks were getting high and having fun, I suspect."

"Sutton, I need you to be frank with me. What's happening in Glenrock?"

"Agent Newman, I don't know. My mother lives in Douglas, a twenty-five-minute drive from Glenrock. And we agreed I'd stay out of it."

Her tone when she said his title told him everything he needed to know about her current state of mind. She was angry with her suspended status and angry with him for not using her title.

"Okay, *Agent* Sutton." He enunciated it heavily on purpose. "I'll be there in a week. Where do you want to meet?"

She told him about the truck stop, picked the night and time, and said she had video coverage and evidence to go after several cops and one particular man, Detective Billings, but wouldn't give Newman anything more over the phone.

"Lay low until I get there. We talked about this. You are *not* working a case at the moment."

"Understood, *boss*."

Sutton refused to lose her attitude toward the one person in the agency willing to listen to her. Yet, that was what he loved about her—that independent streak, that spark, her fire. If she could lie low until the investigation into her incident was completed, she could come back and be a valuable agent with the bureau.

Agent Newman had arrived early in the afternoon, rented a room on the second floor of the Glenrock Hotel, and then went for dinner at the roadside truck stop.

And Agent Sutton did not show up.

He moved across the room, set his glass of rum on the bedside table, rechecked his cell phone, then turned off the light and stared at the ceiling in the dark.

"What have you gotten yourself mixed up in, Sutton?" He closed his eyes, then opened them. "Where are you now?"

He closed his eyes, the rum convincing him it was time to sleep.

He'd stop by the local police station in the morning and formally introduce himself. Maybe he'd get to meet that detective Sutton had mentioned in one of their conversations so that he could size up the man.

Then, he'd visit her mother in Douglas to see if she knew Sutton's location.

He'd find her, he'd look into what she discovered, then he'd go back to work in the Nevada field office, and she'd follow him in another month.

Unless she was on to something that he can't ignore.

If that were the case, he'd bring the entire force of the FBI down on this area and squash any rogue cops who got in the way like cockroaches on a kitchen countertop.

One of his last thoughts before sleep took him was those two guys in that pickup from earlier in the night.

Why pull up and go to a side door? Why not enter the building through the lobby as everyone else does?

He committed their faces to memory but wished he'd taken a photo.

Newman turned to the side and curled up, his final thought a prayer that Sutton was alive and not dead in a ditch somewhere.

Sometimes, an agent saw something they couldn't leave alone. And if this area was rife with drugs, bad cops, and a Satanic cult, she could be dead by now.

He certainly hoped not.

Chapter 16

THE WORLD WAS PAIN. His head, back, and chest all ached from trauma.

He hadn't gone through this much pain since the time he was shot many years ago in Greece. That was before he'd met Sarah, when he had gone after the asshole who killed his sister.

He tried to open his eyes, but the light was too bright. Pain flared in his head until he was moaning.

"The asshole is waking up," a man said.

Then it all came back to him. The detective was shooting at him, and the two cops were rushing him inside the detective's office. He surrendered Billings's gun and was jumped. Something heavy landed on his back and face—the desk, it was the desk, completely upturned onto him.

"What the fuck," he muttered.

When he went to lift his hand to his face, the sound of metallic handcuffs clinked. He checked his left arm. They'd handcuffed him to a bench or table. Even his ankles were cuffed.

When his eyes fluttered open, he had a moment where he could see out of his left eye, but something blocked his right. Was it swollen shut? Is that why there was so much pain?

He was in a drab jail cell; the walls were painted a dull gray.

"What?" He tried to form a sentence but wasn't sure what he wanted to say yet. "Where am I?"

"You're in jail, dickhead," the man said. "Better get used to it. You'll be here for a long time."

"My daughter?"

"With child services. They'll put her in a foster home for now, which will be confidential until Teresa can get in front of a judge on Monday. Once they hear what you did, I doubt you'll see your daughter again for some time, fucking asswipe."

Injured as he was, the fear for Willow, the injustice of what had happened, made him try to sit up again. With his limbs cuffed as they were, he didn't get far.

But that wasn't it. A pain shot through his back like he had a broken bone, and a jagged piece was cutting into the meat surrounding it.

He moaned in pain until he settled back, and the pain subsided off the white-hot scale.

"What charges?" he said in a breathy whisper. "I came in here to report my girlfriend missing."

The man laughed, a full-throated chortle. "'Report your girlfriend,'" he repeated, then laughed again. "That's a good one."

After several moments, Aaron heard the man moving closer.

"Detective Billings went to the hospital last night with a broken nose and a fractured wrist. You stole his weapon and aimed it at my colleague and me. When you're ready to be arraigned, you will be brought up on charges that'll see you in our jail system for years to come. Since you're a Canadian, the flight risk will keep you right here awaiting trial in about a year. Hope you heal fast, idiot." The man moved away again. The distinctive sound of the cell door closing and then locking was easy to recognize. "Because once you're healed, your ass will take a bruising in our prison system. I have a few friends on the inside who owe me favors. Nobody pulls a weapon on us and gets away with it."

There was no use in responding to the man's threats. His thoughts remained focused on Willow, hoping she was okay wherever she was. They'd beaten him and abducted his daughter, and now that she was in the system, getting her back would prove nearly impossible—at least in the short term.

The tears that came to his eyes stung as the salty liquid rolled over his wounds.

How the hell would he get out of here? He needed a hospital, too. Someone had to tend to his wounds.

And where was Sarah?

All he could bet on was Parkman, who promised to arrive that afternoon.

Parkman would raise hell to get him out and to get Willow back.

They'd find Sarah, end this, leave Glenrock, and never return.

At least, he hoped it would be that easy.

He tried to lift his right arm to tend to an itch on his cheek, but it didn't move more than a few inches.

Maybe it wouldn't be that easy after all.

Chapter 17

SARAH BRUSHED OFF THE branches she'd slept under and sat up. A garbage truck backing up with its alarm blaring woke her, and now it was pulling out after emptying the bins at the back of the Glenrock Recreation Center.

She stretched and yawned, then glanced up at the clear sky. It was at least seven in the morning, and she needed a shower.

Early fitness buffs were already parking and assembling by the recreation center's front doors. Sarah had found a spot where she could see the front parking area, but stayed hidden by bushes. This allowed her to watch for pickups—like the one she was in last night—and cops.

Going after Officer Taggart like that would have her name on some wanted list now. Aaron was in trouble with a detective in town, and she had no idea what was happening with Willow.

How could their lives get so fucked up in less than twenty-four hours? And what kind of life was this exposing Willow to?

The purpose of their trip was to get away, heal from Benjamin's loss, stop listening to Vivian for six months to a year, and just live—no more bad guys, no more guns. Aaron had been adamant about it, and Sarah agreed it would be for the best.

Spending a few weeks in Santa Rosa with her parents was suggested as a way to heal their personal wounds. Barring that, they'd take a break from each other. Something was fundamentally wrong with their chemistry, and neither one of them could figure it out—or they were too close to whatever it was and, therefore, blind to it.

Yet, they didn't get that far because, in Glenrock, Wyoming, their little family was pulled into something dangerous and was now torn apart.

"If you don't tell me my next move, Vivian, I'll have no idea how to fix this. Haven't you seen how much trouble we're in with the law around these parts?"

Her sister's answer was simply to *go to church.*

Sarah tongued the hole in her gums and found it wasn't as sensitive this morning. Her face was sore, but she was feeling better. That old saying, *you should see the other guy* was apt here—Liam was dead. Shot in the head in front of her by his own people.

She'd take it if the worst she got was a missing tooth. And she was grateful when she jumped from the loft window last night that nothing had broken or gotten twisted.

She'd made it to the bushes rimming the property before they caught on to her escape and came around the barn in pursuit. On the run for the next two hours, she stayed in the trees until somewhere around four in the morning. Then she came out on a small road called Cedar Street.

There was a church on Cedar, followed by the police station, so she turned left and found the recreation center—whose doors were just opening.

Perfect time for a shower before church.

Why she was supposed to attend a place of worship to get out of this mess boggled her mind, but Vivian was adamant, so she'd do it.

After a pat-down to remove errant twigs and grass, she tied up her hair, wiped her face, and strode toward the recreation center's now-open doors.

Once she paid a small fee—luckily, she had a few twenties in her pocket as she rarely, if ever, carried a purse—Sarah entered the women's change room, disrobed in private to avoid anyone seeing Taggart's weapon, and got into the shower. After scrubbing, she examined her clothes and washed two sections of her pants in the bathroom sink, where she found a small amount of blood. She then got dressed in the same clothes—not comfortable at all, but it would have to do for today.

She made her way back outside and stopped at a large plaque commemorating the man who donated and paid for the recreation center.

It spoke highly of Martin Cohen and his generous ways over the past decade. According to the plaque, the man was a legend around these parts. His family had a history, as they'd farmed the local lands for almost a hundred years. There was a flattering photo of the man, a wide grin exposing a few white teeth.

She wondered what he would think of Glenrock now, with people like Liam, that crooked Detective Billings Taggart told her about, and the man who shot Liam still out there.

The street was void of traffic at this early hour on a Sunday morning. Did that Cohen man own this whole town? Was she on Cohen's farmland last night?

Shaking her head at it all, she jumped off the front steps and headed toward the road.

Eyes forward, watching for police cars, she let her wet hair fall close like a curtain, covering most of her face from each side.

She would have to stop at a thrift shop after church and get a change of clothes.

She turned right on Cedar Street and continued until the Glenrock Community Church appeared on her right.

The area had dozens of cars as the locals arrived at church this morning. Most people were dressed in their Sunday best, which meant Sarah would stand out in her jeans and dirty T-shirt like a vagrant at an opera house.

So, she passed the church and kept walking along Cedar until the end, where she lingered by a tree and waited until services began.

Half an hour later, after whispering a prayer for Willow and Aaron —whether God or her sister was listening, she hoped one of them would intervene—she made her way back up the sidewalk toward the church.

The early morning sun beat down, warming her and drying out the wet spots on her pants. More comfortable in yesterday's clothes, she climbed the steps and wondered if this was a mistake. What if off-duty cops were inside and spotted her? If they had done a little research on Aaron, her face would have popped up online. Half the town could have been given her picture by now, and she was about to be arrested.

But Vivian said this was the plan, so if that became the result, then so be it. They'd figure it all out and survive this—she hoped. They'd survived much worse in the past.

The front doors were wide open as she eased into the shadows of the church. Without taking a seat on one of the pews, Sarah moved to the right and leaned against the wall near an exit sign. A few people met her gaze and nodded. They had no idea who she was and didn't question it. So far, so good.

Once she surveyed the crowd, she estimated about fifty to sixty people were in attendance, with room for everyone. Only a couple of young men, who were volunteers of some sort, were helping to seat people.

One of those men eased the front doors closed, and the din quieted down.

Church was about to begin.

A door at the front of the nave cracked open, and a man stepped onto the vast stage.

Sarah squinted to get a better look at him.

Really?

It was the man from the plaque at the recreation center.

Mr. Martin Cohen himself.

He was their local preacher, too? The rich philanthropist? Or was he taking the stage to introduce the preacher after he did some self-aggrandization? As their local rich guy, his ego was probably the size of Saturn, and these people were its many moons merely floating around him.

"Good morning," he muttered into the microphone at the dais. "I'd like to discuss the criminal element in our society today."

There was a soft gasp that rolled through the crowd like a wave.

Cohen carried himself confidently, staring at the people like they were his children. If she gave the man any credit, he actually looked like he was made for the pulpit.

"When Jesus was nearing his end, the rulers, the soldiers, and even the thief on the cross taunted him. Now, we know that as the Son of God, he had the power to get off that cross. It wasn't the Roman soldiers that kept him there, nor the nails." Cohen's gaze swept the people of Glenrock as he stepped away from the wooden stand he'd been leaning on. "They invited him to prove he was the Son of God, for they said, 'If you are the Messiah, prove it.'" He paused, then raised his right arm. "The greatest miracle wouldn't be that he jumped off that cross and lived. The greatest miracle was that he stayed on the cross." He lowered his arm and moved back to the wooden dais, and then his eyes found Sarah. They stopped for a moment before he looked away. "Jesus died for our sins, and some say that if you don't sin, well then, he died for nothing."

A light ripple of laughter came from the Sunday morning crowd.

"As found in Proverbs 21:15, 'When justice is done, it is a joy to the righteous but terror to evildoers.'"

An *Amen* rose among the people.

Sarah glanced around to make sure no one was paying particular attention to her. Not a single person cared that she stood in the back.

"I speak about evil and crime today because of something terrible and sad that took place in our town last night."

Several people glanced around. Heads leaned toward one another as people whispered.

Was he talking about Liam being killed in the barn? Did someone at the police department inform him?

"There was a shooting at a local barn." Cohen leaned into the mic, which weighed his voice down with bass. "There was a shooting in the police station, too."

Now, he paused to allow the congregation to mutter among themselves.

Sarah's stomach dropped. A shooting in the police station? Aaron was there last night. He said the detective had a gun on him. What the hell?

For some reason, Cohen was working the people up, and it wasn't boding well for the knot in her stomach. Something was wrong here— very wrong.

"Our local detective just got out of the hospital with a broken nose and a fractured wrist." Cohen nearly shouted this time.

Okay, that was Aaron's doing. She was sure of it.

Cohen had stirred everyone up, and now people appeared antsy, restless.

Sarah edged one foot closer to the exit door.

"But the police performed solid work, and the culprit now resides in our holding cells a few blocks from here."

Several people clapped—they actually clapped as if the preacher's words weren't just gospel but were a conviction of a crime. No one knew what happened in the detective's office, Sarah included. But Aaron wouldn't attack the man without serious provocation.

"As it says in Deuteronomy 27:19, 'Cursed be anyone who perverts the justice due to the sojourner, the fatherless, and the widow.'"

A line of sweat oozed down her back as her hands clenched at her sides. She dry swallowed and wondered if he was now speaking to her. Could that message be about Aaron? The *sojourner*? Someone who would stay temporarily? The *fatherless*? Was that because something happened to Willow?

She tightened her teeth together and felt a slight pain from her sore jaw, welcoming it. She'd burn Cohen's town to the ground if something happened to Willow or Aaron.

The large front doors cracked open to her left, and a shaft of sunlight painted the stone floor yellow as several men in black suits stepped inside.

The door closed, and she caught Cohen offering these men a slight nod.

Sarah pushed her back up against the church wall, calming her racing heart with the reassurance of Taggart's gun in her belt pressing into the small of her back.

"Blessed are those who hunger and thirst for righteousness, for they shall be satisfied." Cohen raised his voice again.

The men near the front door were staring at the crowd now as if looking for someone, their eyes studying each person.

She needed to leave. Whatever Vivian wanted her to see, she hoped she'd seen it because a creepy, deranged preacher led this town, and she'd heard enough of his babbling.

"We will root out the evildoers from our town." He slammed down his hand, the sound reverberating throughout the nave. "Romans 6:23, 'For the wages of sin is death.'"

One of the suited men studying the crowd turned her way, but before his eyes fell on her, she slipped back into the recessed area a meter before the exit, spun around, and pushed open the door.

Once outside, she moved quickly across the lawn toward Cedar Street.

When she got to the sidewalk, she glanced back and saw no one pursuing her. In the parking lot, a tall man on a cell phone paced beside a large, extended Land Rover.

Sarah stopped moving. Without a doubt, that was the man who shot Liam in the back of the head last night in the barn. He had the same build and the same height. Even without confirmation from Vivian, she was sure it was him.

Walking into the police station wouldn't work.

Abducting Officer Taggart again wouldn't work.

Hire a lawyer to get out of this mess? Never.

Was he the reason she was supposed to attend the church this morning?

Where was she expected to get answers?

Without proper answers and nothing forthcoming from Vivian, Sarah did the next best thing. She ran along the sidewalk to get behind the man who was still pacing and talking on the phone. His head was down as he stared at the concrete, seemingly lost in thought. The man was upset about something, and whoever he talked to was getting an earful.

The preacher's voice boomed out of the speakers from inside the church. Something about justice and freedom now.

Trying to ignore the voice from inside the church, Sarah moved to the rear of the parking lot and moved from car to car, inching closer to the man on the phone.

He stopped pacing and stared up at the church.

Sarah drew closer still, her hand moving back to the gun.

She was able to hear his words now.

"Work harder, not smarter," he said into the phone.

The anger in his voice resonated with her.

She eased up to the other side of the Rover, his back still to her as she watched him through the SUV window.

He spoke again as she drew her weapon. "Listen to me, Dom, you're now in Liam's position. Prove yourself to me and find that bitch. Why would I need you if I have to find her myself?"

Her eyes widened. Vivian had answered her prayers. This was why she needed to go to church today.

She stepped around the grill of the SUV and raised her gun.

"Drop the phone."

He jumped when he saw her. "What the fuck!"

"Drop the phone and get in behind the wheel. Do it now." Sarah jerked the weapon toward the Rover. "Or say your prayers." She smirked. "I'm sure He'll hear you this close to a church."

The man's eyes brimmed with anger as he glared at her, his mouth half-open. The phone lowered slowly from his ear. "You can't just waltz into my town and—"

She pulled the trigger, aiming to his right. The bullet shot out the window of the car behind him.

He ducked in reflex, glanced back at the car, and then faced her.

She shoved him back against the SUV with her free hand and placed the gun up under his chin. "Don't move." Then she ran her hand over his waist and lower chest. Oddly, he was unarmed.

The church's front doors opened—likely due to the sound of her weapon.

Sarah pushed away from him, opened the back door, and nudged him with the weapon's tip.

"Get in the front, or the next one won't miss."

He nodded twice and opened the Rover's door.

"Hey," someone shouted from the church steps.

Sarah hopped in the back and placed the gun beside the front seat's headrest.

The man slammed his door shut. "Now what?" His words came out garbled, like he was trying to growl.

"Drive."

"Where?"

"Just fucking drive." She glanced to her left. The men in suits who had joined the service late were running toward them. "We'd better be rolling before they get here. I will likely die, but your brains will be on the dash."

The SUV turned on. The man put it in drive—the doors locked automatically once it was in gear—then he hit the gas as one of the men in suits grabbed her door and yanked on the handle.

They eased out of the lot and drove past the police station. A man in an official-looking suit was just getting out of his car at the curb. He watched them pass, then stared at the church. The gun going off likely drew his attention, too.

Was he the detective who was harassing Aaron?

"Hit the highway, then take me to the truck stop."

"The truck stop?"

"Yeah, that's where this all started, and that's where this will all end."

"You planning on killing me?"

"If you're lucky." She placed the gun against his neck. "Just shut up and drive."

Chapter 18

SPECIAL AGENT ANDREW NEWMAN had just stepped out of his car in front of the police station when he thought he heard the sound of a gunshot.

He glanced down the street. The only activity was a Land Rover SUV heading his way in a hurry.

Maybe its engine backfired.

When the SUV was about to pass him, he caught sight of the driver, but the back windows were too tinted to see inside the rear.

He glanced toward the church. People were spilling out and heading toward their vehicles. He shrugged. Church must be over, and everyone was in a hurry to get home and enjoy this lovely Sunday. None of that was his business. He had a fellow agent to locate.

Newman pivoted on his heels and walked up to the front door of the Glenrock police station. Before he could grab the handle, the door was ripped open.

"What the—" he gasped in surprise and stepped back.

Two uniformed officers bolted from the station, one of them apologizing as he bumped into Newman. The men hightailed it to the church.

Newman stood to the side to watch the men sprint up the street.

Maybe it was a gun going off over there.

He shook his head, grabbed the door, and stepped inside the police station.

The contrast from the outside sent a chill through him. Someone liked having the air conditioning on when it wasn't needed.

He strode up to the front desk and glanced through a Plexiglas divider.

"Hello?" he called.

"One minute," a man shouted from the rear office area.

Newman stepped back and took in the place. On the wall to his left were pictures of the officers who had served Glenrock for dozens of years, ending with the photos of the current force. He counted four patrol officers, one K9 unit, a corporal, a detective, a sergeant, and the chief, with multiple communications officers.

The two men who ran outside when he was entering must've been two of the patrol officers.

After briefly looking at the front desk and seeing no one there yet, he moved to the side door and peeked through a square glass window. It looked like a short hallway that led to their holding cells.

"Can I help you?" a man said.

Newman jerked at the sound of the voice and turned around.

A heavyset man in uniform stood behind the Plexiglas divider. Newman frowned, then relaxed his face when he saw the shiner on the side of the cop's left eye.

Newman smiled and strode toward the barrier, his hand removing the ID in his pocket and flipping it open.

"Special Agent Andrew Newman with the FBI." He closed the ID and slipped it back into his pocket.

The man's eyes widened slightly, then stared at Newman's face. "The FBI is in town." Did the cop's voice just crack with emotion slightly? Was he nervous about something? Afraid of something? "What can I do for you, sir?"

Newman was here unofficially, so he decided to lie. It wouldn't do him or Agent Jamie Sutton any good to mention her name just yet.

"I'm investigating a missing persons case."

"Who's missing?"

Newman glanced down at the floor for a moment. Should he be friendly and try to work with these hick cops or strong-arm his way to the information?

By the time he glanced back up, he'd made his decision.

"We haven't been properly introduced."

"Oh. Right." The cop pulled out a chair and plopped down into it. "I'm Patrol Officer Kirk Taggart."

In a soft, caring voice, Newman asked, "What happened to your face, Officer Taggart? Looks nasty."

"Uhm, had a female suspect in custody." His gaze drifted to the left, then down to his lap, where he brushed off the top of his pants. "Didn't see her right hook coming. Got sucker punched." He shrugged and looked up at Newman, then immediately looked away again. "Been up most of the night feeling like a failure as a cop."

"I'm sorry to hear that," Newman said, all the genuine concern he could muster in his tone. "And where is this girl now?"

Taggart met his gaze. "That's the problem. We're all out looking for her."

Newman nodded, watching the cop. None of that made sense. The photographs on the police station's wall showed four patrol officers, yet two ran by him upon entering the building. So how could they *all* be out looking for *her*?

And who was the "her" here? Could the cop be talking about Special Agent Jamie Sutton?

"Is that where those two officers were headed in such a hurry?"

Taggart frowned. "The two officers?"

"Yeah, when I came in the front door, I was almost bowled over by two uniformed patrol officers as they bolted from the building."

"Oh, they were responding to a gunshot fired call at the church down the street."

So, he did hear it correctly. "Weapons fired at a church? Sounds scary for such a small town like Glenrock."

Taggart nodded. "There's a lot of scary in Glenrock."

Now, that was an interesting comment, something Newman wanted to explore further. Perhaps Sutton had been onto something after all.

"Since we're both on the same side," Newman said, leaning up against the Plexiglas, "what does that mean? Isn't Glenrock an idyllic location to buy a house and settle down in a quiet neighborhood?"

"Well, I think every town has its ghosts and demons. But Glenrock got hit by a wave of scary shit last night."

"Oh, I'm sorry to hear that." Newman shook his head slowly, empathizing with the cop. He hoped the man would continue to explain, so he remained silent and waited.

"The girl got away, which is likely a good thing. It's her boyfriend I'm concerned about."

Newman put on his best I-hear-you-and-I'm-with-you face. "Concerned about her boyfriend?" he repeated, not wanting to ask about the girl if it was Sutton. At least not yet. Fishing for more information may produce nuggets otherwise unattainable.

"Yeah, he's in our holding cell at the moment."

Did Sutton have a boyfriend that Newman didn't know about? Could this boyfriend lead him to Agent Sutton?

He devised an idea to dissuade the local cops from thinking he was looking for a woman.

"Do you think I could take a peek at this man in your holding cell?"

"Oh, I don't know," Taggart said. "I wouldn't want to get into more trouble."

"More trouble? Don't tell me your boss shit on you because a woman gave you that bruise."

Taggart nodded. "Yeah, I'm the laughing stock of Glenrock now. I'll probably be manning this desk for months."

"Oh, I'm sorry to hear that." Newman adjusted his suit jacket, glanced at the side door that led to the holding cells, and then faced Taggart. "Look, let me eyeball this prisoner, and I'll put in a good word for your bosses. That ought to mean something coming from the FBI, right?"

Taggart looked up. "You'd do that for me? Why?"

"You look like you've had a rough week. We could all use a break once in a while."

The patrol officer shook his head like he thought of something that disappointed him. "I can't let you back there. What was I thinking?"

He was close—just a bit more prodding. "What, you need to see my ID again? I'm the FBI—the feds. We're on the same side here. You let me eyeball the guy, and we avoid all the paperwork."

"Yeah, I know, but I screwed up once this week. Can't do it again. Let's wait until my boss comes back from the doctor—"

Newman whistled. "The doctor? On a Sunday? Doesn't sound like a regular check-up."

"You must be a detective," Taggart said, his head tilted as he eyed Newman. "That was a quick deduction."

"Is your boss okay?"

Taggart swung his chair to the right, then back to the left. "Yeah, the guy in there did a number on him. Broke his nose and sprained his wrist."

Newman whistled again. "Why'd he do that? Drunken fight?"

Taggart jerked up his shoulders. "Don't know. When I got back here last night, Detective Billings's office was a mess, and there was a bullet hole in the wall."

Newman reared back, staring at Taggart. "Now you're joshing me. No way! A bullet hole? How much gun violence do you guys usually get around here?"

Taggart looked off into space, a dazed expression on his face, while thinking about something. "Well, gee, we really don't get much trouble until that guy showed up last night with his girlfriend and their kid."

Now, he was intrigued. There was no way he was leaving Glenrock until he got the whole story. This was something he could sink his teeth into. And he had to find out if the "girlfriend" was Sutton.

"Those cops earlier, the tall skinny one and the heavier one with the thick mustache, were they working last night?"

Taggart nodded. "I was, too."

"They caught the guy in the holding cell, and you almost caught his girlfriend? Is that how it went down?"

Taggart was still nodding, but now he leaned forward and glanced toward the door. When his eyes looked up at Newman, there was a plea in them. "I don't think it's safe for that guy anymore."

Newman glanced around in a conspiratorial manner to act like he was in on Taggart's paranoia, then whispered loud enough to be heard through the Plexiglas. "Why not? Doesn't he have the same rights as any other prisoner?"

Taggart shook his head. "They took their kid and placed her with child services."

"Because he fought with your detective?"

Taggart nodded. "I think so. But there's always more to the story." Taggart leaned back in the chair. "They never tell me all of it."

"Okay, I'll tell you what. Let me eyeball the guy in the holding cell to ensure he's not the man I'm looking for. Then I'll get out of your hair."

Taggart shook his head. "I've made too many mistakes already. I can't do that."

Shit! Newman pulled out his ID, flipped it open, and placed it against the see-through barrier. "Check it. Call it in. You'll see I'm legit."

"Let's wait until the others come back. They won't be long. If they want to let you in, then fine. I just can't, man. I'm in too much trouble as it is."

Newman decided on another tactic as he put his ID away again. "How long have you guys held this man?"

"Since sometime last night."

"What are his charges?"

"They haven't been filed as far as I know."

"You guys are holding him without charges?" Newman raised his voice to sound surprised. Hick towns often did whatever the hell they wanted. "When's his arraignment?"

"No idea. No one told me. Probably tomorrow, Monday morning."

"If your station violates his rights ..." Newman paused. He wanted to set the hook just right. "Look, I'm with the Federal Bureau of Investigation. When kidnappings cross state lines, it becomes our jurisdiction. I drove up from Nevada to look into a kidnapping. I need to eyeball this man, and I won't be leaving until I do."

Taggart stared at him now, his bloodshot eyes wider than moments ago. The cop likely felt the fear that Newman was instilling with each word.

"If you, Officer Taggart, do not let me inside your holding cells to see your prisoner for all of ten seconds, I will be forced to make a phone call to the FBI. We will have twenty agents in Glenrock before sundown, and I'll be forced to explain to your superiors that it was all your fault." This wouldn't ever happen, but Taggart couldn't know that.

The man looked like he was staring at a deranged alien with antennae and tentacles. Mouth open, eyes wide, nostrils flaring.

"Ten seconds," Taggart managed to squeeze out his quivering lips. He glanced at the door, then back to Newman. "We can do ten seconds. I'll buzz you in."

Newman smiled and moved to the side door. The second his hand touched the knob, the door buzzed. He slipped inside and moved to holding cell number one. The Glenrock cells still had the old-fashioned bars on three of the four sides.

A man lay on a single bench against the back wall. The sight of him made Newman gasp. The only time he'd seen anyone as beat up and bleeding as this guy was at car accident scenes he'd attended.

The man's face was a mess, and it looked like one eye was swollen shut. He was bleeding from several places in his face, and from ten feet away, Newman saw the swelling wasn't confined to his face.

It also looked like he'd pissed himself.

"Hey, you okay in there?"

The man tried to turn to look at him, but moaned in pain.

"Are you able to sit up?"

The man groaned.

"Tap your hand once for no, twice for yes."

The man tapped his right hand twice.

"Is anything broken?"

Two taps.

"Is it your jaw that's broken?"

One tap.

"Your chest?"

Two taps.

"Elsewhere?"

There was a pause, then two taps.

"Are you in pain?"

Two taps.

"Have they had a doctor tend to you?"

One tap.

Newman glanced at the door, then back to the prisoner. "Did they offer painkillers?"

One tap.

He hated the next question, but as dread filled his gut, he asked, "Did cops do this?"

Two taps.

"Fuck," he muttered. "Okay, I'll get you out of here."

Someone shouted something from the central area of the police station. Newman turned toward the door as it burst open.

The tall, skinny cop he'd seen running out past him earlier stood there. "Who the fuck are you?"

"FBI, and it looks like you guys are in big trouble."

Chapter 19

THE BITCH HOLDING THE gun jerked it upward, the tip pushing on the back of his jaw.

"Park at the back behind the truck stop."

Dalton turned the wheel to take them to the back, then eased into a spot between a black van and a pickup hauling a boat.

"Now what? You shoot me, take my ride, and make a break for it?"

"Where's my daughter?"

Dalton looked at her in the mirror. A scared little girl in the back seat, holding a cop's stolen gun. "You think you can kill a man in cold blood?"

"Where is my daughter?"

"It's a tall order to kill someone."

"You're sure making it easy. Keep taunting me, and you'll find out if I've got the balls."

"What's going on here? Why are you in Glenrock?"

The woman in the back let out a short chortle. "We stopped for gas and coffee. That was it. Liam, that asshole you shot last night in the barn pulled me from my car."

Dalton frowned at her in the mirror, his head tilted slightly with the pressure of the gun on his neck. If Liam weren't dead, he'd kill him today. "Then why did you stay? Just leave."

"We didn't *stay*, as you put it. Liam grabbed me, knocked out my tooth, tied me to a chair, and promised to do deranged sexual things to me."

Dalton gripped the wheel hard. "Then I'm happy he's dead. Let's move on. You leave. No more harm comes to anyone."

They stared at each other for a moment in the rearview mirror. "Where's my daughter? Give me my boyfriend. We'll leave."

He watched her eyes and saw intelligence there. She knew the score. She was aware that they were past a truce. He shook his head. "I'm afraid not. You're in too deep. The people I work for won't let this go."

The girl jerked like she had a tic of some kind. Then her eyes had a glassy look about them.

"Now?" she muttered. "But I have him—"

"You have who?" Dalton asked.

The woman's eyes refocused on him. "Nothing. Where's my daughter?"

"No idea." He caught movement in his rearview mirror behind the woman's head. Cohen's men had followed them and were now cautiously approaching the Rover. Good, this bitch would be taken care of soon. "Why don't you put the gun down so we can talk like two rational adults?"

"No deal, and be quiet. I'm listening to something."

Dalton checked the side mirror. Two of Cohen's security vehicles were parked, their doors open. Both men held weapons and were advancing. This would be over in under one minute, and the woman in the back had no idea.

He only hoped he wouldn't be cleaning her blood and brain matter off his seats for the next few weeks.

The woman seemed to have a series of spasms as her head lowered. The gun came off his flesh, and he sat up straighter.

"Fuck," the woman muttered.

She got up, leaned over the seat, aimed the weapon downward, and fired all in one motion.

The impact on his leg was violent. He'd been shot, but there was no pain right away—that would come.

The no-pain thing didn't stop him from screaming, though. Shock, surprise, anger, and several other emotions rolled up into one long scream as he clutched at his leg.

The woman jumped out and was making a run for it. The weapon going off so close to his head left him momentarily deafened.

When the back window broke, he heard that, though.

Cohen's men were shooting at the woman and hitting the fucking SUV!

He ducked down as his leg gushed blood, and the pain rolled through him in waves.

Dalton shouldered the door open and shouted for someone to call him an ambulance.

Once his leg was sewn up and bandaged, he'd kill that bitch. He would send out word that she was his to kill.

Even if it took months to catch her, he would, and then he'd kill her with his bare hands as slowly as possible.

Lightheaded, worried about the blood flowing from his wound, Dalton screamed again as Cohen's men dashed by the Rover, giving chase in the woods.

"Motherfucker," he shouted. "Did anyone call me an ambulance?"

He passed out less than a minute later.

Chapter 20

MARTIN COHEN CONCLUDED HIS business at the church, dismissed the officers who responded to the gunshot in the parking lot, and stepped outside into the sunshine.

"What a glorious day." Even though he spoke to no one in particular, his men nodded, their eyes on the area around them. "Where is Dalton?"

"At the truck stop, sir." Vince, his head of security, turned to face him. "I have a two-man team there now. Also, Dalton has been shot in the leg by the woman who held him at gunpoint."

Cohen wanted to express his joy at what he'd just heard, but decided to show his men no emotion. Dalton had brought all this down on his own head. He kept Liam and Domenick around, trying to give them a break. When one of Liam's victims was found in the North Platte River late last year, he'd warned Dalton to rein that asshole in. Then Liam lost his edge on that situation last night, and Cohen ordered Dalton to go in and kill the idiot before he shot their female prisoner.

But then that woman who punched Officer Taggart jumped from the barn and was lost in the woods.

"The woman." He stared at Vince. "She showed up at church this morning." He shook his head and glanced out at the parking lot. "Ballsy."

"Yes, sir. But we'll get her. She's in the woods again. This time behind the truck stop."

Cohen met Vince's gaze. "Tell your men not to underestimate her. We lost her in the woods last night. Your team may lose her again."

Vince offered him a slight nod as he pulled out his phone.

"And Dalton? He's still at the truck stop?"

Vince nodded. "Passed out in the front seat of his vehicle."

"Is he dying?"

"Ambulance has been called. We suspect he'll make it. Heavy blood loss, but I have one man applying pressure to his leg wound. It entered on the side. Doesn't look like it hit any bone. We'll know for sure when doctors look at him."

"Shit, only a leg wound." Cohen smiled and nodded at a churchgoer as they pulled out of the parking lot. "Okay, tell your man to leave Dalton alone and help find that woman in the woods. Now, take me to the bunker. It's time I have a chat with that woman."

They moved off the church steps with Vince in the lead, mumbling into his phone. Before they reached the car, Cohen's cell phone rang.

It was the police station. He stared at the phone for a moment. With Dalton at the truck stop awaiting an ambulance and Billings convalescing at home with a broken nose, who would be calling him from the police station?

"Hold up," he said to Vince, then stepped behind his Land Rover to take the call. "Cohen here."

"Sir, I'm sorry to bother you." The man's words were slightly muffled, as if he was covering the mouthpiece with his hand.

"Well, go on. What is it?"

"The FBI is here."

That made him spin around and stare down the street in front of the police station. Only one vehicle was parked out front.

This was their greatest worry and what they'd tried to convey to Liam and Domenick last night in the conference room one at the hotel.

The FBI's looking into his business was something he could not allow. That was why the Satanic cult angered him so much. With that kind of sick and twisted attention, who knew what police agencies would show up on his doorstep?

"How many FBI agents are we talking about?"

"One man, sir."

That felt better, more manageable. "Did he state his business?"

"He claims to be working on a missing persons case. Wanted to check in on our prisoner and see if it was the guy."

"So he's looking for a man?" Another bullet dodged. That meant the woman they were tracking through the woods by the truck stop and the woman in his bunker, whom he was about to ask some serious questions, were not on the FBI's radar. The only missing or dead man in this area was Liam, and there'd be little reason for the FBI to be looking for him—unless he were an informant, which Cohen doubted. No man could sexually torture women like Liam had done and be a criminal informant for the FBI at the same time.

"Yes, sir, they're looking for a man. But now he's demanding we bring in a doctor for our prisoner."

"Then bring in a doctor. What harm will it do?"

"But, sir, we were just following Detective Billings's orders to leave Mr. Stevens in the cell for a few weeks without food or water—"

"Is my phone working?"

"Uhm, what was that?"

"I asked if my phone was working?"

"How do you mean, sir?"

"Can you hear me?"

"Yes."

"Oh, then I guess I wasn't clear."

"About what?"

Cohen closed his eyes, inhaled once to calm his nerves, moved around the vehicle to open the back door, and nodded for Vince to get underway.

"Bring a doctor to tend to the prisoner. Make the FBI man happy. I don't care what Billings told you to do. Then I want you to get rid of the FBI man."

The cop gasped. "Get rid of him …"

"No," Cohen shouted. "Do not *harm* the FBI agent. I meant, make him happy, and he'll be on his way. Get rid of him, as in get him out of my town. Do you understand?"

"Yes, sir."

Cohen hung up without another word. He clutched his phone tight, wanting to throw it against the window.

With the FBI snooping around Glenrock, things were getting worse. He needed to discover what that woman, whom he had tied up in his bunker, knew. He also needed to talk to the woman who had just abducted Dalton from the church parking lot and then shot him. He needed to learn so much because his top men were getting beaten up and hospitalized. Usually, Billings would handle these things. And when he couldn't, Dalton would.

But now it was time to get his hands dirty.

"Vince?"

"Yes, sir."

"Send one of our men over to the police station. I want to find out who they have locked up. I want to know everything about that man. He beat up Billings pretty bad last night, and now the FBI is asking about him."

"Yes, sir. On it." Vince tapped away on his cell phone and then spoke quietly into it.

When his call ended, Cohen leaned forward. "Be ready to move once I speak with this woman in the bunker. She will tell us where she's been living. I want to search her place myself. There has to be evidence as to who is behind this Satanic cult shit. We will be putting an end to *The Damned* today. Those Satanic assholes can go back to Hell where they belong."

Vince nodded in support.

With the FBI in town, all the extra noise had to die down. Otherwise, they would catch on to what he was doing and shut him down, and he couldn't allow that.

If that even looked possible, he'd arm all of his men with assault rifles and kill every FBI agent and police officer within a fifty-mile radius.

He'd turn Glenrock into another Waco, Texas.

David Koresh would have nothing on him.

Chapter 21

SARAH DROPPED TO THE ground and lay flat, the gun in her hand under her stomach. One of her pursuers was six feet away—he had stopped to scan the area. Then he surveyed the ground, likely looking at the brush for any sign of her coming through there.

She watched him from behind a branch flush with leaves, breathing through her open mouth. Sweat tickled her face, but she didn't wipe it off.

After what felt like forever, the man got moving again. He mumbled something into an earpiece, then disappeared behind a thick brush.

Go to church? What did that solve?

Her sister didn't answer.

You said it would end at the truck stop, but that didn't happen.

Still, nothing from Vivian.

Just tell me where Willow is, and we can be done with this town.

Her sister entered her consciousness. No matter how often that happened, Sarah never got comfortable with it—a voice in her head, knowing it wasn't hers.

Willow is safe. You'll see her soon.

Okay, then why tell me it would all end at the truck stop?

Because it will.

Then, it dawned on Sarah. *But not yet?*

Not yet.

"For fuck's sake," she whispered, barely loud enough to hear it.

Then why go to the church?

Really? Wake up, Sarah. You saw Cohen's madness. You taunted him by being there. He'll make mistakes now. And Dalton will be out of the picture with that wound—at least until later this afternoon. You're free to finish this. Just don't die in these trees.

"Gee, thanks, sis."

Her heart raced, and a wave of adrenaline rocked her body.

Someone was beside her.

How did she not notice? If listening to her sister got her killed …

Whoever stood there could easily see her.

Without moving, a man's black boot stepped into view.

A radio clicked on. "Wayne calling in."

"Go ahead, Wayne."

"I've got her. Inform the preacher."

"Can you repeat your message and offer a twenty?"

"I've got the runaway. I'll bring her to the parking lot. Let the preacher know it was Wayne who nabbed her."

"Copy that."

Sarah rolled slowly and looked up, a worried expression on her face. "Please, mister. I didn't mean any harm." She kept her grip on the weapon tight, ensuring it stayed under her stomach and out of the man's view.

He had a large pistol aimed at her. "Get up slowly."

"I'm hurt. I can't."

"You're not hurt. Get up slowly, or you will be hurt."

"What will happen to me?" The scared little girl act was hard to pull off, but something in the man's eyes told her he was buying it, even if just a little.

His gun lowered a few inches. "Look, I don't get paid to think. Just get up and come with me. The preacher wants to talk to you."

I'm sure he does ...

She rolled just enough to maneuver the gun toward the man.

His eyes moved toward her stomach—he'd seen the weapon.

She rolled away fast. His weapon fired, chunking up a piece of dirt in front of her face.

Then she squeezed off a round and missed him.

She rolled again, harder, faster.

His weapon fired.

Someone was screaming as she fired Taggart's pistol until it was empty—then she realized it was her screaming.

To be that close to a bullet turned her into a raging lunatic.

When she clamped her mouth shut, the man was on the ground, bleeding from two places—his shoulder and his chest.

She tossed Taggart's weapon aside, then jumped on the gun the man had dropped. When she stood up to slip it into the back of her pants, someone slammed into her, and the gun flew from her grasp.

They both dropped to the ground, a solid tackle that knocked the wind out of her. They rolled as one, and she scrambled to grab the man in some way that would offer her an advantage.

They stopped at the base of a tree with the man in front of her, his hands hammering into her gut.

The tree's roots pushed inward, jabbing her side. She tried to push up off it but couldn't.

She grabbed the guy's hair and yanked him downward, but he resisted, his teeth tight together, moaning deep with the pain, punching her several more times.

She couldn't take much more. She needed a breath, and the man wasn't letting up.

Her vision clouded over, and her peripheral narrowed.

That chunk of something was hurting her back, making her arch upward.

Then she remembered what it was—Taggart's Taser.

Luckily, the man leaned up off her, his hands coming to a blessed stop as he gasped to catch a breath.

She slipped a hand behind her back, gripped the Taser, then rolled to the side far enough to pull it out, aim, and access the trigger.

It shot out two small darts, one slightly higher than the other. The five-second charge incapacitated the man, and he slumped down on her lower legs.

Out of breath and wanting to rest, Sarah did the opposite. She rolled away from the man, got to her knees, then her feet. She watched the man convulse on the ground as she squeezed the trigger for another five-second burst.

With one step, she pulled her foot back and kicked the man as hard as she could in the face.

He rolled onto his stomach, moaning, and she dropped onto his back. A second later, gasping like she was hyperventilating, she tore the gun from the back of the man's pants, flicked off the safety, and held it to his ear.

Somehow, she found her voice. "Say your prayers."

Chapter 22

Special Agent Andrew Newman stood over the prisoner, Aaron Stevens, as a doctor tended to him.

Newman turned to the tall, skinny cop, Officer Paul Grant. "Tell me again how this man sustained broken ribs and a face mangled by fists."

"We aren't sure," Grant said, his tone unfriendly. "Officer Brown and I came in when Mr. Stevens was fighting with Detective Billings."

"And Officer Brown, is that guy with the thick mustache?"

Grant nodded.

"So you're saying Billings did this to the man?"

Grant shrugged and leaned against the wall. "You'll have to ask Billings." He squinted. "But tell me, what's your interest in our prisoner? He's not the missing person you're looking for, right? This isn't a federal case, is it?"

Newman bobbed his head. "I get it." He raised his hands. "I'm not here to stir up your shit. I came as a professional courtesy to let you know I'll be working in the area for a few days. But when I saw this man in such a state …" Newman shrugged. "Well, let's just say respectable police forces don't act in such a way."

"Are you trying to say something about how we're acting?"

Newman gazed at the man momentarily, studying his face and eyes. Was he for real? Didn't he just hear what Newman had said?

"Sir?" the doctor whispered. "I need to take this man to a hospital. He may have internal bleeding."

Grant shook his head. "No way. The prisoner hasn't even been arraigned yet. He stays put."

Newman placed his hands on his hips, about to explain the law to Officer Grant, when Stevens whispered something.

"What's he saying?" Newman asked the doctor.

"He says there's been an abduction."

Newman raised his eyebrows and turned to the cop. "Who was abducted?" He kept his eyes on Officer Grant.

"He says his girlfriend was taken," the doctor offered. "And they stole his child from this police station."

"And he's a Canadian, right?" Newman's eyes didn't leave Grant's face as his cheeks reddened.

"He says his ID is in the car they took."

"If kidnappings cross state lines, the feds get involved, Officer Grant. How about I make a phone call and have a few dozen FBI agents flock down to Glenrock and see what's happening here? How about that? Would that suit you, Mr. Cop?" He slapped Grant on the shoulder, his smile wide. "Sound good to you, old pal?"

"That won't be necessary." Officer Brown stepped into the cell behind his colleague.

The guy could sure use a trim of that mustache. Newman thought a small squirrel had died under his nose, but no one ever told him.

"Now, why wouldn't that be necessary, Officer Brown?"

"We're happy to comply with your requests, Agent Newman."

"*Special* Agent Newman."

"Right," Brown nodded. "Of course. *Special.*"

Grant shot his partner a dangerous look, which had Brown shaking his head at him.

"Doctor, call an ambulance and get this man to the hospital in Douglas."

The doctor pulled out his phone as Newman turned to Officers Grant and Brown. Something was going on here that needed to be ironed out. There was no doubt someone was pulling the strings and leaving a crinkle in the fabric of police work.

Officer Grant wanted to push back. He didn't want the eyes of other officers of the law in his town. Then Brown showed up and rolled out the red carpet, to Grant's chagrin.

So, who did Brown talk to in the other room? If a full-scale investigation were to get underway, he might be able to requisition their phone records, or at least Brown's records, to see who he spoke to this morning.

"Well, gentlemen, I'll escort the ambulance to Douglas and stay with Mr. Stevens for a while. That gets me out of your hair"—he stared at them for several seconds—"for now. If I can confirm what Mr. Stevens is saying, and there has been an abduction ..." He shrugged, raising his hands at the sides. "An investigation into what happened here in Glenrock will be launched. You and your superiors will need to be interviewed." He moved past them, slapping Officer Grant on the shoulder. "So, stick around town. Don't be going anywhere too far."

At the end of the hall, he stepped out into the lobby, pushed open the door, and moved outside. The church parking lot was empty. The roads were clear, and the only traffic was out on the highway.

He withdrew his cell phone and opened the voice memo app.

"There's something strange going on in this town. Sutton was right. We will need to obtain a statement from Mr. Aaron Stevens and submit it to the local field office. Getting to the bottom of whatever is going on in Glenrock might validate Sutton." He stared back at the police station. "Something is wrong here. Something is very wrong here."

Chapter 23

THE LARGE GATES ROLLED apart, and Vince drove onto the Cohen estate grounds. Two armed men nodded at Vince from either side of the SUV, then turned away as the gate closed.

Cohen watched all this from the back seat, stewing on the notion that the FBI was in Glenrock. Was it just some missing person that brought them here? Why did Billings have to go and get himself beaten up? And now Dalton got shot. Either man could have handled the FBI. But now, only the local police could speak with the FBI, and those guys were incompetent.

Too many things had gone wrong in the past twenty-four hours for him to feel settled, calm.

Yet, for some reason, he felt the woman in his bunker was the root of it all.

Miss Jamie Sutton.

Liam had caught her cutting up one of the pigs on Cohen's farm. Another ritual? Some sort of Satanic rite? Was she their leader? How many were in her cult?

Vince pulled up to the front of his house, something Cohen never got sick of seeing. The driveway wove around the vast circular fountain, then aimed back out toward the road. Vince stopped near the front steps that led up to the main foyer. Two of Cohen's men came down to meet them.

His door was opened from the outside, and he exited the vehicle into the early afternoon sunshine.

"Gentlemen," he said to the three men closest to him. "Get me my tools, and let's meet in the bunker. I have information to excavate."

"Yes, sir," came out in a soft harmony from his men as they headed inside the house while Vince walked with him toward the bunker door at the side of the driveway.

Underneath the ground sat an emergency bunker and panic room. It was fully ventilated, with enough supplies in three rooms to last two people several years down there.

When Cohen had it installed, he'd been worried about enemies, people opposed to how he made his money. Instead of the traditional panic room *inside* the house, he had this one built adjacent to the basement so he could get inside before enemies accessed the house. While they were traipsing around the building searching for him, he could either stay in the panic room or exit near the driveway and leave the property through the gate about a hundred yards away.

It was brilliant due to its ability to block sound as well. He'd had to extract information from traitors before, and not one scream was ever heard topside.

Vince lowered to his knees to type in the ten-digit code and then opened the door.

In the well-cut grass, other than a small circular opening that looked like a traditional indent for a sprinkler head, no one could ever tell a fifty-square-meter bunker was hidden beneath the lawn. Even the access hatch was covered in grass and neatly trimmed to blend in with the surrounding yard.

Cohen looked down the stairs into the well-lit hole in the ground— the lights flickered to life when the door opened—and followed Vince down.

"Leave it open. My tools are coming. Once they arrive, everyone should take an hour break. Leave me to my devices down here."

"Yes, sir."

"I need some quality time alone with Miss Sutton." At the bottom of the stairs, he turned to Vince. "It's just after noon. Break ends at two. By then, I want a status report on Dalton, Billings, and the FBI, and I want to know who that prisoner was who attacked Billings. You'll handle all of that for me?"

Vince nodded without hesitation. His loyalty was unquestionable, so he was Cohen's top guy.

"You'll have it for two this afternoon, sir."

Cohen tapped Vince on the shoulder and looked him in the eye. "It's truly a glorious day. One might even say righteous. Hallelujah."

"Hallelujah, sir." A slight grin cracked Vince's face.

Cohen rarely got much of a response from the man, like he was dead inside, so a grin from time to time was nice. He tapped the man's shoulder again, then moved over to the side table where he kept a whiskey cabinet.

"While we wait for my tools," he held up a bottle of the peaty Islay stuff and shook it, "a small drink before the fight will calm me for what I must do."

Once it was poured, he sniffed the liquid, closed his eyes momentarily, and faced Vince.

"You know, there's one thing religious people say when they don't have an answer."

"Sir?"

"The Lord works in mysterious ways."

Vince nodded. If the man wasn't saying *sir*, he was nodding, which worked for Cohen.

"What people don't get is that the Lord does *not* work in mysterious ways. He does as he pleases and keeps his intentions from the minds of the lower-educated." Cohen sipped the whiskey, swallowed, savored it a moment, then gestured with the glass as he spoke. "Liam is dead, for example. He was long past his due date to meet the man downstairs, and that woman in the woods our boys are grabbing helped me see that. Billings got a broken nose because he was callous. He'd gotten lazy, comfortable. Dalton was weak, and a bullet to the leg would strengthen him over time. If he suffers a limp, it's the least he can do in service to our Lord, and it'll be a reminder to walk straighter in his duties or suffer the consequences."

Vince leaned back against the wall by the stairs, arms across his chest, listening.

"You see what I'm getting at?" Cohen drank what was left in his glass and turned to pour another. "This strange woman was thrust into our lives last night to shake things up," he spun around, his glass hand up, a finger raised, "and to bring me the Sutton woman. Without that intrusion, who knows what Liam would've done with Sutton? We sat in the conference room at the hotel, and it took Domenick to spill the beans on who Liam had captive." Cohen shook his head, then drank again. "I thank God that Liam is gone. No more meddling in my affairs. No more dead bodies in the river to bring the heat down on us."

Cohen walked to the base of the stairs and glanced upward. When he saw no one descending, he turned to Vince. "God doesn't work in mysterious ways. Everything he does is preordained. He helps those who help themselves. I'm busy building an empire here, and he sees I'll succeed." Cohen flicked a piece of lint off the breast of his shirt. "Hey, that's how I see it." He snapped his head sideways to look at Vince. "And this FBI intrusion is nothing. It's placed in my path to remind me to maintain a stable workforce of men. Lazy, comfortable men are something I can do without. When things die down, and the Satanists are dealt with—which is God's work, let me tell you—we will bring Billings down here for a talk." Cohen clenched his teeth. "Let's test the man's loyalty." He moved back to the whiskey cabinet and topped up his glass again. "If he fails that test, we can always get another detective, no?"

"Yes, sir."

Footsteps descended the stairs as each man carried a rolled-up canvas knife holder—actually, they were a Chef Knife Roll Bag, but Cohen had removed the word *chef* from their vocabulary.

"Place them on that table there." Cohen pointed. "Vince, see them out. I'll be topside by two. No interruptions."

The men nodded and started up the stairs.

"Vince," Cohen called.

He stopped halfway up. "No interruptions. Understood?"

"Yes, sir. Absolutely."

"Carry on."

The men disappeared, the trap door lowered, and the locks clicked into place a moment later.

He was alone with his whiskey and his tools. Miss Jamie Sutton rested on a dirty mattress in the room adjacent to this one. She was tied down, stripped of her clothes, and waiting for the question-and-answer period of the day.

Cohen stared at the door that led to the other room.

He felt at peace. This was his moment.

A naked woman with answers. And he could do whatever he wanted to obtain those answers, even if that meant he killed her.

"Well, answers first," he whispered to himself. "Then she dies. Every good Christian has blood on their hands."

He emptied his glass and then set it on the table.

"What a wonderful way to spend a Sunday afternoon directly following a church session."

He strode toward the door, tapped the security code, then eased it open.

Her eyes were on him when he entered the room, wide in fear.

Sutton had been recently bathed and allowed to use the toilet. However, a bit of urine and excrement came with the task at times— nothing he couldn't handle.

He strode over and bent to remove her gag.

"Let's you and me have a little chat."

She struggled against the ropes that secured her, shaking her small breasts—something he had no interest in. As a man of God, he enjoyed the sins of the flesh when they were offered and not taken. Sutton's nudity had to do with vulnerability and humiliation, and giving him access to all of her skin. It had nothing to do with perversion or temptation.

"Fuck you," she spat at him.

"As much as I appreciate your willingness to talk, those aren't the words I'm looking for."

Cohen got to his feet, and his smile widened. This was going to be fun. He rarely had the opportunity to inflict harm on those who deserved it. But when it was righteous, it filled him with a sense of euphoria.

He moved back to the other room, grabbed one of the canvas knife bags, and then, cradling it like a baby, strode back into the room with Sutton.

"You sure you don't want to talk freely? Tell me everything I want to know?"

"You're the one who is damned here. You preach God, yet you're working for the Devil."

Cohen laughed, tilting his head back. After calming down to a few chuckles, he unrolled his canvas bag and selected a serrated blade. It was something a chef would cut a Tomahawk steak with.

"This game has currency. Here's how it works. I ask a question, and you give me an answer. We keep doing that, and the knives remain dry. You lie to me, avoid answering, or keep shouting curse words, and the knives get wet with your blood." He held up a hand. "But don't worry. I will avoid the main arteries for several hours. And no, I do not have a doctor on staff, so you'll likely bleed out by tonight, but I suspect I'll know what I need to know by then."

He smirked at her. "You about ready?"

She glared up at him. "I'll see you in Hell."

He shrugged. "I guess we'll see about that."

He lowered the blade to her inner thigh, just below her vagina, where it was most sensitive, then asked his first question.

When she told him to go to Hell again, he started slicing.

No one heard her screams but Cohen.

Chapter 24

SARAH GOT THE MAN to his feet, one hand on the scruff of his neck, the other holding the gun to his brain stem. They were facing the parking lot, staring at it through the trees.

"How many of you are here?" She figured there were just the two men because she'd spent the last minute getting her breath back.

"Dozens of us."

She pulled the weapon away from his neck, then brought it upside his head, the butt of the firearm connecting with his ear.

He jerked away from her, bending at the waist, a hand coming up to cover his ear.

"Fuck, that hurt."

She hauled him back to a standing position, the gun pressed against his neck.

"I'll ask again. How many of you are there?"

"You mean here? Right now?"

She pulled the gun away to smack him again, but he ducked and raised his hands.

"Okay, okay. Just the two of us. Fuck, they just sent the two of us."

Blood trickled from a cut on the top of his ear. She'd hit him hard, which would serve as a reminder of what she had planned next.

"Your partner won't make it. Whether you live to see the sunset will depend on what you do until then."

"Hey, wait for a second." He tried to turn around to look at her. "I'm just doing this part-time. You know, to make some extra bucks."

"Too bad and too late. You're in this now." She frowned and stared at the man. "You came after me, jumped me, and beat me up for a part-time job? Who does that?"

"Cohen pays a lot. I've been unemployed for a long time. Working a few days' security per week is paying the bills."

"What you did to me falls under the heading of security?"

"I hand you over. Job done."

"And he hasn't asked you to murder anyone yet?"

The man half-turned, his mouth making a tsk tsk sound. "Now, why would he do that?"

"Doesn't matter. Start moving." She pushed him by the collar.

"We can't leave Wayne lying there bleeding out."

"Sure, we can. Get moving." She shoved him harder. "Once we're in your car and clear of this area, I'll call an ambulance anonymously. They can pick him up and try to save his life."

They moved through the trees slowly, ducking branches and stepping over upturned roots.

"Where are we going?"

"For now, to your vehicle." Then, a thought struck Sarah. "Wait, did you call an ambulance for the guy I shot in the leg?"

"Yeah, why?"

"Great, then they're already on their way. See, things are looking up for your friend."

The guy tsked again.

"Give me your wallet."

"Why? Is this a robbery now?"

"You want the other ear bleeding, too? Or would you like a hole in the leg to match your friend's?"

He reached into his back pocket.

Sarah eased off him a bit. "Slowly."

The man pulled a wallet from his pocket and extended his hand to her.

She grabbed it and shoved it away into her pocket. "Now, your phone."

"You're robbing me? Really?"

"No, you can have it all back in a few hours. Now give me your damn phone."

They'd made it to the edge of the trees. The concrete of the parking lot was less than five feet away.

Sarah surveyed the area as the man fished out his phone from a front pocket. There were no other SUVs. No more of Cohen's thugs were waiting for her.

The man held the phone at arm's length.

Sarah took it and placed it in another pocket.

"Now, walk toward your car like a normal human being. I'll be right behind you. We're going for a short ride, and then you'll go home. Try to be a hero, and I'll shoot you. Then I'll find out where you live from the ID in your wallet, then shoot whoever lives there, too."

His face slackened at the mention of his home address. That was a sore spot.

"Got someone at home you care about?"

The man was still speechless.

"Good, that'll work well for our conversation. Our relationship will be short-lived but quite beneficial to both of us." She shoved him. "Now start walking and remember what I said."

The man did as he was told, only glancing over at his friend in the front seat of the Land Rover.

From where they were, the man's face lacked all color. His head was back, and his eyes were closed. He'd passed out from blood loss, or he was dead.

"Keep it steady. Act like a normal fucking human being walking through a truck stop parking lot."

"Whatever," he muttered under his breath.

She'd hit a nerve back there, which was good.

Two vehicles were at the pumps, and she counted at least fifteen cars, plus four large rigs scattered throughout the parking lot.

The man she followed, her gun mostly hidden in her belly button area, was headed toward a brown Land Rover.

At the front door of the SUV, he stopped and turned to look over his shoulder. "Keys are in my pocket."

"Get them slowly. Then we enter together. You in the driver's seat, me behind you."

He lowered his head, and his right arm moved slowly to retrieve the keys from his pocket.

As she instructed, they got in the Rover together and closed both doors in unison.

The sound of an approaching siren made her look toward the highway.

"Turn it on and wait."

Sarah leaned up on the seat to watch the man turn on the Land Rover.

Then she looked through the windshield as an ambulance roared into the parking lot and headed toward the SUV at the back.

"When they get out of the ambulance, drive over to them."

"It's your show."

She waved the gun near his cheek so he could see it and be reminded who was making the decisions here.

"Just do what you're told, and you'll go home tonight and likely never see me again."

They watched the ambulance back up toward the SUV with the gunshot victim in it, then Sarah nudged him.

"Go. Now."

He did as she told him, driving across the lot slowly.

"Turn so I can talk to them through my window."

The driver did as instructed.

When they were ten feet from the EMTs, Sarah lowered her window.

"The guy who shot him ran into the woods. We think he got shot, too. Maybe twenty yards in."

The EMTs looked at one another, then back at her. "Thanks."

"Drive," she said, and the Rover moved toward the highway.

"Which way?"

"Toward Cohen's house."

The man gasped and stopped the vehicle. "What? Are you crazy? He'll kill you."

"We'll see about that."

They were stopped at the highway as he stared at her in the rearview mirror. "You have a death wish, woman."

She waved the gun in the mirror. "Drive to Cohen's house. How far is it?"

"About fifteen minutes out of town. It's an old ranch that he had rebuilt into a mansion."

"Then we have fifteen minutes to talk."

"But you won't get in. The entire estate has a huge fence and a large gate. Cohen has armed guards everywhere. You won't get within twenty feet of the place."

"But you will. You're going to escort me inside."

The man shook his head. "No fucking way. He'll kill me."

"Not if I kill him first."

"You're insane," he whispered.

She held up the gun again. "Just drive."

Chapter 25

NEWMAN PACED OUTSIDE THE hospital room at Memorial Hospital of Converse County in Douglas, waiting for the doctor to come out and tell him how Aaron Stevens was doing.

They got to the hospital less than ten minutes before, with Aaron unconscious in the ambulance for most of the twenty-minute ride.

While pacing outside the room wouldn't make things happen any faster, he strode along the hallway, looking for an exit.

Two doctors ran past him, saying something about prepping for a gunshot wound coming in from Glenrock.

What the hell? More gun violence in Glenrock?

Newman exited the hospital through a side door. This would be an excellent time for a smoke, but he gave that up two years ago. The color of his yellowed fingers had faded over time, the smell of nicotine all but gone.

Too many questions ran through his mind, and only a cigarette would calm him.

So he did the next best thing. He called his sponsor, his champion, his wife.

She answered on the second ring.

"What's happening? You okay, honey?"

That was her first response when he was in the field.

He leaned against the wall by the door and stared down at the grass as the afternoon sun warmed his shoulders. "When your girlfriends call, do you answer the same way?"

"With them, I answer with more warmth."

"Ahhh." He tilted his head back and laughed.

"Honey," she whispered into the phone. "I know you, and I know when you call me during work hours, it's because you're stressed—"

"And hankering for a smoke."

"Exactly. So tell me, what is it?"

"I don't know yet."

"Then tell me what you do know. Actually, wait a second. I was just making an afternoon tea."

There was a clunk as the phone was set down. Through the earpiece, he heard the whistle of the kettle.

"Be right there," she shouted, her voice sounding hollow, distant.

The phone was snapped up. "Okay, it's steeping. What's up?"

"You know Sutton, my ex-partner?"

"Yeah, she was up in Wyoming. Isn't that where you are?"

"I am, and I think I stumbled onto something that the local authorities want to keep covered up."

"Are you sure? I mean, don't you always get jurisdictional pushback from the locals?"

"I do, but this is different."

"How so?"

Newman told her about Aaron, his injuries, and the pushback he received at the station, and then they just let him take Aaron to the hospital after Officer Brown stepped in.

"You think this Brown guy spoke with someone on the phone?"

Newman glanced around, his gaze following an ambulance as it pulled out of the hospital. "Yeah, but it could be Detective Billings, the man who fought with Aaron. He could have authorized the doctor to avoid FBI attention."

"So where's the mystery, honey? Some cops are great, some walk a thin line, but not all cops are rogue."

"I know, I know. Oh, and there's a Satanic cult in the area, too. That was what Sutton was trying to expose. Yet she's not answering her phone. I tried her last night, this morning when I woke up in Glenrock, and on the way to the hospital."

"Hospital?" She gasped. "Oh, right, not you. That Aaron guy. Sorry."

"There's something else."

"What?"

"How much gunplay would you expect in a small place like Glenrock?"

"Hmmm, none."

"Exactly. Yet, a gun was fired near the church this morning. I was close enough to hear it. Guns were used last night, and I just overheard that a gunshot victim is coming into the hospital right now."

"Okay, that's too much. Maybe you should get some backup. Is it safe being all alone there?"

"I've considered that, but I want to wait until I've gone to Sutton's mom's place. I want to talk to her and make sure Sutton is okay. Then I'll go back to Glenrock and see what's going on."

"And talk to that Aaron guy, too."

"Of course."

"But you called because you're thinking about having a cigarette, right?"

He pushed off the wall and walked in a circle, then stopped. "I won't smoke, but it was on my mind. Those things always cleared any fuzziness in my head. Helped me solve cases."

"That's what I'm here for, honey. Smoke me."

He heard the distinctive clatter of her small spoon stirring honey into her tea.

"Look, I need to go back in and try to talk to Aaron. Then, in an hour or so, I'll visit Sutton at her mom's place and see if my gut is misfiring or if something weird is actually going on here."

"Okay, but be safe. No need to be a hero. Promise me if it gets too dark, you'll pull out and wait for backup."

"I promise. You know me. I'll give my life for the job, but I won't *give* my life for the job."

She chuckled softly. "That's my man. Call me tonight?"

"Consider it done."

They whispered *I love yous* to each other, then hung up. Then he recalled the men arriving at the hotel last night and entering through the side door. What were they up to? So much was happening without any answers yet.

Aaron would have answers for him. Then Sutton or her mother would.

After that, he'd make his move—whatever that meant.

Newman grabbed the hospital door and stepped back inside. It was time to talk with Aaron Stevens.

Chapter 26

WHEN JAMIE SUTTON SCREAMED, there was something so profoundly moving to the sound of her voice that Cohen worried he'd become addicted to it.

And if that happened, he'd want a woman in his bunker frequently. But wouldn't that make him no better than Liam, that perverted raping scum?

Cohen watched Sutton bleed from the stomach. No, he wouldn't touch their unclean genitals or her breasts. Men sexualized those, even though everyone had nipples. The only difference between a female's nipples was the glands that fed babies, but not the women he brought down here. There was nothing sexual about women in his bunker. That would be un-Christian of him.

Cohen closed his eyes and enjoyed her hoarse scream. The woman's voice had grown rough. Maybe he'd take a break and let her rest until tonight. That gravelly yelling wasn't as pleasing as the high-pitched scream only a woman could produce in abject terror or agony.

He checked his arms for goosebumps and saw them standing up with his hair.

"Oh, what a pleasure you are." He turned back to her as she writhed on the blood-stained mattress. "If I'd known the absolute rapture I get from your screams, I'd have done this years ago."

Sutton closed her mouth, turned her head toward the wall, and moaned deep in her throat, tears streaming from her face.

"How much blood does a body have?" he asked, loud enough to be heard over her guttural whimpering.

The blade in his hand was soiled with blood, so he wiped it on the mattress.

Sutton caught the movement of his knife hand and jerked away from him, the ropes stretching to their limit.

"Take it easy." He touched her thigh with his open palm, and she jerked again. "I was just wiping off the knife. The question about blood was rhetorical. Nothing you needed to answer. Stay calm, my little lamb."

Her groans subsided until she was just crying now.

"All of this goes away with a few specific answers." Idly, as if he had all day to do this, he used the tip of the knife to clean under his fingernails. "How many are there in your Satanic cult? Why are you protecting them? Who's your leader?" He turned to her. "Are you such a believer, Miss Sutton, that you want to die to meet the Father of Lies himself?" Cohen leaned closer to her and lowered his voice. "And how will that meeting go? Hmmm? You think he'll accept you with open arms? Really? The Devil himself? The Lawless One, Lucifer, the Ruler of the Darkness, will simply spread his wings and embrace his lovely child who promoted his name upon the Earth." He snapped his fingers, and Sutton jumped. "My sacrificial little lamb, I'm afraid none of that will happen. You will head down into the great inferno and scream for all eternity. You will suffer for your misdeeds, and I'm grateful that God has brought you before me to enable deliverance of your soul unto the Great Deceiver."

Her head snapped toward him, rage fixing her facial muscles into torment. "You're the one going to Hell, Lucifer's preacher. If I get there before you, I'll tell the big guy *hey* for you."

"No need." Cohen narrowed his eyes and slowly shook his head from side to side. "You are one brave girl. I admire that. I really do."

He traced a finger along her stomach, where one of her wounds still bled. Her thighs didn't look good, but some of the bleeding had stopped. The cuts were thin and small. Only slightly deeper than someone would inflict upon themselves with a papercut. Even though the skin had barely separated and the lacerations he made were superficial, blood still flowed.

Papercuts hurt immensely for how small they were. Due to their tiny nature, he had learned to preserve his victims for days with long— but not deep—cuts along sensitive areas of their flesh.

Sutton did not do well when he cut the inside of her thighs an inch below her labia. She had screamed when he cut around her nipples. Under her arms made her thrash against the restraints. He thought he'd slice a notch deeper between her toes, but that seemed to encourage her against speaking further.

The end result was cutting into her belly button and several sections of her stomach, but that got him nowhere.

"Where to next?" He tapped the knife against his open palm. "Answer these little questions of mine, make me happy, and I'll end your life quickly. The torture will be over." He smiled widely, making sure to smile with his eyes and show his white teeth. "Think about it. Another week down here, bleeding out, shitting, and pissing yourself." He shrugged. "Who wants those memories for their last days upon God's green Earth?"

"I already told you who I am. There's nothing more I can say."

He stared into her bloodshot eyes. "Where does this resistance come from? Tell me, my little lamb—"

"Stop calling me that," she shouted. "I'm not your *little lamb*. If anything, I'm going to be *your* executioner."

Momentarily thrown by her comment, he gaped at her. Then his composure melted away, and he burst into laughter.

"My exec—executioner?" He could barely get the words out as he dropped the knife and held his stomach. It took all of two minutes to reel himself back in and wipe his teary eyes. "That's rich." He watched her with a twisted sort of respect. "You know you're tied up in a locked and secured bunker, right?"

She glared back at him.

"This bunker is like a panic room. You're on my property, surrounded by a twenty-foot fence, with armed men stationed everywhere. You will not be leaving this bunker alive. Even if you answered all my questions, and I verified everything to be true, you'd still die—with much less pain, though, I assure you." He raised a finger to make a point. "But you *will* die. Consider that preordained." He bent over and picked up the knife. "I have over twenty men in my employ. You're a naked woman tied to a mattress." He met her gaze. "I have no interest in taking a woman without her permission, but I have men working here who would love a taste of what you're offering."

"If I'm not offering answers to your stupid questions, what makes you think I'd offer anything else?"

"Oh, sugar, you're a walking vagina. You tempt men by entering a room. The makeup you wear recreates the flushed cheeks of sex, the plump lips after dozens of kisses. The heels women choose accentuate their calves to subliminally show a man what it would look like when you're bent over." He slapped the side of her thigh. "Come on, little one. Men are onto what women do to drive us wild. But hey, I get it." He raised his hands out to the side. "It's in your genes. You make objects of yourselves and then get upset when men objectify you. You claim to want to find a man, have a baby, and procreate." He lowered his hands and traced the knife along her flesh without breaking the skin. "Just don't play dumb. You're a walking sex toy, begging for a man with everything you do. All women are." He stopped and looked up to the side. "Well, perhaps not all women. Some prefer other women, but we know what the Bible says about homosexuality."

"You're a dinosaur. You know that, right?"

Cohen suppressed a laugh. "A dinosaur. Wow, I haven't been called that before."

"All that shit in the Bible was written for another era. Things change, people change. We grew up as a race. The Episcopalians rally in support of the LGBTQ community. They even have Episcopal priests who are openly gay now. Get with the program, old man."

He watched her for a full minute. So long that she turned away.

"Are you trying to end this faster by angering me?"

She didn't respond.

"Enough with the chit-chat. Let's get down to business. Tell me, who else is in your Satanic cult?"

"There isn't a cult, asshole. I already told you."

He applied the tip of the blade to the flesh above her kneecap. "We both know of its existence. Someone slaughtered several of my animals ritualistically and then informed the local media. That has to stop. Just tell me who's involved, and end this."

"Fuck you."

The blade slid effortlessly along her soft, tender flesh.

Sutton moaned until her mouth opened, and a partial wail escaped.

"Who do you work for?"

"*Fine!*" She snapped the ropes and spun his way. "I work for the FBI, as I said when you started. No one at the bureau believed me when I told them about your operation. The drugs, the farming, and what you're doing to the cattle. So, I set it up to draw more attention to your little operation." She spat at him, but it fell woefully short. "I'm a cult of one."

Something about her tone resonated with him.

"FBI agent? That's what you're going with? No way. I don't believe it. You're too careless and stupid to let Liam nab you if you're working for the feds."

"My former partner was supposed to sit in the truck stop parking lot with his car door open last night to get me out of here. I got there early and jumped in the wrong car."

"Oh, fancy storytelling. Do go on."

"When I saw I'd involved a mother and her child, I panicked and let Liam take me. So maybe I deserve to die for all the mistakes I've made." She was openly crying now. "But I know I've done enough to expose you. And when they come looking for me, it'll lead them to you. Unless you can make that mother, the father, and their child disappear, too, and deal with all the cops who handled everything last night, the FBI should be on your doorstep within days."

"You're lying." The words came out of his mouth as if someone else were saying them.

That officer called and said the FBI was in town, but they were looking for a missing man—not a woman. Or did he hear that wrong?

No, he didn't.

When that officer told him the FBI was at the police station looking for a missing person—a man—Cohen had explicitly asked if they were looking for a *male*. He remembered because his mind wandered to Liam and laughed off the thought that Liam could have been an informant.

Calls would have to be made. Who was the prisoner the FBI was so interested in? He had Vince send a guy to check in on him. Perhaps he'd know more soon.

It was time to learn more before he jumped to conclusions, though. He couldn't dismiss Sutton's story as anything more than fear-mongering.

The interrogation would have to be put on hold.

He would have to find that couple with the kid and take care of them if there was even the tiniest bit of truth to what she said.

When he looked at Sutton, she was smiling now, even though blood still oozed out of her body.

"The first tinge of fear just wrapped its arms around your blackened heart, didn't it?"

He jerked forward and placed the knife at her neck just under her ear. "Watch your mouth, *lamb*. Or I'll cut you a Glasgow smile."

The distinct sound of someone typing into the keypad made him turn toward the stairs. "I said I was not to be disturbed," he shouted over his shoulder.

The door opened, and sunlight filtered down, brightening up the bunker.

Cohen jumped from the mattress and set the knife on the side table where the other knives awaited their turn in the canvas bag.

"When I said I didn't want to be disturbed, that's exactly what I meant."

He strode toward the stairs, a knot forming in his stomach.

Which one of his men would openly defy him? Were the police here? The FBI? What could be the emergency?

And then he stumbled and caught himself at what he saw descending the steps.

"The Lord *does* work in mysterious ways …"

Cohen turned and ran for the knives.

Chapter 27

SARAH RIFLED THROUGH THE man's wallet until she pulled out his driver's license.

"Aristotle Hatzis?"

"I go by Aris." Their eyes met in the mirror. "Only my mother uses my full name."

"Where is your mother now?"

He stared forward through the windshield.

Sarah tried again. "You think she'd be proud of her Greek heritage by coming to America and having her son work for some preacher gangster?"

"Look, I already told you. The bank's about to take my house. I have a wife and a daughter, and with my experience in law enforcement, I was told Cohen pays well."

"The whole frog in the boiling water scenario."

"What's that?"

"How old is your daughter?" she asked, ignoring his question.

"She'll be two next month."

"And you want to get home safe to your little girl, right?"

"What kind of question is that?"

Sarah pulled his wallet apart and withdrew card after card. A picture slipped out between two cards and fell onto her lap. She picked it up and examined the faces in the photo.

"This your wife and daughter?" She held it up for him to see in the rearview mirror.

His eyes glazed over. "Yes."

"You want to see them again, right?"

"What kind of question—"

"One I want an answer to!" she shouted. "Fuckin' answer me." She raised the gun. "Or should I smack you with this? Do you want to see them again? Yes or no?"

"Yes," he cried out. "Of course I do."

"Well, guess what. I want to see my daughter again, too. I'm so sick of people separating us from each other that I'm ready to start shooting people on sight."

She leaned back in the seat and looked out the window. After a moment, when her heart calmed while thinking about where Willow may be, she stared at his driver's license.

"I suspect I'll find your loved ones on Hilltop Crescent in Casper, Wyoming, when this is all over."

"I'll kill you first," he muttered from the front seat.

"Or we can work together so both of us can have our families back."

He didn't respond.

"You're either on my side or you're not." Sarah tossed his wallet into the front seat but slipped the license into her pocket. "I'll hold onto your license until this is over."

"So, what, I work with you to save my family from you? Is that it?" He shook his head. "Brilliant. That'll put my family at risk from Cohen, and trust me. He's far scarier."

"No, you work with me and end Cohen's reign. That leaves no one to bother your family." She moved to lean on the back of his seat. "Worst case is you're looking for a new job. No jail time, no one hurt in the Hatzis family."

"Take down Cohen?" He scoffed. "Yeah, right. We have a better chance of kidnapping the Easter bunny and making him shit golden eggs."

Sarah withdrew Aris's phone and dialed Parkman's number. He answered right away.

"Hello?" The greeting was more of a question as he probably didn't recognize the number.

"Parkman, it's Sarah. One second. I'm going to put you on speakerphone." She tapped the button. "Where are you?"

"About twenty miles outside of Casper. I'll be in Glenrock within the hour."

"Don't come to Glenrock right away. I have an address in Casper I want you to go to."

"Send it."

"Don't," the driver said. Tears streamed down his cheeks. "Please don't."

"Who's that?" Parkman asked through the tinny speaker of the cell phone.

"One second, Parkman." Sarah leaned forward and kept all emotion from her voice. "I unloaded Officer Taggart's gun into Liam's chest last night. I abducted and shot that man at the truck stop. I've now abducted you, and I've got men entering Wyoming to finish this job. But Cohen has people working for him who have separated me from my family." She swallowed, fighting the urge to openly weep at what had happened and what she was doing to this man. "You have a unique ability to get me inside Cohen's compound. You're going to do that so I can meet with Cohen, and my friend Parkman will simply walk away. But if you don't help me, my friend Parkman will do damage to your family. They won't be able to walk away from it."

"Give me the address," Parkman said into the speaker, easily catching onto what she was planning.

Aris wiped his tears and shook his head. "But Cohen will kill you, then me."

"I will stop that from happening."

He pointed at a bridge they were about to pass under. "I could ram this Rover into that abutment and end both of us."

"But you won't, and I know this."

That thought had occurred to Sarah, but she ignored it, hoping the man loved his family enough to stay alive.

They passed under the bridge.

"Here's the address, Parkman." She recited it to him.

"On my way." Parkman clicked off.

"He won't touch them, will he?" Aris's voice broke with emotion.

"We're not animals. Your family is safe. But if my family is hurt, all bets are off."

The Rover slowed, and he signaled to turn off the highway. "What do you want from me?"

"I'll lie down in the back. You enter the compound. Find out where Cohen is, and get this vehicle as close as possible. Tell me everything you can about the place, make sure you park so that this rig's back or side door is hidden, and I'll leave quietly."

"That's it?"

"Well, you could stick around if I have to make a run for it."

He turned onto a road that could double as a long driveway.

"This is it. Up ahead." He placed his hand on the seat, palm facing upward. "Give me my phone."

"No way."

"You want in, right?"

She hesitated a moment, then handed it to him.

Aris dialed something, then held it to his ear. "Aristotle approaching. Coming from the truck stop. Wayne is dead. Dalton was shot. We did not secure the asset." He paused. "Where is Cohen now? I will need to report to him directly." Another pause. "Got it. Understood. Open the gate." Aris clicked off and lowered the phone.

Sarah glanced through the windshield at the massive wall in the distance. A large gate was sliding open as they moved closer.

"Aren't you jumping in the back?"

"Don't fuck me on this." Sarah climbed over the seat and tucked herself up in the rear of the Rover, curled into the back of the seat.

"He's in the bunker interrogating that woman from last night. He left instructions not to be disturbed." Aris raised his voice to be heard from the front. "I have the access code to the bunker—we all do in case we need to secure him quickly—so I'll park in a way that this vehicle will block your exit. Then I'll wait one full minute for you to come back up."

The Rover slowed, then sped up a notch.

"Okay, we're through the gate. Keep your head down."

Sarah caught a glimpse of the top edge of the gate as it rolled closed behind them. That didn't bode well for an easy escape.

Was this the right play? Did she make a mistake here? She'd like to think Vivian would've warned her to back off this plan if she did.

The Rover slowed, then stopped.

"I'll open the bunker door. You've got one minute. Then I'm out of here." Aris hopped out of the front seat.

Sarah sat up and glanced around. Two armed men manned the gate. A huge mansion sat to her right. Perfectly tended small trees and shrubs surrounded it with a large circular fountain at the front steps of the vast building.

"It's open," he called.

Sarah rolled over the seat, dropped onto the back seat, and then crawled out of the Rover.

Something resembling a trap door sat open in the grass beside the driveway.

She glanced at Aris, tightened her grip on his gun, then ran down the stairs, bent over.

"When I said I didn't want to be disturbed, that's exactly what I meant," a man said from deep within the darkness at the bottom of the stairs.

A man was walking toward the stairs.

She reached the bottom, and he fixed his gaze upon her, then stumbled and caught himself.

"The Lord does work in mysterious ways ..."

Cohen turned and ran away from her.

Sarah leveled the weapon and fired at him.

Chapter 28

SPECIAL AGENT NEWMAN WAS tired of waiting and pacing. He got up and moved to the nurses' station.

He placed his open ID against the Plexiglas. "I need to speak with a patient I accompanied here from Glenrock."

The woman looked up, stared at the ID for a moment, then turned back to her computer, fingers poised over the keyboard.

"Patient's name?"

"Aaron Stevens."

The woman frowned. "You must be late."

Newman closed his ID wallet and slipped it away, wondering what the woman could possibly mean. "Late?" He shook his head. "How so? I've been here the whole time."

"Someone from Glenrock PD is already in with him."

Newman shuffled back a few steps, his hand tightening on the counter. "Who? When?"

She shrugged. "He claimed to be with the cops."

"And you saw ID?"

The dark-haired woman looked up at him. "I'm a nurse, not security."

"Then tell me, *nurse*, what room number is Mr. Stevens in?"

"I think they moved him to"—she tapped on her screen, taking her sweet damn time—"yup, there it is. Room 204."

Newman bolted from the counter and ran for the exit sign. He'd take the stairs. Mounting them two at a time, Newman tore open the door on the second floor and scanned the hall for room numbers. They worked downward from 210 to 208, going to the left, which meant 204 would be that way.

He made it to the room and shoved the door open.

A man in a white doctor's coat was tapping on a computer beside the bed where Aaron rested.

"Where's the other guy?" Newman asked.

Aaron looked at him.

The doctor turned around. "What other guy?"

"Some guy was just here, claiming to be with the cops."

"Oh, him. Wait, who are you?"

"FBI," Newman blurted without producing his ID. "When did the other guy leave?"

The doctor turned to Aaron, who nodded. "He's legit."

"That *other* guy left no more than a minute ago." The doctor shrugged. "It was no big deal. Just wanted Aaron's particulars to process him."

"What was he wearing?"

"A black suit. Must be undercover or something—"

Newman didn't wait for the doctor to finish. He bolted from the room and scanned the hallway.

No man in a black suit.

He ran for the stairs again, dropped down to the main floor, almost tripped over a janitor's bucket, and ran out past the nurses' station.

The dark-haired woman he spoke to earlier looked up, her fingers raised in front of her face. He must have interrupted her daily nail-painting session.

Newman stared out the window into the parking lot.

"That way," the nurse said.

He spun toward her, and she cocked her head to the left, then blew on her nails.

Newman ran out the sliding doors and turned to the left.

A man in a dark suit was just getting into a brown Land Rover. By the time he took two steps, the Rover was already moving. No way he'd stop the guy now, and no way he'd ID the plate—it was too far away.

He went back inside, nodded at the nurse by way of thanks, then climbed the stairs and stepped back inside room 204.

"You okay to talk?" Newman asked, panting from the exertion of running up and down those stairs.

Aaron nodded. "Sleepy, but can talk. As long as I don't have to move."

The doctor had stepped out of the room.

Aaron was alone.

"They haven't cuffed you to the bed."

"They let me go."

"Let you go?" Newman moved to sit down where the doctor had been sitting. "You were their prisoner an hour ago. What changed their minds?"

Aaron's eyes slowly shut. "My guess is you did."

"You're on painkillers?"

"Yes. Not much they can do for the ribs. Time'll heal that. Small fracture in my cheekbone. Otherwise, all clear."

"Painkillers and don't move works."

"Uh-huh."

"Can you tell me everything? You up for that?"

"Sure. Then I want to sleep."

"Deal. Start talking."

"Someone abducted my girlfriend, Sarah, and Detective Billings tried to kill me when I called it in. After that, a woman named Teresa, supposedly from child services, took our daughter, Willow. Can you help bring us all back together again?"

"I'm going to try." Newman pulled out his cell phone and hit the voice memo app. "Start at the beginning. Tell me what Billings did. Describe this Teresa woman. Give me everything because something is wrong in Glenrock, and I want to find out what."

"I first heard the name Cohen inside the truck stop."

Aaron spent the next half hour fighting fatigue and spelling it all out for Agent Newman.

When Aaron fell asleep, Newman googled Cohen and saw his name everywhere in this part of Wyoming. Even photos of his mansion were online.

Suspected of drug running, money laundering, racketeering, and even rape and murder when a couple of bodies turned up downriver over the past few years. Investigations had been opened but went cold.

Detective Billings had cleared Martin Cohen of any wrongdoing several times.

The FBI has never been involved to date.

Newman got up, left Aaron's room, and made a few calls.

The first one was to his FBI field office.

Once he was on the phone with Supervisory Special Agent Michael Campbell, he told him everything.

"I need help out here, Mike."

"I can't spare any agents. Wish I could help, but you know how it is, Newman."

"Campbell, listen to me. Agent Sutton is still missing."

"What if she's at home having a nap? I mean, seriously, have you gone there yet?"

Newman paused, staring down the length of the hallway. "I'm going there soon, but I know she's in trouble."

"Look, you may not be hearing me. Unless you have evidence of a nuclear weapon on American soil, I can't spare any agents."

"Call another field office. Pull in some favors. Send me a dozen National Guardmen. Come yourself. I don't care how it's handled. Just send me someone, Campbell. Sutton needs our help, and this Cohen guy is filling the Glenrock coffers. A man and a woman driving through the area toward California were beaten up, the woman abducted, and their child taken by child services. Whatever Cohen's doing has spilled out into the public in a bad way." Newman took a deep breath. "Listen, Campbell. I don't ask for much. Six armed agents for two or three days." Before Campbell could object, he added, "Okay, four agents. Even two will help. C'mon, man." He gasped and waited for an answer.

"You've planted enough of a seed that I'm curious to see how this plays out."

"So you'll send me backup?" Newman stepped to the side to let a doctor pushing a patient get by.

"I didn't say that, but I'll see what I can do."

"Anything'll help. Call me when you have something."

As Newman was about to hang up, he heard Campbell still talking about who works for whom, and then the line died.

Martin Cohen will soon get a proper visit from the real authorities.

The Glenrock Police Department would also receive a thorough inspection. Newman wanted to see Detective Billings's desk and take pictures if the office was still in disarray. He needed something to corroborate Aaron's story.

Then, Agent Newman would take Billings's statement.

But first, finding his colleague, Agent Jamie Sutton, took priority.

And who was that black-suited man in the Land Rover?

One of Cohen's men?

He'd wait with Aaron for another hour, then head over to Sutton's place, which was minutes away from the hospital in Douglas.

He'd find her and figure out what was going on with Cohen. And he'd find that child services woman if that's who she really was.

Billings was the answer. Getting him to turn on Cohen was the key.

Like a juicy steak, this case had Newman ready to sink his teeth into what Sutton had implored him to look into weeks ago.

Why hadn't he listened to her?

Newman went back inside Aaron's room, already googling Billings's name.

He wanted to know everything he could about the man before they met.

Shit was about to get real.

Chapter 29

SARAH MADE SURE SHE aimed at the wall beside the door Cohen had just exited. Killing the fake preacher in his bunker wouldn't get her and her family out alive.

The man turned and ran for the back room.

Sarah gave chase, but she was going to be too late.

Cohen slapped a hand against the open door and shoved it hard toward Sarah.

Sarah took her last long stride, then lunged, feet forward, as if attempting to steal third base. She slid along the polished tiled floor, right foot extended, as the door swung closed.

Her shoe caught in the crack between the door and the frame at the last second. She pushed off the floor and shouldered into the door while Cohen tried to jam it the other way.

The door shot open and smacked Cohen off his feet.

When Sarah took in the room—the naked, bloodied woman on the bed, the canvas bag unrolled with several knife hilts sticking out on the stand beside the mattress—it wasn't hard to grasp what Cohen had been doing.

She raised her gun, aimed it at Cohen's head, and applied pressure to the trigger.

"No," the woman from last night in the barn said, her voice weak. "Don't kill him."

Sarah eased the pressure off the trigger as the sick man cowered in the corner, a hand over his face.

"Leave him to rot in prison. Death is too good for him."

Sarah turned to the woman, who lifted her arm. "Cut these off for me. Let's get out of here."

Sarah suppressed every urge to murder Cohen as she grabbed one of the knives and began slicing the ropes from the woman's wrists.

"How did you get past my security?" Cohen asked from the floor, his tone seething with anger. Or was it hatred?

"You don't like sitting on the floor of your dungeon, held captive by women?" She peered at him as she worked on the woman's left wrist.

"Thank her. Otherwise, I would've shot you in the face." The rope snapped. Sarah spun around and dropped to the woman's ankles. "This woman just saved your piece-of-shit life, although I might still kill you. Haven't decided yet."

"It's a bunker, not a dungeon."

Sarah stopped, raised the gun, and held it for a moment, her hand shaking with rage.

"Please," the woman said, gently touching Sarah's wrist. "He needs to rot for decades in prison. I'm Special Agent Jamie Sutton. Trust me. He'll get his."

Sarah blinked, lowered the gun, and looked into Sutton's face. "You're a fed?"

She nodded. "But we need to leave if we want to live. This place is heavily guarded."

Sarah fought hard not to shoot Cohen, then redoubled her efforts to free Sutton.

By the time she got to the last rope, Aris shouted down something unintelligible.

"What?" she yelled back.

"They're watching me. Hurry."

"Doing our best." Sarah faced Cohen. "Give me your shirt."

He shook his head and sneered at her.

Sarah stopped cutting the last rope and pushed up off the mattress. "You have a death wish, Cohen? This woman is naked and bleeding. Look what you've done to her." Sarah snapped her arm out to the right to point at Sutton. "Give her your shirt so she can leave your *dungeon* with some sense of dignity."

Sutton took up the rope cutting and finally snapped the last restraint.

When Sarah went to help her to her feet, Cohen pushed off the wall and made a break for the door.

Sarah's patience ended there.

She raised the gun, assured her aim, and fired.

Cohen dropped hard, sliding along the floor, clutching at his shoulder. He groaned like a truck's engine in a low gear, his head snapping from the wound to Sarah, then back to the wound.

"What have you done?" he bellowed.

Sarah shoved the gun in the back of her pants and ran at Cohen. She kicked him once in the gut to make him shut up and be more compliant. He lay back, dazed, his eyes swimming. When she checked the wound, it was nothing more than a scrape. A gouge about the size of a man's finger was missing from Cohen's left shoulder. Stitches would fix him up.

"Guys," Aris shouted down. "They're coming. We have to leave. *Now!*"

Without responding, Sarah undid the front buttons of Cohen's shirt, yanked his good arm out, and then rolled him onto his side to rip the shirt off his body.

Then she turned around and saw Sutton already on her feet. The woman looked like she'd been through a meat grinder.

"*Guys!*" Aris's tone projected fear now.

"Coming," Sarah shot back.

She draped the shirt—sporting a blood-rimmed bullet hole on the shoulder now—over Sutton, then guided her past Cohen, who was writhing and bleeding on the floor, to the bottom of the stairs.

"We need to leave." Sarah gestured at the stairs. "Can you get up on your own?"

Sutton nodded and ascended the stairs without hesitation.

It took more willpower than Sarah possessed to leave Cohen with one bullet hole. Cold-blooded murder certainly wasn't her thing, but men like Cohen were better off dead. It made the world a cleaner, brighter, and better place to live.

But yet, that willpower got her feet moving, and she followed Sutton up the stairs, leaving Cohen alive.

Aris's Rover was already running when she surfaced, the back door open. As Sutton lowered her head and climbed in the back, Sarah glanced toward the house and saw two armed men—automatic rifles draped over their bodies like someone would carry a guitar—approaching them, frowning.

Of course, they were wondering why Aris parked at the access door to the bunker.

"Get in, get in." Aris's voice took on a pleading tone Sarah had heard before. The voice of someone who knew they were about to die and was praying they'd get out alive somehow.

Sutton pushed across the seat, staying low. Sarah crawled in behind her, then shut the door, and Aris got them moving.

"Stay down. We're not safe yet."

The SUV bounced as it left the concrete and rode onto the lawn.

Sarah withdrew the pistol in case she needed to lower the window and cover their escape.

When she looked forward, the large gate was closed.

"How are we supposed to get out?"

"I don't know." Aris was frantic now. "I know the code, but two men guard it."

Sarah looked behind them at the two soldiers who had been approaching their vehicle, her eyes barely above the edge of the seat. They were running toward the open bunker door now.

"We may have trouble behind us."

"Hold on!" Aris shouted.

Sarah snapped forward to see an armed man in front of the gate, his hand up for them to stop.

Aris slammed the gas pedal down, knocking Sarah off balance and into the back of the seat.

Then, the vehicle jerked to the right, followed by a loud thump. The SUV bounced over something as Aris screamed.

His scream was cut short as they rammed into something hard, knocking Sarah into the back of the front seat, the gun falling from her grasp to the carpeted footwell. There was a heavy puff from the front as the airbags deployed, smacking Aris backward in his seat.

"What the fuck," Sarah muttered, the side of her mouth where the tooth was missing connecting with the seat's cloth. "That hurt."

When she looked outside, Aris pushed the airbag out of his way and climbed from the SUV, grunting like it took effort. Hunched over, he ran around the hood to a keypad on the wall beside the gate.

The scene was easy to deduce. When the armed guard stuck up his hand for them to stop, Aris adjusted his aim and hit the guy, the vehicle bouncing over his body. Then they slammed into the wall, activating the airbags.

Didn't he say there were two guards?

She dropped to the floor and snatched up her weapon as gunfire erupted behind them.

The back window shattered inward, and Aris screamed outside. Sutton curled into a ball, blood smearing the leather seats where it still seeped from her wounds.

When Sarah peeked up to see who was shooting at them, the two men who had gone to the bunker's open door were running toward them now. They had to clear over a hundred yards, but that wouldn't take them too long.

Something caught her eye, and she snapped to the right.

The second armed man who manned the gate slipped out of a small door to the left, his weapon up and aimed at Aris.

"Hey, man!" Aris pleaded. "I got a kid."

Sarah placed her right forearm on the top part of the front seat and adjusted her aim.

"Should've thought of that before you killed Sammy." The guard jerked something on his automatic weapon and raised it, finger inside the trigger guard.

Sarah fired first.

The man's lower jaw disappeared in a spray of red mush.

The weapon dropped from his hands, and he lowered to his knees, his eyes wild and bulging as he tried to process what the hell hit him.

More gunfire erupted from behind them.

"Open the damn gate!" Sarah shouted at Aris.

Then she heard a low rumbling, and the gate began a slow roll to open.

The pinging sounds of automatic weapons kept Aris huddled below the front grill of his SUV, with Sarah lying on top of Sutton, praying a stray bullet wouldn't take either one of them out after getting so close.

They didn't have enough firepower to slow the men coming, and if they didn't leave soon, they'd all die whether the gate was open or closed.

Yet the bullets didn't stop. There were short pauses, but not enough for Aris to come around and get back inside.

Sarah waited for another pause, then hauled herself up and crawled between the front seats.

"Get up on the hood," she yelled through the broken front windshield. The gate was fully open now. "Hold onto something."

She shoved the brake pedal down, dropped it into drive, then jammed the gas pedal down at the exact second the tip of an automatic weapon came into view in the open door.

The man fired, but the movement of the SUV knocked the weapon forward, and bullets riddled the dashboard.

The driver's side door slammed shut with the forward movement as someone screamed. It took Sarah a moment to realize it was Sutton in the back.

Was she hit? What about Aris? Did he grab something to hold onto?

The SUV was still going forward—blindly.

She waited for another heartbeat, then peeked over the dashboard and corrected the wheel to keep it centered on the road.

Sitting higher now, she checked the mirrors, but they were all broken.

"Stop!" Aris yelled. "I can't—hold."

Sarah hit the brakes, and the SUV shuddered and stopped.

Aris popped up in front. "Holy fuck shit."

"Get in!" She spun around, but the armed men were gone. They were likely going for their vehicles.

Aris ran around and jumped into the passenger side.

Sarah hit the gas again, and they made it out to the highway uninterrupted. She yanked the wheel to head toward the truck stop.

"Are you hit?"

Aris appeared to be hyperventilating. He shook his head. "No. Thanks to you."

Sarah jerked a thumb at the back seat. "Check Sutton. Make sure she's okay."

He spun around and looked in the back seat. "You good?"

"Glass cut me."

"Like you needed more wounds," Sarah said loud enough to be heard over the wind coming through the broken windows.

Out of habit, she rechecked the mirrors, saw they were broken, and smacked Aris to get his attention. "Hey, look behind us. Are we being followed?"

"No one yet. Drive faster."

Sarah pushed the gas harder and leaned forward to peer through a smooth windshield piece near the bottom.

"Where are you headed?" Aris shouted.

Sarah hadn't thought that far ahead. "Is there a hospital this way? Sutton will need stitches."

"The closest one from here is in Douglas, about ten more minutes down the highway."

"Keep an eye out back, and I'll get us to the hospital." She pushed the SUV even harder, getting it up to seventy miles an hour. The wind was too loud to talk at that speed as it whistled through a dozen bullet holes. She wanted to ask Aris what he grabbed onto at the front, but that could wait.

Out of what had happened to them since last night, escaping with their lives from Cohen's compound was a miracle. But escaping with an FBI agent was a godsend.

Maybe things were looking up after all.

Chapter 30

MARTIN COHEN GOT HELP getting to his feet. Vince, his head of security at the house, wrapped a thick towel around his wounded shoulder and secured it under his arm to staunch the blood flow while Jacob watched the door.

"We have to get you to a doctor, sir."

"I'm not going to any doctor. That veterinarian we have on staff can fix it up." He started for the stairs. "But not until that meddling woman is dead. Where are they?"

"Gone, sir."

Cohen stopped, his good arm resting on the railing. Seething with anger, the pain irritating him, he looked at Vince as Jacob, another one of his men, came down the stairs. "Gone? You mean off my property?"

Vince nodded. "Yes, sir. Gone."

"How's that?" He glanced at the ground to steady his equilibrium. A wave of dizziness made him stagger. "Wasn't the gate closed?"

"They had help. Aristotle was driving. They killed both guards at the gate, Aris typed in the gate code, and they left."

Cohen looked at Vince, then Jacob. He gestured for Jacob's weapon. "Give me that. I'll kill them myself."

Jacob glanced at Vince, who nodded, then the man slipped the shoulder strap over his head and handed the weapon to Cohen. Once Cohen checked that it was ready to fire, he aimed it at Vince and held the trigger down.

Vince's body shot back several feet as dozens of bullets—or more. Cohen could never be sure how many bullets automatic weapons fired per second—broke the flesh of his upper chest, neck, and face.

When Vince dropped to the floor, his cheeks and nose caved in like a chunk of mangled ground beef, Cohen handed the gun back to the cowering Jacob.

"You're now the head of security for the house, Jacob." He eyed the man. "You okay with the promotion?"

"Yes—" His voice was cut off as he swallowed. "Yes, sir."

"Good. Now follow me." Cohen clutched at his wounded shoulder and ascended the stairs.

In the distance, he saw two bodies lying on the ground by the open gate. "What the fuck," he whispered aloud. "Who the hell is that woman?" He snapped his head to Jacob. "And how did she know to use Aris? What sort of information does she have on me?"

Jacob's face tightened, and his neck corded like he had eaten an olive and swallowed the pit. "Uhm, I'm sorry, sir, but Vince was handling Aris and Wayne at the truck stop. I understand Wayne was shot, and now we know she forced Aris to do ..." he glanced at the gate and gestured with his hand toward the bodies, "this."

Cohen's adrenaline waned, making his shoulder wound throb. He needed painkillers to keep his mind alert and on track.

"Get me to the vet. I need to dull this pain. Then we find that woman. I'll rip off her head, shit on her chest, and burn the body while she's still alive."

"Yes, sir."

Jacob led him to one of the Land Rovers parked near the fountain at the front of the house. Neither man spoke as Jacob helped Cohen in the back, then jumped in the front and got them rolling toward the open gate.

"When we're through, close that fucking gate."

"Yes, sir."

Cohen rested his head back and breathed through his mouth to control the pain as Jacob hopped out and typed in the code to secure the gate. As it began its long roll to close, he detected the sound of an engine revving.

Cohen lifted his head and saw one of his Land Rovers kicking up dust as it raced toward them.

Jacob did not get back in the vehicle. Instead, he leaned across the hood of the Rover and aimed at the oncoming vehicle.

Cohen squinted through the windshield. As far as he could tell, there was one occupant—the driver.

"Hold up," he shouted out to Jacob. "He looks like one of ours."

"That woman was in a hijacked Rover." Jacob pushed off the hood and straightened up. "Just had to be sure."

The other Rover pulled up alongside them, the window lowering as it did so.

"Sir," one of his men said. He thought the guy's name was Bryce or something, but couldn't remember.

"What is it?"

Bryce glanced at the towel wrapped around his shoulder. "Wait, are you okay, sir?"

"Does it look like I'm okay?" Cohen snapped.

Bryce leaned forward and stretched his neck to look at Jacob. "Where's Vince?"

"He's dead. Wayne's probably gone, too, and both gate guards. Aris has been abducted."

Bryce turned back to Cohen. "What the hell is going on?" The man's voice rose in pitch.

Cohen blew out an exasperated breath as the pain rose in his shoulder. "Now that the get-to-know-you stage is over, where the fuck were you when we got ambushed?"

Bryce paled as he leaned back, his face slipping behind the shadow the roof caused. "I'm sorry, sir. I was at the hospital in Douglas. Vince ordered me to get a full ID on the guy who attacked Billings last night."

Cohen ground his teeth, spread his legs in the back seat, and clutched the tops of his thighs, fingers tightening on his flesh. "We're on our way to get me painkillers." His words came out with an edge of rage. If this man—maybe Bryce, maybe not—didn't speak faster, he'd have another dead guard, which was one less salary to pay. Today certainly wasn't costing him money. "With each second you delay me, you're killing me with pain." He glared daggers at the man. "Speak faster. What did you learn?"

"His name is Aaron Stevens, and he's Sarah Roberts's boyfriend."

Cohen had no idea his patience could stretch this thin. "Am I expected to know them?"

Bryce eased forward again, his face back in the sunshine as he leaned out the window. "Sarah Roberts is some kind of psychic witch from the Toronto area. I googled her and saw dozens of cases she's solved. She's also a badass with friends in high places. Her boyfriend is a martial arts expert, and he—"

"Didn't help him with Billings, did it?" Cohen had detected a vein of admiration for this woman and her boyfriend in Bryce's tone, so he had to cut him off. "The detective is at home with a sore nose, and this Stevens asshole is in the hospital."

Bryce nodded. "Right, but I learned this Sarah woman just *knows* stuff sometimes. Cops have requested her help on cases in the past. This woman is formidable. That's why I raced back here to tell you."

Cohen glanced down at his feet. He had to remain calm, or he'd kill the last few members of his security team. Hiring new ones wouldn't be an issue, but it could slow down business, and he had deliveries to make. These men meant nothing to him, so why not use them to better his situation? If they expired in the process, so be it.

"The Lord certainly does work in mysterious ways," he said. After a deep breath to manage the pain, he faced Bryce. "If Sarah *knows* stuff, as you put it, that makes sense. She managed to catch Aris and get him to help her. She entered my compound, walked into my bunker, shot me, and took that woman with her. If she just *knows* stuff, then she knew exactly how to extract that woman and get back out alive."

"Wow," Bryce said, definite admiration in his tone now. "That's insane, sir. Impressive, but insane."

Cohen reached for the gun he had stashed in the pouch at the back of the front seat, then stayed his hand.

"But what that Sarah woman does not know is how I'll respond."

"Wait," Bryce raised a finger out the window, acting as if they were debating a point. "If she's psychic, then she'll be able to anticipate—"

"She's not psychic," Cohen shouted out the window, spittle coming from his mouth. Pain flared in his shoulder to agony. "As stated in Leviticus 20:27, 'Every man or woman who is a medium or a psychic must be put to death. They must be stoned to death because they deserve to die.'"

Bryce's pallid face nodded. This time, his mouth was firmly closed, lips thin and tight against each other.

Oh, blessed silence ...

"Or shall I quote Deuteronomy 18:10 to 12, where God is clear about occult practices? 'Let no one be found among you who practices divination or sorcery, who is a medium or spiritist, or who consults the dead. Anyone who does these things is detestable to the Lord.'" He paused to let that sink in—and to catch another breath. "So, gentlemen, that is why this Sarah bitch is here in Glenrock."

Bryce and Jacob glanced at each other, then back to Cohen. Neither man took the risk of saying a word.

"She's been delivered unto me so I can stone her, burn her, then kill her. God has ordained me to be the one to exile her from our plane of existence and banish her back to the Hell she was spawned from."

"Your arm, sir." Jacob gestured. "It's seeping through the towel."

Cohen rested his head back as his stomach grew queasy. His forehead and hands were sweating hard now.

"Take me to the hospital in Douglas."

"Sir? We're not going to the vet?"

Cohen was tired of fighting. "No, the hospital. They can sew me up and give me painkillers while you two take care of Aaron for me."

"Sir? Take *care* of Aaron?"

He lifted his head off the seat and stared at Jacob. "As head of security, I need you and Bryce to go to Aaron's room and remove him from the hospital. That'll draw that Sarah witch from the lair she hides in. And when she comes out of hiding, I'll end it." He laid his head back.

"Yes, sir." Jacob jumped into the front seat.

"Oh," Bryce said from beside him. "It's Brent, sir. Not Bryce."

Cohen waved a hand. "It's Bryce now. And give me your shirt. That bitch stole mine."

"Yes, sir."

Bryce undid the buttons of his collared shirt, slipped out of it, and handed it across to Cohen.

"Go inside. Get dressed. Then, meet us at the hospital."

Bryce went to say something, but Cohen looked away.

"Go," he shouted.

Jacob hit the gas.

They'd be at the hospital in ten minutes. Aaron would be his prisoner soon after, and he'd have an alibi while getting his shoulder stitched up.

Things were looking better by the second.

He smiled through the pain as the wind rushed through the open window and ruffled his hair.

Maybe he would stone her. That would be something. To throw stones at someone until they died gave him a giddy feeling.

His smile widened. "God is gracious."

Chapter 31

SARAH PARKED THE LAND Rover close to the emergency doors, then hopped out. She opened the back door and looked in at Sutton, who was awake, but she didn't look good—the woman still bled in several places.

With the preacher's shirt over her shoulders, it left her lower regions exposed. Sarah gawked at the damage that man had done to Sutton's thighs—horrendous.

"Give me your shirt so I can wrap it around her waist."

Aris didn't move from the front passenger seat.

Sarah glared at him. "We've come all this way. She needs to be inside." Sarah thrust out her hand. "Give. Me. Your. Shirt. Now."

Aris pointed at her front pocket, where his cell phone now resided. "Call your man off my family."

"My man?" Then she remembered. Parkman was supposed to go over to Aris's house as insurance to get Aris to comply. "My *man* didn't go anywhere. Now, your shirt."

Aris sucked in some air and sat higher in the seat. "What?"

"We don't have time," she shouted. "Now cover this woman up, and let's get her inside—" She stepped back. "You know what? Forget about it. Fuck you."

She ran around the front of the Rover and entered the hospital. At the triage, she slapped the Plexiglas hard.

The woman behind the divider snapped up to look at her.

"I've got an FBI agent who is seriously injured in my vehicle. She needs medical attention *now*."

"Okay, ma'am. Please calm down and—"

"No, *calm down*," Sarah said in a whiny, mocking voice. "This is an emergency. Get someone outside with a stretcher and a blanket. She's been tortured, and she's naked!"

The woman grabbed her phone, hit a few buttons, and dialed out. She whispered something into the receiver, her eyes on Sarah.

"I'll be outside. It's the Land Rover right there."

After pointing at the vehicle through the windows, she'd done her part. Jamie Sutton was safe now—finally. From the moment the woman had jumped into her car last night until now, she was finally safe and out of Cohen's clutches.

When she turned around, she bumped into a man standing too close.

"Excuse me," she said as she attempted to step around the man, but the man grabbed her arm and stopped her.

"Who did you say you brought to the hospital?"

Sarah glanced down at the man's hand, then looked up and met his gaze. "Release my arm, or I'll break your fucking hand."

The man tightened his grip. "I will ask again because I'm a nice guy. Who did you say you brought here?"

Sarah grabbed the man's wrist with her free hand, yanked her arm downward in a jerking motion, and shoved the man backward.

He stumbled, a surprised gasp escaping his lips—likely didn't expect her to react so quickly—then regained his balance, shook his wrist, and rushed her.

She ducked low, jabbed at his stomach twice, then grabbed the wrist of the hand that had held her arm a moment ago and spun it over her head as she twisted her body.

The man flipped around and lifted up off his feet, landing on the hospital floor on his back. Sarah jammed her foot down on his chest, his arm still in her grasp, his shoulder twisted at an impossible angle. Everyone in the room stared at them in dazed silence.

"You're lucky your broken hand will be cast quickly. You know, being in a hospital and all."

She braced herself to snap the man's wrist, but stopped when the man shouted at her.

"I'm an FBI agent." He grunted under her foot, squirming on the floor. "You just assaulted a federal agent."

Sarah stared down at him, then looked over at the triage woman, who nodded. "He's FBI," she whispered.

"I should still break your hand for not identifying yourself." She released him. "And for assaulting me first, dickweed."

The man shook his wrist again as he climbed to his feet. "Where did you learn that?"

"Aaron taught me. My boyfriend."

The man was getting up from his knees when he stopped and stared at her open-mouthed. "Aaron Stevens?"

She frowned as two paramedics burst out of the emergency doors and ran past her with a stretcher, heading toward the Land Rover.

"How do you know Aaron?"

He pushed himself to his feet using the counter's edge. "You must be Sarah Roberts." He went to shake her hand, glanced down at the hand surrounded by reddened skin, and pushed out his other hand.

Sarah didn't shake it. After a moment, the man lowered his hand.

"You said you were bringing in an FBI agent. Where is she?"

Sarah shook her head. "Why did you say my boyfriend's name?" Sarah glanced over the man's shoulder. The paramedics were at the SUV and were easing Sutton out.

"I've been sitting with Aaron, getting his statement. I was just leaving to visit a colleague here in town when I overheard you say you brought in an FBI agent."

Sarah placed a hand on her chest. "Aaron's statement? You mean he's here?"

The man nodded. "He's upstairs in room 204. Who is this agent you brought with you?"

"Jamie Sutton."

The man leaned back on the counter as if he couldn't hold himself up. Behind him, the sliding doors opened, and the doctors wheeled the stretcher inside.

"A man named Martin Cohen abducted her. He was cutting her up pretty badly when I got her out of Cohen's bunker. They shot at us with assault rifles. Just look at that Land Rover."

The man turned to see that the white sheet covering Sutton was already darkening with blood. Aris followed the doctors inside. "That man helped us escape Cohen." She pointed at Aris. "Without him, Sutton would be dead."

"I'm Special Agent Newman." He nodded at Aris. "We'll talk later. You two deserve an award for this." He tapped Sarah on the shoulder before she could smack his hand away, then he ran past her to follow the stretcher deep into the hospital. "We'll talk again," he shouted over his shoulder. "Don't go anywhere." Then he was gone, calling Sutton's name.

Aris sidled up to her. "Who was that?"

"Another FBI agent, likely looking for Sutton."

"You said I helped. You said nice things."

"You did help. And you no longer work for Cohen. I told you, help me, and you'll be out of a job. But that would be the worst case. Better that than spending ten years in prison for Cohen. Your family needs you."

"What about your friend?"

Sarah took a step backward. She needed to get to room 204. "He did *not* go to your house. I told you. I would never *actually* threaten your wife and child."

"Prove it."

Sarah pulled Aris's phone from her pocket and tossed it to him. "Call your wife. She's had no visitors."

Then she turned and ran for the stairs. Sutton was fine. Cohen was fucked. As soon as Sutton told her colleague everything, Cohen would be picked up and arrested.

It was over. She'd get Aaron, and they'd get Willow and get the hell out of Wyoming as fast as the wind.

She hit the stairs running, the gun in the back of her pants digging into her back.

Giving that up wasn't an option yet.

Something told her this wasn't over.

Chapter 32

COHEN OPENED HIS EYES when Jacob slowed the vehicle down as they entered the hospital parking lot. The throbbing in his shoulder had subsided a notch, making it tolerable, but he still needed to go inside and get it looked at. The alibi was solid as his men removed Aaron from the premises.

"Hey," Jacob said as he slowed to a crawl. "Isn't that …" His voice trailed off. "Holy shit. Jackpot."

Cohen sat up, his free hand holding the blood-wet towel in place on his shoulder.

A Land Rover was parked next to the emergency unit's sliding doors. Its windows were shot out, and the side was riddled with bullet holes.

"Well, I'll be." He shook his head. "Sutton and that bitch are here, too. Three for the price of one."

"Three, sir?"

Cohen met Jacob's gaze in the rearview mirror. "Sarah and Sutton are here, as well as Aaron."

"I was thinking four, sir."

Cohen smiled. "This time, you're correct. The Judas, Mr. Aristotle Hatzis, was with them, so he'll also be here. Praise the Lord. He's delivering everyone unto me."

Jacob stopped several parking spaces back from the shot-up Rover in front of them. "What would you like me to do, sir?"

"I'm going to step out of this vehicle and get medical treatment. While I'm in there getting stitched up, you wait for Bryce. Then one of you will find Sutton and that demon witch, Sarah. The other one will find Aaron."

Cohen opened his door.

"And do what, sir?"

He jumped down, closed the back door, and then walked up beside Jacob's open window.

"Kill that Sutton bitch. Shoot her dead. Use a pillow on her face. I don't care. Just make sure she dies. Then kill Aaron, as we won't need him to lure Sarah anymore. But that Sarah witch—bring her to me. I will kill her myself. Oh, and if you see Aristotle, make sure he doesn't leave this hospital alive."

"But, sir." Jacob's voice cracked, and his eyebrow twitched.

"What is it?" Cohen did not soften his voice for the sake of the man's feelings. Asking more questions when he should be running into the hospital guns blazing would piss him off.

"They'll hear the gunshots."

What kind of men did he have working for him? "Then don't use a gun. They're wounded—Aaron's broken up and in a hospital bed. Sutton is cut up and has lost half her body's blood. Neither will resist. Place a fucking pillow over their faces and hold it there for one minute. Surely you can do that, can't you?"

Jacob released the breath he'd been holding. "Yes, that would work."

"Great. Then find a way to get that psychic witch in the back of this vehicle, even if you have to drag her out of the hospital by her hair. I have to be the one who sends her to Hell."

A car screeched to a halt behind them. Cohen looked back and saw Bryce hopping out of the Rover.

"Good, Bryce is here. Fill him in. I'm going inside to get stitched up. Oh, wait. Give me the keys to this Rover. You two take your prisoner in that one." He pointed at the vehicle Bryce pulled up in.

Jacob tossed him the keys, and Cohen walked off, not for a second assuming they'd be able to do as he'd asked but hoping they'd at least kill one of the three before someone stopped them.

When he walked by the shot-up Rover, he thought he detected movement near the rear. Cohen slowed, then stopped, staring at the vehicle. He moved forward, leaning to look around the back.

Nothing.

Bryce and Jacob were talking outside the Rovers when he glanced back over his shoulder.

Cohen moved along the length of the vehicle, peeked around the front, and then entered the hospital.

There was no line at the triage desk when he stepped up. "Ma'am, I need to see someone about a shoulder wound."

The dark-haired woman at her computer seemed a bit pale.

"What happened to your shoulder?"

"My friend and I were doing some target practice, and a bullet grazed me." He offered her a half-smile. "Just need a little help."

"Of course," she said, then picked up her phone.

Cohen turned to look back out the windows at his Rovers.

Jacob and Bryce were jogging toward the side of the building.

Good. Things were looking up.

Chapter 33

ARISTOTLE HATZIS CROUCHED BEHIND the Land Rover. He'd almost allowed Cohen to see him, but the other two idiots were oblivious to his presence as they chatted twenty feet away.

Then, he watched Jacob and Brent sprint toward a set of double doors on the far side of the complex. Once they were out of sight, he bolted from hiding and ran the other way, hoping to find a way inside the hospital.

He came upon a set of open double doors under a sign that read ADMINISTRATION.

Aris stopped running and pulled out his phone. What was he doing? Helping Sarah? Why?—he worked for Cohen. So far, he'd only helped that woman because she forced him to.

His wife was on speed dial, so he hit the button and listened to the phone ring on the other end. He'd exited the hospital and was about to call her when he saw Cohen talking to Jacob by their SUV. So, he hid behind the shot-up Rover and waited.

"Hey, honey," Janice said. "You coming home soon?"

He breathed a sigh of relief. There was no stress in her voice. "Everything fine there, baby?"

"What?" She laughed, and the sound was musical. "Of course, it is. Our little one and I were just about to sit down and watch a Disney classic. Why do you ask?"

Aris leaned against the brick wall. "Just having a bad day at work. I just wanted to hear your voice. I'll be home in a few hours. Love you."

"Love you, too." She giggled into the phone.

"Send love to our little one."

"Daddy says he loves you."

"I wuv Daddy," his daughter said somewhere close by the phone.

"Talk soon," he said and ended the call before she heard the emotion in his voice.

What was he doing working for a man like Cohen? Putting money over the welfare of his family?

Was there a way to change that at this late hour? He could quit, but

Cohen would know he betrayed him. If it weren't Sarah and her people, it would be Cohen who came after him now.

But Sarah hadn't sent her man to his house.

Would helping Sarah go after Cohen end the man's hold he had on Aris? And if it did, how many charges would befall Aris when it was all said and done?

A decision had to be made, and Aris had already figured out what that decision would be.

He had to help Sarah Roberts.

That was the best play here. Even thinking about it made his gut churn up a storm. He didn't want to miss his daughter's early years. Working for Cohen had been easy money. Nothing ever happened in Glenrock, and when it did, Cohen had the cops in his pocket. Also, since Aris was part of Cohen's security team, he had nothing to do with the drug operation Cohen ran out of the farms he owned in the area.

But with the FBI onto him, that would all come out.

Could Aris turn in the state's evidence? Tell them everything he knew and get a free pass along with a witness protection program?

Not helping Sarah wouldn't help that. But what if Sarah's man was sitting outside Aris's house right now?

An idea came to him, and he had to know, even though he was running out of time—Cohen's men were inside the hospital hunting Sutton and Sarah.

He opened the list of the last numbers called on his phone and scrolled to the one before his wife.

The number Sarah called before they got to Cohen's compound.

Aris hit the call button, and acid filled his stomach.

"What else do you need?" the man answered, wind from an open car window in the background.

"Where are you?"

"Who is this?"

"Who I am isn't important. Sarah called you earlier and gave you my home address. Are you on your way there?"

"That doesn't matter. Do what Sarah needs you to do, or your family dies."

Aris tightened his grip on the phone. "Let me tell you something, tough guy—"

"Start talking and telling, asshole. You're running out of time."

"Sarah is at Memorial Hospital in Douglas at this moment. She's in danger. Two of Cohen's security men—call them hitmen because that's what they are—just went inside, and I'm sure they're going after Sarah for what she did at Cohen's compound."

"Why are you telling *me* this? Tell her."

"Well, I'm in a unique position to help Sarah. She does not know they're coming. But why should I help her if you're still going after my family?"

There was a pause on the other end. "How can I trust you'll do the right thing?"

"You just have to. Sucks, don't it?"

"I'm nowhere near your house. Sarah would never *hurt* anyone's family. When she calls and gives an address, I always answer positively so whoever's listening gets the point. We've worked together for so many years—it's code to us. We get each other."

"Motherfucker—"

"But if you know Sarah's in danger and do nothing about it, that'll be cause for retribution—"

"Don't threaten me now." He leaned forward to force those words through his teeth. "How long until you're in Douglas?"

"I'm just entering Glenrock now."

"Then you're thirty minutes away." Aris glanced up at the sky and watched the white trail of a jet as it soared overhead. He yearned to be on it with his family en route to a beach in Mexico somewhere. "You won't make it in time."

"What are we doing?" the man said. "If what you said is true, Sarah needs a warning."

"Who are you?"

"What?"

"I mean, what's your name?"

The man hesitated a moment. "Parkman."

"I'm Aristotle, but everyone calls me Aris."

"Pleasantries aside, what are we doing?"

"Come to the hospital in Douglas. By the time you get here, some people will likely be dead. Let's just hope it's not Sarah and me. I'm heading inside to warn her."

"Then fuckin' hurry—"

Aris ended the call, slipped his phone away, and bolted inside the hospital.

Chapter 34

SPECIAL AGENT NEWMAN REFUSED to leave the room as the doctors sedated and worked on stitching up his former partner. What the hell had Cohen done to her? Sutton would be scarred for life.

And all because no one at the bureau listened to her.

Newman suppressed the rage that made his hands clench, his teeth grind, and an urge to shout.

A doctor bumped into him as he reached for something on a metal cart. "Sir, we need the room."

"I'm *not* fucking leaving."

Several medical team members—four people in total, one woman and three men—looked up at him, then went back to threading up Sutton's flesh.

With a hand on his stomach, Newman wondered if he'd be sick.

He moved to the back of the room and dropped into a chair by the wall. With his elbows on his thighs, he stared at the floor and breathed deeply, hoping his stomach would calm enough for the waves of nausea to pass.

The images of Sutton's horrific wounds, the stitches, and the scars she'd endure would last a lifetime. Who could do such a thing?

The room's door opened, interrupting his thoughts.

A man in a black suit stepped inside.

Newman shot to his feet, his hand twitching to go for his gun. "Who are you?" he asked, thinking this was the guy who interrogated Aaron before he got to him.

The guy watched the doctors working on Sutton, then turned to Newman, his right hand hidden behind his thigh.

"Where's the woman who brought her here?" the man asked, jerking his head toward the bed. "I must speak with her."

Something was wrong with this guy. His body language was off.

Newman moved a few steps to his left to look at the guy's right hand, but it didn't matter—the intruder lifted his arm and aimed a gun at Newman, who instinctively lifted his hands.

"Where's the woman?"

"Hey," one of the doctors said. "What the hell are you doing with that in here? This is a hospital."

The man adjusted his aim. "Last chance. Where's the bitch who brought this woman to the hospital?"

The doctor backed away.

Newman wasn't waiting for someone to get shot. All the bottled-up rage forced his hand back to grip the butt of his weapon, and then he drew it and aimed at the man.

"FBI," he shouted. "Lower your weapon."

The black-suited man didn't hesitate when he swung the pistol toward Newman.

But Newman didn't hesitate either.

The sound of the agent's weapon discharging in the small hospital room was quickly followed by another report as the black-suited man had pulled his trigger as well.

All four doctors working on Sutton ducked, with two of them slamming into the floor.

Due to Newman's bullet hitting the man's upper shoulder, the man's shot missed. His bullet raced by Newman's face and smacked into a corkboard pinned to the wall.

Then Newman was firing again, even though the armed intruder had dropped against a metal tray, knocking all the doctor's implements to the floor in a muffled clanging—his hearing was dulled due to the gunshots.

Newman fired again and again in a wild attempt to neutralize the threat. His fourth bullet tore into the man's elbow—the arm that gripped his pistol—and knocked the gun free from his grasp.

By that point, the man had fired two more times himself. In his peripheral vision, Newman caught sight of one of the doctors grasping at his leg.

Newman pounced when the intruder's weapon dropped to the hospital room floor. He flipped the man onto his stomach and tore his arms backward to secure them.

When the man screamed at the pain—there was a bullet in his shoulder and one in his elbow, which made the elbow bend backward at an odd double-jointed angle—Newman didn't care. The perp had stormed into an FBI agent's hospital room, shot a doctor, and tried to kill a fellow agent.

Sirens were wailing in the hospital now, and men crowded around him. When he looked up, hospital security had stepped in to help secure the man. Out of reflex—muscle memory—Newman swapped magazines, barely aware of what he was doing.

Other doctors entered the room. Over a dozen people now stood in Sutton's small hospital room as they loaded the wounded doctor onto a gurney and wheeled him out.

Then Sutton's bed was unlocked and wheeled to the door.

"Hey, where are you taking Agent Sutton?" Newman shouted.

"Out of the way," a man yelled, pushing Sutton past him.

Newman grabbed the edge of her gurney. "Where are you taking her?"

The doctor looked back at Newman's hand, then up to his face. "Trauma unit. Gunshot wound to the side."

Newman glanced down.

Sutton was bleeding profusely from the side where a hole gushed blood.

He released the gurney in a daze.

Then, her bed disappeared through the door of the room.

Jamie Sutton wasn't getting any breaks. The poor woman would die if those men kept coming.

How was this possible? Where was his backup?

The bureau let this happen.

Still shaking from the adrenaline, unsure his legs would hold him up much longer, Newman wobbled from the room and found a chair in the hallway.

He flopped into the chair, pulled out his phone, and dialed his field office.

He needed a team here yesterday.

And he would stop at nothing to make that happen.

Chapter 35

SARAH HEARD POPPING SOUNDS like gunshots coming from somewhere in the hospital. They stopped when she cocked her head to listen better.

"You okay?" Aaron asked, his voice weak.

"Yeah, I just thought I'd heard something." She adjusted herself against his bed, her hand on his arm. "You were saying. About Willow."

"They gave her to a woman named Teresa with child protection services. Billings orchestrated the whole thing."

"And this was after you called him to say you suspected I'd been abducted."

"Exactly." Aaron opened his eyes and looked at her. "Was that your tooth on the floor mats of the car?"

She opened her mouth and pointed at the hole with her tongue. "The guy who did it died last night in a barn."

Aaron's eyebrows shot up. "You killed him?"

Sarah shook her head. "Well, no, but the guy who killed him is probably somewhere in this hospital because I put a bullet in his leg over an hour ago."

"What the fuck has been going on?"

"Too much to tell you now. I have to find Willow first." She placed a hand on the side of the bed and leaned closer. "Aaron, a preacher runs everything in Glenrock, even the police. I had a chance to kill him, but the FBI stopped me."

"The FBI stopped you?" Aaron's volume rose with each word, and he winced as his chest moved with the intake of breath.

"I'm going to find this Teresa woman and get our daughter back. I'll start with that Detective Billings asshole who did this to you."

"Can you hurt him for me? Just a little?"

"I'm sure when I ask him where Teresa is, he won't answer, so sure …" She stared at the mass of bruises on Aaron's face. "I can break a bone or two—"

The door shot open. Sarah spun around, her hand going for the gun.

A woman dressed as a nurse stepped inside. "I'm sorry, but I'm looking for Sarah Roberts."

Sarah and Aaron exchanged a glance as Sarah relaxed her hand. "Why?"

"There's a phone call for her."

She frowned. "That doesn't sound right," she whispered to Aaron. "No one knows I'm here." Sarah let her hand fall to the side, the weapon no longer needed.

The nurse looked at the phone and then at Sarah. "He said his name is Parkman."

"Well, that sounds right." Aaron nudged her. "Go take the call."

The nurse edged into the room further and handed Sarah the phone.

"Sarah here."

"Guys, you're in danger."

She gave Aaron a slight nod to confirm it was Parkman. "What are we looking at? How many?"

"Two hitmen, according to Aris."

Sarah stood straighter, thinking about the gunfire she thought she had heard minutes ago. "Aris? How do you know him?" She trailed off as it came to her. Aris had his phone back. He would've called his family and found out Parkman never went to his house. He then called Parkman after finding his number in the phone's history.

"We exchanged pleasantries," Parkman said.

"You exchanged pleasantries? What the hell does that mean?"

"Sarah, get out of there. He claimed two armed men—Cohen's men —entered the hospital. Aris said they're pissed because of what you did at the compound."

Sarah spun to stare at the door. The nurse had stepped out into the hallway, leaving it open behind her.

"Anything else?"

"Yeah, Aris was going back inside to help you, but he didn't know where you were, so I called the hospital."

"I think I heard gunfire just before you called."

"Are you armed?" Parkman's tone had turned frantic.

"Yes. How close are you?"

"About twenty minutes away."

"Good. Come pick us up. We'll be out front." She ended the call and tossed the phone on the bed. "We need to leave. Parkman will be here in twenty minutes. He's picking us up out front. We'll get you somewhere safe. Maybe Parkman can check into the Glenrock Hotel, use cash, and get you into a room. Then we can go visit Billings."

"I'd rather be in a hotel. When I'm stuck in this room, everyone knows where I am."

"Where are your clothes?"

"At the police station."

They stared at each other for a moment. "Then you're going to the hotel dressed like that. Is it open at the back?"

Aaron nodded.

"We'll figure it out. Can you walk?"

Aaron nodded again. "My face and chest got hit by a freight train masquerading as a large wooden desk, but my legs are fine. I just can't run, you know. Breathing heavily would kill me."

"Here, let me help you up." She placed a hand behind his neck.

"This'll help," a man said behind her.

Sarah released Aaron, spun around, and drew the weapon all in one fluid motion.

It was Aristotle. He was pushing a wheelchair.

"What?" he said. "Jumpy much."

Sarah lowered the weapon, her finger coming off the trigger. "You called Parkman."

He nodded, watching her. "You tricked me into helping you." Aris moved the chair closer to the bed. "Now that I've killed Cohen's men, I'm dead. This ends only if he's dead or in jail." Aris now stood in front of Sarah. "I want to go home, back to my family. I'll find another job, move away. I don't know, and I don't care. But working for Cohen is over." He moved closer. "Also, Cohen's men entered the hospital, and they may be coming to kill you two." He tapped the wheelchair handles. "We need to leave."

Sarah nodded. "Then we leave together."

Aris turned to Aaron. "Where do you hurt? Legs okay?"

Aaron glanced down the length of his body. "Just chest and head."

"Got it. Let's swing your legs off first. Then we'll sit you up and lift you into the chair."

Sarah moved to the end of the bed and got Aaron's feet over the side. He only winced once.

"Okay." Aris slid his hands behind Aaron's upper body, one at his shoulder blades and the other on his arm. "I'm going to sit you up."

Aaron gritted his teeth. "Do it."

Slowly, Aris brought Aaron into a sitting position. Aaron exhaled through his teeth.

"Now." Aris placed his hands under Aaron's arms. "At the count of three, I'll lift you into the chair. Ready?"

"Just don't drop me. Everyone in Douglas will hear that scream."

"I won't drop you. Now, one"—he tightened his grip—"two." Then he lifted, jerked once, and carried Aaron over open space, softly placing him into the chair.

"Fuck." Aaron breathed the word, his head tilted back as he looked at the ceiling. "I thought you'd count to three." Those six words came out in a growl of pain.

"Who goes on three?" Aris said, a note of humor in his voice.

Sarah was starting to like this guy.

"We ready?" Aris asked.

Sarah nodded and headed toward the door. She peered out into the hallway.

"All clear." She turned back to Aaron, whose face had filled with color at the pain he was enduring. "I'll stay in front." She looked at Aris. "You push."

Aris nodded. "Let's roll."

They exited Aaron's hospital room, and Sarah led them toward the elevator at the end of the hall. She passed other rooms with their doors open, doctors chatting to one another, a nurse explaining something on the phone.

Everything returned to normal after the gunfire on the other floor from about five to seven minutes ago.

She pushed the down button at the elevator, then looked back at Aaron. His color was improving.

"You doing okay?"

"I'll make it."

"Well, that's good to hear." She grinned. Why did something like this have to happen to bring them closer? And why was that so fucked up?

The doors opened behind her.

When she turned around, a man in a black suit was exiting.

She moved to the side to give him room, but then saw the gun in his hand.

And now Aris was yelling something.

Sarah lunged backward and tripped over the front of the wheelchair while her hand was going for the gun at the back of her pants.

When she landed on the floor, her arm got trapped under her, shooting pain up through her right shoulder.

Then, a weapon fired nearby.

Followed by another discharge.

Sarah screamed.

Chapter 36

MARTIN COHEN RECEIVED PREFERENTIAL treatment.

He donated several hundred thousand dollars to this hospital just last year and was well-known for sponsoring high school sports and events.

"How's Michael?" Cohen watched Doctor Fennel stitch his shoulder.

"You remember?" Fennel said. "I'm surprised—you know, for such a busy man."

"Doctor Fennel, your son is the star quarterback. I seem to recall some of the scholarship money I put up last year went to him."

Fennel nodded, his right hand coming up, the black stitch rising with it. "And we're eternally grateful to you."

"And your wife? How's she?"

"Wonderful as always. She's taken up crochet now." He shook his head slowly, eyes on Cohen's shoulder. "The talent that woman has mystifies me at times."

"I wouldn't knock it, Doc."

"Oh, trust me, I don't." He cut the last bit and stood back to admire his work. "All done, but let me dab away some of that extra blood." He unwrapped a gauze, his hands already covered in blue latex gloves, then gently tapped Cohen's wound.

Cohen didn't feel a thing with the two needles of local anesthetic he'd received before the stitching began.

"Once this thing is bandaged up, you'll be good to go." Doctor Fennel moved to the counter and grabbed bandages. "Don't get it wet for ten days. Come see me then, and I'll take the stitches out." He moved back to Cohen's side. "You might feel some pain later tonight or in the morning. Just take some ibuprofen, and you should be fine. Let me know if you need something stronger, and I can call in a prescription."

"Thanks, Doc." Cohen watched as Fennel applied the bandages. "Crazy how many people run around toting weapons nowadays, eh?"

"Yeah, gunshots in a hospital." The doctor stepped back and

removed his latex gloves with a slapping sound. "What's the world coming to?"

Cohen shook his head. "I'm with you there. Why would anyone bring a gun into a hospital?" He hopped off the bed feeling as good as new. The pain in his shoulder was gone as the anesthetic kept it at bay. Too bad he couldn't get his hands on that shit for a few days. "Hey, listen. I wonder if you could do me a favor."

Fennel had moved to a computer screen and was typing something. He stopped and looked up. "Anything."

"A colleague of mine was admitted earlier in the day. Came in by ambulance. Gunshot wound to the leg, I think."

"Oh, right." Fennel snapped his fingers. "Dalton, something."

"Yeah, did you hear his story?" Cohen shook his head as if he couldn't believe what had happened to Dalton.

"Something about being jumped by a crazy woman at the truck stop. Another guy came in with him, but he was DOA."

"Oh, shit. Sorry to hear that." Cohen shook his head. "Dalton and I go way back, and recently, he's been helping my friends around the farm. Just wanted to know he's okay."

Fennel scratched his head and clicked his tongue once. "The wound itself wasn't fatal, but he lost a lot of blood. They gave him blood and cleaned the wound. Last I heard, he was resting on the third floor. He's much better. Won't be here long, but he'll be fine. No bones were hit. More of a hole in the flesh than anything else. He'll go home later with a limp, but that's it."

Cohen smiled and patted the doctor on the shoulder with his good arm. "Thanks. I'll be sure to give him the time he needs before making him throw hay bales around again."

"You do that." Fennel smiled widely.

Cohen moved to the door, then stopped, his hand on the knob. "Third floor? Hmmm, maybe I'll go say hello before I leave."

"He's in 314 as far as I remember."

"Thanks, Doc. Say hi to the wife and that star son of yours."

"Will do, Mr. Cohen."

Cohen stopped and looked back. "Hey, Doc?"

Fennel lifted his head. "Yeah?"

"It's Martin. Just call me Martin."

The doctor smiled. "Martin it is, then."

From somewhere along the corridor, gunfire erupted again—one shot, then a second.

Cohen jerked back into the room, letting the door close.

"What the hell is going on in your hospital, Fennel?"

The doctor's frightened expression almost made Cohen laugh. His men were doing their job, and he wanted to go and let Dalton know that everything was done and over with.

This solid alibi was his top priority, though.

Now that the second round of gunfire was finished, Cohen could move freely throughout the hospital.

"I think I'll go see Dalton, then head home." Cohen tapped the doctor on the shoulder again. "Not sure I want to spend any extra time in this place. Might be bad for my health."

"I don't blame you. But let me call security first, make sure the madmen aren't running down this hallway right now."

Cohen leaned against the wall by the door. "You go ahead. Make your call. Tell them Martin Cohen, your patient, is in here with you, and we're both worried."

"I'm on it."

Doctor Fennel called security and told them precisely what Cohen told him to.

And Cohen smiled once more.

Alibi locked in place.

Chapter 37

SARAH HAD JERKED TO the side, clinging close to the wall, cradling her sore arm.

Aaron had screamed and bent forward in the wheelchair, chest to thighs, but he didn't look hit.

Aris was on the floor behind Aaron's wheelchair, blood coming from his arm, seeping through his fingers.

The gunman from the elevator was still in the elevator, but there was a hole in his neck now. How Aris managed to be that quick on the draw and still shoot the man in the neck was miraculous. The second round had come from the gunman's hand—likely a reflex—and hit Aris in the left arm just above the elbow.

People ran toward them, circling Aris. One doctor dropped to his knees and quickly assessed the gunman, then glanced up. "Get a gurney and rush this man to the emergency department."

A nurse was checking Aaron, and a woman tried to help Sarah to her feet. She leaned in and made sure Aaron hadn't been hit.

"You good?" The frantic tone couldn't be avoided.

Aaron nodded. "I bent over." He sucked in a breath. "Bullet went over my head."

"It hit Aris." She looked up and exchanged a glance with Aris.

"Get out," Aris said to her, his face scrunched up in pain. "Leave this place."

She'd read his lips more than heard him. Sarah nodded and pushed a woman away from her. "I'm fine. That man"—she pointed at the dead guy in the elevator—"came out shooting, and that man"—she pointed at Aris—"saved our lives." Panting and gasping in shock at how close they came to being shot, she could barely get the words out.

Vivian, a little heads up would have been nice—that was too fucking close!

All the attention was on Aris, who was moaning in pain as they led him down the hall, a trail of blood leaking from his arm following him.

Sarah moved behind Aaron's wheelchair. Her legs shook like Jell-O as she pushed him away from the assembled crowd. "Is there another elevator to get my husband to the front doors?"

The nurse nodded. "This way. I'll lead you out."

Thankfully, no one asked them to stick around—she wouldn't anyway. Being here left them too exposed to all the men Cohen could keep sending after them.

"It's the elevator we use for stretchers," the nurse said, her smile stiff as if she were fighting to keep it pasted to her face. She touched her chest, her breath catching and hitching in her throat.

"It's okay," Sarah said, touching her arm as the woman reacted to the trauma. The shake in Sarah's own hand was enough that she pulled back from touching the woman. "It's over. The bad man is dead."

The elevator doors opened, and as Sarah wheeled Aaron on, the woman leaned against the wall outside the doors.

"It's just that it was the second shooting in ten minutes. Some other guy tried to kill an FBI agent one floor below us."

Sarah jumped around the chair and lunged to stop the closing door. "What was that?" The door eased back open.

"Some guy shot an agent on another floor."

"Is she dead?"

The woman frowned. "I didn't say she was a female."

Sarah snapped her fingers. "Hey, I just need to know if she's okay?"

The woman nodded slowly. "Bullet wound to the abdomen. She's in surgery now. I think it was her partner who killed the gunman."

Stunned at Cohen's audacity, Sarah stared at the woman as the doors closed.

Aaron wheeled closer to her. "We need to get Willow and disappear from this place. It's insane here."

Sarah didn't look at him as the elevator descended.

"Sarah? We need to get out of Glenrock. Today. Right?"

Something Vivian told her echoed through her mind. *Leave now, and hundreds of people will die.*

The elevator slowed, then stopped. The doors parted as Sarah stepped behind Aaron and pushed him out into the main lobby.

The coast was clear. No one blocked the doors. No cops held people from leaving.

She leaned down and whispered, "We will get Willow. We will

leave her with Parkman. Then we'll finish this. No way I'm letting Cohen kill hundreds of people. He's too insane to leave unchecked. No fucking way."

Aaron tried to turn around and look at her, but couldn't. "Are you crazy? Where are you getting this *hundreds of people* shit?"

"My sister."

"Oh, great. Just fucking great. We're going to die."

The double doors to the outside parted, and Sarah pushed Aaron out into the afternoon sunshine.

Chapter 38

COHEN GOT TO THE third floor uninterrupted, grabbed an abandoned wheelchair from the hallway, and slipped into Dalton's room.

The man lay out on the bed in his private room, asleep.

Cohen pushed the chair close to the bed, stared at Dalton for all of three seconds, then slapped his face. "Hey, wake up."

Dalton jolted in bed, his arms coming up. He blinked away the sleep and tried to focus on Cohen.

"What … what's happening?" He sounded drugged.

"Shit," Cohen whispered. He shook Dalton's shoulder. "You need to get up. We're leaving."

"Cohen? We're leaving?" Dalton wiped his face, still dazed from sleep. "What? Why?"

"Did they drug you?" Cohen asked, staring into Dalton's eyes.

"Yeah, fuck, man. My leg. That bitch shot me."

"Can you drive?"

Dalton gawked at him, blinking rapidly. Then he wiped his face. "I'll do what I have to."

"You drive." Cohen shook the wheelchair. "We need stones, and we need to get that witch. Then this ends."

"Witch?"

Cohen moved up behind Dalton's head and slipped his hands under the man's shoulders. "C'mon. You're coming with me."

He slid him sideways until Dalton's head and shoulders were suspended in the air, and his butt was still on the bed.

Holding him steady, Cohen used his left foot to push the chair into the right spot where Dalton's butt would fall when he eased him farther off the bed.

Even though it worked perfectly, and Dalton dropped into the chair without an issue, the man's wounded leg smacked the seat of the wheelchair hard enough to make him wince and cry out.

"Take it easy, man," Dalton said, his face reddened with pain. "They shot me up with painkillers, but fuck, that hurts!"

Cohen ignored the whining. Dalton was all he had left at the

219

moment. Sure, he had more security men, but they'd have to be called in from surrounding towns and cities—they worked the night shifts and would likely be sleeping still.

Dealing with that witch was something that had to be handled now.

"What's the hurry?" Dalton asked.

Cohen had pushed him toward the door, but then stopped and moved in front to stare down at Dalton.

"She entered my home, the compound. She kidnapped Aris—that Judas—got the access code to the bunker and shot me." Cohen pointed at his shoulder. Dalton's eyes widened, having seen the bandages for the first time. "She took that Sutton woman and brought her here. Oh, and she killed several of my men along the way. The demon witch woman must be stopped."

Cohen opened the door, then pushed the chair out into the hallway. He spun it to the right and headed toward the elevator bank at the end of the corridor.

"Take me to see that Sutton woman," Dalton said. "I'll end this now."

"She's dead. I sent Bryce and Jacob to terminate her and the witch's boyfriend."

"Wait, what? Then where are we going?"

"That witch won't die. I can feel it. So I'll stone her to death. She needs a biblical ending."

"Okay, I'm feeling that."

The elevator doors opened as Cohen approached them. A man pushing an empty stretcher stepped off, and Cohen maneuvered Dalton on before the doors could close.

He hit the button for the main lobby.

"Where are we going?"

"To the police station in Glenrock. I want one of their SUV cruisers."

"Why?" Dalton's raised pitch flared his anger.

Cohen took a few deep breaths as the elevator slowed and the doors opened. He pushed the chair through a small line of people waiting at the triage, one person coughing, another holding their wounded arm.

Security personnel now stood on either side of the doors as a

Douglas police cruiser pulled up. Two other cruisers followed it.

Once Cohen got them outside and moving toward the Land Rover, he leaned closer to Dalton and talked near his ear.

"I'm taking a cruiser because we're going to the fountain at my compound, where we'll grab twenty or thirty stones from its base. I don't want wet rocks in the back of my Land Rover, and I paid for those police cruisers so they can give me one for the day without an argument."

"Okay." Dalton nodded as they moved uninterrupted toward the back of the parking lot.

Something caught Cohen's eye near a fire exit. Someone else was loading a person from a wheelchair into a car.

Before he looked away, the woman lifted her head, closed the front passenger door, and then dropped into the back of the car.

Cohen stopped walking and stared at the car as it sped out of the parking lot.

That witch, Sarah Roberts, and her boyfriend were leaving the hospital. She'd survived, after all. That had to mean Bryce and Jacob were wounded or dead.

He tightened his grip on the chair's handles. How could this be possible? Who the hell was this woman? And where were they going?

"Cohen?" Dalton muttered. "Everything okay?"

"Where would that witch go?"

"What?"

He released the handles and moved in front of the chair. "I just saw that witch leave in that car." He pointed.

Dalton followed Cohen's finger, squinting. "That car's gone too far to see the plate."

"So tell me, where is she going?"

"There's a kid involved. When she nabbed me, she kept asking, 'Where's my daughter, where's my daughter?'"

Cohen knew there was a reason he kept Dalton around. "And where is her daughter?"

"Billings knows. He took the kid from them."

Cohen moved back behind Dalton and pushed him again. "She's going after her kid, and then she's leaving."

"What are we going to do then?" Dalton sounded sleepy, like he wanted to return to the hospital and finish his nap.

Cohen jerked the chair once, jostling Dalton awake. "We get to her kid before her. That's what we do."

"But how?"

"Oh, Dalton, you are tired." He pulled out the Rover's car keys and clicked the key fob button. The doors unlocked. "We visit Billings after we get the stones. We'll have her daughter inside an hour."

Chapter 39

AGENT NEWMAN WAS TOLD that Sutton would pull through, but he couldn't visit her until tomorrow as she was in the ICU.

While Sutton was in emergency surgery, Newman identified himself as FBI and gave his statement to attending officers, telling them that he'd come by the station tomorrow to review it—he was working an active case. He couldn't be confined to the hospital any longer than necessary. There were others in the room when the shooting took place. The cops could talk to them. Newman had to go.

He strode through the security and police officers at the front of the hospital and walked across the parking lot to his car. Once inside, he hit the gas and left the hospital with his tires squealing in protest.

It took him five minutes to get to the house where Jamie Sutton had been staying—her mother's house.

The street was like any other. Nondescript, unremarkable. He parked by the base of a streetlight and watched Sutton's house for a moment.

He couldn't afford any more surprises. When he saw nothing irregular on the street, knowing he was being more paranoid than he needed to be, Newman stepped out of the vehicle, locked it, and strode across the street, the sun warming his back.

The front steps were well-trimmed. Someone took their time to offer meticulous care to how the grass made contact with the stone steps by gouging out a few millimeters of earth all around the stones. He marveled at the small flower garden under the front bay window. Was that Sutton's doing or her mother's?

When he raised his hand to ring the bell, his cell phone vibrated in his breast pocket, startling him. Newman jumped on the porch, cursed under his breath, grabbed the phone, and turned back to the street, where he walked out to the sidewalk to take the call.

It was his supervisor. "Agent Newman."

"Newman, it's Campbell."

"What do you have for me?"

"Six heavily armed men, as you asked for. We got lucky."

"How so?"

"The six men in one black van were on an operation that got nixed last night. They're only two hours' drive from you."

"How long before they're here?"

"Probably be in Glenrock in an hour."

"Which way are they coming?"

"From the east. One second." Campbell shuffled some papers. "Yeah, east. They'll be in Douglas in just over an hour, and then—"

"Tell them to meet me at the hospital in Douglas."

"The hospital?"

"I want two armed agents to stay with Sutton after they went after her an hour ago. Martin Cohen won't stop until she's dead, or we get to him first. She must have something serious on him."

"Done. I'll call it in and have all six men meet you there. You brief them. This is your case now. Finish it for Sutton."

"I'm on it, sir." Newman hung up, slipped his phone away, then strode back up the manicured stone steps.

He nearly stumbled and tripped on the porch when he saw the front door.

It was open, and an older woman stood watching him from behind the screen.

Newman clutched at his chest. "Ma'am," he said, trying to catch his breath. "You startled me."

"You here to help my daughter?"

Newman stared at the woman's shock white hair and wondered how old she was. "Yes. I'm here for Jamie."

The screen door swung open. "Get in here then. I'll make tea."

"Well, I haven't got much time." He crossed the threshold and entered Sutton's childhood home.

"Yes, dear boy," the woman said in her nasally high voice. "You have enough time to sip a tea and tell me why armed FBI agents are coming to the hospital in Douglas to watch over my daughter." The screen door slapped hard behind him. "I'm thinking you're going to want to tell me all about how the FBI failed one of their aspiring agents." She gestured toward the sofa. "Sit. I'll put on the kettle."

Newman did as he was told.

The woman deserved his respect.
Sutton certainly hadn't gotten it.

Chapter 40

"ALL OF THAT HAS happened since you pulled over at the truck stop last night?" Parkman stared at Sarah in the rearview mirror before his eyes shot back to the road. He moved the toothpick in his mouth from left to right.

Sarah had told him everything, with Aaron pitching in where he could. It also gave her a chance to fill Aaron in on what happened at Cohen's compound.

"That was too brazen, Sarah," Parkman said. "Even for you. Entering an armed compound like that ..." his voice trailed off.

He was right, but she'd been angry. Shooting Dalton, then fighting Aris and Wayne in the bushes, made her so angry she just wanted to kill the man responsible for everything and leave—be done with it.

But that's still murder, and Vivian hadn't sanctioned it.

And she still didn't have Willow back.

"Look, it might have been reckless, but we're here now, alive, and all we need is to get Willow back and end this."

"That's what you want to do?" Aaron asked. "End this? Why not just get Willow back? Full stop."

She stared at the back of Aaron's head as the wind rushed in from Parkman's open window. "What? You just want to leave?"

"Why stay in Glenrock? I was almost killed. They stole our daughter from us through some fucked up legal channels and tried to kill us in the hospital. We aren't safe here—none of us are."

Sarah clenched her teeth and stared out the side window. Her anger with Aaron, the cops, and Cohen spilled over, rendering her speechless for the moment.

"We get Willow," Parkman said. "Leave her with me at a hotel. Then you two go help the cops or the FBI or whoever, nail this Cohen asshole for what he's done."

Aaron was shaking his head. "Sorry, guys, not interested. Also, not needed. This isn't our fight. Agent Sutton knows what's going on. She was awake when you pulled her out of that bunker, cognizant. Once she's on the phone in that hospital, FBI agents will swarm this area and clean up Cohen's mess. We have no more reason to stick around, and I'm serious. Get Willow, then get out. That's it, that's final."

Sarah watched the farmland as they headed back toward Glenrock, refusing to be drawn into Aaron's whining.

But Aaron continued. "I just want Willow out of this shit. After we leave, we report to the insurance company that our car was stolen. Figure it all out from Santa Rosa when we get to your parents. Losing a car is nothing if we're all still alive. I want to leave ASAP."

Sarah turned to stare at the back of his head again. "Then you go."

There was silence in the car for a moment.

"What?" Aaron said.

Parkman kept his eyes on the road, flicking his toothpick from side to side.

"Vivian told me hundreds of people would die if I left Glenrock. So I have to stay, but you don't. So get Willow, then leave."

An entire mile ticked by before Aaron spoke. "What's most important in your life, Sarah?"

"What are you talking about?" She didn't try to mask the disdain in her voice.

"Your daughter? Me? Your family? Or the strangers you risk your life for?" He spoke from the front seat without being able to turn and face her because of his chest injuries, so she couldn't read him well. "Why do you always place strangers above us? Why are they more important to you?"

"There's no *ranking* system of importance here." The disgust she felt at that moment oozed through each word in that sentence. She rubbed the tops of her thighs and tried to calm down before she punched him in the back of the head. "If people need help and I can help, I will do it. I can't see the future. That's my sister's job. I don't know how all these people will die, but my sister does. And one day, when I die, and the Lord asks me what I did with my life, I want to look him in the eye and tell him I did my best to help his children, his babies."

The draft from the open window was the only sound as the seconds ticked by with no one responding to her.

Aaron nodded twice in the front seat, then glanced down at his lap, one hand brushing something on his face.

Is he crying?

"I get it then." Aaron looked up and stared at the road. "Vivian calls. You run. The leash is short."

That was it. That was his problem since day one.

Aaron would never get it. He'd never get her.

She leaned forward and grabbed the back of the seats. "You will never understand my *desire* to help where I can, my personal call to duty. If I could just save one life, I'd stay. Hundreds? Well, now, I don't get a choice." She pushed all those words out with one breath, inhaled, and kept going. "And while sticking my neck out to help, if I break a finger, break an arm, get shot, whatever, but I'm able to save those lives, I do it. We can always heal, but all those people can't heal their deaths." She sat back in her seat hard, her back bouncing once. "When Vivian's involved, I have assurances that she'll be there for me. I have trust. I have *faith*."

"*You* may not have a choice," Aaron said, his voice tinged with emotion. "But Willow and I do. *You* may have assurances, but I don't. And faith? I'm all out."

He wiped his eyes, and Sarah looked away.

There was no happy medium, no place to work from, no compromise anymore.

Aaron wanted out, and that made sense after what happened to Benjamin.

But Sarah would never leave this life. At least not until she was older or Vivian went first.

Parkman slowed the vehicle to make a turn.

They were in Glenrock now, one minute away from the police station.

She hoped Taggart would be there. If not, she'd have to go through a cop to get Detective Billings's home address.

They needed to find out where this Teresa bitch was to get Willow back.

Then Sarah would tell Parkman to drive Aaron and Willow far from here.

And when Cohen was in prison or dead, she'd follow them and begin the process of separation.

Aaron and Sarah, as a couple, couldn't work anymore.
That had been clear for a long time, more so now than ever.
And that broke her heart.
Aaron Stevens and Sarah Roberts would be no more.
It was time to break up.

Chapter 41

COHEN HAD FOUND A way to get Dalton in behind the wheel. The man seemed awake enough to drive, and they were now entering Glenrock in the Land Rover, with Dalton driving.

Cohen had had a driver since his twenties and didn't plan on driving a vehicle himself anytime soon. Emergencies, fine. But a bullet in Dalton's leg wasn't an emergency in Cohen's book. The man still had another leg.

"You're still using your left foot for the gas and the brake?"

Dalton nodded. "I can do it. The drugs are wearing off. I'm feeling some pain, but that means I'm not as sleepy."

Cohen leaned back in the seat to think.

"Are we getting the cruiser first?"

Cohen scrunched up his eyebrows. "You sure those drugs aren't screwing with your brain?"

Dalton looked back at Cohen in the rearview mirror.

"I'm fine. Just want to know where to turn."

"Yes, police station first. Get the SUV cruiser, then head to my compound for the stones." There was more to the plan, but why tell him everything? He'd just forget it.

"Okay, but first, we make a pit stop."

"Pit stop?"

"I need five minutes."

"For what?"

"Unless you want the front seat of your Rover to smell like piss, I need to stop at the truck stop and take one."

"Fine."

Five minutes wouldn't matter in the grand scheme of things.

Questions ran through Cohen's mind about how this would all end. That Sutton woman still hadn't told him about the Satanic cult she was with. Unless she really was with the FBI. That seemed extremely unlikely, though. She was just a dumb woman who got caught cutting up a pig. Liam said so himself. Domenick, too.

"Hey, Dalton."

"What?"

"When the FBI investigates a case, do they lie to fellow law enforcement about it?"

"Where's this coming from?"

Cohen filled him in on his conversation with the Glenrock cops when leaving the church.

Dalton shook his head. "They'd have no reason to suspect any police officer in Glenrock. If the FBI showed up saying they were looking for a man who'd gone missing, then they were looking for a man. End of story."

"Which means Sutton was lying."

"Why? What'd she say?"

"That she was an FBI agent?"

Dalton laughed. "Oh, that's rich. Shit, don't make me laugh." He leaned forward, his face twisted in pain. "I'll piss my pants."

He signaled to pull into the truck stop—the same one where he was shot earlier today.

Dalton glanced at him in the mirror again. "That Sutton woman is a Satanist, through and through. She's a member of *The Damned* in this area. Liam might have been right with her. Maybe she needed a good fucking and then a kiss goodnight before her sleep lasted a lifetime."

"Liam was a loose peg in a wobbly Jenga tower. He could have brought us all down. And who knows, he may be the cause of the missing man the FBI is looking for."

Dalton turned into a handicapped parking spot near the front doors. "How many FBI agents do you suspect are in the area?"

Cohen shrugged. "I only know of one agent for sure."

Dalton opened his door, spun in the seat, and lifted his wounded leg out gingerly. "Nothing to worry about, boss. It has nothing to do with you."

"Worried? Trust me, Dalton. I'm not worried. Whether Sutton is a Satanist or an FBI agent—is there a difference?—she's already dead. And if she isn't dead yet, I'll kill her myself. I just want that Sarah demon. She listens to the Devil and does his bidding."

Dalton looked sideways at him. "We'll get her. Billings knows where her kid is."

"Then hurry the hell up, Dalton. Take your piss, then let's go get this thing back under control."

Without another word, Dalton pushed up and out of the Rover. He limped toward the truck stop's side doors, his face a mask of pain when he used his injured leg.

Cohen checked his phone. He thought about Domenick, Liam's sidekick.

He could use him to help load the stones.

Seconds later, after dialing Domenick's number, the idiot answered.

"Hello."

"Do you know who this is?"

There was a moment's hesitation, then, "Yes, sir, Mr. Cohen."

"I need your help."

"My help?" Domenick's voice cracked.

"How long before you can meet me at my home?"

"The compound?"

"Yes, the compound."

"I can be there in fifteen minutes, sir."

"That would be wonderful. See you there. Oh, and Domenick?"

"Yes?"

"Park out on the road. Don't approach the gates until I arrive. There are no men posted on the gates at the moment. You'll know it's me when I show up."

"How's that, sir?"

"I'll be in a Glenrock Police Department-issued SUV cruiser."

There was a gasp on the other end of the line. "Were you arrested?"

"No, Domenick." He wanted to call him an idiot, but held back. "I'm borrowing it for a small task this afternoon. A task for which I need you."

"Well, okay. I'll be there. Leaving now."

Cohen ended the call, then checked the time. He stared up at the truck stop but didn't see Dalton.

"How long does it take someone to piss?"

Chapter 42

SPECIAL AGENT NEWMAN HAD given Sutton's mother twenty minutes of his time, but now he needed to get up and do what he came here to do. It had been twenty minutes of stories from when Sutton was a little girl. Her mother treated Newman like he was courting her daughter, which wasn't the case. He was trying to keep her alive.

It was all too weird after what he'd just gone through at the hospital.

"Excuse me, Mrs. Sutton," he said, getting to his feet. "But I really need to take a look around your daughter's bedroom."

She smiled at him, showing off her paper-white dentures. "Of course. I don't get many visitors, but when I do …"

"I understand, ma'am." Newman stepped around the coffee table. "She was working a case in Glenrock. Did she mention anything to you about it?"

"No." Mrs. Sutton shook her head, letting out a small giggle. "My daughter never mentions work with me. A woman shouldn't be a cop or an agent, whatever it is she does."

Newman stared down at the older woman. "Why's that?"

"You ever ask yourself what's wrong with society, Mr. Newman?"

"Can't say I do."

"It's the gender roles. They're all reversed. A woman knew her role in the nineteen-fifties, and a man knew his. Hasn't anyone examined the divorce statistics over the past hundred years? It's self-evident what's been happening to us as a race." She placed her hands on her knee, settling in for a long talk. "Let me explain …"

She was dragging him back into a conversation. He didn't have the time.

"Ma'am," he cut in. "You may be on to something, but I really need to leave soon." He moved toward the hallway. "I'll find her room myself," he called over his shoulder as Mrs. Sutton kept talking about a woman's place in society.

The short hallway had three doors. One led to a bathroom, and the other two led to bedrooms. He found Jamie Sutton's room easily enough. It was the one with the FBI jacket on a hanger suspended on the closet doorknob.

Inside her room, he opened the drawers of an old dresser and found nothing but her undies, socks, shorts, and T-shirts neatly folded. Inside her closet was more of the same. Sweaters and oversized shirts were folded on the shelf above the hanger bar, and the bar was stuffed full of light jackets and shirts.

While Mrs. Sutton prattled on in the other room, oblivious that he wasn't listening anymore, he knelt and opened a few boxes on the closet floor. Nothing but knick-knacks and trinkets from a flea market, and in one box, a pile of photos—hundreds of them—from some trip Sutton took in her teenage years.

He backed out of the closet and got to his feet.

Her bed was made like it belonged in a hotel. Maybe her mother did it because the way it was made needed proper attention. The pillow was placed dead center. The covers folded back neatly at the edge of the pillow.

Under the bed? Is that where she'd hide anything she had on Cohen?

The dresser was empty, and the closet was cluttered with clothes and photos.

He dropped to his knees, bent down, and peeked under her bed. Two feet away, a small box sat. He kicked at it with his foot, coaxing it out. Then he sat on the end of the bed and lifted the lid.

Inside, he found recent photos Sutton had taken of a farm. Men were standing around outside a barn. He went to the next photo. It was the same barn with an animal truck pulling in—whether to unload or pick up, he couldn't tell.

Other photos were of the same barn, some taken at night, some during the day. He saw police cruisers parked out front in two photos, officers in uniform directing the large truck as it backed up to the barn.

He ran through the pictures of random men in what looked like downtown Glenrock, then stopped on one with a dead pig, its gut splayed open.

Pulling it closer to his face, he examined every detail. Why get that close to a dead, mutilated pig to take a photo?

"What the hell were you up to, Sutton?"

The following picture was of a dead cow. After that, another pig, but this time, the pig had an upside-down cross carved into its forehead.

"What the fuck?" Newman whispered to himself.

In the living room, Mrs. Sutton had stopped talking to herself about men and women and their role reversal issues.

Newman pocketed several animal photos, then grabbed the notebook at the bottom of the box.

The first page had a date and several notes. When he scrolled through the pages, he counted over one hundred sheets of handwritten notes.

After ten more minutes of reading, he understood what Sutton had been up to.

According to her, Cohen ran a successful drug operation. He'd been muling the drugs all over the state by making his pigs and cows swallow huge quantities in small baggies. Then, he shipped the animals to other farms where the drugs were processed for the street.

The animals that died were victims of a burst baggy. The slicing of their stomachs was Agent Sutton attempting to acquire evidence.

That matched with the photos of the truck picking up pigs in the middle of the night.

He stared at the wall when it all came to him. No one at the bureau had listened to her. No one looked into her claims.

So she cut open the dead animals and left behind Satanic symbols to draw more attention to what was happening in this part of Wyoming. The animals were dead anyway. Might as well use them as a vehicle for attention.

Yet, still, no one came.

"Mr. Newman."

Agent Newman jumped so badly that the box of photos shot from his legs and scattered all over the floor at his feet.

He clutched at his throat. "Damn, you scared me."

"I wanted to know if you'd be having more tea with me."

Newman snatched up Agent Sutton's notebook from the floor and got to his feet. "I'm sorry. I wish I could stay, but I really must be going." He pushed past her at the bedroom door and headed toward the front of the house.

"But Mr. Newman, I have several other stories to tell you about my daughter." She followed him up the hall. "Like when she fell off her bike at the tender age of seven."

Newman opened the front door and turned back. "That sounds lovely. Perhaps the next time I visit."

"Well, I sure hope that's soon, then. My daughter was always a good little girl."

"I'm sure she was. And thank you for the tea."

He hopped down the manicured steps and ran for his car. He'd taken too long in the Suttons' residence. His backup would be at the hospital by now.

They needed to apprehend Martin Cohen and put a stop to his drug operation. Along with that, arrest every member of law enforcement who had been looking the other way—effectively shut down the Glenrock Police Department.

This was a huge case, one that would garner nationwide attention.

And the woman who broke the story was undergoing surgery for the bullets meant to stop her.

Unless Cohen killed all the FBI agents at the bureau, he wouldn't get away with this shit anymore.

"Not if I have anything to say about it."

Newman dropped into his car, tossed the notebook on the passenger seat, cranked the engine, and slammed the gas pedal to the floor.

Chapter 43

PARKMAN ROLLED PAST THE police station, then stopped the car at the corner.

"What now?" he asked.

Sarah was staring back at the façade of the building. "You have to go in. For obvious reasons, it can't be Aaron. And these boys work for Cohen." She turned around to look at Parkman. "He's probably called them after what happened at the compound. They'll be looking for me."

"That's what I was thinking. Got a gun for me in case I need it?"

Sarah shook her head. "I keep the gun. I don't want you walking into a police station armed. Not in this town anyway."

Parkman nodded, tonguing his toothpick. "Who am I looking for again?"

"Detective Billings, but he won't be there. Get anything you can on him. We need to find him today."

"Yeah, it's unlikely I'll get the address, but I'll try to get something —even if it's a phone number."

Sarah pointed out the side window. "See those bushes there? A few feet to the left of the front doors?"

"I see them."

"I'll be in there waiting. If there's trouble, shout something, and I'll come inside."

"You got it." Parkman opened his door. "You okay on your own?" he asked Aaron.

"Yeah, I'm good. Let's just get Willow back."

Sarah tapped Parkman's shoulder. "Oh, and Parkman?"

He stopped and looked back. "Yeah?"

"Sense of urgency. Try to be in and out in a few minutes. We have no idea what's coming our way."

He eyed her for a few breaths. "You'd tell me if Vivian was prophesying something, right?"

"You'd be the first to know."

He nodded at her, exited the car, and headed toward the police station.

The street was quiet for a Sunday afternoon, the only noise a constant din from the highway several blocks away.

Stomach in knots for Willow, not to mention the tension between Sarah and Aaron, he stepped inside the police station and strode up to the main desk.

One man with a thick mustache sat behind the Plexiglas divider.

"Afternoon." Parkman smiled widely. If pleasant didn't work, then unpleasant was on deck.

When Parkman entered the station, the cop stared at a computer screen. As he approached the front desk, his eyes were still glued to it.

"Yes?" the man said without looking up.

"I'd like to speak with Detective Billings."

"He's not here. Come back next week."

The cop still hadn't looked up. What was so fascinating on the screen? Could it be a security camera feed? Did he watch them pull up to the station? If so, maybe he saw Sarah get out of the car and hide in the bushes. Which meant this could be over before it got started.

"Well, I'm afraid I can't wait until next week, Officer"—he glanced down at the nametag—"Brown."

The cop closed his eyes, lowered his head briefly, then opened his eyes and looked up at Parkman.

"Why do you need to speak to Billings?"

Parkman reared back a bit, flicking the tip of his toothpick with his tongue. "Well, now, that's between Billings and me. Bit personal, wouldn't you say?"

"He's off until next week." Brown looked back at the screen. "Come back then."

He needed to speed this up. "Then give me his phone number. I'll call him. Maybe we can meet for coffee."

Officer Brown pushed his chair back from the desk and got to his feet. He sized up Parkman as he adjusted his belt.

"We've had a rough few days here in Glenrock. Look," he punctuated that word with a jerk of his right hand, "Billings is off for a week because some perp broke his nose. So come back some other time, old man. I'm not going to tell you again."

Things have now moved to the unpleasant stage.

"I'll tell you what I'll do—"

"I'm listening," Brown cut in, glaring at him.

"I'll call Billings on his cell phone and keep you out of it."

"Great. You do that." Brown went to retake his seat.

"As soon as you give me his number."

Brown jerked back to a standing position. "What the hell, mister? I'm not giving you shit. Just leave." Brown pointed at the door Parkman had entered through.

Parkman shook his head and crossed his arms. "Isn't this the Glenrock Police Department? Aren't you a police officer?"

"What's that supposed to mean?" Brown shouted in a gravelly voice now—the man's version of a roar.

"Where's your professionalism? I come in off the street, and you stare at that screen. I ask a few innocent questions on how to reach your detective, and you act like I'm asking to borrow a thousand bucks." Parkman tsked twice with his tongue, his toothpick jerking on his lips. "You're a disappointment to the uniform."

"Well, now you've gone and done it. Get the fuck out of my station." Brown was screaming now.

What seemed to infuriate the cop even more was that it made Parkman laugh. He bent slightly and slapped his thighs. When he stood up, Brown's face had reddened a deep shade.

"You are a riot." Parkman gasped out the words. "All bark and no bite. You're a little child in uniform. Just get me Billings's cell number like a good little doggie."

That was Brown's tipping point. He'd evidently had enough of Parkman's taunting as he stormed to the side counter, where he would come out to Parkman's side of the partition.

"You'd best get running, old man," Brown shouted as he rounded the counter and started toward Parkman. "Or you can wait for Billings in our jail for a week."

Parkman raised his hands to the side and waited as Brown approached in a hurry.

The cop shoved his hands out to push Parkman toward the door, but Parkman sidestepped the cop, who stumbled forward and lost his balance. Then Parkman wrapped his arms around Brown's upper shoulders.

In a one-second maneuver, Parkman had his left forearm jammed into the cop's throat and his right hand withdrawing the officer's pistol from his holster.

Brown struggled against him, but Parkman yanked backward, pulling Brown up off his feet, then dropping him hard onto his heels. Once more, another yank backward while Brown clutched at Parkman's forearm, trying to relieve the pressure on his throat.

Already exhausted from the effort of lifting the man a few times, Parkman placed the cop's gun to the side of his head and relaxed his forearm on his throat.

"Breathe, but don't be stupid."

The cop gasped for breath, and Parkman hoped that he wouldn't pass out on him.

"Who else is in the building?"

When Brown didn't answer, Parkman tightened his forearm, choked the man, then released it.

"I saw what you guys did to my friend Aaron."

Brown gasped and struggled anew.

Parkman slapped the man on the side of the head with the gun. "You're unarmed now. Maybe I should pick a fight with you as you did with Aaron. Want me to toss a desk on your head, asshole?"

He shook Brown a few times. His forearm tightened to the point where Brown could not take a breath.

Parkman arched his upper body back, giving Brown no leverage. After seeing Aaron's injuries, something about holding this man made Parkman want to hurt Brown on purpose, yet he fought to control his violent urges.

Then the front door opened.

Sarah entered the building and jogged up to them.

Brown struggled harder when he saw Sarah, and Parkman smacked him on the side of the head with the gun again.

"Looks like you got a gun after all," she said to Parkman.

"Yeah, gonna borrow it while I'm in town." He leaned close to Brown's ear. "You don't mind, eh, big fella?"

"He tell you where Billings is?"

"No, and then he got cocky. Wanted to push me around."

Sarah wagged a finger in front of Brown's face. "Didn't your mother ever teach you manners, dickhead?"

Brown grunted, his hands still clinging to Parkman's forearm.

"Did he at least give you Billings's cell phone?"

Parkman shook his head. "Gave me shit and told me to come back next week." Parkman chortled once. "Then told me that I could spend the week waiting for Billings in the jail cell if I didn't leave."

Sarah's mouth made a circle, and her eyes widened. "Mighty powerful of you, big ego asshole cop. Especially after the damage you did to my boyfriend." Sarah opened her mouth farther and pointed at the missing tooth. "See that? Liam did that, and I killed him for taking one tooth." She leaned closer to Brown as the man's reddened face contorted. "What do you think I'm going to do to you for damaging Aaron?"

The cop pushed into Parkman to get away from Sarah.

"Tell me where Billings is," Sarah said.

Parkman eased his arm off so the cop could talk, but he still said nothing.

Sarah met Parkman's gaze, nodded slightly, then swung hard and wide, driving her fist across the cop's mouth. Parkman had tightened his hold in time to manage the hit.

"Now, tell me where Billings is," Sarah said again.

The fight in Officer Brown had left him. He sagged in Parkman's grasp, moaning now.

"Another?" Sarah held up her fist, making circles with it. "A part of me doesn't want you to tell us. It's more fun mining for information."

Brown removed his hands from Parkman's forearm and raised them in front of him.

"Oh, you've had enough already? I wonder what Aaron would say to that."

"His house is behind the recreation center," Brown managed to get out in a croaky voice. "It's on the corner of Third and Deer Street. It's a beige house. Number 407." He panted and coughed, then added, "Third Street. He's there now. We update him. All the time."

Parkman swung his arm hard to the left, spinning the cop out of his grasp.

Officer Brown stumbled and bumped into the wall but remained upright.

When he looked up, Parkman had the weapon aimed at him. "What'll we do with this guy while we go chat with Billings?"

Sarah looked at Brown, then back to Parkman. "Where was he going to put you for a week?"

Parkman smiled. "Drop the belt, cop. You're going into your own holding cell."

"No, wait a moment. They'll kill me."

Sarah moved closer to him, her fists still clenched. "Should have thought of that when you got into bed with them. Now drop that belt, or I swear I'll punch and kick your face until it needs surgery, and then I'll *take* your belt. I've had enough fucking around for one day in this town."

Brown grabbed the clasp and unhooked it.

"Now go open your jail."

Parkman kept the gun aimed at the cop's gut. He'd shoot him, but he wouldn't go for the head or chest.

"They stole my daughter," Sarah said, emotion lacing her voice. She was working herself up, and Parkman worried she'd lose it on the guy at any moment. "They kidnapped my man and hospitalized him when all he wanted to do was report my abduction. You were part of that." Her volume rose as she followed the cop behind the counter.

"Sarah?" Parkman said, a warning in his tone. "The last time you lost your shit, you killed seven cops." He added that last bit—obviously a lie—so Brown would do as he was told and not say something to provoke Sarah further. As it stood, Brown would be lucky to get out of this with only the one punch.

"I'm trying to remain calm."

Brown tapped something on the keyboard frantically. Locks clicked in a room to Parkman's left. He edged over and peeked through the window of a door.

A small corridor led to three holding cells. When he pulled on the door, it opened.

He held it open with his foot. The closest cell door was now sitting ajar.

"Sarah, hurry. Someone could come. We need to leave."

"No one's coming. We haven't heard the horn."

"The horn?"

"Aaron said he would lay on the car horn if someone approached the front door." Sarah pushed Brown back around the partition to where Parkman was standing. "But that doesn't mean we can waste time." She shoved Brown again. "Hurry the fuck up."

His gun arm tired, Parkman bent over and rested it on the doorknob as they approached him.

Sarah pushed the cop once more, and he stumbled past Parkman into the corridor that led to the cells.

"I'm going to frisk you," Sarah said, walking by Parkman. "Anything sharp in your pockets that I need to know about?"

Officer Brown shook his head. "Nothing. Just house keys here," he pointed at his right front pocket. "And wallet here." He pointed to his left.

Sarah quickly rummaged through his pockets, tossing everything out onto the floor. Then she patted his pants down while Parkman watched.

"Why are you alone?" Parkman asked.

"It's a Sunday. The chief, the K9 unit, and everyone else are at home. We have four patrol officers. The others are at home sleeping after the night shift, and I sent Taggart home because he fucked up. The other officer on duty right now, Paul Grant, is out driving around somewhere."

Brown's face had paled, but there were two red splotches—one on his throat and the other on the side of his mouth where Sarah had socked him.

"He's clean," Sarah said, getting to her feet. She pulled the cell door open wide. "Get in."

Brown stared at them for a brief moment. "You don't have to do this. I won't call and warn Billings that you're coming—"

Sarah moved so fast he wouldn't see it coming. Her right hook was devastating.

Brown's face shot up and to the left. Parkman would swear the man actually lifted off the floor for the briefest of moments.

Then Officer Brown dropped to his knees and sprawled out, moaning, his hands on his face.

"You broke my fuckin' mouff." Brown tried to talk through his hands.

Sarah grabbed his ankles, dragged him into the cell, then stepped back out and slammed the door shut.

"You're getting off lucky after what you did to Aaron. I'm putting you in this cell so I don't kill you. It's not so you don't warn Billings. When I get my hands on the detective, he'll wish he'd never met my family." Sarah hocked up a goober and spat through the bars. "Fuck you, rogue cop asshole. Next time I see you, I'll kill you for what you did to my family."

Then she stormed out of the corridor, past Parkman, and out toward the front.

"Come on," she shouted over her shoulder. "We have a detective to interrogate."

Chapter 44

SPECIAL AGENT ANDREW NEWMAN arrived at the Douglas hospital just as the FBI team pulled up in their van. His timing was perfect.

Once they were introduced and exchanged IDs, Newman spoke directly to Agent Rick Drayton, the man in charge of his six-person team.

He filled him in on everything, right up until the notebook Newman found in Sutton's room. Cohen's operation details were sketchy, but he gave Drayton enough to guarantee an arrest.

"You want two of my men to stand guard in Agent Sutton's room?"

Newman nodded. "Yes. We leave two men here. Martin Cohen has tried to kill Sutton several times. I believe he'll try again. The rest of us head to Glenrock to arrest Cohen. We'll be arresting Glenrock PD officers, too."

"Done." Drayton turned to his men, delegated two to stay behind, and ordered the others to load up.

"Hey, guys," Newman said to the two men heading for the hospital doors. They turned back. "They've tried to kill her several times. Watch your backs. Check IDs. Make sure no one gets access to Sutton until we call and let you know this is over."

They nodded.

"You heard the man." Drayton waved his arms. "Let's hit it."

They started toward the van as a six-man unit now—Newman, Drayton, and four S.W.A.T. team members.

"You riding with us?" Drayton asked.

Newman nodded. "I'll leave my car here. When this is done, I'm coming back to stay with Sutton."

"Understood. Need a weapon?"

"Give me whatever you got."

Drayton opened the back of the van, and after his men jumped up and took their seats, the driver crawled through to the front. He pulled out a black case, flicked the catches, and opened it.

"M4 Carbine," Drayton said, tapping the assault rifle. "We've got eight of these bad boys. Before we stop in Glenrock, I'll have one loaded and in your hands. It weighs just over six pounds and is quite effective in close quarters."

"Works for me. The men we're picking up today are armed and not afraid to shoot federal agents."

Drayton tapped Newman's shoulder. "You sure we're going to make arrests?"

Newman looked inside the van. All eyes were on him. "Arrests are ideal." He looked back at Drayton. "But unless they're unarmed and on their knees, I'd advise we shoot to kill."

"That's all I wanted to hear." Drayton faced his team. "You heard the man. We're going hunting."

He hopped into the van, followed by Newman, and then closed the back doors.

"Hit it," Drayton shouted.

The van jerked forward.

They were on their way to Glenrock.

Martin Cohen had no idea what was coming for him and his little drug enterprise.

It's over, asshole. Newman rested his head back and whispered a small prayer for Sutton.

He marked this as the last time he would not take a fellow agent seriously when they reported suspicious activity.

I owe you, Agent Jamie Sutton.

The men were inspecting their weapons, so Newman did the same.

It felt good to be among a crew ready to do some damage.

It felt good that they were going to clean up the Cohen mess.

And it would feel good to tell Sutton all about it later on when she woke up at the hospital.

Something to look forward to was always a blessing.

Chapter 45

IT HAD TO BE ten minutes before Dalton exited the truck stop, a sandwich in one hand and a juice container in the other.

"Why am I cursed to have such stupid people working for me?" Cohen asked himself aloud.

Dalton limped to the Rover slowly, chewing away on the white bread—probably egg salad.

"Get in," Cohen shouted. "What took you so long?"

Dalton stuck his head in the front seat, still chewing. "I couldn't go to the bathroom in the hospital, so I went here."

"You held your piss that long? What did you do? A ten-minute pee?"

"No," Dalton said. "The other bathroom activity." He held up the juice and the rest of the sandwich. "I was thirsty and hungry, too. Have you ever tried hospital food?"

"Oh, how fucking cliché of you. Just get in, and let's go."

Dalton took his sweet-ass time climbing into the driver's seat, but there was one upside. He was walking on his own and didn't need a wheelchair. The leg wound couldn't have been that bad.

Testing Cohen's patience, Dalton put the Rover in gear and got them rolling.

Cohen contemplated killing Dalton and hiring an entirely new crew when this was over. The man was positively driving him nuts today.

A minute later, they pulled onto the street for the Glenrock Police Department.

Dalton eased to the curb in front of the police station just as a small rental with three people in it pulled away. The woman in the back seat had the same hair as the demon witch, but it couldn't be her.

"Leave the keys under the mat. We don't know what's going to happen later. One of us may have to come back to get the Rover."

Dalton did as he was told, then Cohen got out and stretched. He watched Dalton ease out of the driver's seat and then limp toward the police station, the half-empty juice bottle in his hand. At least he wasn't still eating like they were out for a Sunday afternoon picnic together.

Jonas Saul

The keys under the mat were for Cohen. When this was all over, Dalton might end up with another bullet in him—just not the leg this time. And if that happened, Cohen himself would drive a vehicle again. It couldn't be that bad.

An older model Buick rolled by, the occupants waving from the front seat.

Cohen bent down and smiled, waving back. He was still the town's preacher and had to play the role.

But that meant he needed off the street. Until this was all over and life returned to normal, limiting his public exposure made sense.

So he followed Dalton to the front doors of the police station.

Once inside, they strode up to the empty front desk.

"Hello?" Dalton called, his voice echoing in the empty station.

Cohen frowned as he walked around behind the counter to where they stored the cruisers' keys in a small box affixed to the wall.

"Got 'em," he said, snatching the SUV's keys off the hook.

"Wait." Dalton held up his right hand. "I think I heard something."

They didn't move for a moment.

Then, like the low rumble of a trapped animal somewhere in the building, they heard a grunt.

"It's coming from in there." Dalton pointed at the holding cell corridor.

"Well, check it out." Cohen came around from behind the counter and followed Dalton to the side door.

Dalton opened it a crack and peeked inside.

"Brown? What the fuck are you doing in there?"

Dalton stepped all the way inside, and Cohen joined him.

The man's car keys and wallet were scattered on the floor outside the cell.

"Was this an accident?" Cohen asked, expecting as much. The cops in this area were dumber than a cow standing around chewing cud all day. "You locked yourself inside?"

Officer Brown lowered his hand. He had blood on it, and blood ran over his lips to his chin.

"What the fuck happened to you?" Dalton shouted at him.

"That woman had company. Some mercenary type of guy. Caught

me by surprise, then tossed me in here."

Cohen suppressed a laugh. That car pulling out when they stopped in front of the police station—it was the demon witch—and they'd just missed her.

"When did they leave?" Dalton leaned against the bars.

"A minute before you pulled in."

Cohen slapped Dalton upside the head, making him drop the juice bottle.

Dalton jerked away so fast that he lost his balance, stumbled on his bad leg, and bumped into the wall to avoid falling.

"What was that for?"

"If you didn't take a ten-pound shit for a half hour back at the truck stop, we'd have walked in on that witch *right here*"—he jabbed a finger at the floor twice with those last two words—"and executed her *right here*."

"Geez, sorry. How was I supposed to know?"

Cohen shrugged and dangled the cruiser's keys in his hand. "Doesn't matter. The original plan is still in the works." He turned to Officer Brown. "Any idea where they were headed?"

Brown nodded. "To talk to Billings. They got his home address somehow."

Cohen did an exaggerated nod. "Sure, they did. More like they punched you in the face a few times, took your weapon, searched you, and tossed your shit right there, then threw you in your own jail cell until you gave them Billings's home address."

Brown looked from Cohen to Dalton. "Hey, that's not how it happened. No way. I'm a good cop. I'd never give out shit because of a punch in the face. They found the address somehow."

"Me doth thinks he protests too much."

"Ahh, come on, guys. I said they were some kind of mercenary type. The guy sucker-punched me, taking me by surprise."

"Or the woman punched you." Cohen sneered at the cop in the jail cell, then turned to Dalton. "Let's go, and don't make me wait on you anymore. This ends today."

"Where are we going? To Billings's place?"

"No, why would I do that?"

Cohen pushed the door open and stepped back into the main lobby of the police station.

"Hey, guys, let me out," Officer Brown shouted.

The door closed, cutting off Brown's whiny voice.

"I don't understand." Dalton limped up beside Cohen, one hand on the wall. His pale face glistened with sweat. "If she's at Billings's place, which is a one-minute walk from here, why aren't we just barging in there and shooting her dead?"

"Because I know why she's there, and I know just what to do about it."

"Oh." Dalton watched him for a moment, then looked away. "Works for me. Just tell me what to do, and I'll do it."

Cohen extended his arm, the keys dangling from his fingers. "Take these, get settled in the SUV out back, and wait for me. Then we are going to the compound to meet Domenick—"

"Domenick?" Dalton gasped the word as he snatched the keys from Cohen's fingers. "What the hell do we need that dummy for?"

"I asked him to meet us so he could load the back of the cruiser with rocks from my fountain." Cohen looked up and down Dalton's body. "I didn't expect you'd be interested in lifting all those stones in your condition, and I'm certainly not doing it."

The confusion lifted from Dalton's face. "Oh, right. Great idea."

Cohen patted Dalton on the shoulder. "Go get the cruiser. I've got a phone call to make. Then I'll join you out back."

Dalton trekked down the corridor, then stepped outside.

Officer Brown was still yelling from the holding cell when Cohen pulled out his cell phone and called Billings's number.

When he picked up on the fourth ring—Cohen was wondering if he would pick it up at all—Cohen spoke first.

"Don't tell them who called."

"Uhm, you got it, Mike. No, everything's fine here."

"Do not give them their child back."

"Oh, right. Okay, Mike. That rescheduled meeting time works for me. Next week is fine. Anything else?"

"Yes." Cohen stared at the door that led to the outside. "Tell them to meet me at the front of the church in an hour. I'll let Sarah inside to talk.

Once we agree to end our feud, I'll tell her where her child is, and then they can leave town. Got it?"

"Yes, sir. Understood. Gotta go now."

He thought he could hear whispering in the background. Something hit the phone. Then he heard Sarah's voice.

"Who is this?"

Cohen hung up, then said into the dead phone. "Your worst nightmare, spawn of the Devil."

Chapter 46

SARAH INSISTED THEY LEAVE Aaron resting in the car two houses down, and Parkman agreed. He parked under a large tree for shade and made sure Aaron had a water bottle easily accessible.

Aaron could move, but every position change of his upper body caused him pain. He couldn't fight, he couldn't defend himself—he couldn't even run—breathing too heavily would make him scream.

That left her and Parkman, who now had a gun, as the only two who could speak with Billings.

Outside the car, she pulled Parkman into a hug. "I'm so happy you came." Emotion made her voice crack. "I don't know what I'd do without your support all these years."

"Hey, it's what we do. It's okay." He tapped the small of her back with his hand.

She pulled away from him and wiped her eyes. "I just don't know how these things keep happening to us."

"It's your purpose. Why you're here. Imagine the difference you've made to so many people over the years. That's worth something, Sarah."

"Yeah, like the difference I'm making to Aaron. You heard him in there. We aren't going to make it, you know."

"Sarah." He leaned down and stared into her eyes, his hands on her shoulders. "Whether you make it or not, and I hope you do, Willow needs us. We can't stop now. It's too dangerous. That preacher is coming, and we need to get Willow. Talk relationship shit later."

She nodded several times, sniffling. "Look at me. What a wreck. My daughter is heaven knows where, and I'm crying on someone's lawn in Wyoming."

"We'll chat with that detective, get Willow, then get you guys to safety and figure out what to do next." He pulled out Officer Brown's weapon. "And I've got this now. The officers in Glenrock have been quite generous with their donated weapons over the past twenty-four hours."

A short laugh escaped her, and then her face hardened. "Let's do this. I want my daughter back. I can't believe some people."

Sarah spun around and headed for the front door of the detective's house.

"I'll check out back." Parkman ran past her and disappeared around the side of the house. Once he was gone, Sarah knocked on the front door.

She thought she heard a television from somewhere inside. When she didn't receive a response, she rang the doorbell and knocked again.

The TV lowered in volume.

"I'm coming," a man said through the door.

A lock clicked. The knob turned.

Sarah kept her hands ready for anything, the gun safely stored in the back of her pants.

The door opened to a slightly overweight middle-aged man in a T-shirt and sweatpants. His nose was covered with white bandages, and both eyes were severely bruised. It looked like his face had been rammed into a concrete wall.

The hand that opened the door was fine, but the other had a cast on it.

"Selling something?" he asked, his voice heavily nasal. "Not interested."

"Actually, I came bearing a message."

The man frowned, his good hand moving to the door to close it. Then he stopped. "What message?"

Sarah looked behind her and then back at the man. "It's from the preacher. I must deliver it personally to Detective Billings."

"That's me. Just say it."

Sarah leaned close to the screen and shook her head. "Not out here."

"You can tell me through the screen door. Say what you gotta say or fuck off."

Sarah stepped back and appraised the detective. "You want me to return to Martin Cohen and tell him you kicked me off your porch? With four of his security personnel dead at his house? With more dead at the hospital in Douglas and the FBI looking into things in town?"

Billings's bloodshot eyes squinted and then widened. The man was frightened and wholly unaware of everything Sarah had just told him. No one had been keeping the local detective up to date.

"The message from Cohen," Sarah started in again, "is something you'll want to hear. It'll protect you from the investigation, keep you alive."

The man appeared torn about whether to allow a stranger into his home or tell her to get lost.

Then something changed on his face, like some realization dawned on him.

"Wait, you're that girl ..." He spoke so low that she barely caught the words.

That girl? They'd never met. But Aaron had met with Billings, and Aaron would've shown him photos of her.

Shit!

The detective's arm jerked to slam the door shut because Billings knew who she was now.

Sarah lunged at the screen and tore it open, but it was too late.

The inside door slammed shut, and the lock clicked into place.

Sarah withdrew her weapon and fired two shots into the lock without hesitation. Then she slammed her shoulder into the door once.

Nothing happened.

She stepped back and ran at it, smashing into the door so hard that it buckled near the lock and whipped open.

Once inside, she regained her footing and lifted the weapon.

Billings was beside the couch in the living room, loading a gun.

"Drop it," Sarah ordered.

Billing glanced at her but didn't drop it. Instead, he clicked it closed, tapped something on the side of the gun, and lifted it in her direction.

Sarah didn't hesitate. She pulled the trigger.

Her bullet hit the glass lampshade on the end table beside the detective, shattering it in a wash of decibels.

Having missed the detective, she pulled the trigger again.

Nothing happened.

Her weapon was empty.

Billings had ducked when the lamp exploded, but now he stood upright, gun wobbly in his good hand, a smirk on his face.

"What brings you here, Sarah Roberts?" He moved toward her. "Want to tell me before I kill you for breaking into my home?"

Sarah dropped the empty gun and raised her hands. "I came for my daughter. Where is she?"

Billings stopped in front of her, the weapon close to her chest. "You broke into my home thinking I had your daughter and then shot at me?" He shook his head slightly. "She's not with me, you stupid bitch. She's where she needs to be. You'll be dead, and it'll be a righteous shooting because you already discharged your firearm at me. Your fuckin' boyfriend will rot in prison for attacking me and breaking my nose—"

"They dropped the charges. He's free."

"What?"

"Aaron's out front in the car. I came for my daughter. Then we're leaving your shitty little town."

"Not possible. You're lying through your teeth. Since when did they drop the charges?" His nasal voice rose in pitch until he was squeaking. "What the fuck is wrong with this country? Why would they release him? He attacked a decorated detective."

"Because the FBI is in town."

Billings shook his head, the gun shaking, too. "No fucking way." The cotton or whatever had been stuffed up his nose ruined his chance of maintaining a masculine voice. "Why would they be here? Wait, why am I asking you? I'll call Cohen and end this shit."

He backed up one step, then bumped into Parkman.

Parkman's gun must've been cold because when it touched Billings's neck, he jerked away and almost fell over.

Parkman deftly grabbed the weapon the detective had been aiming at Sarah and twisted the barrel skyward.

"You won't be needing this any longer." Parkman yanked the weapon from the man's grasp and tossed it to Sarah.

She caught it and slipped it away in the back of her pants.

The TV droned on beside her, the volume too low to hear what they were saying over the pulse pounding in her ears. For a second there, things weren't looking good.

Parkman pushed Billings off balance, and the detective dropped onto his sofa.

"What the hell is this? Who are you people?"

Parkman pushed a finger to his lips, signaling to the detective to be quiet. "Tell us how many are in the house."

"No one. I live alone."

Sarah waved a finger at him. "You better not be lying to us."

The man's face creased with multiple lines as he scrunched, then winced in pain. "Who the hell are you people?"

"Where's my daughter?" Sarah moved close to him, and Parkman eased to the side. "I don't have time to interrogate you properly. So make it easy and tell me—"

The phone rang beside Billings.

"Go ahead. Answer it."

Parkman brought the weapon down to rest on the top of Billings's kneecap. "Play nicey nice on the phone. No one needs to know we're here."

Billings glared at them for a breath, then leaned over and brushed the glass shards from the broken lampshade off the phone. He picked it up on the fourth ring.

Sarah detected someone speaking when it got to Billings's ear.

"Uhm," Billings stared up at Sarah. "You got it, Mike. No, everything's fine here." He paused to listen, his eyes not leaving Sarah. "Oh, right. Okay, Mike. That rescheduled meeting time works for me. Next week is fine. Anything else?" Another pause. "Yes, sir. Understood. Gotta go now."

Sarah whispered to Parkman, "That's not some guy named Mike." She leaned in, smacked the phone from Billings's hand, then grabbed it and placed it to her ear. "Who is this?"

The caller hung up.

Sarah tossed the phone aside. "That was Cohen. He knows we're here."

"You want me just to shoot this guy?" Parkman asked.

"No, wait, wait!" Billings shouted, squirming backward on the couch. "That was Cohen." His voice squeaked again. "He wants to meet you to talk."

"We don't care about Cohen, and we don't want to talk to him. I want my daughter back."

"He knows where she is."

Sarah and Parkman exchanged a glance. "Why would Cohen know where she is when you orchestrated her removal from her father?"

"Cohen does everything in town. This is his town. He owns it."

Sarah shook her head. "I don't believe you."

"He just told me to tell you to meet him at the front of the church in an hour. He'll let Sarah inside to talk. Once you guys agree to end this shit, he'll tell you where your daughter is. Then you can leave town."

"For a man who can't be trusted, he offers me no assurances I'm not walking into a trap." Sarah leaned forward and slapped the detective's face. "Just tell me where my daughter is," she shouted at him.

Billings curled up on the couch, covering his face with his hands. He whimpered and moaned, muttering words she couldn't decipher. When he looked up, his bruised eyes were watering at the pain.

"My nose is broken," he said, his voice muffled as if he were talking through a wool scarf. "That fuckin' hurt."

Sarah raised her hand to infer that another slap was imminent. "Where is my daughter?"

"Hold on," Billings said, cowering downward, his hands up to ward off another strike to his face. "I gave her to child protection services. A woman named Teresa Baker. She's legit."

"Then how does Cohen have her?"

"Because Cohen does business that way. He knows your weak spot is your daughter. So he'd call child services and meet with Teresa, and now he probably has her *visiting* him for an hour."

"Visiting? What do you mean? Spell it out."

"He'll implore Teresa to hang around, offer a bonus, or offer to donate money to a children's charity. I don't know. Anything to keep her eating a long lunch or whatever so that he'll know where your daughter is while you're talking to him."

Sarah stared down at the man, knowing they needed to leave. Aaron was out front alone, and the preacher knew where they were now. "Teresa Baker is the name of the woman who has Willow?" Aaron had told her that name, so what the detective was saying rang true.

He nodded. "She's legit," he added.

She smacked Parkman's arm. "We good?"

Parkman stared at Billings, the gun not touching the man's knee anymore but still aimed in his general direction. "What happens in an hour? You go in to talk to that preacher, and this idiot comes up behind us with a shotgun." Parkman shook his head. "I don't like it. Men like this asshole are dangerous because they hide behind their badge." Parkman glanced sidelong at her. "He was going to murder you in his house and file it as a break-in. Sarah, you were unarmed."

"You're right. And look what he did to Aaron."

"Exactly."

"No, no." Billings raised his hands. "I'll stay out of it. I swear."

"Why don't we trust you?"

"You *can* trust me."

Sarah shook her head. "Nope. Don't think so." She slapped his face again.

Billings screamed.

She leaned down close to the detective and shouted near his ear. "That's for what you did to Aaron." Then she stepped on his good hand. "And that's for taking a child from her mother illegally, you fucking piece of shit."

Sarah grabbed his shirt and yanked the man off the sofa. He hit the floor and sprawled out, then tried to curl into a ball, protecting his head and cradling his injured wrist.

She grabbed the phone and ripped the cord out of the wall.

Parkman caught onto what Sarah was doing and shoved Billings onto his stomach. He yanked the man's hands behind his back as Sarah wound the phone cord around Billings's wrists while shouting at them to stop.

The man was literally crying now, but Sarah had no sympathy for him.

When she was done tying up his wrists, she bound his ankles with the cord from the back of his flatscreen TV, that low volume dying along with the screen when she tore the cord out of its back.

Then she leaned down to his ear again. "Men need to do better by women. You wanted to know who I am, so I'll tell you. I'm the woman who beats on men who think they can boss us around, take what isn't theirs, or make decisions about our bodies. Remember, you stepped into my life, my world." She grabbed his hair and yanked his head back, raising it up off the carpeted living room floor. "Don't make that mistake again. Stay out of my world, or I'll kill you next time." She slammed his head down into the carpet and heard something crack.

Billings screeched, and something about it made Sarah feel good. It fed a darkness within her that she didn't want to acknowledge.

When she looked at Parkman, he had grimaced.

"What? Too harsh?"

"Maybe a little."

"No one takes my baby from me." Sarah forced the words through her clenched teeth. "Billings had too much power." She kicked the detective in the side. "Nothing more than a bully with a badge. And now he'll suffer for his actions."

"Okay, Sarah, we get the point." Parkman waved a hand at her. "We need to leave."

"Hey, Billings." Sarah started toward the door. "If I don't have my daughter back before the sun goes down, I'm coming back here to execute you."

Billings just screamed on the floor, writhing in pain and unable to loosen his hands and feet, blood pouring from his nose.

Sarah followed Parkman out the front door, already feeling better about things.

That darkness inside her had been fed. And now it was time to kill a preacher man.

Maybe she was *damned* after all.

Chapter 47

AGENT NEWMAN DIRECTED THE team to the police station. Once everyone was dressed in Kevlar and suited up, all weapons loaded and ready, Newman briefed them in the back of the FBI van.

"We're going in to arrest every police officer in Glenrock. I've tallied the staffing here, and as far as I can tell, we won't encounter too many officers at once. It's a small town with only four patrol officers, and it's a Sunday afternoon."

The team leader, Rick Drayton, got okays all around, then moved to the back door.

"Gentlemen, let's do this."

Drayton opened the back door, and they all filed out and jogged to the front of the police station, passing a Land Rover parked at the front of the building.

Newman fell in behind the team, his FBI vest snug on his chest, with three iconic large letters adorning his back.

Exhilarated, he marveled at how good this felt. They were finally doing something to validate Sutton while she lay in the hospital. He couldn't wait to finish all the arrests in Glenrock and then visit her in Douglas when she woke up to tell her the good news.

Drayton's team entered the station and moved into the main foyer, encountering no resistance.

"Where are they?" Drayton asked Newman as his team spread out, moving behind the front desk.

"No one's here?" Newman whispered aloud, asking no one in particular.

"Hey," a man shouted from behind a door.

All the agents swung their weapons in the direction of the voice.

"Is someone there?"

Drayton gestured with his fingers, and two of his men approached the door.

Newman stayed back to let Drayton's men do what they were trained for.

On the count of three—with Drayton's black-gloved fingers in the

263

air dropping from three to two, then to one—the door was yanked open, and Drayton led the way inside, his weapon at the ready.

"What the hell," a man shouted. "Hey, take it easy."

Newman stepped into the corridor and let his assault rifle drop down so the tip aimed at the ground.

"What are you doing in there?" Newman asked him.

"Oh, it's you. Hey, let me out."

Newman and Drayton exchanged a glance.

"It's Officer Brown, right?" Newman's eyes moved from the wallet and keys on the floor to the cop in the holding cell. "Was this an accident?" He pointed at the minor swelling on the side of the cop's face. "Or were you put in here?"

"Look, that bitch showed up and clocked me one."

"Who else is in the station?"

"No one right now. I was working alone. The night shift officers are at home asleep, and one guy's out on patrol." Brown leaned on the bars. "He's likely sleeping under a tree somewhere."

"What *bitch* hit you?" Drayton asked.

"That Sarah woman. And she had some mercenary-type guy with her. Real badass."

Newman shook his head in a short burst as if none of this made any sense. "Why would a woman show up and assault a police officer?"

"They think I had something to do with taking her kid."

"Did you?"

"No," Brown shouted. "That was all Detective Billings."

Newman nodded exaggeratedly. "And where is Billings now?"

"Probably at home—who the fucks knows. Look," Brown shook the bars, "let me outta here. We can talk out front."

"You can wait until we're done talking."

A look of confusion crossed Brown's face. Then it turned to anger. "What the fuck does that mean? You're the FBI. We're on the same side. Why would you *leave* me in a holding cell?"

"How about this? You tell us everything we want to know, and then we'll talk about getting you out of this cell."

Brown stared at Newman for a long moment, likely contemplating his situation. Then he released the bars and stepped back until he sat on the single bench.

"Do I need a lawyer?"

Newman leaned on the bars. "That's up to you. Did you do something you'd need a lawyer for?"

Brown glanced down at the floor, a hand scratching at an errant nail. "What if I told you everything I know?" He raised his head. "Can I get some sort of deal?"

"I'd have to call that in, but as it stands, you're an accessory to attempted murder, not including all the drug trafficking charges that'll be filed." Newman averted his gaze to examine the size and width of the cell as Brown's face paled and went slack. "This looks like your new home for a couple of decades, Officer Brown, and we all know what happens to cops on the inside." Newman stared at Brown now, waiting for his response.

The man looked as if he was going to cry.

"Get me a deal, and I'll talk."

"Forget it." Newman pushed off the bars and started for the door.

"Wait," Brown shouted.

Newman spun back around. "What?" He lifted his fingers and then dropped one. "We will find Billings." He dropped the second finger. "We stake out Cohen's house." He dropped another finger. "They'll be arrested and charged accordingly." He dropped his hand to his side now. "Financial records will be obtained. A forensic audit will take place. The entire drug operation will be dismantled. With the photos and evidence Special Agent Jamie Sutton acquired, the investigation will be swift, and you'll all spend your golden years in prison. Why should I stand around talking to you? You're already behind bars, right where I was going to put you."

"I'll talk. It'll speed things up."

He glanced at Drayton, then back to Brown. "We're listening."

"You'll get me a deal?" A tear dropped off Brown's cheek.

"Helping us will go a long way for you when you have your day in court. *Not* helping us right now will also be mentioned. Your choice."

Brown pushed up off the bench and walked to the bars. "I know where Sarah went, and I know everything about Cohen's drug business. How he fills the cows and pigs with cocaine and ships them all over

Wyoming."

"Sutton already has that. Photos of the barn, too." He leaned closer to Brown. "I need more. Something I can use now."

"Liam has been raping and killing young women for years, then placing their bodies in the North Platte River. Dalton shot and killed Liam in the barn the other night."

Newman nodded, keeping his face expressionless. This was good. "Go on."

"Cohen has murdered so many people, too. Sure, we get paid a lot of money, but we all work for him out of fear."

"Where can we find Martin Cohen?"

Brown talked for ten more minutes without a break until Newman stopped him and moved out into the main lobby with Drayton.

"Can you leave two men here?"

Drayton nodded. "That means there are four of us now. You, me, and two more guys. Is that enough for what you have planned?"

Newman nodded once. "We're going to Detective Billings's house. Then we're going after Martin Cohen. The woman who saved Sutton might need our help."

"And this guy?" Drayton jerked a thumb over his shoulder toward the holding cell corridor. "The cop. What about him?"

"He stays right where he is, and when the other officers show up here, relieve them of their weapons and cell phones and toss them in there with him. The FBI is policing Glenrock until further notice. Tomorrow, I'll have a dozen agents here."

"We can do that."

Drayton ordered two of his men to stay behind, told them what to do, and then followed Newman to the front door.

"You ready?" Drayton asked him.

"Absolutely. Let's do this." Newman pushed the door open, and they ran for the FBI van.

Chapter 48

COHEN LOOKED FOR ANY sign of Domenick as they approached the gates of his compound.

"That little shit." Cohen yanked out his phone. "He didn't show."

"Who? Him?" Dalton pointed out the windshield.

Domenick stepped around the edge of the gate, his hands in his pockets.

"He looks ready to bolt."

Cohen slipped his phone away. "Pull up beside him on my side." He lowered his window as Dalton eased to a stop beside Domenick.

"I thought I told you to wait back there. Don't approach the gates, I said."

"I was waitin', sir. But then I saw this cruiser coming, and I thought I'se be in trouble because of these bodies here."

"Did you have anything to do with this carnage?"

"Oh no, sir." Domenick raised his hands and stepped back.

"I know, dummy. I'm asking because if you didn't do it, you have nothing to fear." Cohen shook his head. Talking to dummies dumbed down his language skills. "Now, get in behind me. We got work to do."

Domenick opened the back door and hopped in.

Dalton released the brake, and they were moving before the back door of the cruiser closed.

"What are we doing, sir?" Domenick asked, leaning up close to the grate that separated the rear of the vehicle from the front.

"Moving rocks."

"Moving rocks? Well, now, that doesn't seem like much fun."

"It isn't meant to be *fun*."

Dalton pulled them up to the fountain at the front of the house, and Cohen spun around in his seat to look at Domenick. "This is it."

Domenick stared at him, his pallid expression telling Cohen all he needed to know. The boy was afraid but wasn't sure what to fear.

"Get out of the cruiser."

Domenick tried the door, but it wouldn't open. "It's stuck or something."

Cohen glanced at Dalton but spoke to Domenick. "It's a police car, dummy. The back doors only open from the outside."

"Oh. Right. Of course."

"Release the tailgate," he said to Dalton. "Wait here. We'll be loaded in ten minutes."

Dalton tapped a switch on the underside of the dash. Something popped in the back.

Cohen hopped out and opened the back door for Domenick. "Come with me."

Once the back door was wide open, he guided Domenick over to his fountain.

"See all those rocks under the water?"

Domenick nodded. "Yup."

"I want thirty of them in the back of that cruiser. Nothing too small. The ones that are the size of a baseball or slightly bigger."

"Bigger?" Domenick squinted in the afternoon sun when he stared at Cohen.

"Yeah, bigger. Like a man's fist." Cohen held up his fist. "Nothing larger than that. I have to be able to throw them."

"Throw them?"

Cohen sputtered air through his lips in frustration. "Just do it. And hurry."

"Well, can't Dalton help?"

In other circumstances, Domenick would have a broken nose for his attitude, but these were desperate times, and he wasn't about to beat up the one able-bodied idiot who could load the rocks.

"If you must know, Dalton can't help because he's suffering from a bullet wound to the leg after fighting off the people who killed those men by the gate." Technically, that was twisting the story a wee bit, but it didn't matter one way or the other. When this was over, he'd use Domenick tonight to load the drug trucks, then get rid of him and feed his body to the pigs. There was no way he would keep someone so dumb on his team. How he survived this long boggled Cohen.

"Wow, that's rad. Must'a hurt a lot."

"Rad? Really? What is this, the eighties?"

"Oh, sorry. I was watching a show when you called, and—"

Cohen smacked him on the back of the head. "Load the fuckin' stones." Then he stomped off toward the house, thinking about how the meeting with the demon in his church would go.

He would stone Sarah and her mercenary sidekick or whoever the hell he was, finish off that boyfriend of hers, and be done with them. Then, this town could go back to normal. He had shipments due to be loaded tonight. The cargo was to be delivered to Nevada and California, and he was down several men. It would be challenging, but they'd get through it—they always did.

Once inside his house, he went to his weapons locker and selected four handguns. A Magnum, a Beretta, and two Glocks. When they were all loaded and ready to go, he grabbed a few boxes of spare ammunition and then ran back out to the cruiser.

He placed them on the front footwell, passenger side.

"Just in case," he muttered to Dalton.

"No argument here. I'll take two of those when we do this. No one survives the night."

"No one survives the night." Cohen jerked his head toward the back, his eyes not leaving Dalton.

"Got it. No *one* survives."

Cohen nodded once more, then stepped around to the back. It had over a dozen good-sized stones already loaded.

"Good job. Halfway there."

Domenick stood up from the fountain, two rocks in his hands. His arms were soaked, and his jeans showed water strips on the front where he'd dripped onto them.

"I'll keep going, sir."

"Good." Cohen slapped him on the back as he stepped up to the cruiser and dropped the rocks in the rear.

Then Cohen ran back to the house. One shotgun could come in handy. Or maybe he'd bring that assault rifle he'd been dreaming of using on someone.

Assault rifle it is.

He entered his house smiling, overjoyed at the damage he would do to that witch, no longer bothered by the flesh wound on the top of his shoulder.

His wounds would heal.
Sarah's wouldn't.

Chapter 49

NEWMAN DIRECTED DRAYTON TO park on the side of the road right in front of Billings's house. Officer Brown was explicit in his directions—they couldn't miss it.

"We ready to roll?" Newman asked.

Drayton nodded and looked at the other two men.

"Ready, sir," the guy on the right said. Newman had been introduced back at the hospital in Douglas, but couldn't recall the guy's name.

"Look." Newman spoke with his hands. "We're entering a detective's house. He may be armed. We do not shoot to kill unless we have to. I trust Officer Brown wasn't lying on this one. Sarah was directed to this house less than half an hour ago. She has a mercenary-type—Brown's words—with her. Proceed with extreme caution."

Both men in the back nodded. "Ready," the guy on the right said.

Drayton smacked the side of his seat twice. "Let's do this."

All four men jumped from the van and ran toward the detective's house. Drayton and Newman headed toward the front porch, and the other two men sprinted for the back of the house.

When Drayton got to the front door, he stopped and pointed at the deadbolt.

Newman stared at it. Someone had fired a weapon into it.

They exchanged a glance, then Drayton eased the door open slowly. Newman moved to the side of the door, his back to the wall. After a quick breath, he peeked inside the house.

The front foyer was empty.

"FBI," Drayton shouted. "We're coming inside."

"Help," someone moaned in a weird pitch. "I need help."

Drayton led the way inside, followed by Newman, their weapons at the ready.

A man lay on the living room floor, his hands tied behind his back with what looked like a phone cord, and his ankles were tied with an HDMI cable.

Newman caught sight of the side of the man's face and understood why his voice was off. The guy had a broken nose that looked like it was bleeding again.

One of his arms had a cast on it, and both hands had deep red fingers. Whoever tied this guy up went too tight, cutting off circulation.

Sarah?

Newman saw the broken lamp on the end table and the house phone on the floor, then frowned. "What the hell happened here?" he asked.

Drayton's men entered from the rear of the house before the man on the floor answered. One man stepped up to Drayton. "The back door was unlocked, sir, and we found this"—he held up two toothpicks—"stuck in the lock."

Drayton shook his head. "How do you pick a lock with those?"

The guy holding the toothpicks shrugged, then dropped them to the carpet.

Newman looked down at the man on the floor. "Who else is in the house?"

"No one. Just me."

"You're not lying to us now, are you?"

"If someone else was in the house, wouldn't they have untied me by now?"

"Not if it was Sarah and her mercenary friend."

The man tried to look up at Newman. "You know Sarah?"

"We're trying to find her."

"I know where she is. Untie me, and we'll both go and arrest her."

Newman chuckled. "Arrest her? We're not going to arrest her. We're going to thank her."

The man on the carpet—who he assumed was Detective Billings—turned as far as he could and stared up at Newman.

"What the fuck would you thank her for?"

"For saving the life of my former partner at the bureau, Special Agent Jamie Sutton."

Newman watched Billings's eyes and saw it all coming to him.

"I understood the FBI was looking for a missing male in town."

Newman laughed again. "You understood wrong, Detective Billings. Now," Newman lowered to his haunches. "You want to tell me where Sarah is? It would save us the trouble of having to find more law enforcement officials tied up in her wake."

Billings lowered his head to the carpet and closed his eyes. "I want to call my lawyer."

Newman glanced at Drayton. His other two guys had slinked off somewhere quietly—probably gone to clear the house and make sure they were alone.

"You sure you don't want to tell us anything, Detective? It would go a long way when you have your day in court."

Billings kept his eyes and mouth closed.

"Last chance before you lawyer up."

Billings's mouth moved a fraction, mumbling a couple of words.

"What was that?"

"I said, fuck you."

"Suit yourself." Newman got back to his feet as Drayton's men reentered the living room.

"Place is empty. He's alone."

"Load him in the van," Drayton said.

Newman nodded. "We're going back to the police station to speak with Officer Brown some more."

Billings's eyes popped wide at the mention of Brown's name.

When Drayton's men yanked Billings to his feet, they shoved him onto the couch and untied his ankles so he could walk on his own. Then they got him back to his feet and manhandled him toward the open front door.

Billings turned to Newman over his shoulder.

"Brown's a rat?"

Newman lunged out and grabbed Billings's arm, holding the men back a moment. "He's doing the right thing. Gonna make a deal. It's Cohen we're after." He moved within a few inches of the man's damaged face and stared into his bloodshot eyes. "You sure you still want to lawyer up?"

"More than ever."

Newman shoved the man. "Get him out of here."

They all climbed into the van and drove back to the Glenrock police station. It took them a few minutes to settle Billings into his cell, and then they untied the phone cord from his hands.

"Hey, I need medical attention. She broke my fuckin' nose again." He held up his hand. "And she stepped on my wrist. I'll need X-rays, too."

"You can wait until tomorrow."

"What?" Billings shrieked, his high pitch carrying around the hollow cell corridor like a screeching car tire. "If my hand or nose is broken, it'll have to be set."

"They can reset stuff like that." Newman waved him off in a don't-worry-about-it gesture. "We got lots of time."

"You're insane. I'll have your badge for this."

He moved up to Brown's cell and saw that the cop looked like he would be sick.

"You okay in there?"

"Yeah, just reality hitting me pretty hard." He met Newman's gaze. "I don't want to be in here. I'll never last a day in prison. I'm not cut out for doing time."

"Well, I'll tell you what. Squeal on everyone and tell me everything while we wait for more cops to show up here, and I'll speak to the judge personally."

"You mean that?"

Newman placed a hand over his heart and raised the other in the air beside his head. "I swear it to you, and Drayton is my witness."

He detected Drayton nodding beside him.

Officer Brown took a deep breath and started talking from the bench in his cell.

He told them everything he knew within half an hour. But most importantly, he told them where his colleagues would be soon.

Newman had pulled a chair into the corridor to sit and record Brown's statement.

Now, he stood from the chair and addressed Drayton.

"Cohen is driving the only police SUV this station owns. You ready to finish this?"

Drayton nodded. "That's why we're here. Let's do it."

They headed for the front door.

It was time to arrest a bunch of cops and, in the process, take down Martin Cohen, a drug-dealing preacher.

He had to admit that there was an extra pep in his step as he ran for the FBI van.

He'd also garnered a massive amount of respect for Sarah. She pulled Agent Sutton from Cohen's bunker and was now going around town kicking ass.

Who the fuck is this girl?

Chapter 50

SARAH WATCHED THE CHURCH through the windshield of Parkman's rental.

"That cruiser pulled in five minutes ago. You think they brought Willow with them?"

Parkman turned to her from the driver's seat. "Hard to tell because they parked around back in the alley. But I would suspect that is the case. This Cohen guy has to be shaking in his boots after what you and Aaron have done to his town."

"Yeah," Aaron said from the back seat where he'd been sulking for the past half hour. "They took our daughter from us, but we kicked their asses."

"Aaron," Sarah snapped, spinning around. "Lose the sarcasm. We're trying to figure this shit out. You're either with us or you're not. But before you check out, let's at least team up to get Willow." She spun back around and crossed her arms, her hands fisted. "I'm going in to talk to this asshole."

"You have that detective's gun, right?"

Sarah nodded. "I do."

"Okay, once you go in, I'll move around the back and see if I can find a way inside to listen."

"If I'm not out with Willow in ten minutes, break the doors down."

"With what?" Parkman chortled. "That church is barricaded. The front doors are steel, and the side doors are heavy wood. The windows are six feet off the ground, so I couldn't climb inside even if I broke one."

Sarah surveyed the church. "Yeah, there's really no way inside unless the doors are unlocked. Or maybe if you have a battering ram."

"So don't get killed."

"Oh, okay. Great idea." She said this with her usual sarcastic voice, unlike Aaron's hurtful sarcasm. His came equipped with barbs, which was so unlike him.

"Wish me luck." Sarah got out of the car and headed toward the front of the church.

Just before she rounded the corner at the front, a car door closed behind her as Parkman got out and headed toward the back of the church.

They'd get Willow and be done with this town. Maybe Aaron was right. Let the feds clean up Cohen's mess. If that happened, they'd even get out of Wyoming before midnight. The sun was lowering in the west, making this a long Sunday.

When she came around the front of the church, a skinny man with wet jeans and a dopey smile on his lips stood guarding the doors.

She recognized him. This was the scaredy-cat who stood beside Liam in the barn—the guy who grabbed Sutton from her car last night at the truck stop.

His shirt was soaked in sweat, yet it wasn't hot enough to make that much sweat. He had to work out to perspire that much.

"Who are you?"

"Name's Dom."

She gestured at his shirt. "Got hit by a water balloon or something?"

The guy looked down at his wet shirt, then back up at Sarah, and shook his head. "Water fountain stuff."

"I'm meeting with you?"

Dom shook his head, his greasy hair flying up on either side. "Nope. Cohen is inside waiting for you."

Just like he said when he called Billings's place.

"And he has my daughter?"

Dom scrunched up his brow, then released it. "Your bidness with Cohen ain't none of my bidness, ma'am. I'm just supposed to open the door, then close it." Dom grabbed the door, turned the key, opened it, and waited.

Sarah stared at him for a long moment, then peeked inside.

"This a trap, Dom?"

"No, ma'am."

Willow is safe, Vivian whispered.

Sarah jerked. "What?"

"I said no," Dom repeated.

"Not you," Sarah snapped. "What did you say, Vivian?"

Willow's safe. Then her sister was gone.

Dom glanced behind him, then behind Sarah. "Ma'am, there ain't nobody here by you an' me."

Sarah ignored him and stepped inside, emboldened that her sister had her back. Wouldn't Vivian have said that instead if she wasn't meant to enter the church? Besides, this was the house of God, a sanctuary. Wouldn't Cohen consider this neutral territory?

She passed the first few pews when she heard the door close behind her. Then the lock clicked into place, and the key slid out of the door.

The church was empty.

"Hello?" she called out, and her voice returned to her, echoing several times.

She moved to the center of the church and stopped. Cohen had to be here, and he was wounded. She'd shot him in the shoulder, but she'd spared his life. Perhaps he planned on doing the same for her.

But where was he? And where was Willow?

When Vivian said that Willow was safe, was she telling her that because Willow was *not* in the church at the moment? And if so, then where was she? Why not just tell her so they could end this?

"Sarah," a man said from above her.

Sarah spun around and looked up at the balcony railing where Cohen stood looking down at her.

"Where's my daughter?"

"First, we talk."

"I'm not sure we have much to say to one another."

Cohen chuckled, his head leaning back and aiming skyward. "Fair enough, and I'm sure you're right, but I want to know one thing before proceeding."

"What's that?"

Cohen fixed her with a stern glare. "Why did you come to my town and fuck with me and my business?"

"Your ego astounds me."

"What?"

"I didn't come to *your* town to fuck with *you*. I stopped for some gas, and that woman jumped in my car. Liam was chasing her." Sarah shrugged. "Liam grabbed me, too, and now he's dead. That's it. Now, where's my daughter? I just want to leave. You can have your stupid town."

Well, not really. She'd be going to see Sutton at the hospital—see the authorities—to make sure Cohen was stopped, but she needed Willow back before even thinking straight.

"Your daughter is with child services—"

"What?" Sarah shouted. "You said you'd bring her here."

Cohen held up the hand of his good arm. "Hold your horses. I wanted to talk first—just you and me. Then you can have your daughter. Trust me, little witch, I might be considered the bad guy here, but I don't steal children. She's safe."

Sarah looked down as craning her neck to stare up at Cohen was bothering her shoulders. When she looked back up, Cohen held onto a large rock. She frowned, then noticed the pile near his feet.

"What's that for?" She stepped back a few paces. "You going to throw it at me or something? What is this? Sticks and stones can break my bones shit? We in grade school again?"

Rocks up on the balcony of the church? Did he carry them up there with a bandaged shoulder? Then, it all came to her in a rush. The guy out front had carried them up the stairs. But why?

"You know what the Bible says about the occult, about witches?"

"No, and I don't give a damn. The Bible had its place and time. Now, we're in a new age, a new era. Just be nice to everyone, try to get along, and we'll survive down here."

"How very noble of you, but life doesn't work that way."

"Oh, and so you're going to tell me how life works, are you?" She moved toward the front door, then stopped. To get there, she'd have to pass directly under Cohen. "I'm leaving." She pointed up at him. "Don't throw that shit at me. Since you wasted my time here, I will get my daughter back on my own." She moved closer to the door, darted under the balcony, and ran for the front.

There was no thump, no heavy pounding sound of the rock hitting the wooden church floor—Cohen didn't throw it.

She pushed on the door, but it was still locked.

She knocked. "Hey, Dom. Open up. We're done in here."

There was no response.

"Dom," she shouted through the door. "Open up."

No one answered from the other side of the door.

She turned around and placed her back against the door. "Great. They locked me in here with that lunatic."

A gun in her hand made her feel more secure. The time for games was over. She wanted out and wanted Willow back, but this man had placed himself between a mother and her daughter—even if he didn't have Willow, he was stopping Sarah from getting to her.

She stormed back into the main section of the church, darted under the balcony so a rock didn't break open her skull, then spun around and lifted Billings's fully loaded weapon.

Cohen hadn't moved. He stood there with the large stone in his good hand, an ugly smirk on his face.

"Tell your lackey to open the front door. We're done here."

"I don't think so, Sarah Roberts."

She frowned up at him. "What kind of game are you playing?"

"A game where I win. Don't you see all the cards are stacked in my favor?"

"You're delusional. This is a game where you lose everything."

"Wrong, witch."

Something rustled behind her. She barely caught the sound and reflexively lowered her center of gravity as she twisted around to see who was there.

But it was too late.

The man who had shot Liam in the barn had crept up behind her with a baseball bat.

He was already in mid-swing.

She would not get out of the way in time, and she would not be able to fire at him.

The bat struck her left thigh. She yelped and fell sideways, landing out of the aisle, wedged between two wooden pews, the gun gone from her hand.

This is what saved her life, though, because the moment she dropped and grabbed at her thigh to make sure her femur wasn't broken, the stone Cohen had been holding crashed into the church floor less than two inches from her right ankle.

"You'll die in here, demon witch," Cohen shouted.

The man with the baseball bat had disappeared, but the madman on the balcony had thrown another stone.

It crashed into the wooden pew beside her head with a sickening crack.

Sarah had to move—now! But where was her gun?

She pushed up and onto her left leg but dropped back in pain. She didn't think it was broken, but it hurt badly when she put weight on it.

Another stone broke the pew behind her.

"Stop throwing rocks, asshole!" All of her frustration came out in that one scream.

When she looked up, Cohen was about to throw another stone.

She rolled under the pew beside her and covered her face, her heart racing.

The rock crashed into the floor an inch from her ear.

"You'll die today, witch! If there's a Lord in Heaven, hallowed be thy name, I'll stone the witch and spill her blood in the house of God before the day is out."

Cohen tossed another stone, this one even larger.

Sarah screamed.

Chapter 51

NEWMAN STARED AT THE open gate to Martin Cohen's property.

"What do you make of that?"

Drayton kept his eyes on the gate. "Looks like someone left in a hurry."

"And forgot to close the gate?"

Drayton pointed. "And didn't clean up the body."

Newman leaned closer to the dashboard, following Drayton's finger. "Holy shit."

Newman hopped out, and Drayton followed. The other guys got out and followed them on foot to the gate.

"What the hell happened here?"

Near the driveway that led to the front of a large house, some sort of trap door sat open.

His gun aimed in front of him, and Newman headed for the door. Stairs led down into the earth.

"I'm going in," he whispered to Drayton, who came up behind him.

Drayton nodded. "I'll follow you down."

Newman dropped into the semi-darkness of an underground bunker. On the other side of the first room was an open door. He ran up to the wall, placed his back against it, and then peeked into the room.

They were empty. "Clear," he shouted.

Drayton stepped inside the second room as Newman moved to the mattress on the floor.

"Where'd all that blood come from?" Drayton asked.

Newman suppressed his gag reflex when he saw a canvas bag unrolled and several knives sticking out of it. There was blood on a few of them.

"This is where Cohen tortured Agent Jamie Sutton."

"That bastard deserves to die," Drayton mumbled under his breath.

"I second that." Newman backed out of the room. "We need to seal this place off. Forensics will have a field day down here. And those bodies by the gate." He speculated on some of what probably happened. "Sarah was here, too. She got Sutton out."

"You're saying a woman broke in here and killed those guys by the gate, then grabbed Agent Sutton and drove her to the hospital in Douglas? And she stuck Officer Brown in his own holding cell, then beat that detective and tied him up?"

Newman looked at Drayton, nodding. "Because of her, Sutton's alive, so I say bravo."

"Well, I say holy shit, and I'll second that."

They left the bunker, and as Drayton and his men ran to ensure the house was empty, Newman got on the phone.

He needed to explain things to his boss and get an entire team of agents down here by tomorrow.

Martin Cohen was done, finished.

If he survived the day—that woman, Sarah, was hunting him.

Special Agent Andrew Newman dialed out, his hand tight on the cell phone while staring at the bodies left to rot in the late afternoon sun.

Chapter 52

AARON WAS TIRED OF waiting. Sarah had been inside the church for a few minutes now, and Parkman was hanging around at the back of the building.

Where was Willow? Why hadn't Sarah brought their daughter out yet?

He pushed himself up, squinted with the pain in his chest, then opened the car door. It was too warm to sit in the car and wait anyway.

He got out, closed the door, and stood staring at the church.

Front or back? The front might piss off Sarah. She's handling things and wouldn't want her *boyfriend* to screw things up for her. But the back of the church had Parkman.

He chose the back anyway. Maybe Parkman could use a bit of help with something.

Carefully ensuring each step was soft on the concrete, Aaron sauntered across the road and into the alley behind the church. He walked right up to the SUV cruiser and peeked inside.

It was empty.

He glanced around but couldn't see Parkman anywhere.

"Parkman?" he said in a hushed whisper.

Something banged hard inside the church. He ducked down, wondering what was going on inside. Chest pain flared when he ducked, but it wasn't too bad.

Then he thought he heard a scream. Maybe Sarah was shouting at someone.

Aaron lowered to his knees, looked around, and then eased down to lie on the grass beside the SUV. He carefully eased under the vehicle's chassis and withdrew the switchblade knife attached to his keychain.

He wasn't much of a mechanic, so he guessed where the brake line was. Another scream was emitted from inside the church, which made him work faster. He needed to get inside.

Within half a minute, he'd managed to cut several lines, get sprayed by a couple of colorful liquids, and puncture holes in a few metallic surfaces.

The cruiser may turn on, and they may even be able to drive it for a bit, but this baby wasn't going any great distances with the holes and severed lines dangling and dripping now.

Aaron pocketed his keychain and gingerly slid out from underneath the cruiser.

Then he held his breath as he rolled over, got to his knees, and pushed up to his feet.

As fast as he could walk and tolerate the pain, he made his way along the side of the church toward the front, where Sarah had gone inside.

There was still no sign of Parkman.

When he turned the corner, he almost bumped into a skinny guy who didn't look a day over twenty.

"Hey, sorry," Aaron said. "Didn't see you there."

"No problem." The guy moved back off the sidewalk and placed his back against the church doors.

"Actually, I need to be in there." Aaron pointed at the doors. "You wanna step aside?"

"Church is closed. Come back next Sunday."

This was Cohen's security guard? This skinny runt with the dirty hair and the sweat-soaked shirt?

"Maybe you don't understand," Aaron said, moving closer. "My girlfriend just went in there, and I thought I heard her scream."

"Don't worry about it. Just walk away if you know what's good for you."

The guy held up his hands to ward Aaron off. If they were any closer, he would've pushed Aaron.

His eyes zeroed in on the wristwatch the guy was wearing.

It couldn't be—too much of a coincidence.

"Hey, nice watch. That's the Great Wall of China series. The Wonders of the World, right?" It was the *Marvels* of the World, not *Wonders*. But he wouldn't be corrected since he figured this guy was wearing Benjamin's watch, which had been stolen when Sarah was taken from their car at the truck stop. Only the true owner would know the difference.

The guy glanced at it, then back to Aaron. "Yeah, picked it up the other night. Now buzz off."

Something crashed inside again.

Sarah shouted something unintelligible.

"Hey, buddy, I need in there." He moved toward the guy, and the guy took a swing at him.

Aaron blocked the punch with ease, grunted with the pain in his chest, and then drove a fist into the punk's throat. It connected so hard and fast that the guy collapsed against the church's steel door. He clutched at his throat, trying to breathe through a damaged trachea—Aaron didn't think he hit him hard enough to crush the trachea, which meant he should live—as he slid toward the ground.

It took him considerable effort to get to his knees and remove Benjamin's watch from the thief's wrist, but he did it. Once it was back on his own wrist, he pushed up to his feet and leaned his back against the church door, trying to catch a breath. The pain in his cracked and broken ribs made him break out in a sweat.

Something cut into his back. He moved off the door and turned around.

The key was in the lock.

How stupid could this idiot be?

Aaron nudged the man aside with his foot while he still gagged for air, turned the key in the lock, and swung the door open.

Then he stepped inside the church and didn't see the baseball bat swinging at him in the dark interior until it was too late.

Chapter 53

"EVEN IF YOU DON'T want to know what the Bible says about witches, I will tell you."

Cohen seemed to have an endless supply of stones. Hiding under the wooden pew, he'd managed to throw at least ten so far. Most of them had missed. They'd ruined the seats, broken wood, and damaged the floor, but missed her entirely so far. Only one of the rocks grazed her left foot. Nothing was broken as far as she could tell, but it was aching and would be a bitch to walk on. Her thigh was feeling better, but swelling where the bat had hit her. The bruising would be spectacular, but it was a win as long as it wasn't broken.

Injuries notwithstanding, she needed out of here yesterday.

She stuck her head out from under the seat and caught a glimpse of a falling stone. She ducked back so fast that she bumped her head on the wooden frame at the base of the pew. The stone crunched on wood an inch from where her head had just been.

"Motherfucker," she whispered through her teeth.

The preacher wanted to stone her to death.

Even if she rolled out of hiding and ran for the door, it was locked. The back was secured, too. Parkman was back there and would've come in by now if he could.

And where was the guy with the baseball bat?

Afraid to peek again, she waited for another stone to hit the floor. Then she'd roll out and get to her feet. She'd be out of his range at the back of the church.

"Leviticus 20:27," Cohen shouted like he was sermonizing. "'A man or woman who is a medium shall be surely put to death. They shall be stoned with stones; their blood shall be upon them.' So, you see, Sarah, this is all your fault."

The heavy thunk of a large rock crashed a foot away. Sarah rolled out, pushed up on her good leg, then tested her sore ankle. It held her, but she had a limp.

Cohen was already hefting another rock over his shoulder when she looked up. She spun around to run—well, lurch and stumble—but bumped into the man with the bat, the man she shot in the leg at the truck stop.

She grappled with him, hands blocking and jabbing, but he quickly overpowered her and then shoved her to the floor.

When she dropped, she shot a look up at the balcony. A stone was already en route. Instead of rolling to the shelter of the pew, she rolled the other way—and saved her face in the process.

The large stone broke off the edge of the pew and embedded itself in the floor, where she would have been if she'd rolled for shelter.

"Sarah," Cohen shouted. "You can't hide forever. You will be stoned to death in my church." Another large rock dropped, this one missing by several feet. "You are a seer, a witch, a demon. If I run out of stones, Dalton will break your legs with that bat, and then I'll come down there and stone you while you lie at my feet, begging me for forgiveness."

"Do your worst, psycho," Sarah shouted.

Another stone crashed down closer to her feet. This was a dangerous waste of time. But injured as she was, how could she fight that Dalton guy with his bat?

She stared up at Cohen, watching for the next stone. He tossed it, and Sarah rolled away easily.

She sat up and looked for Dalton. He was jogging toward the front doors. Was Parkman coming in that way?

She glanced back up at Cohen. He was holding a rock but hadn't thrown it yet.

Sarah got to her feet, leaned against one of the pews, and moved farther out of Cohen's range.

The front doors opened, and she looked down the aisle at the fading sunlight as it spilled inside the church, her hands on the end of the pew for support.

Aaron stood outlined in the sun, slightly bent at the waist.

Aaron? Where was Parkman?

Then Dalton swung from the shadows to the left of the door and connected with Aaron's chest—a solid *whump* resounded from the front of the church.

Aaron stumbled backward and dropped to the sidewalk outside.

Sarah screamed as Dalton slammed the door shut again and clicked something on the inside to lock the door.

A stone dropped five feet in front of her.

A glint of metal shone from under the last pew on the right, catching her eye.

The gun!

Dalton was limping toward her now, swinging the bat around his right wrist, reminding her of that Negan guy in *The Walking Dead*.

Cohen thundered down the stairs at the side of the church. "Fine, Sarah," he shouted. "Have it your way." Cohen made it to the bottom of the stairs. "Break her legs, Dalton. I'll stone her to death at the base of the cross where Jesus bled for her sins."

Dalton was too close.

She'd never make the gun now.

The sound of an engine revving resonated throughout the church. It was so close that Dalton paused his bat and brought it up two-handed like he was at the plate and ready for the pitch.

Sarah stumbled back, reaching for the next pew to hold onto.

The horror of seeing Aaron, his chest already on fire with pain, taking that hit from the bat made her wonder if he'd survive it. Would he suffer permanent damage, or would he die?

Even with all the rage that enveloped her, she wouldn't be able to fight Dalton, and she certainly wouldn't get past him to her gun on the floor now.

The car stopped close outside.

A door slammed.

Cohen had stopped by all the stones he'd thrown on the floor. "What are you waiting for, Dalton? Break her fucking legs." He bent to pick up two rocks.

Dalton moved forward, swinging left, then back the other way.

"You shot me in the leg, you wench." He swung again, making Sarah bend backward to avoid taking the bat's tip on the chin. Her mind raced with how to dive at him when the arc came through again. "Now I get to watch you die."

Sarah hopped back two paces. She needed more time to think.

Dalton stepped forward and swung again.

"Patience isn't a virtue I possess," Cohen shouted, his voice echoing through the church's cavernous wooden roof.

He dropped a stone, then pulled a handgun out from behind his back.

This was the end. She couldn't think of a play.

In that moment of panic, she screamed at Vivian for help, but nothing came.

Cohen raised his weapon, and Dalton stepped back.

"You messed with the wrong people, demon witch."

Cohen fired his weapon, and glass shattered throughout the church, making all three of them duck down.

Chapter 54

PARKMAN HAD SCOURED THE rear of the church and could not find an access point. His toothpicks—extra-strong wooden ones he had specially made for him—wouldn't work on the back door lock.

He briefly considered climbing to the roof, where he could gain access through the ventilation system, but that would take too long.

Several heavy thunking sounds were coming from inside the building. Sarah screamed something, and then there was more intermittent banging.

What the hell was going on in there?

Quickly walking the perimeter of the building, he checked each basement window, but they were all sealed with metal grates and inaccessible. Stained-glass windows lined the side of the building, but they were all above his shoulders. Breaking one and climbing in was impossible without a ladder, not to mention how exposed he'd be to everyone inside.

"Shit," he muttered to himself.

Letting Sarah go inside that church alone was a mistake.

When he rounded the corner at the front of the church, he jolted to a stop at the sound of the door slamming shut.

The lock clicked before he could react—but the two men on the ground made him clutch at his chest.

A skinny guy with a red face crawled toward the curb, gasping for breath. He had one hand on his throat.

Aaron was on his back on the ground, staring at the sky, his mouth wide, his breath shallow. Something was wrong with his chest—the lower portion near his sternum seemed bent inward somehow.

Parkman dropped beside him. "Are you okay? Can you breathe?"

Aaron moved his head a fraction, his breaths short, shallow.

"What the fuck happened here?"

The other guy crawling away had stopped, half on, half off the sidewalk. His breathing was so bad that Parkman wondered if he was getting any oxygen at all.

Parkman snapped around to look at the door, then got to his feet and tried it.

Bolted shut.

"Okay," he said, more to himself than to Aaron. "You're coming with me."

He grabbed Aaron's hand and eased him up.

His friend screamed on the inside, if that were even possible, like someone trapped in his abdomen screaming in pain.

"If you don't breathe deeper, you'll pass out." He wrapped Aaron's arm around his neck. "We should've never taken you from that hospital. This was a mistake."

He dragged Aaron toward the car across the street.

Halfway there, Aaron passed out and went limp. If Parkman hadn't had such a solid grip on Aaron's wrist, his friend would've done a face-plant on the concrete road.

But now, he could move faster. Parkman half-lifted Aaron and jogged to the car. He leaned him over the trunk, opened the back door, then lowered Aaron's butt to the seat and laid him back.

He ran around to the other side of the car, leaned across the back seat, and grabbed Aaron's wrists, pulling him entirely inside the vehicle.

Then, he checked for a pulse.

Aaron was alive and still breathing.

"Hang in there, buddy."

Parkman slammed the doors, jumped in the driver's seat, his sweat-covered hand slipping once on the gear shift, then revved the engine as he drove across the street and up onto the curb. He parked the rental directly under one of the stained-glass windows at the side of the church, then jumped out of the car.

After one last look around, he clambered up onto the trunk, stepped up to the roof, and tried to peer inside.

A gasp escaped him when he saw Sarah near the middle of the small church, slightly bent over and leaning on the pews in the aisle. A tall man approached her, swinging a baseball bat left and right in his hands.

To Sarah's left was another man.

He held a gun aimed at Sarah.

When Parkman looked back at her, the baseball bat man was stepping back now.

If Parkman could read the scene correctly, the guy with the gun was about to shoot her.

Parkman yanked out his weapon and placed it against the glass, praying that it wouldn't change its trajectory too much when the bullet went through the window.

One last look to aim, and then he pulled the trigger.

The stained-glass window shattered in front of him as the weapon fired inside the church simultaneously.

Chapter 55

THE DRIVE BACK TO Glenrock from Cohen's compound was quick. Newman drove, giving Drayton a chance to call his men at the hospital.

Newman waited until he got off the phone. "What'd they say? How is she?"

"Agent Sutton is out of surgery and in the ICU. She's doing well. The doctor says she'll survive but will be left with scars, a bunch of 'em. They can work on reducing some of the scars, but only time will tell."

Newman slapped the steering wheel. "Cohen will pay for that."

Drayton's phone rang, and he answered it without checking the caller ID. "Yeah." He listened, then said, "Got it," and ended the call.

"What's that?"

"My guys at the Glenrock police station. No other officers have shown up yet, but Officer Brown told them the day shift boys meet the night shift guys and have a bite to eat at the truck stop during a shift change on Sunday nights."

"When's shift change?"

"In ten minutes."

Newman saw Glenrock coming up; the truck stop sign was a beacon in the distance. "We'll be there in two minutes."

Drayton twisted in his seat to look back at the other two men. "Last stop of the night, or at least until we apprehend Martin Cohen. Shift change takes place at the truck stop. We'll arrest all the officers there."

Newman kept his eyes on the road. "Arresting cops at a diner might prove dangerous. We should take them when they're full and exiting the building. That might make them sluggish."

Drayton shook his head. "Take them by surprise when they arrive. The second they step out of their cruisers. That way, they don't have a chance to see our van and recognize it for what it is."

Newman thought about it a moment and decided not to argue the point. Drayton knew what he was doing. This was his team, his show. Newman just wanted everyone arrested.

He signaled and turned into the truck stop.

"Park near those trees at the back. It's getting dark. We could use the cover."

Newman did as he was told. Once they were backed into the spot, he cut the lights, pocketed the keys, and climbed into the back to get his weapon ready.

"Let's try to avoid a bloodbath. But if we can't avoid it, fuck them. Special Agent Jamie Sutton deserved better."

Every man in the van nodded.

Then they waited.

Chapter 56

AT THE EXACT SECOND Cohen's gun fired and glass shattered somewhere in the church, Sarah jerked so hard that she leaned on her sore foot, twisted her ankle, and dropped to the church's wooden floor.

Another weapon fired. Then another.

She tried to hide under one of the pews while still keeping her head out to see who was firing at whom.

Her head tilted back, and she was able to look at the far wall to her left. One of the stained-glass windows had been shattered, and a man hid behind the wall. Only his gun hand came into view when he fired his weapon.

Sarah turned back to the aisle and saw Dalton fifteen feet away, the baseball bat abandoned on the floor as he crawled from pew to pew toward the door she'd entered through earlier.

Cohen shouted something unintelligible, then stood and fired wildly at the man in the window. When he finished, his gun clicking empty, he dropped behind the pews, and the man in the broken window reappeared, repeatedly firing at Cohen.

This time, Sarah caught the man's profile—Parkman!

She pushed herself up and crawled after Dalton, who had made it to the end of the aisle.

Dalton leaned up far enough to see what Parkman was doing, likely waiting for him to stop firing into the church.

Parkman stopped and jumped back behind the wall again.

Cohen stood and fired at Parkman.

Where the hell did Cohen hide those guns?

She was almost at Dalton. Seven feet. Five feet. Three.

She lunged at his legs, but Dalton didn't see her. The second she lunged, he had pushed to his feet and was now running—lurching—for the front door.

Sarah pushed off the pews to her left, rolled once until she bumped into the pews on the right, then dove for the gun she dropped when she got hit by the baseball bat.

She spun around, aimed, and fired at Dalton from twenty feet away just as he opened the church door.

Blood sprayed the side of the door as the bullet hit his arm.

She fired again, but Dalton launched himself out the door and disappeared. Her bullet made a crude hole in the door.

Then she twisted around to face Cohen, who watched her from several rows over. He was on his knees behind a few chairs.

Parkman stepped into view at the window. "Sarah?" he called. "You okay?"

"Yeah," she shouted back. "Shoot this asshole."

Cohen stood near the corner of the church, steadied his arm, and fired at the broken window.

Even though the sun had dipped behind the horizon, Parkman probably couldn't see Cohen, as it was darker inside the church now, and he was still on the outside.

"Look out!" Sarah yelled as she fired at Cohen.

But Cohen was already on the move, ducking low and using the row of pews as cover.

Parkman wasn't in the window anymore.

Sarah pushed up to her knees, rested her arm on the back of a nearby seat, then zeroed in on Cohen. She fired four more shots—all missed him.

Then Cohen disappeared through a door at the rear of the church behind the large crucifix.

Sarah got to her feet and lurched toward the open front door. She could still deal with Dalton, at least.

When she pushed the door open, only one man was lying there—the guy who had let her into the church.

She moved to stand over him, then fired one round into his foot.

The man cried out and pulled his feet toward him.

"You'll limp for a while," she said. "It'll help you remember the mistakes you made today."

Then she moved to the side of the church and peeked around the corner.

A scream forced its way out of her mouth.

Parkman was sprawled out beside their car on the pavement, bleeding heavily from the abdomen. She ran at him, understanding everything now.

He'd been standing on the roof of their car, which was how he'd been high enough to fire through the stained-glass window.

Begging God not to take another life from her, she dropped to her knees, checked Parkman's breathing, and then gasped in relief.

There was too much blood—too much.

Instead of asking where Aaron was, she opened the back door to get Parkman inside—and saw Aaron.

"I'm so sorry, Parkman," she mumbled as she got to work by grabbing his arms and hauling him up into the car as best she could. Blood poured from his stomach area, and she tried not to despair.

Next, she adjusted Aaron onto his side and slid Parkman behind him. Moving unconscious men was like moving dead weight, and it took considerable effort and much more time than she felt she had, but waiting for an ambulance would take longer.

Once they were in position, she bunched up Parkman's shirt at the wound site and eased Aaron backward to rest his body on the shirt. With the door shut, she ran around the car and pushed the front passenger seat back to anchor Aaron against Parkman.

"I'm so sorry," she whispered again as she ran back to the driver's seat.

In less than a minute, she was doing over one hundred miles per hour, heading to the hospital in Douglas, praying for Parkman's life.

Chapter 57

MARTIN COHEN ESCAPED THROUGH the back of the church unscathed but filled with fury.

He jumped in the SUV cruiser and turned the key. The engine didn't sound right. It hesitated, then stopped.

"What the hell is this now?"

He tried the key again, then jumped out of his seat when Dalton slapped the side of the door.

"Trying to leave without me?" he asked, his eyes half-lidded.

"I'm trying to get it started. Get in."

Dalton opened the back door and slid inside behind Cohen.

On the second try, the engine turned over. He jammed it in gear and hit the gas.

"All that damage to the church," he shouted as he swung the vehicle around and headed toward the highway. "All for nothing. Why did someone break that window? The demon witch got away."

"But you shot him," Dalton said from the back seat.

"It looked like it." Cohen checked the dashboard as lights flickered on and off. The engine seemed sluggish, as if it was running out of gas, but the tank was still half full.

"I saw him. Dying in the street by his car."

Cohen checked his mirror. "What's wrong with you?"

"My arm. Got shot."

Cohen adjusted the mirror and saw the blood below Dalton's shoulder.

"Shit, shit, shit." He jerked his body back, gripping the wheel tight. "Who'll help us with the shipment tonight?" Cohen screamed at the injustice of fate. "Why won't that witch just die?"

He slowed for access to the highway and turned toward his compound.

But the cruiser had other plans. Even though he shoved the pedal to the floor, it wouldn't pick up speed.

"What's wrong?"

"No idea. Something's off with this thing."

"Turn around. You're going the wrong way."

"No, I'm not," Cohen screamed so loud that he coughed up phlegm. "We're going to my place to get all the guns in my cabinet. I have to finish this. No more stoning, no more games."

"The hospital is the other way." Dalton's voice had weakened. "I don't want to die."

The truck stop was coming up on their right. Cohen tuned out the whining man in the back seat—who was trapped in there now as those doors wouldn't open from the inside—and pulled into the diner.

"We'll *borrow* another car. This cruiser is a piece of shit. Something's wrong with it."

"I need a hospital. Fuck another car." Dalton sat up and touched the grate, separating them. "Use the cell phone to call an ambulance. Then you do whatever the fuck you want. That wench shot me twice now. I need to heal before I keep fighting. Then I'll pump a hundred bullets into her face, see how she likes it."

"As much as I love that idea," Cohen steered them to a stop beside the access door to the diner, "I'm going to kill her first. She won't survive the night."

"You're going to have to find her first."

Cohen turned off the cruiser, not that it mattered. The engine sputtered and was about to die when he yanked the key.

"You don't think I know where she is?" He watched Dalton in the rearview mirror.

"Do I care at the moment? How about medical attention? That's something I care about." Dalton had wrapped his free hand on the wound, but blood poured copiously through his fingers. "Hey, I'm running out of time."

Cohen turned around in the driver's seat and stared back at Dalton. "It's one woman. Just one." He raised a finger. "Only one. And she's heading to the hospital in Douglas to get her friends looked after."

"Her mercenary friend. He won't make it. He's probably dead already."

"Yeah, because I shot him. And I'll shoot her, too."

"Who cares? The guy was bleeding badly from the chest." Dalton slipped sideways in the seat. "But I will most certainly die tonight if you don't get me to the hospital."

"You'll go, you'll go. Just relax." He adjusted himself to a better angle. "Why are almost all my men dead, Dalton? Where are the cops that I pay for? Where is Billings, and the security he offers that I pay thousands for all year, huh? Why am I resorting to having to run like a scared little boy from my own church, like a common criminal who—"

"That's your own fault. And you are a criminal, although not entirely common. When are you going to wake up to reality? You sell drugs to kids. That new batch that's laced with fentanyl is set to go out tonight. How many kids will overdose and die in neighboring states? But you know what? We will help load the trucks—the money's good. Again, who cares? Now, hospital. *Please*."

Cohen tightened his lips and held his breath. "You have never taken this tone with me before, Dalton." He kept his voice even.

"Hey, I've got a bullet in my fuckin' arm, and we're *chatting* at a roadside truck stop. Are you serious? Get this thing going toward the hospital, or let me out so I can call an ambulance. We can go back to the boss and employee role when I'm all patched up, and I'll be all considerate and nice again."

Cohen shook his head, clicking his tongue. "This is truly how you feel. I can see it. The lack of respect is oozing off you. You do what you're told for the paycheck, not out of loyalty or respect. This is a problem."

"So what? I get the job done." Dalton kicked the back of the seat with his good leg. "Call somebody," he shouted.

Something caught Cohen's eye in the semi-darkness toward the rear of the parking lot. He squinted and leaned forward.

"Holy shit. Four armed men dressed in some sort of battle gear are approaching us."

Dalton sat up and glanced over the back of the seat. "Where the hell did they come from?"

The men were now one row of cars back.

Cohen turned around in his seat and saw several members of the public scattering. A waitress was inside the truck stop, waving for patrons to get down.

"Are they after us?" he asked incredulously. "No one even knows we're here. And this is a police cruiser, for heaven's sake. Why would they approach a cruiser like that?" Cohen tapped the switch to turn on the flashing lights on the roof.

"Maybe that witch—your name for her—called these guys and made up some shit."

Cohen shook his head. "No. Not possible. What happened at the church just went down. She'd almost be in Douglas by now. This is something else."

"FBI," a man shouted from outside. "Get out of the vehicle. Come out with your hands up."

All four armed men had taken cover, their weapons aimed at the Glenrock SUV cruiser.

"This is so bizarre." Cohen couldn't wrap his head around what was happening. "Maybe they're looking for someone else. Why would the FBI come at a police vehicle like this?"

"They're after you, asshole." Dalton sat up and squinted. "You did this. Just remember that. Now let me out. I'm gonna tell them all about you."

Cohen gawked at Dalton, the shock settling over his system at what he had just said. He was mad, losing his mental faculty at being shot. It couldn't be the same man who helped run his enterprise.

"Final warning," the man outside shouted. "Exit the vehicle with your hands where we can see them."

Cohen grabbed his other two handguns and then checked his shotgun. "Okay, here's what we'll do."

"No, not me." Dalton slumped back down. "You're crazy. I need a hospital, then a lawyer."

Discounting Dalton as delirious, Cohen said, "I will slide out my side and open your door. When you slide out, take one of these handguns. I'll cover you with the shotgun."

"You're insane." Dalton's eyes were wide in panic and pain. "Fuckin' certifiable."

"Perhaps I am, but I will not spend a single minute in a jail cell. Not me, the preacher of Glenrock, the savior of this town. I built their only hotel, gave the schools grants, prayed for the citizens, and bought all that new cancer equipment for the hospital in Douglas." Cohen shook his head. "No one orders me around or tells me what to do. Not even the FBI." He turned to the door, hand on the handle. "You ready?"

"Sure, boss."

Cohen opened the door and slipped outside, staying low, using the body of the cruiser as cover.

"Coming," he shouted to the FBI guys. "Don't shoot."

Then he opened Dalton's door and handed him the magnum.

Cohen brought the shotgun up to his shoulder and prepared to fire as Dalton slipped out onto the pavement.

"We're unarmed," he yelled, his entire upper body still behind the back corner of the cruiser.

He took a deep breath, stepped out from behind the cruiser, aimed the shotgun, and squeezed the trigger.

Someone yelled, "*Gun!*"

Even as his weapon recoiled, a hail of angry projectiles smashed into his chest and face, knocking him back several feet until he lost his balance and dropped onto the pavement on his back.

More bullets were fired somewhere to his left.

Dalton dropped beside him, his eyes glazed over, two holes in his skull above his nose.

Dalton was dead, and Cohen was having trouble catching a breath —just like how the cruiser's engine had struggled.

His head lulled to the side as his chest forced its way up and down, waiting for the air to flow.

Wires dangled and dripped under the cruiser, spilling the engine's guts onto the truck stop's parking lot.

Someone had sabotaged their ride to safety. And now his eyes were closing, and he couldn't get them to open.

Men shouted orders around him, but it didn't matter anymore. All he could think about was why anyone would sabotage a police cruiser.

It had to be that witch. She cast a spell on him. And now she would win.

In his final thoughts, as someone touched his neck, searching for a pulse, he asked, *Is there a God?*

He sure hoped so—then his heart stopped.

Chapter 58

THE NEXT MORNING ...

Sarah snapped awake on the chair when someone touched her arm. She sat up straight, blinking sleep from her eyes, her arms up to ward off the attack.

A man stepped backward, a coffee in each hand.

"It's okay," he whispered. "Thought you might want one of these."

Sarah held out her hand, waving her fingers in a give-it-to-me gesture.

The FBI man handed the coffee over. She sniffed it, then popped the lid and inspected it.

"You're safe. It's not poisoned or rancid." He extended his right hand. "I'm Special Agent Andrew Newman with the FBI. We met earlier when you brought in my former partner, Agent Sutton. But now we can be formally introduced."

Sarah looked at his hand, then sipped the coffee. It tasted like medicine. "So, you're with Sutton?"

He lowered his hand, then nodded. "Do you mind?" Newman gestured at the seat next to her.

Sarah nodded, the coffee not far from her lips.

Newman sat, adjusted his suit jacket, and then drank from his cup.

They sat in silence for a few moments while two nurses helped an elderly man along the corridor. Once they were out of earshot, Newman faced her.

"How did you know Agent Sutton was in trouble?"

Sarah stared at the floor, still feeling the effects of the last few days' craziness. She'd barely slept last night, moving from Aaron's bedside to Parkman's.

"Sutton jumped in my car, covered in blood, at the truck stop. She had two guys chasing her. I got involved."

Newman chortled. "That'll do it, I guess." He leaned forward and placed his elbows on his thighs, staring at the floor. "I was supposed to meet her at the truck stop that night. Park at the back. Leave my doors unlocked." He shook his head. "I missed her and stayed the night in the Glenrock Hotel."

Sarah turned to him, frowning. "Hmm, that makes sense. I seem to recall Sutton getting in the car and saying something about all the doors being open and that she thought I was there for her." Sarah glanced back at the floor. "Then she said, 'This can't be happening,' before they dragged her from my car."

"Dragged you out, too, from my understanding."

Sarah nodded.

"Sutton's awake."

Sarah drank more coffee.

"She told us everything you did for her."

"Martin Cohen, that fake preacher, must pay for what he did. All his men need to pay."

"Cohen's dead."

Sarah jerked back and stared at Newman. "Dead? How?"

"He pulled into the truck stop last night with a man named Dalton Janson. When we approached their vehicle, they came out armed. Cohen fired a shotgun at us. It was a righteous kill."

"Both dead?"

Newman leaned a few inches closer. "Sarah, everyone's dead. We had no choice. And if I can be a little honest here, I was happy to be one of the team to shoot the bastard. After what he put Sutton through …" Newman shook his head. "She'll be scarred for life."

"What do you mean, *everyone* is dead?"

"Cohen, Dalton, Liam, Domenick, and Cohen's security team. The only people still employed by Cohen who are still alive are the Glenrock police officers, a few security men who were off duty yesterday, and Detective Billings. But they're all in holding cells awaiting transfer for arraignments. This'll be a long investigation, but they'll all do serious time for their involvement in his drug operation." Newman lifted his cup, held it aloft momentarily like he was performing some toast, and then drank from it.

Vivian had said it would all end at the truck stop. Was she ever wrong?

"What about Cohen's other dealings? His business shit?"

"He's a drug dealer, through and through. Sutton laid it all out for us. He delivers his coke using the animals on the farms he owns. Agent Sutton was working hard to expose him before he sent this latest batch because it was laced with high levels of fentanyl." Newman shook his head. "With Sutton out of the game and you stepping in, are you aware of the hundreds, if not thousands, of lives you saved? We seized quite a few million dollars' worth of heroin and fentanyl from Cohen's farms."

"I knew that there'd be hundreds of lives saved by staying. A little birdy told me."

"You mean your sister."

Sarah looked at him. Their eyes met. "You know about me?"

"Of course. I checked into you."

Sarah lifted one shoulder, then looked away, staring into her coffee cup. "Yeah, my sister told me."

"Did she tell you about the Satanist shit, too?"

Sarah shook her head.

"That was all Sutton's doing."

"How so?"

"When Sutton crept onto the farm property at night to take photos of them loading their drug-filled cows and pigs, she found a couple of them that had died. She was desperate for the bureau to get involved, so when Cohen's people left the area, she opened up the animals, looking for evidence of a coke-filled baggie that burst open. When she couldn't find any drugs in the animals, she covered her tracks by making it look like a ritualistic sacrifice. Then she photographed them and leaked the photos to the local papers."

"I can see how that would piss off Cohen. My sister didn't tell me about that stuff."

"Did she tell you where your daughter is?"

Sarah stopped breathing. She narrowed her eyes and glared at the cup in her hands.

"No. She said she was safe, though."

"Well, you'll be happy to learn that she is safe, and she'll be here within fifteen minutes."

Sarah jerked around and peered at the man beside her with hope in her eyes. "Really?"

He nodded. "A woman named Teresa Baker is bringing her back to you."

Sarah sighed heavily, her hands starting to shake.

"Once we had ironed everything out and learned what happened from Officer Brown, we knew what Billings had done to Aaron. Shit, you were in trouble, and Aaron just wanted to report that to the police. Teresa is legit. She actually works with child services and had no idea Billings was dirty. She would never separate a child from a healthy family. It's just that Billings portrayed a scene that made her take Willow for a few days. Also, you should know. Teresa took care of Willow herself and said they got along smashingly. It was the weekend, so she didn't get to place her with a family."

Sarah suppressed the tears that threatened to flow. Her daughter was coming back to her without a fight. She'd worried for Parkman, Aaron, and Willow all night, and now everything would be okay. She'd have her daughter back shortly, and Aaron and Parkman would pull through. And somehow, Aaron had found Benjamin's watch—he was wearing it in his hospital bed.

"I hear Parkman lost a lot of blood."

Sarah nodded. "They had to give him several transfusions."

"How bad were his injuries?"

"The bullet missed all vital organs. Once he's patched up, he'll be fine."

"And Aaron?"

"Punctured lung, broken ribs, internal bleeding."

"But they got it all? I mean, he'll be okay, right?"

Sarah nodded a few times. "They did. He'll pull through, but it'll be a long road for him." She drank more coffee, then sat back. "Any word on our car?"

"Destroyed. Once Billings had it impounded, he ordered it demolished."

She scrunched up her brows. "Why? It sounds like he was angry about something. We just pulled into town. All we wanted was a coffee at that truck stop."

"It had to do with the evidence inside the vehicle. He could claim it was stolen, and that would be the end of it."

"Shit, now what? No car."

Newman slipped a hand in his pocket and produced a set of keys with a fob. "You and Aaron are now the proud owners of a brand new brown-colored Land Rover."

"How's that?" She stared at the keys dangling from the fed's hands.

"We found an abandoned Land Rover parked in front of the police station, the keys under the mat. When we discovered the Cohen Corporation owned it, we signed it over to you. It's yours if you want it."

Sarah snatched the keys from his grasp. "For all the shit he put us through, we'll take it. Fuck him."

Newman smiled, and they drank their coffee in silence for a moment.

"What the hell happened in that church?" Newman asked.

"Biblical shit. Cohen was trying to stone me to death."

"Ahh." Newman tilted his head back, then forward. "Right, okay. The guy was a megalomaniac, no doubt."

Her cup was almost empty. She could sure use another.

The sliding doors at the end of the hallway moved apart. Sarah looked up, but it wasn't Willow.

"We spoke with Aristotle here in the hospital."

"And?"

"He explained how you guys broke into Cohen's compound and pulled Sutton out. He told us about the guys you killed at the gate."

Sarah tightened her lips and looked at Newman again. "Should I expect bad news now?"

The agent shook his head. "No bad news. They were going to kill you, not to mention they were complicit in the torture and attempted murder of an FBI agent. No, you'll receive no backlash from anything you did to keep Sutton and yourself alive."

She drank the rest of the coffee, set her cup down, and fiddled with the Rover's keys in her palm.

"When Aaron and Parkman are fit to travel, I guess you guys will be leaving?"

Sarah nodded. "We were heading to my parents' house in California."

"Well, feel free to come and go as you please. Your name won't make it into our reports. Sutton is handling everything. We have all the evidence we need to handle the surviving members of Cohen's little crew. You take your family and get back on the road when you're ready." Newman got up to leave. "It's been a pleasure watching you work, Sarah Roberts." He shook his head, a look of wonderment on his face. "Arriving at the police station and finding Officer Brown in his own jail. Then Cohen's compound, and finally that detective tied up in his living room—shit, it felt like I was cleaning up after you all the way."

She lifted a shoulder in a half-shrug. "I was looking for my daughter." She watched his face. "No one should ever come between a mother and her child, especially not a man."

"I couldn't agree more." He extended his hand again. "It was great to meet you, Sarah."

This time, she took his hand and shook it.

"If you're ever involved in this game again, you'll call us and give us a heads up so we can help sooner."

She released his hand. "It's never a *game*, Newman. And I have issues trusting most people."

He grinned. "That is something I can get behind."

The sliding doors at the end of the hallway eased apart.

A tall woman in a business dress stepped through, holding Willow's hand.

Sarah's suppressed tears flooded her eyes as she bolted from the hard plastic chair and ran to her daughter.

"Mommy," Willow shouted.

Sarah swooped Willow up in her arms, spun her around in one circle, and held her tight.

The child services woman was gone when she wiped and opened her eyes.

Agent Newman had left, too.

It was never a *game* what she did. It was real life, real people.

Yet Vivian used that word when she sat vigil by Aaron's bed last night.

She'd said *The Game* hadn't even started yet, but it was coming.

And Sarah had better prepare.

Leaving Aaron behind was step one. She was sure *he* would have no problem with that. But how was she going to tell Willow that her parents were separating?

For now, she held her daughter close. Those were problems for another day. She'd never let Willow go again and fuck anyone who tried to take her away.

No more.

Never again.

Yet, she feared what Vivian meant when she said *The Game* hadn't even started yet.

Something about it scared the shit out of her.

Why did her future have to be so dark? The visions would never stop, would they?

She set Willow down, and they headed toward Aaron's hospital room hand in hand, discussing their weekend.

Willow had a great time in Glenrock.

Sarah, not so much.

Afterword

I can't get enough of the ride Sarah's on and can't wait for the next book in the series, *The Game*.

As far as heartbreak goes, losing Benjamin has taken a toll on Aaron and Sarah—everyone, actually. But at this juncture, Aaron is taking it so hard that he's blaming Sarah, which can't end well.

After what happened to them in Glenrock, we'll have to see how they navigate their relationship in the future, but things are grim.

Hey, there's an upside here. We didn't lose anyone on Sarah's team this time. Right? That's an upside, right?

The idea for this novel began with the image of Sutton jumping into Sarah's car at the truck stop. When I first came up with that idea, I knew the woman was in trouble and that it would pull Sarah into her world, but I didn't know she was an FBI agent. That developed as I drafted the first version of this manuscript.

From the truck stop until we got back to the truck stop at the end—full circle—I wanted it to be a crazy ride without a clear outcome.

And I was happy Aaron got Benjamin's watch back.

I feel I need to mention that Glenrock and Douglas are real places in Wyoming, but everything that happened in this novel is absolutely fictitious. This is in no way a reflection of the police force in Glenrock, as I'm sure they're all upstanding officers. If a philanthropist lives in the area, I doubt he's dealing in heroin and fentanyl.

As always, thank you for reading another Sarah adventure, and now I'm off to start writing the next one. How about we keep doing this for another nineteen novels? Let's go to book fifty, and then perhaps we can take a break from Sarah's life—or better yet, give her a break.

In the meantime, keep reading, stay healthy, love one another, and be generous with yourself.

Sending blessings to you all, with love,

Jonas Saul

The Game

Book Thirty-Two

Chapter 1

WHY WAS HER HEART racing so fast? Sarah checked her hands—there was a slight tremor.

This was a simple snatch-and-grab. Well, of a young girl. Some would call it a *kidnapping*, but it was more of a displacement. At least until the heat died down, then she could let her go.

Sarah Roberts wasn't a kidnapper, but an exception had to be made in this case, according to the voice in her head.

The field across the street was empty. In a few minutes, a small group of teenagers would step into sight and walk across the school grounds. They wouldn't stay long, as the dark clouds overhead threatened rain, but Sarah didn't need long.

Her sister, Vivian, that voice in her head, had filled in all the blanks. She told her where to be and when to go there. She even gave her the girl's name and age. The one thing missing was why Sarah needed to take this girl. To hide her from someone? Was she in trouble at home? Or was trouble coming?

Sarah checked her phone—less than five minutes to wait.

She pushed off the brick wall of the school building and trudged slowly toward the sidewalk. A lazy stroll around the park, then through the field, would bring her right to where the teenagers were supposed to be. How she would separate Amanda Stilton from her group of friends remained to be seen, but where she would take her was prearranged. Once they arrived and were alone, they would talk. Sarah needed to know why Amanda was a target.

On the sidewalk, she slowed her pace and willed her nerves to calm down. When her phone vibrated in her back pocket, she nearly screamed.

Caller ID said it was Parkman.

A quick look around confirmed the field was still empty. The teenagers hadn't arrived yet, so she could take the call.

"What's up?" she asked. "I'm a little busy at the moment."

"Where are you?"

A car turned up the street, heading her way. Sarah stared down at the sidewalk, making every attempt to look like she was out for a late-night stroll.

"I'm in Oshawa, east of Toronto."

When Parkman inhaled, it sounded like he pulled on a cigarette, but it was more of a gasp. "What are you doing there?"

"Something Vivian asked me to do."

The car eased by her position, going too slowly. It made sense when she looked up and saw the school zone sign. Even though it was almost ten at night, people still drove slowly in school zones.

"You alone?" Parkman asked.

"No."

"Who's with you?"

"Vivian."

"Sarah, you know what I mean. Need anything?"

"No, it's a simple job."

Someone laughed, then voices came to her. She spun around to see the concrete path between the houses at the far end of the school's yard filled with people. Four teenagers walked into view, laughing and carrying on like they'd drank too much.

"Parkman, I have to go." Her tone was rushed, short.

"Sarah, wait."

She tightened her grip on the phone, her gaze on the foursome. "Hurry."

"I just heard from your mother."

Sarah glanced down at the sidewalk as another car eased by her. *What's with all the vehicles going so slowly? The school's closed.*

"What's going on with my mother?"

"She wants you to call her immediately."

Sarah frowned as she spun back to look at the group of teenagers. They'd made it to the center of the field and were working their way to the north side of the school, where the main parking lot sat. She had a one-minute window to reach them and extract Amanda from their group.

"Why didn't she call me herself?"

"I asked the same thing. She said she tried you three times. Had me worried, so I called you."

Sarah pulled the phone from her ear and saw that she'd missed five calls—three from her mother and two from Aaron. She put the phone back to her ear. "Yeah, it looks like it. I have it on vibrate. They must've called when the phone was on the seat beside me while driving. Did she say what it was about? I'm kind of busy at the moment."

"She sounded very happy, like *really* happy. It didn't sound bad, so I'm sure it can wait until you're done with whatever it is you're doing in Oshawa."

Two vehicles had stopped by the school's parking lot now. Were they the danger that Amanda was supposed to avoid? Did Parkman's call make her late?

"Shit, Parkman, I have to go. I'll call her soon."

"Wait, Sarah—"

She hit end, slipped the phone into her back pocket, and walked briskly toward the brick wall she'd been leaning against minutes ago, hoping to intercept Amanda before she came into view of the parking lot.

But then, what would she do? Her escape route, her car—the Land Rover gifted to her from an FBI agent in Glenrock, Wyoming—was in the parking lot. Another problem for another time. Getting Amanda separated from her friends would be challenging enough. They could wait until the other cars left—she'd figure it out.

As she closed the gap between them, she saw that the four teenagers had bottles in their hands. They'd been drinking beers. Would liquid courage rear its ugly head with the two boys? Would they try to protect Amanda? Sarah did not want to fight teenagers.

They reached the wall half a minute before she did. Sarah picked up her step as the first raindrops hit her forehead.

One of the boys saw her approaching and slapped the arm of the other boy. They were both looking at her now.

The foursome slowed, and Sarah thanked her lucky stars because they were less than two meters from the corner of the wall, which would've exposed their presence to the idling vehicles parked out front of the closed school.

"Wait up," Sarah called. "I need to speak with Amanda."

The boys and the other girl in their group turned to look at Amanda.

Now Sarah knew what she looked like. *Thanks, guys.*

The tall brunette stepped forward, then bent at the knees to set her beer bottle down.

"Can we help you with something?"

Sarah closed the distance in seconds, then moved to the left of the group and peeked around the corner.

Car doors were opening in the parking lot. The occupants were getting out and looking toward them.

Shit, I have to hurry this up.

Sarah turned back to Amanda and her friends. "Amanda Stilton, we need to talk." Sarah glared at the boys and then at the other girl. "Alone."

"That's not going to happen," one of the boys said, stepping forward.

Car doors slammed shut in the parking lot. Someone shouted a command that Sarah couldn't hear.

They were on their way now.

"We haven't much time." Sarah stepped inside the boy's personal space. As much as she appreciated his efforts and didn't want to dampen his bravery, it was a wasted effort, and she didn't have time to explain why. She stared at Amanda. "Someone's coming, and they mean you harm. We must leave now."

Amanda tried to look cool for her friends by clicking her tongue once and lifting her upper lip in a sneer. An involuntary tremor made Amanda's shoulders shake.

The rain was coming down harder, making them all squint. The girl, who was with Amanda, edged closer to the building, searching for shelter along the wall.

"I'm not going anywhere with you." Amanda shook her head, and water cascaded from her hair. "Who the hell are you anyway?" While trying to sound defiant, her voice cracked.

Footsteps pounded the ground around the corner. The people from the cars in the parking lot had arrived.

And she'd fucked up. This wasn't good.

They were out of time, and running with Amanda to escape this situation wouldn't be an option now.

"Why couldn't I meet her on the street before entering the schoolyard?" Sarah asked Vivian out loud, then spun to greet the newcomers.

Six men came around the corner. The front two pulled their jackets back to reveal pistols in their waistbands.

What the hell?

Sarah backed toward Amanda, staying in front to protect her from these men. "Hey, take it easy. Everything's fine here." Her mind raced on how to protect the teenagers, but more importantly, how to get Amanda away from these men.

The boy who had stepped up to Sarah moments before moved toward the men and pointed back at Sarah. "She said something about taking Amanda with her. That's fucked up, man."

Wait, are these men with Amanda?

Sarah's shoulder bumped Amanda's. She leaned close and whispered, "We need to go."

Why did shit have to go sour so fast? *Vivian, we could've avoided this if you'd been more forthcoming!*

Sarah jumped behind Amanda and yanked out her own weapon, making sure it was visible to everyone.

"We all need to calm down, or someone will get hurt."

"That's exactly what I was just about to say," a man whispered behind her.

Sarah glanced over her shoulder.

A tall man with a thick beard stood there, a large handgun aimed at her forehead.

Chapter 2

PARKMAN STARED AT THE phone for several moments after Sarah killed the call. What could she be up to in Oshawa? What was so important that caused her to miss calls, and why would she speak to her mother later when Amelia clearly wanted to talk now?

After a sip of wine, he snatched up the phone and dialed Aaron.

"Hello?"

"Hey, Aaron, it's Parkman." He eased back in his chair and stared at the ceiling.

"How're things?" Aaron sounded distracted.

"Good. Listen, do you know why Sarah's in Oshawa tonight?"

Aaron cleared his throat. "Whatever Sarah's up to isn't my concern anymore. She's made that very clear. She doesn't tell me shit unless it involves visits with Willow, which we often arrange through her mother now since she's been here."

"Do you know if Alex or Daniel works with her anymore?"

"Not that I'm aware of. She's gone Lone Ranger on us. Back to her roots. At least that's what she told me last month when we returned from Wyoming."

"'Back to her roots,'" Parkman echoed. "What could that mean?"

"She's got her mother here in Toronto taking care of Willow full-time. That frees up Sarah to do little jobs for Vivian. Small stuff. Easy stuff, apparently. Nothing needing backup, nothing dangerous."

"She told you all that?"

"We fought about Willow, about her still putting herself in danger now that she's a mother." Aaron blew out a frustrated breath. "It doesn't seem to stop her from working with Vivian, though."

"Well, whatever she's up to didn't sound easy tonight. She was in a hurry to hang up and even cut me off." Parkman sipped from his wine glass. "Almost since day one, we've been there for her. This just feels wrong somehow."

The sound of Aaron moving into another position came through to Parkman. "What can I do? I mean, I tried to call her a few times tonight, but she didn't answer. I thought she was still mad at me."

"She answered when I called, but as far as I understand it, Sarah wasn't answering her mother's calls either. I'm just worried about her. There was something in her tone."

"Did she give you any idea what's going on in Oshawa?"

Parkman hesitated a moment. "Aaron, that's why I called you."

They both sat in silence for a moment.

"Well," Aaron said. "This is what she wanted. Unless she calls me looking for help, I can't get involved."

The landscape had changed. With Aaron and Sarah separated, everything was different. Did Benjamin's death have anything to do with it? Had that been the catalyst?

No matter what Sarah was up to, she should have some form of backup. And perhaps she did, but she was leaving him out of the equation, and Aaron, too, evidently.

"I passed on Amelia's message. I'm sure Sarah will call her mother soon."

"Amelia left you a message for Sarah?" Aaron asked. "Did it have to do with Willow? I'm heading over there to spend a couple of hours with Willow right now. Amelia asked for my help."

Parkman swirled the wine in his glass, already thinking of his next move. "Amelia didn't say a thing to me. Just that she had something important to tell Sarah, and for Sarah to call her immediately. Amelia sounded excited."

"Okay, then, excited is good. I'll stay out of it, except I'm still heading there to see Willow."

"If I need you, I'll call."

Aaron didn't respond immediately, then he said cautiously, "Parkman, if *you* need me, call anytime. But if possible, keep me clear of Sarah's troubles. She'll grow to hate me if I start showing up unsolicited-like."

Parkman frowned. "You don't think that would show how much you care? To be there for her?"

"I love that woman, but she frustrates the hell out of me. I'm still recovering from our road trip in the States."

"Me too. My bruises have turned an ugly, jaundiced color and seem to take longer to clear with age."

"That'll happen to Sarah soon, too. She's hitting her mid-thirties. When will it ever end?"

Parkman sipped more wine, hoping it would relax him, but it wasn't working. "I wish I knew."

"Look, Parkman, call me if it's life or death, but I need to go." Aaron's frustration came through clearly in this line. "I'm opening the dojo early tomorrow for a special class, and yet I'll be out late tonight. Text me when you hear back that Sarah's okay."

"Will do, and Aaron—" The line died.

That was the second time someone hung up on him in five minutes.

He set down his wine and opened WhatsApp to text Darwin. It was around five in the morning in Italy. Maybe he'd already be awake.

If he were, he'd ask their friend to find Sarah's phone and tell him where she was.

He'd give Sarah half an hour, maybe an hour. If he didn't hear back from her, he'd take Darwin's information and drive out to Oshawa to see what's up for himself.

Once the text was sent, Parkman got up from the easy chair, grunted with the pain in his chest from the wound in Wyoming, and set his unfinished wine on the counter in the kitchen.

He couldn't be drinking and driving.

That wouldn't help if Sarah needed him.

Chapter 3

SARAH EASED HER HANDS out to her sides, her gun in her right hand, aiming at the brick wall now. "There's no need to get riled up. We're just having a chat among friends here."

"Bullshit," the boy shouted, his head swiveling from one man to the next. "You said Amanda had to leave with you. Also, something about meeting her on the sidewalk before entering the schoolyard." The boy's gaze stopped on his friends. "Didn't she?"

The brunette nodded, along with the other boy.

The weapon in her hand was so forcefully torn from her grip that the man bent her wrist back and then shoved her into the wall. He slipped her gun into the rear of his pants.

"I'm going to need that back." She gestured toward his waistline.

"Get them to safety," the bearded man said, ignoring her comment, his weapon trained on her chest.

The four teenagers moved away, with the other men leaving one behind.

She sure wished she'd known the thugs were there to pick up Amanda. Or was this Vivian's doing, some twisted message of hers?

Amanda looked back, her eyes somber in the falling rain, her face drawn. The girl had seen men with guns before in her short life. This wasn't new to her, as these men were her protection detail.

What the hell's going on, sis? Who is Amanda, and what kind of trouble is she in?

The bearded man took a few steps back, slipped his weapon into a shoulder holster, then lunged in and shoved Sarah hard against the brick wall. He didn't need a weapon, with the other armed man watching them from ten feet away.

"You're going to tell me everything," the man said, spitting rainwater that clung to his thick mustache. "Why did you run up to those kids? What's your business with Amanda?"

"Bring her back, and I'll tell her."

The man exchanged a look with his colleague. "Are you fucking crazy? Amanda's gone. You won't get to talk to her, so you can tell me."

Sarah tilted her head and smirked. "Sorry, it's private."

"Private?" The man's voice rose in surprise. "Do you have a problem assessing the situation here? Maybe you're not reading the room too well—"

"Excuse me," Sarah blurted. "My business is with Amanda, not you. Why would I speak with you?" Sarah's smirk turned into a cocky smile.

The bearded man had stuffed her gun in the rear of his pants, and she meant to get it back.

A horn sounded from the parking lot. They were loaded in the vehicles and waiting for their colleagues.

The bearded man grabbed Sarah's arm above the elbow in a vise grip and yanked her away from the wall. "You're coming with us. We'll get you talking."

"Ow, you're hurting me," she moaned, flailing around with her free arm to see how close she could get to the back of the man's pants.

The man who'd been watching them turned away and started toward the parking lot, no doubt happy to get out of the rain.

Sarah took a couple of more steps, then raised her foot and jammed it hard into the back of the man's knee.

He dropped to the concrete hard, all his weight centered on his right knee.

A low groan escaped his lips, the pitter-patter of the rain masking most of its sound.

Sarah spun in a tight circle and bent over to snatch her weapon from the back of the bearded man's pants.

By the time the other guy glanced over his shoulder, Sarah was armed and stepping backward. The bearded man was getting onto his feet, favoring his right leg.

"That'll cost you, Sarah," he whispered, just loud enough for her to hear.

She blinked, stunned into silence for a moment.

How did he know my name?

Her phone vibrated in her back pocket again, and then someone laid into the horn from the parking lot. People had no patience.

"You know my name?"

The men exchanged a glance again, both of them backing up.

"We're leaving now," the bearded man said. "You won't shoot us."

"How would you know that?"

The bearded man turned away and started toward the parking area. "Because only a coward would shoot someone in the back, Sarah, and that's not you."

"Wait, how do you know me?" She followed them to the corner of the brick building and stared across the wet grass at the idling cars.

What's going on, Vivian? Who are these people?

"Perhaps we'll chat again sometime," the man called over his shoulder.

The bearded man and his partner picked up their pace until they were jogging to the parking lot, the hurt knee making the man with the beard limp all the way.

The vibrating in her pocket had stopped. Whoever it was, she could call them back.

The men got in their cars, doors slammed, and engines revved.

Amanda, her friends, and her security entourage peeled out of the school parking lot, their tires slipping on the wet pavement.

Then they were gone.

Sarah put her weapon away. "Well, that was a waste of time, Vivian. Not to mention dangerous." She headed toward her Land Rover. "Any chance you could tell me more? Like, what the hell was this all about, and who are they?"

She picked up her pace. Her clothes were getting soaked, and the adrenaline was wearing off, making her shiver.

Inside the Rover, the heat turned to high, she opened her phone to see who'd called. It was Parkman again.

Instead of calling him back, she dialed her mother, attached the phone to Bluetooth, then got the Rover moving.

Vivian sent her to Oshawa for Amanda. She'd fucked that up, but she'd still stay the night in the hotel she'd rented for the both of them, as it was ten to fifteen minutes away. Maybe by the morning, Vivian would tell her more. If not, she'd return home to her apartment in Toronto, where her mother was taking care of Willow until the morning.

The deal with her sister was that Sarah would only be tasked with easy stuff, nothing dangerous. Vivian was well aware of the arrangement, yet a gun was in her face tonight.

Why's that, my lovely sister? Hmmm? And how come they knew me?

The phone clicked, and her mother's voice came over the Rover's speaker system.

"Sarah?" she gasped. "Is that you?"

"You've got call display, Mom. You know it's me."

"I picked it up too fast." She gasped for air again, then blabbered on. "I was speaking with your father on the other line."

"You sound excited." Sarah turned left onto Cedar Street, heading north toward Wentworth, which would ultimately take her to Highway 401 and her hotel off the north service road.

"Sarah, you won't believe what's happening. I can't believe it myself."

Sarah was tempted to roll her eyes. Not in a losing-her-patience way, but more of a my-mom-can-be-embarrassing way.

"How about you start at the beginning?" Sarah checked her mirrors. No one seemed to be following her. The roads were nearly empty at this hour, and it was raining—who'd be out in this in their right mind?

She'd be at the hotel in less than ten minutes now. A bath, wine, and a good night's sleep were on the menu. Amanda had all the security she needed. Without Vivian explaining more, Sarah was *so* done with this job.

"I don't know where to start," her mother was saying, tripping over her words.

"You sound like you won the lottery. Just spill it, Mom."

"I'm afraid you won't believe me when I tell you, but I *can* verify it."

"Verify what? Now you're scaring me." Sarah checked her gas gauge. She had enough fuel to get home in a hurry if needed. Maybe a night in the hotel room wasn't meant to be.

"I have proof, well, I haven't seen the proof yet, but they're bringing it to the meeting—"

"Wait, what meeting? Who's bringing what to what meeting?"

"Sarah, are you sitting down?"

"Mom, I'm driving, so yeah, I'm sitting." Her stomach twisted into knots. "Please, no more suspense. Just spill it."

"Your sister, Vivian, is alive. Isn't that wonderful? The authorities called to tell me she was never killed all those years ago. Sarah, she's alive and in her late forties. And the best part is, I'm going to meet her tonight. I'll see your sister within an hour."

Chapter 4

D<small>ARWIN TEXTED BACK WITHIN</small> thirty minutes, and Parkman got him searching for Sarah's phone. He sent a screenshot and a link so Parkman could track it from his position.

Then Parkman's phone rang.

"Hey, Darwin, all good over there?"

"Is Sarah in trouble?"

"Right to business."

"Well?"

Parkman set the phone to speaker and then opened the link to track Sarah's phone. "Not that I know of. She was short with me on the phone, and she's listening to Vivian without any backup. I just don't like it."

"None of the boys are with her?" His tone sounded incredulous.

"She keeps to herself most days, does her own thing." Parkman tapped the screen, then spread his fingers wide to zoom in. Sarah was on the 401, heading toward Toronto.

"Who takes care of Willow? Is she with Aaron?"

"Sarah is maintaining custody during their separation. Her mother is here from California for a while to help out."

"There has to be more to it than her being short with you on the phone for you to reach out to me. What got your hackles up?"

"Something in her voice made her seem nervous. Hey, it was just a hunch. The girl had no one with her, so I thought I'd check on her and see where she was."

While waiting for him to respond to his WhatsApp message, he didn't tell Darwin that he'd made some coffee and got dressed to go out into the rain if Sarah didn't answer her phone soon.

"It looks like she was in Oshawa tonight." Darwin whispered something to Rosina, then came back to the phone.

"Say hello to that wife of yours."

"Parkman says hello."

Rosina shouted *hello* from somewhere in the background.

"Sarah's on the highway now. Looks like she's heading back to

Toronto."

Parkman nodded, even though no one could see him. "I'm following her on the link you sent."

"You need anything else? Need me to come to Toronto? Should I consider that as an option?"

"I don't think so. I'll call Sarah back, and if I can't reach her, I'll drive over to her place to see what's going on. Aaron's headed there to see Willow."

"At this hour? Isn't it late there?"

"Yeah, something's up with Amelia. She needs Aaron's help. I'll call you back soon when I know more."

"That works for me. If it's nothing, I still want an update via text, though. I want to know what freaked you out."

"Consider it done."

They hung up, and Parkman dialed Sarah's number.

She didn't answer. He ended the call after the seventh ring, concern gnawing at his gut.

What the hell was going on tonight?

He relocated to the kitchen, grabbed several toothpicks for the road, then stuck one in his mouth. He'd call Sarah back in a few minutes, and if she didn't answer again, he'd get in his car and drive to her place. From where she was on the highway, he'd beat her there.

Then she would tell him to his face why she had worried him so much.

And why was she working with her sister without taking one of the boys with her?

That behavior was too risky. Just too fucking risky.

Chapter 5

"Mom, listen to what you're saying." That gnawing in Sarah's stomach had become a full-on adrenaline shot. "Vivian cannot be alive."

"Your father didn't believe me either. But Sarah, they have proof."

"Who's they?" She sounded hysterical, which was so unlike her.

Sarah glanced at the speedometer, hoping a cop wouldn't pull her over. Breaking the speed limit by over forty kilometers per hour would be a hefty ticket, but if she couldn't talk her mother out of meeting whoever the hell she wanted to meet at this late hour, she would try to force her to stay home.

"Sarah, I *spoke* with Vivian on the phone. I actually reminisced with her."

"How is that possible?"

"Exactly! But it had to be Vivian. No one could know what that woman knew. And it doesn't hurt to see her face-to-face. I can look her in the eye, study her. I'll know my daughter when I see her."

"Really, Mom? After over thirty years? Did she tell you where she was all this time?"

The wipers were slashing across her windshield at full speed, the tires hydroplaning on puddles that had formed in the grooves on the highway. She eased off the gas to avoid being so reckless in her pursuit of getting home. A night in the hotel was out of the question now.

Her phone's screen lit up with caller ID—Parkman trying her again.

Vivian, who is playing this game with my mother? After a moment, she asked, *Is this actually Vivian I'm speaking to?*

Sarah shook her head once. Of course, it was her dead sister she'd been speaking to for almost twenty years. Who the hell else would it be? No way Vivian was alive.

Amelia said, "Sarah, a mother knows. The second I see Vivian, I'll know if she's the real deal."

"And if she's not? Then what?"

"I'll leave and come home."

"Mom, do you really think these people, whoever they are, will just let you leave and come home?"

"Of course I do. I've already spoken with your sister. As I said, she knew stuff no one else did."

"Like what?" Sarah was passing Ajax now. Pickering was next, then Scarborough. If traffic remained light, she would be home in forty-five minutes. The way her mother was talking, that was too long. She needed to get home faster.

"Sarah, it's too much to tell now, but she remembered her childhood, where we lived, and when you were born. She even asked about you. Asked how you were doing and expressed sadness that you missed growing up together."

"Mom, Vivian isn't alive." After saying the words and having spoken to her sister for so many years, it felt off somehow. "What I mean is, someone's playing a cruel joke on you. This is dangerous and reckless. What's Willow saying?"

"She's sleeping."

"You're not taking her with you wherever you're going, you know that, right?"

"I know. I called Aaron. He'll be here in ten minutes to stay with her."

Sarah huffed out a heavy sigh. "Mom, listen to me. Do not go tonight. If my sister has been alive all this time, why contact you now? What's the hurry to meet tonight? Why not tomorrow at noon in a large shopping mall, when I can come with you?"

"Tonight was my idea, honey." Her mother's voice exuded an infectious joy. "After we chatted for nearly an hour, I might add, I asked when I could see her. Sarah, it's been too long. What she told me about her going missing in the mall that day and why Armond Stuart was blamed for killing her made a lot of sense. He didn't do it, honey. She's alive."

Sarah felt like she wanted to pull out all her hair and scream at her mother to wake up. "How could framing someone for murder make any kind of sense? Anyway, just tell me what she said about going missing in the mall."

"It's because of her psychic ability."

"And?"

"She could see things, detect things, just like you. These people approached her and offered her a great life in exchange for using her powers for the betterment of mankind."

"Why does that sound like a brochure at an X-Men school?"

"I wouldn't believe it either, Sarah, but making jokes doesn't help."

"Mom, Vivian died all those years ago."

"You don't know that," her mother shouted. "Wait, Vivian mentioned something else. Remember when that man, Gert, kidnapped you when you were eighteen?"

"Yeah?"

"The FBI had your father and me sequestered in a motel with a department psychologist to help us through the situation."

"And?"

"Vivian called me on my hotel room phone. She'd had second thoughts about being away from us and missed me. She wanted me to pick her up, but the line was too weak for me to make out what she said. By then, she was already in her late twenties, and they hadn't let her go. Somehow, she'd heard you'd been kidnapped and wanted to let me know that you'd be okay. She mentioned that you were together and that you were the same. You're both gifted, and because of that, you'd make it out safe. And look at you now."

"If I'm psychic, just like my sister, then who have I been talking to all this time? A stranger on the other side, even though this stranger has called themselves Vivian all this time?"

"Sarah, I can't answer those questions for you. Once you meet your sister, you can ask her how it works."

"Wait, Mom, just wait. Take a breath." Sarah was entering Scarborough when her phone rang again, with Parkman's name popping up on call display. "Anyone who has access to the police reports from all those years ago could read the entry where you told your department psychologist about that phone call in your hotel room."

"I disagree. Those files are sealed. Tracy was the name of our psychologist, and with patient-client privilege and all that, no one but Tracy knew about that phone call. Well, your father knows, too."

"Mom, you must agree that something smells fishy about this. I mean, you can *feel* that, right?"

"Wait, Sarah, someone's at the door."

"Mom," Sarah shouted. "Don't answer it."

All that came back on the other end of the line was the muffled sound of her mother placing the phone against her clothing. There was a thump as the apartment door closed, then voices.

"Sarah, Aaron's here now. He said he'd wait until you got home instead of waking Willow and taking her to his place. Then he'll leave because he has an early morning class at the dojo tomorrow."

"Mom, please don't go. I'm asking you to wait. Let's do it tomorrow together."

"Sarah, I'll be fine. We're meeting in the lobby of the Royal Oak Hotel. They have security and staff on all night. I'll enter the lobby, and if it's a bad situation, I'll leave. If it's actually her, I'll stay and chat with her. It'll be an in-and-out thing, and I'll know." There was a pause. "Sarah, I *have* to know."

"Put Aaron on the phone."

"Sarah," her mother whispered. Then, as if her mouth was pressed against the phone, she said, "I haven't told him why I need to leave. I don't want anyone else to know but you and your dad. Okay?"

"Mom, put Aaron on the phone." Sarah's tone brooked no argument.

"Okay," her mom said, the exuberance back in her voice for Aaron's benefit. "Thanks so much for calling." The line died.

Sarah stared at the dashboard. Her mother had just hung up on her and refused to hand the phone to Willow's father.

She speed-dialed Aaron's cell phone number, but he didn't pick up. She called the house back but got a busy signal.

"She unplugged the damn phone," Sarah whispered to the empty car.

Then she called Parkman.

"Oh, Sarah, what a relief," Parkman said. "I've tried you several times. Are you okay?"

"Not really. Where are you?"

"Halfway to your apartment."

Sarah frowned. What the hell was going on tonight? "When we talked earlier, where were you?"

"At home."

"Then why are you on your way to my place?"

"Because I couldn't reach you."

Her phone lit up as someone else was trying to reach her. Darwin's name scrolled across the screen.

"I've got Darwin calling on the other line."

"Oh," Parkman muttered. "That would be my fault."

"What? How?"

"I called him to track your cell phone when you hung up on me earlier. I was worried."

As she climbed the access ramp to the Don Valley Parkway heading south, Sarah shook her head. "Okay, Parkman, none of that matters now. I've left one mess, and I'm heading to another mess."

"What are you talking about?"

"Can you turn around and head downtown?"

"Where am I going?"

"Meet me at the Royal Oak Hotel, but don't go in before me. Wait out front."

"I can do that. What's going on?"

"I'd love to introduce you to my sister."

"Your *sister*?"

"My mother just got off the phone with Vivian—supposedly. Get this—she's been alive all this time and working as a psychic for hire or something. I don't know the details, but I'm sure we'll find out soon enough."

"Sarah, I hate to be the one to break it to you, but your sister passed away about thirty years ago. I saw the case files before we met."

"That's what I told my mom, but she's convinced the woman she talked to is actually her daughter, Vivian."

"Impossible."

"Someone's playing a terrible joke on my mother, and I'm determined to get to the bottom of it tonight."

"Why the Royal Oak?"

"Because that's where they're meeting in about a half hour."

"I'll be there in twenty. I'm already turning around."

"See you there."

Sarah hit the gas harder and only eased off when the flashing red lights lit up her rearview mirror a minute later.

"Shit, shit, shit." She slapped the steering wheel. This was not something she could handle at the moment. She *had* to get downtown.

As she pulled to the side, the phone rang again, and she answered without looking at call display.

"Sarah, it's Darwin. You cool?"

"Not really. Shit night just got shittier, if that's possible."

"Talk to me."

"Cop approaching my window. Just got pulled over for speeding. Hang tight."

She watched in her mirror as the officer touched the back of her car with his thumb, holding it there for several moments. Then he stepped up to her window and remained slightly behind her so she'd have to spin in her seat to look at him.

He gestured with his hand for her to lower the window.

Sarah lowered it halfway, her insides a torrential storm of anxiety. She couldn't sit here a moment longer as her mother was having a midnight meeting with some potential extortionist or worse.

"Problem, Officer?"

"Where's the fire, ma'am?"

"Excuse me?"

"You were doing one hundred and fifty in a ninety zone. No one drives like that unless they're heading to a fire."

"Apologies. I can slow it down."

"I'm going to have to ask you to step out of the vehicle."

She spun in her seat to glare at him. "Why's that? I have somewhere to be right now. Just write the ticket, and I'll be on my way." She turned back to look at the time. She'd lost five minutes by pulling over and waiting for the cop to approach her.

"Ma'am, I won't tell you again. Turn off the vehicle and step outside slowly. You were going fifty miles per hour over the posted speed limit. That's an instant seizure and impound of the vehicle, ma'am."

"Like hell," Sarah mumbled under her breath, then slammed the accelerator to the floor.

The Land Rover shot forward, tires spinning.

"Sarah," Darwin shouted. "What are you doing?"

"They can have my car, fucking thieves, but not until I meet whoever is impersonating my sister."

"Impersonat—*what*?"

"My mom has been talking to someone who claims to be Vivian in the flesh," she sputtered out in a rush of words, her voice raised over the sound of the revving engine.

"That's utterly impossible."

"That's what I said."

"And they're meeting you tonight?"

"They're meeting my mother downtown within a half hour." She checked her mirror and saw the cop car hopping between lanes to catch up to her.

"That meeting can't take place." Darwin sounded frantic now. "Your mother does not know what she's walking into."

"My feelings exactly."

"Call Parkman. Get Alex, Daniel, even Aaron if you have to—"

"Parkman is already on his way. Someone will pay for playing this game with my mother." The cop had closed the distance by half.

"I'll call Parkman now," Darwin said. "Just pull over and catch a taxi."

"Not enough time, not enough time."

"Fuck."

"Exactly."

The cruiser was right behind her now, lights flashing, siren blaring.

Her eye caught two more cruisers as they entered the highway, coming in behind the other one.

Sarah slapped the steering wheel twice, swore loudly, and jammed the accelerator into the floor mat.

Chapter 6

DARWIN HUNG UP AND called Parkman. Once he got him on the line, he said, "Sarah got pulled over. I heard the whole thing. I'm not sure she'll be able to meet with you."

"Where is she now?" Parkman asked.

"Running from the cops."

"*Running* from the—shit! That's not good."

"Sarah told me what's happening with her mother."

"Yeah, we don't know who she's been talking to or what she's walking into."

"What can I do from here?" Darwin tapped a pen against a pad of paper in frustration. Before Parkman could answer, he added, "I'll come to Toronto."

"You're always welcome, and we'd love to see you, but don't feel like you *need* to come. We can deal with these charlatans parading around with a fake Vivian."

"Something about this doesn't feel good." Darwin stared at his computer screen, watching the dot representing Sarah on the highway still racing south. "Why was Sarah that far out of town? Was she lured away so someone could get to her mother?"

"Damn, I hadn't thought of that."

"If this is truly Vivian, why call her mother out at night? Why not a dinner meeting or something earlier?"

"I don't like it either."

"You still on your way to meet them?"

"Damn right."

"You armed?"

"Yup."

"You need help? Want Disco to come? I can call Alex."

"For now, I can handle it. If I need him, I can call Alex."

"That may be too late."

Parkman didn't respond right away. Darwin only heard the sound of his engine revving as he headed downtown to a crazy meeting with a girl who was supposed to be dead.

"Okay, call Alex," Parkman said. "Update him that I'll be at the Royal Oak in two minutes and that I'll reach out if I need him."

"I can do that. And hey, Parkman?"

"Yeah?"

"Stay safe."

"Always."

Darwin killed the call and dialed Alex's number. He texted him when there was no answer and then called Daniel's number. He got no answer there either.

He scratched his head, staring at the screen.

After a two-minute internal debate, he used his tracking program to get a read on Alex's and Daniel's phones. Within two minutes, he had them up on the screen.

Darwin snatched the pen off his desk and stuck it in his mouth as he stared at their location.

Both phones were downtown at the Royal Oak Hotel. As far as he could detect, they were somewhere inside the hotel.

"What the fuck is going on?" he whispered to the empty room.

He brought up Parkman's phone, a noticeable tremor in his hand.

Depending on the accuracy of the program, Parkman was standing outside the Royal Oak Hotel right now.

Darwin jammed his finger on the call button to dial Parkman and tell him what he saw on the screen.

The phone rang and rang, but Parkman didn't pick it up this time.

He tried again, his stomach doing flip-flops, a sweat breaking out on his neck. In Europe, in the communications room of his house in Umbria, Italy, he felt cut off from them as if he were in prison somewhere. That's how handicapped he felt. There was zero chance he could get to Toronto in less than twenty hours to help anyone.

On his computer screen to the right, he brought up airfares and typed in the dates and times in search of the earliest ticket to Toronto from Rome.

Then he tried calling Parkman again. It went unanswered.

The dot marked as Parkman's phone was in the vicinity of Alex's and Daniel's dots now.

He texted Parkman, then called him once more.

Nothing.

"What the hell is going on?"

In one last attempt to reach someone, he called Sarah's number. While it rang, the lights blinked out on his screen.

Darwin leaned closer.

Parkman's, Alex's, and Daniel's cell phone locator dots were gone.

He refreshed the screen, entered their numbers, and had his program reacquire the assets, but to no avail.

They had all disappeared.

When Sarah didn't answer her phone, he used his credit card to buy a plane ticket to Toronto.

Then he jumped up from his chair and ran toward the main house.

"Rosina, honey," he called, scared by the panic in his voice. "I have to leave in an hour for Rome. There's trouble in Toronto."

Chapter 7

SARAH COULDN'T KEEP HER eyes off the rearview mirror as the cruisers chasing her ballooned to three cars.

When she reached the base of the Don Valley Parkway and took the ramp onto the Gardiner Expressway too fast, her Rover managed the turn without rolling.

Debating the exit to take, she rechecked her mirror.

Simultaneously, all the police cruisers turned off their lights. They went dark. Then, each one eased back, creating a distance between them.

What made them back off?

She stared out the windshield, trying to see if she was driving into a spike belt or a roadblock, but nothing was up ahead—just an empty, dark, and wet road.

The cruisers were leaving the highway at the Sherbourne Street exit, one by one.

Sarah eased off her gas pedal and moved to the right.

"What is that all about, Vivian? You want to tell me what the hell's happening tonight?" Her voice had a shrill tone that gave her goosebumps.

Another look in her mirror. Not a single cop was in sight.

Did they pull away because the chase was too dangerous? That didn't make sense because the Gardiner Expressway is virtually empty tonight. She could see if it was the middle of the day on tight downtown streets, but not now.

Her phone rang as she stayed to the right to exit on the two lanes descending toward Yonge Street.

It was Darwin again.

She was almost at the Royal Oak. Once she dealt with whoever was fucking with her mother, she'd call him back.

After a quick right on Yonge and then a fast left on Front Street, she gunned it a couple of blocks and pulled up at the front doors of the Royal Oak Hotel.

At this time of night, in this horrid weather, the streets were mostly empty. She could park out front with her four-way flashers on for a few minutes. This wouldn't take long.

Something bothered her more than the jokesters screwing with her mother, though. It had been nagging her for the past hour.

How did that bearded man in the schoolyard know her name? Had they met before? Or did he just know her face from some past trouble?

There were too many strange things happening for it to all be coincidences.

She jammed the Rover into park, hit the four-way lights, grabbed her phone, and hopped out.

Parkman was nowhere in sight. She did a double-take to ensure she hadn't missed him, but he hadn't shown up. Before advancing on the building, she tried Parkman's number. He was supposed to meet her, and she figured he'd be out front, but another full scan of the area came up empty.

She dialed her mother's cell number when Parkman didn't answer his phone.

No answer there either.

Where is everyone tonight?

She moved up to the hotel's front doors and took one last look around the street and sidewalk. Parkman would have beaten her to the hotel, yet he was nowhere in sight. Was he waiting inside?

Her phone was held close, the gun tucked safely in her pants. Sarah entered the lobby of the Royal Oak Hotel.

Her phone chirped that she'd received a text. Before the door closed, she read the text from Darwin: *Don't go into the hotel before talking to me.*

Before typing back a reply, she glanced around to survey her immediate area. The lobby was empty. Even the front desk had no visible staff member.

She tapped back a reply: *Tell me what you know.*

It remained unread for half a minute while she stood by the glass doors. Her hair was still wet from being out in the rain earlier, and she was shivering slightly from the adrenaline rush of the police chase.

Instead of waiting for a reply, she opened WhatsApp and called Darwin. On the fifth ring, without an answer, she hung up.

"Fuck this," she whispered, ending the call and placing her phone on airplane mode. No more calls from people. She'd update everyone once she figured out what was going on.

Once her phone was slipped back into her pocket, she cautiously strode to the front desk and tapped a bell on the countertop.

There was movement from inside an open doorway behind the counter. Then, a young man stepped out.

"Good evening. Do you have a reservation?" He offered her a pasted-on smile, then stared at his computer and tapped several buttons.

"No, I'm here to see my sister." Sarah couldn't believe she'd spoken those words out loud. Fuming on the inside, she said to whoever might be listening, *You have some explaining to do*, then offered her own fake smile and added, "I believe my sister is staying at your hotel. Her name is Vivian Roberts."

The young guy tapped on the keyboard. "Let me take a look." He placed a finger on the screen, lowered it slightly, and then stopped it. "Yes, Vivian Roberts stayed with us until about an hour ago."

Sarah blinked, stunned at what he'd said. This couldn't be a coincidence. "Really?" she asked, her voice cracking on that single word. Collecting herself, she leaned closer to the counter. "Wait, why would someone check out at nearly midnight?"

The clerk met her gaze, lifted one shoulder nonchalantly, and said, "I am not at liberty to divulge our clients' reasons for—"

Sarah lunged across the counter and grabbed the clerk's shirt, yanking him toward her. "I asked, why the fuck did she check out?"

"Family emergency," he stammered, his voice several pitches higher. "She said it was a family emergency. I checked her out myself."

Sarah released the man's shirt. "There, that wasn't so bad now, was it?"

The clerk backed away from the counter, out of reach of her now, his face more red from embarrassment than fear. "You can't just grab people. I'm calling security if you don't leave."

"Fine, call security. I'm going to take a walk around the lobby, then leave. I'll be gone in a minute."

She stepped away from the counter, checked the front doors to see if Parkman was there, and then surveyed the vast lobby, her heart racing.

Vivian Roberts checked out an hour ago due to a family emergency.

How could that be? Who could orchestrate such an elaborate hoax?

What if Sarah hadn't been in Oshawa tonight? How would things be different if she'd been home where she was supposed to be? This would've been dealt with by now.

How about it, Vivian? Why send me out of town for nothing? Who were those armed men?

When no answer was forthcoming—she hadn't felt Vivian's presence at all—she moved about the vast lobby and checked down the corridors to the right and left. The area was rectangular, with an ample open space down the middle filled intermittently with couches and chairs. Sarah walked past a large four-sided clock until she reached the far end and then returned to the check-in desk.

It was as if the entire hotel were empty. Not a single person lounged anywhere.

The clerk at the front desk had regained some of his original color while whispering to someone on the phone.

She was running out of time. Security would likely come to escort her off the property.

There was no reason to stick around anyway. Her *sister* had checked out.

She approached the front desk. "I'm leaving."

The clerk nodded once and lowered the phone. His lips pressed tight together.

"But before I leave," she inhaled to remain calm and remind herself to ask nicely, "*please* tell me what you can remember of Vivian Roberts. What did she look like?"

"I just came on shift at eleven." He shook his head with a quick jerk. "I didn't pay much attention to our client."

Sarah glanced up and to the right, then pointed. "Those cameras would've picked her up." She redirected her attention to the clerk as the elevator opened on the other side of the lobby. "Please pull the security footage to show me what Vivian looked like. Is that possible?" She glanced at the two men in security uniforms coming their way, then back at the clerk. "I'm asking nicely."

"I'm sorry, ma'am." The clerk set the phone down. "I'll be doing no such thing. You're going to have to leave."

She raised her left arm, palm aimed at the security officers. "*Don't* … come any closer."

They slowed, then stopped several feet from her. "Ma'am," one of the security guards said. "If you're not registered with the hotel, I'm afraid you will have to leave."

She stared at the clerk. To come so close to *seeing* what the charlatan looked like, to actually have the person parading around as her sister on camera and be denied the chance to look at her, was driving her insane. The debate raged within her for several seconds about whether to draw her weapon, threaten them, beat them, or walk outside peacefully, but she resolved it by deciding to leave.

"I'll go now."

The clerk let out an audible huff.

Sarah lowered her arm and started for the front doors. "This isn't the last you'll see of me, though. I will be back because I need to see that footage."

"Have a pleasant night, ma'am," one of the guards shouted after her.

She stopped at the door and glanced back. They were just doing their job and would tell their coworkers that they threw out a woman acting like a Karen. It pissed her off, but there was no gain in getting into a fight here or hurting people because she was angry. That was a younger Sarah. She'd grown since those days.

Controlling herself, she emerged from the lobby and moved up to her Rover.

Parkman was still nowhere in sight.

"What the fuck happened to you tonight?"

She pulled out her phone, flipped it out of airplane mode, then redialed him. When he didn't answer, she thought her blood pressure would hit two hundred over one fifty. Next, she tried Darwin again— this time successfully. He picked up immediately.

"*Sarah*," he blurted. "Fucking hell. Where were you?"

"Inside the lobby of the Royal Oak, trying to stop my mother from making a huge mistake, but I didn't see her."

"I was trying to reach you to stop you from entering that hotel."

Sarah took a couple of steps closer to her Rover and then turned back to stare at the row of glass doors leading into the lobby.

"Why would you do that?" Her tone revealed the trepidation she felt.

"Because Alex, Daniel, and Parkman were all just there, like, fifteen minutes ago, and their cell phones all went dark."

Sarah leaned back and bumped into the side of her Rover. "What?" she stammered, her mouth suddenly dry. "Tell me more. I don't think I understand."

"I was talking to Parkman. He asked me to call Alex to have him get ready if he was needed to help. When I got no answer from Alex, I called Daniel. After no answer, I tracked their phones. They were in the lobby of the Royal Oak. So, I tried Parkman again. No answer. But I watched his phone enter the lobby, too. Then they all went dark. I still don't have them on my screen."

"When you say they went dark, I get what that means, but can you explain why that would happen so we're all on the same page?" Her eyes didn't waver from the glass doors of the hotel. Inside the lobby, both security officers were meandering toward the front, likely wanting to ascertain she had left the area.

"Usually, it just means they were shut off. Or it could mean they were destroyed. But it happened to all three in the lobby of that hotel not fifteen minutes ago."

Sarah scanned the length of the empty sidewalk, her nerves shattering second by second. "Darwin, what's happening here?"

"I have no idea. That's why I've booked a flight to Toronto. I'll be there tomorrow evening at seven."

"Wait, can you track my mom's cell before you go? Has she arrived here at the hotel yet?"

"One second. My taxi is almost here. Once I do this, I'm heading to Rome on the train. I'll be there tomorrow." Furious typing sounds came through her cell phone's small speaker. "It's checking. Give me a second—wait, that can't be right."

"What?" She pushed off the Rover, her hand resting on the gun in the back of her pants for comfort.

"Your mom's phone was last seen in the lobby of that hotel, too. It says here that it was ten minutes ago, maybe eleven."

"Darwin, I've been here for at least five minutes."

"Sarah, something's happening in that hotel, and I don't like it. They were all in there within the past half an hour."

"Get here as fast as you can."

"I'm on my way. Running for the cab now."

"I'm going back inside to find out why they're lying to me."

"Sarah, wait! Don't go in alone. If they could get to Alex, they'll get you."

That made her pause.

"Listen to me," Darwin shouted. "Parkman's good, but he's still healing from Wyoming. Your mother isn't made for this shit. Daniel is good, but he could be surprised. Alex? No fucking way. No one gets the jump on him. Whatever's happening in there needs an army to sweep through the place. Wait for me, or at the very least, get Aaron, and I'll send Disco over, but *do not* go in alone."

Hearing Darwin spell it all out like that scared her more than what they were facing. He was right, too. It would be rare for someone to get the jump on everyone in their small entourage.

"Something's wrong here, Darwin. Something is very wrong."

"Leave the area. Come back stronger. You won't fix this alone. You need help."

Those last three words were exactly what she'd been trying to avoid during the separation from Aaron. She didn't want help. She could do it on her own. Or was it her stubbornness in trying to prove something to Aaron?

"Call whoever you want. Call Disco. I'll call Aaron. But we'll raze this place to the ground by the morning if I don't hear from Parkman, Alex, or Daniel."

"Agreed. Then I'll fly in and clean up the mess."

She disconnected the call and stared at the façade of the Royal Oak Hotel. Where did everyone go tonight?

This wasn't the only strange thing that happened tonight. How did that man know her name in the schoolyard? He looked like he said it by accident. And why did the cruisers abandon the chase earlier? Who ordered them off? Was it all connected to this hotel?

Something about this felt *huge*—too big for her. Maybe Darwin was right. If it weren't for him, she would've walked back into that lobby toting her gun and demanding answers. Then she'd hurt people until she got those answers. That was the younger Sarah, though, and she knew it. She was a mother. Things had to play out differently.

Fighting against her will, she walked around the Rover, got in the driver's seat, then connected the phone to Bluetooth and dialed Aaron's number.

When he didn't answer, she leaned over the steering wheel and screamed, clenching her fists. Breathing heavily, she focused on dialing her home line, figuring it would still be busy because her mother had left it off the hook.

But it rang.

On the second ring, Aaron picked it up. "Hello," he said, speaking softly.

"Aaron." She got that one word out. Then her throat seized up at the thought of Parkman, Alex, Daniel, and likely her mother being in trouble.

"Sarah, what's wrong?"

"Aaron," she gasped in a breath. "I think I'm in trouble. Everyone's missing, and I don't know what to do."

"Okay, slow down. Tell me everything."

Sarah told him everything, starting with waiting in the rain for Amanda to show up in Oshawa, right up to getting off the phone with Darwin, along with everything he said. When she was done, Aaron didn't respond for a moment.

"Are you still there?" she asked.

"Sarah?"

"I'm here."

In a tone reserved for shock or surprise, maybe even a slight disdain, Aaron blamed her for everything with four words. "What have you done?"

Chapter 8

AT A COMPLETE LOSS for what could possibly be happening, Aaron packed a bag for Willow. They would meet Sarah downtown at the David Pecaut Square, behind the Roy Thompson Hall, at midnight. Then, they would find a motel in Mississauga that accepted cash and spend the night thinking about what had happened and planning a response.

Either way, staying in Sarah's home made him and his daughter a target.

Darwin was coming, and they'd see if Disco was available.

Why did you pull us all in again, Sarah?

In the meantime, one of the boys would surface—they had to. Alex would contact them or Parkman. Whoever was doing this wouldn't just kill everyone—he sure hoped not—and no one could cage Alex for too long.

Once a bag was packed, he quickly grabbed toiletries, leaving the bathroom a mess. When this was all over, he would clean it up.

Willow was easy to wake, especially once she was told they were going to see her mother and they'd spend the night in a motel together. As sleepy as she was, Willow smiled at the thought and walked on her own to the door, her eyes half-lidded.

"But Daddy," Willow said. "What will we do about the men who won't let us?"

Aaron stared down at his daughter, then shouldered the bag he'd packed. "There are no men who won't let us, honey. No one knows where we are or where we're going."

Willow nodded and yawned, her mouth opening wide for several seconds.

"C'mon, let's go meet Mommy."

He grabbed the knob and pulled open the door.

"But the men won't let us, Daddy."

On the other side of the apartment door stood five thick men. With their tight haircuts, bulging muscles, chiseled faces, and thick pecs, they all looked like retired military personnel.

Aaron shoved the door to slam it closed, but it stopped one foot from the latch. He released Willow's hand and put his shoulder into it, but it felt like he was pushing against a brick wall.

The resistance became an inward pressure, and Aaron was pushed back so hard he lost his balance, tripped twice, and was about to fall when he bumped into the back of the couch.

"I was trying to tell you, Daddy. These men have other plans." Willow yawned again.

One of the men stepped forward. "I'm afraid you must come with us, sir."

Aaron moved to Willow's side as the men surrounded him. Thick sausage-fingered hands gripped Aaron's arms before he could resist, yanking him from Sarah's apartment. Their leader took Willow's hand. She didn't seem bothered by the rough handling of her father.

Asking who they were was a moot point. What would it matter if they were Bob or Doug? So he asked, "Where are you taking us?" He struggled briefly against the men holding him.

"Somewhere safe, sir," their leader said.

"Forcefully?"

"You wouldn't come otherwise."

Aaron pushed off the ground with his feet and tried to flip backward in an attempt to dislodge the hands clamped onto his arms, but they simply righted him in the air, and he landed back on his feet.

"Please don't hurt yourself," their leader said. "Don't fight this, or we have something that will help you sleep through this ordeal." The man looked down at Willow, then back at Aaron. "Is that the memory you want to give Willow here? That her father slept for days while she needed him?"

The man's voice was hardened by years of military service. He had the kind of tone that garnered compliance from the listener.

Aaron glared at him, heat rising to his face. "All of you will pay for this."

The man nodded. "Okay." He offered a half-smile. "Now that we have that out of the way, please collect yourself and enter the vehicle." The man pointed at a black SUV, then bent over slightly to address Willow. "You want to ride with your father?"

"Damn right she rides with me," Aaron shouted, then struggled again.

An arm came around his neck and lifted him off the ground, cutting off his airflow.

"Mr. Stevens, I implore you to avoid testing my men. You won't look so pretty if they lose their temper."

The man holding him whispered into his ear. "It's better for your daughter if you're awake. Last warning, dipshit."

The arm eased off, and Aaron gulped in a few rapid breaths. He nodded his acquiescence.

"I wanna ride with Daddy," Willow said, then moved to hug his leg.

The leader had let her go. "See, now isn't that better?" His grin widened. "A family moment." He met Aaron's gaze. "Worthy of a photo."

One of his men snapped a picture with his cell phone and slid the phone into a Kevlar breast pocket.

"Remove Aaron's phone from his person."

A hand dove into Aaron's pocket and snatched the phone out. Then, it was handed over to their leader. The man held it up to Aaron's face to open the main screen, then rolled a hand in the air. "Load up. We leave in T minus ten."

They shoved Aaron inside the SUV, helped Willow up, then slammed the doors. Two armed men sat opposite them, and the leader got in the passenger seat up front. He spun around and stared at Aaron. "Will we need to restrain you for the duration of the ride?"

Aaron glared back, then shook his head.

The leader nodded and spun back around. "Go."

In seconds, the convoy of SUVs accelerated into the September night, with Aaron hoping he'd see some of his friends wherever they were going. If they were all in the same place, they could cause some significant damage.

These men would regret what they'd done. Willow would make them pay with her unique abilities. At any moment, she could turn off the vehicles, jam their weapons, or even lift them off the ground with her mind.

Aaron glanced over at Willow as she stared out the window, her little eyes heavy with sleep.

Why wasn't she doing anything? She had to know something Aaron didn't, as she was always several steps ahead—like how she knew they were on the other side of the apartment door when she said, "The men won't let us, Daddy."

Maybe she was waiting until the men delivered them to Alex and the others.

That had to be it.

Aaron held his daughter's hand and watched the leader in the front seat as he navigated through Aaron's phone.

Then it hit him. Aaron had texted a pin on a map for Sarah, telling her where to meet him at midnight.

By doing that, he'd condemned her as well.

Confirming his fears, the leader got on the phone and mumbled orders to someone. Aaron distinctly heard Sarah's name and the park by Roy Thompson Hall.

They were all in this together, whether he wanted to be or not. Once attached to Sarah, there was no escape. Even separated, she drew him back in, and she had put their daughter at risk yet again.

He would talk to Sarah about cutting off her sister if they made it out of this in one piece.

The psychic warrior shit had to end.

Or he'd fight for custody and then move Willow far, far away because being this close to Sarah was just too dangerous. Too dangerous.

Chapter 9

HER EMOTIONS PEELED RAW, Sarah turned on the Land Rover and eased away from the front of the Royal Oak Hotel. After all they'd been through, how could Aaron invalidate her yet again? What had she done? Where their friends were had nothing whatsoever to do with anything that she had done or not done.

Vivian instructed her to hold onto Amanda for a couple of days or until she said otherwise. Those were the instructions for tonight. That was it—cut and dried—super simple.

But then her mother called about meeting her other daughter—her dead daughter, miraculously alive now—which had to be bullshit. Sarah wasn't ready to absolutely discount it yet, but she was pretty sure someone was playing a terrible game with her mother's head.

For what gain? To what end? And how was it Sarah's fault?

When Sarah called for help because she'd been too far away to stop her mother, everyone except Parkman seemed to be busy or away from their phones. And now she couldn't reach him.

Darwin was still safe but wouldn't be in Toronto until tomorrow evening. A part of her wished he lived closer, but another part knew that if he did, he might have disappeared along with the rest of them tonight.

Then there was Aaron and his whining. She had agreed to his idea of cooling her heels for the night and looking at everything in the morning. If someone had abducted all of their friends and her mother, they'd be in touch soon. In the meantime, they needed to go off the grid to avoid the same fate.

Two blocks from the Royal Oak Hotel, she turned right onto Simcoe Street, following the directions on the map Aaron had texted her. At the next light, she turned left onto Wellington and saw Roy Thompson Hall to her right. As Aaron said, the public parking was underground and had twenty-four-hour access.

She found it without trouble, angled the Rover onto the ramp, and descended underground.

Within five minutes, she was parked at the lowest level, separated from the GPS by several stories of concrete. She killed the engine and sat there for ten minutes, eyes closed, head back—a short reprieve to catch her breath.

Her phone still had a fifty percent charge. It was enough to last the night and then some if anyone tried to call.

Vivian, are you around?

Her sister's presence in her head had vanished.

What a time for you to disappear. Did you send me after Amanda so I'd be out of town when my mother—our mother—walked into the hands of pranksters?

Nothing.

Then, like the whirl of a breeze stirring curtains, her sister entered her consciousness and whispered, *You still need Amanda.*

Sarah's eyes popped open, and she jerked forward, gripping the steering wheel tight. *What? Why?* "She's a seventeen-year-old girl with more security than Justin Bieber."

Amanda is the answer.

What's the question?

Silence from her sister.

"Vivian," Sarah shouted, all her bottled-up anger in that one word. "Answer me. How could that girl help me with this situation?"

I'll give you Amanda's location soon.

With those final words, her sister departed her consciousness.

"When, Vivian? When will you tell me her location?"

She was talking to no one. Her sister was gone. It was a feeling, like knowing someone was in the house with you versus knowing the house was empty. When her sister was around, she didn't feel alone.

Sarah tightened her grip on the steering wheel, staring at the concrete wall of the underground parking lot directly ahead, silently cursing her sister under her breath.

After several moments of panting like she'd been running, swearing a blue streak, and fighting the urge to scream as her emotional pot had spilled over, Sarah got out of the Rover, locked it, and made her way toward the exit, her footfalls echoing off the concrete walls.

She'd meet Aaron in the square where they'd agreed to meet. They'd find a motel and try to get some much-needed rest.

Then she'd *take* Amanda at all costs and learn whatever the hell it was that Amanda knew.

This would end quickly, and it would end on Sarah's terms.

There was no doubt in her mind.

Chapter 10

SARAH SAT ON THE bench facing the small trees at the center of the park as Aaron had directed. Her phone showed it was a few minutes after midnight, and there was still no sign of him.

Mentally, she calculated the time it would take him to get to her location from her apartment and guessed he would've been here at least fifteen minutes ago.

She rechecked the time, wondering what was keeping him, her stomach in knots. If anything happened to Willow ...

She left that thought unfinished. There was no point because nothing could happen to Willow without Willow's consent. That girl could see into the immediate future and had the power of telekinesis. With only a dark thought, Willow could hurt an entire football team without touching anyone.

A man walking along the sidewalk in a ripped trench coat caught her eye. He stopped before a garbage bin, opened it, and rummaged around inside.

Another man strolled along the sidewalk near the center of the small square, pushing a shopping cart filled with garbage bags, two of which dangled outside the cart.

Even though she didn't expect Aaron to wear a disguise of any sort, neither vagrant matched his physical appearance.

She didn't relish the idea of spending the night with him in a hotel room. He didn't understand her anymore, and because of that, he looked down on her for her choices, even though none of those decisions affected him before tonight. Now that he was involved, everything would be wrong again. He acted as if the whole world were falling apart. Did she start this? Was she the instigator? No, not at all. Someone was doing this *to* her, *to* them, and until she found out who and why, she was powerless to stop them.

What had changed in Aaron? They were a hot team years ago. Aaron was fearless and always there to handle whatever came at him. They'd been to Mexico, Vegas, California, Europe, and several parts of Canada, doing the right thing and making a name for themselves, but then he wanted it all to stop. It cost them their relationship. They'd been close to splitting in the past, but this was an official separation. He even paid a monthly stipend for Willow, for which Sarah was grateful.

That fence-sitting he'd done for years must've finally ended when Benjamin was killed. That had to be the proverbial straw. Or was it earlier, like when Willow was born?

Without reason, a specific trigger, without telling her why, she wondered what caused his about-face.

On the sidewalk, the vagrant pushing the cart disappeared behind the Roy Thompson Hall building. Aaron was almost twenty minutes late now. She scrolled through her phone but found no text, no call, nothing.

Where are you, Aaron?

She got up from the bench and saw someone lying about twenty feet away on the grass. From where she stood, with the limited light afforded her, it didn't look like the man was moving.

It had to be her imagination, but something felt wrong here.

She stepped forward, closing the distance, then whispered, "Hey," but the man didn't respond.

After a quick scan of the area around her, she jogged to the body on the ground. She didn't have to touch him to see he was dead. His throat had been opened, and he'd bled into the dirt. His trench coat had flopped unfastened when he fell. Underneath the coat was a Kevlar vest and several empty holsters. Whoever killed this man had relieved him of his weapons.

Sarah lowered to one knee and surveyed the area. There was no one in sight, no one close by.

What the hell is going on? Who would do this?

She rifled through the man's pockets, but they were empty. Whoever killed him had ensured that all the man's ID was gone.

The meeting location had to change. She would text Aaron. They could meet anywhere else but here.

She stood on shaky legs—something told her it was too late. This man was here because of her, and whoever killed him was likely watching her at that very moment.

She eased out her phone and dimmed the screen's brightness. No one had texted or called. Where were Aaron and Willow?

Frustration led to anger, which quelled her anxiety. What had happened tonight was shitty, and it was starting to piss her off.

Returning to sit on the bench was out of the question, so she took a steadying breath and moved toward the closest building. She walked with purpose, eyes surveying everything.

The vagrant with the cart was back, moving toward her now.

She changed direction, aiming at the building on the left.

When she glanced over her shoulder, two men stood in the shadows by the parking access ramp where she'd taken her Land Rover. She slowed her step as they seemed to be watching her. She squinted across the park at them. They stood at ease, hands clasped in front, legs spread apart. The word *military* came to mind. She couldn't see their eyes from this distance, but would swear they were watching her.

When she turned around, two other men were now standing near the other building, also watching her.

Vivian, wanna tell me what to do here?

She came to a stop. Was she walking into a trap? Two or more men could be behind the next building on Wellington Street.

When Sarah glanced over at the vagrant walking with the cart, he was gone. The cart sat by itself, abandoned.

Did they kill him, too?

Sarah withdrew her weapon and moved toward the Wellington building. When she glanced back, all the men she'd witnessed moments before were now jogging toward her.

It was time to go. This wouldn't end well. And if they were all wearing Kevlar like the dead guy, then it was likely she'd just piss them off by shooting at them. Her aim was good, but she'd have trouble making a headshot from a distance with a pistol.

Before she rounded the corner of the building, she looked back one more time.

The men had disappeared.

A frown knotted her forehead as Sarah slowed her pace, then stopped and set her back against the brick wall.

What the hell happened to them? They had to be hiding because the only body she could see on the ground was the man with no ID. Why weren't they running toward her anymore?

Her phone vibrated in her pants pocket, making her hands jerk and her finger squeeze the trigger. Fortunately, her finger had been on the trigger guard, not the trigger. Gasping for breath, startled out of her wits because she'd thought someone had touched her ass where the phone was nestled in her back pocket, she snatched it out and opened the text.

It was from a private number. *Walk down Wellington! Now!*

She texted back. *Who's this?*

A friend. Go!

Gun still in her hand, she surveyed the area. Two men had stepped out of hiding and were running toward her. They'd be on her in less than twenty seconds.

A new text popped up. *Okay. Don't then ...*

A weapon fired once, then again.

Both men running toward her dropped and slid a few feet. Neither man moved.

"What the—"

Another man broke from hiding, running toward her. One arm pumped as he ran, while the other was raised in front of him, aimed at her. A piece of the brick wall snapped off when his bullet hit directly beside her head.

Instinctively, Sarah ducked. She didn't need any further persuading. She ran around the building and hit the sidewalk on Wellington in a sprint.

This time, she heard the distinctive sound of a high-powered weapon as several bullets were fired above her. When she looked over her shoulder, the man chasing her was facedown on the ground.

Someone had covered her and protected her as she ran.

She put her weapon away and texted back to the private number. *Is that you taking out these men?*

She slowed her pace and jumped behind a pillar to catch her breath.

Three dots jumped and rolled on her screen, indicating someone was texting.

Then, *Yes, it's me. Keep moving.*

Sarah opened her conversation with Aaron as she pushed off the pillar and kept walking along Wellington. Halfway through her text to Aaron telling him they had to meet somewhere else, she stopped at the next block and glanced across the street.

It all made sense now.

A large black Hummer was parked at the curb.

The passenger side door popped open as she stared at it.

"C'mon," a familiar voice shouted. "Get in. We need to leave."

Disco.

Sarah ran for the Hummer, stowing her gun back in her pants. When she glanced inside and saw Disco behind the wheel, she climbed in.

"How did you make it here so fast?" she asked.

Disco hit the gas and lifted a radio. He keyed the mic and said, "Retreat. I've got the package. Rendezvous at the warehouse when I call." He set the mic down and glanced over at her. "It seems the trouble you bring down on your head only gets more and more serious each time."

That felt like Aaron talking, blaming her. She instantly disliked the comment. "You saying I asked for this?"

Disco chuckled. "Not at all. Commenting only on how you seem to level up like you're in some sort of video game."

Sarah glanced out the window. "Well, this ain't no video game, and you didn't answer my question."

"Darwin called me on the way to Rome. He said you might need help and told me where you were. I was parked at Union Station waiting to pick someone up."

She looked in the back seat. "You missed your pick-up?"

Disco shrugged. "Told them to catch an Uber. You're more important." He wore a cocky smile as he drove south toward the Gardiner. "As it turns out, you really did need my help. You'd be in their grubby hands without my boys and me. I dispatched Ape and Water to watch the park."

"Ape and Water? What's that?"

"Their names."

Sarah stared at him for a long moment. "You had others with you?"

"Two others."

"You're always carrying men with weapons with strange names?"

He looked over at her askance. "You know what I do for a living, right?"

Sarah watched him a moment, then said, "Yes."

"Okay then. Next question."

"Who were those guys? The men coming after me?"

"Military, but not ours. Yours."

"You mean American?"

Disco nodded. "These guys are like cockroaches. There are hundreds of them. Step on ten or twenty or fifty, and hundreds more keep coming. What did you do to piss off the US military, Sarah?"

She stared out the windshield as Disco accessed the Gardiner Expressway ramp. "I have no idea."

"Well, they weren't there to play friendly, and we didn't want to take them out, but the guy dressed as a vagrant was a surprise."

"That was you guys?"

Disco nodded. "No choice with that one. We didn't know who we were fighting yet. Once we figured out who they were, we changed tactics and aimed for center mass."

"Their chests?"

Disco nodded. "To wound and bruise but not kill. I do not want the US military on my ass." He glanced over at her again. "So, I'll reiterate —what did you do to bring them all the way up here to hunt you down?"

Sarah lowered her head to check the side mirror. No headlights followed them.

"Sarah?"

She faced Disco. "I have no idea why they're here or what they're doing. But I suspect I know someone who will have some answers."

"Who?"

"A seventeen-year-old girl named Amanda."

Disco laughed. "Man, I've missed you, Sarah. You make what I do fun." He shook his head and whispered to himself, "A seventeen-year-old girl holds the answers."

After a few moments, Sarah said, "This isn't fun. I'm not enjoying myself too much. And hey, where are we going?"

"To my place. No one knows where it is. You can tell me all your troubles and get some sleep. In the morning, we'll find a way to fix this."

Sarah nodded when he looked at her, then she pulled out her phone and finished her text to Aaron. When she was done, she sent it.

"Who was that?"

"Aaron. I told him I'm safe with Disco and that he should also hole up somewhere."

Disco stared at her.

"What?"

"Give me the phone." He held out his hand.

She looked down at it. "No, there's got to be a better way."

"Without a doubt." He waved his fingers in a give-it-here gesture.

She shook her head. "I'll place it on airplane mode and turn it off. Tomorrow, go somewhere random, and I'll turn it on."

Disco lowered his hand. "Why take the risk? It's just a phone."

"Because everyone disappeared tonight."

"And?"

"Whoever made them disappear will reach out to me. I need to be able to take that call." Being cut off from her friends if they tried to text or call wouldn't help get them back. Out here, tonight, she felt truly alone for the first time in a long time. Alone, angry, and despondent. And whatever happened to Aaron and Willow? Why weren't they at the square? Or did they show up, and those military men were holding them? "Did your team see Aaron and Willow at all tonight?"

Disco shook his head. "They would've called that in if they had."

"They may be missing, too."

Disco watched her for a moment, then faced the road. "I'm sorry, Sarah. We'll figure this all out."

She nodded, even though he wasn't looking at her anymore.

"Tomorrow," he added. "Tomorrow's another day."

Chapter 11

AARON CLUTCHED HIS DAUGHTER'S hand as they led them down the tenth-floor corridor of a hotel. They hadn't left them alone for a second, giving him no chance to speak privately with Willow. Attempting to fight this many men was a wasted effort. Even if he could hurt a couple of them, he'd be subdued in seconds as these men were highly trained and on full alert, not to mention fully armed. Questions raced through his mind about who they were and what they would want.

It had to do with Sarah. Of this, he had no doubt. Likely, she'd pissed someone off, someone powerful, and this was vengeance being served. Would these men involve Willow, though? Hurt a child? If so, they were monsters, and he'd die to protect her.

And Sarah be damned for it all.

But for now, he went with the flow and paid attention.

A keycard guarded access to this floor of the hotel. Getting a keycard would be important. A well-placed knife could extract the key code from someone who wanted to live.

The hotel was a popular destination in Toronto. It carried a reputation. The Royal Oak had to extend a courtesy to these men to rent them the entire floor. This led him to assume they were government officials. They were certainly trained like the military.

But if they were government men, how many laws had they broken by abducting him and his daughter?

Near the end of the hall, two huge men stood on either side of a hotel room, staring straight ahead at nothing.

The leader waved for them to enter the room. "Please, this will be your home for now."

Aaron stopped at the threshold, standing between the two burly men on either side. "If we refuse?" He tightened his jaw and pressed his lips together, waiting for an answer.

The leader glanced down at Willow, then back to Aaron. "I think you have to ask yourself what sort of memory of this short visit you would like to give your daughter."

Aaron didn't answer.

The leader continued. "You must always weigh things, Mr. Stevens. A few days of inconvenience or a few months in a hospital." The man's chiseled face softened, and Aaron was sure there was a hint of a smirk at the edge of his mouth. "I wonder what sort of test you'd offer my men." He shook his head. "In any event, we're prepared for all resistance." The man's face returned to its previous hardness—all business again. "Get in the room, Mr. Stevens, and enjoy a few free nights away from your stressful life."

"On whose wallet?" Aaron moved just inside the hotel room. "I'd sure like to thank the people or organization footing this bill."

"I'll pass along your sentiments." A phone rang, and the leader slipped a hand behind him, producing a cell. He read the screen, and his face changed again. This time, he looked furious. "Lock them up," he barked, already tapping a number into his phone. "No one in or out. On my orders."

The man stepped away from the door, the phone going to his ear. "How could this happen?" he said into the phone. "How did she get away?"

That had to be about Sarah. She was pissing them off.

The door closed behind him as Willow yawned and moved over to one of the two beds.

"Can we sleep now, Daddy?"

"Of course, honey. Crawl into bed. Then I have a question for you."

Willow nodded, the small curls in her hair bobbing with the movement of her head.

While she got settled, Aaron tried to open the door, but it wouldn't budge. The keycard would be needed on this side, too. They were veritable prisoners until someone let them out.

He moved to the window and saw they were ten stories up with no balcony and no way to scale the outside wall.

Willow crawled under the covers as Aaron opened the small fridge. It had been stocked with sandwiches, juice, water, apples, several small whiskey bottles, and two little red wine bottles. Behind the apples, he found four cans of beer.

Why not? It'll be a long night.

He grabbed a beer and turned back to Willow. Her little head was on the pillow, her eyes shut.

"Honey," he said softly. "You still awake?"

"Hmm, hmmm." Willow moaned the words.

He sipped the beer and moved closer. "Can I ask you one question before you sleep?"

"Hmmm."

"Why didn't you stop those men from taking us? You could've *done* things to them."

"Because there are too many of them."

Aaron frowned and sat on the bed across from Willow's. "Too many? I saw no more than six, plus the men guarding the room here at the hotel."

Willow's head shook back and forth on the pillow. "There are lots, Daddy—maybe thousands. I don't want to hurt everyone. This is better."

Thousands? What the fuck?

"Mommy is working on it. She'll figure it all out. People might die." Her voice got weaker as sleep took over.

A shot of anxiety burst through his stomach. "People might die?"

"Sleepy, Daddy," she whispered, her voice so soft now. "We're okay for tonight. Tomorrow, everything changes, I think."

"You think?"

"I can't see too far. I just know tonight isn't dangerous ..." her voice trailed off, then she added, "for us."

"Sleep, honey. We can talk in the morning."

Aaron gulped back the rest of the beer, then went to the fridge and pulled out the whiskey. He'd need something more substantial to get any sleep.

Tomorrow was another day, another fight.

Who were these thousands of men? How did Sarah get on their radar? What was going to happen to them all?

He moved to the window and stared out at Toronto at night. After one pull on the small whiskey bottle, he thought about Benjamin.

How many more of his close-knit group of friends had to die to further Sarah's aims?

How many had to die for her to keep *saving* people?

Chapter 12

SARAH ROLLED OFF THE bed and flattened her feet on the polished wooden floor. The sun peeked through the white lace curtains. It had to be at least six in the morning, but she had no way of knowing. She didn't sleep well, drifting in and out, but she couldn't lie in bed any longer.

When they got to Disco's place in Hamilton late last night, she'd entered the home off Upper James and Garth in a daze. So much had happened last night, from Amanda's aborted abduction to having her friends and mother go off the radar—even Aaron and Willow. Distraught with worry as she told Disco everything, he sent one of his men to the Square to see if Aaron ever showed up, and the other man to watch the Royal Oak Hotel. They'd reported nothing before Sarah had fallen asleep from exhaustion.

Disco had convinced her that searching for everyone when she was that tired wouldn't help. The professionals they were up against would either kill her or capture her within an hour of remaining in Toronto. Also, Disco was a colleague no one knew about, an extension of Darwin that didn't exist on paper, a variable they couldn't account for. Sarah had previously worked with Disco, but they only spoke through encrypted means and rarely met in public.

So, it made sense that whoever was after Sarah had taken everyone she knew—but they were unaware of Disco. Which meant that, as powerful as they were, they wouldn't know he lived in Hamilton. Besides, even if they suspected as much, the house wasn't in his name. Ownership was protected by several layers of corporations and a company operating in a European country. Even if top government officials attempted to hunt down the ownership of his house, they'd hit dead ends with privacy laws and end up with companies that didn't even exist.

Sarah pulled back the curtains. Maybe it was seven in the morning. She'd slept longer than she wanted. With Willow missing—she may not be missing, but Sarah had no idea where she was—she wanted to get a head start on the day.

Vivian hadn't been back in touch yet. Sarah wasn't in the mood to talk to her, so she didn't reach out. Her sister—if it were her sister talking to her all this time—would be in touch with Amanda's whereabouts soon enough.

Sarah pushed herself up off the bed and opened the spare bedroom door. The smell of food cooking wafted up to her. There was no need to be quiet. Her rescuer from last night was in the kitchen making breakfast.

She used the bathroom and then made her way downstairs.

"Morning," Disco said when she entered the kitchen. "Bacon and eggs over-easy coming up."

Sarah nodded and took a seat at the table. She rubbed her face and glanced around, really seeing the kitchen in the morning's light. "Does a chef live here?"

"You're looking at him."

The walls were adorned with food art. Gold-colored pots and pans were suspended above a yellow Spanish-style wall unit that filled the far side of the room. The cutting board was still on the counter where he'd chopped green onions and grated cheese for the eggs. On the left was a coffeemaker, the pot warm and full.

"Please pour me a cup when you get yours." He nodded at the coffee.

Sarah pushed up from the table and approached the counter that appeared to be made of one-inch granite.

"Mugs are above the coffee."

She opened a cupboard and saw a collection of matching mugs, choosing two large brown ones.

"Cream is in the fridge, sugar on the counter."

"I take mine black."

"Me too."

A minute later, seated at the table sipping coffee, Disco placed a plate in front of her. It was more than she'd eat for breakfast on any given day, and she was about to protest when he pushed the plate closer to her.

"Eat up—all of it. You'll need your strength. Today, we'll be hunting the fuckers who went after you last night and looking for your friends. Then we will pick up Darwin at the airport tonight. We'll be out all day." He shrugged. "Shit, we may not even have the time to go through a drive-thru, so have more coffee while you can."

He sat opposite her and dove into his eggs. Without protest, she took her fork and cut the yokes free from the whites, then placed the unbroken yoke on her fork and set it on her tongue. Bursting it whole in her mouth was a taste explosion.

"You don't eat the whites?"

She shook her head. "No real nutritional value."

"I spiced them up, though."

She cut a corner of the whites and placed one in her mouth to be polite. Then, she scrunched up her face at him and shook her head.

"Give 'em to me, then. Don't waste that shit."

She tilted her plate over his, shoveling the whites off, then gladly ate the bacon he'd cooked to perfection.

"Thank you."

He shrugged. "Anytime. As you can see, I love to cook."

"Thank you for everything. For pulling me out of that shit last night."

He stopped chewing and stared at her across the table. After a moment, he started chewing again.

"I'll always be there for you, Sarah. Darwin, too." He looked down at his plate and forked the last of the whites. "You guys are family to me now."

To avoid him seeing the tear that leaped to her eye, she glanced around the kitchen and rubbed her face again. Then she jumped up from the table and poured herself some more coffee.

"Want some?"

"Sure, top it up."

She filled his cup, placed the pot back, and then moved to the kitchen window, her cup in hand. "You have such a nice place." She sipped some coffee and swallowed. "I had no idea you were into cooking."

"How could you? With the money I make, there's only so much I can spend it on without getting too much attention. So I had this place renovated to match my hobby, which is cooking."

She turned to face him. "I'm impressed. Would've never guessed."

He set his fork down and wiped at his mouth. "I once knew a fellow merc who was into building model airplanes from World War II. He showed me pictures once. His pride and joy was a huge replica of a P51D Mustang that he flew in airshows. I once knew another guy who killed bad guys at night, then spent all his money on fishing trips, always searching for the best fishing spots, the best lures, the biggest catch." He lifted one shoulder. "Everyone's into something. Keeps us human."

"And sane?"

"That too." Disco got up from the table and set the plates by the sink. "Ready to hit the road?"

"Where are we going first?"

"To a coffee shop in Milton to turn on your phone and check for messages, then to your apartment to see what we can find out. After that, we'll plan our next move based on what we learn or don't learn."

Sarah nodded. "Give me five minutes to shower."

"I already placed a new towel out for you."

Sarah started for the stairs, coffee mug in hand. "I saw it. Thanks."

Fifteen minutes later, they were on the 403 headed to Oakville, where they'd access Highway 25 to go north to Milton.

Disco glanced over at her. "This is probably a dumb question, but can you tell me why the US military is interested in you?"

Sarah stared out at a rig passing them. "It's not a dumb question. I just don't have an answer."

They rode in silence for several minutes, Sarah rolling her cell phone in her hands mindlessly.

"It could be something from my past," she added.

"Could be? Like what?"

She shrugged and glanced down at her lap. "A group this organized and powerful came after me once in Europe."

"Europe?" Disco blurted. "The US military?"

"I was in Hungary looking for the man who killed my sister."

Another gasp from Disco. "Wait, isn't that the one who speaks to you?"

She stared out the window to her right. "Long story." There was silence between them for a moment, and Sarah broke it. "Perhaps one day I can tell you more about my past, but it seems that era is coming back to haunt me."

"How so?"

"When I filled you in last night about everything that had happened, you might recall that my mother thinks my dead sister is alive?"

He nodded. "Could that be possible? I mean, even remotely possible?"

"Not at all—well, I was so young when she died that I don't remember her."

"And you didn't see the body?"

"Hell no," Sarah snapped.

"Right, so you *can't* know that she's dead. I mean, without a doubt."

"Sure, I can."

"How's that?"

"Then where the hell has she been for thirty years?"

"A lot of people take off, disappear. Some never pop back up. What if this is your sister, and she's looking for a little family reunion? It would make sense to reach out to your mother first. Get her blessing, then ease in with the rest of the family."

Sarah shook her head. "I don't believe it. I don't buy it. Someone's playing a game with my mom."

"What could they expect to gain? Are your parents rich?"

"My parents are not rich, and what do these people expect to gain? That's something I have no idea about. We can ask them when we find them because I intend to stop them and whatever it is they're doing."

After another moment of silence, Disco said, "A moment ago, you said something about a group this powerful coming at you in Hungary. What else can you tell me?"

"They were a group funded by the US government called the Sophia Project. A man named Rod Howley was in charge."

"And what were they all about?"

"They studied people with psychic ability."

"Studied voluntarily? Or abducted, and the victim became their guinea pig?"

Sarah stared at him. "What makes you say that?"

"Well, if this is a similar group, they weren't knocking at your door asking for you to sign up and let them do a few tests. These men were there to take you down."

Sarah nodded a few times, her leg bouncing with anxiety just thinking about last night. "Yeah, that would be the Sophia Project men. They take what they want."

"How come they didn't *take* you all those years ago?"

"Rod Howley was killed."

"Ouch." Disco looked at her, then turned back to the road. "Surely he had a replacement."

"He did. I seem to recall that guy's name was Hank something. He's gone, too. They fucked up a lot of shit, and the project died."

"Or did *you* fuck up their shit, and the project died?"

A memory surfaced of how Rod Howley had felt about her and how he'd told Drake Bellamy his thoughts before he died. Rod had even tried to bargain for Sarah's safety in the end, but the Rapturites killed him in a mall in Toronto. She'd barely survived that day.

"You think this Sophia Project group is back?" Disco asked.

Sarah shook her head again. "No, they're gone. It's been over a decade since I heard anything from them. I'm just saying they were as organized as this group is, as powerful, that's all."

"What if they're back?"

"No way, uh uh. Couldn't be, or I'd have to hurt a lot of people."

"Okay, sounds like you have two scenarios to think about."

Sarah twisted in her seat to look at Disco, uncomfortable with what she suspected he was about to say. "Go ahead. Break them down for me."

"The first one is someone claiming your sister is alive. She's either alive or she isn't. If she isn't, then who's fucking with you and why? The second one is, who were these men after you last night? Are they as powerful and organized as the Sophia Project guys? Enough to actually *be* them?" Disco cleared his throat. "If they're something else, then what? That's two dead entities that have come back to life—potentially."

When Sarah didn't answer right away, he asked another question.

"Did your sister possess clairvoyant talents of any kind?"

Sarah nodded. "As far as I know, yes. My parents had a time capsule thing they opened years ago. Inside were prophecies from Vivian."

"Did they come true?"

"They did."

"What if this Sophia group went after her back in the day?"

Sarah looked straight ahead. "Shit, I hadn't thought of that."

"What if they faked *her* death to own her, possess her? And now that she's in her forties, she's free and reaching out to family. It could be that simple. Who knows."

"Then why would they come after me last night?"

"Maybe your sister *broke* out, and you'd be the bait to lure her back in. Or they're trying to get to you so they can set a trap when she contacts you."

Sarah fumbled with her phone again. A memory surfaced like a rake scraping across the detritus of her brain. Her hands dropped the phone as she went numb with the thought.

"Hey, what happened? You okay?"

"Back when they took me," she said, her voice monotone as she worked through the memory, "they faked my death in a car accident. The car was destroyed. My DNA was all over it. When I got free of those maniacs, I had to call my mom and dad and tell them I was okay and wasn't dead. It was a difficult time for them."

"Damn, you may have figured it all out. What if the Sophia Project assholes faked your sister's death, too? And here we are, with everybody back from the dead, haunting you in real-time."

Sarah stared at nothing for a long moment, her mouth open, then leaned down to pick up her phone. "That is one scary thought. If it's them, I'm completely screwed." She thought of Willow and wondered what they'd do to her if they knew all of her talents.

"We'll figure something out. Let's talk to Darwin when we pick him up at the airport tonight, then regroup and solve this thing. Although we may not have to wait that long."

"Why's that?"

"They'll likely be in touch before then, or they're already following us."

Sarah nodded and rolled her phone in her hands as she stared outside at the passing landscape, her eyes going from the mirror to the windshield, then back to the mirror. Aaron and Willow were missing from last night. What if they already got to them?

She fought the urge to turn on her phone to see if there were any messages from Aaron.

Neither one spoke again until Disco pulled into a gas station in Milton.

"This pig sucks a whore-ton of gas. Do you want a Coke? Need to use the can or something to munch on? Now's the time. When we pull out of here, we'll drive to the exit, then turn on your phone. That work for you?"

Sarah nodded and jumped out of the Hummer to use the toilet, her stomach roiling at the thought that the Sophia Project men were back in her life. Hoping that wasn't the case didn't make it so. She just wished it were something else.

But for some reason, that felt like the most plausible scenario.

What if they had Willow?

If they did, the chances of her ever seeing her daughter again were slim to none.

And that thought was enough to make her want to murder every one of them ten times over.

They'd learn to never come between a mother and her child.

They'd chosen the hard way, and she'd be much obliged.

Chapter 13

AARON BARELY SLEPT THROUGHOUT the night, tossing and turning, all the old fears rising to the surface. Everything he had been trying to avoid kept showing up on his doorstep, and yet, just like in the old days, he'd deal with it and move on. What choice did he have?

Why couldn't things change now that Willow was in their lives? That's not how Sarah saw it, though. She led them to this, whatever this was. Even if she didn't piss off some prominent government official, even if she had no idea what this was all about, it was all on her doorstep. Government-type military men in black SUVs don't abduct people on a routine basis. No, this had Sarah written all over it.

He stared out the hotel window as the sun rose above the Toronto skyline, with Willow still sleeping behind him. The days of him taking risks were over. Strategizing an escape with a young girl was madness —unless Willow were willing to help—and would put her in harm's way.

They had no choice but to see what these men wanted and then work from there.

Last night, Willow said there were thousands of them. If she hurt them, more would come, and it would never end. She also said that they were safe for the night.

Did that mean something would happen today?

When a knock sounded from the hotel room door, Aaron launched at least a foot off the carpeted floor, landing in his full stance, arms up. A second later, he relaxed his stance and moved toward the door, his heart tripling in speed.

"Yeah?" he said by the crack in the door. "I can't open it from this side."

The lock clicked, and the door moved an inch inward.

He stepped back and met the eyes of the leader guy from last night.

"Breakfast is being delivered in fifteen minutes. After you eat, how long before you can both be ready?"

"Ready? For what?"

The door opened farther, and the man glanced past Aaron at Willow.

"Her grandmother wants to visit."

Their eyes met, and Aaron crossed his arms over his chest, lowered his head, and stared at the man in charge. "Are you saying Sarah's mother is here?"

The man nodded. "In the flesh."

"And you're going to let her visit us?"

The man watched Aaron for a moment, his expression blank, and then he nodded. "Of course. Why wouldn't we?"

Aaron shook his head. "Forgive me if I don't understand what's happening here, but none of this makes any sense."

The man backed into the hallway. "It'll all be clear soon enough. I'm not at liberty to explain anything, but I will tell you this isn't what you think it is."

Aaron angled away from the man and dropped his arms to his sides. "And what do I think it is?"

"An abduction. Something negative, like we aim to do you harm."

"You don't call what you did to us an abduction?"

The man's face broke into a smile, startling Aaron. That hard veneer cracked, and the military man appeared friendly. "No, this is more like a family reunion."

One of the sentries on either side of the door eased it shut.

"Eat breakfast when it gets here," the man's voice came through the door. "Shower. Clean up. Do what you want, but be ready to visit Sarah's mother shortly after that."

Aaron shook his head, trying to figure everything out. Sarah's mother had been looking after Willow last night. They could've easily met at Sarah's place if she wanted to see them or have some kind of reunion. None of this was making any sense.

He turned around to wake Willow, but she was already sitting up in bed, rubbing her eyes.

"Did that man wake you?"

She nodded.

"They're bringing breakfast, and then your grandmother is coming to see us."

Willow tossed aside the covers and hopped off the bed. Aaron marveled at how mature she was for such a tiny girl.

"They called it a family reunion," Aaron added. "Did you hear that?"

Willow nodded as she glanced out the window. "Daddy, we are so high up."

"Indeed, we are, little one." He moved to stand beside her, resting a hand on her shoulder. "Do you know anything, Willow? Is there anything you can tell me?"

She looked up at him, sleep making her eyes wide and round. "I know what family reunion means." Willow turned and headed toward the bathroom.

"Yeah, meeting Sarah's mother is what he meant."

She stopped at the bathroom door and looked back at him, shaking her little head. "No, Daddy, he meant something else." She flicked on the light.

Aaron frowned at her. "What on earth could he have possibly meant?"

"Vivian, Mommy's sister, is alive, and Grandma met her. It's been a long time. They brought our friends so Aunt Vivian could meet us without upsetting anyone."

Then Willow stepped inside the bathroom and closed the door, leaving Aaron staring after her. His mouth fell open, and a cold sweat broke out on his arms and neck as he reached up to touch his parted lips.

As a heavy feeling hit his stomach, he found his voice. "Holy. Shit."

Chapter 14

AFTER GASSING UP THE Hummer, they drove to another gas station just off the highway, keeping clear of the pumps and the main building. He brought the Hummer to a stop on the side of the exit ramp that would take them back onto the highway.

"Okay, turn on your phone and kill airplane mode. Once that's done, any messages will populate, but whoever's tracking you will see where we are. I'd say we have five minutes max, maybe even three."

Sarah held onto her cell phone, finger on the power button. "You think they can get here in that kind of time?"

"Not at all." Disco shook his head. "But a group this powerful will call to see if a police cruiser is close by and have one at this gas station in minutes if we're that unlucky. So far, they don't know about me or my vehicle, and I aim to keep it that way."

Sarah nodded and pushed the button. Her phone went through its procedures and then asked her to enter the access code. She typed it in, then turned off airplane mode.

The second her phone acquired a signal, two things happened. One, Disco began a countdown, and two, her phone dinged with about a dozen messages.

She opened them frantically, searching for a familiar number, a name, but they all seemed to be from private numbers, which confirmed her worst fears—no one had called her back from last night. Aaron hadn't reached out, Parkman hadn't messaged her, no one.

"What the hell?" she whispered. "That's a lot of private messages."

Facebook Messenger had a red number on it. She wasn't a frequent user of Messenger but opened it anyway.

That was where they'd reached out to her.

"Why would they do that?" she said out loud.

"What happened?" Disco asked.

"Looks like I heard from my mother, Aaron, Parkman, and Daniel on Messenger."

"No, Alex?"

She shook her head.

"Perhaps they didn't nab him." Disco jerked his head once. "What'd they say?"

"I'll open Aaron's message first." She read it and frowned. "This doesn't sound like him."

"What'd he say?"

"To meet him and my mother at the Royal Oak Hotel. They've got great news."

"Do you think that's legit? Or more of those Sophia Project people trying to lure you in?"

Sarah glanced over at Disco and shook her head. "Aaron wouldn't use Messenger. If he did, he wouldn't write to me like this. He'd tell me more. We were supposed to meet at Roy Thompson Hall last night, at that square. He'd at least apologize for not being there and explain what happened. He wouldn't stand me up and then just send a message telling me to meet him in a hotel." She looked back at the messages. "This is too vague and not Aaron's style at all." She scrolled through the messages. "Parkman, Daniel, and my mom's messages all ask the same thing. Everyone wants to meet there." She wiped her eyes. "This makes me feel sick." She faced Disco. "Whoever has them is using their phones to entice me to come to that fucking hotel. Why?"

Disco ignored her question. "There was no mention of Vivian?"

Sarah shook her head. "None."

She closed Messenger and opened iMessage to read the private messages. "These all seem to be coming from the same place, but there's no number."

"What are they saying?" Disco asked, leaning over the center console to get a better look.

"I'll read it to you. It says, We didn't mean to startle you last night. This is a highly sensitive matter, and you must meet us so we can discuss it. We regret the loss of life, as we lost one man trying to bring you in. Your friends surprised us. We didn't expect that level of resistance. We'd kindly ask you to call off the attack dogs and come for a meeting willingly. We will guarantee your safety, and you may leave at any time. Think of it as a meet-and-greet. Once we explain everything, we feel you'll be happy you chose to come in. Respond to this message, and we'll send pictures to reassure you of our intentions."

Sarah looked up to stare out the windshield. "That's it. They sent the same message once an hour for the past twelve hours."

"Okay, respond to them, then kill the phone again." Disco was staring into the rearview mirror. "When we get close to your place in an hour or so, we can turn it on once more and see these pictures they want to send."

Sarah typed, then read it out loud. "I'll consider your invitation. Send the pictures." Then she turned the airplane mode back on and powered down the phone.

She set the phone into the cupholder. "It's done. Message sent, phone off."

Disco hit the gas, and they rocketed out of the gas station. Sarah wondered what she'd find at the hotel and also wondered why they, whoever they were, didn't come out of hiding last night when she meandered through the lobby. She was already in the hotel. Why not approach her and have that "meeting" then?

It seemed like a safe enough place. It was a popular hotel in the center of downtown Toronto. What could they do to her?

Then she reminded herself that if it was the Sophia Project men, they could do a lot to her. They could march her right out the hotel's front door in handcuffs, and people would just think plainclothes officers were arresting her. The hotel would be paid some handsome figure to forget whatever happened, and the world would move on without Sarah.

She could not have known their potential if it weren't for the Sophia Project people. From last night's example, they were well-organized and possibly used American military men to fulfill some kind of contract.

No matter how she looked at it, walking voluntarily into a meeting at the hotel felt like a mistake.

"What are you thinking?" Disco asked.

She snapped out of her reverie and glanced at him. "Just that I could never go to any meet-and-greet they're proposing. That would be too dangerous. I'd be putting them in control of the outcome."

"If you want to meet them, you pick the place. Like, meet at gate C34 in the Toronto Airport in two hours."

She frowned, then understood. "Right, they'd have to go through security, which means they'd be relieved of all their weapons. And two hours wouldn't be enough time to file any sort of paperwork to get them clearance to come in armed."

"Or tell them to meet on the GO train passing through Pickering. We watch the train from the outside, taking photos of everyone. By the time the train stops *after* Pickering, and they think you stood them up, we know how many are on the train and assess how big a threat it is to you. Then you can meet them on the platform as they exit. I'd even have Ape and Water join them on the train to watch them. The point is, you control the narrative, not them."

She frowned at those names, then nodded. "I like that. The airport is my preferred method. Or better yet," she snapped sideways to look at him, "we wear fantastic disguises and check into the hotel as a couple on our honeymoon. Then we have dinner there, have drinks, and investigate the place on our own."

He glanced sidelong at her. "That's even better. I like that idea. Walk right into the bee's nest. I've even got a disguise guy, too. When he's done with you, no one will recognize you."

"Okay, we'll check out my place, get those pictures they want to send, then decide our next move. So far, checking into the Royal Oak Hotel as a married couple on their honeymoon sounds like the best bet."

Disco nodded. "Even better," he said, his voice raised, one finger in the air to punctuate his thought.

"What's even better?"

"We get done up this afternoon and then pick up Darwin at the airport. Let's see if he recognizes us. That would be the real test if the disguises were solid."

"I want to see these pictures they promised before we decide either way."

"That works."

Her hand numbed like it hadn't in a long time.

Vivian?

Whoever had occupied her head for almost two decades entered her consciousness and told her where to find Amanda and why the teenager would be there. Then she heard the time.

"Wait, that's when we're supposed to pick up Darwin," Sarah said out loud.

"What?" Disco asked, glancing over at her, then back to the road.

Sarah shook her head. "Sorry, I just heard where Amanda will be tonight."

"Amanda? How does she fit into all this again?"

Sarah looked at Disco as the entity in her head drifted off. "I'm not entirely sure, but I understand she holds the key to something."

"Didn't you say she was a seventeen-year-old girl?"

Sarah nodded. "I did."

"And you want to kidnap this girl?"

Sarah kept nodding.

"Even though we have enough to go on, and you're in touch with these people?"

"Listening to my sister—or whoever the hell's in my head—has saved my life more times than I can count. Just because someone's claiming that my sister's alive, whether true or not, doesn't change my trust in that voice. I might get angry at that voice and tell her to go away and stop talking to me, I've even drank the voice out of my head in the past, but the only reason I'm ever in these messes is that I listen to that voice."

"Okay, where will Amanda be, and when?"

"At the train station, heading out of town."

"Just out of town? That's all you got? Isn't she here with her parents?"

Sarah straightened up in her seat and rubbed the tops of her thighs. "I'm getting that her parents are separated, and she wants to go live with her dad. But getting as far away from her mother is a start."

"Who's her mother?"

Sarah shook her head. "Don't know that yet."

"Won't she be surrounded by those security men you encountered last night in Oshawa?"

"Not tonight. She will have escaped her security detail, then that's when we step in."

"What time tonight?"

"Just after seven this evening."

"Shit, that'll spread us thin."

"You handle Darwin. Leave Amanda to me."

"Can't say I like that." He shook his head and waved his right hand back and forth. "No, I'll call my guys from last night. Ape and Water can meet Darwin, and I'll come with you."

"Then it's settled."

They looked at each other.

"I guess so," Disco said, turning onto Sarah's street. "Why do we need Amanda again?"

"I don't have all the details. Just that she is a key to what's happening somehow."

"And you don't know her parents?"

Sarah shook her head. "No idea who they are."

"Well, they have to be someone important. Otherwise, who would have two cars filled with armed men to protect her?"

"True."

"Start thinking about these things. Talk to that voice. Find out who she is before we grab her if you can."

Sarah nodded, knowing she'd hear from that voice when that voice was good and ready to talk.

Disco continued. "Let's go check your place, then turn on your phone. I'm eager to see the pictures they offered to send. But first, follow my lead if they're watching your place."

"You think they're that serious? That they have that much manpower?"

Disco lifted one shoulder in a noncommittal shrug. "The guys we danced with last night," he shook his head, "you can never be too sure."

An hour later, he eased the Hummer by her townhouse complex, then drove around the block. They made another pass before he stopped and parked on the street.

After studying car after car, he faced her. "Follow my lead." He opened the glove box, snapped a side drawer open, then withdrew a small pistol and handed it to her. "It's loaded, and the serial number has been removed. Use this one, not the one you're carrying. Shoot to kill if they're firing at you."

"I don't need to be told twice."

"Then let's go."

They hopped out of the Hummer at the same time and advanced on Sarah's townhouse.

Chapter 15

BREAKFAST WAS SERVED, AND after a quick shower, someone knocked on the hotel room door again. There was a ten-second delay; then the door popped open.

"Hello? I'm coming in." Someone eased inside. A man dressed in a white shirt and bow tie, with black pants and shiny black shoes, said, "I'm here to take the dishes away."

"They're on that stand by the door." Aaron pointed.

The man stacked everything onto a tray, lifted it with practiced grace, and then the door was pushed open for him to exit.

"Aaron?" A familiar voice came from behind the door. "Willow?" Sarah's mother, Amelia, slipped inside the room, her face flushed red with life. She looked genuinely happy. "How's my sweet pea?"

"I'm good," Willow said with a shrug. "Just bored."

Aaron waited while they hugged, a thousand questions crossing his mind. The leader man stepped in and closed the door. He rested his back against the door and watched Amelia and Willow.

How could Aaron have a private conversation with Amelia while this man stood over them, watching them?

Aaron moved toward him and saw the man tense, ready for whatever Aaron might do.

"Give me a name," Aaron said.

"Excuse me?"

"What do I call you?"

"How about Tom?"

"Tom?"

The man nodded. "Tom works."

"Okay, Tom, it is."

Aaron turned back to see Amelia whispering to Willow on Willow's bed. "What's this?"

"This?"

He turned back to face Tom. "Why are you guys doing this? What's the purpose of bringing us here to meet Amelia when we could've done that at home?"

"We've already talked about it, didn't we? Before breakfast. Do you remember the part where I said this was a family reunion, not an abduction? I told you it would all be clear soon."

"So this is the family reunion part of the tour?" When Tom didn't respond, Aaron pushed on. "How exactly will it be clear? What could you possibly be hiding to have this all make sense?"

Tom met his gaze. "Just listen to what Amelia has to say. Then you'll see why you're here and how it all makes sense."

"And if we want to leave? What happens if we want to go home? Your boys will just open all the doors?"

Tom's expression tightened. "That won't happen until tomorrow at the earliest."

"Then tell me who else you have here. How about Sarah? Is she here? Parkman? Anyone else?"

Tom raised a hand to pat Aaron's shoulder, but Aaron knocked it aside.

"Don't *fucking* touch me, or we'll have a problem," Aaron whispered under his breath. "My tolerance for this shit is gone. Nobody toys with my family."

Tom eased back, his eyes still on Aaron's. "We are done talking. Step back several feet and listen to Amelia, then make up your own mind." Tom looked away, staring blankly toward the room's large window.

Aaron waited a few heartbeats, then moved over and sat on his bed, watching Amelia with his daughter. He didn't want to interrupt their little meeting, so he watched them talk until Amelia glanced up at him and wiped a tear.

"I have good news—scratch that. I've got *amazing* news."

Aaron glanced at Tom, but he hadn't wavered from staring at the window. He turned back to Amelia and leaned in closer. "What's the news?" He didn't want to say what Willow had told him earlier about Sarah's sister being alive, figuring it would be better for Amelia to tell him.

"Vivian's alive."

He had to act surprised, so he reared back, tilted his head sideways, leaned forward again, and in a conspiratorial whisper, said, "No way!

How's that possible?" He shot a look at Willow, who was also trying to be surprised.

"I saw her with my own eyes." Amelia took Aaron's hands in hers. "I can't believe it."

"But how can you be sure?"

"We spoke about everything. She remembered some of the things we did together when she was a kid before she went missing. She's been watching us from afar, too. But the people she works for couldn't tell us she was alive."

"And why's that?"

"It's a top-secret government thing. She couldn't tell me much, but she explained that her unique talents gave her a good life. I'm just so overwhelmed she's alive."

Aaron stared at Amelia for a long moment, then asked, "Why would they fake her death if she was alive? I mean, if some government agency wanted her for some experiment, why not approach you and Caleb and discuss it?"

"I know it's hard to take all of a sudden, but Aaron, I saw her. This is one-thousand percent my daughter, Vivian. As a mother, I just know."

Movement in his peripheral vision made him turn to look at Tom.

The man had Aaron's phone out, and Tom was snapping pictures of them as far as he could tell. Then the phone disappeared back into Tom's pocket.

Aaron got to his feet. "You going to give that back?"

Tom stared down at him. "When you all head home tomorrow, your possessions will be returned to you." Tom spun around, swiped something in his hand against the door, then opened it.

As he stepped out into the hotel corridor, Aaron fought the urge to make a run for it, already knowing how futile that was with the amount of armed security Tom had as backup, not to mention he wouldn't leave Willow behind.

He turned back to Amelia. "You'll have to forgive me. I don't believe Vivian miraculously appeared out of thin air after all this time."

"Oh, Aaron, that's okay. I understand. It'll take time for everyone to come on board."

"How does Sarah feel about it? What's she saying? Have they met yet?"

Amelia shook her head slightly, her eyes darting to the door and then to Aaron. "When Sarah gets here, the sisters will talk, and then you can take Sarah's word for it."

Did they try to abduct Sarah and miss? "Why all this abduction business then?" Aaron asked loud enough for Tom to hear. "Why not have Vivian come to the house and knock on the front door?"

Amelia patted Willow's knee. "That would be too dramatic, too sudden—"

"And abduction isn't?" Aaron dropped to sit on the bed, bouncing once. "I'm sorry. This isn't your fault. I shouldn't be snapping at you."

"It's okay, Daddy," Willow said. "Mommy's coming to see her sister soon." She offered him a warm smile. Nothing ever seemed to rattle Willow.

If this *person* was, in fact, Vivian, then who was Sarah listening to all this time in her head? That thought sent a shiver through him.

Could the sisters be clairvoyant in the true definition, and Vivian just got caught up with these government people all those years ago? What would that do to Sarah's parents, to Sarah?

But seriously—who the hell was Sarah hearing in her head?

Chapter 16

SARAH STAYED TWO STEPS behind Disco as they approached the front door of her townhouse, both of them watching their backs. They'd done a basic amount of reconnoitering and were confident that no one lurked in the shadows or sat in nearby cars on this sunny early afternoon. With the goal of entering Sarah's townhouse foremost, they headed across the grass from the sidewalk, both of them pulling out their pistols as they approached the door.

Disco pointed at the deadbolt on the door for Sarah to use her keys, then eased to the side.

Instead of reaching for her keys, she thought she'd just try the door. Hand on the knob, she twisted it, and the door opened.

They exchanged a knowing glance, then Disco put his shoulder into the door and bolted inside, hunched over. Sarah entered behind him, her right arm tucked in close to her chest.

Disco had run through the kitchen, turned to the living room, and headed for the hallway leading to the bedrooms. When Sarah followed him down the hall, he stepped out of the master bedroom and lowered his weapon.

"Clear. No one's here."

"Why would Aaron or my mother leave the door unlocked?"

Disco jerked his head toward Willow's room. "They left in a hurry."

Sarah peeked inside and saw Willow's closet open and two of her dresser drawers. She moved to the bathroom. The toothbrushes, toothpaste, and Q-Tips were gone.

"Aaron packed fast to meet me at the square last night."

"And left the door unlocked?"

Sarah moved back to the living room. "They never made it to the square." Her chest wrenched at the thought of where they could be as she let out a frustrated huff. "You don't suppose those men in the square have them, do you?"

Disco nodded, a grim expression on his face. "Aaron's a solid fighter, but a little girl will weigh you down."

"Weigh him down?" Sarah frowned. "His own daughter?"

"Think about it. He can fight two or three men alone and then run. Having to take care of Willow means he has to consider her. He can't just bolt down a nearby alleyway. I'm just saying there's more to account for."

She nodded, glancing around the apartment. Nothing else looked disturbed. "You're right. It just didn't sound good."

"True. When kids are involved, it's never good."

"That helps."

"Sorry," he said, mock indignation in his voice. "Look, turn on your phone in here, check all messages, and then let's leave. If they're tracking you, they'll see you are home now." Disco moved toward the door. "I'll watch our backs. Hurry."

Sarah got her phone powered up, turned off airplane mode, and saw little red numbers populate on iMessage and Messenger. She opened Messenger and saw more messages from loved ones—seemingly fake—imploring her to reach out soon. There was still nothing from Alex.

Then she opened iMessage and gasped, a hand going to her mouth.

"What?" Disco asked from the open front door.

Sarah moved closer and held out the phone for him to see. It was a photo of her mother sitting beside Willow, with Aaron sitting opposite them in what looked like a hotel room at the Royal Oak Hotel.

She angled the phone back to read the message out loud.

"It says, Everyone is safe and waiting for you to come and celebrate the good news. Message us back to arrange a meeting." She activated airplane mode, then turned off the phone. "The photo was time-stamped an hour ago."

Disco moved outside, and Sarah followed, closing and locking the door behind her.

"We need inside that hotel." Disco was already pulling out his phone. "Get in the Hummer, Sarah. I'll arrange for men to watch the building until we get there, for someone to pick up Darwin at the airport, and for us to go under makeup."

They jumped up into the Hummer, and Disco got them underway while jabbering orders into his cell phone.

It was all so confusing. How could everyone be at a popular hotel downtown, having a great time and talking about the good news? Where were the messages from Alex?

Who were these people?

Coming at Sarah and her close friends violently was not a good idea.

And what about Amanda? How the hell did a seventeen-year-old girl have all the answers?

Nothing was making sense, and yet her world was still falling apart.

Which made her sick to her stomach.

Chapter 17

AARON WATCHED WILLOW AS she slept after lunch. How would they ever be able to explain away the attacks on their family, the kidnappings, the abductions, and the violence this little girl has had to endure because she was born to vigilante parents? Would it cause triggers later in life because of the trauma she has had to endure?

His plea for Sarah to stop listening to the voices in her head—he couldn't definitively call that voice *Vivian* without further proof now—had gone unanswered.

And now they were prisoners in a hotel, their future unknown. Sure, Tom spouted off that they would be going home tomorrow. Still, Aaron remained confident that they'd go home when these assholes were neutralized and when Sarah or Darwin or someone in their inner circle that these idiots had *not* abducted would take them down.

Since they couldn't leave now, they were being held against their will—essentially, they were prisoners.

He stared at the ceiling and wondered how these people could act with such impunity. The only explanation that made any sense was that they were the government. They had to be. This was a logical conclusion because Tom and his men were military-trained, and only government officials, under the right pretense, could take ordinary citizens off the streets without explanation.

Based on that presumption, what were their intentions? Was Tom lying about them going home tomorrow? And who was masquerading around as Sarah's sister? Could Vivian *actually* be alive?

His eyes closed as he pondered these thoughts, the warmth of the sun coming through the hotel window on his chest and arms as it moved to set in the west.

Something broke somewhere close by, making Aaron jump in bed. His hands came up in front of him. The light had dimmed in the room. He must've fallen asleep.

Beside him, Willow was sitting up in bed and reading.

"What was that?" he asked.

"Glass broke somewhere down the hallway," Willow said.

A thump followed her words, then more glass broke. Someone shouted a command. That sounded like Tom.

"What's happening out there?" Aaron swung his legs off his bed. "Can you tell me?"

Willow shrugged and turned the page of her book. "I think men are fighting in another room."

Think men are fighting? That wasn't like Willow. He didn't know what to make of it. She could usually tell exactly what was happening around them, confident about the next five to ten minutes. She would usually say things with more certainty.

He leaned close to her. "Do you *know* what's going on?"

She kept her head angled down at the book but moved her eyes to look at him. A slight nod, almost imperceptible, told him she knew *everything* but wasn't willing to share.

Should he push and demand answers? As soon as the thought came to him, he squashed it. She'd tell him if he needed to know. In the meantime, involving her more was something he had begged Sarah to stop doing.

There was another bang from somewhere down the hall, followed by more glass breaking. Someone was putting up a huge fight, and it sounded like Tom's men were losing.

A gun went off, making him jump.

"Come on," he said to her. "We shouldn't be out in the open like this."

"Where are we going?" Willow asked as he lifted her off the bed. She clung to the book, bringing it with her.

"To hide in the bathroom until that noise stops."

"But why?"

"What if someone opens our door, and that fight spills into the room? Sitting on our beds won't help us."

Willow didn't ask any more questions as Aaron lowered her into the bathtub.

"Sit in here until whatever's going on out there is over, okay?"

She nodded and opened the book, reading the lines with her fingers.

Aaron moved to the bathroom door and listened. He heard nothing. It sounded like it was over.

He glanced out the window and saw that the sun was in the final stage of setting. How long did he sleep? He hadn't meant to sleep, but there was nothing wrong with being well-rested in situations like these.

After a glance back at Willow, he moved to the hotel room door and placed his ear against it to listen.

Other than the sound of footfalls in the hallway, the distinctive racket of fighting had ended. He wondered if they'd finally gotten Sarah, and she attacked them before they were able to place her in one of the rooms. Or maybe it was Alex fighting back. Daniel could fight, and so could Parkman, but they wouldn't take on military men as Alex or Sarah might. Well, unless they felt their lives were at risk.

Willow tapped his leg, making him jump. His nerves had been shot since this all started.

"Honey," he whispered, leaning closer to her. "It's better if you're in the bathroom."

She held up four fingers, then lowered one. Then another. And finally, someone knocked on the door when she lowered the last finger.

"Time to go," someone shouted through the door. "We are relocating to another hotel for the evening."

"The hell we are," Aaron shouted back.

The door clicked open, and four men spilled inside, their bodies wrapped in Kevlar. Each man had a pistol in a holster on their belt and a knife stashed in a sheath strapped to their legs.

Aaron stepped back, his hand out in front of Willow. Before he could say anything, Tom moved inside the room. The man was bleeding from the mouth. Someone or something had made contact with his lips, mashing them against his teeth, which cut the flesh on the inside. When he opened his mouth to talk, his teeth were framed in red.

"We're leaving now. Grab what you can. You have one minute."

"How about you guys leave, and we'll take a taxi back home?" He waved once at Tom. "It's okay. We got this. We can handle ourselves from here."

Tom stepped forward, and Aaron did the same, moving into his personal space. There was a rustling behind Tom as the men withdrew weapons.

What the hell happened in the hallway that has them all on edge?

"You will come with us willingly and offer zero resistance," Tom said in a stern voice, his eyes darting to Willow, then back to Aaron. "Or your little girl will watch her father be hogtied and carried out of here. I can call another dozen men if you feel I don't have enough men in this room. Are we clear?"

Aaron glared at the man from less than a span of four inches, his heart in his throat. Something had changed. These men were on edge. They were afraid.

"Sarah got you on the run?" he asked. "Is that it?"

"You will be free to go tomorrow, but tonight you will remain in our company." Tom closed the distance to one inch, their noses almost touching. "Or would you like to test us, Mr. Stevens?"

"Daddy," Willow whispered in her soft voice. "Let's go with these men. It's okay."

Like butter in an oven, Aaron melted at the sound of her voice. He eased back from Tom and placed a hand on the back of Willow's head. "You're right, honey. We will go with these men *willingly* for now. Perhaps tomorrow, we'll change our minds."

Tom stared at him a moment longer, then nodded and pivoted for the open door. "Be downstairs and loaded up to go in under two minutes."

"Sir, yes, sir," one of the men shouted.

Aaron grabbed their bag, stuffed their toiletries into it, grabbed Willow's book, and headed for the door.

In the hallway, with two men leading them and two men trailing, he caught sight of the debris two doors down. A stretcher sat empty in the hall as a group of people worked quietly in the room.

Something big happened there, and it spooked Tom and his crew.

Was that Sarah's doing or something else?

The bigger questions were, where were they going? And would they ever see Sarah again?

Chapter 18

SARAH AND DISCO HAD a late lunch, found a great spot to park the Hummer close to the train depot, then wandered down to Union Station to watch the ticket booth. According to that voice in Sarah's head, Amanda would be heading back to Oshawa on the GO train several minutes past seven that evening. It was close to six-forty now, and Sarah found a spot to sit where she could watch the ticket window and still see the main concourse.

Disco moved to mingle with the public and was lost to sight. Five minutes later, she picked him up, wandering by the exit on the far right, then lost him again to the rush of evening foot traffic.

Trains leaving and their designated track numbers were announced over the speaker system in a tinny voice while more and more people clambered for tickets at the wicket.

The idea that a seventeen-year-old girl could help with what was happening to Sarah and her inner circle of friends confounded her, but when had that voice ever been wrong? Even if it wasn't Vivian, the voice in her head had saved her life more times than she could count.

So they showed up. They were here. And if Amanda came into view, they were taking her this time.

The benefit was that there would be no security detail. According to that *voice*, Amanda had ducked out, and her detail wouldn't know she was gone for at least an hour. Something had weakened their numbers drastically this afternoon, which gave Amanda her chance.

Again, no idea how that connected to anything. What choice did she have, though? Sarah was willing to go with it, as was Disco.

She checked the time on the clock on the far wall. It stated they were one minute past seven.

Amanda was bound to come into view at any moment.

Sarah waited, her heart rate elevated. That anticipation never got boring. She'd been doing this since she sat under a bridge waiting for a car accident to happen at 10:18 a.m. with a hammer beside her as an eighteen-year-old. Looking back, she was just a kid then. What she'd been through from that day forward was insane, and how she made it this far was to the credit of that voice from the other side, always telling her what to do and when to do it.

She blinked and came back into the room. Reminiscing wouldn't help her see Amanda in the mass of people strolling past her location.

Her eyes darted to the clock as she rocked from foot to foot, a tingly, pins-and-needles feeling coursing through her left leg now. It was four minutes past seven. She tried to see where Disco was, but the man had disappeared from her view.

One more look at the ticket booth offered up no results.

Amanda was nowhere to be seen.

"Come on, come on," she whispered to no one in particular. "Where are you?"

That girl from the schoolyard in Oshawa had not shown up.

Her eye wandered across the moving crowd, then stopped on a man in the middle staring at her.

Disco raised his hands in a where-is-she gesture, and Sarah responded by mouthing, *I don't know*, her hands out to her sides as well.

Then Disco waved for her to join him. She pushed off the wall where she'd stood for almost half an hour without results and met him in the center of the mass of people heading home, with the younger crowd heading the other way, no doubt on their way for a night of drinking and partying.

"The train heading to Oshawa is on track two."

"And?"

"We must've missed her somehow." Disco pulled Sarah with him. "C'mon. Maybe she already bought tickets and is sitting on the train."

They hopped the turnstiles, and no one tried to stop them. At the train, with four minutes before departure, Sarah slowed and grabbed Disco's arm.

"Listen, I know what she looks like. I'll walk the interior, and you walk the outside, shadowing me. I'll flush her out to you if she's already on the train."

He nodded and backed off to watch the train cars as Sarah jumped on the first car. She scanned the passengers as fast as she could and raced through the first car. Once she got through the connecting doors and started down the second car's center aisle, she heard the final announcement to board as the train would be leaving in a few minutes.

Shit, we're running out of time, Vivian. Why send me on this wild goose chase if she isn't here?

Sarah hit the third car, then the fourth.

Through the window to her right, she saw Disco jogging along in concert with her. He held up one finger.

They had one minute left.

On the sixth car, she finally saw a familiar face.

At the moment the boy saw her, his face hardened, and he mouthed, *No way*, but Sarah wasn't close enough yet to hear him speak.

The boy leaned forward, grabbed someone's arm, then pointed at Sarah.

Amanda lifted in her seat and spun her head around to look at Sarah, her eyes widening.

Sarah pointed at them without looking at Disco, knowing he'd see Amanda sitting up now.

The boy grabbed Amanda's arm, and they bolted from their seats about fifteen meters ahead of Sarah.

They would exit the train car by the time she got to the middle.

So Sarah stopped and ran back to the door she'd just passed.

A buzzer sounded, and the doors began closing as Sarah jumped onto the platform. She landed like she was in the middle of a sprint, taking three more steps to slow down.

When she looked left, the boy was staring back inside the train window in search of their pursuer.

The train nudged forward, and the boy laughed.

It was Amanda who saw Sarah first. She tugged on the boy's shirt, then pointed.

"Oh shit," the boy said loud enough to be overheard by the train's noise.

The train was underway now, leaving them behind.

The boy grabbed Amanda's hand and turned to run the length of the platform, but bumped into Disco's considerable bulk, stopping him short.

Sarah even heard the grunt when they made contact as she started toward them.

Disco locked the boy's arm behind his back and held him in place.

"We need to talk." Sarah was close enough for them to hear.

"We got nothin' to say to you, crazy woman." Even though the boy was in an iron grip and couldn't budge, all of his bravado remained intact.

"You can come willingly." Sarah spun sideways to show them her gun. "Or unwillingly, but you're both coming with us either way."

"Fuck you," the boy said.

Disco tightened his hold until the boy grunted in pain, his face as red as a ripe strawberry. Sarah noticed the boy's feet had come off the ground.

"I know you're trying to protect your honor and all," Disco said into the boy's ear. "But that's no way to talk to a lady, now is it, kid?"

The boy shook his head in a desperate jerking motion.

"Apologize."

The boy's eyes darted from Sarah to Amanda, then back to Sarah. "Sorry." The word came out in a huff of compressed air like he was holding his breath to manage the pain.

"Hey, you there?" someone shouted from the other platform.

"Mind your fucking business," Disco shouted back, easing up on the boy until his feet were back on the ground.

"Amanda?" Sarah moved closer. "No harm will come to either of you if you just come with us." Sarah sidled up beside her. "But if you refuse, we have a team of men who will descend on this platform, and you'll be handcuffed and taken by force. Understood?"

Amanda met the boy's gaze, then turned back to Sarah. "It's because of my mom, isn't it?"

Since Vivian hadn't told her what this was all about yet, other than Amanda having some answers they needed, Sarah had to guess that Amanda's mom was deserving of this statement.

"I'm afraid so."

Amanda moved closer to the boy. "We have to go with them, Brody. I'll explain later." She stared at Disco. "You won't hurt him?"

"Not if he watches his mouth and comes with us without a fight. There's no need to break any bones today."

There was a slight rise of Brody's eyebrows that leveled back out so fast that Sarah almost missed it. The boy wanted to look tough and protect his girl. Admirable as that was, Disco was a professional. The boy wouldn't last ten seconds against someone like Disco as an opponent. Better to let it go and move on to live another day.

The moment Brody realized that, Sarah saw it flicker over his face. A shadow of resignation, his eyes aiming downward.

The tough-guy persona was wiped clean, and to give Amanda credit, she saw it too because she nodded at Disco to ease up.

When Disco looked at Sarah, she said, "It appears Brody won't be a problem after all. I'll call off the ambulance."

Disco released the boy's arm, and his face lost color, going from beet red to ghost white.

"The ambulance?" he muttered.

Sarah nodded. "We only need to talk to Amanda. Everyone else was supposed to get broken kneecaps." When Brody stared at Amanda, Sarah winked at Disco. "Since you're willing to join us without trouble, my friend here will leave your bones intact."

Brody, completely cowed now, nodded once at Disco and muttered a *thank you* under his breath.

The foursome marched along the platform—under the watchful gaze of several passengers waiting for trains—and headed out to the main concourse.

Sarah led the way to the front doors, and then, after a quick left, they approached the Hummer.

"Hop in," she ordered. "But first, surrender your cell phones."

They exchanged glances, then pulled their phones from their pockets and handed them over.

"You'll get them back when this is all over."

Sarah turned off both phones, placed them on the dashboard in the front, then turned to look at the Royal Oak Hotel across the street. Two ambulances were parked at the front entrance, with one exiting onto Front Street, its lights flashing.

"See? They aren't needed." Sarah said this to back up her earlier claim about calling ambulances for people who gave them trouble. Still, her stomach was knotted up at why so many ambulances were needed at the hotel where she understood her mother might be, along with her daughter and everyone else important to her.

Once they'd all climbed into the Hummer, Disco got them moving.

"Where are you taking us?" Brody asked.

"For a chat," Disco said.

"Why does that sound scary?"

Sarah spun in her seat. "Answer the questions, and you'll be fine. Since you missed your train, I'll even give you the money for a taxi to Oshawa."

"You'd do that?" The teenagers in the back seat looked at each other. "That would be, like, well over a hundred bucks."

"It's the least we can do for inconveniencing you." Sarah righted herself in her seat as Disco took them to his warehouse on Richmond Street. It was only a few blocks away, and Disco could park the Hummer inside.

On the way there, Sarah wondered what her reserved spot in Hell would look like for kidnapping two teenagers and threatening them with violence they'd never follow through with.

The illusion of pain was a great motivator. The idea that it was easier to talk than be tortured was as old as time.

Yet, she had no idea what Amanda knew or how she could help them. The only clue so far was that it involved her mother—potentially.

Disco turned onto Richmond Street, and Sarah was eager to get the teenagers talking.

They had a makeup artist coming within an hour to get them ready for their grand entrance at the Royal Oak Hotel.

Patience wasn't something Sarah prided herself on having, so needing to wait an hour to find out why all those ambulances were parked out front of the hotel was going to drive her mad.

They entered the warehouse with the large garage door descending behind the Hummer.

"Get out," Disco ordered.

The interrogation was about to begin.

Chapter 19

DARWIN WATCHED THE LIGHTS of Toronto as the plane descended toward Canadian soil. Rome to Toronto was a direct flight, which he was grateful for, but it was still long—too long.

As he aged into his late thirties, there were more aches and pains from previous injuries. The torn skin and muscle damage he'd endured at twenty-six years old when the Toronto mafia kidnapped his new wife at the time had healed many years ago, but had it? He still felt aches on cold nights by the fire, on rainy days in Canada, and when he sat on ten-hour flights from Europe.

Regret wasn't something he suffered from, meaning he did it once, and he'd do it again. That didn't stop the muscle spasms, the cramps, and the use of ibuprofen on long flights.

He yawned, then stretched out his legs and yanked the thighs of his jeans to loosen the tightness from sitting. He would need several hours' sleep before he could be effective in any way for Sarah or anyone else, which wasn't reasonable because he'd be expected to hit the ground running, so to speak.

His watch told him they were landing half an hour late. The pilot said something about a headwind, but Darwin had been trying to sleep in the last hour of the flight—sleeping on a plane was almost unachievable. Age limited the actions of the young as the years around the sun increased.

The plane thumped down softly, and he stared outside as the plane slowed. It taxied off the main runway, then turned toward the terminal.

Red lights caught his eye as the plane moved in a wide arc to finish the turn, then they were gone, hidden by the fuselage.

Without notice, the plane came to a stop. Passengers stared at one another, likely wondering why they'd stopped this far from the terminal.

The speaker system engaged, and a flight attendant reminded everyone to remain in their seats until they had taxied into the terminal and the captain had turned off the seatbelt sign.

After waiting a minute, the passengers got antsy, and the captain came onto the speaker system.

"Good evening, ladies and gentlemen. This is your captain speaking. I apologize for the delay. As soon as the tower clears our gate, we'll taxi in, and we can begin to deplane the aircraft. Please remain seated with your seatbelts fastened until we arrive at the gate. Thank you."

Darwin tried to catch a glimpse of those emergency lights again, but they were now on the other side of the plane. The reflections of the red and blue splashed across the tarmac and bounced back from the windows of a nearby aircraft taxiing for takeoff.

Something more than a gate clearance was taking place.

He'd bought economy plus, which gave him more legroom. These seats were near the front of the plane, right behind first class. This allowed him to notice when the flight attendant took a phone call, which flustered her.

She immediately went to work on opening the door to the consternation of the passengers around Darwin as they watched the door being cast aside.

The flight attendant stepped back and waved a hand in a welcoming gesture to someone out of sight.

One after another, four men wrapped in Kevlar and heavily armed, like they were preparing to storm the plane, entered the aircraft. They wore balaclavas and helmets, cargo pants littered with pockets for weapons, and an iron gaze that swept the front rows of seats as if looking for a threat. These men oozed a yearning to shoot someone, to enter combat, or find a confrontation to be a part of.

A collective gasp rose around the front seats when they entered. People spoke in whispers, with some of them lowering in their seats.

Darwin watched as the lead man spoke quietly with the flight attendant, their heads bent close. They had to be working on a tip that a member of a Mexican cartel, the Italian mafia, or someone equally dangerous had smuggled themselves into Canada via this particular flight.

Since his problems with nefarious organizations were well over a decade old, he used his legal passport for this flight, the one with his real name on it. They remained in hiding in Italy for the most part, as his name was old news to crime bosses on this continent. So these men couldn't be here for him, could they?

Did the Toronto mafia's reach extend to government officials and government databases? If so, he'd be in more trouble than he ever thought possible.

Even if their reach extended that far, could they dispatch a team to stop a commercial airliner filled with members of the public at the Toronto airport to apprehend him?

That didn't seem plausible. If these men were indeed here for him, it was connected to Sarah's trouble because her friends were disappearing, and men like this could make that happen without a trace.

His fears were realized when the flight attendant checked a handheld tablet, scrolled down the screen, stopped and tapped it once, then turned and locked eyes with Darwin.

She pointed at him, and every passenger in the front of the cabin followed her extended finger to stare at him as the armed military men strode down the aisle to form a semi-circle around him.

"Mr. Kostas, please get to your feet. We are escorting you off the plane."

Trying to pretend he wasn't Darwin Kostas was a waste of everyone's time, so he just stared straight ahead. "Yeah? Why's that? Under whose authority? Gonna charge me with something?"

"Get up now, or we'll drag you off this airplane."

Darwin glanced over at his seatmate. "Apologies." He undid his seatbelt and pushed up to his feet. "Men in uniform often lack manners."

They grabbed his arms and dragged him toward the exit.

"Hey, take it easy. What about my carry-on bag, my luggage?"

"That'll be offloaded and brought to you," the leader said.

They escorted him down a set of stairs, then applied handcuffs and shoved him toward one of the waiting SUVs with their lights still flashing.

As precise as expected by the highly trained military, they had him off the plane and racing toward the exit in the SUV in under five minutes.

He caught a glimpse of the plane he'd just disembarked as it got underway, heading to their assigned gate.

At least the passengers would have a story to share with their friends and family. All Darwin had was a headache and a burning need to take a piss. He'd held it thinking he'd use the airport toilets before clearing customs and meeting with Disco or whoever came to pick him up.

That raised a question. "I guess clearing customs isn't necessary with you guys, eh?"

No one moved, looked at him, or did anything to indicate that they even heard him speak.

"Well, you bunch are about as much fun as a handful of sand in my underwear while running a marathon."

That elicited a half-smile from the man sitting across from him.

Darwin glanced outside as they accessed Highway 427, heading north. With no idea where they were going, he leaned forward.

"Okay, pull over and remove my handcuffs, or I can guarantee you won't be very happy."

The man who spoke with the flight attendant earlier turned around in his seat. "You're in no position to issue threats. Shut up, sit back, and relax. We're in for a ninety-minute ride."

"That wasn't a threat. If you don't pull over soon, I'm gonna piss a couple of liters all over myself, this seat, and these boys on either side of me."

The man swore under his breath, then issued an order to the driver that Darwin couldn't hear.

After a minute, he asked, "Well? Piss time coming, or not?"

"Wait ten minutes. We're stopping for coffee at a Timmy's up ahead. Piss then."

Darwin smiled widely. "That sounds amazing. Maybe we'll get donuts, too, eh, guys? Mark me down for a couple of toasted coconuts and a Boston cream."

The man in the front seat just shook his head.

Darwin sat back to wait, hoping he wouldn't piss himself—it was getting that serious.

Chapter 20

SARAH STOPPED PACING IN front of Amanda, her finger tapping her lips. "So, your mother's name is Janice Stilton, and you don't know what she does for a living?"

"She works for the US government. That's all I know."

"What department? What does she do for them?"

Amanda shrugged, then her arm jerked like she was cold. "We don't discuss her work. She says it's top secret or some shit."

"Are you cold? Need a jacket?"

Amanda shook her head.

"You jerked. Was that a tic?"

"I get that sometimes. It's a side effect of some meds I have to take."

"Meds?" Sarah faced her, a worried thought racing through her mind that they had kidnapped a girl who needed insulin or some heart medication, and she'd die if she didn't get it.

Amanda stole a glance at Brody, then stared down at her lap. "Can we not talk about that?" Her shoulders vibrated once.

Sarah recalled seeing the muscle tremor in her once by the school last night. "Well, I need to know about these meds in case something happens to you while you're with us. How serious is it?"

She looked up and met Sarah's eyes. "My mother has me on something called clozapine. I have an overactive imagination, which got me in trouble when I was little. This keeps things calm, and the side effects are mild."

Clozapine? Sarah thought back to when doctors prescribed her Zoloft for depression when she was eighteen. She didn't suffer from depression, so she avoided taking the drug, along with other meds that came next. Although, that didn't stop her from researching the side effects. She would have to look up clozapine when she was on her phone again.

Sarah tapped her chin for a moment, then started pacing again. "Tell me about your dad. Where does he work?"

"That's easy. He works at the Pentagon."

Sarah stopped moving, shifted her gaze to Amanda, then went back to pacing. "And what does he do?" Sarah watched her from an angle.

Amanda shrugged again. "I don't have particulars, but it has something to do with defense."

"So, American parents who work for the American government, and you're in Toronto. Do you know why your mom brought you here?"

"I wish I knew." She raised her shoulders and thrust out her hands. "Vacation?"

"You're not being obtuse, are you?"

"Obtuse?"

"Thick-headed, slow-witted, whatever you want to call it. You're not *trying* not to answer my questions, right?"

She exaggeratedly shook her head, her face a mask of pleading. "Never, no way. You have to trust me. I'm pissed at my mom right now. We never see eye to eye."

Sarah checked the time. It was creeping up on eight in the evening. Where was the news that Disco's men had picked up Darwin at the airport?

She snuck a glance at Disco, who was watching over Brody in the corner. They'd opted to avoid tying him up as long as he didn't try anything stupid.

"Darwin?" Sarah said, hands out at her sides. "Anything?"

Disco glanced at the screen of his phone and shook his head. "Nothing yet."

Her attention shifted back to Amanda; she rolled her hand over and over. "Tell me why you're pissed at your mother."

"Because she won't let me see my new friends in Oshawa."

"Is that why you two were going on a train and not with your armed security?"

Amanda and Brody stared at each other from twenty feet away, and then she turned her attention back to Sarah. "My security is always two or three guards. About an hour before we ran for the trains, they reduced it to one guard. I haven't had one guard in a long time." She paused, looking down at her hands where she was prying at a nail. "I waited until he went to the bathroom, then ran from my room and called Brody on the run. He was already downtown as we were supposed to meet

422

tonight."

"So you two got together and ran for the train?"

"Yeah." Amanda's shoulders slumped in resignation, another involuntary twitch of her shoulders shaking her. "I just wanted a night out without minders, without anyone watching over me. If I stayed in Toronto tonight, they'd likely find me."

"Does your mother approve of you drinking?"

Amanda shook her head.

"And she was pissed after I met you in Oshawa, correct?"

Amanda nodded. "She was so angry. I don't know why. My handlers were there. We were safe the whole time."

Relatively safe. I was there to abduct you. "Also, you'd been drinking. That'd make most moms flip their lid."

"I'm old enough," Amanda said, a sulky note to her voice. "Europeans drink at fourteen and sixteen. These laws are stupid."

Was I ever this young? Sarah asked herself.

"Wait," Amanda said, staring at Sarah. "How did you know I'd be on that train? I'm rarely without my handlers when we travel out of the country. I slipped away and was on that train within thirty minutes, then *boom*, there you were." She studied Sarah with a quirked eyebrow. "How could you know?"

"Hold on a second." Sarah started pacing again, mindful of the time and completely ignoring Amanda's question. "Earlier, you said they reduced your guard to one. Why?"

"The others were needed elsewhere. Something went wrong, and they were short a bunch of men."

Could that be Darwin's doing?

She glanced back at Disco. "Anything on the plane yet?"

Disco shook his head. "I'll check with my guys, though. Give me a few minutes. Also, the makeup artist is coming in twenty minutes. Wrap this up."

Sarah gave him a curt nod and refocused on Amanda. "Do you know why the guards were needed elsewhere?"

Amanda shook her head.

Sarah stopped and lowered to her knees in front of Amanda. "Help me out here. Should I know your mother? How about your father? Have you ever overheard my name?"

Amanda seemed to think about it for a moment, then shook her head. "I honestly can't think of anything. Truly, I just don't know."

Sarah touched Amanda's knee with a reassuring tap and returned to her feet. "Well, Amanda, let me tell you what's happening in case it sheds some light on what you don't seem to know."

Amanda nodded, a worried look on her face.

"My mother went to meet my sister last night and disappeared. My ex and my daughter also disappeared last night. We were supposed to meet downtown. They didn't show." Sarah turned to look at Disco as he spoke into the phone. "As far as I can tell, my friends Parkman, Daniel, and Alex all went missing last night as well."

"Oh, I'm so sorry, but what's that got to do with my mom or me?"

"That's what I'm trying to figure out."

"I'm confused."

Sarah turned back to her. "How so?"

"If you have no thread tying my family to that group of people who went missing—"

"My family," Sarah cut in.

"*Your* family, who went missing, what led you to want to talk to me? Back to my question. How did you know I'd be on the train?"

Sarah thought about how to answer that. "Well, let's just say I have good intuition."

Amanda shook her head. "No, there's something you're not telling me. No way intuition would have you kidnapping teenagers of US government officials to find out how they're connected to people gone missing in Toronto without a basis." Her voice rose when she added, "Why would my mother be involved in abductions? She works for the US government. She isn't running a criminal organization."

"Well, that depends on how you look at it. Government can be criminal."

Amanda clucked her tongue.

Sarah waved her hand. "Another conversation for another time. For now, I need to know the connection because I believe there is one."

"And what if there isn't?"

"Sarah," Disco called.

She spun around. "What is it?"

"Bad news."

Her stomach filled with lead. "Tell me."

"Government officials met with Darwin's plane out on the runway and removed him from the plane. They landed late, and Darwin wasn't there when they finally got to the gate. Several passengers reported that four armed men boarded the plane and took Darwin away in SUVs. He's gone to the wind."

They stared at each other for a long moment until Brody broke the silence.

"What does that mean? Who's Darwin?"

Disco turned to him. "It means the people we are up against are more powerful than we anticipated. They've been ahead of us every step of the way."

Sarah tightened her fists at her sides. "We change that tonight. When we hit them hard, they'll regret coming at us."

Disco's phone chirped. He glanced down at it.

"What?" Sarah said after a moment. "What is it now?"

"Take it easy. It's the makeup guy. He's at the door." Disco got up from his chair. "I'll go let him in." He waved at Brody. "You can come, too. I'm not leaving you alone yet."

Dutifully, Brody got up and walked beside Disco as they left the center of the large warehouse, headed for the door that led to the road.

Sarah released an exasperated rush of air and spun back to Amanda. "I'm all out of questions. I cannot, for the life of me, figure out how we're connected."

"What if we're not connected?" Amanda said. "And this was all a mistake? You know, we could use that cab fare. It's not too late to forget this whole thing." Amanda leaned forward and stared up at Sarah. "Let us go now, and we won't tell my parents about any of this."

Sarah was nodding at Amanda, that voice in her head coming back into question. What if Vivian were alive? Then who was in her head? And if it was a stranger talking to her, then why have her kidnap two teenagers and threaten them with violence? Could this be the end of her life as a vigilante, and the voice made her abduct a high-profile teenager to solidify that ending, to shut her down for good?

Amanda was on her feet now beside Sarah, looking across the warehouse at Brody and Disco. "If I'd spent more time with my mother, maybe this wouldn't be happening. What I mean is, if she *understood* me better. She never listens. She never takes the time."

Sarah heard the plea in Amanda's voice and swore she'd be there for Willow when her daughter was in her teens. Amanda longed for her mother to listen, console her, and hear her; evidently, her mother was career-focused and missing out on her daughter's formative years.

"Blah, blah, blah," Amanda went on, her tone imitating a child's. "This associate, this business friend. Everyone is *so* important, but what about me?" She raised her hands to Sarah. "And no offense, but for a kidnapping, this was pretty lame."

"Lame?" Sarah's brows rose as high as they'd go.

"Yeah, I mean, you took us off the train, brought us here to ask a bunch of questions that I couldn't answer, and you're going to pay for a taxi so we can go to Brody's place for the night. I mean, all you did was save us a train ride and a half-hour walk. Now we can take the taxi right to his place."

Sarah pursed her lips. She was certainly softer since Willow was born.

The door at the far end of the warehouse slammed closed, and three people started toward them. The makeup guy had arrived.

Amanda glanced at the floor. "My mom's friend consumes all her time, too." She slipped her hands in her pockets and raised her shoulders. "I thought coming to Toronto was supposed to be a shopping trip, a short vacation, but all they've done is hole up in that hotel across the street from the train station."

Sarah's eyes widened. "The Royal Oak Hotel?"

"Yeah," Amanda said, nodding slightly. "You know it?"

Sarah nodded back, afraid to say anything else that might stop Amanda from continuing her venting.

"That's why my security detail drove me to Oshawa to meet Brody. We met on an app called Discord, and we just wanted to meet in person. My mom was against it, but her friend said it would all work out. So we went."

"Is this friend female or male?"

"Female." Amanda nearly spat the word, as if her mom having a male friend was repulsive.

"How long has your mom known this friend?"

"Why? Does that matter?"

"Well, for her to travel to Toronto with her, she'd likely be a grade school friend, right? I mean, they'd have to have history."

Amanda stared at the three men who were almost upon them. "I've only met Vivian a few times, believe it or not. Shows how much my mom brings her friends around the house. But yeah, they've known each other for at least ten years or more. They met at work, so she's more of an associate who became a friend."

It was like someone gut-punched her. Sarah stumbled backward and dropped onto the chair Amanda had just gotten up from.

Disco was close enough to see her hit the chair. "Sarah, you good?"

Unable to find her voice at the moment, she shook her head.

Disco jogged the fifteen feet separating them and placed a comforting hand on her shoulder. "Talk to me."

Amanda and Brody gawked at her, and the makeup guy stood with two suitcases, one in each hand, staring at her with a look of bewilderment.

"Repeat that last bit," Sarah muttered to Amanda.

"What bit? I was just complaining about my mom's lack of interest, is all."

Sarah pushed up from the chair. "Your mom's friend."

"Right, that woman Vivian who takes up all her time."

Disco snapped his head sideways to stare at Sarah.

She met his piercing gaze. "Amanda's mother has been hanging around with *Vivian* for about a decade. And get this—they're staying at the Royal Oak Hotel."

"Wait, is that important?" Amanda's shoulders jerked once as she stepped backward, as Brody wrapped an arm around her.

Sarah flicked her head at the young couple, and Disco moved to stand behind them.

"It appears this kidnapping won't be so lame after all."

Amanda stared at Sarah, then looked at Disco. "What are you talking about—wait, what's happening?"

"You'll be staying with us for a little bit longer."

Amanda shook her head, and Brody squeezed her shoulders. "No, you can't do that," Amanda whispered, her voice catching in her throat.

Disco already had zip ties in his hand. He grabbed Brody's arms first and secured him without resistance.

"It appears you are a connection to what's happening after all." Sarah had collected herself, forcing the following words to roll out of her mouth. "Your mother, the group she hired or works for, has kidnapped all of my people, my daughter included, and I intend to get them back because I've got the best leverage."

Amanda and Brody exchanged a worried glance. "Leverage?" Amanda repeated the word.

"Yeah. You."

The makeup guy set his cases down. "Who's getting a transformation? I'm here to do makeup. Otherwise, I didn't see a thing."

Disco grabbed Amanda's hands and zip-tied them, too. "Don't worry, Sarah. Charlie here knows how to keep his mouth shut."

"Good, then let's get started. We've got a hotel to crash."

Chapter 21

THEY DROVE FOR OVER an hour, passing through Orangeville north of Brampton. Aaron watched the signs to know where they were headed in case that information was needed later. Shortly after driving through Shelburne on Highway 10, the SUVs pulled into an extended motel that resembled a strip 'mall called the Sky View Motel, according to the pylon sign out front. The place was in the middle of nowhere, with vast empty fields in all directions. Perhaps the motel derived its name from the area because there wasn't a single obstruction to viewing the sky.

Once they unloaded, Aaron and Willow were taken to room number two and secured inside. They weren't given a key, and the door was locked from the outside.

Willow was tired from the time in the SUV, so she sat on her bed to flip through the pages of the book she had been reading and eventually lay down, the book held up, suspended over her head.

"Honey," Aaron said, moving to sit on the edge of her bed. "Can you tell me what's happening? Are you *seeing*"—he used air quotes on that word—"anything?"

She glanced at him and lowered the book, her eyes blinking heavily with sleep as it was past eight in the evening now. "I only know some of what's happening."

"Can you tell me?"

She shrugged as if it were no big deal. "Not sure how it'll help."

"Try me."

"They have us as prisoners."

"Willow," Aaron said softly. "Can you tell me something I don't know?"

"Someone's coming to meet us soon."

"Who?"

"The person running this operation." She paused on the last word. "Isn't an operation something that happens in a hospital?"

Aaron nodded, leaning on his hands to ease closer. "Yes, doctors perform operations. But the military also does operations. For them, that's what this would be called."

"Oh," Willow said, then directed her attention back to her book.

"How soon?"

"Minutes."

Aaron turned to face the door, then looked back at his daughter. "Who else is here?"

She closed her eyes, then after a moment, she opened them and looked at him. "I'm feeling Uncle Parkman, Daniel, my grandma, and us."

Aaron frowned. "Your mom isn't here?"

Willow rolled her head back and forth on the pillow.

"No Alex? No Darwin?"

She kept rolling her head. "Alex is in a hospital."

"Hospital?" he blurted. "Why? Is he okay?"

She shrugged her little shoulders, pushing the pillow upward. "I can't see that far into the future—only little bits. And I can sometimes hear the thoughts of the men outside."

He collected himself and took a breath. "Where's Darwin?"

"Darwin's on his way."

"To get us out?"

She shook her head again. "He's with them now."

Aaron frowned. "They captured Darwin? How?"

She looked at him and lowered her book. "I'm tired, Daddy. Talk to the operations manager. They have more answers than I do."

He patted her head lightly. "Of course, my little one. Sleepy, sleepy."

Aaron moved to the window and eased back the curtain. At least they weren't on the tenth floor of a hotel tower anymore. Smashing the window and getting out of there was more of a reality now.

He glanced back at Willow, curled up on top of her bedsheets, hands tucked under her chin. He'd need a vehicle as he couldn't expect his daughter to run across fields and escape into a copse of trees.

Someone rapped lightly on the door when he moved to his bed to rest. Then a key was inserted, and it clicked open.

"Aaron?" a man said.

"Yeah?" Aaron got back up and moved to the door. "What's up?"

The man motioned for Aaron to step outside.

"I'm not leaving my daughter alone in here."

"She'll be fine." The man gestured at the other soldier beside him. "He's stationed outside your door and will not move until you return."

Aaron shook his head. "Have whoever wants to talk to me come to my room. I'm not leaving my daughter."

Aaron made to shut the door, but the man blocked him and withdrew a weapon, pressing it up under Aaron's chin. "I'm used to getting my own way," the soldier whispered. "I'm sick of your whining." The man jerked his head, gesturing for Aaron to come outside. "Move."

Aaron raised his hands out to his sides and tilted his head back from the pressure of the gun on the underside of his mouth. "If something happens to my little girl while I'm gone, I'll hold you personally responsible."

"Nothing will happen to her, asshole. Just shut up and do what you're told so we can end this shit and all go home."

They started down the length of the motel. Aaron glanced back once. "What's pissed you off?"

"Shut your mouth and keep walking to the last room."

Aaron slowed at the door and glanced back at room number two. The guard still stood sentry outside Willow's door. With Willow asleep, he reasoned it was like leaving her alone in her bed while they were in another room watching a movie. Well, not exactly, but rationally it was in the same ballpark.

The door was opened, and the man pushed him inside.

This room was much bigger, with a desk at the back and a short sofa on the left side against the wall. There was still enough room for a king bed to ensure everything else fit. The bathroom was set back in the room, separated by white frosted blocks piled high as a makeshift wall. It was something out of an '80s motel he'd expect to see in a movie.

A single lamp illuminated the woman sitting behind the desk, her head down, scouring a document. Two soldiers stood at ease, flanking her on either side. One was tapping something on a phone—playing a game? Writing a message?—and the other was picking at a fingernail.

The door shut hard behind Aaron, making him jump. He glanced over his shoulder, but the man who escorted him here had stepped back outside. When he spun back around to the woman, she was looking at him. She had to be in her late forties, well-coiffed like she'd just come from having her hair done. The woman sported the kind of slim figure that only discipline produced.

"No," Aaron said, shaking his head. "You're not Vivian." He leaned down to get a better look at her face, then stood back up. "No way in hell you're Sarah's sister."

The woman clasped her hands together in front of her chest, her chair creaking as she leaned back. "I've never claimed to be Sarah's sister, Mr. Stevens. Vivian Roberts is here, though. She's in another room. We didn't bring you over here to discuss her at the moment. She's a conversation for later."

Aaron looked at each man behind the desk, then back to the woman. "Then why are we here? Why kidnap us and hold us against our will?" He crossed his arms over his chest. "And who the hell are you people?"

"Why would a name be important?" She seemed amused by her own question, with a slight smirk lifting her mouth. "What if I said I was Margaret Smith? Or perhaps Judith? How about Alexandria, but I go by Alex? Would it make any difference who I am or who we are?"

Aaron nodded once. "Sure, it makes a difference. It would be better than the name I have in my head for you, which starts with a capital C." He fought the urge to spit on the floor of the motel. "What kind of a *woman* is involved in kidnapping children?" He stepped toward the desk, and both soldiers stood more at attention. "I mean, who the hell does that?"

"Before you pass further judgment, I'd like to ask you the same thing."

Aaron frowned. "What?" That one word was all he could think to say. "That doesn't make any sense."

The woman pushed away from the desk and got to her feet. "My daughter is missing."

"How is that my problem? Wait, someone kidnapped your daughter, so you kidnapped mine? For what? That two-wrongs-don't-make-a-right shit not click when you were in the first grade? How about this? Take us home, then focus all this energy and resources you have at your disposal on putting your own family back together again."

She moved around the desk to lean against the front of it. "My daughter went missing within the past few hours, and I suspect Sarah Roberts, a woman you know well, was the person who took her."

Aaron scoffed, clicking his tongue. "Why would Sarah take your daughter? My ex is not in the kidnapping business." Calling Sarah his "ex" was something he'd never gotten used to, yet they weren't a couple at the moment, so it was time to move on.

"She tried to abduct my daughter in Oshawa earlier last night but failed. Luckily, my men were there. They had to stop her, forcefully, I might add."

"Was that before you came to Sarah's apartment and grabbed us?"

"I'm afraid so."

He stepped closer, punctuating each word with his right arm jerking forward. "Are you saying Sarah started all this? You know, tit for tat? She went after your daughter, so you grabbed hers? Is that it?"

"Not at all. I'm merely stating that she tried once, failed, then was successful earlier this evening."

Aaron righted himself and adjusted his shirt, satisfied for the moment that Sarah *didn't* start all this—one less thing to blame her for later.

"Okay, what now? Keeping us here doesn't find your daughter."

"Sure it does. I need your little psychic daughter, Willow, to tell us where they are, and you can do that for me."

A kick in the stomach with concrete shoes would have felt better than the sentence this woman just said. They know about Willow. They knew she was *special*. Their precious daughter was now on the government's radar, or whoever these sick people were.

"How would Willow know where her mother is?" Aaron asked, his voice breaking as he spoke. "She's been with me since last night."

He couldn't hide his fear on this one—the fear of losing his little girl. They'd both worried about this, so they'd tried to keep Willow a secret, always stressing the importance of never letting anyone see what she could do.

Yet, no matter how much they tried, someone saw something, and now these people knew what Willow could do, and they had her in their own little prison. Maybe that's why Willow didn't try to break them out or damage their weapons. Aaron had wondered several times why she was just going along with everything. Perhaps she knew these people and what they wanted since they knocked on the apartment door last night, which would explain her reasons for not putting on a show for them. She didn't want to give them front-row seats to her psychic abilities.

"Aaron, we were listening." The woman's smirk was definitely one he'd want to slap off if he hit women.

Everything he feared was coming true. A powerful agency was interested in Willow. This was the beginning of the end, and it all had to be placed at Sarah's doorstep—all of it.

"Listening?"

"Willow knew men were fighting down the hall when she had not left your room. Your daughter counted down on her fingers to the second before my men knocked on your door. She even whispered to you that Sarah would visit her sister soon. Just now, she listed off who was here and who wasn't. I mean, my men just grabbed Darwin. How could she know that?"

Aaron swallowed, his throat dry. They were *listening* and *watching* them.

"Aaron, you can drop the I'm-so-surprised act. We all know of Willow's unique abilities. How about how she handled the Wagner Group's weapons several months ago?" The woman clucked her tongue. "Come on, the time for games is over." The woman pushed off the desk, walked around it, then settled back in her seat. "Talk to Willow. Get me some answers. You don't have long. My men will talk to her if you're unsuccessful, but be clear about one thing. I want my daughter back unharmed, and I intend to get my daughter back. If anything happens to her ..." She paused, blinking up at Aaron, a vein pulsing on her forehead. "Let's just say Hell hath no fury and all that shit." She waved a hand, dismissing him. "Now go, get out of my sight."

The door to the motel room opened. Men stepped in to escort Aaron back to his room. He felt numb all over, his limbs moving on their own accord. But he was able to turn back. "I never did get your name. What should I call you?"

The woman stared at him for a long moment, her men waiting for her to say something. Finally, she said, "Janice. But why does it matter?"

"It matters because if anyone enters my room to speak with my daughter about anything, I'll make them regret it. Then I'll come for you, *Janice*, and being the gentleman I am, you will—"

"Dispel with the threats, little boy. You're in no position to threaten anyone. I snap my fingers, and your body will be tossed into a ditch up north somewhere. Now fuck off back to your room, and remember to get my information. Otherwise, this'll drag on and on, and no one wants that."

Aaron seethed, his hands forming fists. He calculated his chances of hurting some of these men and still getting back to his daughter in one piece, and didn't like the odds.

Tom moved into the room, and Aaron noticed his mouth was swollen, with bruises forming above his lips. "What's the holdup?"

"They were still talking," the man on the right said.

Tom glanced at Janice. "You done with him?"

She nodded and waved a hand. "Get him out of my sight."

The men grabbed Aaron's arms so hard and tight that they lifted him off the ground and out to the walkway that ran the length of the motel.

Room number eight's door slammed closed.

He struggled, but it was useless. Fighting men like this were relatively easy to take down, as he would use pressure points while remaining fast on his feet. As soon as they got hold of you, though, things got more complicated. To have them restraining his arms as they were at this moment immobilized him to some degree.

Someone had parked one of the SUVs up on the walkway, right against the building. To access his room, they'd have to walk around it, out into the parking area.

Drawing near, he saw what they'd done. The truck acted as a barrier for the window of his room. If he broke the glass to escape, he'd be faced with the side of the vehicle.

"I hope you didn't wake my daughter when you guys moved that in place."

"We were quiet, Mr. Stevens."

When they got to his room door, Tom stepped in to unlock it. He peeked inside, then turned back. "She's still sleeping, but under the covers now. Go in quietly."

They released Aaron, and he stepped inside the room. The door closed quietly behind him, the lock engaging.

He shook off the filth he felt from that conversation as he moved to his bed. After lying down, he stared over at Willow's inert form and wondered if she would be able to see where Sarah was because that wasn't one of her specialties. At least not one he thought she possessed.

Knowing he had about twenty minutes to talk to her on his own, he got up and whispered her name.

He leaned over and shook her sleeping form when she didn't respond.

Something wasn't right. Her shoulder was too soft.

Aaron pulled back the covers. Underneath were just rolled-up towels and pillows.

Willow was gone, taken from him.

Aaron screamed.

Chapter 22

"WHAT WAS THE NAME you left for the reservation?" Sarah pushed her new brown hair over her right shoulder. The makeup applied in a hurry was overdone, but she could live with it for an hour or two. "Will that name stick?"

"Of course." Disco eased to a stop on the side of the road, then killed the engine. "Why wouldn't our reservation stick? I have a credit card in that name and a driver's license."

"I know. I'm just pissed that we have to go under this disguise."

He watched her for a long moment. "Not your style?"

"If I'm entering a building, I walk through the front door and deal with it. This isn't about my ego. It's about doing the right thing with your chin held high." She stared out the windshield at nothing in particular. "If wearing a disguise—this wig, these clothes—gets the job done, then so be it. Otherwise, pretending to be someone else just feels like a lie."

"You've never worn a wig?"

She thought back to when she covered her hair with a bandanna, but that was different.

"I've dyed my hair before if that's the same thing." She glanced over at him. "I mean, to disguise myself. So there's that."

"Nothing wrong with being upfront when dealing with your enemy. But this time, those guys are too trained, and there are too many of them to walk in the front door, guns swinging."

"Yeah, and I don't want to do that either. Too many people would die senselessly, and we still have no idea what their intentions are, except wanting to play a game by telling me my sister is still alive."

Disco clucked his tongue. "The way I see it is we would need cartel enforcers to take over the hotel if we weren't going in like this."

Sarah nodded, then grabbed the door handle. "Let's do this and find out what we can about them, then get back to Amanda and Brody."

After exiting the Hummer, Sarah waited for Disco to come around to her, then she held onto his arm. Playing a couple, she had to be in the role all the way to the front of the hotel until they got into their room.

"Will those kids be okay with your hair guy?"

"Of course. He's ex-special forces, turned hairdresser. I've got the guys who missed Darwin at the airport on their way to relieve him. Nothing will happen to those kids."

As they strode along the sidewalk on Front Street, her gut twisting at the knowledge that Darwin was missing now, too, no one paid them any extra attention. Near the front of the Royal Oak Hotel, in the pickup and drop-off area, the ambulances were gone now.

"Wonder what happened earlier," Sarah mumbled for Disco to hear.

"Hope it has nothing to do with the people you know."

"If it does, screw this disguise. I'm hurting someone."

"Just try to stay calm as long as you can. We need to get in and get out, and in between, learn as much as we can without hurting anyone. It's a lot of hotel to cover, and we have no starting point."

"Got it. Stay as calm as a summer breeze."

They turned toward the lobby, and Sarah dropped into the act by swinging her hips more than usual. She popped a gum into her mouth and chewed with her mouth open as Disco yanked open the lobby doors.

Thankfully, the clerk from last night wasn't behind the counter, which made sense. He'd been working the night shift, and these clerks were on the evening shift.

"How can we help you?" the clerk asked as they approached the front desk.

"We've got a reservation for tonight," Disco said, wrapping an arm around Sarah's shoulders.

"The name, sir?"

"Sung."

"First name?"

"Sam."

Sarah didn't think she'd lose it when he said the name, but when a short chortle rose in her throat, she warded it off by making a bubble and smacking the gum off the roof of her mouth.

The clerk glanced up briefly, then stared back at his screen. "And you're an additional guest, ma'am?"

"Yeah," Sarah said.

"Name, please."

"You need my name?" She acted stunned and turned to Disco. "I thought the room was rented in your name, Sam."

"Ma'am," the clerk said. "The room is rented in Sam Sung's name"—even the clerk paused when he *said* the name aloud—"but we like to know who's in each room."

"Just call me Angel, honey," she said, chewing her gum around the words.

The clerk typed in her name, and she hoped that was it. They did not have an ID for Sarah. Actually, Disco didn't have a spare ID in a female's name at all because, as a man, when would he need it?

"I have you on the ninth floor this evening, overlooking the city toward the water."

"Great," Disco chimed in.

"I'll need a driver's license and a credit card for the deposit."

"Of course," Disco said, fishing in his pocket to produce the cards.

Sarah released his arm and stepped away from the counter to avoid any more probing questions. Scanning the large lobby gave her nothing. She hadn't heard from whoever was in her head—her sister, as far as she was concerned—and they hadn't turned her cell phone back on yet. They were going to do that inside the hotel when they planned on leaving.

She moved over to a cushioned seat and sat down to watch the front doors while listening to the clerk finish with Disco. After another minute of the clerk explaining the pool hours, the exercise room, the check-out time, and several other details, Sarah tuned out. Disco obtained two room keys and turned around.

"Sir, can our bellhop assist you with your bags?"

Disco whirled back to the clerk. "We don't have any bags tonight."

"Very well. Enjoy your stay, sir."

Disco turned back to Sarah. "Angel? Ready to head up to the room, or are you too comfortable?"

The clerk gave her an odd look that suggested he didn't approve of her style, her hair, or the entire package. This energized her to become slightly more irksome, but she chose to be nice. Being nice didn't raise alarm bells later.

She pushed up out of the plush chair and moved closer to the counter. "I have a quick question for you."

The clerk looked up, a broad smile revealing white teeth, his brow raised, and that odd look from a moment ago vanished.

"Of course. Fire away."

"We walked by about an hour ago and saw several ambulances parked out front." She leaned in and looked at him with her head lowered. "You can tell me. Did something happen? Someone get into a punch-up? I mean, are we safe here?"

"A punch-up?" the clerk stammered, acting surprised that something like that would happen in this hotel. "I wouldn't know what happened, as I'm just the front desk clerk, but they brought quite a few men down from the tenth floor." He raised his hands, palms aimed at her. "That's all I know. As I said, they don't tell me nothing."

She slapped the counter once. "Well, there, I thank you for that. Makes me feel much better."

She stepped away to join Disco, and they walked to the elevator together.

"What floor are we on again?"

Disco checked the room key card, pointing at the small numbers written in pen at the top of the little card. It said they were in room 912.

"Wonderful," Sarah muttered as the elevator doors opened.

They stepped aside to let two couples exit, then got on and pushed the ninth-floor button. Neither spoke as they got to the ninth floor and found their room. Disco used the key to give them access. Once they were both ensconced inside the room, Sarah let out a deep breath.

"Did you hear what that clerk said?"

Disco nodded. "Yeah, some sort of fracas on the floor above us."

She narrowed her eyes at him and put her hands on her hips. "A *fracas*? Really?"

He shrugged. "Why not? Call it whatever you like. A fight, a brouhaha, fisticuffs, scuffle, brawl, melee, a dust-up, and even a free-for-all. I had to use something different after you called it a punch-up. I mean, really? A *punch-up*? How is that staying in character?"

"You're hilarious." She threw her head back in mock exasperation. "Come on. We have to get onto the tenth floor to see what happened."

"Agreed." Disco walked past her and opened the door.

She thought she heard him whisper *punch-up* as he moved down the hallway. It was punctuated by a slight shake of his head.

"You're having too much fun with this," Sarah called after him.

"Nothing wrong with that, right?"

She couldn't argue there, even though she felt guilty for enjoying even one second of what they were doing while an unknown group was holding Willow and everyone else important to her.

They hit the stairwell and quickly ascended to the tenth floor. Disco stopped, pointed at the access card reader, and then tried the ninth-floor card. A red light came up, indicating no access to the floor.

"Shit, now what?" Sarah asked.

"Wait, listen." Disco put his ear to the door and stared at nothing while he listened. "Someone's in the hallway talking."

Sarah lunged forward and knocked on the door hard.

"The talking stopped." Disco waited a heartbeat, then jumped away from the door. "I think they're coming," he whispered.

Seconds later, the door clicked open. "Yes?" a tall man said.

Disco grabbed the door and opened it wide. "We're with the insurance, and they gave us cards programmed for the ninth floor." He stepped past the man dressed in the hotel uniform polo shirt, shaking his head. "I'm still not sure if that was an accident or on purpose."

The man who opened the door gawked at them. "Well, head back down and get a new card." He shook his head and blinked twice. "Wait, insurance for what? And why would they give you the wrong card on purpose?"

Disco looked at Sarah, then back at the tall man, glaring at him. Sarah thought the man looked a lot like Josh Brolin.

"I am not going all the way back down to the front desk to get a new card like this one"—Disco shook it in the air as if he was getting ready to throw it—"only to come right back up to this floor to stand in this exact same spot. We are with Fairmont Insurance and are here to survey the damage to see if it's covered under the hotel policy. Otherwise, the previous tenants will have to pay, as we won't accept the claim. Regarding your second question, they might have given us the wrong key on purpose because I told the front desk clerk and manager, and don't ask me for names because I suck with names, that the likelihood of us accepting this claim was pretty near zero. That wasn't an answer they enjoyed hearing. How does that sum it up for you?"

Sarah wanted to start clapping. What a performance.

"Well, I can't let you on the floor without a proper card, sir."

"Oh, fuck your card." Disco handed it over. "I'll survey the damage while you run down and get this card switched out. I am not going back down. Besides, we'll be done in a few minutes anyway."

It looked like the tall man—Brolin—seriously contemplated taking the card down to the front desk, then figured it would be a waste of time.

"Now, which room or rooms were damaged?" Disco walked away, glancing into open doors.

Brolin pointed down the length of the corridor. "Room 1010 was the only one hit."

"Hit?" Sarah asked as they got moving down the hall. "What do you mean by 'hit'?"

"There was a skirmish of some kind."

Sarah stared at Disco from behind and wondered if he cracked a smile. That was one of the synonyms he hadn't used.

Brolin continued. "I think ten men were taken to Toronto General just north of here."

They stopped in front of room 1010 to see that it was a total wreck. The window was cracked, the desk chair was in pieces, and the desk unit that had been previously connected to the wall was shattered on the floor and stained with blood.

Sarah stepped inside the room to see that the bathroom was worse. To her eye, the fight started there. The back of the toilet had been used as a weapon and was now broken in two, with small pieces of bone, hair, and blood matted on it. Someone was either dead or would suffer a massive headache tomorrow.

The sink was sprayed with blood, as if someone had taken a can of dark red paint and punctured the side of it. The bathroom mirror was shattered, with several pieces scattered about the room, as it looked like someone had used those pieces as a knife.

All the bedsheets were scattered throughout the room, needing a fire to cleanse them, as it would be too challenging to get the blood stains out. In one area by the mini fridge, a small pool of blood had collected where someone had sat bleeding for some time.

Sarah could only hope and pray that none of her friends were a part of this fight, but she knew deep in her heart that one of them had to be involved. Would it be asking too much for whoever it was to be still alive?

"You said they were taken to Toronto General?" Sarah asked.

The man nodded, a frown creasing his brow. "Aren't you going to assess the room?" He waved a hand at the mess.

"Nothing to assess," Disco said. "We would never cover this claim."

"Oh?"

Disco nodded. "When guests offer their credit card, then break up the room, they can pay for it." Disco started toward the door at the end of the hall that led back to the stairs.

Sarah quickly caught up to him. "We have to go to the hospital," she whispered.

He snapped his fingers as if in a mad rush. "Turn on your phone. Check for messages. Do it here, on this floor. If they track you, we want them to see exactly where you are."

Sarah did as Disco directed, liking the way he thought.

"There's one message."

"What's it say?"

"That Vivian wants to meet me and to reach out when I'm ready to set something up."

"A bit vague, no?"

"Yeah, fucked is the word I'd use. No way my sister would send such casual messages after all this time. Someone's playing a game with all of us for sure."

"You may be unable to avoid playing their game if these are the people who have your daughter."

"True, but I have Amanda."

"You'd use her to bargain?" Disco sounded surprised. "A seventeen-year-old girl?"

Sarah looked into his eyes to see if he was joking. "Disco, I'll do anything to get my family back. I won't *hurt* Amanda, but she isn't going anywhere until Willow and everyone else are safe."

"Hey," the tall man called after them. "I just called the front desk. They said they didn't send up any insurance people."

"Did you speak with Dwayne?" Disco shouted back, his tone a warning in and of itself.

"Well, no, I don't know who I spoke with."

"Call back. Ask for Dwayne. He's in charge of the claims. Anyway, it doesn't matter." Disco waved dismissively at the man. "We're denying the claim."

"I thought you said you suck with names," the guy yelled back.

He ignored the man, grabbed Sarah's hand, and shoved open the door to the stairs. "Turn off that phone again."

"Already done."

On the ninth floor, he used the second room key to access their floor, then they jogged to the elevator. It came quickly; moments later, they were outside the front of the hotel and heading to the Hummer.

"I'll check on my guys to see how Amanda and Brody are doing on our way to the hospital."

"I was hoping you'd say we were headed to the hospital," Sarah said. "I need to see if anyone I know is injured."

"We will be inside that hospital in under ten minutes." He placed a comforting hand on her shoulder, then pushed away to run for the driver's side of his vehicle.

They hopped in the Hummer and were underway in seconds.

Sarah rubbed the tops of her thighs. "It doesn't look like anyone is at the Royal Oak anymore. Someone at the hospital will know where they went. And what a great place to hurt people for information. They're already in a building littered with doctors, nurses, and all the equipment they'll need to help people in pain."

"Unless we have to kill a few of them."

They exchanged a glance.

"Well, there's that. But hospitals have morgues, right?"

"That they do, that they do."

Chapter 23

AARON RAN TO THE hotel bathroom, looked behind the door, then dropped to the carpeted floor and searched under the beds.

Willow was nowhere to be seen. The bastards had tricked him. They'd separated him from his daughter, and he fell for it, thinking she was safe to be left alone for a few minutes.

He was breathing too fast, his heart racing a mile a minute. His skin tingled, and he fought dizziness to remain upright.

"*Why!*" he shouted, then ran to the door, smashing into it with his shoulder.

The door wouldn't budge. He spun around, searching for the desk chair, then jumped over to it.

"Stay calm, Mr. Stevens," someone shouted through the door. "She will be back shortly."

A distant part of his brain told him it was Tom's voice, but Aaron was too focused on the task. He grabbed the chair, lifted it over his head, and twisted at the waist, sending it sailing through the air at the large window.

It hit with a solid thunk, then dropped to the floor, the window unmarred.

"Aaron!" Tom yelled. "Do not break the glass, or we will come in there and subdue you."

Aaron was already picking up the chair for another swing at the window. He infused as much torque as he could muster this time, throwing the chair at the glass with all the pent-up rage at what they were doing to his daughter.

Even as the chair connected with the glass, the door shot open, and four men barged in, diving on Aaron before he had a reasonable chance to fight them off. Their combined weight and formidable strength were enough to force him onto his stomach as he wailed and thrashed. His arms were wrenched back, and metal cuffs were slapped on, but he barely felt the bite of metal on his skin as he jerked under their weight like a wild cat in the claws of a predator.

Something landed hard on his legs, forcing his knees in a way they refused to bend. The pain was immediate and intense, dissolving all the fight in him in a blinding flash of white-hot agony.

The freedom his lower extremities once enjoyed was restricted by something on his ankles.

Aaron screamed in pain until the pressure relaxed, then he took in the room and his current position, breathing hard to stay awake and not pass out, frothing at the mouth like a rabies-infected animal.

The men had gotten up off him, but he couldn't move. Arms and legs bound, he remained on the floor, his shoulders aching with the strain.

"What have you done with my daughter?" He forced it out through his teeth, the rage in him a seething breath of words. Untied and on his feet, he'd kill every one of the men watching him.

Each face revealed nothing. There was no hint of empathy, no compassion, no nothing. Dead expressions of men who'd seen battle and were just doing a job for a paycheck, the money of which would buy them booze and weed. His life, relationships, and the trauma they were causing in Willow were all for a few measly dollars that would be drunk or smoked away.

How was this possible? How could people be so heartless, so empty?

He tried to roll but couldn't. Curling into the fetal position didn't help.

"Aaron," Tom called. "Relax. Calm down. Willow will return in a few minutes. It didn't have to be like this."

Aaron screamed at the mention of her name. Gasping for a breath, struggling against what bound him, he glared up at Tom with a raging hatred. "You will all pay for this."

"Your threats hold no weight, little boy. This ends tomorrow. You go back to your life, and these men go on another mission." Tom lowered until he was squatting in front of Aaron. "You see how this all works? We're professionals, and you're a common citizen. So, watch your little mouth, or you might get hurt." Tom slapped Aaron's face twice. It enraged Aaron to snap his teeth at Tom's hand. "If you'd like a beating, these men will oblige. Then you could recover with your friend Alex at the hospital. These men wouldn't mind giving you a few broken bones. After all, Alex almost killed a few of their friends." Tom slapped Aaron once more, but this time much harder. Heat rose to the cheek that Tom had slapped, and Aaron tasted blood where his teeth had cut the inside of his cheek. "I'm the only one keeping them off you because we need you to take care of Willow until Sarah arrives. Then we don't need you." Tom pushed up to a standing position again. "I'll drive you back to Toronto myself, or I can call an ambulance for you. Either one works for me. So, if I were you, I'd watch my mouth until Sarah arrives."

"Fuck you," Aaron managed to say, then spit blood-tinged saliva at Tom's shoes.

"Wow, some people are just asking for it." Tom nodded once.

One of the men pulled back a foot and kicked Aaron in the gut like he was punting a football for the end zone.

The air whooshed out of Aaron's lungs. He lay there, mouth open, trying to breathe, but nothing was coming or going.

Man after man filed out of the room, and the door closed and locked.

Only when the door was completely closed did a smidgen of air traverse his airways. Then more came. The darkness at the edge of his eyesight eased off, then disappeared as he began to breathe again, tears escaping his eyes.

He'd kill them all. Each and every one of them for hurting Alex, for hurting Willow, for doing this to his family, his people.

They picked the wrong group to fuck with.

This was no game. If it were, the visiting team would lose.

He would make sure of that.

Now he was happy Sarah had taken Janice's daughter. Maybe now, that woman Janice would know how it felt.

Sarah was coming, just like Willow told him. And when she got there, all hell would break loose, and he'd be there to help.

To kill as many mercenaries as possible.

Chapter 24

ALTHOUGH IT TOOK LONGER than expected to find parking, they eventually found a spot two blocks from the hospital.

Sarah felt antsy, bouncing her leg and fidgeting with her hands. Everything seemed so out of her control, yet she couldn't accept the blame for any of it. They came at her, not the other way around. This wasn't her fault.

"You okay?" Disco asked when he turned off the Hummer.

"Yeah." She looked over at him, her hand on the door handle. "Why?"

"Because you're like a junkie jonesing for a fix."

Sarah's leg stopped moving. "Is it bothering you?"

"What the fuck do I care if you're a bouncy girl?" He laughed briefly. "Just checking in."

"Well, I'm pretty fucked up right now. Aaron and Willow were supposed to meet me almost twenty-four hours ago, and I have *no* idea where they are. Darwin got taken off his plane by the authorities. For what? How did they even know he was coming? I mean, Darwin has some old enemies. He won't see tomorrow if they learn about him being in Toronto."

"Darwin can take care of himself." Disco tapped Sarah's shoulder in an attempt to comfort her, but it didn't work. It only made her want to yank her shoulder away, but she resisted.

"And who the fuck is masquerading around as my sister? What kind of sick and twisted game are they playing? This stuff just gets so frustrating at times. I'm so sick of powerful people doing and saying whatever they want. I saw that photo they sent of Aaron, Willow, and my mom chatting in the hotel room. At least I know they're okay, but that photo was taken in the Royal Oak, so where are they now?" She jerked her head toward the hospital once. "And who will we find in there? Is Parkman on life support? Aaron? Alex?"

Disco stared out the windshield, looking at nothing, his gaze distant. He blinked once, then faced her. "Well, they want to meet—"

"So we'll meet."

"And you've got Amanda."

"Two can play their game."

"And you've got that voice, whatever the hell it is, in your head."

"Unreliable at best lately."

Disco frowned. "Really? I thought whoever that is has saved your life countless times."

"It did in the past. Over the last few years, the conversations were sporadic at best, and the information was limited. I follow what they say as best as I can, but it's been slowing down. I miss the days when Vivian—I have to call the voice Vivian because that's how it's been from the beginning—would *chat* with me."

"You know, most people would call that schizophrenic."

They stared at each other for a stretch. Then she cracked a smile. "True, and it does sound funny, but that's my truth."

"What's next?"

"Next?"

"I mean, after the hospital?"

"I text back that I'm willing to meet this imposter, this *Vivian*, but it has to be tonight."

Disco checked the time. "Then we'd better hurry because it'll be ten soon."

"We can meet at midnight or one in the morning. I don't care. But we are meeting tonight. If it's my sister, she'll understand me."

"Without *knowing* you, you think she'll understand you?"

Sarah nodded. "Sure, it's in our DNA."

"Yeah. Right." Disco jumped out, and Sarah followed on her side.

They jogged to the front of the hospital, ran inside through the automatic doors, and then headed to the triage to ask about the men brought in from the Royal Oak Hotel.

When the woman behind the Plexiglas looked up, Disco said, "We just had a dear friend get admitted and want to check on them. Can you tell us where the people from the Royal Oak Hotel went? What floor?"

The woman typed something on her computer, then looked up again. "I'll need a name."

Sarah leaned forward and said Alex's full name. It was the most logical, as only he could be the one who put that many men in the hospital. Parkman and Daniel could put up a solid fight, and Aaron would be excellent, but Alex would be relentless. Was it ten men? Military trained? Mercenaries? Had to be Alex.

"I have Alex on the third floor. His doctor is Dr. Green." The woman picked up her phone and tapped in a number. "There's a note here to call him if anyone shows up. It's best to speak with Dr. Green, and he can bring you to see Alex."

The hospital had a casual feel as people were milling about. It reminded her of an airport minus the luggage. Men and women in long white coats and scrubs strolled by with purpose. Members of the public ambled by, some with injuries—a cast on a broken arm, a sling and tensor bandage for a sprain, a plastic contraption covering a foot, crutches—while several others were weeping.

Sarah hated being in a hospital. It brought back all the injuries she'd sustained over the years, making her adjust her weight to ease off the foot that was broken by a mad woman who ended up being a cannibal in Kelowna many years ago.

She shook her head to break the reverie and glanced back at the desk.

"Dr. Green will meet you both on the third floor. Elevators are that way." The woman pointed down the hall. "But wait, take these visitor passes. You've got about a half-hour left."

Dr. Green was waiting for them when the elevator opened on the third floor. "Are you here to see Alex?"

Sarah nodded. "How is he?"

"What relation to Alex are you?"

"Sister."

"Your name?"

Her patience was thin, and she almost screamed at the man. Instead, she took a calming breath and said, "Sarah, and this is Sam. He's with me."

"Come this way."

They followed the doctor past two nurses' stations, around a corner, and to the end of the hall to room 314.

Dr. Green opened the door, and Sarah followed him inside, with Disco coming in behind her.

A blanket pulled up over his sternum, Alex lay on the hospital bed. Above that, his left arm was in a cast already, and there were heavy bandages on his left shoulder area. Sarah took in the bandages encasing his head and had to fight back the tears.

She covered her mouth with her hands and stepped closer. His face was ruined. Both eyes were puffy with swelling, and his nose was twice the standard size, even though it was covered in bandages. Bruises were already forming intense colors like purple, dark blue, and black, some framed in yellow.

"How bad?" Disco asked the question on Sarah's mind.

"Well," Dr. Green spoke softly. "The pain was hard to manage. Either that or it was his anger. We had to give him a sedative to calm him down."

"You gave ... him a sedative?" Sarah asked, finding her voice. "Don't be in the room when he wakes up, Doc."

"I'm not sure he'll be able to do much harm. He's got cuts and bruises, scratches and lacerations like someone in a bar fight. He's also got a broken left clavicle, a broken left arm, a nasal fracture, a possible concussion, and several pulled muscles and tendons. I'm not sure this boy should have another bar fight until at least Christmas."

"You said bar fight twice." Sarah glanced at Disco, then back to the doctor. "Didn't this happen in a hotel?"

"We responded to a report of multiple victims at a bar in the hotel lobby. A brawl had taken place over who would buy the next round."

"Yeah," Sarah said sardonically. "That sounds about right."

"This is a clear case of *you should see the other guy*, though," the doctor said, changing the pitch of his voice to say the popular cliché.

"How do you mean?" Sarah moved closer to Dr. Green. "The others are worse?"

"Where do I start?" Dr. Green shook his head as he stared at Alex. "I've got two men in a coma, and several men have collapsed lungs from someone stomping on their chests. Either that, or they got kicked *very* hard. Internal bleeding, bruised organs, two punctured lungs with a piece of a mirror still inside one man, a ruptured spleen, two broken kneecaps, and in three cases, bones were sticking out of flesh when the men arrived. One even had a broken femur, which is one of the most painful bones to break. I could tell you about the broken jaws, orbital bone fractures, and missing teeth, but I want to find out how all that happened, and yet no one wants to press charges."

Sarah exchanged a glance with Disco, then lifted her shoulders. "That is odd."

"Yeah, and most of the men I worked on remain nameless with some major corporation's blank cheque footing the bill for meds." He gestured toward Alex. "This guy got the least damaged, but he's still in a bad way."

"Anything permanent?"

The doctor shook his head. "From what I can see, he'll recover fully. Eventually. It'll take several months for the bones to fuse, heal, and stop hurting. Although, his anger will take much longer. A broken arm or not, this guy was a challenge to work on. No one could touch him. He kept smacking people." Now it was the doctor's turn to shrug. "I didn't know what else to do. I had to sedate him. Tying him to the bed would've been more detrimental to his broken arm."

"Is that why you met with us, why you have a message on his name to call you if anyone came asking about him?"

The doctor faced her. "Of course. I wanted to be forthcoming with the family or friends so you'd understand our intentions, as all we wanted to do was help him."

"Doctor, it's okay. We understand. Under any other circumstances, no one touches Alex unless he lets them." Now she was consoling the doctor and assuring him of no upcoming lawsuit. "When can we talk to him?"

"Oh, sorry." The doctor breathed in past his tightened teeth, making a wet, breathy sound. "He'll be out until the morning at least, and visiting hours will end soon."

"Okay, we'll come back another time. Although, I have a question for you."

The doctor faced her. "Shoot."

"What is clozapine, and what's it used for?" She caught Disco frowning beside her, likely wondering where this was coming from.

Even the doctor seemed taken aback. "Clozapine? Hmm, that came out of left field."

"I'm sorry. Short of googling it, I thought I'd ask you since we're in a hospital."

Dr. Green nodded, seemingly happy to bestow his knowledge upon them. "It's an antipsychotic drug, but not the first one that's recommended. We use clozapine when Risperdal, Seroquel, and several others aren't effective enough. Even though Clozapine is ideal when other meds aren't helping, but there's an issue with white blood cell counts that needs to be monitored."

"Can you tell me some of the side effects of taking clozapine?"

The doctor moved around her, heading closer to the door. "Well, I'm not sure I have time for that, as there are so many. Everyone reacts differently, and there are so many side effects like dry mouth, dizziness, blurred visions—"

"How about tics?"

The doctor stopped at the door, his hand on the knob. "Why are you asking these questions?"

Sarah glanced at Disco, then back to the doctor. "Because I'm worried about someone who is on clozapine. Someone close to me."

The doctor seemed to think about something, as if he had some sort of moral dilemma, but then he nodded again. "Yes, involuntary muscle movements are a strong side effect. Actually, the longer an individual takes antipsychotic meds, the higher the chance they'll develop TD."

"TD?"

"Tardive dyskinesia. Fancy words for repetitive, involuntary movements of the body. Many of the side effects of antipsychotics dissipate when the medication is stopped, but TD can worsen and remain permanent in an individual's life." The doctor seemed agitated now, having spent more time with them than he wanted. "Anything else?"

Sarah shook her head. "Thank you." She gestured at Alex's sleeping form. "Just give us a minute with him."

Dr. Green nodded and stepped out of the room, the door closing whisper-soft.

"Whoa, what the fuck was that all about?" Disco whispered.

Sarah stared at Alex before she answered. "Amanda said she was taking clozapine, and I witnessed her having what looked like mini seizures. Without much time to look it up, I figured the doctor could fill us in."

Disco stared at her a moment longer. "So she's on antipsychotics?"

"Looks that way."

He shook his head in dismay, then turned to look at Alex. "Sounds like Alex kicked ass hardcore."

"And paid the price for it. He'll be so pissed off with a broken arm and collarbone. He'll lose three months of training, at least. And that nose?" Sarah moved closer, the tears harder to fight off. "My poor Alex, what were you fighting for? Trying to escape?"

"How about we ask the others?"

Sarah wiped her cheek and turned back to Disco. "Let's do it before they kick us out of here."

They left and moved to the next room, which had an open door. Sarah peeked inside and saw that this one wasn't private like Alex's. Three men with military haircuts were connected to various machines, with one man's heart rate being monitored.

A woman was typing something into a laptop when they entered.

"Can I help you?" she asked.

"You their nurse?" Sarah moved closer to her.

"Visiting hours are almost over."

"We won't be long."

The woman closed her laptop as Sarah moved to the foot of the bed, where the man was watching them.

"Are you family?" the woman asked.

Sarah nodded. "Shhh, it's top secret," she whispered.

The nurse scrunched up her brow. "What?"

"Do you have names for these guys?"

"No, that's what I was trying to determine."

"You'll never get their names. It's all top secret. That's why we can't tell you our names." She made a shooing motion with her hand. "Now, run along and give us a few minutes with our family."

The nurse hurried out, likely to call a doctor or run to security.

"We haven't much time." She moved around the bed of the man whose eyes were half open. His leg was in a cast, his face was a mess, and they'd applied quite a few bandages to his chest and side. "What happened at the hotel?"

He tried to open his eyes, was partly successful, saw Sarah's face, then blinked several times. Sarah put a hand on the man's chest and applied a small amount of pressure.

His eyes widened, and his mouth opened.

"What happened at the hotel?"

"He's probably all drugged up, Sarah. You won't get much from him."

"I can try." Anger welled in her that these men had held Alex against his will. "Where's my daughter?" She slapped the side of the man's swollen cheek. "Wake up, asshole."

The heart monitor to her right beeped faster. When she looked over at the other patient, he was staring at her, a look of fear on his face.

Sarah moved away from the sleepy guy and smacked the other man. "Where's my daughter? Speak up."

"She's gone," the man said, his heart racing now. That machine's noise was bound to bring doctors running.

"Gone where?" Sarah smacked him harder this time. "Don't fuck with a mother. Ever."

The man angled his head to look at her, hatred in his eyes. "We'll kill that little punk when we get out of here. Then that asshole Parkman, Aaron, and everyone else. They're all dead—"

Sarah clamped a hand over the man's mouth.

"Sarah?" Disco breathed the word. "What are you doing?"

"What am I doing?" She grunted, forcing her hand to remain over the man's mouth. "I'm doing. Him. A. Favor."

The heart monitor lit up like a slot machine, announcing a jackpot.

Disco tugged at her shirt. "We have to *leave*. Now!"

Sarah leaned in close to the man. "Anything happens to my family, and I execute your entire family, then kill you." She lifted her hand and then drove it back down onto the man's mouth, knuckles first. When she spun around, she unplugged several cords from the wall, and the heart monitor flicked off.

Then Disco was dragging her toward the door.

Outside in the hallway, names were being called over the speaker system, and a group of people was coming around a corner up ahead in a hurry.

They walked toward a door marked EXIT, then turned back.

Sarah saw the same nurse from moments before, waving her arms outside the room.

"They were just here," she cried out. "A man and a woman. I think she was wearing a wig. It didn't look natural."

Sarah ducked into the stairwell, and before the door closed, she heard a man shout, "Find them."

"We need to hurry."

"No shit."

Chapter 25

SOMEONE KNOCKED, THEN THE motel room door opened.

"Why bother knocking?" Aaron asked. "It's not like I can open the door for you in this condition. You guys fucking left me tied up."

Tom stepped in with the same four men from before.

"How long has it been? Ten minutes?" Aaron asked. "Missed me already?"

"No idea why you're trying to be funny." Tom stood over him, hands on his hips. "You're an asshole, but Vivian is important to us. And since you are Willow's father, we are supposed to be nice to you."

"Well, if this is being nice to me, I'd hate to see your mean."

"Control yourself around us, and you won't see our mean side. Remember, I said Vivian is important to us, not you. But we will let you live."

"That's a step up."

"Without being shackled."

"What's the catch?"

"Your daughter is being brought back to this room in a few minutes. Do you want her to see you like this, or would you prefer to wait patiently in that chair over there?"

Aaron didn't have to think about it, but had to delay his answer because his breath was caught in his throat. They were bringing Willow back to him. He didn't expect that so soon, if ever.

"I'd rather the chair." He shook his hands and rolled to give them access.

"So, the catch is, when we release you, there's no fighting. The second we detect any aggression, you're tied up for the rest of the night."

Aaron glared up at Tom. They knew they had him because of Willow.

"I'll remain calm when I have my daughter. Take her again from me, and I can't make any promises."

"We do not need to take her from you a second time." Tom nodded at his men, and they went about unlocking the cuffs and ankle restraints.

Once they were done and Aaron was freed, he rolled onto his back and stared at the ceiling while massaging his wrists.

Tom stared down at him. "You still have it all wrong, don't you?"

"Me?" Aaron searched above him until he met Tom's gaze. "How do I have it all wrong?"

"We're friends, and—"

"Yeah, right. I abduct and tie up all my friends. You're quite convincing with that argument."

"If you would let me finish."

Aaron grunted in response.

Tom exhaled a heavy sigh. "Vivian Roberts has been released from her position with the US government. Effectively, she's retiring. Because she's a valuable asset, we were brought in to help her make contact with her family. So we had to look into the people she would be integrating with. That means we know your history. We know about Sarah." He paused, likely to let that sink in. "Since we thought Vivian's story would be hard to believe, Janice wanted us on board. It was a simple case of contacting the mother, Amelia, and bringing her in first so she could help us win the others over. But Sarah fucked that up."

Aaron sat up and leaned against the bottom of the bed. "Are you actually believing this fiction?"

"We've got another minute or so before Willow comes back. I will explain as much as possible, then you can hear it from her. Whether you believe it or not, it's true."

Aaron took in the men lingering behind Tom, their expressions dead serious. "You guys should win an award for this performance." His chest hitched up as he took in a huge breath, then released it along with the tension he'd been carrying. "Really, I'm serious. Bravo." He clapped twice.

Tom went on as if Aaron hadn't said a thing. "Vivian's death never happened. The agency she worked for didn't even make it up. Vivian went missing when Amelia and her daughter were shopping at the mall. That was supposed to be it, end of story. At the time, there was a group of people trafficking little girls, and when they went to plant evidence of another girl, she looked almost identical to Vivian, so the people Vivian worked for left her DNA at the crime scene instead. That wasn't supposed to happen."

"And that's how Sarah's parents heard their daughter was raped and murdered?"

Tom nodded. "Regrettably so. When they try to cover their tracks, they don't make it that traumatic for the parents."

"Sarah has told me all about Armond Stuart and how he admitted to killing Vivian. How can you explain that?"

"The ravings of a lunatic who raped and killed dozens of girls, if not hundreds, in his lifetime. Do you think he could recall every girl he violated by name? Sarah went after that monster righteously and did what many people couldn't do. But did he touch her sister, Vivian Roberts? No, he didn't because Vivian is waiting to talk to you in another hotel room."

Aaron glanced at the open door. If what they were saying was true, that would be a massive win for Sarah. These people would have to deal with Sarah if it weren't true. He'd want to stay out of that fight.

"Well, where has Vivian been all these years? Why not reach out earlier?"

"She dedicated her life to the service of her country, and that service has ended. She's retiring with a full pension and protection for the first few years."

"Protection? What would she need protection from?"

"Sarah, mostly."

Aaron jerked his head back and frowned. "Why? If they're family, that wouldn't make sense."

"We know that Sarah thinks it's her sister she talks to in her head —"

"You guys know a lot for strangers."

"We know this because we've been effectively briefed on the file. Vivian has watched you all from afar. Do an extensive Google search, and anyone will see who Sarah is and how her story has played out from Gert when she was eighteen to Vegas, Los Angeles, Mexico, Europe, and recently in New York."

"So what?" Aaron thought about what Tom had said. "If Vivian isn't inside Sarah's head, who is it then?"

Tom shrugged. "How would we know that? Do we even care?

Sarah is the one who will have an existential crisis on that point. Maybe she just hears voices. Maybe she is clairvoyant. Who knows? All I'm telling you is Vivian Roberts is alive. Your daughter just met her, and Vivian wants to see you soon, too."

"Great, I'm always open to meeting new family members. Although usually, it's at Thanksgiving dinner or Christmas time. Can't say that an abduction to a family reunion is the most popular method of endearing oneself to the new dynamic."

Tom didn't move from his position. He stared down at Aaron with something like disappointment. "Your attitude could use an adjustment. That sarcasm seems to be a family trait. You're not listening well, either. Faked death. She served her government in a top-secret program. It's like she's being released from a witness protection program. None of you could know. That's just the way it is. This wasn't personal, so don't take it as an insult."

Aaron rubbed his face and blinked up at Tom. "You take us from our home, kidnap my family and friends, and then comment on my attitude? Understandably, I'm a little ruffled here."

Tom gawked at him. "Look, we've brought half a dozen people back home to their families in a similar fashion, and they were all happy to get a government escort to a fancy hotel where they met their long-lost loved ones. There are many emotions tied up in these sorts of reunions, so we like to control things until everyone's calmed down."

"And to avoid lawsuits, right? Isn't that what you're really saying?"

"No, we do it this way because sometimes people are angry ..."

"No *fucking* kidding."

"... and you bunch are the worst. We knew you and wanted to control the narrative, but we underestimated Alex."

"Yeah, how so?"

"I've got ten guys in the hospital because Alex tore through them."

"Well, maybe you should've been briefed better. Guys like Alex don't take kindly to being abducted."

"We realize our mistake and won't make the same one twice. Stay calm, stay cool, Mr. Stevens, and you'll be home tomorrow." Tom backed toward the open door, and his men filed out around him. "Meet with Vivian when Willow goes to sleep tonight, then make up your own mind. If you still refuse to believe she's Sarah's sister, go home tomorrow and continue your life without Vivian in it. Maybe Sarah will see the truth. Her mother knew her daughter when she saw her." Tom shook his head. "Even after all these years, her mother knew."

Tom snapped his head sideways, then stepped aside. "Please, go ahead," he said to someone out of sight, gesturing with his hands, and Willow stepped into the doorway.

Aaron pushed up off the floor and opened his arms. Willow ran to him, and they hugged, the room's door closing them in alone, the lock clicking into place.

He pulled her away from him and sat on the bed to stare into her face. "Are you okay, honey? Did they hurt you?"

Willow shook her head from side to side, then stopped to stare at him. "They gave me pop and chips, and I met Mommy's sister."

"Wow," Aaron said, letting Willow believe what she wanted at the moment. She said the same thing when they'd talked with Amelia in the Toronto hotel room. To discount Willow's story might hurt her. But that didn't stop him from asking questions. "What did she look like? Was she nice?"

"She's tall like Mommy and has the same nose and eyes. She even talks like Mommy a little."

Aaron reared back, surprised. "You mean she swore in front of you?"

"No, silly, I mean, she sounds like Mommy."

Aaron drew Willow close and stared into her eyes. "Can you tell me," he whispered just loud enough for Willow to hear in case anyone else was listening, "that it was Mommy's sister for sure? Like, using your abilities to know?"

Willow stared back. "I don't want to be in trouble for using my abilities."

"It's okay. You won't be in trouble. But could you tell whether it was Aunt Vivian or not?"

Willow nodded with her face aimed at the ceiling, then her chin tapped her chest in the way kids like to exaggerate a nod. "It's Aunt Vivian. There's no doubt, Daddy. Now, can I go to bed? I'm so tired."

Chapter 26

DISCO HIT THE GARAGE door button, then pulled into the warehouse off Richmond. Once the door was down and secured behind them, Sarah and Disco joined the two men, who were sitting with Amanda and Brody.

The man on Sarah's right was gigantic. There was no other word for it. His upper body was massive, with arms as thick as steroids would produce, and a chest like a barrel. The problem was that the guy resembled a light bulb because his legs were bone thin.

The other guy was thin everywhere and reminded her of Alex. His expression spoke volumes about never underestimating him.

"Sarah, this is Ape, and this is Water."

She looked from one man to the other, finally meeting the man whose name had intrigued her since she first heard it earlier in the evening. "I can see why you're called Ape, but why Water?"

"Because of Bruce Lee," the man said.

"Bruce?"

"Be water, my friend. Be the water." The man stared at her a moment longer, then added, "You've not heard his famous speech on being water?"

"Can't say I have."

"YouTube has it. He talks about how water transforms into the item carrying it and how water can crash and yet be formless."

Disco waved his hands. "We've all heard this speech a million times. When this is all over, you two can have the Bruce Lee chat. In the meantime, we have to fix this mess."

Water nodded. "Right. Of course."

"When can we leave?" Amanda asked.

"We're all leaving within the hour." Sarah moved closer to Disco. "I've got an idea. How many men can you gather on short notice?"

"To do what?"

"To aim a weapon."

"Aim a weapon? What about firing it?"

Sarah shook her head. "That probably won't be necessary."

He eyed her a moment. "I could rustle up a dozen men or so."

"Within an hour?"

"It'll take a few phone calls, but it can be done. And it'll be expensive. Some of these guys don't come cheap, especially at this hour."

"Do what you can, and when this is over, Darwin and I will figure out the expenses."

"Where should we meet them? It can't be here. This warehouse is only known to a few of my closest people."

"I'll give you the details in a few minutes." Sarah stepped away. "Wait for me here." Then she turned and ran for the door.

Once outside, she ran up to the next block, stopped on the corner of Spadina and Richmond, turned on her phone, and flicked off airplane mode.

She quickly sent a message back to the people who'd contacted her. *I want to meet my sister. I'm ready.*

Patience wasn't something she had in abundance, but she couldn't *make* them respond, so she had to wait.

It didn't take long.

We are glad to hear that. Would you come to us?

I want to talk to you first, Janice, Sarah typed back.

The message showed that it was read. Then there was no response. She waited an entire minute until her phone vibrated with a phone call from a private number.

"Janice?" Sarah said, placing the phone to her ear.

"Nice to finally speak with you, Sarah. How's Amanda? Faring well?"

The woman's voice was clipped, tight. Sarah imagined her lips pursed, anger on her face, her free hand clenched into a fist.

"Everyone's fine here," she said. "How about over there? No more outbursts from your captives like the Alex issue?"

Janice didn't respond, yet Sarah detected an intake of air. Someone spoke in the background, but Sarah couldn't pick up what they said.

"Janice? Are you still there?"

"Yes, although I'm saddened at the response we're getting from your people."

"Saddened? Hmm, is that the right word? I thought surprised would be more appropriate." Sarah stepped back to lean against the brick wall of a closed clothing store.

"Did you want to see your sister, or did you want to take shots across our bow?"

"You've misread me. I'm willing to play your little game—"

"It's not a game, Sarah. Your sister has completed her contract and is retiring. Family integration is routine. I've known Vivian for over a decade. She's a family friend, so I agreed to help her meet you all. That's all this is."

"I'd love to say I believe you, but then we'd both be wrong."

"Have it your way. Don't come then. But know this: I'm not the only one saying that this is truly Vivian, your real sister, alive and well."

"Oh yeah? Who else agrees with you?"

"Your mother and your daughter."

That hit her in the sternum. They had Willow and Aaron. She didn't know where they'd gone for sure and had assumed that these people had them, but Janice just confirmed it.

Everything came together as Sarah stared up Spadina Avenue at nothing. That was why the voice told her she needed Amanda, Janice's daughter. They had to trade kids to get their lives back.

"Sarah? Cat got your tongue?"

"I just needed a moment to think. No one plans first-degree murder out loud."

"Are you always this sarcastic?"

"Sarcasm is like punching you with words. Makes me feel better since you're not right in front of me."

"My, aren't you delightful? Well, I can already see you're nothing like your sister."

"How so?"

"She's kind and loving and has a big heart. All she wants to do is help people, even complete strangers."

"Like you know me from a newspaper clipping or this two-minute conversation. Fuck you, lady."

Now Janice was silent.

"Where's Parkman? Where's Darwin? How about Daniel and my

mother?"

"They're all here with us. Everyone's safe and sound. It's a big family reunion. We've been trying to get a hold of you. We even sent pictures to reassure you. We're above board, Sarah. Everything's on the up and up."

Yeah right. "Okay, I'll come to your little get-together, but on one condition."

"I'm hesitant to ask, but what is it?"

"I want to hear from Daniel, Parkman, Darwin, Aaron, Willow, and my mother. I need to hear their voices. I need to hear it from them that they're all fine. Otherwise, you're playing some elaborate game with me, and it's one you will lose."

"Sarah, it's late. Some of them will already be sleeping."

"Wake them. And tell me where I'm supposed to go."

"We're at the Sky View Motel on Highway 10 north of Orangeville. Don't come armed. Innocents could be hurt on both sides."

"Orangeville? Shit, that's over an hour's drive from here."

"You want me to send someone to pick you up? That can be arranged."

Sarah pushed off the wall and started moving up Spadina toward Richmond. "I'll come. And I'll be unarmed. But only after I speak to everyone. I need assurances."

"Okay, I'll call you back in fifteen minutes. Have your phone on this time. Oh, and Sarah?"

She turned the corner to Richmond and stopped walking. "What?"

"I want to speak to Amanda, too. No games. You get your people. I get mine."

"Just have everyone ready, or this deal dies along with you."

Sarah ended the call, checked the time, then turned off her phone.

She ran back to the warehouse with a plan and almost no time to execute it.

Chapter 27

THE SUVs SLOWED AND pulled into what looked to be a motel.

"We stopping over for the night?" Darwin asked.

He set his empty cup in the cupholder, wide awake from the caffeine. They'd stopped at the Timmy's as promised, bought him a large coffee, a sandwich, and a donut deal—the Boston cream he wanted—and then drove north for the past hour.

During the trip, no one answered his questions, except to say he wasn't a prisoner and that everything would be explained soon. So far, nothing had been explained, and he still felt like a prisoner.

Once the SUVs stopped, a small group of men came out to meet them. Once Darwin was helped from the SUV, he was directed to a room with the number four on it.

"What's this? My prison cell for the night."

"You're not a prisoner."

"Then I'll be on my way." He moved to the left toward the road, but two men stood in front of him.

"Darwin," the leader guy from the front of his SUV said. "We brought you here to meet someone."

"This is not my go-to method for setting up meetings, but go ahead. Who am I meeting?"

"You'll see soon enough. In the meantime, go inside and have a chat with Parkman."

"You guys have Parkman here?"

The door opened, and they shoved Darwin inside. The door closed behind him and locked.

Parkman was lying on the bed, feet crossed, arms at his side.

He sat up and gawked at Darwin. "Is that you?"

Darwin nodded. "Hey, I missed you, man."

Parkman jumped off the bed, and they embraced.

"Bring me up to speed." Darwin pulled away. "I need to know everything."

Parkman told him all he knew, including his short visit with Vivian. "If I didn't know any better, I'd swear it was Sarah's sister."

"What makes you think she isn't?"

"Everything."

Darwin laughed. "Convincing argument."

"Well, the truth is, it's just too damn hard to believe."

"Sometimes it's hard to believe because it's not real."

"There's that." Parkman's face hardened.

"What is it? What's bothering you?"

"Did anyone tell you about Alex?"

Darwin shook his head. "I've heard nothing."

"He's in the hospital."

Darwin's mouth fell open. "What? Really?" He paused, then, "How?"

"He fought almost a dozen soldiers. They're in worse shape."

"Oh, okay, that makes sense." Darwin moved to the window and peeked outside. "What's going on here? This doesn't add up. Why are they going to all this trouble?"

"I was thinking the same thing. If Vivian really is Sarah's sister, I think they were worried Sarah would end up hurting her before she learned the truth, or worse. If she isn't Sarah's sister, then they're up to something else, and they need us all neutralized to execute that plan."

"And Sarah would end up killing her then, too."

"True, so either way, here we are."

"You think we're bait to get to Sarah?"

Parkman shook his head. "With this much manpower and training, they could just hunt Sarah down and be done with it."

Darwin moved to sit in the chair by the desk. "This is a lot to take in, yet so much doesn't make sense." He studied the room. "These are places you take a captive. You tie them up, hold them until they go back in the trunk of your car, and you drive somewhere else. In the end, you're forced to kill them because they've seen your face."

"I have a strong feeling that's not the case with these people." Parkman moved back to sit on the bed. "They remind me of the Sophia Project men we met in Hungary and then again in Toronto. They had far-reaching power and did as they pleased."

Darwin rested on the arms of the chair and leaned forward. "You think the Sophia Project is back and interested in Sarah? If so, they're in for a surprise. They'll never tame her. They couldn't then, and they won't now."

Parkman shook his head. "No, I think whoever these people are, they're interested in something else."

They remained silent for a stretch, lost in their thoughts, until someone pounded on a door. "Phone call in five minutes," the person shouted. A moment later, they pounded on Parkman's door. "Phone call in five minutes." The distant pounding started next door, then moved to the door after that, getting softer as the person made their way down the line.

"What's that all about?" Darwin asked. "Is this a regular event?"

Parkman shook his head. "First time."

Darwin got up and surveyed the room, walking into the corners and checking for hidden cameras. "Are we being watched?"

"Not that I'm aware of. They moved us here quickly after the big fight with Alex at the other hotel."

"So they had no time to wire the place."

"That's my guess."

Darwin moved over to sit on the bed beside Parkman. "You said Alex was in the hospital."

Parkman nodded.

"So he fought a dozen men and survived?"

"Well, eight to ten men, but yeah, as far as I know, he made it."

"They didn't kill him?"

Parkman studied Darwin's face for a moment. "What are you getting at?"

"That we shouldn't be here."

"I'm open to ideas."

"Well, they're not going to kill us, right?"

"We don't know that for sure."

"I've got a theory."

"Shit." Parkman adjusted himself on the bed to be more comfortable. "Am I going to like this theory?"

"Probably not, but if I'm right, we all walk away unscathed."

"You remember, they're the ones with the guns, right?"

Darwin nodded. "I got that."

"So what's the plan?"

Darwin whispered it to him in under a minute.

"That could work." Parkman stared at the curtained window, then looked back at Darwin. "Or it might get us killed."

"If given a chance, it could work very well."

They both jumped when their door shot open, and four men stormed inside the room.

"We need you both to come with us," the man Darwin recognized from the SUV said.

"Why?" Darwin asked.

"Because Sarah's on the phone and wants to talk to you both."

They looked at each other.

Darwin shrugged. "That's a good enough reason for me."

"Me too."

Both men got up and followed the soldiers out of the motel room.

Chapter 28

"How about the Stopover Roadhouse Diner?" Sarah asked. "Would that one work?"

They studied it on Google Maps with that little guy at the street level scanning the front of the roadside diner.

"Yeah, it could work. And it's a 24-hour joint."

"We'll make it work with eight to ten guys," Ape said, his voice deep. "If you have more, even better."

Sarah itched to ask Ape if the steroids had affected his voice, but thought better of it. He was helping her, so she'd reserve her shit talk for someone else.

Water pointed his skinny finger at the screen. "It's about a ten-minute drive farther north of the motel they're staying at."

"How long before we could get there?" Sarah asked.

Disco scrolled with the mouse, typed on the computer, then looked up. "We could be there by midnight, maybe a little past."

"Okay, so we set this meeting for two in the morning."

"Really? You think they'll go for that?"

"I won't give them an option." Sarah pushed away from the table. "I want my daughter back, and Janice wants her daughter back. I'm not too sure how much of this I can take, so it has to end tonight." She ran for the door. "They're going to call me back. I'll be on the phone for at least five minutes, and then we'll head north." She stopped at the door. "Disco, get as many men as you can to head to the Stopover Roadhouse Diner. Bring as many guns as possible. Without knowing what to expect, we need to be prepared."

Disco shot a look at Amanda. "It's okay," he said. "No one will shoot your mom. Sarah wants her daughter back, and sometimes weapons help people better understand your intentions."

Amanda nodded, and Brody placed an arm around her.

Then Sarah was out the door and running up the street, turning her phone on as she ran. Earlier, Sarah had pulled Amanda aside while the guys were busy looking for a suitable meeting place before they brought up Google Maps and found the roadhouse diner. After a brief chat, she recorded a twenty-second video on her phone of Amanda talking to her mother, telling her she was fine and that they were being kind to her. If Janice refused to agree to Sarah's terms without speaking directly to Amanda, which was expected, they could get back on the phone once they were on the road heading north.

There was no way Sarah would turn on the phone and have Amanda speak to her mother from inside Disco's warehouse.

Back at the corner of Spadina Avenue, Sarah stared at her phone. It had been fourteen minutes since they last spoke to one another. Hoping Janice didn't lie to her and had already sent a team of soldiers to pick her up, Sarah watched every dark corner, every car, but nothing looked out of the ordinary.

When her phone rang in her hand, she jumped. "Yeah," she said, pressing it to her ear.

"Who do you want first?"

"Is Willow awake?"

"Everyone's here, Sarah. You're on speakerphone to make it easier."

I'm on speakerphone, so you can hear if I tell my group a plan.

"Not much privacy, eh?"

"How about Amanda? Is she there with you?"

"You'll get your chance. Willow? You there?"

"Yes, Mommy. I miss you."

Sarah's heart melted and then hardened at the same time. Who could do this to a little girl? Even if everything were on the up and up, she'd hurt Janice just for spite.

"Are you coming to see your sister soon?" Willow asked.

"Yes, honey." Sarah's voice cracked for all the room to hear. "I'm coming soon. Janice and I are going to arrange it."

"That's good, Mommy. I'm sleepy."

"I know, baby. You can sleep soon." She waited a moment, her heart racing. "Aaron? You there?"

"Yeah, right here."

"All good?"

"Right as rain."

"Parkman?"

"Yeah?"

"No issues?"

"None. Well, other than Alex. That's an issue."

"I visited him at the hospital." Someone gasped on their end. "He'll be okay. A few broken bones, but he'll be as good as new in a few months."

"Good to hear," Daniel shouted from somewhere farther away.

"You doing well, Daniel?"

"All good, Sarah. Hey, even Darwin's here."

"They got you off the plane safely, Darwin?" Sarah asked.

"Yeah, a little heavy-handed, but we're all here in one piece."

"Mom? You there, too?"

"I'm here, Sarah. Your sister isn't here, but she'll be along soon."

There was a pause, then Sarah asked, "Mom, tell me in front of all these people. Do you think it really is Vivian?"

"Absolutely. I have no doubt. It's her, Sarah. She even remembers what we did the day she went missing."

"Has anyone else met Vivian yet?"

"I have, Mommy."

Sarah heard her little girl's voice and couldn't believe they'd exposed her to all of this shit.

"And what's your verdict, my tiny Willow?"

"She's your sister, Mommy. It's in her face. I can see."

"Wow, good for you." Would Willow lie that easily in front of all those people? If not, then it had to be Vivian because there's no way they could hoodwink Willow, not with her ability to *see* things.

No way in hell.

"Now," Janice cut in. "You've had your chance. You've heard from everyone." There was a click as the phone went off the speaker. "We're all good here, just waiting for you to conclude our big family reunion." Janice's voice was loud in her ear. "And I need to know Amanda is okay."

"Of course. I'm a mother, too. Call me back without blocking your number."

"Sarah, what are you up to?"

"You want this to work? Then we have to have trust."

There was a pause. "And? So?"

"You know my number. Let me see yours. Then I have a video to send you. I can't send a video to a private number."

"What video?"

"You're wasting time. If you want to see the video, call me back." Sarah hung up and walked left, then spun around to the right. At the corner of Richmond, the phone rang with a number on the screen.

Sarah answered it. "Give me a moment." She pulled the phone away from her ear, brought up the short video she'd shot of Amanda and Brody, then hit the share button and sent it to the number she was speaking to. "There, check your phone."

"Checking now."

Sarah gave her the time to watch the entire video. When she came back on, her voice had changed.

"This wasn't supposed to involve her. And why do you have that boy?"

"Brody was with Amanda when they were escaping Toronto on the GO train."

"What made you say, 'escaping Toronto'?"

"Because that's what it was. They were running away."

"And you just happened to bump into her?"

Sarah leaned down, her free hand on the brick wall beside her. "Janice, I can tell by your tone that you're not happy. You think I like this?"

Janice grunted something into the phone. Was she about to cry? "Nothing will happen to her."

"Of course not. I don't hurt kids."

"That wasn't a question."

There was an extended silence between them. Sarah didn't mind, as it gave Disco more time to arrange what was needed.

"When are you coming to meet Vivian?" Janice asked, her tone hard now. She was back to business.

"Once you've let everyone go."

"Excuse me?" she shouted. "I don't think I heard you correctly."

"Sure you did." Sarah moved backward to a recessed doorway and sat on the steps. "Here's how it'll work. Send everyone away and give them their phones. Tell them to call me when they're clear, and I'll know they're clear because they'll speak freely. Once they're all gone, I'll bring Amanda to you and meet Vivian. Nice and easy."

"No *fucking* way," Janice screamed.

"Think about it. If this is truly just about everyone meeting Vivian, then you don't need my friends anymore. Keep Willow and Aaron, and I'll bring Amanda to you so you have something of mine and I have something of yours. I'll meet Vivian, we can reunite you with your family, and all will be right with the world again. Although, if you try to hurt my people, you'll have another Alex situation on your hands and never see Amanda again."

Sarah smashed the button to end the call. She checked her battery power and saw it was under twenty percent. They needed to wrap this up quickly. She could charge it in the Hummer on the way north.

A minute went by, then another. She tapped her foot, standing on the street corner with one arm across her chest, her hand clasped to the elbow of the other arm, waiting for the phone to ring.

Then it rang.

"What?" Sarah said.

"I'm keeping Aaron and Willow." Janice's voice was stern before. Now it was steel. "The rest can go. They will call you soon."

"That makes sense. After all, wasn't this whole thing to help integrate Vivian back into our lives? Now that they've all met her, you don't need them."

"You have Amanda. I have Willow. Come meet Vivian, and we'll make sure all the families are reunited."

"You have a deal. But I am not leaving Toronto until I receive a call from Daniel, Parkman, Darwin, and my mother."

"They all came with us. None of them has a car."

"That's fine. Put them all in one of yours. I'm sure you have a spare SUV somewhere. Don't all of you guys drive black SUVs? Or is that just the FBI? Anyway, they can all leave together and then call me on their way back to Toronto. When I get that call from *them* that they're safe and long gone, I'll load Amanda and Brody and head your way."

"How can I trust you?"

"Blind faith? It's in the stars? Because you have to? I have no idea and don't care. Just do it if you want to see Amanda again. Also, if this backfires for any reason—which it won't—you saw how easy it was to nab all of them. You can just pick us all up again. You've got the resources. Right?"

"They're preparing an SUV as we speak."

"Brilliant. I expect to hear from them soon. Then I'll be on the way north."

"You know where you're going, where we are?"

"I do." Sarah pushed up off the step and started toward the corner at Richmond.

"And you'll bring Amanda?"

"If I get that call that everyone's safe and they've left the premises, I will bring Amanda. You have my word as a mother." She turned the corner and started back toward the warehouse.

"Don't come armed, Sarah. That won't look good when meeting your sister."

"Why would I need weapons at a family reunion?"

"Vivian has been important to us for a long time. My men will search you."

"And I'll let them search me. If my mom and daughter both tell me this is Vivian, then it's the real deal. I won't need any weapons." She walked faster. It was actually happening. "I'm hanging up now to take Parkman's and Darwin's call that they're safely away."

"See you soon."

"I'll be there by one or two. Stay awake."

"We'll be waiting—"

Sarah cut her off by hitting the end button, then stopped walking.

That voice in her head whispered something that made sense. Sarah stared at nothing for a long moment, then completely understood.

She quickly googled the American embassy in Toronto and called the after-hours emergency line. When it was picked up, she told them everything. After five minutes, she was transferred to the person in charge, the consul general, who was awakened at home to receive the call. Once she spilled everything again, embellishing a few things, the consul general told her what to do next.

Within ten minutes, she was running back to the warehouse. She needed to know how many people Disco had confirmed for the ambush.

Tonight would prove to be quite the explosive family reunion.

Chapter 29

BACK IN THE WAREHOUSE, Disco had already outfitted the Hummer with over a dozen guns and several knives, much to Amanda's dismay.

"Are you guys going to hurt my mom?"

"Sarah?" Disco said, gesturing to Amanda. "She's not listening to me. You tell her."

"Amanda, come sit with me. You too, Brody." Sarah gestured at the chairs they'd set up on the side when Ape and Water watched over them.

Once they were seated, Sarah checked her phone, but Parkman or Darwin or anyone hadn't called yet. She'd thought about turning it back off, then changed her mind. If they were tracking her phone and zeroed in on them in the warehouse, they'd be gone before long. Would Janice take those kinds of risks while Sarah had Amanda?

Sarah didn't think so.

But why were they taking so long to call her?

She held the phone up in the air and shook it. "I'm waiting for an important call. Once we receive it, we leave."

Amanda nodded. "All of us?"

"Yes, you're coming with us."

"What are all the guns for?" Brody asked, wrapping a protective arm around Amanda. It appeared he was doing that more and more. Maybe he subconsciously figured he could control her TD, those jerking tics. If he thought that, he'd be wrong.

"The people your mom has working for her can be dangerous. The guns are for our protection. I assure you that no harm will come to you or your mother. We intend to get my daughter back unharmed."

"I still don't understand. Why would my mom work for people who would kidnap your daughter?"

"I'm as lost as you are. Your mom and dad sound like good, career-oriented people. They are clearly trying to ameliorate a sensitive situation and don't claim they kidnapped anyone. They've merely *picked up* my family to have a reunion of sorts."

Amanda seemed confused but appeared willing to go with it.

"Look, I can promise you we mean no harm regarding your mother. I want you there when we meet her so that nothing will go wrong." This wasn't entirely true. They'd be stopping before the rendezvous at the roadhouse diner to drop Amanda and Brody off somewhere, but now wasn't the time to tell them that. "Also, I'll be unarmed as a sign of good faith." She gestured over her shoulder at the guys loading the Hummer. "These guys are my protection. That's it. They will be backing me up."

Sarah rechecked her phone. No call. *What the hell? Was Janice playing hardball?*

This made her nervous. Could something have happened to them?

"Earlier, you said I was leverage."

"You are and will still be. I want my daughter back, and your mom wants her daughter back. It's a win/win."

"Can I ask you one more question?"

Sarah glanced down at her phone, her leg tapping a mile a minute. "Sure. Go ahead."

"The more I stare at you, the more you look familiar."

"How so?"

"My mom's friend, Vivian …" Amanda glanced over at Brody, then back to Sarah. "You guys could be related. Are you?"

Sarah's leg stopped moving. She stared at Amanda, unflinching, her hand tightening on the phone wrapped in her fingers.

What if it was *actually* true? Could she even entertain the idea for a second that her *real* sister was alive? Even Willow confirmed it, so it had to be the case, right?

"Sarah?" Amanda whispered. "Did I say something wrong?"

Sarah snapped out of it and opened her mouth to respond, but then her phone rang.

Call display said it was Parkman. She raised a trembling finger. "I have to get this. Don't move."

Sarah jumped up from her chair and answered on the third ring.

"Hey, you guys all good?"

The sound of a vehicle's engine could be heard in the background.

"Yeah, we have left them behind at the motel. Darwin's beside me, and Daniel is in the back with your mother."

"Hi, Sarah," her mother said, the sound coming through like she was talking into the wind.

"Brief me on them. What am I walking into?"

"They've been kind, fed us well, and as long as we didn't protest much, we were handled well. Alex fought back, and you know how that went. Aaron protested when Willow met your sister, so they had to secure him, but he's fine now."

"My *sister*?" Sarah stared at the far wall of the warehouse, wondering if she'd ever believe the unbelievable. "Parkman, is it possible?"

"Last week, I would've said absolutely not, but I didn't meet her. According to Willow and your mother, it's definitely Vivian."

"It's her, Sarah," her mother added. "I'm sure of it."

"And no one else is in the car with you guys? No one is listening? You're not under duress?"

"No duress, Sarah," Darwin jumped in. "We're free and clear. However, it was hard to leave Aaron behind. Knowing you were coming helped us leave."

"What took you guys so long? I figured you would've called before now."

"Janice had to get a vehicle ready. All the SUVs were armed and had some personal effects. They emptied this one and gave it to us."

"You think they're tracking you?"

No one answered right away. Then Darwin said, "It's likely. But to what end? They want you to meet Vivian, and Janice wants Amanda back."

Something bothered her about how long it took to get the SUV ready. Something wasn't right. As a mother, Janice would have ordered them into the SUV and torn out the stuff they wanted to keep. Why did it take twenty minutes to empty just a few bags?

"Where are you guys now?"

"Ten minutes south of the motel."

"Okay, here's what I want you to do. Drive to Orangeville, find a motel, and leave Daniel with my mother. We'll meet them after this is over."

"Why, Sarah?" her mother asked.

"Because this isn't over, and I need as many men to help as possible."

"I can help," Daniel shouted.

"You are helping by staying with my mother. We need this abduction shit to stop."

"Got it," Daniel said, his voice more subdued.

"Then what?" Parkman asked.

"Head back toward the motel on Highway 10, and drive past it for about ten minutes."

"Ten minutes? Why? What's up there?"

"You're going to stop at the all-night truck stop diner called The Stopover Roadhouse Diner."

"And?" Darwin chimed in. "Do what? Order some food? I'm hungry."

"Sure, order food. What you're doing there is waiting for us. We'll meet you there."

"When?"

"We should show up by one or one-thirty. But there's something else."

"What's that?"

"Don't stay in the SUV. If they're tracking it, park it on the road and walk the last hundred meters as if it ran out of gas."

There was silence again.

"Would you rather we change cars in Orangeville?" Darwin asked.

"Car rental agencies won't be open at this hour."

"I didn't say *rent* one. I said *change* one."

"No, they won't do anything to you guys until they see us, and they won't see us until two in the morning."

"Okay, I've got the Stopover Roadhouse location on my phone," Darwin said.

"Great, we're on our way."

"How will we know it's you?"

"We'll be in Disco's Hummer."

"Oh, right, easy. See you soon."

Sarah hung up, slipped her phone into her pocket, and spun around. Amanda and Brody were still watching her.

She walked over to them and placed her hands on the back of the chair she'd been sitting in before the phone call.

"In response to the last thing you said, yes, Vivian is my sister." She raised a finger to make a point. "My *alleged* sister." She lowered her hand back to the chair. "That remains to be seen." She clapped her hands once. "How about it? Let's take you home to your mother and meet my sister."

Chapter 30

AFTER SECURING DANIEL AND Amelia in a motel that accepted cash in Orangeville, Parkman and Darwin headed north on Highway 10. Parkman cut the lights as they approached the Sky View Motel and drove by in the dark.

None of the vehicles had been moved. Everything was exactly as it was when they'd left earlier. Several hundred yards up the road, Parkman turned the lights back on, and they drove the ten minutes until they got to the roadhouse diner.

At this late hour, there were only a few cars out front with eight long-haul rigs parked at the side of the building, several with engines running. Parkman drove past the diner, then eased to a stop about a hundred yards north and pulled off onto the shoulder.

Without a word, they got out, locked it up, and started the short trek back to the diner.

"I'm starving," Darwin said. "All I've had since they fed us on the plane, which was a *long* time ago, was a donut."

"I can't think about food at a time like this."

"Hey, if we've got an hour to kill, and we're in a truck stop, why wouldn't we eat?"

"What about that plan you whispered to me in the motel?"

"That was meant to get back at them for what they did to Alex and to get out of there."

"Well, we're free." Parkman pointed at the diner. "About to order some food. So, I guess that plan is dead?"

"And?"

"I'm just asking because we'll see those guys again soon. Do you want to stick to the *getting back at them* part?"

"I'd wait to see what Sarah has in mind. She may have already covered that."

"True."

They walked up the three wooden steps at the front and entered a truck stop built in the 1950s. It still had the long counter with round, swivel chairs running the length of the back. Tables that could seat four people ran the length of the windows, each chair on its own individual swivel. Everything was red—red cushions, red countertop, even the ceiling was painted red.

A waitress behind the counter was pouring coffee into a man's cup. She smiled at them when they entered, nodding once.

"Evening," she said. "Take a seat anywhere."

Darwin gestured toward a table in the far corner that would allow them to see the road without being observed. Menus were already on the table. Darwin grabbed his and scanned it quickly.

The waitress brought over the coffee pot and glasses. "Two coffees?"

They both nodded.

She set the mugs down and poured into both of them, then nodded toward the creamers and sugar packets on the table.

"I'll need a cheeseburger and fries," Darwin said without preamble.

"And you?" The waitress set the coffee pot down, flipped open a pad, and jotted down Darwin's order with jerky motions of her pen.

Parkman stared at the desserts on the menu, then pointed. "Give me the apple pie."

"With ice cream?"

"Sure. Vanilla."

She nodded, slipped her pad away, collected the menus, then leaned over the table and dropped them into their holder. Once she had the coffee pot in her grip again, she hurried away, saying, "Coming right up," as she headed toward the kitchen.

"Fast service," Darwin said, glancing around the place.

"Not too busy at this hour. How many patrons in total?"

Darwin's head bobbed slightly as he surveyed the restaurant. "I count eight." He checked his watch. "By the time Sarah gets here, half of them will be gone. They're already eating."

"More might come."

"True. But it's late. Even if more come, eight might be the high-end number."

Parkman leaned forward. "It's good to see you, Darwin. We didn't get a formal hello." He leaned back in his seat and placed both hands on the table flat-out. "I'm happy you could fly in to help."

"I'm happy to be here." He scanned the restaurant again. "I didn't like how Janice's people acquired me, though. Somewhat nerve-wracking."

"What happened?"

Darwin filled him in on how they stopped the plane and walked him off. "The big question is why?"

"How do you mean?"

Darwin scanned the restaurant, then leaned his elbows on the table, playing with a sugar packet. "Why go to all that trouble, get clearance to stop a plane on the tarmac just to drive me here and let me go?" He met Parkman's gaze and saw the worry in the man's eyes. "The power these people have is immense. What are they playing at?" He pointed out the window. "They took too long to get that SUV ready for us. Then Sarah told us to park far from the diner." He shook his head and looked down at the packet of sugar. "Something is still coming. Something bad."

"I feel it, too. This isn't over by a long shot." Parkman shifted in his seat. "They waited until I parked my car, then nabbed me as I entered the Royal Oak Hotel."

Darwin tossed the packet aside and picked up his coffee, sniffing it. "Tell me something."

"What?" Parkman grabbed his coffee, too.

"Looking at things from a different angle, what are the odds that someone's fucking with Sarah?" Darwin's eyes narrowed. "Could Vivian be alive?"

Parkman shrugged. "Everything rational says no way, and even Amelia's assertion that it's Vivian wouldn't be enough for me to believe it." Parkman stared down at his coffee cup. "But Willow. That's a different story."

"Could Willow be lying?"

Parkman shook his head. "That girl doesn't know how to lie."

Darwin's brow tightened, and he shook his head slightly. "Can you explain that?"

"If someone were masquerading as Vivian, Willow would be able to see through it. She has unique abilities. I do not doubt Willow. If she states emphatically that it's Vivian Roberts before her, I'd never ask for a DNA test."

"I hear they have one and are saving it for Sarah."

Parkman reared back. "What? Where'd you hear that?"

"Amelia told me. They asked her to provide a DNA sample and showed her the results today. They've got irrefutable proof of Vivian's existence."

Parkman stared at Darwin open-mouthed. "Wow," he managed to say. "Sarah won't be able to deny it then."

Darwin sipped his coffee, watching Parkman over the lip of his white cup.

"What?" Parkman asked. "What else is on your mind?"

"The question everyone is thinking."

"Which is?"

"Who's been talking to Sarah all this time? You know, in her head?"

The door opened, and Parkman turned to see two large men enter the diner. Both men could be stereotyped as thugs. They looked like they were part of a gang with their neck tattoos, tight T-shirts, and angry expressions.

"Looks like someone's pissed off with the world," Parkman said.

Darwin tapped the table twice. "We're up to ten people now."

The men seemed to be studying the entire diner. Once they were done glaring at everyone, they chose seats on the far side of the diner.

Parkman turned back to Darwin. "You were saying? Oh, right. The voice Sarah can hear." He shrugged. "I have no idea. That will be something Sarah will need to ask that voice. But whoever it is *can* be trusted. After all we've been through, that voice has saved us countless times."

Loud motorcycles rumbled in the distance.

"What's that?" Parkman turned toward the window and stared out into the darkness, cupping his hands on the glass. "Harleys?"

"Sounds like it."

When he glanced toward the front doors, everyone in the diner looked out the window as four Harley-Davidsons pulled off Highway 10 and eased to a stop. The riders killed their engines, removed their helmets, then got off their bikes and stood in a huddle for a moment. Some of the diners returned to eating, but Parkman and Darwin remained glued to what the men were doing.

The waitress interrupted them by setting down two plates. "One cheeseburger and fries, and one apple pie with ice cream. More coffee?"

"Sure, warm it up." Parkman nodded, and the waitress moved back to the counter for the coffee pot.

The bikers were ascending the stairs now. All four wore leather cuts, pants, and shin pads. Parkman could've sworn they were wearing Kevlar vests under their cuts. Chains secured their wallets to their person, and all four carried knives in sheaths on their right sides.

The waitress was back with the coffee pot. "Oh, don't worry about those boys." She'd noticed they were staring at their food without touching it yet. "We get all types here, but everyone's after one thing."

Parkman looked up at her. "What's that?"

"Food, honey. It's the food."

Parkman nodded. "Right. Of course."

The waitress laughed kindly, her smile gentle.

The four bikers settled at a table by the door as the waitress sauntered over to them.

Parkman turned to look at Darwin. "Is this Janice's doing? Did they track the SUV?"

Darwin stared a moment longer at the bikers, then over to the two gangsters who walked in before them. When he faced Parkman, he lifted his cheeseburger.

"Let's eat up before shit gets crazy." He took a large bite and moaned, explaining to Parkman that he should've ordered a cheeseburger, too, while talking with his mouth full.

Parkman shook his head, playing with the pie with the end of his fork. "Sugar keeps me alert and ready. A cheeseburger would put me to sleep." He waited until Darwin had swallowed, then asked again, "Is this Sarah's doing? Or Janice's?"

Darwin opened his mouth to take another bite, then stopped. "It's neither."

"So they're not part of this."

Darwin waited another moment, the cheeseburger in front of his face. "Oh, they're part of it, all right. These men are here because Disco called them." He took another large bite of his burger and chewed, his cheeks puffed out. "That's my guess."

"How would you know that?"

After Darwin swallowed again, he wiped his mouth and set the burger down. "Because I dealt with a biker gang many years ago. It was run by a man they called H. That was it, one letter. I forget his full name now, but I don't forget a face, and two of those four bikers were close to H."

"So they're on our side?"

Darwin nodded. "They were then and likely are now. Disco only works with the best."

"So it's all happening here? We're not waiting for Sarah to call, and we'll go pick her up?"

Darwin lifted the remains of his burger. "You're probably right. Disco has set up a meeting here. Then we all descend on Janice and her people and end this."

Parkman dug out a large chunk of his apple pie, held it up in front of his face, and looked across at Darwin as grease rolled down his friend's chin.

"I'd sure like to find out the truth. Like, why grab me? Why grab you?"

"Looking around, my guess is Sarah would, too."

After eating his pie and scooping up the melted ice cream, Parkman looked around the diner. "There are two gangsters and four bikers, plus us and Disco and Sarah." He looked back at Darwin, who had almost eaten the entire burger in three bites. "Is that enough to be effective against Janice? Doesn't she have over a dozen armed and military-trained men?"

The heavy rumble of motorcycles approaching in the distance made him look out into the night again.

Darwin followed his gaze.

"I think you have your answer."

They hurried to finish eating.

Chapter 31

THEY DROVE TO ORANGEVILLE, and as they entered the city limits, Sarah brought up the police station on her phone's GPS.

"What's that?" Disco asked.

Sarah looked over her shoulder. Amanda was asleep with Brody's arm wrapped around her. His head was back, but she figured he was awake and just resting his eyes.

"It's the Ontario Provincial Police detachment."

"Why would we go to the cop shop?"

She kicked her head back once. "To drop them off."

Disco scratched his ear, then rubbed the lobe. "Wait, what?" He stared at her, studying her for a long moment, then turned back to the road. "Sarah, you'd be giving up any leverage you have."

"They won't know that, though."

"So, what will you tell this Janice woman? That you just gave her daughter to the police?"

"I'll tell her that her daughter is safe in Orangeville, and if she wants to see her again, she'll do what I tell her to do. Also, I suspect they're tracking the SUV Parkman and Darwin are in."

"And?"

"They'll see that they drove to a hotel in Orangeville, then went to the diner north of them."

Disco understood when he said, "They'll assume you left Amanda with Daniel and your mother."

Sarah nodded. "They will."

"Okay, but why the cops?"

Sarah righted herself in the front seat. "For starters, I don't want to be charged with kidnapping or abduction. As far as I know, Amanda was on the run from her mother. We picked her up, kept her safe, then dropped her off at the OPP detachment."

Disco shook his head. "That's why I love you, Sarah. You're so fucking unpredictable. I did not see this coming."

Outside the detachment, Sarah roused Amanda. When she sat up and rubbed her eyes, Sarah said, "Well, this is it."

"Where are we?" Amanda asked.

"At a police station. This is where you get off."

"What?" Amanda and Brody looked at each other, concern on their faces. "Why would you leave us here?"

"This is where you'll be the safest. When this is over in a few hours, your mom can pick you up here."

"Wait, where are you guys going?"

"To speak with Janice and get my daughter back."

Something about this idea seemed to make Amanda happy as she was already reaching for the doorknob. "Okay, this works. I didn't really feel like going with you guys with all those weapons anyway. I had a bad feeling about it."

Sarah understood exactly what she was saying. "I do, too."

They hopped out, and while Disco waited in the Hummer, Sarah escorted Amanda and Brody inside the building. She explained who they were and why she was dropping them off, and once they were settled, she jogged back out to the Hummer, and Disco got them onto Highway 10, heading north.

Sarah glanced at the GPS, then watched the dark road ahead, only lit by the Hummer's powerful high beams.

"We'll pass the motel on the left in a few minutes. They don't know about you. You're an unknown addition to the mess they created, so they won't know your vehicle."

"And?"

"Drive by slow, like seventy or eighty, so I can assess the place."

"What are you looking for?"

"No idea."

"Hmph."

"You remember we talked about the Sophia Project?"

Disco glanced her way. "Yeah. You didn't think this was them."

"I didn't say it *wasn't*, just that they died off and stopped bothering me."

"Maybe they figured they couldn't own you."

"Who knows, but something's bothering me. Something scary."

"What's that?"

"When I left Oshawa last night, I spoke to my mom, and she was heading to meet Vivian." Sarah stared at the darkness, waiting for the lights of the motel to materialize on the left. "I called Parkman to help, then called Aaron to meet me downtown."

"And I heard from Darwin. He was going to fly in to help like Tarzan."

She managed a smile. "Right, and I'm grateful."

"Well, what's bothering you? What could be scary, other than the obvious—all of this can be scary for a mother."

As I was speeding down the Don Valley Parkway, I got pulled over. The cop said it was an instant seizure and impound of my vehicle because—"

"You were going fifty over the posted limit."

"Exactly."

"So, what happened?"

"I took off."

Disco looked at her again, surprise all over his face. "And?"

"Other cruisers joined in the chase."

"And?"

"Then they backed off."

"Were you entering a populated area? Maybe the chase got too dangerous."

Sarah shook her head. "I was still on the highway. They just slowed down, then exited and disappeared. I didn't see them again."

"Okay, that is weird."

"The only people I've ever dealt with who had absolute authority over law enforcement agencies in all the days I've been doing what I do were the Sophia Project people. They were even granted permission to work in Europe."

"That's some high-level shit, Sarah. I mean, there's got to be a treaty or something on that. How would they even know the cops were chasing you?"

As they crested a hill, lights on the left came into view.

"There it is," Sarah said, leaning forward and pointing. "That has to be it."

Disco eased off the accelerator.

Sarah studied the nondescript motel with the SUVs parked out front. The main office was dark, and the sign said NO VACANCY, yet there were at least ten rooms and only three vehicles out front.

"They've taken over the place."

"Likely rented out the entire property for a night or two and paid twice what it was worth."

Three rooms had lights on inside. She stared at the one with the curtain pulled back and could've sworn she saw Willow watching them, her little hand waving.

"Hey, look." Sarah pointed. "Is that a little girl waving?"

Disco let off the gas again and stared. "Actually, I think it is."

Then they had passed the motel, and Sarah's heart sank.

Disco added gas and got them back to their regular speed. Not ten minutes later, they were pulling into the Stopover Roadhouse Diner. Disco drove by all the motorcycles parked near the front, then around two large black vans, moved to the far end of the parking lot, and placed the Hummer between two large rigs that looked parked for the night.

Sarah spun in her seat. "Looks like everyone's here." They exchanged a look. "Let's go inside, get settled, then I'll call Janice and tell her where we are."

"And I'll speak with the boys and tell them what's up."

Sarah and Disco hopped out and closed the distance to the entrance in seconds.

It was time to set things right.

Chapter 32

THEY ENTERED THROUGH THE diner's front door, saw Darwin and Parkman, and made their way over to their table.

"Sarah," Parkman said, wrapping his arms around her.

Darwin and Disco hugged, slapping each other's backs.

"Thanks for taking care of her, man," Darwin said, his voice muffled by Disco's shirt.

"Always. I'd take a bullet for Sarah." He caught her looking, then added, "Well, I wouldn't want to, but you know, if I had to."

She punched his arm lightly, then turned back to Parkman. "Everyone okay? Did Willow look good? Aaron?"

"They've treated everyone well. Fed us well, too. All the while operating under the auspices of a family reunion."

Sarah shook her head. "Why wouldn't they just call us up, set a time, and meet for a picnic?"

"Because we'd all come ready to fight or shoot someone?" Parkman shrugged. "I have no idea why they did it this way."

"I have my suspicions, but for now, I'm ready to meet Janice and the woman calling herself Vivian."

"Sarah, there's something you should know." Parkman's tone had lowered. He sounded serious, making her stomach drop.

"Tell me. What is it?"

"Your mom agreed to a DNA test."

"And?"

"They tested Vivian's blood. The results came back positive. According to DNA, this woman is her daughter, and she only had two kids."

"Then the DNA test was doctored. I don't trust these people at all."

Parkman pressed his lips together and rubbed the back of his neck. "Doctoring a DNA test would be hard to do. Like, impossible."

"Hmmm, I think anything's possible with these people. Now, we don't have much time. Disco and I have an idea of how to end this. It's simple and will take two minutes to brief you on it."

"Go ahead then."

"Coffee, anyone?" A waitress stepped in beside Sarah as Disco was about to wave her off. "Wait, yes, I'd love a coffee."

"Anyone else?"

Two more coffees were ordered, and Sarah and Disco laid out their plan while waiting for their beverages.

"It's perfect," Parkman said. "But if there's resistance, it could take more time than we have."

Disco raised a hand. "That's where I come in." He turned to Darwin. "Come with me. Let's go brief all the boys who are already here. Then we'll get the weapons I've stored in the back of the Hummer."

"Then?" Parkman asked.

"Well, then it will be showtime."

"Wait," Sarah said, raising her hand. "I still have to call Janice to set it up."

"True." Disco nodded. "How about calling her as soon as we've briefed everyone?"

"Perfect. It'll give me time to have a coffee."

Disco and Darwin walked away, and Sarah took Darwin's seat. "I'm so happy to see you're okay," she said.

Parkman reached across the table to take her hand. "How's Alex?"

"He'll be fine. Beat up pretty bad, but as the doctor said, you should see the other guys."

Parkman reared back. "The doctor said that?"

Sarah nodded. "The other guys are all worse."

He jerked his head up as if a thought had just struck him. "Where's Janice's daughter?"

"That's part of the plan we didn't mention. We dropped her off at the OPP station in Orangeville."

"You did *what*?"

"It's the safest place for a seventeen-year-old."

Parkman leaned across the table. "But what if they won't give you Willow without Amanda?"

Sarah frowned. "I'm concerned, but I think Willow's safe."

"I'm not too sure."

Sarah stared at him. "What makes you say that?"

Parkman glanced around the diner, then leaned across the table. "Sarah, this feels a lot like the old days. Do you remember Budapest? And then the ball game in Toronto with Drake Bellamy?"

She nodded. "Like it was yesterday."

"Rod Howley could do whatever he wanted to get whomever he wanted. You got them off your back. What if they took Vivian, and now they want Willow?"

Sarah's eyes didn't leave his face. *Willow?*

"Have you considered that?" he asked.

"Great minds and all that."

"Was that your theory when you said you have your suspicions?"

"It was."

"Which means you're preparing for every eventuality, right?"

"Yes, and Willow will *not* be part of the deal."

"So then what?"

"I guess I'd have to kill them all."

"Sarah ..."

"That's where Amanda comes in." Sarah glanced around the diner. "You'll see. It'll all work out."

"I hope so."

The waitress stopped at their table. "This is one busy night," she said. "Haven't seen this many folks at this hour in a long time." She poured a few coffees and topped up Parkman's even though he waved her off.

Disco and Darwin nodded at Sarah from across the diner. Everyone knew what they were going to do.

They were ready to go.

"Will you be eating tonight?" the waitress asked.

"Actually," Sarah said. "There is something we'd like to talk to you about."

"What's that, sugar?"

The diner's lights went out, plunging everyone into total darkness for an instant, before the emergency lights flickered on.

And Sarah told the waitress what was happening and what was about to happen.

Chapter 33

SARAH STEPPED OUTSIDE THE diner, and the cooler night air caused her to shiver. The next few hours were crucial. She would meet her sister, or the woman pretending to be her sister, and get Willow back. And she would try to do all that without a single person getting hurt.

She searched her consciousness for that voice that's always been in her head, but heard nothing and felt nothing. The entity was there when she needed them. If they weren't there, they weren't required. It was that simple, and she urged herself to trust that.

Her fingers shook when she typed in Janice's number. What she was about to do was risky, but her options were limited. She needed several things to go well for it to all work out, starting with the diner meeting.

The woman answered right away. "Where are you?"

"Waiting for you."

"Cut the bullshit, Sarah. Do you want Willow and Aaron back or not?"

"Is that a question you'd want me to answer?"

"Then bring Amanda to me. We can talk, you will meet Vivian, and everyone can go on their way."

"Works for me. Although I prefer somewhere more public."

"Public?" Janice blurted out the word like it was contagious. "The motel is a public place."

Sarah put her back to the highway and stared up at the diner. "I don't think so. We drove by there about twenty minutes ago and only saw your SUVs parked out front. Janice, it looked like you rented out the entire building."

Janice didn't respond at first. The sound of her drinking something came through the phone.

"You were *here*?" Janice cleared her throat. "Why didn't you stop in?"

"Hello?" Sarah said. "Are you there? Did you hear what I said?"

"Sarah, don't lose your patience with me, or it won't be the only thing you'll lose."

Sarah held in her initial retort by tightening her lips closed. After a few calming breaths, she said, "Are we reduced to threats now?"

"Where are you?"

"At the Stopover Roadhouse Diner, ten minutes north of your location, having a bite to eat and a drink. I thought Willow would be hungry before we drove her back home."

"Don't move. We'll be there shortly."

"Bring my daughter. Don't come without her. No tricks."

"Oh, I assure you, I won't be alone."

The line died.

Sarah checked the time. They'd be there by two in the morning. She could only hope and pray that everything would mobilize in her favor.

There was one more call to make, and then she'd be ready.

Her eyes on the windows of the diner, she dialed the number, praying everything would work out well, but knowing beforehand that lives would be lost tonight.

And it wouldn't be her fault.

Chapter 34

SARAH SAT TWO TABLES from the door, her right side leaning against the diner's window.

The lights were back on once all the staff were informed of what was happening tonight. The last few customers were asked to pay their bills and take the rest of their food to go. All that remained were half a dozen trucks parked in the side area where the truckers had fallen asleep for the night. As long as none of them woke up in the next half hour and interrupted the events about to unfold, none of them should be in danger.

The waitress explained that traffic from two until four in the morning was the lightest. Even if someone pulled in, they could be easily dissuaded from entering the premises if Disco had one of his men monitoring the parking lot.

As it turned out, Disco had already placed most of his men in the parking lot, keeping them hidden well.

The Harley-Davidsons were all moved around to the back of the building so they'd be out of sight. The only vehicles that weren't touched were the cook's and the waitress's.

Parkman and Darwin were stationed in the far corner with a clear sight of Sarah. Both men were armed, as Janice's soldiers would be armed, but Sarah was unarmed. She expected to be patted down when Janice and her soldiers arrived, yet a pistol was strapped under her seat if she required one.

The confrontation that was about to happen settled over her system. It reminded her of stage fright. The same nerves were firing, the same acid filling her stomach. The butterflies in her gut felt as if they'd escaped from a nuclear waste dump—radioactive bastards roiling around in her abdomen. Ginger might work to help calm her insides— that or copious amounts of whiskey—but being on edge honed her skills, gave her better reaction time, and that was something she needed for Willow.

Even if everything worked out well, she'd have to deal with Aaron's wrath if they all saw the sunrise. Pulled into her world again, unwillingly, he would be fuming that their daughter became a pawn in some government game. But his wrath would be misplaced. This was all Janice's doing, whatever the hell it was she sought to gain.

"It's time," Darwin said.

The sound of engines came to Sarah at the exact moment he spoke those words.

Both sounds—the engines and Darwin's voice—multiplied the butterflies in her stomach and pushed her heart rate to over one-fifty. Nerves weren't much of an issue in the past, but now that she had a daughter, they played a more intense role in everything she did. And when Willow was involved, her nerves were frayed.

Hands placed flat on the Formica table, she slowly clenched them into fists, then released them, spreading her fingers flat again.

The vehicles stopped out front.

Sarah turned to her right and studied the men exiting the SUVs. They formed a perimeter around the front SUV before the passenger door opened, and a woman in her fifties stepped out. Their eyes met, and Sarah knew this was Janice.

The woman leaned into the closest soldier, and then he jogged to the second SUV and spoke to the driver.

After Janice studied the diner's windows, she made a sweeping motion with her hands, and three soldiers ran for the main doors.

The waitress, already briefed on some of what was happening, turned toward them as they entered, a pot of fresh coffee in her hands.

"Good morning, gentlemen. Care for some coffee?"

They ignored her as one soldier ran to examine the bathroom, another invaded the diner's kitchen, and the third roamed the dining area, passing the table with three men eating and stopping at Darwin's table.

"Hey, Tom," Darwin said. "Long time no see."

Darwin and Tom looked at Sarah. Then Tom focused back on Darwin. "Why are you here?"

"When this is over, whatever this is, you guys gave us an SUV, and I think Sarah might need a ride home." Darwin offered Tom a warm smile. "What are friends for, right buddy?"

Tom leaned a few inches closer. "I'm not your buddy."

Darwin regarded him with disdain. "Then step back. Even my friends don't get this close."

Without missing a beat, Tom held out his hand and waved his fingers in a give-it-to-me gesture. "I want the keys to the SUV we supplied you."

"Why?"

"It was a loan. We didn't *give* it to you."

"How will we drive to Toronto?"

"Not my problem. Don't make me *take* the keys from you."

Darwin held up his hands. "I don't have them."

As much as Tom thought he was being lied to, he looked ready to play along. "Then who does? Sarah?"

"No." Darwin pointed at Parkman across his table. "He does."

Tom addressed Parkman. "You interested in causing trouble, too?"

Parkman held up the keys. "Absolutely not. Once those women talk about their kids, we'll find our own way home."

Tom tore the keys from Parkman's grip, then stormed to the front door where the other two soldiers were waiting.

"All clear?" Tom asked.

Both men nodded. "Bathroom's empty," one said.

"Kitchen has a cook and a waitress. That's it."

Tom glanced at the three men eating and talking in whispers. "Are they going to be a problem?"

"We saw several rigs parked at the side. You think three big truckers will cause us problems?"

Tom looked back at Sarah from about ten feet away. "I don't like this. It's all too simple. Feels too clean."

"Looks like, feels like, probably is," one of his men stated.

Tom nodded and handed the SUV keys over. "Fine, do the transfer and bring them in."

One soldier stepped outside and waved at Janice as he descended the steps.

Janice Stilton walked with confidence to the front door of the diner and stepped inside, surrounded by two more soldiers, which brought the number up to four surrounding her now.

When Sarah glanced outside, the man with the SUV keys had

disappeared in the darkness by the highway, no doubt gone to get the SUV they'd given to Darwin. With Parkman and Darwin in the diner, Tom would know that their SUV was on the premises. But how did they know where it was?

So they *had* been tracking them on GPS.

Janice moved closer to Sarah's table, but Tom stepped around her and waved for Sarah to stand.

Without preamble or demanding that he ask politely, she eased off her seat and allowed him to pat her down.

"She's clean." Tom stepped back, and Janice took a seat opposite Sarah. Then her men moved into position to best guard entrances and exits.

Now it was just two women with an agenda.

"I don't see Daniel or your mother," Janice said, her eyes darting over to Darwin and Parkman. "I was wondering who they'd dropped off at the hotel in Orangeville."

Of course, they were tracking them, and she wasn't shy about letting Sarah know.

Outside, the vehicle Darwin and Parkman came in lit up about a hundred yards down the highway, then performed a U-turn and raced toward the diner.

Sarah cleared her throat. "As much as I'd love to chit-chat, just tell me where Willow is, and we'll do the exchange."

"Slow down, Sarah." Janice reared back, acting surprised. She reminded Sarah of someone who reveled in histrionics. "Don't you want to meet your sister first?"

"Why is it you people never understand? Why can't you get it?"

"Enlighten me, Sarah. Get what?" The smirk that eased onto Janice's lips invited Sarah to smack it off, but she declined the invitation—for now.

"You want me calm? You want me to meet my sister and welcome her with open arms? Then don't kidnap my entire family to do so. Otherwise, I won't be calm."

Janice matched Sarah's composure by leaning back on the seat and placing her hands on the table. "That's exactly why we wanted to control the narrative. We know all about you and your crew. Your exploits around the world have been reported in dozens of papers over the years. Your sister has admired you from afar." She leaned in. "We *knew* how you'd respond to Vivian being alive and worried you would try to hurt her or worse. Bringing these men"—she pointed at Tom— "and collecting your family to meet Vivian was the most secure way to do it." She grinned. "And I mean secure for everyone involved."

"But that backfired, didn't it?"

"You mean with Alex?"

Sarah stared at her without answering, the pain for what Alex endured rising as an emotional storm centered at the base of her throat, temporarily cutting off her ability to speak.

"That was unfortunate." Janice glanced at Parkman and Darwin's table. Then she studied the rest of the diner. "Why hasn't that waitress offered us a coffee?" She snapped her head back to Sarah, suspicion written all over her face. "Have you done something?"

Sarah forced her face to soften. Then it was her turn to smile. "Of course not. What could I possibly do to a public diner?" Sarah clucked her tongue. "She offered your men coffee, but you'll have to understand something. Your men stormed in here, walked every inch looking for a trap, which included invading their kitchen, and then they invited you in here. I'm sure she's scared out of her wits to move out from behind that counter."

Janice seemed to have been working herself into paranoia, but she visibly deflated, slumping in her seat. Then she waved at the waitress. "Could we get some coffee over here?"

"Where's Willow and Aaron?" Sarah said, tired of waiting. "Let's get right to it."

"Safe."

"Bring them in. Let them sit with Darwin and Parkman." Sarah sat back. "Unless your pretenses are false."

"My pretenses?"

"You said you picked us all up for a family reunion. I'm here. Bring in Vivian. Now that my daughter has met her aunt, there's no need to keep them apart. Unless, as I said, you've abducted my family for another purpose."

"Well, now, things changed when you snatched Amanda. Produce her, and I'll produce Willow."

Sometimes the urges on the inside were harder to fight than the person in front of her, but somehow Sarah kept her hands on the table and didn't ball them into fists to pummel the woman.

Outside, she caught sight of the SUVs parked side by side, their doors open. There was activity between them as they transferred someone into the vehicle that Parkman and Darwin had used.

"What's happening outside?"

"None of your concern at the moment."

The waitress stepped up to the table. "Cream and sugar's right there." She pointed at the small tray that held both as she poured coffee with the other hand. "Menus are there if you want to eat."

Janice waved the woman away like she was a nuisance.

"This is your party." Sarah crossed her arms. "You set this up. What's the plan? Where's my alleged sister?"

"Did you know we did a DNA test and can confirm without a doubt that Vivian is your sister?"

"Great. Tell her to come on in and bring her niece."

Janice wrapped her hands around her coffee mug and stared down into it. "You still don't believe it, do you?" She looked up and wiped a wisp of hair to the side.

The woman wasn't holding her age well. Whether it was stress from the demands of her job or too much sunshine, crow's feet had formed behind her eyes, with a subtle hue of purple in the bags suspended underneath. In any other situation, Sarah would feel sorry for the woman with what was about to happen.

"I'm done talking to you. Bring my daughter to me, or I will go and take her from you."

"Now, now, Sarah." Janice waved a finger in the air, and Sarah again fought the urge to grab it and snap it back. "Temper, temper. All in good time."

"I don't have *good* time, nor do I have patience."

"I haven't seen Amanda." Janice swiveled left and right, pretending to search for her daughter. "Where are you hiding her?"

A movement made Sarah glance to her right again. The vehicle Janice arrived in moved across the parking lot to wait at the exit. The one parked beside it for several minutes—the SUV Parkman and Darwin had used—remained there with two men standing on either side of the front passenger door. In the window, she saw Willow clambering to wave at her.

Sarah's eyes widened. "That's Willow." She pointed. "Right there in that SUV."

"And you can have her the second you produce my daughter."

Sarah glanced back at Janice, wanting to stall so Disco's men could take out the soldiers and grab Willow. "What about meeting Vivian? That's not happening now?"

Janice shook her head. She still hadn't touched her coffee. "No, I told your sister what you did, and she wasn't too happy with you." Janice glared at her, then leaned across the table, speaking in a low voice. "Sarah, she's blood. I have proof. And after what you did, she's disappointed. No, she thought you were better than that. Maybe you'll meet in a year. Maybe never."

Janice's phone dinged. She pulled it from a pocket, read the message, then scoffed.

When she put her phone away, she returned to shaking her head.

Are there awards for self-restraint? If so, Sarah was confident she'd win gold for not slamming Janice's head into the table.

"You've been a bad girl, Sarah."

"I'm always bad."

Janice slid her coffee to the side. "Like Alex, I guess I underestimated you."

"How so?" She was itching to slide her hand under her seat, grab her weapon, and make Janice scream for all she'd done to her family.

Janice's face had taken on color. A vein throbbed on her forehead. The woman's visage gave off an angry feeling.

What could that text have possibly told her?

Headlights on the road pulled her attention away. It was a large FedEx truck easing into the diner's parking lot. The driver angled the rig to back in between two other rigs at the far end.

"You brought your own army with you."

Sarah focused on Janice as more weight was added to her stomach. Pins and needles coursed through her fingers. "What are you talking about?"

"I thought we could work this out, but it's obvious I can't negotiate with the likes of you."

Whatever Janice happened to know, there was no way Willow would be leaving with this woman. No way in hell.

Janice pushed up from her chair and stared down at Sarah. "The only way out of this is to tell me where Amanda is. Tell me now."

Sarah glanced outside at the SUV. Both soldiers who had stood on either side of the passenger door were gone now. The SUV with her daughter sat alone in the parking lot. That's how they learned about Disco and his men. They'd already taken out several of Janice's soldiers, and she needed to leave. Tom probably messaged her to get out of there. That had to be what the text said.

This was the moment Sarah had been waiting for. "Amanda is with the Ontario Provincial Police." She shrugged. "I didn't want to be charged with abduction. My story is that Amanda ran away, so we picked her up to keep her safe and then dropped her off at the OPP detachment in Orangeville. Amanda thanked me for helping her." She slapped her hands together twice. "End of story."

While she spoke, Janice's nostrils flared, and her breathing got louder.

"You made a *huge* error, Miss Roberts." Her volume had doubled. "One you'll pay dearly for."

Sarah lifted out of her chair, done with playing nice. "Okay, how about shut the fuck up, you pretentious bitch, and give me back *my daughter*!"

Sarah's hand dropped beside her leg and reached for the gun suspended under the seat when Janice forced a fake smile onto her face.

"Say goodbye to Willow, you conniving bitch—"

The explosion shook the building as the SUV outside that had Willow's smiling face only moments before was reduced to a pile of burning metal. The shock wave shattered several windows in the diner, plunging it into darkness as the electricity was cut off. This time, it wasn't Disco's team who did it.

Someone screamed from the back of the restaurant. A weapon fired outside as the shock rolled over Sarah's body.

Did Willow get out of the SUV? Could she be alive?

Janice was almost at the exit. Someone was calling Sarah's name. Everything was happening too fast.

Then Tom was marching Darwin after Janice, and two other soldiers passed Sarah's table with Parkman's wrists already zip-tied.

Sarah shook her head to clear it. Something had to be done, but it was like life had been sucked out of her very being.

Her little girl. Gone from this world on the whim of another. How could this be possible? How could the voice in her head allow that to happen without warning?

Something banged so loud that Sarah jumped in her seat, her hands coming up.

A man stood beside her, yelling in her ear. He was one of Janice's soldiers, shouting for her to get out of her seat.

When she glanced at the table where the three men had been eating —Disco's men—the table was empty.

The soldier grabbed her arm and tried to drag her from the seat.

Sarah yanked her arm out of his grip and ducked so low and fast she bumped her chin on the table, clamping her teeth together painfully.

Her hand reached for the gun taped under her seat, but it wasn't there. The explosion must have knocked it loose because they'd left it barely suspended by the tape, so it was an easy rip and tear.

Then the hand was on her arm again, dragging her from the seat.

On her feet now, they tied her wrists and shoved her toward the door.

She caught sight of the cook in the back, his arms wrapped around the waitress whose face was a mask of fear.

Willow was dead, and it didn't make any sense. How could that be allowed? That wasn't a move she anticipated. At worst, these were the Sophia Project people, and they were after Willow. At best, it was the Sophia Project people, and they really were reintegrating Vivian back into their lives.

Why did they have to kill my baby?

Outside now, it wasn't the cool night air that made her shiver. It was the sight of the burning SUV and the thought of what was inside it.

The soldiers pushed her toward the SUV waiting by the exit.

Janice stood by the open door, her arm pointing to Sarah's right. "Sarah, witness the group of men brought here to save you."

In her dulled state of anguish and loss, she turned to the right and saw the bikers standing beside Disco, Darwin, Parkman, Ape, and Water. They were lined up against the wall of the diner with six of Janice's soldiers standing opposite them, assault rifles in their hands.

"No," she stammered, but it came out as a whisper.

When she turned to walk that way, one of the soldiers flanking her shoved her forward, and she stumbled for several steps until she found her balance.

"Come on, Sarah," Janice yelled. "We don't need to be witnesses to the firing squad. We've seen enough death for one day. I need you with me when we pick up Amanda."

The soldier shoved her again until she got to the SUV, tears streaming down her face.

It was over.

It was truly over.

They'd won, and she didn't even want to play.

The soldier pushed her inside the SUV so hard that she bumped the side of the bench seat with her chest, grunted in pain, then dropped to her knees on the pavement beside the vehicle.

Someone grabbed her and tossed her onto the seat like she was a bag of air. Her mouth open, her mind consumed by grief and guilt like a heavy, dark blanket, Sarah stared at nothing.

Doors closed, and the vehicle got underway.

From somewhere far away, Sarah heard Janice speaking.

"Kill them all, then join us. I've called ahead. We have a helicopter picking us up in Orangeville. We all fly out of Toronto at eight this morning. I'm done with this fucking country. I've got what I came for."

Less than half a minute later, in the not-so-far distance behind them, Sarah heard the roar of automatic weapons as they unleashed death in small metallic increments, killing her bullet by bullet without touching her.

Chapter 35

PARKMAN STOOD BESIDE DARWIN after being paraded out to the lineup already formed against the side wall of the diner. His mind raced on how to get out of this, but nothing was coming to him. Running would be rewarded with a bullet in the back. These weren't the kind of men who could be negotiated with. He'd worked with mercenaries enough to know. Even offering them more money, which Parkman didn't possess anyway, wouldn't work unless that figure was astronomical. Millions might save their lives tonight, but none of them had millions.

He glanced to the side and saw Disco seemed calm, as if this was just another day at the office. Darwin also stood with poise, shoulders back, head held high. Did they know something he didn't?

That explosion had rattled his fillings, and he was still getting his hearing back. The soldiers may have endured the same hearing issues. If he were to get Darwin and run behind the diner and into the dark, there was a chance the soldiers might not hear them.

When Parkman leaned in to whisper to Darwin, one of the soldiers stepped close.

"No talking," he shouted and shoved Parkman several feet from Darwin.

On the left, the woman Sarah had been talking to walked by them, followed by Sarah with her hands tied behind her. Two soldiers made up the rear as they all headed to the SUV parked by the exit. The soldiers hit Sarah's shoulder, making her stumble. She hadn't looked over at them yet.

The woman Sarah had called Janice now stood by the door, pointing at Parkman and the dozen men on either side of him.

"Sarah, witness the men brought here to save you."

Sarah turned, then stopped walking as she took them all in. "No," she stammered, her mouth forming the word, but it wasn't loud enough for Parkman to hear.

She stepped toward them, but the soldier shoved her again, and she almost dropped to the pavement. It took her a few steps until she righted herself.

"Come on, Sarah," Janice yelled. "We don't need to be witnesses to the firing squad. We've seen enough death for one day. I need you with me when we pick up Amanda."

The soldier shoved her again, harder this time. She bumped into something, dropped to the pavement, and then they pushed her inside. The SUV's doors closed, and the vehicle got underway.

Before their taillights disappeared, Tom answered his phone and listened for a few seconds. Then he closed his phone, slipped it into his Kevlar vest pocket, and lifted his weapon.

"Orders are to kill them all." Tom shouted loud enough for the people in the retreating SUV to hear them. "They killed one of us and injured ten more. Gentlemen, pick your target and shoot to kill—"

"*Freeze!* Drop your weapons. We have you surrounded."

As men stepped out of the bushes, those words were emitted from a bullhorn. These newcomers were dressed in military fatigues, helmets, goggles, high-powered weapons, and shiny black boots.

His knees were weak from the ordeal—being that close to dying by firing squad tends to make a man piss himself—Parkman lowered to the ground. Darwin did the same beside him.

Then one of Tom's men fired at the advancing army and was immediately blown off his feet. Two more of Janice's soldiers fired at the advancing army but were quickly dispatched. Weapons were fired at different intervals, with some firing behind the building.

Parkman looked over at Darwin, who was also flat on the ground now. His mind raced with questions. Who were these new men? Where did they come from? Why couldn't they have been here moments before?

Then Tom and one other soldier dropped their weapons, shoving their hands above their head, and were quickly subdued. They were pushed to the ground and cuffed.

Parkman curled on his side into the fetal position, pushed himself up onto his knees, then stood, his hands still locked behind his back.

"Who's in charge here?" he called out.

"Sergeant Karen Doolittle, sir," a woman shouted from the side of the building.

Everyone turned to look at her as she strode around the corner.

"Everyone okay?"

Parkman nodded as Darwin was getting to his feet.

"How did you know to be here?"

"Sarah Roberts called us several hours ago to set this up. We got here as soon as we could. She briefed us on how we'd be entering a situation with well-trained soldiers—mercenaries for hire—so we *borrowed* a FedEx truck to bring to the truck stop. By the time we got the place surrounded, one of the SUVs had blown up out front."

"Yeah," Disco said. "Wish you could've gotten here a bit sooner."

"We came south out of Barrie. Got here as fast as we could for this time of night. We were doing joint training exercises at CFB Borden with the Canadian Armed Forces. Otherwise, you'd be hard-pressed to find American forces on Canadian soil."

Parkman turned to have his zip ties cut off. "Why American forces?"

Doolittle faced him. "We were called in to support from the American embassy. I'm afraid that's all I know at the moment."

"We lost Sarah in the vehicle that drove away three minutes ago."

"We saw the SUV leave the premises. It was that bomb that slowed us down by at least a minute. And that other SUV on the far side of the parking lot. We had to be careful as a child was in that one."

Parkman and Darwin looked at each other.

"What?" Darwin said. "Did you say a child?"

Sergeant Doolittle nodded. "A child and her father. We ascertained that two men were watching them. We observed them sneaking from the SUV that had just blown up. Once they were secured in the other vehicle, we took out both soldiers. The father and daughter are secure."

Parkman wanted to cry right there on the spot. Aaron and Willow were safe. They were safe. Everyone made it without a scratch. Then a thought occurred that made him gasp.

"What is it?" Darwin leaned close.

"Sarah saw the explosion and will likely think Willow is dead."

"Oh ..." Darwin stared off into the distance.

"She might have heard the gunfire after Tom took that call to execute us." He grabbed Darwin's arm. "We have to get to them, stop them. Sarah is convinced everyone in her life is gone."

"Well, except Alex." Darwin raised a finger.

Parkman swatted his shoulder. "This isn't funny."

"Sir, we have a chopper in the air." Doolittle moved close to them. "We'll find them and bring Sarah home."

Parkman shook his head. "Why would you come all this way with this much firepower from a single phone call from Sarah? What could she possibly have said to get a response like this?"

"Sir, we followed orders from the consul general at the United States embassy in Toronto. I understand she called them. We were given orders, sir. I didn't question them, nor was the reason explained to me."

Parkman nodded his understanding as Darwin stepped forward. Before anyone could stop him, Darwin shot a right hook into Tom's face. Blood shot from the man's nose as he bent over, his hands of no use as they were already cuffed behind him.

"Take him away," Doolittle shouted.

Her men got Tom moving alongside his comrade.

Aaron came around the corner holding Willow's hand. "Where's Sarah?" he called to Parkman and Darwin, who massaged his hand after decking Tom.

Parkman closed the distance between them and bent to hug Willow first. Then he pulled Aaron in close.

"Janice took her." Darwin showed up at his shoulder. "I think they're going to Orangeville to pick up Amanda. That would be my guess."

"Then we need to go after them." Aaron glanced around as if he were looking for a car.

"Sir," Doolittle said, moving closer to them. "Our chopper has them in sight. Could everyone please come with us? We understand a clean-up crew will be here shortly to assess the damage. We don't need to be here when that happens."

Sergeant Doolittle, followed by Parkman, Darwin, Aaron, and Willow, all hopped in one of Janice's SUVs, with one of Doolittle's men driving.

"Get us there fast," she ordered. "Willow's mother needs to know her daughter and her friends are safe."

The tires squealed as they exited the diner's parking area.

Chapter 36

SARAH ADJUSTED HERSELF TO sit up on the seat, then shifted to remain on the edge, legs tucked under her. If she didn't, her tied hands behind her would be squeezed between the small of her back and the seat.

The lights of Orangeville could be seen in the distance. They'd be there in five minutes or less. What would Janice do when she couldn't get Amanda back? There was no way Sarah could allow Amanda to go anywhere with Janice.

"Why did you do this?" Sarah asked. "*How* could you do this?"

"Oh, come now, Sarah. Bleeding hearts unite." She turned in her seat to look at Sarah. "People die. It's a fact. Get over it. Everyone loses someone close to them in the course of their lives. This was your turn. That's it. You're not special. You're just like everyone else." Janice turned back to face the road. "Doesn't matter anyway. You'll be joining them as soon as I get Amanda back." She looked over her shoulder. "You're only alive because I don't entirely believe you. If she's at the police station and we get her back without trouble, I don't need you anymore. If she's somewhere else, you're my bargaining chip."

"Why do you insist on calling her by her name? You only ever say, Amanda? You've never said the word, *daughter*."

Janice didn't respond right away. "How about minding your own business?"

Fidgety, appearing bothered by that line of questioning, Janice tapped her phone's screen, held it to her face, then dialed out. After a moment, she lowered the phone and stared at it. "Hmm, that's odd. It went to voicemail." She glanced at the driver. "Why wouldn't Tom have his phone on?"

"Try him again," the driver said. "That is odd."

She dialed again, this time on speaker so the driver could hear. It went right to voicemail.

She shot a glance back at Sarah. "Did you do something?"

Sarah shrugged. "How could I do anything? I've been with you."

"Sarah, you and Alex have made this operation quite frustrating. I can't have that, and I can't leave loose ends. People will ask questions.

People will investigate. *People* become loose ends."

"What?" Sarah stared out at the road as street lights raced by, her mind on Willow. They were entering the city limits of Orangeville.

"After we get Amanda," she looked back at Sarah, hatred in her eyes, or was that madness? "My *daughter*," she turned around to face forward, "we'll go to that hotel where we watched your mother and Daniel get dropped off. They won't even see it coming. How's that for meddling in my business?"

"They won't see what coming?" Sarah asked, afraid to hear that this evil woman was telling her she would kill her mother, too.

"Come now, Sarah. You think I can leave your mother alive to search for Willow? She'll recognize her in a heartbeat."

"Recognize Willow?" Sarah repeated the words as if in a daze. "Wait, *search* for Willow. I don't understand ..."

Janice glanced at the driver. "Should I tell her?"

But Sarah had already zoned out.

They were going to kill her mother. Everyone else was dead. There was no way she could let the killing go on.

With Aaron and Willow gone, what did she have to live for? Suicidal thoughts weren't in her DNA. Her will to carry on was in Aaron's embrace, and hope in life was found in Willow's eyes. Now that both had been extinguished, the least she could do was hurt the people who hurt her.

Hurt people hurt people, and it felt good.

Even though her world ended back in that diner's parking lot, it didn't have to end for her mother and Daniel, too.

"Sarah, we are almost out of time." Janice was speaking again. "We should talk about your extremely talented daughter."

Sarah leaned close to the soldier in the back seat with her, then shot her head forward and head-butted his nose so hard that his head smashed into the passenger side window. He slumped forward, moaning and cursing and holding his bleeding nose.

Janice started yelling something as Sarah angled between the front seats and pushed off with her feet. Even as she slammed into the driver, her upper body coming to rest across his arms, she thought she heard the deafening sound of a chopper's blades.

The driver shouted something, trying to get his arms out from under Sarah's weight. The SUV jerked back and forth on the deserted highway as Janice screamed, lunging at Sarah, her hands about Sarah's waist, trying to yank her off the driver.

But it was too late.

The SUV left the road, hit the ditch hard, then became airborne, twisting sideways in the air.

The thump when they came back to earth was on Janice's side, which placed Sarah in an almost standing position as the airbags deployed, jamming her violently into the driver, and her feet into Janice's face.

Then the SUV stopped sliding.

At first, there was moaning, then the sound of the helicopter was all she heard.

Janice said a helicopter was coming to pick them up and take them to Toronto. As more of Janice's people arrived, Sarah struggled to breathe. The airbags deflated behind her, and she slumped sideways until she was leaning against the driver's legs as he hung unconscious at the extent of his seatbelt.

Sarah glanced down at her feet—they stung from the impact, but nothing felt broken—and saw Janice's face. It was smeared with blood where her lips had mashed up against her teeth. The woman's nose gushed blood like a thin river.

Sarah reached out to that voice in her head, but it went unanswered.

No one was there.

Would that entity be there when she died and transitioned to the other side?

Would it be her sister?

Chapter 37

VOICES CAME CLOSER. MEN could be heard as they mounted the side of the SUV. The door above Sarah's head was torn open and propped up by a piece of wood.

"Is everyone okay in there?"

Janice moaned as she slowly came to. The driver was still unconscious. Sarah's shoulder hurt where it had connected with the driver's jaw when the airbag had jammed her into him.

"Hold on. We'll get you out."

Someone lay on the side of the SUV, leaned their head and shoulders down into the vehicle, wedged past the steering wheel, and clutched Sarah under the arms.

She was lifted up and out, where other men grabbed her and eased her down to the grass.

"Someone put zip ties on her wrists," a man said.

"Cut them off. Now," another man ordered.

The cold steel of a knife caressed her skin. Then the zip ties were gone. Blessedly, her arms came around to the front, and a pain shot through her shoulder from the strain.

She winced, a moan escaping her lips. With her right arm, she pushed up into a sitting position. Other than a throbbing pain in her ankles where they'd smashed into Janice's face, she'd survived the crash without any broken bones.

They unhooked the driver next, then lifted him out.

Sarah looked out at the road as an ambulance screeched to a halt. Coming from the other way, from the roadhouse diner, one of Janice's SUVs stopped nose-to-nose with the ambulance.

Another chopper hovered nearby. When Sarah glanced up at it, they were already pulling away, the blinking taillight heading off into the distance.

"Where is that bitch?" Janice shouted as they eased her out of the vehicle.

Sarah lifted her right leg into her chest, held it there momentarily, then did the same with her left. Then she pushed up off the ground and stood on the grass in a daze. So much had happened in the last half an hour. A decision flitted through her consciousness. Should she run or go after Janice?

"There she is," Janice said, pulling one hand away from her ruined face to point at Sarah.

Half a dozen uniformed men came around the SUV that lay on its side, most of them having disembarked the helicopter. Now that the damaged vehicle had been emptied, they no longer needed to climb on it.

Sarah stared at the driver, who was still unconscious. She hadn't checked to see if he was alive when they were inside the SUV. Maybe the accident killed him.

The paramedics were being directed to him first.

"Arrest her," Janice shouted. "I'm Major General Janice Stilton with the United States Army, and I demand that you arrest that woman." She was pointing at Sarah again.

So that's her name and rank. Maybe she should've googled the woman's name earlier.

Sarah waited for the zip ties to be put back on her wrists, but then the men dressed in military fatigues converged around Janice—two in front, two to the side, and two men behind her. Without warning, Janice's arms were wrenched back as zip ties were secured in place.

"Hey, what the hell—how *dare* you!" Janice raged at the men. "Release me at once. Take these wretched things off me. I'll have you all demoted. Your careers are over. You'll never work again." When no one moved to remove the restraints, she screamed, "*Take these things off!*"

One of the men from the helicopter moved to stand in front of her. "Janice Stilton, you are under arrest for kidnapping, false imprisonment, and the abduction of Amanda Smith, as well as …"

Sarah didn't hear another word as Darwin stepped around the damaged SUV. She couldn't believe her eyes.

Then Parkman stepped into view.

"How?" her mouth said, but she didn't hear the word come out. She might have lost her voice at that moment.

Threatening to give out, her knees barely held her as she stepped toward them. When she saw Aaron move out from behind Parkman, she gasped and choked on the air as her throat closed with emotion.

Aaron's arm was held at a forty-five-degree angle, clinging to something she couldn't see yet, and even as she took another step toward them, her mind registered what it would be.

Then Willow stepped into view, her face lighting up at seeing her mommy.

And Sarah dropped to her knees too hard, her forward momentum making her hands come out to break her fall. Pain raged through her wounded shoulder, but she ignored it and looked up as Willow closed the gap between them, her eyes already blurring with tears.

Then her daughter was in her arms, and nothing else mattered.

Sarah hung onto her too tightly.

She would never let her go again.

They dropped onto the grass sideways, and Willow giggled.

"I love you, Mommy."

Chapter 38

Sarah sat in a chair at the head of Alex's bed in the hospital, her hand on his good shoulder. They'd been chatting for an hour, covering many of the basics of how he ended up in that bed and how he would be discharged later that day.

Parkman and Darwin sat on chairs by the window, sipping coffee.

Sarah checked her phone. "We have about fifteen to twenty minutes before they get here. So, since it's still just the four of us, I wanted to thank you, Alex, for attacking those men in the hotel."

"Thank me?" Alex said, quirking an eyebrow. "You're welcome, I guess. Painful choice, though. Thought I could deal with it all, then help the others leave."

"As much as we think you're Superman," Parkman said, "you're still human."

Alex kept his attention on Sarah. "Why thank me, though? Did something come of it?"

Sarah nodded and tapped his shoulder lightly. "Because Janice had fewer *staff*, for want of a better word, she had to pull the security detail off Amanda. With only one guard watching Amanda, that left her free to escape, which put her into my hands."

Darwin leaned back against the wall, his right arm resting on the table. "Whatever happened with Amanda? Will she be sent back to her dad?"

"Why don't we wait until Sergeant Doolittle joins us in fifteen minutes? She can explain it better." Sarah frowned. "Although something was bothering me with this whole thing, and now I think I figured it out."

"What's that?" Darwin asked.

"Do you remember when we were talking on the phone that first night and I got pulled over by the police?"

Darwin nodded and lifted his coffee cup. "I certainly do. I called Parkman to tell him you may be delayed."

"Well, I took off, and the police gave chase. By the time I got to the bottom of the Don Valley Parkway, I had three cruisers on my tail."

"How did you lose them?" Parkman asked.

"That's the thing." She shrugged. "I didn't. They just killed their lights, slowed down, and exited the highway one after another." She slapped her hands together twice. "Chase over. Just like that."

"Okay." Parkman stared at her with open interest on his face. "You said you think you figured it out."

"Janice was a major general, and her husband is Brian Stilton, the assistant to the deputy secretary of defense at the Pentagon. With her clout, she had usurped twenty men to join her in Canada on this little venture."

"And?" Parkman said, leaning closer.

"I understand, through diplomatic channels, that she let the Canadian authorities know she was here on official business, but she wasn't." Sarah raised a finger. "If anything went wrong, she'd be on her own. At least that's how it was understood."

"Okay, how does that connect to a police chase?" Darwin asked.

"Janice's people were following me, saw me get pulled over, then called in to have me left alone as I was a party they were interested in obtaining. By the time the call was authorized and got to the right people, then dispatched to the cruisers, we'd made it to the bottom of the Don Valley Parkway."

Parkman was nodding. "That makes sense. She was wielding the power that the Sophia Project people used to wield."

"Funny you should bring that up." Sarah offered them all a wicked grin. "That project officially died with Rod Howley. They tried to keep it going, but they failed miserably. Janice was in charge of their records, and her job back then was to place the children they'd *stolen* from their families back to their original homes, to reintegrate them."

"Even the families where they'd faked the child's death?" Parkman asked. "That had to be hard. I mean, there had to be lawsuits."

Sarah picked up her water bottle and twirled it around in thought. "There were a few. But in the end, the families were more overjoyed to get their kids back than to think about lawsuits. A few tried, but several million dollars shut them up, and nothing hit the press."

"So these people weren't the Sophia Project?" Darwin asked. "Nothing to do with resurrecting the old ways of thinking? Because they faked Willow's death."

"Yes, and you know what Janice said in the SUV before the crash?"

"Tell us," Alex said beside her.

"She spoke about loose ends, and how people were loose ends, and how she couldn't have my mom asking questions or investigating too deeply because she could recognize Willow."

"*Recognize* Willow?" Parkman said, emphasizing the first word.

Sarah nodded. "When I asked what she meant, thinking Willow was in that SUV when it exploded, she turned to her driver and said something like, 'Should I tell her?'"

"Oh," Parkman said, understanding everything. "But how did they get the bomb into the vehicle so fast? Darwin and I were watching what they were doing outside the whole time. They took the keys from us, drove it back to the parking lot, transferred everyone into it, then left it alone in the parking lot."

"And after I saw Willow inside that SUV, Janice got my attention focused back on her as they extricated Willow from the other side and ran her and Aaron to the SUV parked by the back entrance. Once everyone was clear, they blew it up."

"Okay." Darwin leaned forward in his chair, a confused expression creasing his features. "So, they just happened to be carrying bombs with them?"

Sarah shook her head. "Are you sure you want to hear this next part?"

Now they all looked confused. Before anyone said anything, Sarah raised her hands. "Wait, back up a moment. Remember when Disco and I were at his warehouse on Richmond, and I had negotiated your release? You guys were supposed to call me when you were clear of the Sky View Motel?"

"And we did," Parkman said.

"And I asked you what took so long."

"They were getting the vehicle ready ..." Parkman stopped talking as it dawned on him.

Darwin leaned back hard, smacking the wall. "They were getting it ready, all right. They planted the bomb under the SUV and set a cell phone to it. One call, and boom."

"Remember how I told you guys that Tom, real name Tom Middleton, was going to do a plea deal?"

"Yeah," Parkman said. "You told us that yesterday."

"Well, Sergeant Doolittle gave me a copy of his entire statement."

"And?"

"He said the bomb was planted, and they were supposed to blow it up with all of you in it as soon as Janice saw me with Amanda. No loose ends, remember. *People* are loose ends to her."

The room was silent for a moment as everyone contemplated how close they all came to being killed.

"Because you guys stopped in Orangeville, then drove back to that diner and parked up the road, you were no longer in danger. Janice was the one who decided this was a brilliant opportunity to stage Willow's death. When they first got out of their SUVs upon arriving at the diner, she ordered her men to set it up."

Darwin rubbed his face. "That explains their little huddle when they first got there."

"What about Tom Middleton?" Parkman asked. "Just another mercenary for hire?"

Sarah shook her head. "All the men Janice brought with her were US Army men. They were on leave or took leave to join her on an international mission to obtain an asset."

"What?" Parkman blinked twice in an exaggerated manner, leaning forward. "Damn, where's a toothpick when you need one?"

"That doesn't make a lot of sense," Darwin said. "They lined us up to kill us against that diner's wall. We'd be dead if Doolittle's team hadn't dropped in to the rescue. The US Army isn't recruiting murderers."

"Let me explain," Sarah said, the water bottle still in her hand. She unscrewed the cap, took a swig, then tightened the cap back on. "When I was supposed to meet Aaron by the Roy Thompson Hall that first night, Tom and his men were waiting for me. Disco pulled me out of there." She looked from Parkman to Darwin, then to Alex. "One of Tom's men was killed as Disco thought they were hostile mercs. When his men checked the body and saw the deceased was a US Army or the equivalent, they fired at the Kevlar to wound and hurt, but not to kill after that. Tom explained in his statement that the man killed that night was a childhood friend. They'd served together. Tom wanted us all dead after that, but no one was willing to murder anyone except Tom and Janice."

"What changed?"

She nodded at Alex. "After ten men were hospitalized, some with grievous wounds, Tom was able to rally the troops and get some more men on board. Then Janice threatened them beyond an inch of their Army careers, dropping her husband's name at the Pentagon. They'd be court-martialed upon return to the States if they didn't finish the job as per her exact orders."

"Whatever happened to all those wounded men in this hospital?" Parkman asked. "I heard they were cleared out, but some were still badly wounded."

Sarah nodded. "They were all arrested and taken by air ambulance to a place where they wouldn't hurt anyone else for some time."

"You mentioned Disco's name," Parkman said. "Where is he? I haven't seen him in a few days."

"On another job near Ottawa," Darwin jumped in. "Someone is trying to kill a high-ranking government official, and he's been tasked to stop it."

Parkman turned to stare at Sarah. "No Aaron today?"

She shook her head. "He's spending the day with Willow, so I could be here to meet with Sergeant Doolittle and help Alex get home."

"How's Daniel?" Alex asked.

"Happy as fuck." Sarah spun in her chair to look at Alex. "He's back at the dojo from open to close and even doing some of Aaron's classes so Aaron can spend more time with Willow."

"Your mother?" Parkman asked. "How's she handling everything?"

"Because she wasn't sure who these people were, she played along until I was supposed to get there. At one point, she started to believe it was actually Vivian." Sarah shrugged, her hands raising off her thighs. "I mean, she met the woman, and she resembled her daughter. Then Willow said it was, and that DNA test solidified it, although we later learned that it was doctored after all. She's disheartened but will survive this. To some degree, it's like losing Vivian twice."

All three men nodded their understanding.

"And you met this woman, Vivian?" Darwin asked, leaning forward in his chair.

Sarah nodded. "I did."

Parkman leaned forward, too. "What was that like?"

Sarah sighed heavily. "It was weird because the woman could really be a dead ringer for Vivian. She had some makeup done to add size to her nose, and they made her eye shape resemble mine, but after getting arrested, she admitted to the entire scheme that Janice was paying her handsomely to be a part of." Sarah adjusted herself, uncomfortable at the thought that someone could *pretend* to be a dead person without regard for that person's mother or extended family. "Apparently, Janice hatched the plan over a year ago with her husband and asked their family friend to *act* for them. A free trip to Canada, all expenses paid, plus a hundred grand, all to act like Vivian Roberts for a week or less."

"You said Willow confirmed it was Vivian." Parkman frowned, his brow scrunched up. "Can't she *see* things before they happen? Can't she interpret someone's intentions on the spot?"

"Absolutely, and she determined that the people who abducted them were only interested in her. Since Aaron and I told her from day one not to let anyone see what she can do, she did her level best not to use any of her abilities."

"So she lied to Aaron and her grandmother."

"The lesser of two evils. I'm happy she lied in this case. She was able to keep things moving along smoothly until the end. If she'd shown everyone what she could do, the hired Army men might have bought more of Janice's bullshit earlier."

"So," Parkman said, getting up from his chair to move in front of the window. "All of this was to abduct Willow, fake her death, and take her back to the States?"

Sarah grabbed her bottle again and took a sip. What she was about to tell them was nerve-wracking. It had come too close.

Meeting Parkman's gaze, she spilled the rest. "When Janice was cleaning up the Sophia Project files and returning children to their homes, she was fascinated with their accomplishments and openly asked why the project was being dissolved. She was convinced there would be a military application to the project. Over ten years later, she'd advanced her career to major general with aspirations to become the first female deputy secretary of defense. Since her husband worked at the Pentagon, they planned to take Willow and show their superiors what she was capable of and how it could be studied, harnessed, and used to the Army's benefit."

"Now I'm worried," Alex said beside her.

"Why?"

"How many people know about this plan? In other words, how many people know about Willow?"

"The only ones are dead or in jail. They picked up her husband and arrested him as an accessory after the fact and on a conspiracy to commit something or other."

"But who did they tell about their abduct-Willow plan?"

"No one. This was something they needed to do quietly to maintain plausible deniability. Once Willow was secured away and performing like a circus monkey, they would produce results that would win their superiors over. According to Tom Middleton's statement, Janice was always ranting and raving that her bosses only wanted results."

"And we're waiting for Sergeant Doolittle to explain something else?" Parkman asked.

Sarah nodded.

"Like how she knew to come to the rescue?" Darwin said. "That's what I want to know. We're still breathing because of her."

"How's Amanda holding up?" Parkman asked. "This has to be hard on her." He shook his head. "Both parents are in jail."

Someone knocked on the door.

"Speak of the devil," Sarah said, pushing up off the chair to go answer the door.

When she opened it, Sergeant Karen Doolittle was in civilian clothes. They hugged warmly, then Sarah invited her inside and formally introduced her to Alex.

"I can't stay long as I'm being transferred back to the States for a couple of weeks."

"Oh?" Sarah raised her brows. "I hope that's a good thing."

Doolittle smiled widely, her teeth showing. "I'm going back with Amanda to help her integrate back into her family."

Parkman gasped, and Darwin reared back.

"I haven't told them that part yet."

"Oh shit." Doolittle placed a hand over her mouth. "I'm sorry."

"It's fine. We were just getting to that part. Go ahead. Tell them about Amanda."

Doolittle adjusted her shirt and stood with her legs apart like she was on duty. "Amanda Smith was stolen from her parents by the Sophia Project when she was three years old. Once dental records confirmed her death in a fiery car accident, there was a funeral, and everyone moved on with their lives. When Janice Stilton got to Amanda's file, she decided not to send her back. Amanda was still so young that Janice told everyone she was her dead sister's daughter, her estranged dead sister. Over the years, Amanda started calling her mom, and the rest is history."

"Amanda isn't even Janice's daughter …" Darwin said out loud, stunned at what he was hearing.

"And she's clairvoyant," Sarah added.

"Was that something you picked up on?" Parkman asked.

"Not at first, no. I noticed she had a tic when we were talking in Disco's warehouse. She would twitch uncontrollably at random times. I asked her about it, and she said it was a side effect of a drug called clozapine."

"Clozapine?"

"It's an antipsychotic, sometimes used to quell the voices. People with schizophrenia are known to use it. With Amanda, it stunted her psychic ability. Janice didn't want her to be psychic all the time, so she and her husband had Amanda on clozapine for the past ten years, off and on."

"That long on an antipsychotic?" Parkman said, shaking his head.

"Which caused the tics."

"But wait," Darwin said, adjusting his attention to Doolittle. "Off topic a bit, but how did you know to come to that diner in a FedEx truck? We're eternally grateful and all, and we know you came from the

Barrie area, but how did you know?"

"We received orders from the consul general at the US embassy in Toronto." Doolittle pointed at Sarah. "They'd heard everything from her."

Sarah nodded. "Once I found out Amanda was on antipsychotics, I wondered if it was because she was clairvoyant. And if so, could she be like Willow? Following that logic, was she *actually* Amanda Stilton? So I made some calls on a hunch. I told the embassy I'd located an American citizen who had been missing for over a decade. I identified myself as an American, which I am, and told them that a high-ranking American official was on Canadian soil creating havoc. They'd already kidnapped my daughter, my mother, and some of my friends. This official"—she used air quotes—"had likely kidnapped Amanda, and people were dying. Then I embellished a few facts and told them where I'd meet Janice and when. On the way to Orangeville, they called me back. They'd looked into my story, who I was, and who Janice Stilton was, and decided they'd send Doolittle's team. I told them to come armed and ready for a war but arrive covertly, or Janice could potentially hurt the people she'd abducted."

"And so we did," Doolittle finished for her. "We even had a chopper in case of a car chase."

Sarah looked at Doolittle. "Who was in that other chopper I heard at the scene of the crash? Did you ever find out because Janice said she had one, too?"

Doolittle nodded. "We tracked it to a local airport, and the men were arrested peacefully in their hotel rooms."

"Sounds like everything is all wrapped up and tied in a bow." Sarah leaned against Alex's bed, tired from all the talking.

"Not everything," Doolittle said. Then she turned toward the door. "Come on in," she shouted.

The door opened, and Amanda Smith entered the hospital room, her face lit up with a smile.

"Amanda," Sarah said, her arms open for a hug.

They embraced, and tears slipped from Amanda's face when she pulled away.

"I'm sorry," she cried. "I told myself not to cry. I said it over and over."

"It's okay." Sarah rested a hand on Amanda's shoulder.

"They found my parents, and they're still alive."

"Wow, that's such great news."

Parkman and Darwin echoed her words.

Amanda wiped her eyes and took a deep breath. "Sergeant Doolittle is escorting me back to the States. She'll take me to my parents' place. I'm so grateful to have her." Amanda waved her hand quickly in the air. "Oh, and guess what?"

"What?" Sarah said, matching Amanda's tone.

"I'm off all those meds that woman Janice used to make me take, and the tremors have lessened."

"That's great news."

"But the voices are back," she said in a lower voice, looking around the room in a conspiratorial manner. Then she broke out laughing. "I'm kidding!"

Sarah laughed along with her. It felt good to laugh.

"The truth," Amanda said, her face pensive now. "Some of my older abilities are coming through. I just have to figure it all out. Yet, something tells me this isn't the last I'll see of you." She stared into Sarah's eyes without wavering.

Sarah rubbed Amanda's upper arm. "I'm sure we'll see each other again."

Amanda was shaking her head. "I can't believe you kidnapped me to prove I wasn't Janice's daughter. You dropped me off at a police station, and here we are."

"And we have to leave," Doolittle said, checking her watch. "Or we'll be late for our flight back."

Amanda shot forward and hugged Sarah again. "Thank you for everything," she whispered in Sarah's ear. "I'm eternally grateful. You gave me my life back. This is something I can't repay. Just know I'm beyond grateful."

They pulled apart, and Sarah held onto Amanda's arms. "Just don't get into trouble with boys. And no sneaking out."

"Sarah, I'm almost eighteen."

"Oh, right." She shook her head. "Forget what I said. Do what you want, but be careful about it."

Everyone laughed, and everything was right in the world for a brief moment. There were no gunmen, no one was abducted, Willow was safe, and Alex was leaving the hospital today.

That voice in her head, the one she'd taken to calling Vivian again, had dropped in last night to ask, *How could you ever doubt me?*

Her sister had been pulling away over the past few years, but promised last night to be a bigger part of Sarah's life in the future.

She also told her that *The Game* was done. She'd won with her own wits.

What worried her was *The Decoy*. It was coming, and she'd need Vivian more than ever.

Even as she waved at Sergeant Doolittle and Amanda as they left the hospital room, even as she brushed a tear from her cheek, she knew the danger coming in *The Decoy* would be a lot to handle alone.

Aaron wanted no part of her life anymore and threatened to take her to court to secure full custody of Willow.

Daniel needed to be at the dojo, and Disco said he'd remain on call for Sarah but hoped he wouldn't come that close to dying next time.

Darwin was heading back to Italy soon, leaving Sarah with Parkman because Alex would be out for several months, healing his broken bones.

This meant she'd need Vivian if they were going to keep doing this shit together.

After all, they'd started it as a team, so they had to finish it as one.

That didn't stop the churning in her gut at what was coming, though. According to Vivian, it would test her skills in every way, and Sarah hated tests.

She detested them.

Afterword

DEAR READER,

Kidnapping and abductions seem to be common themes in Sarah's life. While writing this novel, I was struck by the realization that this has been an ongoing theme, and I feel we need a change. Therefore, starting with book 33, *The Decoy*, I will write several Sarah Roberts books without kidnappings. I say this in case several of you are getting as bored with that theme as I feel you might be.

In this vein, I want more of Vivian in Sarah's life as well, like back in the first dozen books. So, going forward, you will see them acting more as a team like never before. They've been through a lot together in thirty-two books, and I plan on taking them to many more crazy places in the subsequent eighteen novels. (Remember how I said I wanted to get to book fifty eventually?).

I used Oshawa in this novel as an homage to the city I was born in. In April of 1969, I was born in Oshawa General Hospital, and I grew up in South Oshawa, moving to North Oshawa for my high school years. I also lived in Hamilton in the 1990s, where Disco lives off Upper James and Garth. Disco's warehouse in downtown Toronto was modeled after a company I did business with back in the nineties, right on Richmond, a block from Spadina. They say we should "write what you know." It certainly makes it easier.

The schoolyard where Sarah was waiting for Amanda in the first few chapters was modeled after the first school I ever went to, although it's no longer there. The school was torn down many years ago, but I still recall the yard, the brick building, and where the parking lot was situated. It was a rough elementary school. In grade one, I was rushed to the hospital for stitches in my forehead after splitting my skin in a fight. In the second grade, I got my front teeth broken in a tumble with another boy named Rueben, which I mentioned in a previous book. These were the days in southern Ontario when the principal could still give students the belt. He had to call the parents and ask for their permission after explaining the infraction. With as much trouble as I got into back in those days, my mother never let the principal touch me. For that, I was thankful. When I got home, my gratitude dissipated quickly as the trouble my parents gave me was worse.

I'm sure anyone raised in the 1960s and 1970s is familiar with the punishments dispensed back in the day. Today, our parents would be charged with a criminal offense, but that didn't happen back then, either.

I moved out at sixteen, started my first business at seventeen, and never looked back.

This novel's Roy Thompson Hall was used as an homage to a fantastic venue. Back in the early 1990s, I saw an Australian band called Crowded House play there, and I absolutely loved it. This author has fond memories of that concert.

The Royal Oak Hotel does not exist.

Part two of the afterword will deal with gratitude.

A very special thank you has to go out to my author wife, Rania Stone (Synodinou), for her immense help with the plot of this novel. When I was stumped on the plot, Rania proposed the idea of Vivian coming back in some way. I was initially against the idea, but then we discussed it further, and the early signs of a plot began to take shape. After many hours of bouncing ideas off each other and a bottle of tsipouro (a delicious Greek beverage), the ideas could not be contained further. You've just read the result of those long conversations, making me eternally grateful for the woman in my life who knows what it takes to write a wicked thriller and how plots need to come together. Her novel, *The Unjustified*, is an example of that—a wicked thriller with an intense twist.

Thank you, honey, for everything.

I want to thank Karen Doolittle for allowing me to use her name in this novel. Sending gratitude your way.

I want to thank Sheri Whitewolf Doll for coming up with the title of this novel. I ran a contest in 2017 to determine the titles readers would like to see in the Sarah Roberts Series, and this was the last title selected from the top ten names. So, thank you, Sheri.

This novel is dedicated to Sheri and Karen.

Finally, I want to share with you a novel I've written that's out now. It's called *The Woman in the Woods*, and I'm excited to share the blurb with you here. A release date has not been set yet, but I am working on it and will post about it on social media as soon as one is selected.

Hit the "Follow" button on Bookbub and Amazon to stay updated when books are released.

Here's the blurb for *The Woman in the Woods*:

Something is wrong—horribly wrong—in the deep woods of Oregon.

People age at accelerated rates, then disappear. Hundreds of disappearances have occurred in the area for decades—a veritable Bermuda Triangle on land. Even the authorities sent in to investigate the disappearances have gone missing. After that, the government stepped in and fenced off the entire area.

But when a group of four strangers misses their train and wanders onto the site searching for shelter, they discover what was left behind. After one of their four goes missing, they decide to leave the area. Something's toying with them, something ancient and malicious, and it doesn't want them to leave.

It's wise enough to understand them and powerful enough to control them.

It's also hungry, and it needs to be satiated.

Until next time, thank you beyond words. I'm eternally grateful to you, the reader.

I love you all.

Take care of yourself and each other.

Yours,

Jonas Saul

The Decoy

Book Thirty-Three

Chapter 1

THE ENEMY WAS TIME—the clock didn't stop for murder, it didn't stop for Sarah Roberts. It certainly wouldn't stop for the bombs planted in several downtown locations.

If this were about a madman causing general mayhem, why couldn't Sarah's sister just tell her where the bombs were? That could tidy up things faster.

But no, Sarah didn't have a sister who thought like the rest of the human race. She always had her own plan, her own way.

Innocent people would be killed. Funerals would be arranged, with all that pain and suffering to endure—and for what? How was she supposed to stop it with just a name and a short message? The bomb threats were supposed to be called in at ten this evening—fifteen minutes from now.

Sarah Roberts spun the steering wheel to the right and raced along Queen Street. At least Aaron had agreed to take Willow for the night. She couldn't leave her daughter alone at home, and when Vivian shouted for her to get up and get out of the house, Sarah responded with a sense of urgency. To her surprise—although she shouldn't be surprised—her daughter was packed and ready to stay with her dad for the night before Sarah even opened her bedroom door.

"How did you know?" Sarah asked. "My sister messaged you, too?"

Little Willow shook her head.

"Right. Why do I always forget?" Sarah tugged the backpack higher on Willow's shoulders. "You can see what's coming up to thirty minutes before it happens." Sarah lowered to her haunches until she was eye-to-eye with her daughter. "So you saw me coming and packed?"

Willow nodded. "I would love it if Aunt Vivian talked to me, but she doesn't."

Sarah studied her daughter's face for a moment, knowing she was wasting precious time but wasting it anyway. "I'd love that, too."

Now, two blocks from Aaron's new apartment above his dojo, she snatched her phone off the seat beside her and dialed him.

"Yeah." He sounded gruff, put out.

"Meet me outside."

"What's this all about—"

Sarah ended the call, cutting him off.

She got behind a slow-moving delivery truck, waited until the dojo came into sight on the right, then eased back and slipped into a spot in line with the front door.

The interior lights flickered to life, and then Aaron unlocked the entrance from the inside.

Her heart caught in her throat at the sight of him. A longing coursed through her for the better days, back when they weren't living apart and negotiating a separation agreement for some arbitrator to sign off on. At least Aaron hadn't made good on his threat to go to court regarding Willow—yet.

In the brief seconds comprising her delay, Willow opened the back door and jumped into her dad's arms. Aaron kissed her cheek, and Sarah glanced away to stare at the clock on the dashboard.

It was 21:54.

She had five minutes to make her call and send the message. If she didn't, people would be murdered, but with the short time she had left, there was no guarantee someone wouldn't get hurt.

The clock truly didn't stop or even slow down an iota—she was desperately running out of time.

She put the car in gear, but a knock on the passenger side window kept her foot on the brake.

Aaron stood there, bent over, his hands outstretched in a what-the-fuck gesture.

Sarah lowered the window, catching her last glimpse of Willow as she ran inside the dojo.

"What's going on, Sarah? You call me all harried and out of breath, drop off our daughter, and if I'm not mistaken, you were about to squeal out of here. Got a hot date?"

Why did that hurt more than missing him? Her interest in men was staring at her through her open passenger window. Years would disappear on her calendar without a single *date* being recorded, as she had no interest in *other* men.

"I've just got something to handle, and I couldn't leave Willow alone."

"Something to handle?" Aaron lowered to his haunches, his forearms resting on the door. "Vivian again?"

They locked eyes briefly, and Sarah broke the look with a subtle nod.

"Will you be safe?"

She nodded again without saying, *I hope so.*

"You've got Parkman's number if you need something. He's still in town."

And there it was. Aaron's refusal to be a part of this life and his refusal to mention Alex's name, even though he had just left the hospital and was still recuperating after that hotel fight weeks ago. No mention of Daniel's name either, and Darwin was out of town. No one knew where Disco was or what job he was working.

How could she blame Aaron, though? They'd lost Benjamin. Aaron lost a finger years ago to a cartel. They'd lost so much. And in the end, they even lost each other.

Yet Sarah continued to do her sister's bidding. At what cost? Was it an addiction? That's what Aaron had called it. Like a drunk who loses their job, marriage, and ultimately their family, Sarah was living that same path with Vivian. All she had to do was quit Vivian, and they could be a family again.

A family.

That's precisely what Vivian said this bomb threat was all about, which made zero sense. But when did anything ever make sense with Vivian?

She didn't have time for this. It was 21:57 now. That phone call had to take place by 22:00, or she would already screw this one up.

"I need to go." She glanced back at him and suppressed the urge to wipe the wetness building in her eyes.

He stared at her a moment longer with a look in his eyes she couldn't make out. Longing? Sadness? Or was it disappointment?

Aaron pushed off the door and stepped back. "When will you pick her up?"

Sarah leaned down to look up at him. "I'm not sure yet. Tomorrow afternoon?"

"Leave her with me."

She stared at him for a long moment. "What does that mean?" She would not voluntarily give up custody if that were what he was talking about.

"Until this thing, whatever it is Vivian has you doing, is over. Then call and come get her. We don't want any part of it."

And there it was again. Another smack when she was down. He didn't have to use *we* when referring to himself. Including Willow in his decision might be a father thinking he was protecting his daughter, but it made Sarah feel ganged up on.

To avoid a fight, to escape the pain of harsh words exchanged, she moved her foot off the brake and hit the gas, pulling away from the curb with barely a look over her shoulder.

One block later, she turned right to drop down to Leslie Street, then pulled over and grabbed her cell phone to make the call.

Save people's lives tonight. Then work on saving her own life tomorrow.

On the third ring, at precisely 21:59, the phone was picked up.

"Hello?" a man said, more a question than a greeting.

"Heath?"

There was a pause, then, "Who's this?"

"Are you Heath?" Sarah asked, not willing to answer his questions yet. There was no time for chit-chat.

"Yeah, who's this?"

"Listen to me and do as I say."

"Who the fuck *is* this—"

"*Listen!*" Sarah shouted. "Bomb threats will be called in very soon. Disregard them. Avoid them. They are a waste of time. The bombs that detonate shouldn't harm anyone if you avoid them—"

"Bombs?"

"You're not *listening*. Fuck the bombs. Leave them. It's a diversion."

"Diversion? Like a duck?"

"A duck?" Sarah scrunched up her face as she watched the clock on her dashboard flip to 22:00.

"Yeah, a decoy."

"Look, I have no idea. All I have are names. Leslie Barns, Greg Brown, Harris, and Mills. But that's not important. What is important is the bombs are harmless as long as no one responds to investigate any of them—"

"Hold on. Someone's on the other line."

"Wait! Do not waste resources. Sending people will get them killed. Are you listening? Do not ..." she paused.

He'd put her on hold.

And now people were going to die.

He should've listened better.

Sarah hung up and tossed her phone onto the seat beside her. She had a woman walking along King Street to find.

Vivian talked to her more lately, but she still wasn't forthcoming. Her sister had no idea what *full disclosure* meant.

That would have to change if this arrangement were to continue.

Otherwise, maybe she would quit this gig and get her family back.

Vivian did say this was all about family—perhaps she meant Sarah's.

"There you go, Vivian," Sarah shouted to the empty car. "You've listened in on my rationale. Work your shit out, or I'm going back to my family."

Sarah got the car headed in the right direction as Vivian popped into her head and explained how to hurt the woman on King Street once she located her.

This was not going to work out well. Why did the woman need to be injured?

"What the hell is going on?" Sarah asked the empty car.

There was no answer.

Her night was just getting started, and it already sucked.

Chapter 2

TOM HEATH FLICKED OFF his TV, bored with how the series was going, then pushed up off his recliner to get the bottle of whiskey. Once his glass was refilled, he moved to the living room window without the aid of lights. The drapes were pulled apart enough for him to stare out at the empty cul-de-sac. At this hour on a Friday night, only the odd car moved through the dark, headed to some unknown destination, in a life with purpose.

He'd know because his life once held purpose. He'd once aspired to be a somebody, doing extraordinary things, making good money, and building his career.

But all that ended with his suspension from duty without pay. Two dead bodies can do that to a detective with the Toronto Police Department.

Well, two dead bodies he created.

Tom sipped from his glass. Even the whiskey didn't taste as good as it had last month before he killed that couple.

How was he supposed to know they weren't the perps? He did the training, followed the rule book, made a choice, and now an example had to be made at his expense.

So, lounge at home until the hearing. Stay out of the public eye. Leave his badge and gun with the boss. In other words, discard his entire career in the double muzzle flash of an accident, pure and simple.

Disregarding the ugly taste, he jerked his head back, swallowed the rest of the whiskey, and headed over to the cabinet for more. It may not go down as well as in the past, but the effect was the same. Medicating with alcohol was a dangerous road to take, but where was his life going anyway? Barely mid-thirties, single, jobless—or rather career-less now —with bills stacking up and no idea where to start.

He filled his glass, already regretting the headaches and hangover that would inevitably have him swearing off booze tomorrow morning and drinking again by tomorrow evening.

Maybe he could apply for some private security firm. Perhaps he could be a doorman, given the hours he put in as a rookie cop, combined with his experience working undercover on several occasions, before being promoted to detective.

How could life change that fast? One minute, his career was being fast-tracked; the next, it's that proverbial house of cards, but they're on fire and burning everyone associated with him—the ultimate version of career HIV.

He moved back to the window to look at the world he once protected.

Before he took another sip, his phone rang.

A frown scrunched up his face and affected his vision. Who would be calling him on a Friday night? Not a single colleague that he had gone out with months ago was in his corner. No one wanted to associate with him, understandably. Career suicide can be contagious.

The caller ID came up unknown, even though he could read the phone number.

On the third ring, he brought the phone to his ear and whispered a tentative, "Hello?"

"Heath?"

He tried to place the voice but couldn't. "Who's this?"

"Are you Heath?"

The woman on the other end of the line sounded angry, like a school teacher he once had. Feeling chastised, even though he hadn't done anything wrong, he said, "Yeah, who's this?"

"Listen to me and do as I say."

"Who the fuck *is* this—"

"Listen! Bomb threats will be called in very soon. Disregard them. Avoid them. They are a waste of time. The bombs that detonate shouldn't harm anyone if you avoid them—"

"Bombs?" he cut in. Why was she calling him? No police department this side of Hell employed him anymore. Wait, how did she get his number?

"You're not listening. Fuck the bombs. Leave them. It's a diversion."

"Diversion? Like a duck?" He stared at nothing as he set his full glass of whiskey on the side table.

"A duck?" the woman asked, sounding confused.

"Yeah, a decoy," he mumbled. *How does she not know what a decoy is?*

"Look, I have no idea. All I have are names. Leslie Barns, Greg Brown, Harris, and Mills. But that's not important. What is important is the bombs are harmless as long as no one responds to investigate any of them—"

A beep sounded on the line. "Hold on. Someone's on the other line."

"Wait! Do not waste resources—"

He smacked the button to go to the other line. "Hello?"

"Heath, it's Doyle. You hear from the sergeant yet?"

"Doyle?" He may not be sober, but he was fully awake now. "Why would I hear from Sergeant *Amanda* Miller?" He didn't mean to, but her name came out with sarcasm dripping from it.

"We received a credible bomb threat."

Heath's stomach churned, and he dropped into the recliner. "Yeah, seems I heard about that."

"Wait, what?"

"A woman just called to tell—"

"So you heard from Miller?"

"No, some woman called. I have her on the other line."

There was a pause. "Heath, are you drunk?" Doyle whispered the words as if someone was listening in.

"No, Doyle, I'm tired. Just trying to wake up." Would the lie pass muster? "Someone called and told me something about bombs, then said it was a diversion, a decoy."

"She actually said it was a decoy?"

"Well, I said, 'duck,' then she repeated my word, and I said, 'decoy.' Anyway, what's this got to do with me?" He blinked twice, but the room spun slightly, listing to the side like a boat nudged by a wave.

"Heads up. Amanda Panda is walking into her office. No, not walking, storming across the room to her office. She has just received clearance to return your badge for this job. Get suited up. You're coming in tonight."

He hadn't heard the sergeant's nickname for weeks, as he hadn't been out with the boys for drinks since he was suspended.

"Why's she calling me in? I'm suspended pending the investigation of manslaughter charges. She's got you and an entire force of officers."

"I'm sure she'll explain that, but I have to hang up. Wait, one more thing. Who called you to tell you about the bombs? That's fucked up, man."

"I don't know. Some woman. She sounded angry at me."

"What else did she say?"

"She prattled off a bunch of names—"

"Names? What kind of names?"

"She said Leslie and Banks or something. Some guy named Greg, and Harris, and …" He stopped. "Oh, shit. She said Miller, too."

"By any chance, did she say Greg Brown? What about Leslie Barns and not 'Banks'?"

"Right, that's it. How did you know?"

"It's Mills, not Miller."

"How the hell, man? She call you, too?"

"Heath, listen closely. That is where all the bomb threats are located. Greg Brown College Campus, Leslie Barns, the TTC depot, RC Harris, the water treatment site, and the Victory Soya Mills Silos have been abandoned since 1991. And we've only got fifteen minutes between detonations, with the first one going off twelve minutes from now."

"*What?* Holy shit, dude." Heath sat up, eyes wide and blinking at the streetlight pouring in through his living room window.

"You're drunk, Heath. I know you. Also, the sergeant is on the phone, so she's likely trying to call you in. Piece of advice?"

"Yeah, man. Hit me."

"Find out who called you with the bomb locations and why. Find out how they're connected, and I suspect you'll stumble upon the bad guys. This is important. You nail this; the odds of your career washing back *up* the drain it flushed down might increase."

"Counting on you for advice is like buying a pizza at Taco Bell."

"What? They don't sell pizza, dickbreath."

"Exactly."

"That doesn't make sense, you drunk ass. Take a cold shower to wake up. Then find that woman because we have no leads over here."

"Wait, call in a favor. Here's her phone number."

"What? She didn't block her number?" Doyle sounded shocked, his voice rising with each word.

"Write this down." Heath held the phone out, brought up the recent calls, and recited the number. "Find out who owns that cell and triangulate the number. I'll call her back in ten minutes with this phone."

"I can't do that shit on such short notice without a warrant, and you know that."

"You want to solve this shit before it even starts? You said so yourself. 'Find out who called, and you find the bad guys.' Just call in a favor. I know you know Jimmy, and he can do it undetected."

"Fine. Call her back in ten minutes and keep her on the line, but you'll owe me for this." His old partner ended the call without a goodbye.

Heath tapped the button to go to the other line, but it was dead.

The woman had hung up.

Chapter 3

SARAH PULLED OVER AND parked, leaving the car idling. According to her sister, the woman would hurry along King Street toward Jarvis on the right side. Even though her sister had popped into her head, Sarah was still left wanting. Would she ever get a whole, real conversation out of Vivian? Maybe that was asking too much.

She killed the lights and waited. The woman had to come along within ten to twenty minutes. Then Sarah was done for the night. Probably. Likely. But one could never tell with Vivian.

Several cars passed her, but otherwise, this area of town seemed uneventful. A small amount of foot traffic, with a few stores still open, catering to the night crowd.

The passenger seat, Vivian whispered into her inner ear.

Sarah frowned. *What the hell for?*

Just do it. I'll tell you when she's coming. Minutes away now.

Sarah turned off the engine, pocketed the keys, moved her cell phone to the console, then got out and walked around to get back in the car on the passenger side. She adjusted the seat to watch the mirrors, keeping an eye on the rear of the vehicle.

When her cell phone rang, she nearly jumped out of her seat. A startled yelp escaped her lips as she fumbled for it on the center console.

"What?" she barked into the phone without checking to see who was calling.

"Who is this?" a man asked.

"You called me, dumbass. If you don't know who you called, then I'm hanging up."

"No, wait!"

Sarah paused, her eyes fixed on the sports mirror, watching the people on the sidewalk coming her way. "I'm waiting."

"You called me about ten minutes ago—"

"Heath?"

"Yeah."

"Oh, now the information I have is important? Is that it? You put me on fuckin' hold."

"Who are you?"

Sarah shook her head. "Why would knowing my identity solve anything? There are four bomb threats. A few of them will detonate, but not all of them. I can't see how many, but stay away, and no one gets hurt. Send colleagues to validate the bomb threats, and people will die."

"That's not my call, and I certainly can't do that on an anonymous tip. How do you know about these bombs? How are you connected?"

"Connected?" Sarah laughed. "I'm not connected in any way. I was just minding my own business when I heard things. So, I'm relaying information to save lives. That's it. Look, I gotta go."

"Wait, why would people die if we respond?"

Sarah released an exasperated breath. "Because, Mr. Critical Thinker, you will have emergency crews too close to the explosion. They'll be advancing on the site, then *boom*. You know what I mean?"

Sarah glanced at the clock. It was 22:15. The first bomb would detonate—

Heath was about to say something, but stopped when he heard it, too.

Sarah ducked lower in her seat as the explosion sounded like thunder from a distant storm. A couple strolling by her car paused in their step, exchanged a glance, looked skyward in unison, then kept walking, but quicker now.

"What the hell was that?" Heath nearly shouted.

"Oh, now you're listening. There are three more. Stay away." Eyes on the mirror, she was sure the woman she was waiting for was one block back and coming her way. When she faced forward, a black van pulled to the curb one block in front of her, its headlights off before it came to a stop.

Why would they do that? *Vivian, is that van part of this?*

"You still there, Heath?"

"Yeah, one second."

Sarah glanced into the mirror again. The woman was on her phone, walking slowly. "I don't have much time. Besides, I've done my job. I've delivered the message. Now it's on you people to steer clear while trying to determine what these guys are up to."

"Right, the decoy thing."

"Okay, bye."

"Wait!"

"For what?" Sarah gripped the door handle, ready to jump out as the woman moved even closer.

That's her, Vivian whispered. *Hit her.*

"Gotcha!" the man shouted into the phone.

Several thoughts raced through Sarah's mind until she latched onto the correct one.

"You were tracing this call, or whatever they call it? Triangulating my phone?"

"Sarah Roberts," he said. "We now have officers responding to King Street. Then you can come in and explain to us why you set the bombs—"

She hung up on him, slamming her phone onto the center console harder than she wanted to. Vivian had given her an hour's notice. She hadn't had a spare phone to use as a burner.

"Shit," she mumbled as she stared across the intersection at the black van.

The doors had opened, and four men piled out, balaclavas on their heads. This was shaping up to be too dangerous too quickly, with too many unknowns.

"Why do I get involved in this shit, Vivian?"

She glanced over her shoulder as the woman walked by her trunk and then the back door.

Sarah shoved her shoulder into the car door, viciously slamming it open. The woman couldn't avoid bumping into it with her knee.

The woman reared back, hopping on her good leg as she moaned, her hands clutching at her leg. She jumped over until she was leaning against the back of Sarah's car.

"I'm so sorry," Sarah said. "Here, let me help you."

"No," the woman groaned, "it's fine. Just hit my knee." She winced. "Shit, that hurts."

"Here," Sarah opened the back door, "take a seat in my car."

"Really, it's fine." The woman tried to push her away, but Sarah persisted.

She glanced over her shoulder at the black van. The men were running across the street toward them now, all eyes on Sarah.

That confirmed it. They were involved somehow.

"Get in the fucking car," Sarah said and shoved the woman backward.

The woman's head smacked the roof's edge on the way down, but she landed solidly on her butt in the back seat. Before she could protest or fight back, Sarah grabbed the bottom of the woman's pants, lifted them, and shoved her legs inside. The woman shouted in pain, but Sarah cut it off when she slammed the door.

The men were twenty meters away and closing fast when Sarah reached the driver's side door.

And now several police sirens wailed in the distance—no doubt coming after her as promised by Heath.

She dropped into the driver's seat, jammed the key in, cranked the engine, and had it in gear in seconds. The car lurched away from the curb, slamming her door shut.

One of the men got close enough to slap the trunk of her car, and then she was gone, watching them in the mirror.

From a distance of a dozen meters or more, she couldn't be sure, but one of the men pointed his hand at her as he pantomimed a gun going off.

Who the hell were they, and who was the woman in her back seat?

A police cruiser skidded around the corner two intersections ahead, followed by another.

Red and blue lights lit up her rearview mirror.

"Hold on," she shouted as she cranked the wheel to the right.

What's going on, Vivian? she shouted in her head as the woman in the back seat screamed in pain.

Chapter 4

NEIL KRAMER RIPPED OFF his balaclava and motioned for his men to do the same.

"Nonchalantly, saunter away," Kramer said under his breath. "Get back in the van."

Jason rushed up to walk beside him. "What do we do now, sir?" He folded his mask and stuffed it in his pocket.

Kramer turned to stare at him as they crossed the street, then looked back at James and Jack. "Nothing changes. We'll breach the building without her."

"Who was that other woman?" Jack asked. "She got in our way."

For his formidable size—at almost seven feet tall—Jack had an incredibly high voice. He spoke in falsetto but shouted in baritone.

Cruisers raced by, their sirens screaming and cutting off any chance to reply. Once they were gone around the corner, the noise died down considerably.

"I don't know who she is." Kramer picked up his step as more cruisers sounded in the distance. "But she sure as hell knows us."

"What makes you say that, sir?" James asked.

James didn't live up to his moniker. For this weekend's heist job, Kramer gave them fictional character names. James for James Bond, Jack for Jack Reacher, and Jason for Jason Bourne. With all the names starting with the letter J, he wondered if he'd get confused, but Jack was tall and strong like Reacher. Jason was from Europe, where he evaded the Mossad after they came after him—he was still on their wanted list —and James looked the most like Bond, but he was woefully lacking in the gray matter department.

Without answering James, Kramer got in the van and slammed the door. The other three men hopped in the side and slid that door closed.

He produced a burner phone from the glove box and dialed the number from memory. It was time to call Detective Tom Heath again— he'd called minutes before to warn him of the first bomb, and now another one would detonate.

"Heath here."

"Did you enjoy the show?"

"Are you the guy who called me a few minutes ago? Why are you doing this?"

"I want you to know another bomb will light up the Toronto sky in minutes." He paused as two more police cruisers buzzed by their location.

"Why are you doing this?" Heath asked again. "Why call me twice? I can't do anything about it. How did you even get my number?"

"Tonight is a trial run for the big bang. I will get what I want and not stop until I do."

"Then tell me what it is you want." Heath's tone sounded one part exasperated and one part furious. "Can't we arrange to get it to you without bombing shit?"

"I will supply my list of demands soon, but the first thing I want is that woman."

There was a pause. "What woman?"

"The police are chasing a woman in the King and Jarvis area."

Heath gasped on the other end. "How do you know that—"

"She interfered with my plans. She should not have gotten involved. Now I blow the second target early because of her. I pray you've moved your men back already."

Heath's voice could be heard as if he were speaking to someone else at arm's length. Kramer barely heard him on another phone ordering people to get out of there, and then he was back on the line.

"What's the target?" Heath asked, the desperate tone to his voice triggering Kramer into wanting to blow the entire city to smithereens. "There are fire and bomb squad men en route. They may already be there. Look, whoever you are, you don't want to do this."

Kramer's hand tightened on the phone as he pressed it against his head. "You don't know me, nor do you know what I want and don't want. You think lives matter? One life? Twenty?" Kramer laughed into the phone, then stopped abruptly, his face dropping. "Nothing matters, Detective Heath. Just like that couple you killed with your service weapon, the people that die tonight will be buried and forgotten. Isn't that how it works?" When there was no response, Kramer said, "Goodbye, Detective Heath. I'll call again soon, but in the meantime, let's have a blast, shall we?"

Kramer lowered the window, then, without ending the call, he lobbed the burner phone into a pile of dirt at the base of a tree that lined the sidewalk. Let them trace it to this location, right where that interfering bitch in her car was. That'll make them think she's involved with us.

With the window up, he checked both ways, then performed a U-turn and drove one block, where he killed the engine and vacated his seat, joining the fictional characters turned mercenaries in the rear of the van.

"Here's how we're going to do it."

He laid out his plan in under a minute, got nods all around, then grabbed the detonator and blew up the Toronto Transit Commission's depot called Leslie Barns. The loss of life would be minimal, but the loss of the TTC trains for the weeks ahead would be catastrophic.

His objective was clear, and no filthy woman would stand in their way.

For her interference, strapping a bomb to her would offer him great pleasure, something akin to orgasmic bliss.

Perhaps that was what he would demand once the city was under siege.

Give him the girl, and he'd go away.

The stirrings of a plan formed, and he smiled at how he could incorporate her into taking the blame for everything. Even that cell phone he tossed away would help.

When he laughed to himself, his men turned to look at him. This wasn't part of the original objective, but it was now.

That woman should never have interfered.

Now it will cost her—dearly.

Chapter 5

DETECTIVE HEATH STOOD OUTSIDE his home waiting for a taxi when his phone rang again.

"What?" He shouted into it.

"Detective Heath," Sergeant Amanda Miller shouted into the phone. "When will you get to the station?"

"I'm sorry, ma'am. I'm waiting for a taxi."

"You couldn't *drive* in?"

"I had, I mean, I drank something with dinner. I shouldn't be driving."

There was a heavy exhalation on the other line. "Are you *fucking* kidding me? *Get in here, now!*"

"Yes, ma'am." Heath glanced back at his closed garage door too fast, lost his balance slightly, then took an extra step to remain standing. Driving anywhere was out of the question. "I'm sure the taxi will be here soon."

"Bombs are lighting up Lakeshore Boulevard, and you're waiting for a taxi." She grunted like she'd been punched in the stomach. "We're in the middle of a full-blown crisis, and I can see the camera zoom in on you tapping your foot on the street corner with elevator music playing in the background." She scoffed. "Waiting for a taxi." She repeated his words in a mocking tone filled with disdain. "You have got to be fucking kidding me."

"Am I being reinstated?"

"Do I have a choice?" Amanda shouted. "These assholes called you, according to your ex-partner, Chip Doyle—twice now, minutes apart."

"He told you that?"

"Doyle's loyalty lies with the department, Heathcliff. When he traced the call that you asked him to, he saw the name Sarah Roberts pop up and briefed me on everything while sending units to pick her up, but guess *what!*" Those last three words were nearly screamed as she uttered them.

"What?" was all Heath said.

Headlights flashed at the end of the street. He narrowed his eyes and saw it was a taxi, but the idiot stopped at the house numbered 69. Heath's house was 96. How could they possibly switch the numbers?

"Miss Sarah Roberts," his sergeant droned on in his ear as he jogged toward the waiting taxi, "bolted when police approached her. Now, why is that? She calls in the bomb locations to you, boldly doesn't block her number, then answers the phone when you call her back. When officers come to bring her in to learn more, she runs." Sergeant Miller paused. "Only the guilty run, Heathcliff."

He hated it when she called him that. Back in high school, he hated that Brontë book, *Wuthering Heights*, too, but they made him read it. His classmates called him Heathcliff for years. He figured a serious job in law enforcement would disavow him of that name, but it wasn't to be. To be fair, everyone called their sergeant Amanda Panda because she has a child's panda bear on her desk and watches *Kung Fu Panda* at least once a month.

"My taxi is here," Heath panted into the phone as he ran across the last driveway, waving at the driver.

"Good. Get in here and explain why Sarah called you, and then you can tell us all why whoever is doing this called you twice, too."

"Wait, how do you know they called me?"

"Have you been listening to me at all? We all know Jimmy, the cell phone hacker, and Detective Heath. Your ex-partner told me about the trace on Sarah's phone. Then I ordered a trace on yours, too, in case she called back. Jimmy just sent me the transcript of your call with a man claiming to be the bomber and that he has demands."

Heath's legs weakened as he reached the taxi's back door. He fumbled with the handle, opened the door, and almost fell into the back seat.

"Where to?" the driver asked.

Heath told him the station address, then pressed the phone to his ear. "Sergeant, I have no idea how I'm involved. They just randomly called me."

"Yeah, sure they did. Okay. Of course, I believe you. Get in here and explain yourself."

"Explain what?" he asked, but the line was dead.

The driver met his gaze in the mirror. "Hey, man, none of my business, but are you a cop, or am I delivering you to their holding cell?"

Heath turned to stare out the window. "Both, I think."

,

Chapter 6

"WHO ARE YOU?" SARAH blurted out as she tried to make a right turn without hitting anything.

"What?" The woman righted herself in the back seat.

"Why are you important to those men?"

"Wait, who the hell are you, and where are you taking me? This is kidnapping. I'd call the police, but …" The woman jerked a hand over her shoulder. "Seems like they're already after you."

"Yeah." Sarah shot a look in the mirror, then back to the road. "There's that."

"What men are you talking about?" The woman leaned forward, and her shoulders moved rhythmically—likely rubbing her wounded knee.

Sarah eyed a narrow alley coming up on the left, debated the odds, then gave up. Why she was running from the authorities in the first place didn't make sense. They tracked her cell phone. They knew who she was. Officers would have already gone to her house—luckily, Aaron lived separately now, and he had Willow with him.

Would they go to the dojo? Probably not until tomorrow if they didn't stop her tonight.

"Who are you?" Sarah asked again, wanting to know at least that before she stopped the car.

"I'm not sure how my name will mean anything to you, but I'm René."

"René, what?"

"René Atchison."

Sarah took one more right turn heading south. The cops would have a roadblock up soon. She'd pull over before that.

"What were you doing out so late? Why walk King Street alone?"

"How's that any of your business?"

"Look," Sarah stared at her in the mirror as she slowed down. "I'm trying to figure out why my sister pegged you and what those men in the black van wanted with you."

"What men in what black van?"

Sarah eased to the curb and turned off the car as at least six cruisers fanned out behind her.

"Looks like we'll figure this all out at the police station. I'm not getting shot over this shit."

Sarah opened the door, got out with her hands visible, then slammed the door shut with her hip. Before the officers jumped out of their cruisers and ordered her to, she lay on the concrete on her stomach, hands flat on the cold ground above her head.

"Stay down," a man shouted as doors opened and officers jumped out.

Half a dozen footsteps approached her in a rush.

"Don't move," another man said.

A knee dropped onto the small of her back, and another pressed down on her shoulder blades.

"Arms behind your back," a man grunted as he grabbed her forearm.

Her cheek was forced into the pavement, and she could barely mutter, "I was told not to move."

"Smartass bitch," someone mumbled.

Her right arm was wrenched behind her back, then her left. Handcuffs were slapped on, and someone counted to three.

Then several men lifted her to her feet.

Officers were helping René out of the back seat. The woman rested on a cop's shoulder as she hopped to the nearest cruiser.

"It won't take long," a cop was telling René. "We just need to take your statement."

"That woman hit me with her car door, then threw me in the back of her car like some sort of abduction shit. You Canadians are crazy!"

"You can tell us everything at the station, ma'am."

Then Sarah was ushered out of earshot as she was manhandled into another cruiser. They're never too kind when you make them chase you. A female cop who helped Sarah into the back seat wasn't really helping as much as body slamming and shoving. A bruised shoulder, a bump on the head, and a smacked ankle, but no broken skin.

Vivian, what the hell is going on?

No answer.

You want to tell me why I just did all that?

A large officer dropped into the driver's seat and slammed his door. He left the lights flashing as he got underway.

"You're in a hell of a lot of trouble, Miss Roberts."

She stared out the window, wondering what her daughter would think if she saw her now. But she wouldn't see her now because Willow was with her father, likely sound asleep and already dreaming about fun things.

Even in the worst of times, small things offered comfort in this world.

Sometimes …

Chapter 7

KRAMER PARKED IN FRONT of Gold Run Jewelry without concern for surveillance cameras on the neighboring businesses. The van would be blown apart into unrecognizable bits of metal within a few hours.

"Suit up. We go in with explosives and the drill."

All three men nodded and collected their tools.

"On my count, we exit the van and get to work." Once they all nodded again, he pushed the button for the third detonation. Somewhere along Queen Street, near Nursewood Road, the RC Harris Water Treatment Plant, a historic building on a slight hill, just lost its southern corner of concrete and windows.

Three of the four bombs had detonated. The abandoned silos south of Lakeshore Blvd., the TTC train car depot, and the water treatment plant were all likely on fire now. Lucky for them, Toronto fire stations were close, with fire station #326 literally across the street from the train depot.

His last bomb of the night would detonate at the Greg Brown Campus. That one would cause the most damage, but if they got what they were coming for quickly, he might save that one for tomorrow afternoon's job.

"Detonation confirmed. We move now."

All four men jammed balaclavas over their heads, then Kramer checked the van's mirrors and gave the okay to exit.

Once on the sidewalk, Jack got to the jewelry store door first. He brought out his lock-pick kit, which was just his concrete drill.

He powered through the door's hinges while Kramer kept an eye on the street.

As he suggested it would, the door slipped off its moorings in under thirty seconds.

No alarm sounded. Perhaps it was a silent alarm. Didn't matter, though, because every cop, firefighter, paramedic, and bomb squad officer was currently busy, and an alarm at a jewelry shop wasn't a top priority at the moment.

What was of enormous concern for the authorities was the last bomb. If Kramer and his team were trapped inside the jewelry store with the authorities responding faster than he anticipated, he had that last bomb to negotiate their free pass. After all, hadn't he proven his willingness to detonate without compunction?

Once inside the store, Jack drilled into the door that would access the back room while James and Jason smashed the cabinets and filled large velvet sacks with every bit of jewelry they could find.

Kramer moved to the side to dismantle the alarm system's box as red lights flickered with their movement. The hammer worked well, ripping into the wall in the top right corner and tearing the small panel out with three hits with the claw end.

"I'm in, Boss," Jack shouted, likely because his hearing had been affected by the sound of the drill.

Jack shouldered the door out of the way and stepped into the back room.

"We leave in less than two minutes," Kramer shouted at the other men.

Whether they heard him or not, they didn't acknowledge it. They just kept filling bags with jewelry.

Kramer stepped into the back room and saw what he was looking for—the safe.

"Step aside, big guy."

Jack moved toward the small desk that held a loupe on an extendable arm. That same loupe was likely the one that the jeweler used to survey the Cullinan diamond sitting in the store's safe.

The Cullinan, initially weighing in at over three thousand carats, was the largest rough diamond in history. Some say its worth was over four hundred million dollars.

Instead of entrusting it to the safety of several large vaults in the city, the brain trust got together and suggested it be moved to a secure location that no one knew about until it was unveiled in a special ceremony at the visiting dignitaries' luncheon happening Saturday afternoon.

Before they could change their minds or regret their decision, the diamond was moved to an unknown safe location, then to a simple safe in a small jewelry store where no one would be the wiser.

Only two people knew where it was at the moment.

Well, except Kramer.

He was the third person.

He set small squibs on the front of the safe, knowing the diamond was inside a sealed Kevlar, bomb-proof case on the interior. He could blow the safe to tiny bits, and the diamond would remain safe inside its separate enclosure.

"Okay, leave this room now."

Kramer followed Jack out to the front, where the other two had left a mess. Glass crunched underfoot as he strode out to the front door.

James and Jason were already back inside the van, watching the street. Not a single cop car could be seen. Not even a security guard patrols.

Kramer moved to the other side of the van, then, without a second's more delay, he smashed the button to blow the safe.

The explosion shattered the store's front windows, along with neighboring windows, causing a massive amount of noise as glass rained down on the sidewalk.

Kramer bolted back inside, yanking a flashlight from his side pocket to illuminate his way through the dust and debris.

The safe was mangled open, and as suspected, a black case was inside.

The Cullinan.

He wrenched the case out through the jagged hole that had almost torn the safe in two. Damage to the walls was extensive. He'd hoped the entire building wouldn't collapse with the explosion, but he'd figured that wouldn't be the case—he'd been willing to take that chance—and he'd been correct.

Kramer ran back out to the van with Jack on his heels and hopped in the driver's seat. Opening the Kevlar case was something they'd do at the warehouse when he had all the time in the world.

A distant siren came to them.

They'd done it without blowing up that last bomb at the campus.

"I think I'll leave the campus bomb for tomorrow," he said to no one in particular as he hit the gas and eased away from the curb.

One block up, he turned north toward Bloor Street, where he'd head

Jonas Saul

over the bridge and drive up to the Don Mills area. That got them far away from the carnage of all the bombs along Lakeshore. Once on the Don Valley Parkway heading north, they were free.

"We did it," he whispered. "That wasn't too bad, eh, guys?"

A few mumbled acknowledgments came his way. When he checked the mirror, the three of them were inspecting the loot in the velvet bags.

That was all for them—their payment for today's job.

The Cullinan was his and the ultimate prize from tomorrow's job.

The practice run was successful, proving tomorrow's task would be a breeze.

Although tomorrow's job involved more people dying. But what did that matter in the grand scheme of things? Everyone dies eventually.

He knew that firsthand when he saw his family killed by the man who raped his sister and mother. Any empathy he ever felt in this life died with them. Or it morphed into apathy. Whatever—it didn't matter.

Killing a few of Canada's men in uniform would make him feel good instead of triggering the trauma he lived with every day.

Maybe tomorrow, he'd kill a few extra just for good measure.

Neil Kramer smiled to himself as he drove the black van toward his destiny. It was time to set things right for his family and to get rich doing so.

Chapter 8

THEY MANHANDLED SARAH INTO an interview room and locked the door. It had to be past midnight before the door opened again. Two men and one woman, all in suits, stepped inside with a small cardboard tray of coffees.

One guy's eyes were seriously bloodshot. Was that from lack of sleep, or had he been drinking?

"You guys gonna let me go home now?"

The woman scoffed, then left her mouth open as she stared at Sarah. "You've got some nerve, little lady."

"Temper," the man with the bloodshot eyes muttered.

"Seems I've heard that thing about my nerve before." Sarah shrugged, then leaned back, knowing this could go bad for a while but also knowing they had nothing that would stick to her long-term. "So, what's the charge? Gotta charge me with something or let me go. Isn't that how this works? Or should I lawyer up?"

The woman glared at her with an iron face, each muscle rigid, unmoving. Her look was so street-tough that Sarah wondered if she struck a match across the woman's chin, would it light?

"Intimidation won't work." Sarah glanced at Bloodshot Eyes. "Good cop, bad cop won't work. Just tell me what's up, and I'll fill in what blanks I can. Then we can all go home and get some sleep." She nodded toward Bloodshot Eyes. "Looks like you need to sleep off some extra brewskies."

The woman glared at Bloodshot Eyes, then chairs were pulled out, and all three visitors sat.

The third man was casually dressed and seemed more like wallpaper to the other two in the room. So much so that she didn't even glance at him until they took their seats.

The woman cleared her throat. "I don't usually partake in these interviews myself." She did that glaring thing at Sarah again. "But when I have a suspect in my station who may be torn apart by officers that I'm responsible for, I think all conversations will have to go through me."

Something stirred in Sarah's stomach. A small nervous shot of acid mixed with her dinner from four hours ago. She leaned forward on her elbows. "Torn apart? Why would cops want to hurt little ol' me?" She looked from one cop to the next, then back to the woman. "What's going on here?" *Vivian, what have you gotten me into?*

"I'm Sergeant Amanda Miller." She pointed at Bloodshot Eyes. "This is Detective Tom Heath and his partner, Detective Chip Doyle." All three of them stared at her. "And you're an hour away from being charged with the murder of four police officers, two firefighters, and one bomb squad officer, not to mention the countless injuries of over another dozen men in uniform." Miller's eyes watered as she spoke those last words. "I've got seven men in the hospital, with two of them critical. Six city workers at two locations were injured, too." Miller slapped her hands on the table, her facial muscles were no longer firm —they twitched in anger—and said, "Try to talk your way out of us charging you on multiple counts of murder. I think you've got less than an hour before you'll never see the light of day again."

The air in the small room seemed to thicken. That shot of acid in her stomach opened into a geyser. This was wholly unexpected. Could they pin all that on her? Could they prove anything?

She faced Heath, her own jaw twitching now. "I called you—" She swallowed, her mouth suddenly quite dry. "I called you to warn you."

Heath nodded once. "Why set those bombs, then call to warn us, and still detonate them—"

"I *didn't* set those bombs!" she shouted, cutting him off. "My guess is those guys in the black van did it."

Doyle grinned. "'Guys in the black van,'" he repeated. "Sure, we've heard that defense before. The guy in the hat did it. That guy in the suit jacket." He shook his head. "Is that the best you've got?" He clucked his tongue once, then scoffed. "You're in a fight for your life, for your freedom. Come on, Miss Roberts, you can do better than that."

The room descended into silence while Sarah contemplated calling a lawyer, but she'd never done that before and always weaseled her way out of a mess. These three were convinced she had something to do with the bombs—or were they? Was this some sort of interrogation trick they were playing on her, and she was falling for it? Only Heath didn't look convinced, but it appeared he was on his way to absolute.

"How about this?" Sarah said after a few moments of contemplation. "I'll tell you what I know. No bullshit. Then you tell me who that woman was."

"In the interest of saving time, since you're clearly out of it, her name is René Atchison," Sergeant Miller said. "There, you know who she is, so tell us everything."

Sarah shook her head twice, her eyes on Miller. "I meant *who* she is. Why is she connected to the men in the black van, and what they wanted with her—?"

"There's the black van shit again," Doyle cut in.

Sarah glared at him. "Why is it always a circus with you types?"

Doyle went to stand, but Miller shot him a look, and he remained in his seat.

Heath leaned forward. "Why call me? Tell me how I'm connected to all this?"

Without further deliberation, Sarah told them everything she knew, from hearing his name and phone number from Vivian to stopping Atchison in the street. She described the black van and their immediate response to her snatching Atchison off the street.

"Wait, who's Vivian? Your phantom sister?" The sergeant shook her head once, then waved a hand. "Don't answer that. Your crystal ball isn't here." She inhaled deeply, then leaned forward. "Tell me this— why run when Heath triangulated your cell phone to that block? If you did nothing wrong and felt you were protecting this woman, why not meet the officers and explain the black van to them?"

"Because I wanted to learn why Atchison was involved myself." She shrugged. "I didn't get that chance because she wasn't too forthcoming, and the officers in pursuit were surrounding me."

They all stared at each other for several moments.

"Heath." Sarah broke the silence. "I told you people would die if you sent teams to investigate these bombs. I told you to stay away, that it was a decoy of some sort, a diversion." She fixed her gaze on the sergeant. "I called in the warning. This isn't on me if you people don't listen to warnings. Also, Miss Atchison has something to do with the decoy shit. Since I didn't figure it out, it's on your heads."

Miller's face was twitching again. "So the death of our officers is on us?"

Sarah didn't respond for a moment, not wanting to incite the woman further.

"What's this about a decoy?" Doyle asked.

Grateful to get the subject off dead cops, Sarah said, "The bombs were placed in locations where damage would be caused, but with minimal loss of life. Responding to the bomb threats, knowing they'd detonate, was a suicide mission. It makes me think the people responsible for planting them wanted uniforms to get hurt, presuming they—whoever they are—called in the locations themselves. Anyway, the perpetrators did this for another reason as well. A theft? A murder?" She shrugged once more. "I wasn't told that information, but I suspect it involved Atchison because the guys in the van"—she held up her hand when Doyle opened his mouth to protest—"came running after me when I grabbed her off the street." She lowered her hand to the table. "Atchison is involved somehow. Find out how, and you'll be closer to those guys in the van, which will lead you to the *real* bombers." She stared at Heath. "I just sent a warning, a message. Don't shoot the messenger."

The detectives exchanged glances with their sergeant, who then stared at the table momentarily.

No one had touched a single coffee cup since they arrived.

"Is one of those for me?" Sarah pointed.

Heath nodded. "Hope you like it black."

Sarah pulled one toward her.

Miller looked up to glare at her, a muscle under her right eye twitching. "You have a long history with this department. Some here respect you; some despise you. You're a hero to others and an interfering *bitch* to the rest."

Sarah lifted the coffee cup to hide her expression, then sipped from it. Bitter, but better than nothing. She closed her eyes, swallowed, then blinked once to enjoy the moment of peace—and to suppress her smile at the word 'bitch.'"

"I'm from the group of personnel who despise you, and I do not want your example of vigilantism to become popular, not to mention

I'm an unbeliever in your psychic shit." The sergeant leaned forward. "I *know* you make it all up for some self-esteem award or popularity or some shit. There is no other side, no psychics, and no way you could know about those bombs without being a part of it somehow. So, now that we all *know* the facts, we know you're involved in murdering police officers, we know you're lying, and we know your ego is huge, you have one hour to confess to everything in writing, or we'll charge you will multiple counts of first-degree murder—this was planned, there was foresight, forethought, of this, I have no doubt—and you'll never see the light of day. Well, except for an hour a day when they release you from the hole you'll occupy until you die."

Miller shot up from her seat, smacked on the door hard, waited until it was opened, then nearly jumped into the corridor as if whatever Sarah had could be contagious.

Heath and Doyle followed, then the door was slammed shut and locked.

"Hey, don't I get a phone call?" she shouted. "Stupid bitch."

The door remained closed.

At least they left all the coffees.

Vivian, give me something.

And Vivian did. She explained why Heath was involved. She told Sarah that without Heath, she would die.

This was the end of the road for Sarah without Detective Heath.

It's him. Or death.

"Motherfucker," Sarah muttered as she grabbed another coffee cup. "I'm fucked."

Chapter 9

KRAMER PULLED UP TO the warehouse door on Hillmount Road near Major Mackenzie and Highway 404. They exited the van, with Jason and James hauling their bags inside the warehouse without a moment's hesitation, eager to divide their loot.

Jack watched Kramer get out of the van, then approached him and extended his hand.

"It's been a pleasure, sir."

They shook.

"Where are you off to now, Jack?" Kramer didn't care, as his three mercenaries would be dead as soon as he left the premises, but small talk with soon-to-be-dead men was polite.

"With this job, I think I'll take a break. Count my lucky stars."

How ironic. Kramer smiled. "You should do that."

They stared at each other for a long moment, and then Jack backed away.

"I'll head inside to ensure I get a fair share."

"You do that. I'll be leaving the van for whoever wants it." Kramer leaned across the front seat and grabbed his diamond and cell phone. He turned back to Jack, who now stood at the back of the van. "Keys are in the ignition."

Jack nodded and again stared for a fraction too long.

What's he thinking? Could he know he would be dead in minutes?

"Be seeing you," Jack said, then turned, walked behind the van, and disappeared inside the warehouse.

What the fuck was that?

Kramer placed the box under his arm and started across the parking lot toward his black Suburban SUV. He checked over his shoulder once but saw no one following him, even though he felt like he was being watched.

The night's success—even though that stupid bitch interfered with the jewelry store keyholder—gave him a dopamine high like never before. God willing, the rest of his plans would culminate in avenging the deaths of his family.

But he couldn't let the success go to his head.

If he did, mistakes would be made.

Kramer unlocked the SUV, placed the diamond case in his back seat, closed the door, and glanced back at the warehouse one last time.

The side door was closed. The van sat untouched.

All three men were inside, divvying up their share.

But something was off. Something bothered him.

He opened the driver's door and climbed into the driver's seat, leaving the door open.

He waited several seconds, listening to the night and only hearing a distant truck on Highway 404 as it lumbered north.

What was making him so paranoid? They had one setback, but it did nothing to alter the success of tonight's mission.

He retrieved his cell phone from his pocket and dialed the number, which would detonate the leftover devices inside the warehouse.

James and Jason would've emptied the loot on the table where he'd built the improvised explosive devices over the past week. The same table that had two large IEDs strapped beneath it.

By his calculation, all three men would be hovering over that table at that very moment.

No witnesses. No one left to point at him in a lineup. No one around to rat him out.

He'd been an explosives expert with the Afghan Army, trained by the United States. When they pulled out, and it looked like the Taliban would take over again, he had no reason to remain on Afghan soil.

The family he once shared a home with were all dead and buried, and he'd taken his grieving out by building bombs that would execute their murderers—Canadians.

Nice Canadians, governed by a soft, whiny prime minister whose only strength is his world leader neighbor to the south.

It was a Canadian soldier who broke into his home when he was at work. By the time he got off the night shift and returned home, his mother and father were dead, their throats cut with a blade like a pig before the spit.

He burst inside the hovel and was jumped by men standing behind the door, their pants off as they waited for their turn. Held down and then handcuffed to a pipe in the kitchen, Kramer wailed and cried behind his cloth gag as they ravaged his sister for several hours. One of the men even fucked his dead mother's body, claiming she was still warm.

After the Canadian soldiers were tired, claiming their dicks were rubbed raw, they slit his sister's throat in front of him. He'd locked eyes with her as she inhaled her final breath, and he watched the longing for life leave those eyes as something peaceful entered them.

Moments later, his sister's eyes were lifeless.

Kramer swore he'd make Canadians pay for their transgressions against his family, even if he died doing it.

So here he was, a refugee turned landed immigrant to the great nation of Canada, a retired Afghan explosives expert, and a man on a mission since that day—the day they made a mistake by letting him live.

James and Jason were two of the Canadian soldiers in his home that day. He'd tracked them down and hired them for this job so they could repay him with the diamond and their death. Both men had quit the military and become mercenaries, and Kramer convinced them to do this diversionary mission with him.

Without further delay, he hit the dial button on the phone in his hand and stared back at the warehouse roughly two hundred meters from his position to watch the detonation.

But nothing happened.

He frowned and looked down at the cell phone.

It had dialed the correct number, but the IEDs didn't blow.

"What the—" He stared at the warehouse again. Nothing like this had ever happened before. Could one of them have defused the IEDs? If so, how was that possible? Nothing in their combined dossiers suggested bomb intel.

He tapped his chest to reassure himself that his Kevlar was intact, then pulled two pistols from the glove box, stepped back out of the SUV, shut the door, and locked it.

After one more look around, he started back toward the warehouse.

What if there was some sort of delay, and he was walking to his own death? Could this be a trap they set for him?

He shook his head. These guys were killers for hire, wannabe professionals. They couldn't make it in the rank and order of the Canadian military, so they retired to kill for profit. No way they were able to outsmart him.

There was one more device under the van that had to be detonated. He could not leave the van behind. Not with his prints and DNA inside.

But first, three mercenaries needed to die.

Other than the distant sound emanating from the highway, he heard crickets, as it was around midnight, and this particular industrial area was dead at this hour.

Back at the van, without seeing or hearing anyone, he took a calming breath, placed one of the pistols in his right hand, and moved to the warehouse door, a bead of sweat oozing down his back.

He pushed the door open, stepped inside, slipped to the right, and dropped to his knees.

One light lit the center table where the velvet sacks of jewelry now sat.

How could they have been onto him? What did he do to give himself away? It was impossible that they recognized him from Afghanistan over a decade ago. He'd changed too much, and they were too dumb.

He pushed up to his feet and moved along the wall in search of the three mercs he needed to kill, praying those IEDs didn't explode now that he was inside the building.

Chapter 10

Sarah had drifted off, her head on her arm, when the waiting stretched to hours.

Sergeant Miller and Detective Heath reentered the interview room with a bang on the door. She jerked her head up, glanced around, then eased back in her chair and crossed her arms.

"The coffee didn't help keep you awake?" Heath asked. "How could you be tired and not panicking about how much trouble you're in? What about your future?"

"You guys took a long time." She uncrossed her arms to rub her eyes. "And the future is not something I've ever really worried about." She offered him a quick smirk, then dropped it.

"So, you're a smartass, too," Miller said.

"I've been called worse." Neither one took a seat. "You came to let me go because you have nothing to hold me on?"

"Far from it," Miller said. "We spoke with Atchison. She said you hit her with your car door, then virtually abducted her off the street by tossing her into the back seat of your car."

Sarah nodded slowly as if thinking about it. "Hmmm, I'd say that about sums it up."

Heath leaned forward, placing his hands flat on the table. "So you're confessing to abducting her?"

Sarah kept her gaze trained on Miller. "Yes, for what reason, I don't know yet, but I suspect we'll find out soon enough."

"What's that supposed to mean?" Miller asked, lowering into a chair.

"Whether you believe in the other side or not, Miss Fancy Police Sergeant, I hear things from my sister and act on them."

"Sarah, if you're hearing things and acting on them, you might escape a life sentence after your trial."

"How's that?"

"Insanity plea. You're clearly schizophrenic."

They stared at each other for a long moment. "I can't tell if there's humor in your comment or if you actually believe your own bullshit."

"Trust me. There's no humor. Only pity."

"Look," Heath cut in. "Can we dispense with the hatred being flung around?"

Sarah's gaze remained unwavering. "I didn't kill your men tonight. I tried to save their lives by calling him." She jabbed a finger in Heath's direction. "I'm not the bad guy here, and Atchison is involved in some way."

"We'll get to Atchison. But first, why call Heath?"

Sarah broke her gaze, blinked a few times, then looked up at Heath. "Because Tom is a good detective with a bright future." She wasn't going to add the part Vivian said about saving her life in the future. That would have to be a surprise for everyone.

Heath's cheeks reddened.

Miller looked at Heath, then back to Sarah. "He's currently suspended."

"Yeah, I know. But it was an accident. Reinstate him. You need him." *I need him.*

"An accident that cost two innocent lives."

"Come on." Sarah scoffed. "When it gets to trial, the jury will exonerate him. It was a domestic dispute, or wait"—Sarah closed her eyes and tapped the side of her head—"a home invasion. Mr. and Mrs. Huxley had empty guns strapped to their wrists with duct tape, and their mouths were gagged. How could they warn him? Any cop on this force would have taken the shot."

Something melted in Heath's face. Likely that was the first time he'd heard someone in his corner telling it like it was.

"Did you see the future?" he asked. "I mean, do you *know* the jury will exonerate me?"

"Enough," Miller shouted. "This circus act of a psychic fair ends now." She shot to her feet. "Tell us something we can use, something about the bombers if you're so psychic, or lawyer up, or rot in a holding cell for all I care. I'm so fucking done with your bullshit crystal ball and the childish parlor tricks."

Miller spun away and knocked on the door. It unlocked, and she yanked it open.

"Sergeant," Heath said. "Wait."

Miller spun back around and glared at him. "What?" That one word came through her teeth and sounded more like a warning.

"How could Sarah know about the Huxleys?" Heath asked without looking at his sergeant.

"Who knows, and who cares?" She turned to leave. "Come on. Leave her to her fantasies. I'm done with the fucking games."

"Wait!" Detective Heath raised his voice.

Miller pivoted so fast that Sarah thought she'd lose her balance. Then she stepped completely back into the room.

"Have you got something to say to me, *Detective*?" Miller's tone came out like a reprimand, cautioning him to monitor his words carefully.

"Yeah, I do, *Sergeant*."

"You are one inch away from being thrown out of this building." Miller's cheeks puffed out, colored red, and a vein throbbed in her neck.

"My case is sealed, ma'am. No one but those directly involved knows the Huxleys' names. That duct-tape detail is an even lesser-known fact, so don't tell me she could've googled it." Heath faced his superior officer. "And we haven't even covered how she got my phone number and chose me to call. My number's unlisted, and she didn't block her number, even taking my call when I phoned her back."

Miller seemed to ponder things for a moment, struggling with Sarah, the enemy, versus Sarah, the helper. She shoved the door closed, then placed her hands on the back of the chair and faced Sarah.

Apparently, having come to terms with some of Heath's rationale, she said, "René Atchison is the keyholder for a jewelry store one city block from where you snatched her off the sidewalk."

When Miller stopped talking, no one spoke to fill the void. Sarah was doing better by letting the two cops do all the talking for her.

Miller continued, "She was on her way back to the store because her boss said she forgot to set the alarm, and could René go in and do it for her."

"A lone woman, at that hour, going to set the alarm at a jewelry store? Doesn't sound like a smart idea."

"Isn't it better to have the alarm on than no alarm at all? The likelihood of someone breaking in during the few hours it was unarmed was low."

"Or this was a setup to call her in. Once she's unlocked the door and about to activate the alarm at eleven at night, the bad guys can take whatever they want without interruption. No alarm means no security or cops."

The detective and his sergeant exchanged a glance.

Heath leaned back against the wall and crossed his arms. "Five minutes after you abducted her, the jewelry store she works at was robbed. They virtually cleaned it out."

Sarah snapped her fingers. "There's the connection. Find her boss. She's in on it." Sarah glanced away, then back to Heath. "I sure wish my sister had told me that earlier." She rubbed her hands on her thighs. "Wait, why go after Atchison if they can just break in anyway? There's more to that. Also, you'll want to pull cameras from local businesses. You'll see the black van and the men in balaclavas."

"Sarah, please." Sergeant Miller held up her hand. "Don't tell us how to do our job."

"Our response time to the jewelry store was over an hour due to the carnage left behind by the three bombs that detonated."

"Three? Not four?"

"Just three." Heath nodded.

"There's one more out there in a dangerous location. We need to coordinate the names I gave you, and then we can find that last—"

"You won't be involved in any of that," Miller cut in. "We already wrote down the names, and three of the locations matched the bombings. The final one is the Greg Brown St. James Campus on Frederick Street. We have a team with bomb-sniffing dogs scouring the evacuated location as we speak."

"Don't," Sarah snapped. "Haven't you been listening? Pull them out now. That bomb could go off at any time."

Miller got up from the table. "I don't think so, Sarah Roberts."

She glanced from Heath to Miller, then back to Heath. "Talk to her. Get her to see reason—"

"There's nothing to see, Miss Psychic. It's clear we have a leak in the department. They told you what you wanted to hear about Detective Heath and his case. Then you set the bombs and called them in to divert attention from yourself so you could abduct Miss Atchison and let your team work the jewelry store. I've watched your escapades for some time from the sidelines in this town, but now officers are dead, and you're the only suspect, not to mention the vast knowledge you seem to possess concerning the crimes that took place tonight." Miller knocked on the door. "I'll have the murder charges drafted up soon." She motioned to two men outside the interview room. "Take her to holding until I come for her. No one speaks to her but me. Is that understood?"

Two uniformed officers entered the room, acknowledging Sergeant Miller's statement.

"Get to your feet," one of the cops said, his tone flat and full of hate.

"You're making a mistake, Miller."

"Then it's one I'd happily make over and over." She marched away down the corridor as one of the officers turned Sarah around and slapped cuffs on her wrists.

She winced at the sharp pain as they were playing rough on purpose.

"Heath, you have to do something."

"I will. I'll work on things out here."

"I'm going to need a phone call. Tell that bitch I'm going to lawyer up." They shoved Sarah toward the door, then out into the corridor so hard she body-checked the opposite wall. "This is fucked, Heath. And that hurt."

The officers shoved her again.

This was going to be another shitty night with the gang in blue.

Chapter 11

HE COULDN'T SEE A damn thing. Three men, all hired murderers, hiding in the dark. They likely knew he intended to kill them, that this had turned into a double-cross, and that he'd make off with the diamond worth four hundred million.

The diamond.

Did they plan this? *Could* they plan this?

Which one had explosives training? None of them had that in their dossiers. Was this a ploy to get him inside the warehouse, then blow it up so they could split the four hundred million, or did his devices simply malfunction?

With so much internal debate, he was aware that he was stalling while listening to his surroundings—stalling where he was unseen and still relatively safe. His back pressed into the wall in an attempt to merge with it and disappear in the darkness in this section of the warehouse.

He was also aware that he'd have to find a way to outwit these soldiers, who were better trained than he was with weapons. He would beat them a thousand times over with explosives, but hunting humans with guns was their playground.

Or he could just leave. Walk away. Finish tomorrow's job and be done with it. He already had a buyer lined up for the diamond. Four hundred million would change his face, his life, his soul. He gave himself a year for the changes to settle, then fifty years to sail the seas, live in penthouses, eat the best food, and fuck as many women as Gene Simmons.

With that thought, he suddenly wanted to be back outside. He needed to get to his SUV and drive away. He couldn't let them have it if they were after the Cullinan diamond. His freedoms would be limited without it, and eventually, the authorities would find him, hence the new face and identity the diamond would afford.

He inhaled, slowly wiped the sweat from his brow, and slid along the wall toward the warehouse door.

Should he stay and fight, risking his life? Or leave and kill them on sight later?

Easy choice.

There was a chance they weren't even after him, and he was paranoid because of a device malfunction. But if that were the case, where were they? Why weren't they taking their loot and leaving?

As he moved toward the door, he thought back to when they arrived and recalled seeing them running in the door, not five meters from him. Even the velvet sacks were still on the table under that one light across the warehouse floor.

No, they were here, and they meant him harm.

And he was stupid enough to walk into their trap.

He flipped off the safety on his weapon and placed his index finger across the side of the trigger guard as he moved up beside the door.

Should he use a different door? They were probably waiting on the other side, guns trained on him the second he stepped outside, bullets eager to open him up.

But he had to use this door. He suddenly needed to get out of this building. It was like the air had already left, and he was stuck inside, struggling to breathe.

After mouthing a silent prayer, he twisted the knob, shoved the door open, and stepped back.

No bullets hit the door, and no one stood on the other side.

Where are they?

He hopped outside and dropped to his knees, his back to the wall. The cooler air made his sweat-covered back and face cold, causing a slight shiver to escape him.

The black van was parked where he'd left it, about five feet to his left. Loaded with a large explosive device under the driver's seat, one phone call would destroy the evidence found within, along with anyone driving it. He'd hoped all three mercs had piled in before he left the area so he could end things quickly, but that didn't happen.

He pushed up, sliding his back along the wall until he was in a standing position.

Where the hell are they? This was a waste of time. He needed sleep. Then he had to confirm everything was ready for tomorrow's job.

Were they hiding on the other side of the van?

He dropped to his knees again, then leaned over to peek under the chassis.

Nothing.

Kramer frowned. They'd all disappeared.

He got back to his feet and edged around the van.

The parking lot was empty.

These guys were playing an expert-level game where he was the mouse, and they were the cat.

His odds of survival were thinning the longer he remained stationary.

He had to leave and face the consequences.

Kramer marched across the parking lot, his head on a swivel. The SUV was twenty feet away, then fifteen, and finally ten, and he still heard nothing and saw nothing.

Seconds later, sweating profusely as he waited for a bullet to enter his back, he reached the SUV's door and yanked it open.

The SUV was empty. His men were all still gone, and now so was the diamond case.

"No, no, no …" he whispered to himself as he hopped up onto the seat, then wrenched around to look behind him.

His free pass on a new life was gone.

They had conspired against him to take the diamond.

"You *fuckers*!"

He set the gun on the passenger seat, then gripped the steering wheel with both hands, staring at the empty seat beside him, willing his eyes to be wrong.

"Looking for this?" Jack shouted from somewhere across the parking lot.

Kramer jumped in his seat, bumping the tops of his thighs on the bottom of the steering wheel, and spun around so fast he felt a muscle in his neck protest.

Jack stood by the side wall of a warehouse to the right—some telecom building occupied that one.

The Cullinan diamond case had been cracked open, the top of the diamond exposed to the air. He could see the parking lot lights reflecting off its surface from about forty meters.

"What are you doing—wait, how did you—"

The tip of a gun came into view on his left. "Step out of the vehicle slowly," Jason said. "Make sure your hands are empty and raised so I can see them."

"Do as the man asked," James said from his right, about ten feet away. His arms were extended, a weapon in his grasp.

It was like James and Jason had materialized out of the darkness. Where they'd hidden was beyond Kramer's understanding.

Both hands out in front of him, he lowered out of the SUV and eased sideways to move around the open door, his gut clenching at how stupid he'd been.

Jason's weapon nudged his shoulder. "Move toward Jack."

Kramer started walking, and James came up beside him on the right.

It was over. All the planning, tomorrow's big hit—everything ruined because of mercenaries turned thieves.

"What, you thought you could just blow us up and drive away?" Jason asked. "We were onto you since the beginning. We watched everything, studied your every move."

James scoffed beside him, and Kramer detected the man shaking his head. "How do you think we've stayed alive this long? We knew who you were since the day we met you. Fuckin' idiot thought getting older was a disguise."

"Why?" Jack asked as they got closer.

"Why what?" Kramer said, a sense of peace coming over him now, even as his body entered a panic phase, knowing death was coming. He'd be with his family soon. The suffering would be over. Perhaps underestimating these men was a blessing.

"Why all those bombs to steal this fake diamond?"

Kramer stumbled once, then caught himself and stopped walking. "Fake?"

Jason shoved him from behind, and he got walking again.

"Before this job, I spent some time stealing diamonds." Jack shrugged as they pulled up in front of him. "This Cullinan is a fake."

Dumbfounded, Kramer stared at what he now thought was cubic zirconia. If that was the case, it wasn't a diamond, and it wasn't worth much at all. Or maybe it was moissanite, which is currently one of the most sought-after fake diamond stones.

But that didn't make sense. The *real* Cullinan was supposed to be in Toronto for tomorrow's dignitary event. He'd tracked it. He knew where it was supposed to be, thanks to two sources on the inside.

"How do you know it's fake?" His anger at being duped—twice— once by the informants on the location of the Cullinan, and the second time by his own men, he now stared in awe at the diamond, fake or otherwise, oblivious to the weapons pointed at him.

"See the scratch marks?" Jack pointed at an area that appeared to be scuffed.

Kramer nodded. "I used sandpaper on it."

"You what?"

"Come on, Kramer." Jack set the diamond on the ground at his feet. "On the hardness scale, diamonds are at the top of the list. A real diamond can't be scratched by sandpaper. Only fakes can. That's why they have to use another diamond to cut one because nothing else is as hard. Besides, I did the line test."

"The line test? Did you see it?"

"Clearly."

"What's the line test?" Jason asked.

Jack turned to him. "When you place a real diamond onto a black line, the line disappears because light bends when passing through a diamond. When looking at a fake, you'll still be able to see the line." He glanced back at Kramer. "This diamond is as fake as a stripper's implants, and I'm not a fan of implants."

Kramer blinked once, then stood straighter. "What now?"

"Do you know where the real one is?"

They locked eyes briefly, and Kramer tried to see what was on Jack's mind, but the man remained a mystery.

One thing was for sure, though. He had to *admit* he knew where the Cullinan was—he suspected where it could be, but didn't know definitively—in order to stay alive.

Forcing his head to move, he nodded slowly. "Yes, I suspect I know where it is now."

"Good." Jack pulled out his weapon and placed it against Kramer's forehead. "Because I didn't believe for a moment that they'd leave such a treasure inside an easy-access jewelry store like the one we just walked in and out of in minutes."

In his peripheral vision, his eyes wide, waiting for the bullet to decimate his brain, Kramer saw Jason and James lower their weapons and slip them away.

"You're going to tell us where the diamond is in one minute."

"Why-why"—he gulped in a breath—"one minute?"

With speed unbecoming of a man his size, the weapon pulled away from Kramer's forehead and fired twice, once to his left and once to his right.

Kramer felt a warmth cover his crotch as his bladder loosened. At that exact moment, he became conscious of James and Jason on the ground.

Each man sported a red dot near the center of their forehead. Neither man died immediately, but the death throes were upon them.

Jack slapped Kramer across the face. "Hey, wake up. Help me carry these assholes to the van. Then we'll take that IED you left inside the warehouse and place it under the van. When that's done, we'll go get the Cullinan."

Kramer heard his words, but not much was registering.

Jack slammed another open palm across Kramer's face. The sting made it feel like a swarm of bees had landed on his cheek and were thrusting their barbs into him.

"Wake the fuck up." Jack grabbed James's arms and started dragging the body. "Grab Jason and follow me."

In a daze, Kramer did as he was told, his heart in his throat.

Once both men were inside the back of the van, Jack ran through the warehouse door and returned with the two velvet sacks over one shoulder and the defective bomb in his other hand.

"I pulled the wire to defuse it."

Kramer stared at Jack for a long moment. "Explosives expert wasn't in your dossier."

Jack glanced up at him. "Dude, there was a lot that wasn't in my dossier. I'm considered top secret." He set the sacks down gently, then focused on the explosive, his fingers already gripping the loose wire.

"Go, get the SUV and drive around to the front of the warehouse. I'll meet you there."

Kramer couldn't believe his luck. "I'll put these in the back of the SUV." He grabbed the sacks and started toward the SUV.

Before he got five feet, Jack spoke up. "Hey, Kramer."

He stopped and turned around slowly. "Yeah?"

"Don't try to fuck me again."

Jack stuck a small flashlight between his teeth and went back to work on the explosive in his lap.

With nothing left to say, Kramer shambled to the SUV, placed the sacks filled with jewels from the heist in the back seat, then hopped in the front.

He eased his cell phone out and brought up the number that would detonate the bomb under the van's driver's seat, surprised that after all he'd been through tonight, he was back in the driver's seat, metaphorically and literally.

Jack would never know what hit him.

Kramer glanced back at the van and saw the flashlight moving in the dark in Jack's mouth beside it.

Something was off. Why was the guy suddenly so trusting? Kramer could hit the gas and drive away with the sacks.

The sacks.

When Jack had exited the warehouse with the velvet sacks of jewelry, he'd set them down gently.

The IEDs from under the table. How stupid could he be?

It was time to take action.

Kramer grabbed his guns and jumped out of the SUV. When he glanced back at Jack, the man was gone.

"Shit." Kramer ran twenty meters, then called the phone number on his phone to detonate the bomb under the van's driver's seat.

But it wasn't under the van's driver's seat anymore.

Jack had found that one, too, and placed it conveniently in the velvet sacks.

The SUV Kramer had vacated seconds ago blew up in a tremendous display of shattered glass and twisted metal.

He was knocked off his feet, landing hard on his ass and crying out in pain as the gun in the back of his pants dug into his flesh and pressed against bone.

After rolling onto his hands and knees and catching a breath, he pushed up to his feet, one of his guns in his hand.

The flames billowing out of the SUV lit up the night sky.

Emergency crews would be coming soon. He needed to get out of the area. Dead bodies and explosives would have him jailed for years as they tied it all up in a neat bow in their court system.

The van. That was the only way out of here fast.

Eyes peeled for Jack, he started toward the van, his gun extended out in front of him.

Within three steps, the van exploded, knocking him off his feet again. This time, the gun wasn't in the back of his pants. It was in his hand, and it flew from his grip, hitting the pavement and rolling in a clunky fashion like a fallen football.

He stumbled on his knees to the gun, grabbed it, and rolled onto his back, aiming it back toward the van.

Jack had disappeared.

Both vehicles burned, their shattered remains a reminder of how badly his plan had culminated into a disaster.

He had underestimated Jack. Outwitted in this business meant you died.

An engine roared behind him, and his brain entered panic mode before he could turn around. He got to his feet and dove to the grass on the left, landing hard on his shoulder just as the front grill of a Mustang missed him by less than one foot.

When he righted himself, he fired several bullets at the fleeing vehicle.

Jack was gone, and with him, the loot from tonight's heist.

James and Jason were dead, their corpses burning in the destroyed van.

At least most of his plan worked.

He collected himself and moved away from the carnage as he heard the Mustang's engine revving in the distance.

He needed wheels. Then he needed that diamond and knew exactly who could tell him where it was stashed.

That woman who got away might have something to do with it—René Atchison.

And how he got to her was through the bitch that snatched her off the road in front of them. He just had to make one phone call, and everything was back on track. After careful consideration, it all came to him as he walked away from the warehouse and the burning vehicles.

Getting to that bitch would be the perfect decoy for the rest of his plan tomorrow.

Everything could stay on track.

Except for Jack. He'd have to deal with Jack.

Who the hell was that guy anyway? *Top secret, my ass.*

Kramer could never be outwitted by him again. The instant he saw him, he'd shoot him before he could utter a word.

Nothing could stand in the way of tomorrow's plan. Today had just been the test run.

Tomorrow was the real deal.

And now that woman would make it all come together much easier.

Kramer hopped a fence and ran across a freshly mowed field, excited about tomorrow's prospect. Or was that excitement disguised as exhilaration that he was still breathing?

After twenty minutes, he pulled out his cell phone, grateful he hadn't dropped it, and called the police station.

It was time to put the new plan into action.

Chapter 12

SOMETHING SMACKED THE CELL bars somewhere in the corridor, making her jump. It took several moments for Sarah to remember where she was as she rubbed the sleep from her eyes and yawned. Then she sat up on the filthy mattress, her head hanging, eyes closed, and waited for whoever made the noise to show themselves at her barred door.

"Wakey, wakey, little bitch." A uniformed officer stepped into view. Another moved around him, dangling a pair of handcuffs from his index finger.

"Hands through the bars right here." The officer with the cuffs pointed at the rectangular opening.

"You guys gonna let me make my phone call?"

"Hands. Through there." He pointed again as both officers exchanged a glance.

"Should I pack all my stuff, or will I be coming back to this cell?"

"What?" The cop looked genuinely confused. "You don't have any *stuff.*"

"Whatever." Sarah got up and walked over to the bars, where she turned around and shoved her hands through the hole for the cuffs to be attached. "I was just wondering if you guys were taking me somewhere I'd never return from, but my sister just told me I was safe to go with you."

The guy doing the cuffs paused for a moment, then continued. "If it was our choice," he whispered close to her ear as the second cuff was clamped on, "we'd all take a turn on that sweet snatch of yours, then slit your throat for what you did to our boys today."

Even though none of this was Sarah's fault, and she made an effort to warn them, everyone across Toronto—no, the province, the country —would blame her. She was the easy target. At least until the truth came out, which she hoped would happen soon.

The cell door popped open.

Sarah turned around and stepped out without looking at either man. "You might want to call an ambulance."

"Yeah, why's that?"

"If you speak to me like that again, you'll both need a hospital."

They laughed, but there was an undercurrent of wariness in their tone.

Both men flanked her as she headed for the exit.

Several minutes later, she was cuffed to the center of the table in the same interview room she'd been in hours before. When the cops were leaving, the one with the foul mouth blew her a kiss, then the door closed.

Still sleepy, she lowered her forehead until it rested on the table, but then lifted it as the position was too awkward on her shoulders with her arms locked to the table in front of her.

The waiting was shorter this time. Something important had happened, and they needed her now. Vivian was around, but she kept saying this was a good development.

There was a knock before the door opened, then Sergeant Miller stepped in, followed by Detective Heath, who looked like he could use a week's sleep.

"Even though that mattress sucks, I was enjoying a catnap." Sarah watched them closely, wondering what they wanted from her. "Why'd you drag me back in here? Another chat?"

Miller pulled out a chair, the edge banging on the table leg. She seemed quite pissed about something.

"How long have you been working with the guy setting off these bombs?"

She suppressed her surprise while searching for Vivian on the inside to see if she could obtain any insight into where this was going. What new development had come to light? Why would they ask something like that?

Yet, they were serious and waiting for an answer.

"Oh," Sarah blurted, jumping forward in her chair and yanking on her wrists simultaneously so the cuffs would create a loud clanging sound. "You were being serious." She shook her head and widened her mouth to express surprise. "I had no idea you'd ask me something so ridiculous. How about asking something worthy of an answer so we don't waste each other's time, hmmm? Otherwise, let me go back to my cell so I can sleep some more."

Heath pulled out a chair now. "The man claiming responsibility for the bombings threatened that more are coming."

Miller shot Heath a stern look.

That told Sarah everything. Miller still thought Sarah was guilty of something, an outsider not to be trusted. At the same time, Heath was warming to her and wanted to include her in some way to end this.

"Are you asking me if I can predict locations again?" She looked between Miller and Heath. "Because I have no idea where the next ones will hit. It's like they don't have an address, a name. The others did."

That got Miller because her eyes narrowed. "So you do know more than you're letting on."

Sarah frowned. "How so?"

"The bomber called an hour ago and told us a twenty-eight-foot truck is parked downtown somewhere. It's full of firecrackers and cases of bullets, but no bombs."

"Well, that's good, right? No bombs." She grinned at the sergeant, waited a moment, then dropped it.

Heath shook his head. "This could be worse."

"How so?" Even as she asked, it came to her. "Fire."

Miller nodded. "If he burns the truck, it'll ignite every single firecracker and shoot many, if not all, of the bullets inside. Like a shrapnel truck from Hell. In other words, it'll be a disaster for anything and anyone close by. If we don't locate that truck, more people could die."

"Wow, this guy has planned a lot of shit out."

"Sarah, come clean. Just confess to your part in this, and we'll definitely go easy on you. Tell us everything."

Sarah scoffed. "If you don't want to believe who I am and why I got involved tonight, why are we talking?"

"You were the decoy, right?" Miller stared her down. "You make these wild calls, you pretend to predict locations, and have us running around while your colleagues rob the exact jewelry store of the woman you kidnapped off the street. Then you ran from the police. C'mon," Miller shot a hand out in a pleading fashion, "you look guiltier than most of the convicted felons in our system at the moment." Miller produced a folder and set it on the table. "Write your confession here, then give up the other locations before more people die." Miller leaned forward as a warmth entered her eyes. "I can make it easier in prison for you. We can arrange for you to get some sort of protective custody on the inside." She raised her hands in an I-give-up gesture. "Life on the inside is tough, and for what you've done, I can't guarantee you'll live through the prison sentence the judge will pass down."

Sarah didn't move as she stared back at the sergeant for several heartbeats.

Then she cleared her throat and sat up straighter. "Take me back to my cell. I wanna sleep more. You're a boring bitch." She yanked her cuffs again.

Miller just stared her down, and Heath moved his head back and forth.

"Okay, the game's over," Miller said. "I'll lay my cards on the table, and I hope you'll do the same."

"Shoot." Sarah suppressed a yawn, but it still made her eyes water.

"I don't like you. Never have. You're a meddling bitch. I'm absolutely convinced you're involved in some way, and what I'm about to tell you bolsters my convictions about you."

"This is getting interesting." Sarah leaned forward. "C'mon, do tell."

"An hour ago, when we took the call from the alleged bomber, he asked for you."

Sarah didn't move so she could avoid revealing her surprise. "He asked about little old me? How sweet."

"Has that attitude kept you alive all this time?"

Sarah's brow tightened, then loosened in a half-frown. "You're a strange one, Miller."

"He asked to meet with you."

"Did he say why? I mean, what would be the purpose, really?"

"No, can't say that he mentioned any motivations."

"Well, set it up. Tell him I'll meet him. Then you guys swoop in, make the arrest, and save the day."

Miller shook her head. "Not going to happen."

Sarah glanced at Heath but gestured at Miller with a flick of her hand. "This one seems defective. Can you take it back to the store for a return? I don't want a refund. Just get a replacement, another sergeant to work with."

Heath shook his head. "Trolling her as you are won't endear you to her, Sarah."

When she glanced back at Miller, the woman's cheeks had darkened with a shade of red.

Heat rose to Sarah's face. "I'm not trying to endear anybody to anybody."

Miller blew out a puff of air. "I will not be dictated to by the man who murdered our officers, nor will I use as a civilian—you, Sarah—as some sort of bait to make an arrest."

"Even if that civilian is a willing participant?"

"Even if."

"So, why am I here? What do you want from me if you won't use me?"

"I was hoping you'd put an end to this charade and just tell us where he is in your confession."

Sarah let her mouth hang open for a moment.

Miller nodded at her. "I know, surprise, surprise. You got caught."

"Caught?" Sarah muttered.

"You can't see why I'm convinced you're involved? Remember, a moment ago, I said what I was about to tell you bolstered my convictions about you." Miller got to her feet and stared down at Sarah. "Your partner is asking to meet you so the two of you can walk off into the sunset. You got caught. That wasn't part of the deal, and he needs you. So, tell me, Sarah, is it Aaron? Parkman? One of Aaron's students? Which one of you came up with the plan to rob a jewelry store by setting up all those bombs as diversions?"

Sarah glanced away, shaking her head. "You're a sick puppy."

"It's so convenient that the *psychic* girl calls in locations, expecting us to believe her because she has a track record and not send officers to their deaths. Then they detonate the bombs, kidnap the keyholder, and rob a jewelry store. If it weren't for Detective Heath, your plan would've been golden—or diamonds, as it were. But Heath was able to locate your phone and send in officers." Miller knocked on the door. "Interview's over. I'll leave you here for the night, cuffed to the table, the lights on. That way, when you're ready to confess, you can still write to some degree."

The door opened, and Miller slipped out into the corridor.

"You wanted cards on the table," Sarah said so loud that Miller stuck her head back in the room. Heath stopped by the door. "I've been doing this shit probably longer than you've carried a badge." She adjusted herself to get comfortable. "Your threats mean nothing to me. The intimidation doesn't work. I'm as calm as a butterfly flitting around a spring garden." She adjusted her gaze to meet Miller's. "More people will die, and it'll be on you for your inaction. I don't know who the asshole is or why he's doing this. If he wants to meet me and you don't pursue that, then I'm thinking he'll make good on his threat to blow up that truck full of firecrackers." She shrugged. "Who knows, perhaps he has several trucks parked strategically around the downtown core. What are you going to do? Evacuate the entire city?"

"I'm bored. Your point?"

"Any single injury or death that occurs due to your inaction, Sergeant Miller, will be on your head."

"Are you trying to persuade me to release you and set up some sort of criminal meeting? If so, it's not working. I do not negotiate with homegrown terrorists."

"I said everything I wanted to say because I know through there"— she pointed at the two-way glass—"this is being recorded. I wanted everything I said documented so that when this is over, you'll have consequences to deal with. You're letting your personal grudge or hatred, or whatever it is you feel toward me, cloud your vision. That's a conflict, and it's unbecoming. You're not doing what's best to solve this crime and get the bad guy. You're doing what's best for you." Sarah shrugged and dipped her head. "And that's fine because you've earned that sergeant title. But it can all be taken away. Those stairs to success that you took, one step at a time, can also be descended. That's why I asked Detective Heath for someone else to work with. You're not playing the game properly—Heath is."

Miller's cheeks twitched, and that throbbing vein was back on her forehead as she glowered at Sarah.

"Go along now." Sarah waved a hand. "Try to convince yourself you've made the right choice. I'll be here if you change your mind. You're dismissed, pissant sergeant."

Sergeant Miller's head jerked backward, out of view. Then Heath exited the room, and the door slammed shut.

"For fuck's sake," Sarah whispered, shaking her head. "Amateurs."

Chapter 13

Neil Kramer, whose real name was Abdul-Kabir, meaning servant of God, woke up on the motel bed he'd paid cash for the night before. He'd grabbed a taxi and had it take him to Dundas and Dixie in Mississauga, then he walked several kilometers to a motel near the bottom of the 427 Highway.

It was impossible for anyone to find him here. No one could track his cell phone because the one he carried was only ever used to call his explosive devices to activate them.

But no amount of self-convincing could calm his irrational worry about Jack and what that man could do. Vetting each mercenary he hired wasn't just something he did for security or to make sure they did the job—it was necessary fieldcraft. Outside of anything top secret that he couldn't get his hands on, he wanted to know as much detail as he could on every person who worked for him.

Yet nothing in Jack's dossier revealed training with explosives.

Nor did it mention his superior intelligence and wit.

The man knew he'd been double-crossed. But not just that, he knew diamonds, and he wanted his cut, so to speak.

But Jack didn't know what this first job was all about—he couldn't have known. His interference now could cost Kramer today's job. That was why all three mercs were supposed to die in the warehouse last night. Having Jack out there roaming around posed a risk—a small one, but still a risk.

Kramer rolled out of bed and got to his feet. Within a half hour, he'd performed his morning prayers, did some stretching to limber up for the day's activities, then used the motel phone to call his brother.

"Hello?"

Kramer stared at nothing; the phone pressed to his head. "Is it still scheduled?"

"At the moment, it is."

"Do you think they'll cancel after what happened last night?"

"Hard to tell." His brother sighed. "They have a woman in custody, so everything will likely go on without rescheduling."

Kramer thought about what to say next. "It was supposed to be the other woman."

"I know, but what I don't know is how you pulled that off."

Sweat made his palm slip on the phone, and he tightened his grip. "I'm not directly responsible, but it worked out in our favor, and now I'll use that to my advantage."

"Everything work out at the warehouse last night?"

Kramer chastised himself for pausing again, but so much went wrong last night that he didn't know how to spell it all out without looking like a complete fuckup.

"To some degree, yes. There's one still out there."

His brother gasped. "Will that become a problem today?"

"I suspect not."

"You *sus*pect?"

"There'll be no problem if you do your part because I'll surely do mine."

Kramer listened to his brother's breathing on the other end of the line, as he no doubt was listening to Kramer's.

"Do you have the Cullinan?"

"No, it was a fake."

Another pause, then, "What are we going to do?"

"Once we get today's package, we get the money. All we'll ever need. We must stay on course."

His brother cleared his throat. "Godspeed, my brother. Yes, let's stay the course."

"Stay the course," Kramer repeated.

"Tonight, the world will revere our names, and our families will have their stories told. Their cups of vengeance will be overflowing."

"Yes, my brother. Nothing will stop us."

The line died.

Kramer set the phone down and rubbed his face. The planning was all done. The heavy lifting, as it were, had been completed.

Today would be when they just went to work, did their job, and came out on top.

And Canada would rue the day they set foot in his country and tore apart his family.

Today, he would get his revenge, and neither Jack nor that woman in custody would stop him.

Even God was on his side.

If he were to be stopped, God would've already taken him out. There were countless chances last night, yet here he was, in the final stages of the biggest military exercise of his career.

There was just one added bonus—that woman in custody.

He had to ensure the authorities would arrange for her to be given up, which would provide an additional layer of safety and security, guaranteeing today's exercise would be a success.

Time to check out of the motel and get downtown.

There were calls to make, people to kill, and bombs to detonate.

It was going to be a fantastic day in Toronto.

He could already feel his dead sister and mother smiling down at him.

Chapter 14

VOICES CALLED HER NAME several times as she drifted to consciousness. Sarah fluttered her eyelids open, squinting in the bright light.

"Turn it off. Too bright."

"Not going to happen," Miller stated.

"Oh, you again." Sarah lowered her forehead to rest on the table, her eyes closed. "Have you come to bore me with your *evidence* and *theories* that I'm the big bad wolf?"

Something slapped the table, making Sarah look up. Another folder was filled with paper.

"What's this?" she asked. "Wait, let me guess. You wrote my confession for me, and all I have to do is sign it, right?" Sarah nudged the documents with her elbow as far from her as she could with her limited mobility—they'd left her cuffed to the table. "I wonder if leaving me cuffed like this could be construed as cruel and unusual punishment by a good lawyer. Hmmm, you think I could sue the department?"

When no one answered, she looked up, forced to blink in the light.

Detective Heath was there, and his partner, Doyle. Two other men in suits stood behind Sergeant Miller.

"What's this?" She forced herself into a sitting position, not concealing the wince when her shoulders protested the movement. Locked forward as they were while she slept on the tabletop had inflamed the muscles.

"These men are with the Royal Canadian Mounted Police."

"Count me impressed. The RCMP always gets their man."

"I'm thinking they won't tolerate your brand of jokes or sarcasm or whatever it is you spew."

"Oh, fuck off, lady. I'm beyond done with your bullshit. Where's my phone call? Where's my lawyer? I'm thinking I don't want to talk to you anymore."

"Then talk to us," one of the men in the suits stepped forward.

"Sure." Sarah watched him, her eyes having adjusted better now. "Let's talk. But can any of you do a coffee run? And while you're at it, I need a toilet. Is that possible?"

The men in the suits nodded and stepped out of the room. A female officer came in, undid her cuffs, and then escorted her to the washroom while Sarah rolled her shoulders to increase blood flow. When she returned to the room, a large coffee cup with small creamers and sugar packets sat in front of her seat.

"No cuffs," she said.

The man in the suit nodded.

Sarah took her seat, then shoved the creamers and sugar to the side. "What do you guys want to talk about?"

Detective Heath got a nod, so he stepped forward and flipped open the folder Miller had dropped on the table five minutes before.

"We obtained footage of the area from security cameras." He produced a photo of the black van, then slid it aside and showed her a picture of four men running in the street wearing balaclavas. "These men ran at your car here." He pointed at the third photo, where Sarah was easily seen behind the wheel. "In these last two photos, a Kwik Copy shop captured you hitting René with your car door here"—he tapped it—"and you driving away while they tried to stop her here." He revealed the final photo.

She looked up to meet Miller's eyes. "Has anyone shown the sergeant this yet? Funny how everything I said is now being corroborated, huh?"

Heath collected the photos, tapped them against the table, placed them back in the folder, then stepped back.

One of the men in the suits moved forward. "A warehouse north of Highway 401 got hit by a bomb last night."

Sarah frowned. "North of the 401? That wasn't on my list."

"We know."

She met his gaze. "And?"

"The van in those photos has been destroyed."

Understanding dawned on her. "Of course, and any further evidence inside that warehouse will also be gone."

"We did manage to recover two bodies." The besuited man stood straighter.

Sarah eyed them for a moment, waiting for someone to continue, yet she suspected what they would say.

The other man in the suit spoke for the first time. "The bodies belonged to two of those four men in balaclavas." His voice was deep, matching his rugged appearance. The man's build and five-o'clock shadow with an angular jaw made her think he'd tossed his lumberjack jacket aside in favor of the suit and better pay.

"Bullets to the head." His partner nodded once.

"Dead men keep secrets," Sarah whispered.

"We were hoping you could shed some light on the jewelry store heist."

Sarah scanned the faces in the room. *Now*, they wanted her help? "What happened to the confession you're all waiting for me to sign?"

"Sergeant Miller," the RCMP man said in his deep voice. "Exit the room. Detective Heath, stay."

Sarah could not believe how red Miller's face got before she fled. The door shut and locked quietly after her departure.

Coffee cup in hand, Sarah sipped from it. Something about the coffee—it tasted better suddenly.

"We pulled a man named Parkman out of bed. We went after Aaron but couldn't locate him."

"He's in a new apartment. No one knows where he's staying." She sipped again. "So, why hassle my friends?"

"We needed information on you, and we got it."

She lifted one shoulder. "You could've asked me."

Ignoring her comment, the RCMP guy continued. "We're leaning toward believing you and," he paused, "working with you, if possible."

"You sure about that? Because you don't sound sure. And what's 'if possible' mean?"

"If you'll work with us."

"Depends on what you want from me. I mean, after the way I've been treated—"

"Sarah," Heath cut in. "Please, we need your help. I mean, isn't that why you called me in the first place?"

She nodded, keeping the coffee cup in front of her face. It was going down so good.

"There's a huge diamond in Toronto—"

"How large?"

"It's called The Cullinan Diamond and is considered the largest rough diamond in the world."

Confused, she leaned forward and placed her cup on the table. "And this large diamond was supposed to be at René's jewelry shop?"

"Well, not exactly. It's in a secure location. But it was *rumored* to be at her shop."

"Rumored?" She tilted her head. "Why is it rumored?"

"Because it's supposed to go on display today at the Toronto Metro Convention Centre, as there's a large event taking place, and we've been tasked with keeping it safe. So, to find the mole within our ranks, we let it slip that it would be moved from one jewelry store to another at random, never staying in one spot for more than eight hours."

"And no one stopped to think there's more danger in transporting something of that sort of value rather than keeping it locked in a gigantic vault with a hundred armed men?"

"The delivery vehicle between locations is better equipped than a Brinks truck, stronger than a tank, and has men leading and trailing it in bulletproof vehicles with enough artillery to fight off a small militia."

"Okay, so yeah. Someone did think about it." She grabbed her cup and drank more, waking more with each sip. "So, what do you need me for?"

"We placed fake Cullinan diamonds at a dozen locations, with René's shop being one of them. The real one is still secure."

She glanced from Heath to the RCMP men. "So you think those bombs last night were all a decoy for a huge diamond heist?"

"We're sure of it, and we think you tried to stop it by snatching René off the street. How you came by the information you possess isn't our concern." The RCMP men exchanged a glance. "Let's just say it isn't something that we can add to any of our reports, and presumably, we can go so far as to say you saved René's life last night, at the very least."

Without acknowledging the compliment, Sarah went on. "So, to sum this up, the heist wasn't successful, two of the four guys are dead, and the bomber guy is at it again today?"

They nodded.

"Meaning he's likely going after the diamond still?"

They kept nodding.

"And he wants to speak with me?"

"Sort of. He wants to *meet* you."

She searched their faces. "Why me? Did he say?"

They shook their heads. "Can you tell us anything?"

"Like what?"

Heath leaned closer and spoke in a conspiratorial manner. "He means, can you tell us anything from the other side?"

"My sister has an attitude. She does what she wants when she wants."

The angular-faced RCMP cop half-smiled. "From their file on you here, I'd say that's a family trait—no offense."

"None taken. Where will the diamond be today?"

No one answered.

"Okay, I'll ask in a different way. Is the diamond at a safe location?"

"Yes, with several dozen armed men guarding it." Angular Face adjusted his suit jacket. "Would you be willing to help us?"

"Sure, but I don't want Sergeant Miller involved in any way. She'll compromise whatever we do. Oh, and Detective Heath gets fully reinstated."

Mr. Angular frowned. "Why does that matter to you? Why not negotiate for something else?"

"I don't need anything else. Well, besides that bomber guy dead or in jail."

"Hey, guys," Heath said. "Give the girl what she wants. We need her."

"Yeah, but what's your connection to Heath?" The RCMP man placed his hands on his hips. "I'm suspicious when someone goes out of their way for someone else without some sort of benefit. This world is controlled by money, greed, power, and fame. Yet, you sit here willing to help with a dangerous bombing case—likely a homegrown terrorist —and all you want is Detective Heath back in the saddle. That just doesn't add up."

"It matters to me because of something my sister said."

"What'd she say?"

Mr. Angular's phone rang. "One second." He held up a finger. "Richmond here." His jaw clenched as he listened. Everyone in the room watched him. He sighed, mumbled something like a grunt, then ended the call and slipped the phone away. "We need to leave. Now."

"What happened?" his partner asked.

"It started."

"What started?" Sarah asked, even as Richmond smacked his fist on the door to be let out.

"There's a truck on fire on Yonge Street by the Eaton's Centre. It's already broken out all neighboring windows as bullets and firecrackers make a complete mess of the area. No one can approach the truck to put the fire out unless they're wrapped in body-covering Kevlar." The door opened, and Richmond rushed through it, followed by Detective Heath.

Richmond's partner held back, staring at Sarah. "Well, aren't you coming?"

"Are my meager terms accepted?"

The man nodded vigorously. "Of course, whatever you want. Heath is back in the saddle. Just hurry."

Sarah bounded up from the chair and bolted out into the corridor to follow Heath and Richmond.

As they hit a stairwell, she asked, "Hey, did this little operation expose that mole you were looking for?"

"No," Richmond shouted over his shoulder.

"Well, I've been told you'll discover the mole today."

Richmond stopped and turned to look down at her on the stairs. "Anything else?"

"Yeah, my sister just said he works for the RCMP, but he doesn't work in the department or detachment or whatever you guys call it that you're thinking of. He's in another section."

"What does that mean?"

Sarah stared up at him, hands out to the side. "I have no idea, but I'm thinking we'll find out soon."

Richmond turned away and jumped to the next floor with Heath close behind him. Several minutes later, they entered a control room of sorts where leather chairs surrounded a long table, and boxed sandwiches covered the table in front of each chair.

Sarah grabbed a tuna sandwich and dug in, thinking they'd let her make a call now. Perhaps she'd be able to talk to her daughter soon.

"Any idea why this guy"—she swallowed—"is setting off these trucks?"

"He called in asking to meet you," Richmond said.

"I knew about that. Miller told me."

"Yeah, well, did she tell you that you were supposed to already be on the train, and if not, he'd set a truck on fire in a populated area?"

Sarah stopped chewing, swallowed what was in her mouth, then stared at the RCMP guys. "No, she didn't say any of that."

"She figured you were working with the guy, and it was his way to break you out of custody, so she refused to negotiate with the terrorist."

"And now we're negotiating?"

"Yeah, you said you'd help. Our team is ready to wire you up and send you to the train station in minutes. They're out front."

"You're sending me to meet this bomber guy terrorist asshole?"

Everyone stopped what they were doing and turned to look at her.

"What other option do we have?" Richmond asked. "He claims to have two dozen trucks planted all over the city. Hundreds of people will die, perhaps more. We send you in, track you, then storm the area—whatever area he's taking you." When Sarah didn't respond immediately, he added, "You said you'd help. But you have to know how dangerous this is. Are you still okay with that?"

She tore into the sandwich and bit off so much that her cheeks filled like a chipmunk storing nuts for winter. Everyone waited for her answer. Five new men ran down the length of the hall beside the conference room and stopped at the door.

"We're ready, sir," one of the men said, panting for breath.

"Well?" Richmond eyed her, an eyebrow quirked up. "Are you in?"

"Fuckin' A, I'm in. Let's stop this bastard." She grabbed two more sandwiches and ran for the door, with everyone following close behind. "But I'll need a gun," she shouted. "And don't be surprised if I kill the bastard before you storm the place."

"Not a chance. This guy must be taken alive, Sarah."

"That's your problem, not mine."

"Sarah, everything's your problem now."

She didn't respond as she was already biting into the second sandwich on the run.

Chapter 15

DRESSED AS A COURIER, Kramer sat behind the wheel of his courier van across the street from Union Station, his four-way flashers on. He'd just received confirmation that the authorities would send that meddling woman—Sarah Roberts—to the train station as he had requested. It took them a truck exploding on Yonge Street to listen to him, but how stupid could they be? Send her or don't send her. He'd still light up every truck he had loaded with ammo before the sun began its descent in the evening sky.

Nothing would stop him; nothing could get in his way—well, except for Jack. That man mystified him and surprised him.

He checked the time and saw that he had four hours left. In five hours, he would be safe and secure with the package. Then the real negotiations would begin, the entire reason he was doing any of this in the first place.

Front Street was busy at this time of day, especially since several roads were blocked by traffic because of the visiting dignitaries arriving at the Metro Convention Centre for their summit.

He waited to see if his specific instructions were followed, and right on time, four dark-colored SUVs raced up to the train station's entrance and stopped. Doors on all the vehicles opened, dispersing men in suits with sunglasses as they scanned the area.

The bitch from last night stepped out and was surrounded by three men, likely giving her last-minute advice.

Kramer checked his mirrors, then focused back on Sarah and her entourage. One of the men patted her back, then Sarah strode away from them all without looking back.

The men jumped in their SUVs, with three of them leaving the curb and merging back into traffic.

One SUV remained parked at the curb until Sarah disappeared inside, then it did a U-turn and pulled to the side of the road to observe the front entrance.

"Smooth, boys, but it won't work."

Kramer made the call. The man answered on the first ring.

"She's coming in now," Kramer said, then went on to describe what she was wearing. "Got it?"

"Yeah, Mister, I got it. You don't need to worry about a thing. I got this, sir."

"Do this, and you'll eat like a king for a month."

"Gee, thanks, man. I could sure use a steak."

"Watch for the girl. Her name is Sarah. She'll buy a ticket to Oshawa. Make sure she takes the phone, and you can have as much steak as you want."

Kramer hung up and waited for Sarah to call him.

He didn't have to wait long.

Chapter 16

THE LISTENING DEVICE IN Sarah's ear was uncomfortable, making her want to pull it free, but it was the only connection to the RCMP on the outside, so she left it where it was.

Her thoughts meandered on why the bomber would want to meet her. Only one reason made sense—to kill her for interfering. Yet, Vivian seemed to think this was a good idea, so Sarah had to agree. Besides, it got her out of that damn police station and away from Sergeant Miller.

She pushed through the doors and scanned the interior of the massive building, looking for the train schedule board. The original instructions were to buy a ticket to head to Oshawa and be on the train by 10:10 a.m., but she missed that one, hence the truck fire on Yonge Street. The next train was supposed to leave by 11:10 a.m.

She had twenty minutes to buy her ticket and board the train.

From the electronic schedule board, it appeared the train was on time.

A man and a woman walked toward her, chatting about a baseball game. She watched them, turning slowly to follow their path while scanning around them to see if anyone was watching her. No one, in particular, stood out. Everyone in the building was on the move, heading toward the trains or away from them, except for the few people sitting on the benches lined up in the middle of the waiting area.

She headed toward the ticket window, skirting the last row of chairs. At the booth, the woman looked up and nodded at her.

"I need to get to Oshawa," Sarah said through the Plexiglas.

"Next train's ten minutes after eleven."

Sarah nodded. "That works."

They exchanged money for a ticket, and Sarah stepped away.

"Hey," a man said to her left.

Sarah stopped moving; her hands raised slightly. A vagrant on a bench about five feet away watched her, his head tilted slightly.

"You talking to me?" she asked.

"You just bought a ticket to Oshawa." The man looked away, fiddling with something in his hands.

"So?"

He looked up. "What's your name?"

"What's it to ya?" She scanned the immediate area and saw no one watching them.

The man held up a cell phone. "I'm supposed to give this to Sarah, but I have to confirm it's you so I can eat my steak. Man said you'd buy a ticket to Oshawa about now. And yous dressed the same as he said on the phone."

A cold chill passed through her. *Said on the phone* could mean this vagrant was in touch with the bomber, and if so, then the bomber was watching the entrance. He'd seen her. He'd seen how she was dressed.

"Yeah"—Sarah glanced around once more—"that's my name, and I just bought a ticket to Oshawa. See?" She held it out for him to examine, but he didn't look at her. His eyes remained glued to the cell phone.

Sarah whispered into the mic in her ear, "Are you guys getting this?"

"We are, and we're already looking for him out here."

The vagrant lifted a shoebox onto his lap. "See this?"

Sarah nodded. "What you got there?"

"New shoes. The man was nice to me."

Sarah moved a step closer and took in his disheveled appearance. The man's pants were covered with countless stains and torn and frayed near the bottom. His T-shirt had a hole near the neckline, and his jacket hung loosely off one shoulder. What stopped her from advancing closer was his stench. The poor man likely hadn't showered in months.

"That man who gave you the shoes was nice to you?"

The vagrant nodded, and Sarah would swear she saw his eyes glaze over. "Nicest man I've met in a long time. No one is kind anymore." He looked up—yes, his eyes had watered. "He gave me a job, and I'm determined to do it."

"A job?" Sarah couldn't avoid turning her head slightly to breathe, so she didn't take on the full rancid stench wafting off the man.

"He said, give this cell phone to Sarah after she buys a ticket to Oshawa, and I can keep my new shoes and the money."

"Money?"

The man's face hardened, and his stare turned to a glare. "That's not your business. I'm keeping the money. You can't have that."

She raised her hands. "It's okay. I don't want your money." She nodded once toward the cell phone in his hand. "That's for me?"

The man looked at it. "Yeah. Here." He held it up.

Sarah took the phone and examined it. An older Nokia that didn't need Face ID, passwords, or fingerprints to turn on. The screen lit up, and she hit a few buttons until she tapped the last number redial.

The phone rang. She placed it to her ear—where the RCMP's hidden mic still irritated her—so the RCMP boys outside in the SUV could listen in.

"I get to keep it, I get to keep it," the vagrant repeated as he hugged the shoebox.

The line rang twice, then was picked up.

"Sarah?" a man asked. "Nice of you to call me."

Her stomach twisted at the sound of his voice, and her grip tightened on the phone.

"Why?" slipped out of her mouth in her effort to be professional because the RCMP was listening. Other words flitted through her mind, but suppressing snide remarks left her almost speechless.

"Why what?"

"The bombs. The bodies. For what? *Diamonds?* Are you for real?"

Shit, here comes snide.

"Sarah, remove all tracking devices from your person. If you're wearing a wire, take that off, too. You must be electronically naked but for the phone in your hand."

She stepped away from the vagrant as he ran his hands over the shoebox like someone summoning a genie from a bottle.

"I'm not doing anything you tell me without getting something from you."

The man snorted into the phone. "That's not how it works, woman. But tell me, what do you want? And hurry because we're running out of time."

"Running out of time?" She moved to the side wall where no one would hear her. "What are you talking about?"

"If you don't do as I say when I say it, devices will explode throughout the city. I'd say that's a fair description of running out of time."

"Just tell me why you're doing this."

"The why will reveal itself by the end of the day. Discussing it now is pointless—I can't be stopped—and it will cost lives to waste time. Do as I say, and I'll stop the countdown on the next device. Keep talking about nothing, and people will die."

Sarah fought to keep her next words on the inside. Everything about a man like this, an adversary, was infuriating. Of course, he'd know that the RCMP wired her. Of course, he'd watched them drop her off. And he made it clear that he wasn't afraid to set ammo-loaded trucks on fire in populated areas when she didn't show up for the earlier train due to Sergeant Miller's negligence.

"We have less than a minute before the next truck explodes near an elementary school where a thousand young students are doing a fundraiser outside. You wouldn't want children to die, now would you, Sarah?"

"You fucking—"

"Monitor your temper, or I'll blow two trucks to prove how lethal I can be. This isn't a game. Consequences are real. And I love killing people. Testing me infuriates me."

Sarah suppressed the urge to scream. She wanted to wail, hit something, and balk at the injustice of it all, yet her anger immobilized her.

"Sarah, that vagrant's currency was money, new shoes. Your currency is human lives. I've looked you up, and I'm impressed. So much so that I think we'll work together just fine. But if you don't acknowledge that you've removed the RCMP's devices immediately, I'll have no choice but to end this call and kill more women and children than you could count at a public fairground on a Saturday."

The doors at the front of Union Station burst open, catching her attention. Two men in suits bolted inside.

Angular Face and his partner—the RCMP—she never did get the partner's name.

They made a ripping gesture by their ears, and Sarah understood immediately.

"Okay. I'll do it." She pulled the phone from her ear, then reached inside and tore out the listening device, letting it drop to the floor, where she stepped on it. "The device is on the floor. I stepped on it."

"One second." The man tapped something in the background. "Done. Okay, the next truck will not ignite. For now."

She stared across the tiled floor at the two RCMP officers, waiting for the bomber to speak.

"Now, you need to head toward the train tracks, and when you get there, you will lose Laurel and Hardy, those two detectives who just ran inside to follow you, whoever the hell they are. You know the men I'm referring to. They bolted inside because they were listening to us. Oh, and Sarah, I'm watching everything. If you approach them and they give you a new device of any sort, I'll blow up the train station."

"You're awfully confident for an asshole. I don't believe you because when did you have time to plant bombs in Union Station?"

"You underestimate me, and the mistakes you make today will have consequences. That is something I've said twice now. I won't be warning you again. One more comment of insubordination from you, and I'll just blow a truck or two."

"Okay, chill. I'm walking away from those guys and toward the tracks. But we both know there aren't any bombs in here."

"You might remember the vagrant."

Sarah glanced back over her shoulder. The vagrant was opening the shoebox and rubbing the sides of his new shoes—they looked like Reeboks.

"Yeah, you made him so happy."

"In this business, the device at the bottom of the shoebox is called a squib."

Sarah stopped walking and turned around.

"Keep moving, Sarah. If you take one step toward the vagrant or shout anything, he will die needlessly, and you'll be injured or killed."

She angled the phone up away from her mouth so the bomber wouldn't hear her panting, in one part anger, the other fear.

"Sarah? Do I need to offer you a demonstration?"

"No."

She turned back toward the tracks and got moving again.

"I assure you the squib is harmless unless I call the small device. It will remain harmless as long as you do everything I ask of you."

"Why me?"

"Because you interrupted my crew last night. You got involved. This is on you."

"But obviously, you've made plans for some time. Adding me at this late stage could backfire."

The bomber sighed through the phone. "Adding you has increased the odds of success for today's job."

She entered the platform and searched for her track number. "How so?"

"You'll know in a few hours. Now, I need you to lose those guys."

"When I get on the train, they will, too. How do you propose I lose them?"

"You won't be getting on the train."

Sarah stopped and stared at nothing for a moment. "I won't?"

"Please, don't play dumb with me. You're trying my patience. You're a smart girl. Figure it out, but lose them. The train ticket was a ruse."

"So, where am I going?"

"There's a Speedy Courier truck parked one block over on Bremner Blvd. The keys are hidden in the visor. Run. Get to that truck. Lose those two cops in suits. When you get there, turn it on and start driving."

"Where do you want me to go?"

"Toward Mississauga on the Gardiner. I'll call you back soon. Just do this, and keep driving until I call."

"Why?"

He sighed loudly. "My patience is see-through; it's that thin. I'm getting you to do this so I can watch who is following you. If I see one cruiser, marked or unmarked, following you, I blow up the city. Now go! You've got four minutes to get to the truck."

"I can't make Bremner in four minutes!" She glanced around to see how to exit the station.

"Then a lot of people will die in your name."

Sarah hopped down onto the tracks and ran. People shouted at her, but that just made her run faster.

A large man studied her from the platform. The guy must be seven feet tall and built like a mythical god. His eyes didn't leave her as she ran.

Then she hopped the tracks and ran for the grassy area on the side where she'd jump a fence.

When she looked back, the huge man was gone.

Seconds later, her step faltered when she heard a loud bang.

Did he blow up the shoebox anyway?

Just run, Sarah, Vivian said. *Nothing you can do now.*

Chapter 17

KRAMER FOLLOWED THE TWO suits as they exited onto the platform. He'd already hung up with Sarah and wanted to see which cop would chase her as she ran, but neither one did.

Instead, they watched her from the platform and pulled out their cell phones to call it in.

So he called the shoebox squid.

Enough playing around. Once their attention was diverted, he could get back to business.

He pressed his back to the brick wall and waited a few seconds until the device blew inside the train station.

Those few seconds were enough for the two cops to speak animatedly into their phones, gesturing wildly in the direction Sarah had run.

When Kramer tried to find Sarah in the distance, he couldn't.

She was gone.

Then the squid blew.

Screams emanated from inside the station.

Why did that make him smile? Was he covering up the pain of hearing his sister's screams?

Never, not even once, did he ever question his quest for revenge. Because he hated Canada and everything and everyone on Canadian soil for what happened to his family on the other side of the world, pity, shame, regret, or empathy were nonexistent in his heart. All he wanted to do was blow up as many buildings and people as possible.

Innocents? No one was innocent in this world. Even their Bible called it Original Sin.

Everyone had blood on their hands, and soon, everyone would literally have blood on their hands.

He pushed off the wall to go inside and see the commotion firsthand.

That feeling of being watched made him stop and turn back.

Sarah was long gone, with only a minute or so left to reach the truck on Bremner. The platform was emptying as people ran to investigate the noise inside the station. No one was watching him.

Still, he needed to be more diligent. That final mercenary from last night, Jack, was still out there. The odds of him being at the train station at this exact moment were few and far between, but it was possible.

Kramer shook his head and checked the time.

Two hours left before his brother did his thing, then their prize was within sight.

He entered the station and saw a commotion over by the ticket booth—exactly where the vagrant had waited for Sarah with his fancy new shoes.

What he saw didn't make sense, though.

Someone was escorting the vagrant to the side wall to sit down. There was no blood, no one lying on the ground wounded, nothing.

He moved closer to have a better look as the RCMP guys in suits were now hovering over the vagrant.

Did the vagrant throw the shoebox in the garbage? That had to be it because the black, metallic garbage bin ten meters to the side of the ticket booth was blown to shit, and there was damage to the wall beside it, but that was it.

Yet something else bothered him.

The man consoling the vagrant. He recognized him.

It was one of Sarah's friends. It took him a second to remember the name, but he was pretty sure it was Parker or Parkson.

Parkman. That was it. Parkman.

What was he doing here? How did he know about the squib? Did Sarah truly remove all the listening devices?

He dialed another number. This one was a large white cube van parked in the Square One Shopping Centre in Mississauga.

Sarah would learn that he wouldn't tolerate her disobedience.

What she didn't know was that he would call all thirty trucks parked around the Greater Toronto Area within a few hours, except one —the one that would hold the package, the result of the final heist.

He just needed Sarah to be his little decoy for a few hours.

She got herself involved, and now he would use her to get the authorities out of the downtown area en masse.

Kramer shook his head as he walked toward the exit, mystified at how Parkman got involved.

He rechecked the time, slipped between the crowd gathering around, then took one last look back.

There was one face watching him, one face looking his way and not toward the carnage.

Jack's face.

Kramer ducked and bolted through the train station's door.

"What the fuck?" he whispered to himself. "How did he get here?"

Kramer ran for his delivery truck like a demon was on his tail.

He'd die today; that much was likely. But he had to die on his terms and not at the hands of Jack the mercenary.

One more heist, then glory.

It was the final heist that would guarantee his glory and an end to his suffering.

Some people choose suicide, exiting this Earth alone.

When he proposed his idea to his brother all those years ago, they agreed this was the best way to do it.

A combined effort with a higher purpose.

He dodged traffic on Front Street, made it to his truck, cranked the engine, and sped out of there.

When he passed the front doors of the train station, he took one more look over.

Parkman was outside now.

Watching him …

Chapter 18

PARKMAN PULLED OUT HIS cell phone and called Aaron. The delivery guy got to his van as the phone rang, then Aaron picked it up.

"Did you find her?" Aaron asked.

"Yes, she was at Union Station, just as Detective Heath said she'd be. When I entered the building, Sarah was talking on a cell phone beside some homeless guy."

"What happened?"

"Sarah took off toward the trains, and the two RCMP guys followed her."

"Those are the two that Heath said would be watching her?"

"I guess so." Parkman stared at the delivery truck as it raced by him, glaring at the driver, who looked back just before he passed him. At the next street, the driver turned left and disappeared from sight. Parkman leaned back against the wall. "There was a bomb in a shoebox."

"Like the shoe bomber?"

"No, because those bombs were in shoes. This was in a shoebox, and it was relatively small. Big enough to kill within a two-meter radius, though."

"What happened? Did anyone get hurt?"

"I ran over to see if the homeless guy heard what Sarah was saying, and he went on about some deal he made."

"Deal?"

"Yeah, give Sarah the cell phone for a new pair of shoes and enough cash to eat steak for a month." Parkman shaded his eyes from the sun as the two RCMP guys in suits burst outside and ran for their SUV. "The guy showed me his shoes, and I noticed the shoebox was a tiny bit larger than most, so I asked if I could see it."

"And he gave you the box?"

"He did, but it wasn't empty. There was a false bottom with something small stashed inside. So, I stuck it in a metal receptacle, then pushed the garbage can into a corner and went back to the vagrant. That's when it blew up."

"Blew up?" Aaron sounded worried.

"Whoever wanted Sarah to get that cell phone also wanted no witnesses, but I think I know what he looks like now."

"How?"

"There were two guys not gawking at what happened. I can tell when someone's genuinely not interested as they're preoccupied with a phone call, or they're late. But these two guys were different. It was like they knew what had happened and didn't have to stare after it to see."

"Where are they now?"

"I followed the shorter one outside. He ran for a delivery truck and took off."

"That could be the guy. What about the other man?"

Parkman shrugged, even though Aaron couldn't see him. "No idea, but I'd recognize him without a problem if I saw him again."

"What's he look like?"

"He's a monster. Easily seven feet tall and about as thick as the Hulk."

Aaron fell silent for a moment. "Look, Parkman. I appreciate you doing this. No one wants anything to happen to Sarah, but is there any way you can just bring her home? Why not let the police handle this bomber guy?"

"Tell that to Sarah. Something tells me she's quite involved at the moment, and she doesn't have anyone's support but the authorities, and we both know how supportive they can be."

Parkman pushed off the wall and moved along the sidewalk back toward the lot where he parked his car.

"What do you want me to do?" Aaron asked.

"Nothing. You've got Willow. Stay with her and stay safe."

"Want me to call someone to help? Darwin's gone back to Italy. Disco is on a job somewhere. Alex is still recovering from multiple broken bones from that fight in the hotel, and Daniel is running the dojo while I'm here."

"I got this. I'll call Heath back and see what he knows."

"But Sarah's gone to the wind. How can you help her if she's disappeared? Even that delivery truck guy is gone, right?"

"Yeah, everyone's gone."

"So, what's next?"

"I need to get inside the Metro Convention Centre."

"Why there?"

Parkman rounded the corner and headed south. "Because that's where they're having some political summit."

"What? I'm confused. How's that related to all this?"

"Heath said Sarah grabbed that woman, Atchison, off the street, and then her jewelry store was looted."

"And?"

"They were looking for a rare diamond called a Culligan."

"Culligan? The water guy?"

"No, wait. Maybe it was Cullinan. Anyway, they didn't get it. Fakes were placed in several stores downtown. The real one is in some secret city vault."

"What's that got to do with the convention center?"

"It will be on display for one hour after lunch for the visiting dignitaries, and something tells me all this bomb activity is to deflect from the real job—a diamond heist."

Aaron exhaled heavily. "Seriously? You think they just want to steal a diamond?"

"Dude, it's a big fucking diamond."

"Parkman, even if it was as big as a car, who the hell would try to steal a diamond that size in the middle of the day at the convention center where well-guarded dignitaries are visiting? That amount of security would be immense. That sounds like a logistical nightmare for even a seasoned thief."

"And yet I still think they're going for it."

"Let's suppose you're right. How's Sarah involved?"

"No idea, but I intend to find out."

"How?"

"By having a chat with the woman they released about an hour ago. The employee of that jewelry store whom Sarah abducted briefly."

"What could she know?"

"The real question is, why her and her store? Something seems off here. If fake diamonds were placed in several locations with the real one in a secure vault ..." he trailed off as he stopped walking and looked skyward. "Motherfucker."

"What?" Aaron blurted. "What is it?"

"Heath told me something about a mole in the RCMP. That's why they did the whole cloak and dagger thing with the diamond."

"And whoever knew about that Atchison woman's store would be the mole? Is that what you're thinking?"

"That could be, but wouldn't they have figured that out already?" Parkman started walking again. "They kept the information very limited."

"Wait, are you suggesting that the Atchison woman told someone, who then blabbed to the bomber guys?"

"I have no idea. Look, I need to go. I need to call Heath. They're putting the *real* diamond on display in a few hours. I need to figure some shit out before that happens."

"Call me when you can, and if you need me, I can leave Willow with Daniel."

"Aaron, right now, I'd prefer to leave you out of this entirely with what's happening between you and Sarah."

"Parkman, I still love her. I just want her to stop all the dangerous stuff."

"And you know she won't."

"Which is why we are where we are at the moment."

"And why you will stay where you are until this is done."

"Just call me if you need me. I'd rather have Sarah angry at me than dead."

"Well, there's that. Gotta go."

They hung up, and he dialed Detective Heath as he reached his car.

"Heath. Go."

"It's Parkman. I might have something."

"Speak to me."

Parkman laid it out for him in two minutes, then obtained René Atchison's home address.

"You didn't get that from me, you hear?"

"Heath, I'm a private investigator. Her address would've been mine in an hour or less, but we can't waste time today. If she asks, I'll remind her what I do for a living, and that's that."

"Make up some shit reason for interviewing her. She seems sweet. She'll listen. When you're done, call me. I want to know what the hell is going on."

"Give me an hour, tops. Maybe two."

"Just hurry."

Parkman killed the call, tossed his phone onto the passenger seat, cranked the engine, and took off for the Danforth and Pape area where Atchison lived.

This had to do with the mole, and once they found the mole, it would lead them to the bomber and end everything.

At least, he hoped so.

Chapter 19

SARAH FOUND THE DELIVERY truck unlocked on Bremner, just as he said it would be. She jumped in the front seat and turned to the white wall behind her. A small door led into the back, but it had a padlock on it. She tugged on the lock, but it was solid.

"What is the cargo?" she asked out loud, but Vivian was gone again. "Am I sitting in a bomb on wheels?" She glanced up and looked around. "Vivian, you'd tell me, right? I mean, is this how the guy gets rid of me?"

No answer.

"Fuck it." She popped the sun visor, and the truck's keys dropped into her other hand.

Once the door was slammed shut, she cranked the engine and pulled away from the curb.

"He wants me to drive toward Mississauga, so I'll do what he says, just like a good little girl." She suspected talking to herself was due to nerves, or maybe it was so Vivian could hear her. "Hmmm, you listening to me here?" She took a left and headed south toward the Gardiner. "Where am I going? What am I doing, Vivian? I could use some help. I'm on my own out here."

Minutes later, she ascended the ramp to the Gardiner Expressway and quickly got up to the speed of traffic. By the time she was passing the Kipling Avenue exit, the cell phone rang.

"What?" she spat into it. "Where am I going?"

"You're not a nice person, are you?"

Sarah slowed the delivery truck, then pulled to the shoulder. "Nice person?" She spoke through her teeth. "Are you fucking kidding me? *Nice* person? After what you spent your Friday night doing, you want to talk to me about being nice?"

"Okay, you've made your point. Where are you?"

"Halfway between losing my mind and driving this truck into Lake Ontario to make all the bombs on it soggy and useless."

"You're not driving a vehicle with devices."

"Oh, how reassuring." Even though her tone was sarcastic, she shuddered with relief, hoping he wasn't lying.

"I need you to do a pick-up for me, but not for another hour or so."

"I'm not picking up anything for anyone."

"Oh, I think you are. Again, do I have to remind you of the consequences?"

She stared out the windshield, listening to the traffic race by at over a hundred kilometers per hour—and just like that, she was back to controlling her verbal responses.

"Sarah, stay with me a little longer. We're almost done."

"Haven't I complied with everything you've asked of me so far?"

There was a pause. "Hmmm, let me think." Another pause. "To some extent, I would say yes, you have done as you're told. Well, that and no further bombs have gone off, so that's your confirmation."

"Then why did you detonate that shoebox bomb and kill that vagrant and whoever may have been too close to him?"

"The vagrant is alive. No one died, Sarah."

There was something in his tone like he was lying. Or was that regret that others didn't die?

"Why can't I believe you?"

"I got the bomb into a metal garbage container, then detonated it to avoid having those cops chasing you. It was something of a decoy."

"Sure you did. I'm convinced you're lying."

He released an exasperated sigh in her ear. "Believe what you will, but I think the news stations are covering it. When I have time in the next half hour, I'll send a link to that phone with a video clip from the scene."

"For someone who is lying, that's bold. What, are you going to edit the video yourself?"

"Then I'll message you a link to watch what the media is posting. In the meantime, I need you to get on the 427 heading north and exit at Airport Road."

"What's on Airport Road?"

"The International Centre. You will park there and await further instructions. Any deviation will result in a dozen trucks going up in flames."

"How do I know you're not bluffing?"

"Two reasons. One, you can't take the risk, and two, wait until I send you the link. Then perhaps you'll trust me that the vagrant is alive."

"That's only one reason because I am a risk taker."

"Not with other people's lives, you're not. This is not the time for you to take risks. I have a GPS tracker built into the truck you're driving. I can see you parked on the side of the Gardiner by Kipling at the moment. Deviate from what I've told you, and trucks will explode, killing countless civilians. Then I'll release everything to the media. I'll say that Sarah Roberts murdered them by simply driving down the wrong street."

"*Bastard*," she whispered.

"Excuse me?"

"Faster. I said I'll drive faster."

"That's better. Run along now, little girl."

She ended the call and merged back into traffic, her heart pounding, palms sweaty.

"Help me out here, Vivian. What's going on?"

Still nothing …

Chapter 20

PARKMAN FOUND A SPOT to park on the side of the road one block up from Pape Avenue. Atchison's house was on Eaton Avenue, less than a two-minute walk from his car.

The first thing that hit him anytime he was in this area, which was aptly titled "Greek Town," was the smell of gyros cooking. Restaurants along the Danforth offered everything from moussaka to pastitsio, dolmades, and saganaki—all the best Greek food this side of Athens. With over fifty thousand Greeks having settled in Toronto, it was no wonder that the best Greek food was in Greektown.

He made his way past a couple of tavernas, resisting the urge to get a gyro to go, and walked up Eaton until he got to Atchison's front door.

This stretch of buildings resembled brick townhomes. They were much newer than the houses in this area, and René kept her yard work up. The small, neatly cut lawn, with vibrant flowers in a tiny garden by the door, just under the front window, made it look welcoming.

Parkman rang the bell and, after a moment, heard someone approaching from the inside.

"Who is it?" A woman bellowed from behind the door.

"Name's Parkman." He pulled out his PI license. "I've got ID. I'm an ex-cop turned private investigator."

The door opened a crack, and the woman's long, dark hair cascaded over one shoulder as she peeked out through the screen door at his ID. "What can I do for you?"

"I'd love to have a word with you, Miss Atchison."

"Everything I had to say, I already told the cops. Can't you ask them for a copy of my statement?"

"Afraid not, as I'm working privately."

"Then who hired you? Who would be interested in me?"

"Sarah."

Parkman waited for a response, and then the door opened more.

"Why would Sarah hire you to investigate me?" She leaned against the doorframe as they spoke through the screen door.

"I'm going to be honest with you, Miss Atchison—"

"René, please."

"René then." Parkman nodded. "Sarah and I have worked together since she was an eighteen-year-old still living at her parents' home. Now she's out there on her own, and I'm worried about her. What I want to find out is why she targeted you."

René frowned, then pushed a stray hair back behind her ear. "We already know why she targeted me. Those thieves wanted to break into the jewelry store where I work."

"Right, well, there's that. But why did they pick your store?"

René's frown deepened. "Didn't anyone inform you about the diamond that's in town? My friend's store was picked as one of the ones that would receive a fake diamond. They stole the fake one."

"I'm afraid it goes deeper than that, Miss Atchison—René."

"How so?"

"May I come in so we can discuss this at the kitchen table or perhaps in the living room?"

René looked him up and down, then clicked something on the screen door and stepped back, her arm sweeping inward.

"Come in. I'm sorry, normally I would've already invited you inside. It's just, with what happened recently and all—"

"I understand completely." Parkman stepped inside the foyer. "What's that smell?"

"I'm baking brownies. It calms my nerves to do something, so I put a mix together."

He glanced to the left and saw two suitcases and a carry-on. "You going somewhere?"

"Please," she gestured toward the couch, "come sit. We can chat for a few minutes before I have to take out the brownies."

Parkman took a seat, his back facing the front window, with René taking the chair to his right.

She crossed her legs, placed her hands together on top of her knee, and looked past Parkman out the window behind him. "I'm leaving tomorrow."

"Tomorrow? That's sudden, isn't it?"

René glanced down at her hands, then fidgeted with a nail. "You know, to my friends, I'm considered resilient. I'm pretty fearless." She looked up and met his eyes. "I've done a lot with my life. I sang with the Colorado Symphony for years. I performed backup vocals on Broadway in New York for the Disney live movie *Beauty and the Beast*, yet I've always dreamed of being a photographer."

"And now you live in Toronto?"

She shook her head. "Not necessarily. I moved to New York at forty-three, in pursuit of a dream that ultimately fell apart. To take a break, I came up to Toronto a few months ago to help out a friend, the owner of the jewelry store." She glanced down at her hands again, shaking her head back and forth slightly. "I never thought I'd say this, but I'm moving back to New York, where I'll be safer. Canada sucks."

"I'm an American, too. So is Sarah. She stayed because the man she fell in love with lives in Toronto. Canada can be a pretty place to visit, but it does suck to live here sometimes." Parkman cleared his throat. "Can you tell me a little about your friend, the owner of the jewelry store?"

"Who? Meredith?" Surprise colored her tone. "How would she be involved?"

Parkman lifted one shoulder. "She may not be, but perhaps there's something you can tell me about her that'll help us understand why they chose her jewelry store."

René swept her arms out. "This is her house. I'm staying with her and helping manage the jewelry store until she's done with the committee."

"Committee?"

"Yeah, she's hyper-involved in some board or committee downtown that has kept her very busy for the past month or so. That was why I came north." René adjusted her legs, then crossed them again and placed a hand on her knee. "Tell me something."

Parkman nodded. "Sure, if I can."

"You mentioned they *chose* Meredith's jewelry store."

Parkman nodded again. "That's right. It would appear so."

"How would anyone know why anyone chose any particular store to rob unless you ask the idiots who trashed her store? What I mean is, why say it that way?"

"I spoke with Detective Heath at the Toronto Police Department this morning. He said the diamond they were looking for is in a secure vault in the city. It's going on display in a few hours." Parkman checked his watch, then met René's eyes. "To deter security risks, fake Cullinan diamonds were placed in quite a few jewelry stores, with yours being one of them."

"I was told that, but was also told it was kept under wraps. That no one really knew about it."

"Yeah, that." Parkman brushed a piece of white fluff off his pants. "Apparently, a mole in the RCMP leaked the information, and your store was targeted. For some unknown reason, someone thought the *real* Cullinan was in Meredith's store."

"Wait." René held up a finger. "Why Meredith's store if there were others?"

"That is the million-dollar question. That's what I'm trying to figure out. Somehow, the mole discovered the diamond was hidden in a store, and they targeted Meredith's store. But why her store in particular? Why not the one on Keele Street, or the one on Lawrence Avenue, or even St. Clair?"

A buzzer sounded from the kitchen.

"Please, give me a moment to take out the brownies."

"Of course."

René got up and headed to the kitchen as Parkman pulled out his cell phone—no missed calls.

It made him sick to realize that Sarah was out there fighting this all alone without any backup. Everyone was busy with their own lives. If Darwin were here, he'd help. Disco too. Even Alex would be in the thick of things. But the last few months have broken the team up with injuries and Benjamin's death.

He rechecked his watch.

Limited in what he could do to help without more information, once he was finished speaking with René, he'd head to the police station and pour several large coffees and wait for Detective Heath to give him more. When the time came, and Sarah surfaced, he needed to be there.

"Mr. Parkman," René called from the kitchen. "Can I offer you a coffee or tea?"

"No, thank you. I'll be leaving soon."

"How about a piece of warm brownie?"

"Well, there's something I can't refuse."

A moment later, René returned with two pieces and two small glasses of water, placing one in front of him and the other in front of her.

"Please, dig in. Let me know if they're worthy of Meredith. I made them for her as well."

Parkman sampled the warm, moist piece and moaned. "Wow," he said with his mouth full. "This is delicious."

They ate in silence for a moment, then René rubbed her hands together over her plate, swallowed her last bit, and leaned back in her chair.

"Please convey my thank you to Sarah for saving my life."

Parkman raised his brows. "Saving your life?"

She nodded. "According to the detectives, two of the jewelry thieves were found dead last night. They suspect that since Sarah is some sort of psychic, she stepped in to save me. They would've robbed the store with me or without me, evidently. Who knows what would've happened to me."

Parkman used a napkin on his fingers. "I can confirm Sarah has a psychic ability. I'll let her know what you said." He drank some water, then rechecked his watch. "I really should get going, but something's still bothering me about the jewelry store." He shrugged. "Until we find those responsible, I doubt we'll ever discover *why* they felt the diamond was in that location."

He got to his feet, and René did as well.

"Thank you for seeing me today, especially after what you went through yesterday."

"You have a kind face. The ID could have been fake, but I got this *trusting* vibe from you."

He raised his brow. "You trusted me because of a vibe?"

"Well, not exactly." Her cheeks reddened slightly.

Parkman tilted his head. "Oh?"

"Detective Heath told me about Sarah and Aaron, and your name came up a few times. When I got home, I googled her and saw your picture, too."

"Ahh," he nodded, "that makes sense."

"I was sure you were Parkman, with or without your ID, and after what Sarah did for me, if there was anything I knew that would help her, I had to try."

Parkman stuck out his hand. "Well, thank you for trying."

They shook hands, then Parkman moved to the front door. This had gotten him nowhere. He wasn't any closer to learning how they chose Meredith's jewelry store because the woman involved, René Atchison, was visiting the city and helping out a friend. That meant René wasn't likely connected to a criminal element, didn't know anyone in the police department or with the RCMP, couldn't be speaking with the mole, and she didn't strike him as the kind of woman who would run with diamond thieves.

As far as he could tell, René had nothing to do with what happened last night, and Sarah saved her life *because* she had nothing to do with what happened last night.

He stepped outside and turned back to her. "Is there any way I could get in touch with Meredith? Even just to speak with her for five minutes?"

René raised a finger. "One sec, let me get my phone."

Parkman spun around to stare out at the street. *Where are you, Sarah?*

"I'll give you her number." René was back at the screen door, tapping on her phone. She recited the number, and Parkman typed it into his phone's contacts, then added her name.

"Thank you again," he said, waving once as he walked out onto the sidewalk, his gut twisting with all the unknowns.

He dialed Detective Heath as he walked. There had to be some update on Sarah, or he'd go mad.

"Heath."

"It's Parkman. Anything new?"

"You're not going to like it."

"Then don't spare me the details. Just tell it like it is."

"The team watching Sarah lost her."

Parkman gasped and stopped walking to tighten his fist and purse his lips. "How? I saw Sarah running, and the two guys watching her called it in."

"She pulled her tracking device, and they—"

"Incompetent bastards," Parkman shouted, then got moving again.

"She bought a train ticket to Oshawa but didn't take the train."

"And they couldn't follow her down the street?"

"She was too fast, but she didn't do it alone."

"How so?"

"The entire time, she had a cell phone pressed to her ear. They suspect the bomber guy coached her on what he wanted her to do."

"Not *coached*. The word is *coerced* her by threatening her with another bomb or something."

"True—like he did when we refused his demands to bring Sarah to the train station."

"Now what?" Parkman got to his car and dropped inside.

"Now we wait."

This wasn't Heath's fault. The RCMP took the case from him. But he wanted to shout at Heath like there was no tomorrow.

Sarah was out there all alone, dealing with some mad bomber who had the city in his sights while everyone went about their business. And what for? A diamond?

Something wasn't adding up.

"What's next, Heath? There has to be something the authorities can do?"

"That bearer of bad news thing is coming."

Parkman hadn't turned on his car yet. He stared through the windshield at nothing and waited for Heath to continue.

"Until we hear from Sarah or the bomber, there is absolutely nothing we can do."

"Well, the real diamond is going to be on display today."

"Yeah, at the Metro Convention Centre for about an hour."

"What time exactly?"

There was a shuffling on the other end of the phone as Heath was probably pulling up his sleeve. "At one this afternoon, so ninety minutes from now."

"After what happened last night, why are they even bringing it out on display? Isn't that hyper-risky?"

"Some visiting dignitaries from Africa, Asia, and Europe are here for a quasi-NATO summit of sorts. The diamond was discovered in 1905 in South Africa and was bequeathed to Queen Elizabeth in 1953. It's part of her personal collection. And hey, I know I sound like *Wikipolicia*, but I looked that shit up."

"You sound like you know a lot about this diamond."

"The case was ripped from my hands. What else do I have to do?"

"Then answer me this. Why the fuck is it going on display?"

"After the queen's death, it's part of a collection that came to Canada for the Nato summit thing at the convention center. Also, don't forget that Canada is still a British territory. It's called a monarchy, and they've got a Governor General who still reports to the homeland and shit."

"Thanks for the history lesson, but now you know where your bomber will surface. That's what he wants. The queen's collection."

"We're way ahead of you. Every member we could spare from soldiers, cops, detectives, armed Brits, and a few squads the Canadian military could scrounge up are guarding that damned diamond today. No one is getting to it without a fight. Also, that's not my fight anymore anyways."

Parkman shook his head. "Something doesn't fit." He tapped his fingers on the steering wheel. "Have you considered this could all be a ruse?"

"A ruse?"

"Yeah, like the bomber is up to something else, some other reason to have everyone focused on the diamond."

"Like what?"

"I have no idea."

"Where are you?"

"Still on the Danforth. I just had brownies with René Atchison."

"*Brownies?* What the fuck?"

"I asked her why Gold Run Jewelry was targeted, but she came up empty. She's an American who has only been here a few months. I thought that store was hers, but it's not."

"You could've just asked me those details. We talked to her for over twelve hours and got nowhere. She was only helping out a friend."

"Yeah. Meredith."

"It's a dead end, Parkman. Come on in, so you're with us when we hear more about Sarah."

"On my way."

He ended the call and quickly dialed Meredith. She answered in a hurry.

"Hello, who's calling?"

"My name is Parkman, and I wanted to ask you a few questions about—"

"I'm sorry, but I haven't got the time today."

"When's a better time to call you back? An hour from now?"

"How about next week? We can do an interview then."

"Interview?"

"You're with the press, no?"

"No, I'm a private investigator pursuing an angle on your jewelry store."

"Oh, well, there's nothing to pursue there, and I'm too busy to chat today."

"I can come to you—"

"You wouldn't get past security on such short notice."

"Security?" Parkman frowned. "Where are you?"

"At the Metro Convention Centre. Look, Mr. Parkman, I have to go."

Then he heard something in the background before she ended the call.

Someone called Meredith, identifying themselves as an RCMP officer. Without contemplating what it all meant for too long, he called René Atchison's number.

"Hello?"

"It's Parkman again."

"Did you forget something?"

"I'm sorry to bother you, but something strange just happened."

"What?"

"I called to speak with Meredith, and she was too busy to take my call."

"That wouldn't be strange." René let out a short chuckle. "This is the weekend they've all been working toward. That's why I was helping at her jewelry store."

"At the convention center?"

"Yes, she's working with the RCMP, involved with the security detail for Canada's minister of defense who's visiting. Think Secret Service in America."

Parkman's eyes widened as his grip on the phone tightened.

"René, I have to go."

He hung up and dialed Detective Heath back.

"What's up?" Heath asked.

"It's not about the diamond," Parkman whispered. "It's not about the diamond."

"What are you babbling about? You just said that's where the bomber would surface."

"He's making it about the diamond, but it isn't."

"Then what's it about?"

"It has something to do with the dignitaries, specifically the minister of defense."

"What makes you say that?"

Parkman filled him in on his call to Meredith and then René. "There's the connection."

"What connection?" Heath asked, sounding completely perplexed.

"Meredith is working with the RCMP at the convention center—where the diamond is—and she owns the store that was robbed last night."

"Wait, you think Meredith is going after the diamond?"

Parkman rolled his eyes, then turned on the car. "Heath, listen. The RCMP said they had a mole and leaked information on where the diamond would be stored overnight."

"Yeah ..."

"And Meredith's store was one of the decoys for the diamond."

"I'm with you so far."

"So the leak isn't with the team guarding the diamond." Parkman hit his blinker and merged into traffic.

"Where's the leak, then?"

"The leak is with the RCMP team guarding the dignitaries, namely the minister of defense, since they're working directly with the jewelry store owner who got hit last night."

Heath didn't say anything for a moment. "Are you saying you want to hunt the mole within the RCMP, with the team guarding Canada's minister of defense? Today?"

"No, what I'm saying is they're looking in the wrong spot, number one. And number two, it's not about the diamond—as I said earlier. It's about the dignitaries."

"The dignitaries?" Heath's voice rose as he spoke the word. "You mean like an assassination attempt or something?"

"I have no idea, but whatever it is, it'll happen within an hour or two, and it'll take place at the Metro Convention Centre when everyone is hyper-focused on the diamond."

Something banged on the other end of the phone. "I just ran from my office." Heath was already panting into the phone. "Where will you be?"

"At the convention center in ten minutes."

"Meet you there."

"Bring me a gun."

"Not a chance," Heath shouted into the phone. "I just got fully reinstated. I'm not doing anything to risk that."

Parkman swerved around a slow-moving pickup. "Bring me a gun, or I'll steal one."

"I didn't hear that. Bye." Heath ended the call.

Parkman shoved the phone on the seat between his legs, wishing his car had sirens and lights so he could drive faster.

Something was going down at the convention center today, and he didn't want to miss it.

Sarah would be involved in some way as well—he just knew it.

Yet, he hoped they all lived through it—whatever *it* was.

Chapter 21

NEIL KRAMER DROVE AIMLESSLY to waste time. Until his brother called him, there was nothing to do. He'd stopped for a coffee and had something sweet to keep his blood sugar levels high.

His eyes were often glued to the clock. He hated waiting; patience was not his strong suit. Too much had gone into the planning of this operation. And now he'd added that woman, Sarah, into the mix, thinking this was a good opportunity.

Why not use her? He had plans for her, and when the authorities came after them, and he knew they would, he could use her to get his pursuers off his tail.

Last-minute changes could derail everything, but there was something about this new idea that made the entire plan better.

And, if things went terribly wrong, it was Sarah who would die.

His phone rang, and he nearly jumped out of his skin. He fumbled with it, almost dropped it, then hit the button and smashed it to his ear so hard it hurt.

"Are we on?" he said into the phone.

"We are," his brother whispered. "Make the call. Set off the devices. Make sure they know you're serious. The rest will fall into place from there."

"Okay, doing it now—"

"Wait."

"What?"

"Are we still set up for a pick-up?"

"Of course. The truck will be waiting. In approximately thirty minutes?"

"Thirty minutes. Set the clock. Go."

The line died.

"Finally," Kramer said to himself.

He dialed the phone Sarah had with her.

"Where's my video clip?" she asked.

Shit, he forgot to send it. "I've been busy. You're just going to have to trust me." Kramer set the phone on speaker, then accessed the tracker to make sure the truck Sarah was driving was still parked on Airport Road at the International Centre.

"But I *don't* trust you. That's the problem."

"Sarah, when this is all over, I'll leave Toronto, I'll leave Canada, and I promise never to hurt anyone ever again. But that's tomorrow. So, for today, do as I say to avoid further bloodshed."

He was rewarded with deep breathing over the phone.

"Good, now I need you to drive back downtown—"

"*What?*"

"Head back downtown and pull into a parking garage off Lower Simcoe Street, just south of Front Street. It's easy to see from the road and can be accessed whether heading south or north. On either side of the entrance, you'll find large TV screens advertising monthly parking available. To the right is a hotel sign that says, Intercontinental. Do you know where that is? Can you do that?"

"Yes, I know where that is." Her tone was so sarcastic, he wanted to call one of his devices to prove a point, but held off—for now.

"Good, drive there and unlock the vehicle's doors, keep the engine running, then don't move. I won't call again, but I'll be watching by GPS."

"So you want me to be your driver for a diamond heist? No fucking way."

"Sarah, if I wanted you to be my taxi driver for a diamond heist, a beer run, or a drive across the country, you'd do it because hundreds of people, Mr. and Mrs. Joe Public, are relying on you to do this for me. Now, we are running out of time. Be there in half an hour, or I'll start blowing shit up. Oh, and just to clear your conscience, this isn't a diamond heist."

"Sure, it isn't. Then tell me what it is. I mean, after last night, I think everyone is clear on what you're after."

"You're doing this to save a life."

"Yeah, and I'm your uncle. Fuck you."

"Sure, Sarah, fuck me. But it'll be a huge fuck you when those devices light up Toronto on a busy Saturday afternoon. Do as you're told and do it now, or hundreds of dead people will haunt your dreams."

He waited a moment, staring at the GPS app, but the truck still wasn't moving.

"I don't see the truck moving."

"I was stretching my legs, you fuck. Walking back to it now."

"I'd suggest you run."

He ended the call to avoid raising his blood pressure further. It was either he'd explode at her over the phone, or a few trucks would explode. Better to just hang up.

It took a full minute, but the GPS tracker showed the truck pulling onto Airport Road and heading toward the 427 South.

Good. Sarah Roberts was on her way.

Now for the next part of the plan.

Kramer grabbed another burner phone and dialed the number he committed to memory when the plan was formed.

"Toronto Police Department. How can I direct your call?"

"It's time." Kramer kept his voice low. He didn't have to disguise it or worry they'd be able to track the phone.

"What time is it, sir?"

"Bomb time."

"Excuse me?"

"I hope you're recording this."

"Sir, can you speak up?"

"The bomb promised last night will ignite in five minutes."

"Sir, please wait. Let me get you someone to talk to."

"I placed it at the Greg Brown campus, but you guys evacuated the wrong campus. It's at the waterfront campus on Dockside Drive. You've got five minutes."

"Can you give us more time?" When the woman spoke this time, he could easily tell he'd been placed on speaker.

"Whoever else is listening, please gather around and listen closely."

A general din came from the other end of the line as people used cell phones, someone muttered something to someone else, and there was a pounding like footsteps down a hallway in the background.

"I hate Canada. I hate your government, your politics, and most of all, I hate all Canadians. Today, you *fucking* Canadians die."

"But sir, you're talking about innocent lives here—"

"I don't care about Canadian lives. Not after what you filthy fuckers did to my life. Now, listen, and listen closely, as this is the only time I'll say it."

No one spoke on the other end of the line.

"Once Greg Brown campus is destroyed, I will set off a few more devices, then leave the city. After today, no one else will have to die. But I will have my vengeance, and I chose today for that."

"I understand," a man said. "I'm Detective Doyle. Is there anything we can do—"

"There's nothing you can do but send fire trucks and ambulances to the bomb sites. Today, your job is to clean up. You will be cleaning the mess you made in my country."

"Greg Brown is one site. Can you help us prepare for the other sites by telling us where they are?"

"Stay on this phone. I'll call back in twenty minutes with the second location."

"Why not tell us now?"

"Because I want the campus bomb to blow first. Then you'll know how serious I am."

"Sir, after last night, we're quite aware of how serious you are."

Kramer clenched his jaw and spoke through his teeth. "You know nothing about me or how serious I am. But you will know just *exactly* how fucking serious I am when there are a thousand dead Canadians on your conscience. Now fuck off."

He hung up the phone and immediately dialed the Greg Brown campus bomb.

A five-minute warning was too long. That Doyle guy pissed him off. The Greg Brown bomb would blow now.

"Fuck 'em. Fuck 'em all."

The line connected. He heard the click. The line died.

The bomb exploded.

And Kramer smiled.

It was going to be a good day.

Chapter 22

SARAH HOPPED IN THE driver's seat and got the delivery truck—roughly the size of a brown UPS truck—going toward the highway to drive back downtown.

There had to be a way out of this without people dying, but until she could figure that out, she had to do what the asshole told her to do.

Why did he get her to drive to the airport area only to drive back downtown? Was that to avoid her being located by those RCMP dicks who were supposed to be following her?

She merged onto the 427 heading south, a hand on her stomach in a futile attempt to quell her nerves. Where was her sister now? She'd been so talkative recently, but now that she needed her, Vivian was gone.

What about Willow, Vivian? You're not just accountable to me anymore. Remember that.

Luckily, traffic was light heading into Toronto, and she was on the Gardiner coming up to the Spadina exit in just over twenty minutes, praying the asshole would call her back before he triggered any devices.

At the bottom of the ramp, she hung a left, raced up Lower Simcoe Street through another light, and saw the large sign for the Metro Convention Centre on the left.

This is where traffic got tight. She was stopped under a long bridge, the left-hand turn she needed in sight.

Tapping her fingers on the steering wheel impatiently, Sarah stared at the phone in her hand, willing it to ring. She'd done exactly as he'd asked, but her timing was slightly off.

Emergency sirens sounded in the distance somewhere.

"You'd better not have …" she muttered.

The phone rang. She jumped and almost dropped it, even though the call was expected.

"Yes! What!"

"Where are you?"

"Track me, bitch. Use that GPS thingy."

"Tell me where you are and dispel with the name-calling. This is the last time I'll warn you. The next time, I kill people in your name."

You fucking animal. I'll kill you! almost slipped out, but Sarah was able to slap her mouth closed with her free hand to squelch the protest.

She eased her hand away from her mouth. "I'm under a bridge." She inhaled deeply. "Stuck in traffic. Waiting to move forward."

"That tells me nothing. There are many bridges in Toronto. So, I'll ask again. Where are you?"

"The parking garage you want me to pull into is in sight. I'm fifty meters from the entrance but stuck under this large bridge on Lower Simcoe Street."

"Okay, now I know why the GPS couldn't pick you up. You're under the train tracks exiting Union Station. How long before you're in the parking area with your doors all unlocked?"

"The traffic isn't moving. One minute. Three minutes. Maybe ten."

"No. That won't work. Be inside in one minute, maximum ninety seconds. If you aren't, I can't control the outcome."

The line died.

"*FFFuuuucccckkkkk,*" Sarah screamed.

Chapter 23

PARKMAN CALLED HEATH BACK, but the man didn't pick up the line. For some reason, likely the visiting dignitaries, several roads were closed, and traffic in front of the convention center was being redirected.

He had to drive four blocks away to find parking.

Once on his feet and running toward the large building on Front Street West, he saw the police barricades with officers directing people away from Front Street.

This event's security must have tripled since last night's heist and bombings.

He made it to Lower Simcoe and Front, but that was as far as he could get without an invitation or a press pass.

A crowd had formed at the barricade, some chanting about the economy, others calling the Canadian government a cult, while others demanded the prime minister's resignation for embezzlement and lying, calling him Castro's child.

Parkman squeezed through the crowd, getting an elbow in the chin for his efforts, and made it to the front with a few protestors shoving him hard.

"Officer," he called. "I'm here to meet Detective Heath."

A cop looked over at him and shook his head. "I'm no secretary." The cop pointed at the barricade. "No one gets past this line unless I'm told otherwise by my superiors."

"Just call Heath and tell him Parkman is waiting for him."

The cop shook his head and waved Parkman away dismissively. "I don't know anyone named Heath." The cop raised his voice to be heard over the chanting that seemed to increase in volume. "Call him yourself. Get the invite. Then they'll tell me, and I'll let you in. That's the only way it works. Now go away."

The cop stepped sideways to shove a man back who was trying to jump the sawhorses they had placed on the asphalt.

"Everyone, step back," the cop yelled.

Other officers converged as backup. This was a hotspot, a mob mentality, and it would get Parkman nowhere.

He eased back and moved along Lower Simcoe Street in search of an opening, but found nothing.

Exasperated, he leaned against a building and called Heath again. This time, the man answered.

"Where are you?" Heath asked.

"Outside the convention center, but I can't get in."

"No one can get in at the moment."

"Why? What the hell is going on?"

"The Greg Brown campus just blew up. No reports yet on the number of dead."

"What! I thought they'd scoured it with bomb-sniffing dogs, and nothing turned up."

"There are *two* Greg Brown campuses. They searched the wrong one. No one thought it would be the waterfront campus. Luckily, it happened on a Saturday. Only cleaning staff are usually inside on a Saturday, but most of them took today off."

"Why, did someone tip them off?"

"The Greg Brown campus was being searched by bomb dogs last night. The other campus staff got freaked out, and everyone took the weekend off. Last I heard a couple of minutes ago, security was still in the building. They're trying to put out the flames and locate the guard."

"So they just locked down the convention center? How does that work?"

"Someone called in a bomb threat to this very location two minutes ago."

Parkman stared across the street at the imposing building. "You're kidding."

"I wish I were. They're not keeping me looped in, but I heard from a reliable source in the department that the bomber called them twenty minutes ago to taunt them."

"Taunt them?"

"Yeah, like he holds all the power, all the cards. In summation, he said something to the effect that he wants mass casualties, so they're not taking any chances in the convention center."

A horn sounded to his left. Parkman turned in time to see a white delivery truck squeeze past a small Tercel, scrape along the concrete wall, sending sparks flying, then bounce off the curb and back onto the road.

The driver leaned on the wheel hard, making a left turn into the open maw of the parking garage.

In the seconds it took for the driver to career off the wall and enter the garage, Parkman was barely able to get a glimpse of the driver through the glare of sunshine bouncing off the windshield.

As far as he could tell, it looked like Sarah Roberts.

"Parkman, are you there?"

"Holy shit," he mumbled.

"What the hell is going on?"

"That's what I'd like to know." He moved down the sidewalk to get a better look inside the garage.

"Parkman, talk to me. Were you even listening?"

"A white delivery truck just got damaged as it maneuvered around another car on Lower Simcoe, then barreled inside the parking garage under the Intercontinental."

"What?" Heath's voice rose in volume. "I think that's where they're evacuating some of the dignitaries."

"I caught a glimpse of the driver."

"What did he look like? Could you recognize him if you saw him again?"

"Yes." Parkman got to the end of the crowd and was able to look inside the parking garage. The delivery truck was too deep to see from the road.

"Well? What did the guy look like?"

"It wasn't a guy. It was Sarah Roberts. Heath, I'd swear it was Sarah."

"What the hell is she doing in a delivery truck barreling inside that parking lot at this specific time?" Heath's voice rose in time with Parkman's blood pressure.

"That's exactly what I am going to find out."

"Parkman. Wait!"

But Parkman had already pulled the phone from his ear and was slipping it into his pocket.

Then he bolted across the street and slipped behind a parked car to approach in stealth.

Knowing Sarah, she was here to help someone, and he didn't want to get in the way.

Chapter 24

RICHARD BROCK TOOK THE call as the lead of the VIP Protective Detail (VIPPD) of the RCMP that worked to safeguard Canadian and foreign dignitaries at home and abroad. They were an elite branch of the RCMP's Protective Policing Service, Canada's equivalent of America's Secret Service, protecting their president.

Today's task was simple: ensure Canada's Minister of National Defense, John Williams, arrived safely at the Metro Convention Centre, delivered his one-hour speech, and then exited safely before being escorted to his private jet and flown back to Ottawa.

But today's task had gone to shit in the past few minutes, as Richard was informed that another bomb had been detonated in the city. They had moved to a conference room on the second floor to debate logistics.

The question was: should the speech go on as scheduled, which was what the defense minister wanted, or should it be canceled?

"Keep the diamond in the vault," Defense Minister Williams said. "Remove the artwork. Take away all the temptation for these thugs, and then guard the perimeter." Williams threw up his hands. "It can't be too hard to maintain a perimeter. No one in or out except our guests."

Richard nodded. "Yes, sir. But, if a threat to this building—"

"I'm not running with my tail between my legs because someone blew up a bomb ten or twenty city blocks from here." He stomped over to the window and stared outside. "Look, they're already blocking off the streets out front. This is good."

"But, sir. We have a contingency plan in case a threat is imminent —"

Williams spun around and glared at Richard. "Brock, what kind of minister of defense do I look like if I can't be defended?"

"Yes, sir."

"Do whatever you have to do in your playbook, but keep here, and keep me alive."

"Yes, sir."

The defense minister turned back to stare out the window.

Lead agent Richard Brock stepped out into the corridor and stared at his four highly trained men. There were four more, but they were guarding the doors at each end of the corridor.

"He has ordered us to remain in the building."

His men moved closer, listening intently.

"He won't leave because of that campus explosion. He won't leave for a bomb threat." Richard suppressed an exasperated shake of his head because he didn't want to look insubordinate. "We remain on-site at all costs, but be prepared."

"For what, sir?" Jenkins stepped forward. "You think he's the target?"

"I do not, but if this goes south fast, and we have to evacuate, then we evacuate. We're tasked with keeping the minister alive, which means going against his direct order to do so. He wants to stay, so we stay. But if staying puts his life in danger, I'm making the final decision about his safety, not him. Understood."

His men nodded, each one repeating, "Understood."

"Relieve the men at the doors. I'll call the coordinator and see if the speeches are still on or if any of the other guests are off-premises."

Brock's phone rang. He tapped the earbud. "Go ahead."

"We've got a bomb threat, sir."

"Excuse me?" Richard Brock said into the phone loud enough so his men would hear him. He held up a finger for them to stop, then waved it for them to come back. "Can you repeat that?"

"We're investigating now. It may be a hoax, as there are protestors out front. With all the bombs going off yesterday, someone may be calling in a copycat."

"What makes you say that?" Brock asked.

"Sir, the building was swept yesterday. Routine security procedures are in place due to the dignitaries' arrival. It has been locked down for almost a week. If there's a device inside this building, it would've been planted weeks ago and somehow remained virtually undetected all this time. An unlikely scenario."

"I can't risk the minister of defense's life on a theory of *unlikely*, sir."

"I understand that." The caller's voice hardened. "We are sweeping the building again."

"I'll inform the minister." He clicked off.

"Gentlemen, we have a bomb threat in this building now. It looks real, and it looks imminent. Prepare to evacuate. Tell the others. I'll inform the minister."

Brock spun on his heels and knocked on the conference room door.

"Come," the minister shouted from the other side.

Brock stepped inside and slammed the door shut. "It's time to evacuate, sir."

Williams raised a finger and jabbed it in the air. "I thought I told you I wasn't leaving. Even if there is a bomb threat, isn't this building secure? Didn't they say everyone was vetted, checked, and double-checked?"

"Yes, sir. But I'm afraid this bomb threat isn't only a threat."

Williams's brows touched above his nose as his face scrunched. "How would they know something like that? If they've located the device, simply send in the bomb squad."

"Sir, someone along the chain of command has confirmed we are less than a minute away before this device goes off, but there's something else."

"What's that?" Williams crossed his arms over his chest. The ego of the man was often untenable. He wanted to deliver a brief speech in front of the other world leaders to get his name on the map. The little Canada on the international playground, always following in the military shadow of their southern neighbor, had damaged Williams's ego in a way that could never be fixed. So, his little speeches on strategy and the military situation abroad always bolstered him and made him feel better.

"The bomber named you as the target."

Minister of Defense John Williams's face paled as the realization of what Brock had just said settled in over him.

"Me?" he asked, his voice cracking on that one small word. "Why me?"

Brock nodded, happy the minister bought his lie. "I'm sorry, sir, but we must leave."

Williams turned away, likely to hide his embarrassment at almost pissing his pants, and stared down at the crowd on Front Street.

"What will happen to all those people?"

"My concern is you, sir, not them. It's unfortunate, but I can't protect everyone. Now, please, we must be on our way."

Williams didn't move from the window.

Brock checked his watch. Half a minute had gone by. Every second they wasted was another second against making it out alive.

"Sir?"

"I said," he shouted without moving away from the window, "I'm not going anywhere—"

Something rumbled outside, then the window blew inward, showering the minister of defense in bits of glass. He scrambled backward, bumped into the conference table, then dropped out of sight behind it.

"Sir!" Brock shouted, running toward him.

The sound of the explosion hit him as he took his first step toward Williams.

Brock leaped around the end of the table and grasped the defense minister by the arm. When he helped him to his feet, the man's face and neck were spattered with drops of blood.

"Sir, can you see okay?" The man was blinking and trying to rub at his eyes with his right hand. Brock leaned back to survey the man for further injuries. "Sir, bits of glass have embedded themselves into your face and arms, but nothing appears to be deep enough to hit an artery or need stitches."

Something else exploded outside, making more glass break behind him.

"Sir, we *must* evacuate the building," Brock shouted. "*Now!*"

Defense Minister Williams nodded. "Go," he said, even as he got one eye open, blood oozing from the other. "Get me out of here."

Brock led him forcefully around the end of the conference room table and out through the door as alarms throughout the building lit up.

"Evacuate now." He barked the two words loud enough to be heard over the alarms. Several of his men gaped at the sight of the defense minister. "Toward the parking garage of the neighboring hotel. Go *NOW!*"

No one questioned his decision, yet Brock waited for the minister to speak up.

Like American football, his team formed a shield in front of him and led the way, prepared to block any interference.

"Why not out front?" Williams asked close to his ear. "My armored car is parked out front."

"Sir, your vehicle is gone, destroyed. Whoever is after you went to great lengths, and now you must hide in the garage until we can secure you something nondescript."

Jenkins, Brock's second, looked back at Minister Williams quickly. Brock was able to read the surprise in his eyes. They'd never seen the minister of defense covered in blood.

"He was standing at the window, looking out into the street," Brock offered as an explanation. "The window blew inward."

Whether Jenkins heard him or not, he nodded while holding a door for them.

They hit the stairwell and jogged downward as fire alarms raged much louder in the enclosed space.

A pile-up of people on the first floor slowed their advance.

"Move, move, move," Brock shouted at his men.

Two of them shuffled people aside—manhandled them—and made a path for Jenkins to lead Brock, who still clutched at the defense minister's arm, down to the garage level.

Then his men were lost to a flow of human bodies attempting to exit quickly, hoping to get out before the whole place blew up.

Brock glanced back once over his shoulder and saw Jenkins with two others, but the rest of his team was lost.

The fire alarm sirens canceled any chance of him hearing their call for him, or vice versa, so he set his primary focus on getting the minister into the parking garage.

Jenkins jumped the railing on the final turn, landing two steps in front of Brock and the minister—whose face was a mask of red now as the minor forehead cuts were bleeding profusely—and ripped open the door to the first level of the underground parking.

"There!" Brock shouted, nodding at the white delivery van parked ten feet away. "Get inside the back. I'll direct the driver."

"Yessir," Jenkins shouted, the words blurring into one with the volume down here.

They hobbled toward the van, approaching from the rear.

Small plumes of smoke emanated from the exhaust, telling him all he needed to know. There was a driver inside, and likely not moving because of the fire alarm.

It was perfect.

Just as Jenkins reached the back door and ripped it open, the brake lights lit up. But then he turned and helped Brock lift the defense minister inside.

Three more of his men formed a semi-circle around them as they got the minister settled in the back, then Jenkins hopped up, followed by the three men.

Brock pulled out his weapon. "I'll go have a talk with the driver. Get everyone secure. I can't guarantee how bumpy it'll get. Also, turn off your phones and refrain from communicating with anyone. We don't know if we're being tracked."

"Roger that."

Brock shut the back door as they were all pulling out their phones. He twisted the handle, effectively locking it from the outside.

No one was getting out of the back until he let them out.

Then he walked along the side of the truck toward the passenger seat, flicking off the safety.

The driver would do as he wished, or the driver would die, and Brock would drive.

It didn't matter to him.

His job was done.

Chapter 25

SARAH HELD THE PHONE in her hand as she waited, the engine running. She'd kept all the windows up in the cab to avoid smelling the exhaust, hoping the asshole would call her and tell her what to do next.

She was unarmed, unaware, and unsure of what the hell was going on. Her sister's presence was close; she could feel it, giving her a sense of peace, which translated to Sarah that she was exactly where she was supposed to be.

Did that mean being in the driver's seat of a delivery truck, waiting on a package that would likely involve her in some criminal activity, was precisely where she was supposed to be?

"I have no backup plan, Vivian." She hadn't totally gotten used to speaking out loud to her sister, but sometimes she felt it was the only way Vivian truly heard her. "No one knows where I am, and there's no way for me to get out of this—"

Something made a huge bang outside the underground parking. Even with the engine running, she was sure she heard glass breaking somewhere.

Several buildings in the area featured glass façades, so glass breaking made sense if a bomb went off.

She leaned down to check her mirrors, then stared out at the road, which was lit up like a movie screen from the sun, the rectangular opening at the end giving her the impression of a drive-in theater.

People ran by the opening. Then, more people were running.

Sirens in the building came on—the fire alarm, and she glanced down at the phone.

Nothing. No call.

She checked the battery percentage. It had less than twenty percent.

"You'd better call me and tell me what to do, or I'll fucking walk out of here," she said, her eyes not leaving the phone.

Threats of blowing shit up if she walked away were over if that's exactly what the asshole had done out front.

She looked up at the people running down Lower Simcoe Street, some with blood on them.

"You will die for this," she whispered.

She stayed a moment longer because she wanted to tell him herself when he called her back. Besides, where would she walk to? Why not take the truck and drive to the police station, where she could give them the phone and explain everything?

She wanted to find out if that vagrant was still alive, too. Or was that a lie to keep her compliant?

People were spilling into the underground parking area from the stairs, running for their cars. She was parked with her nose aimed at the exit. As long as no one clogged the exit, she had a clear run out of the area.

Still no call.

Could that GPS tracker *see* her inside so much concrete? It couldn't find her under that bridge earlier. Did he *know* she was in there?

She set the phone down and put her foot on the brake to put it into gear and get the hell out of there—it was time to leave.

Then the truck moved like something had bumped into it softly.

Someone was doing something at the back.

She leaned down to check both side mirrors, but saw nothing. Whoever it was, they were entirely hidden from view.

The back door slammed shut.

She grabbed the door handle, her heart racing. Did the bomber just toss a device in the back?

A man moved along the passenger side, advancing on the cab, his shoulder rubbing the truck as he moved forward. Something was clutched close to his chest.

If this were the bomber, she'd kill him.

Sarah placed the cell phone between her legs on the seat, then gripped the steering wheel with both hands as the passenger door ripped open.

The man hopped up into the passenger seat. "Drive," he said, like a military man barking out an order. "Now!" He revealed what was in his hand.

A gun.

"Where?" Her mind raced with questions. Was this the guy on the phone earlier? Was he the bomber? His voice didn't match. Did he just load the diamond and was now forcing her to be part of his heist?

"Hit the gas, or I'll shoot you and drive out of here myself." The man raised the gun until it touched her right breast, then he angled it slightly so the bullet would tear a hole through her heart and lungs.

Sarah dropped the truck into gear and hit the gas.

A man jumped into the center of the road up ahead, but she couldn't see his face as he stood at the threshold between the outside sunlight and the darker interior.

The passenger lowered his window, stuck his gun out, and fired twice at the man standing in the way.

The man jerked like he got hit. Bent over, he stumbled to the side.

"Run him over if he doesn't move," the man ordered.

Sarah pushed the gas harder.

At the last second, she smacked the horn, and the man jumped out of the way.

But Sarah caught a glimpse of his face—Parkman.

Then they were on Lower Simcoe Street and heading south, and Sarah wanted to vomit at the thought that Parkman was shot, and she almost ran him over.

How the hell did he know to be there? Why would he try to stop her?

As much as it consoled her to know he had her back, she was sick with worry now. It took everything in her soul to keep driving and not pull over to see how Parkman was doing.

Well, everything in her soul and a passenger with a gun that was back to pointing it at her right breast.

"Get on the Gardiner Expressway and drive toward the airport."

"Again?" Sarah said, exasperated with all the driving.

The man stared at her. "Do you know who I am? Or better yet, who is in the back of this delivery vehicle?"

"I have no fucking clue." She took the ramp to the Gardiner a little too heavy, the delivery truck almost going up on two wheels.

The man pulled out an ID wallet, then flipped it open. "RCMP. Protective policing. We're providing personal protection for Canada's Minister of Defense, John Williams. When that bomb went off, we had to evacuate immediately. The defense minister's armored car is out front."

Sarah caught a glimpse of the man's ID, then averted her gaze back to the road. "You've got to be fucking kidding me." It was more a statement than a question. "Then why shoot at that man back in the garage?"

"We were under an imminent threat. If someone stands in our way, they're removed. It's that simple. Those were warning shots."

"It looked like you hit him."

The man shrugged. "Could've been a ricochet." He lowered the gun to his lap. "You did this country a great service today. Thank you."

The phone rang between her legs. "Shit, the guy on the other end of this phone won't be too happy."

"Answer it and tell him the RCMP has commandeered you. We'll cover all damages and loss of wages. Just don't tell him where we're going."

Sarah grabbed the phone and hit the button. "Yeah?"

"Where are you?"

"On the Gardiner, heading west." She pulled the phone away from her ear. "He can GPS the truck. I can't lie." She put the phone back to her ear.

"Did you pick up a package?" the bomber asked.

"Yes, you could say that."

"And you have someone in the front with you?"

"Yes." She snuck a look over at him.

"Let me speak to him."

Sarah held out the phone. "He wants to speak with you."

The man took the phone. "Brock here."

The RCMP officer listened, nodding a few times, then extended the phone to Sarah. "He wants to speak with you again."

Sarah took the phone. "Well done," the bomber said. "You saved the minister's life. Follow his instructions and get those people to safety. Then your job is complete."

"What?" Sarah asked, completely baffled, but the line was dead.

She set the phone down between her legs again.

What the fuck is going on? The bomber asshole is one of the good guys?

Chapter 26

PARKMAN SLIPPED OFF HIS belt and tied it above the elbow. The wound was minor, nothing more than a graze, but the bleeding wouldn't stop, and now he'd need stitches.

Once the belt was secure, he called Detective Heath's number. It rang ten times before he hung up and redialed.

"Detective Heath," came through the phone on the second ring this time.

"It's Sarah." Parkman swallowed breaths in gulps as the pain in his arm increased.

"What? I can't hear you with all those alarms in the background."

"One second," Parkman shouted into the phone, then got to his feet and shuffled outside, where he turned down the street to saunter away from the building and that incessant alarm.

"Is this Parkman?" Heath asked.

"Yes, and it was Sarah. She's driving a white delivery van—"

"Plate number?"

"I didn't get it."

"Wait, what? How's that? You were a cop, and now you're a private investigator. How do you not go for the plate like a magnet?"

"I got shot."

"*What?*"

"Well, grazed is a better word, but I'm bleeding too much." Parkman was far enough away from the sirens that he stopped to sit on a concrete ledge. "It was Sarah driving. The passenger shot at me."

"Driving what?"

Parkman rested his head back against the concrete wall and closed his eyes. "A white delivery van. Same size as a UPS truck. It said 'speedy' something on the side. Like 'speedy courier,' I think."

"That helps." The sarcasm was evident in his tone. "There could be one truck like that or a hundred. I'll look them up and see if we catch a break. Where are you going?"

Parkman's heart rate was calming, the throbbing in his arm still constant. "Nowhere. Maybe to sleep."

"I meant, which hospital are you going to? I'm with Meredith right now in the convention center. Once we're done talking, I'll come to you."

"I don't know which hospital." The effort to pull his head off the wall exceeded his expectations. He stared up the street. "I'll go to those ambulances. They will help. I'll call when I'm all stitched up."

"Stitched up? It sounds like you were stitched up. Listen to me. I'll be down there shortly. Then we'll go find Sarah. Deal?"

"Yeah. Deal."

"Parkman, you don't sound good."

He glanced down at his arm. The belt had loosened, and blood flowed freely from his arm. Was there an artery in that spot? Was he bleeding out?

The belt didn't have holes that far up, as he had tightened it around an arm and not a waist, so, of course, it would loosen. He pulled it tight again, stuck the end in his mouth, bit down hard to secure it, and straightened his head.

That did it. The bleeding slowed to a small stream.

He pushed up to his feet, slipped the phone into his back pocket, and put one foot in front of the other as he started up the street.

A wave of dizziness hit him. He took a step to correct it, slipped on the curb, then dropped to the pavement face-first.

The belt popped out of his mouth when he grunted with the impact.

His eyes closed.

He was so tired and in so much pain.

Perhaps a small sleep would help block all the pain.

Just a few minutes and he'd feel better ...

Chapter 27

SARAH HELD THE WHEEL tight, thinking this had been her fate all along. If so, no wonder Vivian wasn't getting involved, as she was now working for the good guys.

But there were a few things that still didn't make sense.

As she checked her mirrors and took the ramp to drive north on the 427, she glanced over at the RCMP man—Brock. He'd holstered his weapon and was typing something into his phone.

"Do you know that man who called five minutes ago?"

Brock looked up from his phone, then nodded. "He's my brother by blood. We've been working together to ferret out the mole in the RCMP."

"The mole?"

Brock set his phone down and stared out the windshield. "Someone has been trying to kill the minister of defense for some time. Someone on the inside." He glanced at her. "They got close today."

"Then why did the guy on the phone, your brother, make me run from the RCMP at the train station? Why threaten that he'd blow shit up if I didn't?"

"He had to do something, and since we can't trust anyone who works for the RCMP, he couldn't have you trailed by them."

She stared forward, changing lanes to avoid driving behind a large truck, lost in her thoughts.

That all seemed to make sense. But were they connected to the heist last night? She saw four men in balaclavas. Two were confirmed dead in that warehouse fire. Their van was gone.

She glanced back at Brock. Could these *brothers* be the other two?

"Where were you last night?" She stared forward again as she made the wide turn over the 401 to remain heading north on the 427.

"Setting up a perimeter at the hotel to protect the minister of defense." He glanced at her, a frown on his face. "Why?"

"Your boys in the back will verify that, I'm sure."

"Why does where I was matter to you?"

"Something doesn't add up."

"None of this is your concern. You're just a driver, a fill-in. Once you drop us off, you can go home. I've got a minister to protect, a job to do."

He was lying. She could feel it.

His goal was her compliance. If she felt hope blooming that this would all be over soon, why would she do something reckless?

Without Vivian whispering in her ear, she had to go with her gut, and her gut said this was all wrong.

"Take this exit," Brock said, pointing to the right.

"Let me guess. The International Centre on Airport Road."

"Yes, where my brother had you drive earlier. If we needed you to extract us, he needed to know there'd be no issues with the location."

She slowed and stopped at a red light, putting on her blinker. "Why me? And how would you know you would need an extraction in the first place?"

"Why all the questions?" Brock's tone suggested genuine interest.

She turned to stare at him. "Because I don't trust the authorities, which means I don't trust you."

Someone honked a horn. Sarah turned forward and saw that the light was green.

"That's probably a healthy approach to life, but I'm sure you'll feel really good when cops respond to your house after calling them about a prowler, eh?" He scoffed. "All these people living privileged lives, going to afternoon barbecues, seeing a movie on a Friday night, sleeping in on a Sunday, and taking vacations at leisure, easily shit on the authorities when one cop does one thing wrong." He shook his head, typing on his phone again.

"You don't know me. My distrust runs deeper."

"Whatever. Talk to your therapist, not me. Just drive the fucking truck or get shot, and I'll drive. Protecting the minister is all I care about."

So much for instilling hope. They were back to being enemies, which left her with nothing to say.

When she got to the building where she'd parked earlier, she pulled in and slowed the vehicle, glancing at Brock for further instructions.

"Drive around to the back and park by hall number four." Brock pointed to where he wanted her to go. "My brother will meet us there."

Sarah did as she was told, her stomach roiling as this might be the end of the road. On the final turn toward Hall Four, it was a dead end. In this section, the large building formed a rectangular alcove, hiding the truck, everyone, and everything from public view. Even the parking lot was elevated, which blocked random passersby from seeing this area. Lining the back of the property were train tracks, so it was improbable anyone would happen upon them unless they were working in Hall Four today.

"It doesn't look like anyone is having a convention here today."

Brock looked at her as she slowed, then stopped the truck. "Are you trying to be funny?"

She smiled at him and shrugged. "Just making an observation. The parking lot is empty. That led me to conclude no one was here. Well, except for security. I'm sure there's security in a building like this."

"None of that concerns you. Your job is done. Once my brother gets here"—he tapped his phone to check the time—"in a few minutes, I'll introduce you to the boys in the back and the minister of defense, and then we'll call you a cab." He smiled back at her. "That about work for you? Will that instill trust in the authorities again?"

She frowned. "Nothing will ever do that for me. I work with them out of need, but I always watch my back."

"Work with them? What's that mean? Are you working for them now or in general?"

Resting her hands on the top of the steering wheel, she stared out at the parking lot. "In general."

Brock leaned forward so he could stare at her face. "You work for the police? In *general*? Who the hell are you?"

She averted her gaze to stare back at him. "In the past, yes."

"Were you working for the police last night? How about yesterday? Are you working for them now?"

She shook her head slowly. "I'm working for myself now."

The sound of an engine came to them, and they both looked forward as another delivery truck, virtually identical to the one they were in, went around the corner and parked nose to nose.

Brock typed something into his phone again, then slipped it into a pocket on his jacket.

"You're a confusing woman," he said. "Doesn't matter, though. We get out now—time to meet everybody. Be polite, Sarah. Be polite."

Sarah opened her door and stepped down. Did she offer him her name at any point?

Vivian, I'm still asking you—what the hell is going on?

Chapter 28

DETECTIVE HEATH WAS LOSING his patience and his mind. Locating Parkman had become a logistical nightmare with over a dozen ambulances on site and several already gone to neighboring hospitals.

"Who's in charge here?" he shouted as he roamed through the multitude of people crowding around the wounded and the wailing on sidewalks and curbs.

Then, twenty meters away, he saw two men he recognized and shoved his way to them.

"Inspector Sean Richmond and his partner, Inspector Chris Stone. I'm sorry to see you two here."

They turned away from a screen where they were watching a video, looked at him, and then exchanged glances. "Not a friendly way to welcome the two RCMP inspectors who got you fully reinstated when we worked our deal with Sarah."

"*Sarah* got me reinstated. She added it to the deal."

"Potatoes, tom*ah*tos." Richmond waved him off. "Go back to your detachment and let the big boys do their investigation."

"The big boys?" Heath's tone edged into anger.

Both inspectors turned back to face him. "Is there a problem?" Stone asked.

"The *big boys* lost Sarah. The *big boys* have screwed this operation from the beginning. And the *big boys* are screwing it up by not involving us little guys."

Stone crossed his arms. "How's that?"

"I know the truck Sarah's in because Parkman saw it. I know about the mole in your ranks and might even know who it is now. I also know why Meredith's jewelry store was burgled."

"Meredith? Who's that?"

"My point exactly."

"If you've got a point," Richmond said, leaning forward, "spit it out or fuck off. We're busy."

"My point is, Meredith picked the stores where the fake Cullinan diamonds would be kept, hers included. Then she informed the protective policing service of the RCMP, as they required a list. No one else knew."

They exchanged that look again. "Should we ask some probing questions here? Or will you just continue?"

Heath blew out a breath and controlled the urge to slap them both. "The only people who knew where the diamonds were were two men with the RCMP. Since Meredith didn't like that, she told them the real diamond was in her store so no one would attack the other stores unnecessarily and to protect the real Cullinan, which was in a vault one block from here."

"So, let me get this straight," Stone said, tapping a finger on the bottom of his chin. "Someone high up on the protective detail, someone working with VIPPD, which are the lads who protect people like prime ministers and visiting dignitaries, risked everything to steal a diamond? That's your story?"

"There's a mole within the RCMP, and he's connected to Meredith. That's why her store was targeted. After I spoke with her, that's what we learned." Heath shook his head in exasperation. "Whatever. Why am I telling you idiots? You'll just fuck it up like you lost Sarah."

Stone waved his hand in dismissal, tilting his head back and squinting his eyes. "Run along, little boy. We have work to do."

They turned their backs to him, tapped the tablet's screen, and went back to watching a video that looked like some sort of security footage.

Fighting with them would get him nowhere. He needed to find Parkman to ensure he was okay, then figure out what to do next.

He strode away, yanking out his phone to see if he had missed a call. He hadn't.

The thought of calling half a dozen hospitals looking for a man with one name sounded maddening. Why didn't he get Parkman's first name? When he looked up Sarah online, any reference to Parkman only used the one name.

With this many people gathered around, talking, tending to the wounded, people coming and going, he was feeling overstimulated. He needed to step away from the center of it all and think.

At the corner, he turned down a side street and took a deep breath, the mid-afternoon sun drawing sweat from him, dampening his shirt.

His phone rang, and he pulled it to him. There was no caller ID.

"Detective Heath," he barked into it.

"It's Sergeant Miller."

"What can I do for you, Sarge?"

"We may have a problem."

Heath moved farther down the road to hear her better. "What sort of problem?"

"Where are you right now?"

"Outside the Metro Convention Centre."

"We have new intel, but this is RCMP territory."

"Them again?"

"It doesn't have to go to them. You could work it on your own. I just can't authorize anything as they're currently mobilizing a team."

Heath stopped walking and stared at the bridge in front of him, seeing nothing. "What's this intel you have?"

"Can anyone hear me?"

"No, I'm alone."

"We think Canada's Minister of Defense, John Williams, has been kidnapped."

"What? From where?"

"From the convention center. Camera footage was sent to us by their security team before the RCMP seized everything. The minister was taken out through the hotel's parking area. He was covered in blood, as if someone had stabbed him and shoved him into the rear of a white delivery van. And guess who the camera saw behind the wheel."

"Sarah Roberts."

There was a little gasp. "How would you know something like that?"

"Because Parkman was there. He tried to stop them, and the passenger shot at him."

"Well, that woman seems to be quite involved in everything. She ditched her RCMP tail and has now kidnapped a high-ranking official. She'll burn for this one. We have every available officer out looking for that van."

"Holy fuck, I have to find Parkman."

"You'll do no such thing. Get in your car and find that van before the RCMP do. I want the collar on this. I can't wait to see Sarah's face when I read the charges to her."

"I'm on it," Heath said into the phone, then ended the call, figuring Sarah had nothing to do with any kidnapping or abduction. His "I'm on it" referred to him being on the case, but not Sarah's case.

A second later, he was running for his car.

"SARAH," THE OTHER VAN driver said upon seeing her. "It's so good to meet you finally."

His voice was definitely the same as the man she'd been calling the bomber. To confirm that, she asked, "Are you the man behind this phone?" She held it up for him to see.

He nodded. "I've been directing you to my brother to help out the good guys, and you did a fine job."

"Then why do I want to jump on you and pound your face into the concrete? You threatened to use bombs on innocent people. How could you possibly be connected with the good guys?"

He glanced at his brother, and the smile on his face made her want to hurt him badly. When he fixed his gaze back on her, the smile faltered, then vanished.

"If I asked you nicely, would you have helped?"

Someone banged the back door of the delivery van Sarah had driven. All three of them ignored the sound.

"If anyone read your profile," the man continued, "they'd quickly learn that you don't do what you're told. You don't listen to authority. You have always done it your way. Then there's respect. If you respect someone, you'll do things for them, but we've hardly had the time to get to know one another, let alone earn any sort of respect."

"So you threatened to kill innocent people to *make* me drive your truck?"

He stuck his hands out at his side. "It worked, didn't it?" That smile was back. "And you saved the minister. It's been leaked to the media, too."

"Leaked to the media?" She couldn't contain the hysterical sound of her voice. "They hate me."

"Sarah, that parking garage had cameras. The media will write their spin on things, but they caught you driving the truck out with this cargo." He pointed at the truck. "Because they saw my brother here"— he slapped Brock on the shoulder—"escorting the minister out of the building."

"It's a win all around," Brock said.

Sarah crossed her arms. "So why are we hiding out in a parking lot near the airport? Why didn't we just drive to the local cop shop or RCMP detachment?"

"You don't listen well." Brock pointed at his brother. "I told you about the mole when we left the downtown area, and Kramer here has been helping me to find them. If we drove to an RCMP detachment, we'd be inviting another attack by the mole."

They were lying. Something else was wrong. A lot of what they said fit, but it didn't fit exactly.

"You said you had footage of the vagrant, but I never saw it."

Kramer snapped his fingers. "Oh, right." He moved closer to her and produced a cell phone. "This was taken by a bystander and uploaded to TikTok. The media grabbed it and shared it."

Sarah watched as he scrolled to a video, then pressed play.

When she saw Parkman enter the camera screen, she didn't react. Parkman spoke to the vagrant, then took the shoebox from him, examined it a moment before placing it in a garbage can, and shuffling the can into a corner. By the time Parkman moved back to the vagrant, the black metal garbage receptacle had exploded.

It took everything inside her not to grab the guy, shove him to the ground, and stomp on his head. There were two of them, and they were armed, so she had to wait for the right moment.

"I sent that man in to make sure the vagrant wasn't hurt," Kramer said, that annoying smile back on his face. "See? We're the good guys."

Her stomach twisted with what to do next. She was trapped. Running wasn't an option. They'd shoot her in the back before she got ten feet.

They were lying, but why? What was their gain? She was already their prisoner, doing as they demanded.

Unless something worse was coming.

Just hang in a little longer, Sarah, Vivian whispered.

Sarah jerked when her sister popped up in her head. *Where have you been?*

You need to be here at this time. It's the only way to save countless lives.

Sarah uncrossed her arms and moved a few feet away from the brothers as they whispered something to each other.

What about my life? Am I going to live through this?

That's not something I can see.

You can't see it? What the hell does that mean? I always thought that with your help, my safety was a given.

There was no answer for a moment.

Vivian? Sarah screamed the name in her head.

It's never a given, but I'll do what I can to help. There was a pause. *When I can.*

How comforting.

Like a gust of wind dying down, Sarah felt her sister whoosh out of her head, leaving her with that empty feeling.

It was perfect timing, anyway. The people in the back of the delivery van sounded agitated. Someone was banging on the wall continuously now.

"C'mon, Sarah." Brock waved at her. "Come meet the crew."

Something about this still didn't feel right, but she felt slightly better having had a moment with her sister.

She followed the brothers to the back of the truck, where Brock opened it.

A heavyset older man sat near the front, his back against the wall leading to the truck's cab. What struck her was the amount of blood on his face and hands.

"What happened to him?" Sarah asked, barely loud enough for anyone to hear.

Standing over the bloody man were four more men dressed similarly to Brock.

"Jenkins, no phones were used?" Brock asked.

A man standing to the right shook his head. "No phones."

Brock nodded and pointed at him. "Everyone, meet Sarah. She's the one who got us out of there without harm. That man on the floor is Canada's Minister of Defense, John Williams, and to his right is my second in command, Bryce Jenkins."

"Are you mercenaries?" Sarah asked. "Or real RCMP guys?"

Jenkins's brow scrunched up. "Mercs? Where did that question come from?"

"Any of you own balaclavas?" she asked, turning to stare at Kramer.

When their gaze met, he knew she knew.

The game was up.

Kramer pulled out a weapon and flicked off the safety all in one fluid motion.

The gun had gone off when Sarah backed up one step.

Then Brock pulled his weapon and fired as well.

Sarah's knees gave out, and she dropped to the pavement hard amid the cacophony.

Chapter 30

Once in his unmarked cruiser, Detective Heath googled Aaron Stevens's dojo, then called the number.

"What can I help you with?" a man answered.

"Isn't this a place of business?" Heath asked.

"Sure. What do you want?"

"Answering the phone that way could cost you business. Don't you answer, like, Aaron's Dojo, how can I direct your call?"

"If I wanted advice on how to run a business from the local police, I'll be sure to call you."

"Oh, shit. Call display."

"Yeah, you didn't block your number, and we all know the name Heath today. So, I'll ask again. What do you want?"

"Who is this?"

"Does it matter?" There was a pause. Then, "My name is Daniel. Now, will you tell me what you need, or will I hang up?"

"Sarah's in trouble."

"When is she not in trouble?"

Heath ran a hand through his hair. "That's an odd response from a friend."

"True, but if we dropped everything and ran every time Sarah was in trouble … well, let's just say we wouldn't have a life of our own. Those aren't my words; they're Aaron's. And because Alex is still recovering from the last time Sarah was in trouble, Benjamin is dead now, and Aaron is taking care of his daughter, I'm the only one at the dojo doing classes. Over twenty students are learning discipline and technique on the mats in the other room. Sarah's a big girl and can handle shit better than all of us put together. So, if there's nothing else to discuss, I'm returning to my class."

"Parkman was shot."

Another pause, with only breathing coming through on the other end.

"Did you hear me?" Heath asked.

"Yeah, I heard you." Daniel's voice was softer, more caring. "How bad?"

"I have no idea. I was on the phone with him, then he faded out. I don't know if he made it to a hospital or if he's lying in an alley somewhere bleeding out."

"Holy fuckshit."

"That's what I was thinking."

"Why call me?"

"I was looking for Aaron, but if he's got his daughter …"

"I can take care of Willow if you need Aaron."

"That thing you said a moment ago. You said they were Aaron's words. Will he help me?"

Daniel cleared his throat. "Doesn't hurt to ask, but Sarah is Willow's mother. As much as he hates what she does, Aaron isn't an asshole if she needs him. He'll go to bat for her."

"Then I need Aaron."

"Why him specifically? I mean, I have to tell him something convincing because he'll just tell me you have hundreds of cops to help Sarah. So, why him?"

"Because Sarah is in deep shit and is out there alone."

"What kind of deep shit?"

"We're wasting time, but I'll explain it all as succinctly as possible." Heath told him about Sarah getting picked up for abducting René Atchison off the street, then running from the cops. Then, her negotiated release, how she lost the RCMP tail, and finally, how the cameras caught her driving the getaway vehicle with the Minister of Defense in the back. "So, after those officers died at the bomb sites, I suspect every cop this side of Alaska is hunting for her, and likely they've got shoot-to-kill orders." That last part was Heath putting on more peanut butter than palatable, but he needed people on Sarah's side. Otherwise, she'd go down for a long time if she lived through the next few days.

"Fuck me," Daniel breathed into the phone. "I'll get Aaron. Where can he find you?"

"Give him the number on your call display. I'm in my car, driving to the closest hospital. I need to find Parkman before someone else does."

"Hold on. I know a guy who can trace things like that in minutes. Wait, what time would it be in Italy at the moment?"

"Italy? Why does that matter?"

"Never mind, it's breakfast time there. He'll be awake by now." Heath detected movement on the other end of the line. "Someone will call you back. Keep your phone on and charged, but don't waste your time driving to hospitals aimlessly. My guy will call. He'll know where Parkman is in minutes."

"Okay," Heath said, feeling slightly out of his depth. "When should I expect—"

Daniel had already hung up.

Chapter 31

SARAH HAD COVERED HER head, but she lowered her hands after feeling no impacts from bullets—and no pain except from the pavement when she hit the ground hard on her tailbone.

The brothers stood over her, staring into the back of the delivery truck while someone moaned from within.

"What the fuck was that all about?" she mumbled, trying to get her shaky legs curled under her so she could stand. A moment ago, she was convinced Kramer would shoot her dead, making her insides jelly-like. The adrenaline that shot to her muscles now gave her an aftereffect similar to when someone ate too much sugar.

"You figured it out too soon," Kramer said, reloading his weapon. "We never meant to let Brock's men live, but when you asked about the balaclavas, we had to execute them so they wouldn't get suspicious." He clicked his weapon shut, then stared down at her. "It was us or them." That horrid smile again. "We chose them, naturally."

With her feet under her, Sarah pushed up and leaned against the back of the truck. Then she forced herself to look inside to see who was still moaning.

All four men she'd been introduced to a moment before were clearly dead. Blood was splattered across the van's interior, and bullet holes were scattered on the cheeks, foreheads, and throats of the men who dropped haphazardly like rag dolls about the floor. Only one man had been able to pull his gun, but it never got fired.

The moaning came from the minister, who was still scrunched up on the floor, his back to the wall, his head buried in his arms.

"Jump on up there, Sarah. We need you for something."

"Fuck that." She shook her head violently back and forth, then stopped as a wave of dizziness swept in. "I ain't going in there."

Brock moved fast. He was definitely the creepy one of the two because he was back with the gun against her breast, but this time it hurt, and she had to pull back.

"I will blow off this tit. I will give you a mastectomy right here in the parking lot. Then, as you writhe on the ground bleeding out and screaming, I will fuck you until you die." He jerked his head once toward the back of the van. "Avoid that sort of mess by jumping up in there. The second option is much easier and a lot less trouble."

She stared at him open-mouthed, then found her voice. "Holy shit, you're one twisted individual. When the time comes for me to kill you, you know I won't hesitate. You just made it something I look forward to."

"Likewise, now get in the fucking truck." The gun pressed into her breast again, hurting so much she swatted it away. When she stepped toward the back of the truck, Brock slapped her ass.

When she snapped back around to break the hand that touched her, the gun found its way to her eye. Brock tried to jam it into the socket. She had to rear back to save her vision and ended up stumbling backward into the back of the truck.

"I do what I want when I want," Brock said. "You and your kind are nothing more than a plaything, dead or alive. Be a nice girl and do what you're told, and I promise to violate you *after* I kill you."

"Comforting," she muttered through clenched teeth. *Oh, Vivian, please let me tear off his balls and decapitate this man.*

Sarah turned away from him, grabbed the side handle, then planted a foot and climbed up into the rear of the truck.

"Here, take this." Kramer tossed his weapon to her, and Sarah quickly caught it.

The weapon slipped into her palm as if it were made for her hand, and she pointed it at Brock.

"Fancy that." She gritted her teeth. "A dead man."

Brock lowered his weapon and smiled that highly creepy grin that gave her goosebumps.

An electronic snapping sound, like someone taking a photo, broke her focus on Brock.

When she turned to Kramer, he had a cell phone in his hand, and it was aimed at her.

"Thank you, Sarah. You're now wanted for the murder of four decorated RCMP officers who work for the VIPPD team."

"Yeah, whatever. I saw you reload this gun, and I'm sure it'll wipe that smile off your face." She aimed it at Brock and pulled the trigger without hesitation.

Nothing happened.

She checked the safety. It was off.

She aimed and pulled it again.

"There's nothing in that gun." Brock stared at her like a predator might. "My brother wasn't *loading* it. He was making sure that even the chamber was empty. But that gun is important now. It'll match ballistic reports to those dead bodies, and it'll have your prints on it, not to mention the lovely photos we have. And the cameras at the underground parking lot have you racing out with the minister of defense as your prisoner." Brock quirked one eyebrow. "You don't see how this is shaping up to look?"

Sarah examined the gun once more, saw that it was indeed empty, then rubbed it on her pant leg and dropped it to the floor of the truck.

"The minister will know the truth." She stared down at them, her gut-wrenching so much she felt sick now. "I have nothing to worry about."

Brock laughed and shook his head. "What makes you think the minister will live through this? Sarah, we want you to live. We really do. Because when this is all over, they'll find you holding the smoking gun over the dead body of the minister, and we'll be long gone, disappeared into the sunset and richer than Jeff Bezos. But we could also fuck you and kill you. That might be fun, too."

"Well," Kramer slapped his brother's arm, "maybe not as rich as Jeff Bezos, but close."

"Give me the phone so I can upload those photos with our demands."

Kramer handed the phone over. Then Brock stepped to the side.

"Come on down, Sarah," Kramer said. "Try anything stupid, and he'll shoot to maim." He glanced sidelong at his brother. "You don't want to be maimed around him. That would be like a wounded impala around a hungry tiger. He'll rip you apart from the vagina outward." Kramer extended a hand. "Trust me, I've seen him do it countless times. He's addicted to rape now."

Repulsed by everything she saw and heard, she understood why Vivian had recently remained silent. None of this would've gone over well if any of it had been whispered to her.

She hopped down and stood to the side, waiting for what would be next.

"Mr. Williams," Kramer called. "You're next. Get up and walk out of here. We are leaving these bodies behind."

The minister didn't move.

Brock stepped closer and stared in at the wounded man. "Minister Williams. Either come on your own two feet, or I'll come in there and drag you out by your few gray hairs. Then I'll cut off one of your hands or something." Brock glanced at Kramer. "Maybe I should cut off his tongue so he can swallow all his blood."

Kramer chuckled. "You are deliciously sick, my brother."

"Coming," the man mumbled. "I'm coming."

"Be aware, Mr. Williams," Brock said, "that since you won't live to see tomorrow, I have no issue cutting pieces off you. So, please, don't make me. Just do as you're told when you're told."

How could God make men like this? Or were they created by a greater evil? The psychopath versus sociopath argument.

The minister made it to the back of the truck. In the light of the afternoon sun, Sarah could see all the minor cuts that only broken glass could make.

Kramer helped him down—probably because Brock would likely shove him off the back.

The sound of an engine revving came to them, and instead of freezing on the spot to see who was coming, Kramer jumped up and grabbed the door, then smacked it closed and sealed it from the outside.

Whoever was coming wouldn't see the bodies now. They'd just see the brothers protecting a bloody old man and a woman.

The car came careening around the corner and aimed right at them.

A security vehicle.

Of course. There was no trade show today, but security guards were working.

Sarah wanted to wave the man off, warn him somehow, but it was too late. He was already pulling to a stop.

Brock moved in front of Kramer to shield him.

The vehicle's door opened, and the man who stepped out had to be seven feet tall. The guy was a monster, either that or an NBA player.

Wait, wasn't he the man she saw at the train station—watching her?

It all happened so fast that Sarah barely had time to register what came next.

Brock jumped to the side as the security guard raised a weapon he'd concealed behind his leg.

The gun fired rapidly, bullet after bullet entering Kramer's stomach. Then he adjusted his aim and shot Kramer in the legs.

A painful scream burst from Kramer as he slumped to the ground.

The security guard holstered his weapon as he moved to stand over Kramer. "You were going to kill me, motherfucker."

"Jack," Kramer said, blood bubbling up from his mouth. "Why?"

"Brock here called and told me your plan months ago." Jack kicked him. "You're one sick fuck."

"*I'm* sick?" Kramer whispered. "What?"

"Yeah, you're sick. Hire the three of us only to kill us, and you keep all the diamonds. We didn't even get the Cullinan." The security guard glanced over at Brock, then back to Kramer. "Now Brock and I will get the Cullinan, kill the minister, rape that bitch, and disappear. You? You'll just die like the pig you are."

Brock moved to stand over Kramer. "This idea, this plan you had, my brother, doesn't bring back our family. Our sister was raped and murdered by a Canadian soldier, yes. Our mother, too, well, after she was dead. But that happened because you weren't there. I've wanted to kill you ever since that day, but out of respect for our mother, I didn't want your blood on my hands."

Kramer tried to say something, but his breathing was becoming more ragged.

The minister clutched at Sarah's arm, leaning into her, and she let him.

"When you called me with this plan, I agreed," Brock continued, "then I let Jack here in on it, and we came up with this new plan." He swept his arm wide. "But you fucked it up with René. She was supposed to be the one who drove the truck. It was her body we were supposed to leave behind with the minister. Everyone would be convinced René was the insider for the jewelry store heist. The only thing you didn't fuck up was convincing the authorities to release Sarah and then getting her in that driver's seat." Brock clapped his hands twice. "I gotta hand it to you, my brother. When you had to come through, you came through. Now *we* will finish the job"—his hand waved between him and Jack—"our family gets their revenge, and you can head off to Heaven or wherever assholes go. If you see Mom, tell her I said hey."

Brock pulled a weapon and shot Kramer in the face three times, the man's head bouncing on the pavement with each impact as his cheeks caved inward.

Then both Brock and Jack turned to Sarah and the minister.

"Get in the back of the truck my brother drove. Now. Or die right here. I don't give a flying fuck." Brock cocked his weapon and aimed it at Sarah's face from three feet away.

She held up her hands and backed toward the truck.

The minister followed.

This wasn't going well at all.

For the first time in a long time, Sarah wondered if Aaron was right.

Why the hell was she involved in any of this? Then she remembered René Atchison and knew why.

She was here for the innocent lives out there. And she'd find a way out of this.

She had to.

Willow needed her.

Chapter 32

THE PHONE RANG FIVE minutes later, and Heath snatched it off his dashboard, answering it without looking at who was calling.

"Detective Heath."

"It's Aaron Stevens. You called, looking for me."

"Yeah, I might need help, or rather, Sarah might need help."

"Is there a time when she doesn't?"

"Excuse me?"

"Nothing, look, I've left my daughter with Daniel. What can I do?"

"First, help me find Parkman."

"Done."

"Meaning what? You found him, or you'll do it?"

"Found him. He was rushed to Toronto General. Minor surgery on an arm wound. Because he was shot, they reported it to the police. He's stuck there until the authorities arrive."

"Shit, I'm on my way." Heath cranked his engine, put it in gear, and hit the gas. "I'll get him out of there."

"What can I do?"

"Meet me there. We have to find Sarah and end this shit."

"When I get there, be prepared to tell me everything. Leave nothing out. You want my help, then I'm all in. That means you're all in, too. No games."

Heath hugged a corner, the car bouncing up on the curb. "Why does that sound like a threat?"

"Sarah's the mother of my daughter. If I work with you, you're on Sarah's side. This means it's not about arresting her or bringing her in. It's about helping her survive this ordeal."

"Yeah, yeah, I'm on your side. Sarah isn't doing all this. She's the only one trying to stop it."

"And what have the authorities been doing?"

"Cleaning up after her."

"So, the usual." There was a moment's pause. "I'll be there in thirty minutes."

The line died, and Heath jammed the gas pedal to the floor.

Chapter 33

THE BACK OF THE second delivery truck was set up like the interior of a small recreational vehicle. The walls were covered in paneling, eggshell white. Two short sofas faced each other with a gorgeous coffee table bolted to the floor. A drinks table with glasses placed in holders so nothing would move while the vehicle was on the road was quite impressive.

"Did you guys steal the show vehicle for an RV convention?" Sarah asked.

"Funny." Brock pushed her shoulder. "Get inside and help the minister up. Then we're on the move."

Sarah climbed in and turned to grab the minister's hand. Whether quiet by nature or subdued by the abduction and murder he'd witnessed, Sarah wasn't impressed by Canada's minister of defense. He wasn't *defending* anything so far.

He was overweight with a bulbous nose, likely from too much alcohol at evening galas held in the nation's capital. The hair on the top of his head had died decades ago, and the thin sides were used in a terrible, thin combover.

The man was the stereotypical appointed government employee getting fat off the hog while holding office. She had her opinions and many things to say about those sorts of people, but he didn't deserve to die simply because of his position. If what she heard was true—that Canadian soldiers had raped and killed Brock's and Kramer's family—then she understood their need for justice, revenge.

But then, those men in the back of the other truck, all four VIPPD members, didn't deserve their fate, either.

She helped Williams take a seat on the couch, and she dropped onto the other one as the back door slid shut. The front doors opened and closed, and then they were moving.

"We'll get out of this," she said to him.

He met her gaze, his eyes bloodshot. "I'll kill him with my bare hands."

"That's anger talking. They've got the guns."

"I trusted Agent Brock with my life; now he may take it." Williams leaned forward. "That man was vetted by the best the Canadian government has. How was I supposed to know he was a rogue officer, bent and bound on my paying a debt for something soldiers did in the field years ago?"

Sarah shook her head. "I'm inclined to believe the debt is a side gain."

"A side gain?" The contempt in his voice was almost tangible.

"This is about a large diamond heist, and you're their negotiating piece, like chess. You're being maneuvered into position."

"I'll be no one's pawn."

"Not sure you've got a choice at the moment."

"Miss, there's always a choice."

Now Sarah leaned forward. "What does that mean? Have you come up with something you'd like to share?"

The minister glanced around the back of the truck as they jostled with the movement, his left arm holding tight to the armrest.

"If what he says is true, that I'll be dead by tomorrow, then letting them move forward with their plan and offering them a chance at success is pointless."

"Meaning what? Suicide?"

"No, nothing so ruthless and selfish."

"Then what?"

"I challenge Brock, piss him off, make him come at me, and when he's busy with me, you leave. Run for the hills or something."

Sarah shook her head. "That's a dumb plan."

Williams jerked back as if she slapped him, but probably because no one had spoken to him in such a way in a long time. "Why is that dumb?"

"Because all we'd end up with is me going home, you dead, and two bad guys on the loose."

"Yeah, but I'm dead either way. And you get out. Let the authorities handle these guys."

Sarah shook her head again. "No, I'll find a way that they both die, get arrested, or end up in a hospital for several months, and we both live."

"How? That's impossible. Did you see that guy—Jack? He's a walking tank."

"Not sure how yet, but I'm sure my sister will have a plan."

Williams scrunched up his face. "Your sister? How is she involved?"

"Trust me, she's involved big time. She's here with us. She's always around somewhere."

The minister glanced around the truck, then back to Sarah. "Are you okay, lady?"

Sarah widened her eyes briefly, tilted her head, flicked her hair off her shoulder, and said in a high-pitched voice, "Of course, why wouldn't I be?"

Williams seemed to sink lower into the sofa.

The truck slowed, then stopped.

A red light? Or had they arrived?

A second later, the truck advanced forward again.

Sarah studied the back. There had to be something she could use as a weapon. She leaned to the side and grabbed one of the glasses, but it was plastic and bolted to the table. After touching everything on the cabinet and pulling on the drawers, she understood it was all just a weightless prop. Even the couches were secured to the floor, and the cushions were part of the main couch. She could tear the fabric, but to what end?

"Brock wouldn't leave something in here for you to use against him." Williams's eyes hadn't left her. "He passed all the advanced exams with his IQ topping out at genius level. The man's a strategist, a professional, and a psychopath. When he had a plan, we all listened. When he had an idea, it was usually brilliant."

"So why pick this life? Why kidnap his boss for a diamond?"

The minister shrugged. "I can't speak for him, but it's likely because he was bored."

"All this because he was *bored*?"

"There have been allegations, rumors, that he went too far with a few women he met in the past. Online dating sites."

"Now there's something I can believe."

"They all disappeared."

"Of course, the allegations would dry up. He'd make sure of that."

"No, you misunderstand. The women saying he did terrible things literally disappeared."

She sat forward. "And no one suspected him?"

"Every time, he had an alibi. A fellow officer, a colleague, even his brother, on two occasions."

"Did you think his hands were clean?"

The minister glanced off to the left in thought. "Without proof, without evidence," he faced her, "there was nothing anyone could do."

She leaned back, disgust on her face. "Why does this remind me of the church or an old-boys club? The men are rallying around to protect their own while more and more women suffer. Didn't he just say to me, 'You and your kind are nothing more than a plaything, dead or alive,' or something like that?"

The minister didn't respond.

"See why I can't walk away from this or *run* away, as it were? I'm now here for the women. I'm here for each and every woman he has hurt or will hurt. I've already spared René Atchison this fate, and I will die to spare another woman that fate. I will bide my time, but let me assure you, Minister of Defense, your Agent Brock will be dead before this is over, and it'll be by my hand."

They sat in silence for several minutes until the truck came to a stop. This time, they'd reached their destination because both doors at the front opened and closed.

Then the back door slid up.

"Wakey wakey, lovebirds," Brock said. "You're the stars of our traveling band. It's time to put on a fucking show."

He hopped up into the back as sunshine filled the truck.

When he produced a Samsung tablet, the screen was already lit. He was unarmed, but when Sarah glanced past him, Jack was still on the pavement at the rear, a weapon resting in his hand.

"Take a look at this." Brock pushed play, and the volume echoed in the cavernous truck.

The interior was filled with the sound of a female news anchor. "Authorities are on the lookout for this woman, Sarah Roberts." The screen changed to a picture of her driving the delivery truck out from under the parking garage on Lower Simcoe Street, then it zoomed in on her face. "She's considered armed and dangerous. If you see her, do not approach. Please call the number on your screen. We also received breaking news that the delivery van was located off Airport Road with multiple casualties in the rear of the truck." The screen changed again to the photo Kramer had taken of her before Jack shot him. "We have blacked out the gruesome details in the photo's background, but we're led to believe this was the weapon Sarah used to end the lives of all the officers found in the truck she'd stolen. The photo was uploaded to Twitter anonymously, but the authorities suspect Sarah did it herself to gloat." The image changed back to the anchorwoman doing the news broadcast. Her head was down as she wiped at one eye. When she glanced up, her jaw clenched. "We would like to remind you all that this is the same Sarah Roberts who has terrorized this city before. Some have grown to love her, some hate her, and others think she's a spawn of the devil because she claims to be psychic—"

Brock pointed at the screen, his grin stretching from ear to ear. "I love this part. So emotional!"

"Whatever your particular thoughts on this woman, she must be stopped. We have heard from a reliable source that the authorities will apprehend Miss Sarah Roberts very soon. When they find her, they'll put an end to her reign of terror on the streets of Toronto—"

Brock pressed a button, and the screen went dark. "Isn't that fantastic? You're burned, bitch." Brock laughed hysterically. "Wait, I should have said, you're a burned witch." Then his laugh turned uproarious. "I'm brilliant. This plan is absolutely better than I ever thought possible." He glanced back at Jack. "My brother sure came through for us with this bitch, eh, Jack?"

"Sure, Brock. Can we just get the recording done now? I want my share, then I'm out of the city."

"Of course, of course. Just hold your horses." Brock turned back to Sarah as she stared over his shoulder, trying to determine where they were. Brock caught her gaze and looked outside, then back to her, then outside again. "You trying to figure out where we are, little girl?"

They looked at each other from five feet away. "Looks like a nice field out there."

Brock nodded, a goofy smile on his face. "Yes, a large field. We're not far from the airport because as soon as we get what we want, we have a plane waiting to take us somewhere no one will find us."

"You won't be on that plane."

Brock's smile faltered, then it disappeared as he stared at her. "Well, holy shit, Momma, we have a firecracker with us today." He slapped his leg, spun around to face Jack, then did some kind of clunky laugh. "You are one spicy woman. I sure wonder how you taste."

Sarah glared at him, wondering if she could kill him before Jack shot her. Perhaps now was the time. She perched on the edge of the couch, her gaze unwavering.

Brock's lips twitched as he stared at her. "I think it's time we do our last bit of business, and then we'll be off to our earned permanent vacation, and you'll be counting the bugs in your eye socket as you rot several feet below ground."

"Sounds delightful."

"Sarah." The defense minister's one word made her snap out of her reverie. She was so focused on Brock's face and throat that she had been seconds from leaping at him.

She blinked and turned to face him.

"Soon," he whispered. "Not now."

"Whoa, ho, ho," Brock yelled in the confined space. "Shit, man, why did you do that, Williams? I was taunting her. I saw that look in her eyes and was waiting for her to land on me. Dude, don't break her spell like that. We could've had a delicious tussle." Brock slapped his hands together again several times. He had to be addicted to the sound of his own clapping. "I have never met a woman with so much spite and spice. Too bad we weren't working on the same side. I could use someone like you, and when I say *use*, I mean *use* if you know what I mean."

"What the fuck, man?" Jack said from the door behind Brock. "Can we get on with it?"

Brock waved his hand behind his back without taking his eyes off Sarah. "Give me the heater."

"Now?" Jack sounded surprised. "I thought that was only if she *didn't* cooperate."

Brock stood to his full height, his facial muscles relaxing, his hand lowering back to his side. "Jack, *please* give me the heater."

"Whatever, man." Jack set a small handheld device on the truck floor, then shoved it toward Brock. It stopped at his feet.

"That field out there means no one will hear the screams." Brock picked up what looked like a soldering gun. "This little beauty is such a pleasure to use because it injures and heals simultaneously."

"You're head isn't on straight." Sarah felt a coldness come over her and waited for Brock to continue.

"If I cut off a finger, a hand, you would bleed and bleed, and it would be relatively painful and bloody messy. But," he held up the device, "my little handheld blowtorch causes even more pain as it singes hair and melts your skin, all while cauterizing the flesh at the same time. See? No stitches needed. You feel tremendous pain, and you don't bleed all over me, the floor, and the furniture, nor do you need a doctor. Well, not immediately. I mean, if you were to live when I'm through with you, a doctor can help ease the pain with salves and painkillers, but that won't matter in this case."

"Why?" Williams asked, drawing Brock's attention to him. "Why are you doing this? Revenge? Is that it?"

Brock's awkward smile was back, and it hit Sarah why it was so awkward—because it was pasted on, acted as if he didn't actually feel joy, happiness, or even amusement. He was *acting* that smile. He'd seen how others smiled and learned to use those facial muscles. The man was emotionless. He felt nothing, yet he was trapped in an emotional world. Sarah forgot what the exact percentage of psychopaths mingling with society was, but seemed to recall the number was quite low, like under three percent.

"You think this is about revenge?" Brock bodily turned to face the minister.

"I'm listening to you talk to the man I've worked with for quite some time, the same man who was in charge of keeping me alive, and I'm wondering where the break with reality came, or rather, *when* it came. That said, I merely asked if it was revenge. By asking, it should tell you that I don't know. But if not revenge, then what? Money?"

Brock pushed the button on the blowtorch, and a small blue flame shot out of the tip. Then he released the button, and the flame disappeared.

"This is about too many things to discuss now—"

"I hear that," Jack muttered behind him.

"—but we can boil it all down to money."

"Money?" Williams said. "You want money?" He moved to the edge of the couch. "Give me your banking details, and I'll transfer half a million dollars over immediately, with more to come. Let's discuss this like civilized men. Let the girl go, and I'll make you rich."

"I'm not going anywhere," Sarah whispered. "Not until this man has stopped breathing."

"Does that work for you?" Williams asked, trying to speak over Sarah's voice to drown her out.

Brock angled his head back, staring at the truck's ceiling as he tapped a finger against his chin. "Hmmm." He looked back down at Williams. "Tempting, but the diamond is worth hundreds of millions. I already have a buyer, and you could never give me that amount. Not to mention working with you would mean I'd be looking over my shoulder for the rest of my life—"

"As long as I'm out there," Sarah said, "you will still be looking over your shoulder. I mean, *if* you survive the night."

Brock turned to her, flicking the blowtorch on, then off, then on again. "Wow, you are the best woman I have ever met. I'm going to love destroying that little body before we hop on the plane. I'm already so hard for you." His eyes gleamed with madness as they roamed her body. "All you're doing is marinating the meat for me. Please, keep it up. I may fall in love before the night's over, and that's not something I could ever imagine."

"Are all men born monsters, or do they become one? What keeps a man civil?"

Confusion crossed his face. "What?"

"Were you born this way or violated as a little boy?" She sneered at him. "Oh, shit, I'm sorry. It was the local priest, right? Oh, wait, was it Kramer, your own brother? Is that why you killed your own flesh and blood? Because he played with your little wiener—"

Brock screamed and jumped at her, but then was yanked off by Jack, who had quietly climbed up into the back of the truck.

Jack was a large man—very large—and completely overpowered Brock, lifting him over the couch and depositing him on the truck's floor near the opening to the outside.

Sarah panted, her hands up, hair in her face.

"Kill her later," Jack shouted. "We need her intact. She can't do the video with blood on her face, or worse, dead. I want my fuckin' money. Now stand up, fuck off, and get the job done, or I'll kill you myself, you fuckhead dickstain."

Brock collected himself by rolling to his knees, his stomach bulging and contracting like he'd been running for ten minutes.

Was this the breaking point? Would he go for his gun?

Everyone waited to see what was next, and then Brock nodded slowly. "You're right. She taunted me one too many." Brock got to his feet and turned on the torch. "I've never met a woman with a mouth like that. She's quite alluring." He shook his head, then cleared his throat and swallowed. "In a few hours, when this is over, I will jam this blowtorch up your snatch and turn it on to warm your insides for my cock. Then I'll use it on your eyes and your—"

"Dude," Jack shouted. "The video."

Brock blinked like he was coming back to the room after a powerful hypnosis. "Right. Of course."

He produced a piece of paper, handed it to Jack, then walked over to stand beside the minister of defense.

Jack handed the paper to Sarah. "Read this slowly. Read every word, line by line, exactly as it's written. I'll be holding the camera. Don't try to message anyone, don't do anything stupid, and don't fuck around. Just read it into the camera, and no one will get hurt."

"Fuck you," Sarah said, scrunching up the paper and tossing it away.

Jack scoffed and ran after it, then unfolded the thing.

Brock laughed as he clutched Williams's wrist with his hand and jammed a knee down on the man's elbow, securing the man's appendage to the couch's armrest.

He flicked on the blowtorch and applied it to the minister's flesh, which seemed to wave under the assault of the heat like water, the flesh already peeling back and turning dark.

The minister of defense screamed a high-pitched wail as every orifice in his face widened, and he jerked back, punching at Brock with his free hand. But Brock held him in a vice grip as he leaned his body weight into his knee. The minister's flesh continued to melt off his arm below the elbow without resistance.

The screams pierced Sarah's consciousness in a way that made her see red. It was the sudden act, the absolute evil intent, and the subtle rationalization that she caused this by throwing the paper away that made her dive at Brock.

Then all hell broke loose in the back of the truck.

Chapter 34

DETECTIVE HEATH FOUND PARKMAN'S hospital room quite easily. When he entered, a nurse was just turning on the in-room TV for Parkman. She nodded at Heath, handed the remote to Parkman, then exited the room with the door closing softly behind her.

"What the hell?" Heath said, staring at the thick wad of bandages on Parkman's arm. "You got shot." He stated the obvious—something they were both aware of—while staring at him in a daze, shaking his head.

"Yeah, and the cops want to know why Sarah would shoot at her friend. They're pissed at me by association."

"I'll get that cleared up."

"No matter how many times I told them the passenger shot at me, they think I helped Sarah get out of that parking garage, and this bullet wound was meant to deflect blame from me. You know, assisted robbery shit. Accessory after the fact."

"What?" Heath shook his head again. "Talk about imaginations running wild. Fuckin' guys should write a book or some shit. I mean, that's all fiction."

Parkman stared at the TV, flipping channels until he got to the all-news station. "At this point, they aren't discussing any charges." He exhaled hard. "There's zero evidence of any wrongdoing."

"Not to mention there are cameras down there."

"Hey," Parkman said, pointing at the TV with his good arm, the one holding the remote. "There she is."

The volume increased as Heath pivoted to watch the TV.

The anchorwoman said the authorities were looking for Sarah Roberts. The screen changed to a picture of her driving the delivery truck out from under the parking garage; then, it zoomed in on her face. "She's considered armed and dangerous. If you see her, do not approach."

"What the fuck," Parkman whispered. "Why do they always twist shit against Sarah. That does her more harm than good—"

"Shhh," Heath said. "I want to hear this."

The anchorwoman talked about multiple casualties in the rear of a truck. The screen changed to a photo with blacked-out details in the background. Apparently, that photo had been uploaded to Twitter anonymously, but the authorities suspect Sarah did it out of pride. The image changed back to the anchorwoman weeping softly and clenching her jaw. She summarized with the usual bullshit, and then the channel took a commercial break.

Heath turned back to Parkman, who was lowering the volume, then he hit the mute button. "Shit, she's in trouble, my friend."

"I'm quite aware of that, but have no idea what I can do now."

"What can I do?" a new voice asked as the door popped open. Aaron stepped into the room and closed the door.

"You brought Aaron along?" Parkman asked, staring at Heath.

"Not exactly. I called him to see if he knew where you were, and some guy named Daniel said they'd figure it out. Aaron called me back and told me about this hospital. So, here we are."

Parkman and Aaron nodded at each other.

"Give me a quick update," Aaron said.

Parkman told him what he knew, starting with his talk with René and finishing with how he got shot.

"You're not trying to take Benjamin's place, are you?" Aaron nodded once toward the bandages.

"Funny, not funny." Parkman sneered at him. "Also, too soon."

Aaron tapped him on the shoulder. "You're right. I'll wait until you're shot again to repeat any comments in honor of Benjamin."

"What's that mean?" Heath asked. "What are you guys on about?"

"Nothing." Parkman waved him off. "You don't want to know."

Heath looked at Aaron. "Let me add a few points to what Parkman told you." Heath explained how Sarah was being held for abducting René and running from the cops, and that they were building a case against her as an accessory to the jewelry store robbery when the bomber called to negotiate Sarah's release.

"And now she's seen running from the underground parking garage and shooting at me," Parkman added. "Well, according to the authorities."

"We can't trust anything they say." Aaron raised a hand at Heath. "No offense."

"None taken."

"What else?"

Heath crossed his arms. "They now think Sarah killed all the people she abducted from the Metro Convention Centre because of a leaked photo on Twitter."

"Meanwhile," Parkman said. "Sarah's probably out there trying to save everyone from the murdering thieves, and she's getting no support from anyone."

"Which is why I'm here." Heath jerked when his phone rang. "One second." He answered it and moved to the side. "Heath here."

"It's Sergeant Miller. We just got a development."

Heath looked up at Parkman, then Aaron. Both men were staring at him.

"What sort of development?"

"The perps sent a short video to the RCMP in charge of visiting dignitaries. They're called the VIPPD."

"What kind of video?"

"I'm sending it to your phone now."

"How did you get it?"

"They asked for backup. Just thought I'd let you know that this case is solved. We're leaving now, but I can tell you that they won't be giving up the real diamond."

"What?" Heath's phone dinged as a text came through. "What's this about the real diamond? Shouldn't it remain locked in the vault?"

"Just watch the video. The case is over. I'll fill you in on everything tonight."

The line died, and he pulled the phone away to open the text.

"What was that all about?" Parkman asked. "What real diamond?"

"My sergeant just told me it's over, and they won't give up the real diamond or something."

"And that means what exactly?" Aaron asked.

"No idea, but she sent me a video." Heath opened it but didn't press play. He held up the phone so the other two could watch it with him, then raised the volume.

"Ready?"

Parkman and Aaron nodded, even as all three could see Sarah on the screen.

"Holy shit," Parkman muttered. "What's Sarah doing?"

Heath hit the play button.

Sarah stood on camera in what looked like a motel room with two small couches behind her while reading from a white piece of paper.

"There is no one left." Sarah glanced up, then back at the paper. "My partner and I have killed everyone but the Minister of Defense, John Williams." The camera flashed to the right to a man sitting on one of the couches, his face beet red with blood and his eyes bulging as he clutched at his forearm. Then the camera was back on Sarah. "We will wait two hours, but after that, John Williams will die." She frowned, then looked at the person holding the camera. "Really?"

Parkman sat up straighter. "Where is she?" he muttered out loud.

No one answered him.

On the screen, Sarah glanced back at the paper. "Have Meredith Whitlock of Gold Run Jewelry deliver the Cullinan—the *real* Cullinan —to the Vaughn Mills Mall north parking lot. She will park by the Tesla Supercharger stations, then walk away and enter the mall. She will be watched. Leave the vehicle there without tracking devices. Once my colleagues retrieve the Cullinan, the minister of defense will be released without further harm. If this isn't done within two hours, the minister will die a horrible death, and every truck with bombs, fireworks, and bullets will be ignited across Toronto like the demonstration I performed in front of the Metro Convention Centre." Sarah stared at the camera directly. "You've got two hours." The camera feed died.

"What the hell is she going to do now?" Heath asked. "There's no cop this side of Saturn that won't shoot her dead on sight. Those uniforms who died in the explosions last night sealed her fate. Now the VIPPD officers' deaths will crush her."

"What's VIPPD?" Aaron asked.

"It stands for VIP Protective Detail. Canada's version of the US Secret Service."

Aaron looked up from the cell phone, his cheeks a pale off-white. "I wonder how many cops are racing to that mall at the moment, hoping to be the one to shoot her, too?"

"Something isn't right," Parkman said, staring at the phone in

Heath's hand. "Why the mall? Why in public like that?"

Heath shrugged. "Maybe it's so when the car is approached by whoever's behind this, or Sarah herself, they don't unload a fusillade of bullets and cause collateral damage by killing members of the public."

"But they won't get away with it." Parkman stared at the single window in his hospital room. "Aaron, you must go to the mall, find Sarah, and protect her."

"I'll do that, no question, but how close will I get without getting killed? The cops'll lock it all down."

"Heath, get him two Kevlar vests."

"Two?"

Parkman turned to Heath. "Yeah, Sarah will need one when Aaron gets to her."

They ran for the hospital room door.

"Wait," Parkman shouted.

Both men stopped and turned back to look at him.

"Something's not right here. Heath, keep your phone on and turned up loud. I'll call you when I work out what's bothering me."

Heath nodded, ripped open the door, and the men disappeared into the hallway.

Chapter 35

SARAH HAD LANDED ON Brock's side, her knee jamming him just below the ribs, her fists pummeling his upper body, all for two seconds before Jack yanked her off and tossed her bodily onto the opposing couch.

Then he shoved Brock off balance, knocking the man into the wall of the truck so hard that his legs collapsed, and he dropped to the floor.

Sarah righted herself, pushed to her feet, and took one step toward the downed Brock when Jack brought up a hand in front of Sarah's face.

The hand with a gun.

"Don't," he said. "Just leave it."

Sarah panted in and out, her hair in her face, her eyes on Brock. Everything in her being wanted to tear the man apart, but that gun in her face sent images of Willow to her. She couldn't get shot—well, at least not in the face.

Two more breaths and she straightened herself, unruffled her shirt, and looked at Jack. "Take that thing out of my face. I'm good."

Jack lowered the weapon but kept his finger inside the trigger guard.

A clapping sound resonated throughout the back, then another.

"Bravo," Brock said, clapping faster now. "I'm beyond impressed."

"Get him to stop clapping." Sarah pointed at Brock. "Or we're back to fighting."

Brock clapped harder, louder—like a child rebelling after being told to stop whining.

"Brock," Jack shouted. "Let's do the video, then we can get what we came for, and you can do as you please."

The clapping stopped. "I can do as I please any time I want."

His icy tone sent a shiver through Sarah as Brock glared at Jack.

"Yeah, okay, you can do whatever you want at any time, but right now, we need that video. This fucking around is costing us time." Jack handed Sarah the crumpled paper. "If you don't want more flesh being burned off this man's forearm, read what's on there into the camera." He glanced at Brock, who was getting to his feet, then back at Sarah. "Can you do that for me?"

Sarah stuck out her lower lip and blew a wisp of hair out of her face. "You control the monster." She glanced at Brock. "Or I'll kill him."

"He's fine now. It was just a demonstration to show that he doesn't bluff."

"I don't either. Control him, or he dies."

"Sarah," Jack said. "Comments like that one don't help. He might lose it again, and he's the one in control here."

She met Jack's gaze. "Next time, stay out of it so I can finish the job."

He gave her a subtle nod, then looked at the paper. "Will you save the minister more pain? Will you read that?"

Sarah looked at the minister, who seemed to be in terrible pain as he rocked on the couch slightly, a hand on his burned arm. The man's face still looked grotesque as they'd done nothing to wipe the blood off him. At least most of the cuts stopped oozing blood, though.

Her heart swelled for him. She needed to read the damn note. "I'll do it. Just keep Brock away from both of us."

Jack looked at Brock, who raised his hands. "I'm cool now. But no promises once we send that video."

"Deal. No promises."

Brock stared at Sarah while licking his lips. Then he moaned deep in his throat. "Gonna tie you down and eat you all up. It's going to be a wild ride tonight." Brock clapped his hands twice.

Jack clenched his eyes shut, then opened them. That clapping thing was riding his nerves, too.

Sarah read the note over once. "What the hell is this? Who is Meredith? Is she René's boss at the jewelry store?"

"Doesn't matter," Jack said, raising the cell phone camera and aiming it at her. "I'm recording. Just read it."

Sarah looked down again, then up, and read it line by line. When she was done, she tossed the paper on the floor.

Jack ended the recording, did something on the phone, then handed it to Brock.

"I've edited out the first part where my voice was on it, and I've selected the share button. Just type in your boss's number and hit send, and we're good to go."

Brock did as he was told, then returned the phone to Jack. After a moment, Jack nodded. "It's showing sent and delivered."

Then Jack dropped the phone on the truck's floor and stomped on it until it was in a dozen pieces.

"Well," Jack said, looking from Sarah to Brock, then back to Sarah. "That about wraps up this leg of the journey. Hope you all had a pleasant stay."

"What does that mean?" Sarah asked.

"It means we don't need you anymore." Brock pushed off the wall.

"Well, we kinda do."

Brock stopped halfway to Sarah to look over at Jack. "Why?" He sounded quite stymied with the notion.

"Since she just admitted compliance, along with the photo proof everyone has, leaving Sarah to run keeps them off our backs for a while. If they find her body today or tonight, they will want to know who else was behind everything. See? She needs to stay alive."

Brock shook his head back and forth slowly. "No. Not part of the deal."

"Deal? What deal? We had no deal regarding Sarah. She's an add-on."

"There's an unwritten law regarding women in general around me." Brock stared her down like a hungry wolf. "I claim them, devour them, ravish them, then watch the life leave them while I'm inside their worthless husk of a body."

Jack stared at Brock for a long moment. "You know your mother was a woman, right?"

Brock's cheeks reddened, making Sarah wonder what was coming next.

"I'm just saying," Jack added. "Not all women are to be tortured, raped, and murdered. I mean, aren't some women sanctified in your world?"

"Gee, thanks for your support," Sarah said.

"Some bring life into this world," Jack finished as if Sarah hadn't spoken. "There has to be some you wouldn't touch."

Brock lowered his hands to his side, then leaned against the wall.

"Let me explain something to you all."

Jack nodded. Sarah stared at both of them, waiting for a chance to get the gun or jam her thumbs into Brock's orbital sockets.

"I know I'm a predator. I'm self-aware." He cleared his throat. "I was born a predator. Ever since I was a young boy, I knew who I was, what I was, and I accepted it. But I'm smarter than most predators." He tapped the side of his head. "Guys like Harvey Weinstein do it too publicly and get caught. How about Ron Jeremy, the Hedgehog? He worked in the porn industry for decades because he was a sexual predator, but even he got caught and is sitting in prison now." Brock shook his head. "No, the best way for a lecherous sexual predator to do as he pleases and never get caught is to be a criminal, a mercenary. So, the women I work with rarely survive, and my female hostages never do —which is why I never got caught. If the witnesses are dead, there's never a trial, never any charges laid. And I have done all this while donning the RCMP uniform daily. Brilliant, no? That's how I never got caught, how I have never had to face the music."

Sarah clapped her hands, making Brock jump. "Until now."

They all stared at each other in silence, which was only broken by a moan from the minister of defense as he held his arm.

"My brother was weak," Brock said.

"Oh, I thought you were done." Sarah rolled her hand in a circular motion. "Carry on."

"My brother was weak, so I killed Canadian soldiers in my village, stole a uniform, and dressed like one. I killed my parents, then covered my face with a mask to tie him up and rape my sister." He shrugged. "Then I raped my mother's corpse in front of him. Once I slit my sister's throat, I just walked away. A little while later, I re-entered the house without the uniform or the mask and acted shocked at what had happened. By the time I untied him, my brother was more of a man."

"You made him into what he was?" Jack asked, his tone incredulous.

"As I said earlier, I do what I want when I want. Always have." He stared at Sarah like a vampire who hadn't fed in months. "A vagina is a vagina. My mother's, my sister's"—he shrugged—"who cares. A hole's a hole." He stepped toward Sarah. "Besides, I had to kill my family. My sister told my mother I'd been violating her for as long as she could remember. They'd called my brother home for a family meeting to see what to do with me." He shook his head. "I couldn't have that. So, I jumped between her legs for one more kick at the can, then added my mom to see what it would be like to fuck the dead, then came back to check on my brother." Brock laughed to himself, shaking his head. "The look on his face that day was priceless, and he died never knowing what I'd done." He moved within reach of Sarah. "And now I will rip your holes open with my cock, my fist, and eventually my blowtorch until I've torn you in half—"

A gun was fired in the confined space of the back of the truck, making everyone jump.

Sarah couldn't suppress the short yip that escaped her lips.

All eyes turned to Jack, the weapon in his hand.

Then Sarah looked down, but nothing had hit her. When she faced Brock, the man was leaning on the couch an arm's length from the minister of defense, blood rushing from a wound in his thigh.

"What the fuck, man?" Brock shouted. "You shot me."

"I couldn't listen to another second of that shit," Jack said. "Don't you see what's happening here? You're one sick fuck, and you don't deserve to leave this truck alive. I'm thinking this is where Sarah steps in."

Brock stared at him, his face a deep shade of red, but his eyes roving the back of the truck, likely already working on a plan.

Sarah suppressed the urge to clap heartily.

"When you came to me with the plan," Jack continued. "I saw how sick you and your brother were. Then you told me that Kramer was going to kill me, along with James and Jason. So we formed our own plan, with me knowing you wanted Kramer dead. Now Kramer is dead, and I want you dead, too."

"Wait," Brock said, barely able to lift a hand. He seemed to be weakening fast. "What about the diamond? What about the plane out of here?"

"You may be a predator, soon to be a dead predator, but you aren't that smart."

Brock sat on the couch's armrest, no longer able to hold himself up.

"Then explain it to me."

"I already have the *real* Cullinan. It's in the trunk of my Mustang."

Brock seemed as confused as Sarah was, but she didn't ask for more, feeling Jack was already in a telling mood.

"Meredith and I have been working together for over a year now. What are the odds that you and your brother would reach out with a plan to steal it? Of course, I wanted to get involved—so I could make sure Meredith and I could keep the diamond and blame you two. But then you told me Kramer had to die, and you planned to blame everything on Meredith's American friend, René. And we all know how Sarah stopped René, blah, blah, blah."

"How do you already have the real diamond?" Brock's face was now yogurt-white with a green tinge—his body was going into shock.

"Meredith planted fake diamonds in several stores, ensuring the real one was put in her store so I could take it. A fake was given to me so I could show it to Kramer and complain that we were double-crossed. I did everything you asked, but now when Meredith drives another fake diamond to that mall, she'll go inside the mall and lose anyone following her because they'll all be hyper-focused on the car in the north parking lot. I'll be waiting in the Mustang for her in the south lot. We have our own flight out of here, thank you very much. I don't need you, nor do I want to work with such filth any longer. You're disgusting, man."

"You'll pay for this."

"I doubt it." Jack stepped backward until he was in the truck's opening, where the door was still rolled up. "I'm going to leave this gun here, on the truck floor, for whoever gets to it first."

Sarah stepped forward but stopped when Jack aimed the weapon at her.

"Make it fair, Sarah. Wait until I jump down."

"How is this fair?" Brock protested. "I've lost a lot of blood and can't use this leg."

Jack grabbed the door over his head, then hopped off the back, dragging the door down with him, which cut off a lot of the sunlight. He flicked a switch on the side, turning on the interior light, then faced them.

"Who survives today is no longer my problem, but I have a feeling it's Sarah who'll walk out the victor." He laughed. "Get it, *walk* out."

He laughed again, the door strap in one hand, the other holding the gun. After a moment, he set the weapon down and pulled the door shut, metal clanking on the other side, confirming they were locked in.

Sarah took two long steps and dove for the gun, sliding along the floor of the truck, snatching it up, and hitting the closed door with her shoulder. When she spun around, she was surprised Brock hadn't also come for the gun.

Instead, he'd grabbed his blowtorch and had wrapped an arm around the minister's head. The blowtorch was now aimed at the man's left eye, which was blinking rapidly like he was trying to get water out of it after swimming.

"Go ahead, Sarah." Brock's evil smile covered his face. "Shoot me. I hope you're a good shot and don't hit the minister. You'll blind him, though. Because if you don't put that gun down, I'll use this torch on his face. More specifically, his eyehole. Once his eye is removed, I can use this hole to fuck his brains out." The man's laugh was maniacal, something reserved for circus funhouses.

Brock was too far away to jump on and too far to guarantee the shot. In the seconds she considered what to do, Brock continued talking.

"All I ask is you put the gun down, then take off your pants and panties. Allow me to fuck you once, nicely. Then I'll leave you both alone. Promise." He shrugged. "We have sex, and everyone lives." The edge of a smile played across his blanched face. "I'm offering orgasms and freedom. How could that be an offer a rational human being would pass up? Come here and sit on my face, gorgeous."

"Fuck you," she whispered.

"Well, I'd rather fuck you, but if that's how you feel, I'll *take* what I want—I always do. But don't say I wasn't fair and didn't offer."

The blowtorch flickered to life, and the minister screamed as he jammed his head back with the blowtorch moving closer.

Sarah aimed the gun as she ran at Brock across the length of the truck, then pulled the trigger.

Nothing happened. No bullets spit out the tip. It didn't fire.

The blowtorch turned off, and Minister Williams slumped on the couch, passed out from the pain. The area around his eye melted into his head, dripping red and white pus around bubbling flesh.

She checked the gun in her hand.

It was empty.

Jack had used it to shoot Kramer multiple times. Then he fired a bullet into Brock's leg. Was there another click after that? A dry click? How many bullets had been in the magazine in the first place?

She tossed the gun aside in time to see Brock almost on her. She went to brace for impact, but it was too late.

He hit her with all his weight, and they went down, the wind escaping Sarah in a rush. His leg had a bullet wound, but his upper body strength and hands weren't affected as he jammed an elbow into her throat and pinned her to the floorboards of the truck while the other hand wrapped around her breast and squeezed, the pain an immediate agony which felt ten times worse than any mammogram.

She tried to scream with the pain, but her airways were blocked.

"We're locked in here together," Brock said. "I'm going to fuck you for hours, then paint these walls with your blood."

Sarah was able to twist her head back and forth.

"What's that?" he asked. "You're trying to say something to me?"

He released the pressure on her throat enough that she could take a deep breath. Then she coughed, her throat raw from the abuse, and forced more air inside her lungs.

"You trying to tell me something?" Brock's hand roamed down her body and cupped the triangular area between her legs.

"We're not locked in here together," she said, her voice hoarse. "You're locked in here with me."

She swung her legs to the side, wrapped them around his wounded thigh, then squeezed, locking him in a scissor hold over his wound.

The hand between her legs was squeezed out, and her thighs quickly soaked with the blood gushing from the pressure. But the best part was his shout of pain.

"Oh, you bitch," he bellowed.

Brock fumbled with something behind him, then produced a knife, raising it in his right hand high over her face. "I'll fuck your corpse. I'll fuck your skull. I don't need you alive, you whore's daughter."

His arm swung downward with nothing to block the blow because Sarah's arms were locked under Brock's weight.

She squeezed her eyes tight, but the knife didn't penetrate her flesh.

Instead, Brock dropped the knife and screamed even louder than the moment before.

And then, just like that, he rolled off her, writhing on the floor, his hands clutching at something near his ankle.

Sarah sat up on her elbows to see what had happened, still trying to catch her breath.

The minister of defense had woken up, and somehow, his one good eye wide with rage, had grabbed the blowtorch and used it on Brock's ankle. As she watched, the defense minister dropped off the couch and landed on Brock's lower leg.

The man screamed again, which would usually make Sarah cringe, but something about Brock's screams satisfied her and gave her a feeling of contentment.

How many women had he made suffer during his life? How many innocents had he killed? By his own admission, he was a predator who destroyed his own family.

Perhaps it was time for him to go to Hell if there was one. The planet had enough evil on it. She couldn't let this man continue to breathe. Some people *should* die ... something she'd always believed.

The minister flicked on the blowtorch again and applied it to Brock's lower leg. The man thrashed and kicked, but the minister was a large, heavy man. His weight alone kept the wounded leg where he needed it to be.

The minister crawled up Brock's body, then pushed the end of the torch into Brock's stomach.

Blows rained down on the minister's head and shoulders, but it didn't seem to bother the man as he lifted the torch farther and jammed the flame into the crook of Brock's neck.

That silenced the screams, the fight all but gone from Brock.

A moment later, the minister passed out again and rolled off the predator.

Sarah got up and stood over Brock's damaged and burned body.

His eyes found her as he struggled to breathe through all the pain and the burned flesh of his throat. His odds of survival were pretty good if he got to a doctor soon, but that throat wound didn't look so good.

She leaned over him. "For every single woman who ever came within a hundred meters of your evil presence, for every woman you hurt, for every woman you killed."

Sarah raised her foot and brought it down on his throat, crushing it.

Then she did it again. And again.

And she screamed as Brock died under her boot.

"For all the women ever hurt by a *fucking* man," Sarah screamed and stomped both feet onto his ruined face, denting his skull inward.

One more predator erased from the Earth.

Thousands more to go …

Chapter 36

DETECTIVE HEATH DROVE LIKE a maniac, with the sirens wailing as he headed north on Highway 400.

"It's clear up ahead." Aaron pointed out the windshield. "At this hour, you can get around those guys in time."

"And?"

"Kill the sirens." He flicked switches on the dashboard, but nothing changed.

Heath slid a switch sideways, the sirens died, and the lights turned off.

"I'm just saying we don't need to announce our arrival since this isn't your operation."

"I don't want to be late, and getting out of downtown by using Yonge Street to go north, then the 401, was taking too long. We lost over an hour."

"Too late now, but that's why I use Mount Pleasant to Lawrence."

Heath tapped the dash by the clock. "We've got forty-five minutes until Meredith is supposed to drop off the diamond, and we're ten minutes away. We'll make it."

"Where are you planning on parking?"

"The south lot, somewhere hidden if possible."

Heath's phone rang, and he hit the button on the dashboard for it to go to Bluetooth. "Go ahead."

"How close are you guys?" Parkman asked.

"Ten minutes away," Aaron said. "Almost there."

"Something was bothering me, and I think I figured it out. Heath, didn't you say they wouldn't be taking the real diamond to this drop-off thing?"

"Yeah, my sergeant said they're doing the Meredith-drop-off-the-car thing, but the diamond they're leaving in the car will be a fake."

"Do you know why?"

"Why?" Heath looked at Aaron, then back at the road. "Likely because it's an expensive diamond, one of a kind. They'll do what they can to save the minister of defense's life, but a diamond worth half a billion—nope."

"Well, I've got a hypothesis to pass over you both."

"Go ahead," Aaron said as Heath changed into the right lane.

"They aren't delivering the real diamond because they don't have it."

Heath and Aaron looked at each other.

"Then who has it?" Aaron asked.

"The thieves. The bad guys responsible for all this."

"What?" Heath laughed. "How many painkillers have you taken, buddy? Why would they ask for the diamond and go through all this shit if they already have it?"

"Look, here's how I see it. A mole within the RCMP discovered a top-secret plan to divert the Cullinan diamond, moving it through various jewelry stores instead of keeping it safely locked away in a vault. Only a few people knew about this plan, and Meredith Whitlock was one of them."

"Okay, following so far. Keep going."

"Well, she worked with the mole to make sure the *real* diamond was in her safe. Unaware of that, she had René involved to take the fall, but Sarah stopped that. The one thing I can't work out is why the thieves didn't just peace out, and all I can come up with is that Meredith is involved."

"Meaning?"

"They set this drop-off thing up so everyone will be watching the car with the *diamond* while Meredith walks away and into the thieves' car and disappears."

"Dude," Heath said. "That's pretty far-fetched. I don't think so. Meredith Whitlock has a great reputation with the convention center and owns a jewelry store. Why not just keep a few diamonds for herself from her own store?" Heath shook his head. "Your theory doesn't feel right to me."

"Me neither," Aaron said. "There's got to be something else."

"Guys, do me a favor then."

Heath hit his blinker and eased into the exit lane for the Vaughn Mills Mall. "Sure, what is it?"

"There will be a hundred cops watching that car with the fake diamond in the north parking lot, and hardly anyone watching—"

"You want us to tail Meredith?" Aaron asked.

"I'm sure she'll have a tail already, someone escorting her to a cruiser, but I suspect she'll lose them and disappear. If you see anything suspicious, then I'm right."

Aaron and Heath exchanged another glance. "Doesn't hurt," Heath said. "What else will we be doing, anyway? This isn't my case. I just want to ensure they don't execute Sarah if she's there."

Heath pulled into the parking area near Bass Pro Sports, then turned south to find a well-hidden spot.

"We're here," Heath said. "We're parking by the large Vaughn Mills Mall sign in the south lot. It's in an area titled 6B."

"Okay, stay in touch," Parkman said. "I want to know how this turns out."

"We'll call the second we know something."

"Guys, I think I'm right about this."

"That's good enough for me," Aaron said. "It doesn't make sense if they already have the diamond, but we'll watch Meredith for any fuck around."

Heath ended the call, backed into a spot, and then killed the engine. "We've got thirty minutes."

"This is a huge parking area and a huge mall."

Heath nodded. "True. I have no idea how we're going to handle this."

Aaron wrung his hands together in his lap. "All I'm focusing on is they'd better not kill Sarah. Then watch Meredith. Everything else comes after that."

"I sure hope Parkman's right about Meredith."

"Yeah? Why's that?"

Heath glanced sideways at him. "Because if he's wrong, the perp will come for the diamond. But if he's right, this deal is about Meredith, and Sarah won't be here at all. This is a mall that'll be crawling with hundreds of cops in no time, which is the last place on earth Sarah should be today."

"Meaning she'll survive this."

Heath nodded. "Meaning she'll survive this."

"She'd better, or I'll kill her."

Chapter 37

SARAH HAD TRIED EVERYTHING to get out of the back of the truck, but she was running out of time. After Brock died, she'd taken the time to dress the minister's eye wound with cloth from Brock's shirt, but the minister would need a doctor for a proper dressing. His heart rate seemed to spike, then drop to where it was almost undetectable, then spike again, and she hadn't been able to wake him since the fight with Brock.

Back on her feet, she stared at the access door to the truck's cab, which was locked. The back door was sealed from the outside. Unless she could pound through the thin side walls, they were stuck in the back until someone came to let them out, wherever they were.

The immediate problem was the heat. With no ventilation, the afternoon sun permeated the thin roof and positively baked them inside.

What if Brock and Jack had taken them to an abandoned farmer's field, and they wouldn't be located by anyone for days, weeks, or months?

She had to think. There were two couches bolted to the floor. Each sofa was made of thick material. She could work on breaking one, ripping the fabric, then finally render herself a club from one of the wooden supports, but for what purpose?

The coffee table between the couches would give her a wooden club faster, but it was also bolted down, and kicking it for a few hours to break off a piece felt like a waste of time.

The blowtorch.

Was there enough fuel in that handheld device to burn a hole in the side?

She grabbed it and hefted its weight. The little thing definitely had some juice left, but she'd have to pick her target well.

The back door? The sides?

She spun back to stare at the small white door that led to the truck's cab. The little lock appeared to be made of steel.

It could work. Maybe.

Once she had the minister lying on his side in the recovery position on the truck's floor, wedged between the coffee table legs and the base of the couch, she ran to the little lock, flicked on the blowtorch, and applied the flame to the keyway.

The flame of that blowtorch is over one thousand degrees, Vivian whispered. *It'll get you where you want to go.*

Sarah kept her hand steady as the lock showed signs of melting. *So, now you show up?* Sarah asked. *To offer blowtorch specifications?*

I was always here. You just didn't need me.

A tear leaped to Sarah's eye. "I needed you, Vivian. I've always needed you."

There was no response.

The center of the lock oozed drops of metal to the truck's floor as Sarah held down the trigger on the blowtorch, forcing the flame into the center for several more seconds.

Then the torch sputtered and died.

She clicked the switch repeatedly, but nothing happened.

It was empty.

She tossed it aside and pulled on the door. It took some convincing as the rest of the locking mechanism fell out of the burned hole where it once sat, but after a few more minutes of playing with it, the small door popped open.

After one last look back at the minister of defense, who hadn't moved, Sarah crawled through to the front and saw the keys in the ignition.

"Are you fucking kidding me?" She gasped at the air, which was even hotter in the cab, with all the windows amplifying the sun's heat like a magnifying glass. "Something finally went in my direction."

She dropped behind the wheel, cranked the engine, saw the gas tank was over half full, and had to laugh to herself. Maybe things would work out after all.

It took her seconds to turn the delivery truck around to see where she had parked.

A farmer's field was accurate. They'd come in on the road and only parked just a few feet onto the crops under a large tree. She was able to back it up and get on the gravel track in seconds.

Once out on the road, she guessed they were in the Kleinburg area. A sign came up at the next intersection. She was on Teston Road and

Pine Valley Drive, less than fifteen minutes from the Vaughn Mills Mall.

She hit the gas, wondering if she should be going to a hospital first so the minister could get medical attention. But wouldn't there be ambulances at the mall, as the exchange with Meredith was expected to happen anytime soon?

An exchange she couldn't let happen.

Otherwise, Jack and Meredith would ride off into the sunset, and everything would have been for nothing.

The minister of defense would understand.

She hoped …

Chapter 38

JACK PARKED NOSE OUT at a corner spot near the far back, giving him access to an exit with two lanes. Once he got Meredith, all he had to do was hit the gas.

They were almost home free.

Since no one knew what he looked like, he exited the Mustang and crossed the parking lot to enter the mall. They had half an hour left, which was enough time for him to use the bathroom and get an ice cream.

Fifteen minutes later, he stood outside a store called Urban Planet with an ice cream cone in one hand and the last phone with the final detonation code in the other, while staring at the Tesla Supercharger stations.

Whether Meredith managed to escape the men assigned to watch her or not, he would blow the only truck Kramer had armed, which was programmed to this phone. The rest of the trucks around the city would never blow, now that Kramer was dead, and would eventually be towed and discovered by the authorities. But he couldn't let this last one off the hook. Every bit of distraction he could get kept eyes off him.

People wandered by, oblivious to what was about to happen, their hands laden down with bags from various stores within the mall. Others were strolling toward the mall doors.

Jack took a seat on a bench and enjoyed his ice cream, wondering how Sarah and that asshole Brock made out with their fight over an empty gun. His bet was on Sarah as she was a strong woman—Brock was strong, too, but he was wounded and bleeding. That gave Sarah the advantage, and he prayed she could utilize it.

If not, the final explosive device would obliterate all of them as it was planted under the chassis of that last delivery truck. Kramer's idea of destroying the evidence was one of the most attractive clauses he brought to the table when offering Jack a place in their diamond-stealing business.

And why wouldn't he join the Afghanistan boys? Meredith saw it as a way to keep tabs on what they were doing and to feed them shitty information. It worked, and as much as Jack didn't like to kill needlessly—he wasn't a monster like Brock—he knew both men needed to die for him and Meredith to walk away with the diamond, which gave them anonymity. Even if Brock beat Sarah, they weren't getting out of the back of that truck anytime soon, and everyone would die when he blew it up.

So, kill Kramer as Brock wanted, then wound Brock and leave him locked in the back of the wired delivery truck to fight and eventually die, regardless of who won their fight.

It was unfortunate that Sarah had to die with him, but when they found Kramer's body, the gun in Sarah's hand, and Brock, Kramer's brother, with the burned body of the minister, Jack figured it would all be put together as the ultimate double-cross.

Brock killed Kramer, and Kramer blew up Brock.

The minister of defense and Sarah were collateral damage.

Jack bit into the ice cream cone, savoring the quiet moment on the bench and thinking about the people who didn't have to die but did anyway.

He'd kill a lot of people to be half a billion dollars richer. There was no question in his mind.

And he was doing it for love.

Meredith Whitlock was the one for him, and weren't diamonds a girl's best friend?

He got her the best damn diamond in the world—the Cullinan.

Jack finished the cone, tossed the bottom in the garbage can beside him, then stood to stretch, all the while taking in the unmarked cruisers that were getting into position in and around the Tesla Supercharger station.

The Urban Planet store had windows that looked out into the parking lot. He'd go in and spend ten to fifteen minutes shopping to kill time. With pants draped over his arm, keeping a watch on the vehicle that Meredith would exit wouldn't be too challenging.

Then, once she was in the mall, he'd help her lose her tail, they'd jump in the Mustang, and the rest would be history.

Jack entered Urban Planet with a smile on his face.

They were almost home free.

Beaches in South America—here we come.

Chapter 39

SARAH ARRIVED AT THE Vaughn Mills Mall parking lot to find it nearly full. She eased the delivery truck into the south lot, assuming Jack wouldn't park in the north lot where all the cops would be watching the bait vehicle.

Even though it wasn't a "bait" vehicle as usually set up by the authorities to trap car thieves, this was similar in theory.

Where the hell would Jack be hiding in this sea of vehicles?

She angled the delivery truck along the back road that accessed the parking area and drove slowly, staring at all the cars and the people walking by, but no one looked like Jack, nor were they as tall.

Halfway down, she saw an empty spot beside a Mustang and pulled in to park beside it.

Jack's words came back to her. *It's in the trunk of my Mustang. I'll be waiting in the Mustang for her in the south lot.*

Sarah hopped out and placed a hand on the hood to feel for engine heat. It was relatively hot, possibly due to the sunshine, so she touched the car next to it, and the temperature was about the same.

She hopped back in the delivery truck and moved along the rows of vehicles looking for more Mustangs. She stopped to touch two more, but they were all the same—nothing indicating the car had been driven recently.

This was a crazy and useless way to locate Jack's car.

Any help would be appreciated.

But as expected, Vivian didn't answer, which likely meant one of two things. One, Sarah was on the right path. Or two, Vivian was being a little bitch.

Sarah sat behind the wheel, staring out at the cars. Where would Jack park to ensure easy access for a quick escape?

It had to be the final rows, backed in, so the nose of his car would be aimed at the exit.

She drove the delivery truck along the back rows and only saw one Mustang in such a position.

There was a spot right beside it, too, so she backed in as close to the

Mustang as possible, leaving barely an inch between her passenger side and the Mustang's driver's side. If Jack came running to jump in and drive away, he'd be disappointed, as he'd have to get in on the passenger side, and a man of his size would struggle to hop over the center console with the small interior of the Mustang.

Sarah killed the engine and instantly heard knocking.

The minister.

She pushed the small door aside that gave access to the back and peeked in.

"You're awake?"

The minister had pushed himself up off the floor and was sitting with his back against the couch, his head resting on the cushions.

"I have a massive headache."

"You need a doctor, and I'm sorry I haven't taken you to one yet, but I couldn't let Jack get away."

"Understandable." The man's mouth hung open, his good eye closed. "When can I leave—?" He stopped talking, and Sarah stared at his chest as he seemed not to be moving. Then he gasped for some air and said, "This vehicle?"

"Here's what we're going to do. I'll go inside the mall and tell them you're out here and to send an ambulance. They'll open the back door and tend to you. In the meantime, I need to find Jack and end this."

"That works for me. Just hurry. I don't feel so good."

"On it," Sarah said. "Stay with me a little longer."

He waved a hand, and that was enough for Sarah. The man needed medical treatment immediately. Weighing his health and life in pursuit of Jack had been a decision she had to make, as she was likely the only one who knew what Jack looked like. And what was an extra thirty minutes without seeing a doctor? Sure, for some, it could mean life and death, but she'd take the risk in this case unless Vivian told her otherwise.

Sarah got out of the cab of the delivery truck, pocketed the keys so no one would move it away from the Mustang—she had to pray it was Jack's at this point—and jogged toward the mall entrance on a high.

When was the last time she'd eaten? Given it had been over a day, where was all this energy coming from? Could this be what those intermittent fasting people experienced when not eating? Her mind was clear, her energy high—exactly what she needed as this was her final chance to stop Jack.

She pulled the mall doors open and ran inside, heading through the food court toward the doors on the other side by a store called Urban Planet, the whole time looking for a security guard.

Then she saw one talking to two girls by the doors to the mall.

She ran toward him. "Excuse me," she said, slowing down. "I need to talk to you in private."

"One second, ladies," the guard said, turning to give Sarah his attention. "What can I do for you?"

"I need an ambulance called to attend to a wounded man out in the parking lot."

"What?" The guard seemed surprised as he fumbled for his radio. "What happened to him?"

"He's badly wounded and sitting in the back of a white delivery van —"

It was unexpected and completely out of her line of vision, but something broadsided her so hard she flew sideways several feet before smacking into the wall.

The area went dark by the time she hit the floor.

Chapter 40

JACK WATCHED THROUGH THE store window as several cars parked by the charging station. But then his heart skipped a beat when he saw Meredith get out of a large four-door sedan.

She used the key to lock the door, her black hair swinging slightly with the soft breeze as she shouldered her purse and started toward the mall.

They'd done it. They were home free.

All she had to do was get in the mall, walk toward the south side so he could see who was following her, and they'd be done—providing they didn't stick some sort of tracking device on her.

A couple strolled to their car. Another couple left the mall after an afternoon of shopping. Nice and easy, while dozens of law enforcement officers stared at the car with the fake diamond in it for hours, waiting for someone to show up and try to take it.

They'd be on the private jet he'd hired before they ever figured out no one was coming for the diamond that was supposedly in that car.

Once they realized they'd been duped—the biggest decoy ever— and began looking for Meredith, she'd have a new identity and a new life.

Jack placed the pair of pants he'd been holding on a table with folded T-shirts, then moved toward the entrance to the mall so that when Meredith walked by, he'd be in a position to watch for someone following her.

But then he heard something he didn't think was quite possible.

"Excuse me," that girl, Sarah, said, running up to a security guard at the doors to the outside, not ten feet in front of him. "I need to talk to you in private."

How the hell did she get here? That's impossible, but holy shit—this girl is resourceful.

Jack was close enough to hear their exchange without them seeing him as he edged beside a wall of dress pants that towered over his head at the mall entrance of Urban Planet.

"One second, ladies," the guard said to two girls he had been speaking with, and turned to Sarah. "What can I do for you?"

"I need an ambulance called to attend to a wounded man out in the parking lot."

"What?" The guard seemed surprised as he quickly reached for his radio, almost dropping it, then held it in front of his face. "What happened to him?"

Jack couldn't let the security guard make that call. It would attract too much attention to the mall, particularly to *this* side of the mall.

Jack pushed off the wall and ran at Sarah from an angle that kept him slightly behind her.

"He's badly wounded," she was saying, "and sitting in the back of a white delivery van—"

He hit her as hard as he could, lowering his shoulder and rising into the body check. Sarah lifted off the mall's tiled floor and flew into the side wall several feet away, then crumpled to the floor, her eyes rolling back in her head.

Outside, Meredith was almost at the mall doors. This was going to shit fast.

He needed another distraction. But before he could pull out that final cell phone to blow up the delivery truck, the security guard had stepped back to appraise the man, looking him up and down in fear, stammering about calling the police.

When Jack pounced, the guard had his radio in his hand and was bringing it to his mouth.

Two solid fists smashed the radio against the guy's ear and broke his nose virtually simultaneously, and it only took a second.

The guard dropped to the floor, moaning and holding his nose as blood gushed from it.

The girls who had been talking to the guard backed through the mall doors and ran outside, disappearing around the corner.

It was too late. He couldn't contain all the fallout as shoppers stopped what they were doing to gawk.

He needed to get Meredith and run for the Mustang. Their escape was assured if he could get her in his vehicle. It was a minute's run from where he now stood.

Meredith slowed her pace as she watched those girls run from the mall doors.

"C'mon, c'mon," he muttered, staring at her. "Get in here."

Sarah mumbled something from her position on the ground. He glanced over at her as she pushed herself into a sitting position and tried to focus on him.

"You resourceful bitch." He moved closer to her, the people around them not getting involved as the security guard still writhed and moaned on the floor to his right. "Where is the delivery truck? Where's the minister?"

Sarah raised her hands to ward off another attack. "I parked over there," she said, pointing to the east lot.

"You parked that way?" he asked, gesturing in roughly the same direction.

She nodded and pointed again, but this time it was the south lot.

"Where's the fucking truck?" he asked, his teeth grinding together.

"Over there. The minister is still in the back."

"Jonathan?" Meredith had stepped inside the mall. "We need to leave."

"One second," Jack/Jonathan said, standing to his full height, a cell phone in his hand. "One last device to blow."

He tapped in the numbers and hit send.

Sarah seemed to realize what he was doing and kicked at his legs. "No. Don't. The minister is in there. You'll kill him—"

A loud boom sounded somewhere to his left as the cell phone connected to the device and detonated it.

"We're done here now." He reached for Meredith's arm.

Sarah's pathetic attempt to kick him felt like small twigs on his shins. He stepped sideways and kicked her face once as he pulled Meredith with him.

"Who was that?" she asked, clutching his arm like a vise grip.

"A problem that will now take the fall for everything."

"Why? How?"

"Long story, honey." He glanced at her. "It's so good to see you. Let's get out of here. We finally did it."

"Hey!" someone yelled.

He had to expect some members of the public to want to be heroes.

When he glanced back, a man was trying to help Sarah to her feet, blood pouring out of her mouth from his kick to her face.

"We should hurry," he whispered.

Sarah pointed at him just before they scurried around a booth and entered the food court.

Then two men ran toward them.

"Run," Jack said, half-lifting Meredith along with him.

She held her own pretty well, and they got to the exit doors to the south parking lot so quickly that the two men were still twenty feet back.

Outside, he'd hurt both those men, and they'd no longer be a distraction.

But when he glanced at the fire in the distance and saw what was left of the white delivery truck, the same one he'd left Sarah and Brock in to fight it out, he understood what she had done.

It was parked directly beside a car that was fully engulfed in flames as well.

His escape vehicle, his Mustang, the very same one with a half-billion-dollar diamond in the trunk.

"That bitch," he screamed.

And then someone jumped him from behind.

Chapter 41

AARON HAD USED THE facilities, washed his face to wake up, grabbed a sugary donut for energy, and met with Detective Heath to walk back to the doors leading to the north parking lot. As they walked, they both heard elevated voices.

One look at each other, and they ran toward the mall entrance.

A huge man strode by them, half pulling a woman with him. Heath was staring straight ahead, his eyes on the carnage by the mall doors.

Aaron paid little attention to the large man as he turned and saw Sarah crumpled on the floor and a security guard clutching his bleeding face.

"Hey!" he yelled, running for Sarah. He dropped to his knees in front of her. "What the hell happened?"

"That big guy," Sarah pointed, "has the diamond, the girl. He killed everyone."

Aaron tried to help her up but ended up settling her against the wall. He glanced over and saw that a large man was dragging the woman out of view around a booth.

"Stay with her, Heath. Fucking protect Sarah with your life from your colleagues." Aaron ran after the big guy.

"Wait! Where are you going?"

Aaron didn't wait to answer. Heath's footsteps pounded behind him, but he didn't stop to get him to turn back because he couldn't let that large guy out of his sight.

Lucky for him, the large man and woman stepped outside and stopped moving as they stared at something in the distance.

Aaron plowed through the mall doors and heard "That bitch" from the guy as he jumped onto the man's back, wrapping his forearm around the guy's throat and his legs around the man's abdomen.

The man bent at the waist with the impact and grabbed Aaron's forearm, but he remained immovable as he redoubled his force on the man's neck.

Screaming for Aaron to get off him, the woman jostled around them, trying to get in Aaron's face.

Then the man did something unexpected. He straightened his body and jumped backward.

They went sideways in the air—Aaron still clinging to the man's neck, his legs still wrapped around his waist—and landed on Aaron.

All the man's upper body weight bore down on Aaron's torso, knocking the wind out of him and forcing his arms and legs to shoot outward as if he were doing a snow angel.

In the split second after they landed on the concrete, the back of the man's head shot toward Aaron's jaw and mouth, and he twisted sideways quickly, his cheek taking the brunt of the hit.

While still gasping for air, the big man rolled over and drove an elbow down toward Aaron's face. He blocked it, and pain shot through his arm. The man twisted around and delivered a left hook that caught Aaron in the uninjured cheek, dazing him momentarily as he tried to breathe after the initial concrete hit.

The incessant woman wouldn't stop yelling as the big man hovered over Aaron now, blocking out the afternoon sun.

The man's fists were like hammers as they drove into his chest—convinced each hit cracked a rib.

If he didn't move out of the way of Andre the Giant, he'd die here, leaving a shattered body behind for an easy autopsy.

The big man bent his arm inward to drive Aaron's face with an elbow, but Aaron was able to see the move in time and jerked sideways to avoid the hit while raising his right leg.

The leg connected with the big man's groin, making him emit a heavy groan. It was either that or the groan came from when the elbow connected with the concrete.

Aaron tried to launch a comeback in this uneven match, but his jabs and punches held no power because of the pain in his chest. There had to be broken ribs because each movement made his body scream on the inside.

He had to go for pressure points. Incapacitate the man, weaken his resolve.

The big guy was already pulling back for another punch when Aaron shoved his thumb upward and into the crook of the guy's neck. Then he jammed it toward the trachea, hoping it was enough to choke him but not collapse the tube.

That decision weakened the man's punch, which only grazed Aaron's chin, and caused the man to lean to the side, gasping and clutching at his throat.

When Aaron tried to maneuver out from under the big guy as he was preoccupied with catching his breath, the man just lay down, pinning Aaron to the concrete with two hundred and fifty pounds of sheer muscle.

"Get off him," a man shouted.

The corners of Aaron's sight dimmed. Was he losing consciousness?

"Don't shoot my Jonathan," a woman shouted.

The dimming increased. He wasn't breathing. What was on his chest? Someone was coughing. Something jolted the thing on top of him.

A weapon fired.

The body on him jerked.

The woman screamed.

And the weight left his chest. Aaron sucked in air like he was a free diver coming up from a seven-minute dive. His vision cleared rapidly, allowing him to take in the scene, pain throbbing from his chest and face.

Detective Heath stood over him, legs spread, arms extended, a weapon in his hands. The woman was crying and whispering *no* over and over, and the big guy was clutching a leg wound that seemed to be oozing blood rapidly.

"Step aside," a man yelled, moving into Aaron's vision. "I'm a paramedic."

He lay his head back, thinking the guy would tend to him, but then looked back up as the paramedic wrapped a belt around the man's leg while calling someone on the phone.

Heath identified himself, claiming this couple was wanted for multiple murders. Then he snapped a handcuff on the woman's wrist with the other end on the big guy's wrist.

"Jonathan, I'm so sorry," the woman whispered to the man.

Aaron was surprised he could hear her with the throbbing and ringing in his ears. He sat up and winced at the pain.

Then two other police officers in uniform ran up to the group and pushed their way through the small crowd of onlookers.

"What's going on here?" one asked.

"Detective Heath. This couple is wanted for multiple murders around Toronto. My colleague here"—he gestured at Aaron—"was able to subdue the man but was quickly losing the fight. I had no choice but to use my firearm."

"I'm calling this in," one of the officers said. "We know this woman. She's involved in something on the other side of the mall."

"Yes, it's Meredith Whitlock," Heath said, turning back to Aaron. He must've seen the concern on his face because he leaned toward him and whispered, "What is it?"

Aaron drew in a breath, winced, then was able to croak out, "*Sarah.*"

Understanding dawned on Heath's face, followed by concern. He addressed the cops. "Don't let them out of your sight. I'll be right back."

"Sir," one of the cops said. "I'd appreciate it if you didn't leave the scene of a shooting, even if you feel it's a righteous one."

"Thanks for the protocol lesson." Heath rolled his eyes at Aaron, then he bolted inside the mall.

Aaron lay his head back down, praying that Sarah made it through the next few hours.

Chapter 42

THE BLEEDING HAD SLOWED to a stop in her mouth by the time those two girls who had been talking with the security guard came back. The mall doors opened and closed, and Sarah glanced over to see the girls surrounded by at least six police officers. They all looked at the guard's ruined, bloody face and then gazed at Sarah.

Several of them gawked at her, blinking like they couldn't believe what they were seeing.

"Holy shit," one cop with graying hair said. "I feel like I'm seeing a ghost. That's the bitch from Twitter and the video the sergeant sent us." He stomped toward her, followed by his brethren. "She's the bomber, the one who got out of custody." He pointed at her. "The same whore who killed those VIP Protective Detail officers."

"Yeah, Sarah Roberts," another cop said as they formed a circle around her. "She killed our brothers. She's trying to get to the diamond that *she* arranged to be dropped off here."

Another cop shook his head. "Beat up by a security guard."

The cops laughed.

"Wait, sir," one of the girls said. "That's not what happened—"

"Everyone step back," the gray-haired cop shouted. "We're arresting this woman. Look, she's already resisting."

"Wait." Sarah had tried to raise her hands. Her wounded mouth emitted a sound more like *ate* instead of *wait*. However, no one heard her plea over the general din of the mall.

"Stop resisting," several cops shouted. They roughly flipped her onto her stomach. Someone pulled her hair back. Someone else landed on her legs, driving her kneecaps into the hard floor.

She grunted and tried to move away from that pressure as the pain was too intense.

"Still resisting arrest?" A cop yelled in her ear. "*Really?*"

Her arms were forced back behind her as someone's knee dropped on the back of her neck. The force of that impact jammed her wounded face into the floor—right on the same spot the monster, Jonathan/Jack, had belted her.

The pain increased in intensity as more bodies piled on her back. Breathing became a struggle. She tried to move out from under the oppressive weight to catch a breath, but there was no play here, nowhere to move. Agony rose in her shoulders as they wrenched her arms back to lock up her wrists.

Someone rolled her sideways, and she caught a glimpse of uniforms. So many uniforms, at least a dozen now, all wanting to hold her, hurt her, for what they think she'd done.

Even though she couldn't breathe a moment before, rolling her over eased the pressure on her lungs, and she gasped in some blessed air.

Hands roamed her body roughly as her legs were bent back, her heels almost touching her butt.

A cop leaned in close, a gun in his hand. "If you don't stop resisting, we will have no choice."

Something hard was forced under her.

The pain made it difficult to focus. Someone was yelling that she hadn't done anything. His words came to her, but she couldn't understand why he said *she dies on that floor*. Wasn't he trying to help her?

She tried to curl into a ball, but her arms and legs were all locked up. A wall of uniforms completely surrounded her. Not a single member of the public could see what they were doing to her. No one protested the brutality of it all.

And whatever had been shoved under her was digging into her abdomen.

Then someone yelled one word that made her body freeze like she'd been dropped into a polar bear dip at a frozen lake.

"*GUN!*"

They'd slipped a weapon under her body.

The cop closest to her face pointed his gun in her direction and whispered, "Die, bitch. This is for the cops you killed today."

A gun fired.

Chapter 43

DETECTIVE HEATH RAN THROUGH the mall, jumping around people and getting through the food court in seconds. When he turned the next corner and saw a group of fellow officers making a semi-circle wall around the area where he'd seen Sarah only minutes ago, he understood what was happening immediately.

He grabbed his cell phone, opened the voice memo app, and then pressed the record button.

"Hey," he shouted, slipping his phone back into his pocket. "Stop."

But no one even looked his way as he ran toward them all.

A group of onlookers had made their own semi-circle half a dozen feet back. Heath pushed through them, shoving and jostling until he got to the cops in uniform, standing shoulder-to-shoulder around Sarah.

Barely visible through their pant legs, he witnessed at least five or six other cops restraining Sarah into some sort of hogtied position.

"Guys, step aside," Heath yelled, flipping out his ID badge.

One cop shoved him away. "Fuck off. We're making this arrest."

"She didn't do anything. It wasn't her." His protests fell on deaf ears.

Lost on what to do, he ran at them, but they gelled at the right moment, pushing him off like an adult's game of British bulldog.

He drew his pistol and aimed it at the mall's roof. "If she dies on that floor, I will shoot her murderer," he yelled. "This is not how we arrest an unarmed woman."

Then someone holding Sarah down yelled, "*GUN!*"

Heath fired his weapon.

Chapter 44

DETECTIVE HEATH GOT THE desired reaction.

The officers who had formed a line in front of Sarah parted and dove out of the way to avoid getting a stray ricochet, while drawing and aiming at him. Most people's reaction was to bolt away from a man who fired a weapon, but not trained officers. He was just hoping to get enough room to reach Sarah.

He holstered his pistol and dove through the broken line onto the melee, scrambling for Sarah's arm as other officers drew their weapons. Men in uniform punched and kicked at him, but he was able to lock an arm around Sarah's just below the elbow.

Someone grabbed his hair and yanked him back.

Heath lashed out, screaming, but instead of hitting and punching this many men, he snatched a pair of handcuffs off an officer's utility belt, yanked his hair out of the hand of whoever was pulling him back, and deftly swung the cuffs onto Sarah's lower arm, then latched the other one to himself.

Several fists hit him before the man in uniform closest to Sarah got them all to calm down for a second.

"What are you doing?" the gray-haired cop asked him, spittle flying from his mouth as he spoke.

"Risking my life."

The cop nodded. "I can see that. Who the hell are you?"

"I'm Detective Heath, the man Sarah called to warn about the bombs. I'm risking my life to protect her just like she risked hers to protect us."

"Bullshit." The man slapped Sarah's head. She barely grunted as her face was still jammed into the corner where the wall met the floor.

Surrounding Heath, three officers held Sarah's legs, and two were still pushing down on her upper body, with one on her neck.

"She better be able to breathe, or I'll have all of you arrested for murder."

The cop who seemed in charge looked aghast. He leaned in closer. "Arrest us? After what she did?" He horked up a goober and hocked it on Sarah's hair. "Fuck her, and fuck you. Why don't you let us do our job and take out the garbage?"

More noise came from the mall doors. People were leaving in groups or entering, but it was slowly becoming a mob out there. If more officers joined this cop, Heath would have a genuine problem on his hands.

"Sarah didn't do what you think she did."

"I call bullshit. She knew where the bombs were. She set them off. She kidnapped the minister of defense. We have her on camera driving the delivery truck. The cocky bitch even sent those videos with her face demanding that she get that big diamond. And we found her delivery truck, with the gun that killed those men in the back of it, at the convention center on Airport Road. If this isn't a perfect case, then I'm a monkey's uncle. And what about the men we lost in the first explosions she caused yesterday?"

Heath gasped for breath. "I've got proof she didn't do any of that —"

"We don't care about your proof." He leaned in closer and whispered, "She dies today."

More noise came from outside the newly formed circle the uniforms had made.

"Then you're taking me with her." Heath held up the cuffs linking his arm to Sarah's. "Shoot me, too, and you'd be killing a fellow officer."

The cop looked at his colleagues as even more noise, pushing, and shoving came from outside the circle.

"Fine, we'll load her up, drive her outside of town, and execute both of you then. Better for us that we don't do it here, anyway. Too messy."

The cop lunged toward Heath's midsection but didn't hit him. He retrieved a small handgun that had been hidden under Sarah's hip bone. The gun disappeared into the cop's pocket, and he pushed to his feet.

"We got her, boys," he shouted triumphantly.

"Fuck, you really are a relic from the sixties," another cop said as he watched the gun slip into the other cop's pocket.

Several officers nodded as the human chain they'd made broke up.

Inspector Sean Richmond and his partner, Chris Stone, stuck their heads in and saw Heath.

"What the hell are you doing here, Detective Heath?" Stone asked.

Heath exchanged a glance with the gray-haired cop. "Just helping to make an arrest."

They helped them both to their feet, with Sarah needing extra help to stand. Her mouth was bleeding, and her face was a dark red, with bruising forming anywhere skin was exposed.

"What the hell happened to her?" Richmond asked, glancing at the gray-haired cop. "Looks like she got hit by a truck."

"She resisted arrest. We had to hold her down."

"Bullshit," Stone said. "Get the fuck out of our sight."

The gray-haired cop didn't move. None of the uniforms moved.

"Who owns these cuffs?" Stone yelled, holding up Heath's and Sarah's bound hands.

A man stepped forward, the key in his hand.

"Why'd you cuff a decorated detective to the suspect?" Richmond asked.

"He did it to himself," the cop said, undoing Heath's wrist.

Stone and Richmond turned to Heath.

"They were going to kill her." He glared at the gray-haired cop.

Stone and Richmond understood everything.

"Leave the cuffs with me," Stone said, pushing the cop away before Sarah's wrist was unlocked. He took the end that was on Heath's wrist and clamped it onto his own. "Walk me out of here," he said to his partner. Then, with his voice raised to a shout so everyone could hear him, he said, "The RCMP has taken over the case. This is our collar."

Richmond led the way as Stone helped Sarah toward the mall doors.

The gray-haired cop turned to Heath. "She won't make the week."

"I'm sure she'll do just fine."

"And even if she makes the week, someone will get her on the inside."

"You keep telling yourself that, asshole."

He rolled a hand in a circle. "As these boys are my witnesses, that bitch won't survive lockup, whether in holding or after sentencing. We all have people on the inside. All you did was delay the inevitable." He shoved Heath hard, knocking him back against the wall.

Heath drew his weapon. "Back the fuck off," he shouted. "Touch me again. I fuckin' dare you."

The gray-haired cop leaned closer as his fellow officers placed their hands on their weapons. "This isn't over, is all I'm saying. You'll have your day, too." He blew him a kiss. "We're coming for you, Detective Heath. You're batting for the wrong team now, asswipe."

Then they dispersed as if nothing had happened. All the uniforms strode toward the mall doors, leaving Heath with his back against the wall, his heart racing, and his gun still in his hand.

Once his gun was holstered, he pulled out his cell phone.

The recording was still going.

He stopped it, then saved the file. A moment later, he pressed play and heard himself yell, "Hey," and then, "Stop." He slid his finger along the line at the bottom to fast forward and stopped it at a random spot, hearing, "… explosions she caused yesterday?" Then Heath's voice responded with, "And I've got proof she didn't do any of that—" He was cut off by, "We don't care about your proof." The man's voice lowered when he said, "She dies today," but he could still hear it with the phone pressed to his ear.

He stopped the recording and pushed off the wall, ignoring the stares.

They lost a lot of cops with those bombs, and that made people act crazy. But when crazy turned officers into murderers, he couldn't let that go.

The police force would be losing a lot more cops in the coming days; he was sure of that. As soon as the right people heard his recording, heads would roll.

He picked up the pace to a jog. Aaron needed to hear the good news.

Sarah was safe but in custody.

They'd work everything out.

Eventually.

Chapter 45

SARAH STARED ACROSS THE hospital room at the blank TV screen as Parkman set flowers on a table by the window.

Then he turned to face her. "You doing okay?"

She blinked once. "As good as can be expected. They still haven't let me see Willow."

"It's been almost a week." Parkman shook his head. "Callous bastards."

The edge of a smile lifted her lip.

Parkman gestured toward the door. "They've got two assholes in uniform guarding the access to your room."

"There are four in total."

"Four?" Parkman gasped. "Why?"

"Who knows who'll come to take a shot at killing me next? They only needed a few more seconds on that mall floor."

"Good thing Heath showed up when he did."

She looked at him. "See? My sister knew I'd need Heath involved."

"What?"

Sarah told him about calling Heath about the bombs and how she added a condition that if they were going to use her as bait at the train station, Heath was to be fully reinstated. "He stayed on this case until the end, working with you and Aaron."

Parkman moved closer and pulled on the handcuffs that secured her to the hospital bed railing. "They locked you to both sides?"

"They aren't taking any chances."

"What if you have an itchy nose?"

Sarah shrugged. "Shout for a nurse?"

They looked at each other for a long moment. "They have a lot of charges laid against you, Sarah." Parkman pulled away, grabbed the chair by the window, and pulled it closer. "Any plans on how to deal with this?"

"You wanna be my lawyer?" Her tone raised, suggesting humor.

"I wish. We'd be a great team. But seriously, what's the next step? These kinds of charges could get you in prison until you're in your sixties or later."

Sarah closed her eyes. "It's been five days. I'm covered in bruises. My jaw has a hairline fracture, which is why I'm here. They sent me for an X-ray because the pain won't go away. I've lost a tooth from getting kicked in the face, and I miss Willow. Have I thought about fighting these charges yet? No, I haven't."

They sat in silence for a moment.

"Where's Aaron?" she asked. "I haven't seen him since all this ended."

"He's here, likely still trying to get clearance to see you."

"Clearance?"

"Well, he's part of the other side of this thing."

"The other side? Sounds like there's more to the story."

Parkman nodded, absentmindedly touching the bandages on his arm where Brock had shot him. "Aaron attacked Jonathan Black. You know him as Jack. The other side's story is that Jack orchestrated everything, using the Abdul brothers as pawns."

"Abdul brothers?"

"Right, after everything went down, their real names were published. Abdul-Kabir, otherwise known as Neil Kramer, and his brother, Abdul-Sayeed, otherwise known as Brock. So, Jack and Meredith were a team working on stealing the Cullinan diamond when Kramer and Brock approached Jack, looking for someone to help steal the diamond with them. They even claimed to be working with a woman who would help them pinpoint where it would be—Meredith."

"But Kramer and Brock, the Abdul brothers, wanted to kill the minister of defense."

"They did." Parkman nodded. "So they combined the whole thing, with Brock and Jack working together to remove Kramer."

It was Sarah's turn to nod. "I watched Jack, I mean Jonathan, kill Kramer. Then the minister of defense helped me kill Brock, who was a seriously sick fuck, by the way."

"Right, well, this drop-the-diamond-in-the-mall-parking-lot shit was a decoy for Jack and Meredith to leave. They already had the diamond in the trunk of their Mustang."

"But Aaron jumped the guy, and he got arrested, right?"

Parkman tapped Sarah's hand. "Right, but someone parked a particular delivery truck right beside their Mustang."

Sarah raised her eyebrows. "The one that blew up?"

"The very one—which ruined the Mustang."

"And they found the body in the back of the delivery van?"

Parkman looked sidelong at her. "They did. All burned up."

"Shit." Sarah averted her gaze.

"The idiot blew it up while standing over me in the mall. He had no idea I'd parked beside him. He even asked me where I parked, and I just pointed in a random direction." She stared at him. "Wait, how do you know all this? Did Jonathan and Meredith confess? And if so, why are all my charges still pending?"

Parkman shook his head. "Jonathan didn't confess. He's remaining tight-lipped."

"Then who?"

"Meredith Whitlock confessed after they threatened her with twenty years in federal lockup."

"Holy shit."

"She's got aiding and abetting to murder and so many more charges. As of this morning, they're offering her a deal to walk them through it all."

"What will that mean for me?"

The hospital room door banged open.

"Fuckin' idiots," Aaron said as he stepped inside. He looked at Sarah and Parkman, took in the handcuffs, and then stared at her face. "Are those really necessary?"

"Tell that to the assholes in uniform outside that door." Sarah jerked her head at the door once. "See how far you get."

He moved over to the bed, gently wrapped an arm over her shoulders in a half-hug, then pulled back. "You doing okay?"

"As can be expected. My jaw still aches, but talking doesn't hurt much as long as I limit movement. How about you?"

"A few ribs were cracked, and my ego bruised heavily, but I'm okay. I'm just happy Jonathan Black is behind bars, as well as Meredith."

"She might be getting out," Parkman said. "I heard from Detective

Heath that she's cutting a deal this morning."

Aaron smiled. "Did you hear what else happened this morning?"

They both shook their heads.

"Heath had a recording of Sarah's arrest"— he mock-coughed into his hand—"excuse me, I misspoke. It wasn't an *arrest* but an attempted murder by police officers."

"He what?" Sarah gasped, lifting her head, then wincing in pain and resting it back down. "He recorded all that?"

Aaron nodded. "And he played it for his superiors, who played it for theirs. Finally, the names of every officer involved were gathered, plus a video recording of them entering the mall to arrest you. Witnesses have been interviewed, including the mall security guard who was injured. By the way, he said you did nothing to him—it was Jonathan who attacked you both."

"And?" Parkman asked. "What are they going to do to those officers?"

Aaron watched them a moment, a smile on his face. "They rounded them all up an hour ago. Over eighteen cops were arrested and suspended without pay for trying to kill Sarah Roberts."

Emotion rose in her throat, and she took a moment to suppress the feeling, or it would turn into tears, and she didn't want those right now.

"Things'll change fast now," Parkman said. "My bet is your charges will be dropped very soon."

"I fuckin' hope so," Aaron said.

"Where's Willow today?" Sarah asked.

"With Daniel."

"How's Alex healing?"

"Much better. He's coming back to the dojo for light exercises in two weeks. All his broken bones from that hotel fight are healing well."

"Good, because Vivian's been telling me about a disappearance soon, and something tells me Alex needs to be involved."

Aaron gave her a hard look. "Sarah, after all this—" he stopped when Parkman adjusted in his seat to glare at him.

"Aaron. Now's not the time." Parkman wrapped a hand around Sarah's. "Let's get Sarah home, find a way to remove those charges from her record, and heal. Then we can discuss the future."

Aaron raised his hands. "Of course, but this merry-go-round of violent criminals and broken bones should have a best-before date, is all I'm saying."

Sarah stared up at the blank TV. Parkman remained tight-lipped.

"Okay, okay." Aaron looked away. "I just can't promise to always be there when—"

"Aaron," Parkman said, a warning in his tone. "Spat's over. Seriously, man."

Voices rose in the outer hallway. Someone shouted at someone else. Then a voice rose over all of them, and what sounded like a serving tray or a clipboard banged to the hospital floor.

Aaron started toward the door.

"Wait," Parkman said, getting up. "You have broken ribs. What are you going to do?"

"*Cracked* ribs—and you've got a bullet wound in your arm."

"Okay, then, together."

The men approached the door, but before they got there, it banged open, and a man in a Canadian military uniform stepped inside.

He kicked his leg up, stomped it down, then stood there staring at nothing.

Parkman and Aaron exchanged a glance.

Then another soldier entered the room, followed by yet another. In moments, six men in uniform formed a line in the hospital room, making Parkman and Aaron ease back to stand by Sarah's hospital bed.

The man who was doing all the yelling in the corridor got closer.

Then a wheelchair was pushed into the room.

The man in the chair wore a baseball cap, and he had huge gauze wrapped around one eye, the other one rolling in his head as he took in the scene.

Sarah sat up straighter, unable to move too far because of the handcuffs.

"What the fuck," she muttered. "Is that really you, sir?"

"In the bloody flesh," John Williams, the minister of defense, said. "And I have you to thank for that."

His one eye widened so far that Sarah wondered if it would pop out.

"Why the *hell* is she cuffed to the bed?" He bellowed in his authoritative military voice. "If she isn't uncuffed within one minute, you will spend the rest of your career in a hard labor prison in North Korea before I'm through with you."

The cops who'd been guarding Sarah's hospital room door were shoved inside by two other men in military uniforms.

They ran over and undid the handcuffs, then ran for the door.

"How dare you?" the minister shouted. "Get out of my sight before I end your careers."

The men ran, their footfalls echoing down the corridor.

"Sarah Roberts," the minister said, wheeling closer. "I have you to thank for saving my life."

"Sir, it wasn't all me. Without your help with that blowtorch."

Aaron snapped his head toward her. "Blowtorch?"

"Excuse me, sir. How impolite." She introduced Aaron and Parkman.

"This is one tough woman," the minister said. "I had front-row seats as she challenged those men. I would've sworn your mouth would get you killed." He shook his head, his one eye never leaving her face.

"That's our Sarah," Aaron said, a half-smile on his face. "Even her mouth gets her in trouble."

Sarah caught the look Parkman gave him, and Aaron's smile died. He mouthed, *What?* to Parkman, his hands out at the sides.

"How did you get out of the delivery truck?" Sarah asked, rubbing her wrists. "They found a body in the burned wreckage ..." She stopped as it hit her. "Oh, shit. That was Brock. He was still in the back."

The minister nodded. "You drove to that mall and parked, so I figured you were going after the people involved in all this shit. Since they made you read that recording, of course, you would know where they'd be."

"I'm sorry I didn't take you right to a hospital. I ranked finding them and stopping them as number one and figured under other circumstances, you'd agree."

"I do agree, even under our current circumstances. But I didn't have to sit in the back. It was too hot, and I wanted help. So, I crawled out that little door, rolled into the passenger seat, then dropped out of the truck. I had trouble walking, so I crawled away. About two car lengths from the delivery van, two women found me and called mall security. Minutes later, I was picked up in the small SUV they drove and taken to their office, where an ambulance came and got me." He extended his hands. "And here we are."

She shook her head, amazed and happy to see him. "Here we are."

They stared at each other for a long moment: two people, a common bond shared after having endured a tragic event.

"I'll have you know that I'm recommending a medal of some kind."

"Sir?" Sarah gasped out the word. "But I have a plethora of charges —"

He waved his hand. "Every single charge ever placed against you has been dropped. No one will pursue you for anything. I've already sworn in my entire statement as the minister of defense of this great nation. I was there during the kidnapping. I listened to Brock. I saw them murder their own and take that photo of you. These are facts, undeniable facts. Sarah Roberts, you're free to go anytime you like"— he raised a hand—"after you sign off on your full statement. And I swear that not a single member of the policing community will even think about pulling you over or approaching you for anything in the near future unless it's to protect you from a crime. The truth of what happened has been explained to every department and detachment. They don't look at you as the enemy now. They see the woman who stopped this madness at the risk of her own life." He paused to catch a breath. "Now, we only request one thing from you. That statement you gave to the police—we need to make sure it's accurate."

The tears she tried to suppress threatened to leak over her eyelids. "Of course. I can do that." The elation running through her body was overwhelming.

"I understand they tried to kill you. They didn't take your statement yet. The RCMP asked for your version of the story, but a full statement is needed. They've had you locked up for four days in a hole and only now brought you to get checked out at the hospital." He wiped at his eye. "I will hold every last one of these men accountable for your mistreatment. I'm already overseeing the arrests of all the cops who sought vengeance for the killing of their own. I understand their motivations, but they were making a grave error. They cannot act as a judge or the jury, as they had their facts wrong. I've placed Detective Heath in charge of everything, and even though I don't generally get so involved in the inner workings of a police department, I've asked for an executive order to do so in this case, and I got it."

Now Sarah had to wipe her eyes.

"Thank you, Sarah," the minister added. "Truly. I'm alive today because of you. I'd be dead right now if you didn't stomp on Brock's throat. You truly are one of a kind. I only wish you'd serve as a personal bodyguard for me, but I'm aware that doesn't fall under your sort of purview."

"Sir," one of the soldiers said.

The minister spun his chair around.

"I've got Detective Heath on the line."

He spun back to Sarah. "In another life, we will work together, dear. Heal up, and go home to your daughter. I'll have a couple of my soldiers drop by for your statement. You won't be giving it to police officers."

"Thank you, sir."

"No, it is I who must thank you." He placed a hand over his heart, leaned forward, and closed his eye. Then he was wheeled away to take his call.

"Holy shit," Parkman whispered. "It's over. Just like that?" He clapped his hands once.

"Parkman?"

"Yeah?"

"Don't clap your hands. *Please*."

He lowered them to his lap. "Sure." Then he pulled out a toothpick and popped it in his mouth. "So, what's next?"

Aaron shot his head around to stare at Parkman.

"I mean," Parkman shrugged, "tell me more about this disappearance thing. Maybe we can stop it before the person disappears."

Sarah rested her head back and closed her eyes. "I'm scared, Parkman. This one feels personal, like it'll happen to one of us."

"Any idea who?" Aaron asked, suddenly interested.

"No idea yet. Just that it's coming in a few months, and as talkative as Vivian has been lately, she's now gone quiet on this one. Something about serial offenders, and the crimes are horrific."

"Great. More shit on the menu."

She opened her eyes and stared at Aaron. "I won't stop. I can't. René Atchison would be dead right now if I hadn't gotten involved. A lot more people would've died." She lowered her head and closed her eyes again. "I'll never stop until Vivian stops. And when that day comes, it will truly be the end."

Afterword

And now we have finished another Sarah journey—the thirty-third book!—and all is well that ends well. Book thirty-four, *The Disappearance*, will continue with devastating consequences soon enough.

As mentioned by Sarah in the final chapter of this book, when she said, "I'll never stop until Vivian stops. And when that day comes, it will truly be the end," the final book in this series will be called *The End*. That book will be book number fifty. So, we have about seventeen more to go until we get to *The End*.

I used the Metro Convention Centre in this novel because it's an excellent location for the plot's purposes, and I've been there before. I walked the entirety of that building for a golf show once and loved it.

I've also visited the International Centre on Airport Road for trade shows in the past, and I wanted to feature that building because of its unique parking at the back, which offers a limited public view due to the rarely used train tracks and elevated parking area. So, Brock and Jack could execute the rest of the team without worry of being seen.

Finally, I chose to use the Vaughan Mills Mall (notice the spelling in the novel was "Vaughn Mills," though, to avoid an exact match) as the public location for the final showdown because I've walked the corridors of that mall dozens of times since it opened. It's one of my favorite malls in the Greater Toronto Area, and I've bought many pieces of clothing from Urban Planet.

There are more spelling issues; the existing campuses in Toronto are called George Brown, but I'm calling them Greg Brown.

Although Greek Town is an actual location in Toronto on the Danforth, and I lived off of Pape Avenue back in the mid-nineties— actually, if you ever read the book I wrote called, *The Threat* with Drake Bellamy, then you got a tour of the house I lived in on Hunter Street (near Pape) because Drake's parents lived there in that novel.

Even though I now live over nine months per year on a Greek island with my lovely Greek wife and fellow thriller author, Rania Stone, Toronto has a place in my heart as I grew up in its environs and spent over thirty years on its roads, in its malls, and enjoying its golf courses.

Allow me to correct a few mistakes now, as I intentionally made them, knowing exactly what I was doing. In Canada, the police departments and the RCMP do not use the word "detective" to describe their investigators. They use other names, chief among them "inspector" and "division commander." I used "inspector" for the RCMP guys, but chose to stick with "detective" for Heath because "detective" is more widely known, and frankly, I prefer it over "inspector."

The other issue isn't a mistake, but people might be confused, so allow me to explain it. The word "centre" is British English, and "center" is American English. So, in this book, when you see "center," it's because I write all my novels in American English. But when I'm using a proper noun like the name of a building in Canada, they use British English, so I have to call it by its correct name.

To avoid confusion, the "International Centre" and the "Metro Convention Centre" will use the British spelling "centre" because that's the official name. Everywhere else, I'll write "center" in American English.

Now, to the acknowledgments!

René Atchison—thank you so much for allowing me to use your name in this book. You were a great sport and even gave me personal information about yourself to make the character very real. Everything I wrote about her living in New York, singing backup vocals on Broadway in New York for the Disney live movie *Beauty and the Beast*, and how she's always dreamed of being a photographer is true for the real René. I'm honored you would allow me to include you in Sarah's adventure.

Until the next time, I want to thank you, the reader, for continuing to pick up another volume of Sarah's life, and I can't wait for you to read *The Disappearance*, book thirty-four. There's still so much fun and craziness to come for Sarah's life before book fifty, *The End*.

Take care of yourselves and each other.

Get caught reading.

Love you all,

Jonas Saul

About Jonas Saul

Jonas Saul is the bestselling author of the Sarah Roberts Series—over two million copies sold—and more than sixty published thrillers. His work has outranked Stephen King and Dean Koontz on Amazon and has been optioned for television and film by MadRiver Pictures.

A sought-after speaker and teacher, Jonas has presented at international writing conferences and film festivals around the globe. He is the creator of Imagine Greece Retreats, hosting annual writers', screenwriters', and readers' retreats on the sun-drenched shores of Greece, where he now lives. His teaching focuses on creating unputdownable tension and emotion, building a sustainable writing career, and avoiding the pitfalls of the publishing industry.

An acclaimed freelance editor, Jonas works with several publishers and offers private editing services to authors worldwide. His editing site features glowing testimonials from clients who credit him with elevating their books to the next level.

For speaking engagements, jury work, or to connect:

jonassaul@icloud.com | jonas@imaginegreeceretreats.com

Linktree – Find me here | Amazon Follow | BookBub Follow | Facebook (most active)